BOOKS BY

REYNOLDS PRICE

THE COLLECTED
STORIES

REYNOLDS PRICE

THE COLLECTED STORIES

ATHENEUM

NEW YORK 1993

MAXWELL MACMILLAN CANADA   TORONTO

MAXWELL MACMILLAN INTERNATIONAL
NEW YORK   OXFORD   SINGAPORE   SYDNEY

Some of these stories appeared in *American Short Fiction, The Archive, Encounter, Esquire, Harper's, The Kenyon Review, The New Yorker, The Paris Review,* PEN Syndicated Fiction Project, *Playboy, Prairie Schooner, The Red Clay Reader, Shenandoah, Southern Exposure, The Southern Review, Story, TriQuarterly, The Virginia Quarterly Review, Vogue,* and *Winter's Tales.* Some appeared in limited editions published by Albondocani Press and by North Carolina Wesleyan College Press.

Atheneum
Macmillan Publishing Company
866 Third Avenue
New York, NY 10022

Maxwell Macmillan Canada, Inc.
1200 Eglinton Avenue East
Suite 200
Don Mills, Ontario M3C 3N1

Macmillan Publishing Company is part of the
Maxwell Communication Group of Companies.

Library of Congress Cataloging-in-Publication Data
Price, Reynolds, 1933–
  [Short stories]
  The collected stories / by Reynolds Price.
    p. cm.
  ISBN 0-689-12147-4
  I. Title.
PS3566.R54A6   1993   92-36807
813'.54—dc20

Macmillan books are available at special discounts for bulk purchases for sales promotions, premiums, fund-raising, or educational use. For details, contact:

Special Sales Director
Macmillan Publishing Company
866 Third Avenue
New York, NY 10022

10 9 8 7 6 5 4 3 2 1

Printed in the United States of America

CONTENTS

TO THE READER

Except for three related stories published in 1991 in *The Foreseeable Future* and one college story never published, the fifty stories gathered here are what I've written in adult life by way of fiction shorter than the novel. Like many children raised among books and compelled to write, I began with the story in adolescence—"The Ring," a supernatural tale finished and illustrated with a snaky death's-head in 1948. The oldest story here though is "Michael Egerton" from 1954; the newest is "An Evening Meal" from 1992. Half of the fifty appeared in my prior volumes, *The Names and Faces of Heroes* in 1963 and *Permanent Errors* in 1970; then for almost twenty years I attempted no stories. Apparently the narrative and lyric forces that had surfaced in stories moved instead into poems and plays; and by a principle of mental physics, those forms consumed the available energy. But once I needed—for unknown reasons in a new and radically altered life—to return to the story, it opened before me like a new chance.

It's often remarked that, while the story's technical and emotional demands are more strenuous in some ways than the novel's, its short distance is paradoxically the event first entered by most young narrative writers. The choice is understandable. A young writer's perspective and stamina, his literal breath, are short and can hardly sustain a longer trek. The knowledge and reflection over which he has sufficient depth of command are recent, often unconfirmed by repetition and are mostly

xi

deprived of the long submergence which fiction wants in the shaping dark of the unconscious mind.

So while the good story is a hard event, its prime needs prove to be the young writer's birthright since first it demands a shortsighted eye, an eye set on the foreground, and a close-bounded subject. If for me the broad subject of novels has been the action of time—its devastation and curious repair—the story has charted briefer stretches of concentrated feeling, and it always speaks an intimate language. Because of its single-minded intent and the narrow ground from which it looks, the story is more likely than the novel to issue straight from a writer's home—the crow's nest from which, at the rates of his body, he gauges the riptides between him and land. So the story shorter than, say, fifty pages is the prose narrator's nearest approach to music—duo, trio, quartet, serenade, dance or the deeper reaches of song: the lean lament or ballad of hunger, delight, revulsion or praise.

A collection like this then, from five decades, will show a writer's preoccupations in ways the novel severely rations (novels are partly made for that purpose—the release from self, long flights through the Other). John Keats's assertion that "the excellence of every Art is its intensity" has served as a license and standard for me. From the start my stories were driven by heat—passion and mystery, often passion for the mystery I've found in particular rooms and spaces and the people they threaten or shelter—and my general aim is the transfer of a spell of keen witness, perceived by the reader as warranted in character and act. That aim inevitably feeds a hope that any sizable group of stories will be consumed by the reader at a measured pace—one that grants the form's tendency to fever and its risk, in the hands of any writer, of inducing exhaustion (a reason the story has often been unpopular with American readers; however limited their time, they mostly choose a less probing novel).

To sort old stories is to meet selves, lost or long-since abandoned. Like a search through old snapshots, such a look back soon calls for change—temper that young man's burdened frown and the dialect of his early compulsions, the words and grammar that once were common as lines in his hand but that now look strange. Far more closely than in the novels, these stories clung to the shape of the ground my life was crossing at a given time. Some of the ground was rough underfoot and tested whoever I was that month. I've resisted the chance to remake those selves. The man who wrote half these stories is no longer me, but I was once him. He did what he meant, and I've left him at it.

With only a few corrected proof or spelling errors—and with no attempt to reconcile my evolving attempts at a clear minimal system of punctuation—the older stories stand as they first appeared in volumes. Throughout, at this late point, I note the recurrence of a few indelible sights, names and actions, that struck me early and have followed me always. Most of the recent stories have undergone the useful discipline of magazine appearance and stand here, minus editors' quirks. All of them stand in a new order—one which attempts an alternation of voices, echoes, lengths and concerns that would prove unlikely if I held to the order of prior volumes or set the stories by date of completion. My hope is the reader's well-tended pleasure.

Finally the seven stories in *The Names and Faces of Heroes* were dedicated to the memory of my father Will Price, to my mother Elizabeth Rodwell Price and my brother William. The eighteen stories in *Permanent Errors* were dedicated to Eudora Welty. The force of those thanks is strong with me still. In its new order, and with many new stories, this volume bears its own dedication.

R.P., 1993

FULL DAY

Early afternoon in the midst of fall; but the sun was behind him, raw-egg streaks of speedy light from a ball-sized furnace in a white sky. Buck even skewed his rearview mirror to dodge the hot glare that would only be natural three hours from now. *Am I nodding off?* He thought he should maybe pull to the shoulder and rest for ten minutes. No, he'd yet to eat; his breakfast biscuit was thinning out. One more call; then he'd push on home, be there by dark. But he took the next sharp bend in the road; and damn, the light was still pouring at him, redder now.

Buck shrugged in his mind and thought of a favorite fact of his boyhood—how he'd searched old papers and books of his father's for any word on the great Krakatoa volcanic eruption in 1883. He'd heard about it years later in school—how an entire island went up that August in the grandest blast yet known to man. The sea for miles was coated with powdered rock so thick that ships couldn't move. And for more than a year, sunsets everywhere on Earth were reddened by millions of tons of airborne dust. Buck's mother would tell him, each time he asked, that the night before her wedding in 1884, the sunset scared her worse than his father did.

Like boys in general, he'd consumed disasters of all shapes and sizes but only from books and the silent movies of his childhood. Otherwise he often thought of himself as an average tame fish, safe in his tank.

I

He'd missed the First War by only a month and was several years too old at Pearl Harbor; so even now, at fifty-three, he'd never witnessed anything worse than a simple crossroads collision, one death with very little blood. He suddenly saw how the light this afternoon was similar to that, though hadn't he watched the wreck in springtime? Early April maybe—surely dogwood was blooming.

Buck had sat at the Stop sign in what felt like a globe of silence and watched, slow-motion, as an old man plowed his toy Model A broadside into a gasoline truck, which failed to explode. Buck had got out and joined the young truckdriver in trying to ease the trapped old man (a country doctor, named Burton Vass, crushed by the steering wheel). Awful looking as he was, pinned into the seat, Dr. Vass wouldn't hear of their trying to move him till an ambulance came. But a good ten minutes before it appeared, the doctor actually grinned at their eyes. Then he said "I'm leaving" and left for good. So yes, Buck was maybe a fish in a tank. *Whose tank?* he wondered. But since he mostly thought about God in his prayers at night, he dropped the question now. God knew, he spent his life in a tank, this Chrysler gunboat, working to bring electric ease to country wives—stoves, steam irons, washers, freezers, fans.

He turned the mirror down again and tried the sun. It was now even stranger; and the leaves, that had only begun to die, were individually pelted by light till they shivered and flashed. Buck slowed and pulled to the narrow shoulder by a tall pine woods. He'd pushed too far but, on the back seat, he had a wedge of rat cheese, a few saltines and a hot bottled drink. That would calm his head.

The next thing he knew, a voice was speaking from a great distance, toward his left ear. *It's nothing but your name. You're dreaming; dream on.* But the voice was only saying *Sir?* Eventually a second voice, young and hectic, echoed the word—*Sir? Please wake up.* Something in the pitch of the *please* helped him rouse. But he didn't reflect that the tone of the voice was much like the younger of his two sons at home.

It was almost night; he thought that first. But then he realized his eyes had cleared. It was dimmer, yes; the sun was tamer. He glanced at the clock—a quarter past four.

Then from as far off as in his sleep, the older voice came at him again, "Are you all right?"

He looked to his left and was startled to see a woman and a child. Young woman, boy child—maybe thirty and ten. They were two steps back from his side of the car; but at once their faces made him want them closer, though both were tense with doubt and fear. He lowered the window. "Good afternoon."

The woman was the one who retreated a step.

Fearless, the boy came on to the car.

Buck could have touched him. But he settled for touching the brim of his hat, a worn World War II bomber's cap. "Was I snoring too loud?"

The boy said "I'm Gid Abernathy. No sir, I just thought you were dead."

It struck Buck cold. He actually put a hand out before him and flexed his fingers; then he worked them quickly one by one as if at a keyboard, running scales. He smiled at the boy. "Thanks, Gid, but not yet."

Gid's worry wasn't spent. "The schoolbus sets me down right here. Ten minutes ago, when I got out, I saw you slumped at the wheel and all; so I knocked on your glass and you didn't budge. I even tried to open your door—"

Buck noticed that oddly he'd locked it on stopping, a first time surely. It didn't strike him as brave or risky that a child tried to help so trustingly. This time and place—1953 in the coastal plain of North Carolina— were slow and safe; everybody knew it and moved accordingly. Gid was curious and very likely kind, not heroic. Still Buck thanked him and started explaining how tired he'd got from skipping lunch. He should have known not to mention hunger in a woman's presence, not in those times. Maybe in fact he did know it and, half-aware, brought down the rest of the day on himself.

The woman was wearing a clean house dress with short sleeves that showed her strong, but not plump, arms. Her face was an open country face; surely she also had never met with harm or deceit. While Buck thought that, she stepped up slowly through his thoughts and rested a long hand on Gid's bony shoulder. "I'm Gid's mother, Nell Abernathy. He always eats an after-school sandwich. I'll fix you and him one together, if you like." It seemed as natural, and she seemed as ready, as if they were in a cool kitchen now and she were slicing homemade bread and spreading butter that her own hands had churned.

Buck fixed on the best of her homely features. She had an amazing abundance of hair, not the new rust-red you saw so often now since the war but the deep auburn you imagine on women in daguerreotypes, the hair that looks as if each strand bears a vein that pipes blood through it. He'd never seen the like in his time; and he wanted to say so but thought it would sound too forward, too fast. He felt he was smiling anyhow and that now was the moment to say his own name, open the door and stand up at least. But while his eyes had cleared in the nap, he suddenly wondered if his legs would obey. They felt long gone, not asleep exactly but not all there. He tried it though.

A half-hour later he'd drunk buttermilk, eaten a thick tomato sandwich on store-bought bread and said what he thought would be goodbye to Gid. Gid said he was due at a touch-football game a mile due north in the woods from here. As he shook Buck's hand, the boy made his plan sound natural as any town child's game. Only when his thin short gallant frame had shut the porch door and run down the steps did Buck recall his own country boyhood. *Whoever played football in the woods?* But he quickly imagined a clearing big enough for two pygmy teams. And for the first time, he thought of a father, *Who's the man around here? Is he dead, run-off or still at work?* But it didn't seem urgent to ask for him yet.

So he looked to Gid's mother, here at the sink four steps away. Her back was to him, and he knew on sight that now she'd literally forgot

he was here. Plain as she was, she was that good to see, that empty of
wishes for him to perform. All his life he'd tried to show women the
boundless thanks he felt for their being. From his long-dead mother
on the day he was born, to Lib his wife just yesterday morning, Buck
tried to tell each woman who helped him the strongest fact he knew in
life, *You're reason enough to stay on here.* He honestly felt it and toward
most women. To be sure, he knew there were bad women somewhere;
he'd never met one. So he always meant the praise he gave them,
mostly selfless praise with no hopes of any dramatic answer. And here
past fifty, still he fell in love several times a month, with a face in a
diner or crossing the street ahead of his bumper or dark on his back in
a hot hotel room, staring at nothing better to see than a ceiling fan and
old piss stains from the room above. He knew, and still could cherish,
the fact of love-on-sight whenever his mind saw a winning girl; it would
gently lie back on itself and tell him, *Buck, rest here for good.*

Not that he had. When he was twenty-seven he married Lib and
had touched no other woman since, not with a purpose warmer than
courtesy. That never stopped the joy or his ceaseless thanks. Hell,
women had not only made him but named him—*Will* from his
mother, *Buckeye* in childhood from his favorite sister. Now he fished
out his pocket watch—quarter to five, Lib would be starting supper.
He'd be half an hour late, no major crime. He folded the paper napkin
with a care due Irish linen, and he said "I'm going to be late for supper."
But his legs didn't move to stand and leave.

Buck's guess had been right; Nell jerked at the sudden sound of his
voice and looked around, wild-eyed for an instant. But calm again, she
said "You sure?"

"Of what?" Now his legs were trying to stand.

"That you can make it home?"

"Do I look that bad?"

She took the question seriously enough to move a step toward him
and study his face. "You look all right. I just meant, you being dizzy
on the road and sleeping so deep in the car when Gid found you—"

He was upright now but his head was light. "I could drive this last stretch, bound and blindfolded."

She looked again and said "You may have to."

Buck meant for his grin to force one from Nell. But no, it didn't work; she was solemn as church, though better to see. Could he look that bad? He tried to remember where his car was parked. Had he driven on here from where he pulled off? Had he left it there and walked here with them? And where was here? He looked all round him—a normal kitchen in a well-worn house, maybe sixty years old, a high dim ceiling, heart-pine floor, white walls smoked to an even gray. He said "Did we leave my car by the road?"

Nell seemed to nod.

So he looked to the door that Gid had walked through and aimed for that. At first he thought he crossed half the distance, but the final half then doubled on him and kept on multiplying the space till each further step was harder to take; and he thought his feet were sinking through the floor, then his calves and knees, his waist and chest, till even his mouth had sunk and was mute before he could call on Nell or God or the air itself for strength or rescue.

It felt like a healing year of nights, endless dark with heart-easing dreams. But when his eyes opened, it looked to Buck no darker than when he had tried to leave the woman's kitchen. He heard a clock tick, it was near his face, it said five forty—a black Big Ben, with the bone-rattling bell that he used to wake up early to beat. His mother solemnly gave him one, the day he left home for his first real job. But surely he'd told Lib to chuck it, years back. Or was he doing the thing he'd done so often lately—dreaming he was young, in his first big boarding house, strong as a boy, with the body to prove it in daylight and dark?

He was lying on his stomach on some kind of bed, under light cover. With both dry hands, he felt down his length from the top of his butt to nearly the knees. All that skin was bare; and upward, the sides of his chest and shoulders were warm but naked too. And when he felt beneath

himself, his dick and balls were warm and soft. Still what surprised
Buck was the calm soul in him—no fear, no regret in a mind as fearful
as any not locked in a state institution. He shut both eyes and gradually
searched the sheet beneath him, far as he could reach. His right hand
soon met a block that was big but soft. His fingers stopped against it.

A woman's voice said "You know you're safe."

Buck's eyes were still shut. In the hope of knowing whether this was
a dream, he thought *In three seconds I'll open my eyes, I'll look straight
ahead, then shut them again.* He counted to three, looked, saw the
same clock—five forty-two—and shut them again. It proved he was
alive, awake and sane, though apparently stripped in a woman's bed.
Nell, he finally thought of the name; then the memory of her face.
He firmly believed he still hadn't touched her. *Two things may have
happened. I fainted, somehow Nell got me in here, but why am I
stripped? Or I've been here days, maybe years, and am sick.*

He had not been prone to wild thoughts, not in his life till now at
least; and he halfway liked it. He suspected he smiled. *But Gid—oh
Christ. Is Gid on hand?* Buck tried to see if his hand could lift off the
pillow—yes. He held it up and listened to the house. No sounds at all,
not even from Nell. He settled back, brought his right hand to his face
and felt for beard—the normal stubble of late afternoon. So he told
her "It feels very safe. Thanks, Nell. But did I collapse? Am I someway
sick?"

She had seemed to sit on the edge of the bed, facing out from him
toward the door—Buck saw the open door and a blank hall beyond it.
And now she gave no sign of moving, surely not toward him. She said
"You had a little sinking spell. You may have blanked out, but you
didn't fall hard. I helped you in here. You slept half an hour."

"With you here beside me?"

"I just got back," she said.

"From where?"

"The phone. I called your wife."

"How do you know her?"

Her voice was smiling. "You'll have to excuse me, but I searched your pocket and found her number. I didn't know what—"

Buck said "Don't worry. But what did you say?"

"That you stopped by here, just feeling weak. That I thought you'd be back on the road soon, but did she know anything I ought to know?"

Buck almost laughed. "Such as, am I a killer?"

Her voice stayed pleasant. "Such as, do you have seizures? Are you diabetic?"

"What did Lib say?"

"Is Lib your wife? She said you were normal, far as she knew, just maybe exhausted."

Buck smiled but, on its own, his mind thought *Exactly. Nobody but Lib's allowed to be sick.* Lib was having what she herself called "the longest menopause on human record." Good-hearted as she was till five years ago, in the midst of that winter—with no word of warning— she suddenly balled up tight as wax till, for weeks on end, Buck could hardly see her, much less touch and warm her. Next she seemed to grow in-turned eyes, set all down her body, to watch herself—her own long stock of pains and self-pity, when he'd been the famous complainer so long.

By now they could sometimes laugh about it; and everywhere else in her life with others—their sons, her friends—Lib seemed to be waking from a long hard dream. She'd yet to welcome him truly back. And even if she did, the harm was done now and might never heal. She'd turned from his care and need so often that Buck was permanently lonesome in ways he hadn't felt since boyhood, roaming the deep woods north of his house and pressing his lips to dry tree-bark, just for something to lean his body against, some living thing to know that young Buck was clean and warm and could be touched with pleasure.

His right hand had stayed where it found Nell's hip. Three layers of cover kept them apart; he'd never probed or tried to stroke her, and she'd never pressed back into his fingers. As he went on waking, he began to like their balked contact. It gave him a trace of the friendly warmth of his sister Lulie, who was less than one year older than he and with whom he'd slept till his sixth birthday—pups in a box, warm and moving like a single heart.

He thought the next question and asked it clearly, "Whose room is this?" Before Nell could speak, he thought of the several answers he dreaded—her husband's and hers, even young Gid's. Not that he feared their linen and blankets, he just hoped to be in an open space, one he could rest in from here on out. He felt that happy and it sprang up through him in a peaceful flow.

Nell said "My father built this bed, oh sixty years ago. He and Mother used it, all their life together. She died and he came here to live with us, brought nothing much but his clothes and this bed. He helped us a lot till he went, last winter."

"He died?"

"Pneumonia."

"So it's you and the boy, on your own now?"

"Seems like," she said. She gave a little chuckle as if she sat alone on the moon and watched her distant amazing life.

"How do you live?"

She laughed out brightly. "Like squirrels in the trees! No, I sew for people. Gid works in the summer, on the next farm over. My dad left us a small piece of money. We do all right, nothing grand but enough."

Then the lack of a husband and father was sure. *I'll ask to stay.* Buck understood that the thought should have shocked him. It didn't. The calm poured on through his chest, and for several minutes he napped again. When he came to, his right hand was back by his side; and he spoke without looking, "Why am I naked?"

She said "Remember? It was your idea. You had a little accident, when you blacked out."

"Oh God, I'm sorry."

Nell said "Forget it. It was just in the front, a spot the size of a baby's hand."

"Did I wet my shirt too?"

"Not a bit," she said. "That was your idea; I tried to stop you."

Then I have to stay.

She said "I've got you some clean clothes out."

"You're a lightning seamstress." But then he thought *Her husband's clothes.*

"My dad's," she said. "You're his same size."

"I couldn't accept them."

"Oh he'd be thrilled. He couldn't bear to waste a half-inch of string. And Gid'll be way too tall when he's grown."

"You good at predicting the future?" Buck said.

She laughed again. "Height runs in his family, most of the men—"

Buck rushed to stop her before she clouded the good air between them with a useless name, "I'll be much obliged then, for one pair of pants."

Nell said "They're laid out here on the chair, khakis as clean as cloth ever gets and a clean pair of step-ins. I'm bound to go now and start our supper. You think you feel like trying to stand?" She seemed unhurried but as bent on leaving as if a walk to the dark heart of Africa faced her now.

Never, no ma'm, I'll lie right here. But he tried to move both legs and they worked. And his eyes were clear. All that refused was his mind, *Stay here. You're actually needed here. Not so, she and Gid are doing all right. Ask her though; just see what she says.* Buck heard his voice say the reckless thing, "Nell, what if I said 'Please let me stay'?"

He expected she'd wait to think that through. And at once she rose from the edge of the bed and took three steps on the bare wood floor. Then she said "We had this time, here now. Your own supper's cooking, up the road, this minute."

As her low voice moved, Buck knew she was right. She seemed to know much more than he remembered; whatever had happened, if anything new, it hadn't changed the tone of her voice. So at least he could trust that he hadn't been cruel or made a promise that he couldn't keep. Then he saw his course clearly. The decent thing was to try standing up, getting dressed, saying thank you and heading on home. So he turned to his side and threw off the cover. He saw his bare body; then said "*I'm* sorry" and reached again for the sheet at least, to hide his lap. For the first time, that he remembered here, he looked toward Nell.

She stood by a tall mahogany wardrobe and was half-turned away, lifting a bathrobe from the high-backed chair. She was naked as he and had been naked all that time she was near him. Before she could cover herself, Buck rushed to print her body deep in his mind. She was still young everywhere, with firm pale skin and no visible scars (Lib's side was pocked by the cavernous scar of a ruptured appendix). And the hair of her crotch was the same high color of life and health that she showed the world on her striking head. Then she was hid in the faded robe; and with no further look or word, she brushed on past him and left the room.

Buck went to the same chair, found his pants in a clean ragged towel, his shirt on a hanger—Nell had managed to iron it—a pair of blue boxer shorts and the khakis she mentioned. He put on his socks first, the shirt, then the pants. They were stiff with starch and two inches short. He thought of his mother's old comic greeting for outgrown pants, "Son, I see you're expecting high water" (they lived twenty miles from the Roanoke River, a famous flooder).

Was this time-out, here under this roof, some high-water mark in all his life? With the tender mind and heart he got from his mother at birth, Buck had wanted an unadventurous life. And except for Lib's three awful labors (two live boys and one dead girl), he'd virtually got it. His chief adventures had come in his head. Alone on the road, he sometimes lived through active nights with imaginary women. But mostly he still enacted each possible threat to life and limb, any time his family stepped out of sight. And his own body, strong till now, had always seemed a rickety bridge over too deep a gorge for a confident life in some place hard as the present world.

So sure, whatever had happened here—if nothing but what Nell owned up to, a fainting spell and a half-hour rest—was like a splendid volunteer, the giant flower that suddenly blooms at the edge of the yard, where you least expect, from a secret hybrid in last year's seed that has bided its time. When he'd tied his shoes, he stepped to the dark old mirror and smoothed his tangled hair. *Nothing visibly changed, not to my eyes—and who knows me better? Well, Lib but she won't see this time, whatever happened here. And if anything did, it was gentle and finished.* He could hear Nell drawing water in the kitchen. In less than an hour, if fate agreed, he'd be in his own house, among his first duties. He bent again to the peeling mirror and awarded his face a final grin. Then he went out to thank Nell Abernathy for one happy day.

In four months Buck will die from a growth that reached decisive weight in his body this full afternoon and threw him down.

His elder son has made this unreal gift for his father on the eighty-ninth passing of Buck's birthday, though he died these thirty-five years ago.

THE WARRIOR
PRINCESS OZIMBA

SHE WAS the oldest thing any of us knew anything about, and
she had never been near a tennis court, but somewhere around the
Fourth of July every year, one of us (it was my father for a long time
but for the past two years, just me) rode out to her place and took her
a pair of blue tennis shoes. (Blue because that was her favorite color
before she went blind and because even now, opening the box and not
seeing them, she always asked "Is they blue?") We did it on the Fourth
because that was the day she had picked out fifty years ago for her
birthday, not knowing what day she had been born and figuring that
the Fourth was right noisy anyhow and one more little celebration
wouldn't hurt if it pacified my father who was a boy then and who
wanted to give her presents. And it was always tennis shoes because
they were the only kind she would put on and because with her little
bit of shuffling around in the sun, she managed to wear out a pair every
year. So now that I was doing it, the time would come, and Vesta, who
was her daughter and had taken her mother's place and who didn't have
much faith in my memory, would look up at me from stringing beans
or waxing the floor and say, "Mr. Ed, Mama's feets going to be flat on
the ground by next week," and then I would drive out, and it would
be her birthday.

My mother goes out very seldom now, so late in the afternoon of
the Fourth, I took the shoes and climbed in the broiling car alone and

headed down the Embro road where she lived with Vesta and Vesta's husband, where she had lived ever since she took up with Uncle Ben Harrison in the Year One and started having those children that had more or less vanished. (My grandfather asked her once just when was it she and Ben got married. She smiled and said, "Mr. Buddy, *you* know we ain't married. We just made arrangements.")

All the way out there the shoulders of the dirt road were full of Negroes dressed up in a lot of lightcolored clothes that were getting dustier by the minute, walking nowhere (except maybe to some big baptizing up the creek) slow and happy with a lot of laughing and with children bunched along every now and then, yelling and prancing and important-looking as puppies on the verge of being grown and running away. I waved at several of the struggling knots as I passed just so I could look in the mirror and see the children all stop their scuffling and string out in a line with great wide eyes and all those teeth and watch my car till it was gone, wondering who in the world that waving white man was, flying on by them to the creek.

There was still the creek to cross that I and a little Negro named Walter had dammed up a thousand times for wading purposes. It would follow along on the left, and there would be that solid mile of cool shade and sand and honeysuckle and the two chimneys that had belonged to Lord-knows-what rising from the far end of it and the sawdust pile that had swallowed Harp Hubbard at age eleven so afterwards we couldn't play there except in secret and always had to bathe before going home, and then on the right it would be her place.

About all you could say for her place was it would keep out a gentle rain, balancing on its own low knoll on four rock legs so delicate it seemed she could move once, sitting now tall in her chair on one end of the porch, and send the whole thing—house, dog, flowers, herself, all—turning quietly down past the nodding chickens and the one mulberry tree to the road, if she hadn't been lighter than a fall leaf and nearly as dry. I got out of the car without even waking her dog and started towards her.

She sat there the way she had sat every day for eight years (every day since that evening after supper when she stepped to the living room door and called my father out and asked him, "Mr. Phil, ain't it about time I'm taking me a rest?"), facing whoever might pass and the trees and beyond and gradually not seeing any of them, her hands laid palm up on her knees, her back and her head held straight as any boy and in that black hat nobody ever saw her without but which got changed— by night—every year or so, a little deaf and with no sight at all and her teeth gone and her lips caved in forever, leaving her nothing but those saddles of bone under her eyes and her age which nobody knew (at times you could make her remember when General Lee took up my grandmother who was a baby and kissed her) and her name which my great-grandfather had been called on to give her and which came from a book he was reading at the time—Warrior Princess Ozimba.

I climbed the steps till I stood directly in front of her, level with her shut eyes and blocking the late sun which had made her this year the same as every year the color of bright old pennies that made us all pretend she was an Indian when we were children and spy on her from behind doors and think she knew things she wasn't telling. I wasn't sure she was awake until she said, "Good evening to you," and I said, "Good evening, Aunt Zimby. How are you getting on?"

"Mighty well for an old woman," she said, "with all this good-feeling sunshine."

"Yes, it *is* good weather," I said. "We'll be calling for a little rain soon though."

"Maybe you all will," she said, "but it's the sun and not the rain that helps my misery. And if you just step out of my light, please sir, I can take the last of it." So I sat down on the top step by her feet that were in what was left of last year's shoes, and the sun spread back over her face, and whatever it was my great-grandfather thought the Warrior Princess Ozimba looked like, it must have been something like that.

When she spoke again it seemed to confirm she knew somebody was with her. "I been setting here wondering is my mulberries ripe yet?"

I looked down at her knobby little tree and said "No, not yet."

"My white folks that I works for, they littlest boy named Phil, and he do love the mulberries. One day his Mama was going off somewhere, and she say to him, 'Phil, don't you eat n'er one of them mulberries.' So he say, 'No ma'm' like he swearing in court. Well, I give him his dinner, and he go streaking off down the back of the lot. That afternoon I setting on the kitchen steps, resting my feets, and Phil he come up towards me through the yard, no bigger than a mosquito, and ask me, 'Aunt Zimby, what you studying about?' I say to him I just wondering if them mulberries back yonder is fit to eat yet. And he don't do nothing but stand there and turn up that face of his, round as a dollar watch and just as solemn but with the mulberry juice ringing round his mouth bright as any wreath, and he say, 'I expect they is.' "

I thought she was going to laugh—I did, softly—but suddenly she was still as before, and then a smile broke out on her mouth as if it had taken that long for the story to work from her lips into her mind, and when the smile was dying off, she jerked her hand that was almost a great brown bird's wing paddling the air once across her eyes. It was the first time she had moved, and coming quick as it did, it made me think for a minute she had opened her eyes with her hand and would be turning now to see who I was. But the one move was all, and she was back in her age like sleep so deep and still I couldn't have sworn she was breathing even, if there hadn't been the last of the sun on her face and the color streaming under the skin.

I sat for a while, not thinking of anything except that it was cooling off and that I would count to a hundred and leave if she hadn't moved or spoken. I counted and it seemed she wasn't coming back from wherever she was, not today, so I set the shoe box by the side of her chair and got up to go. Vesta would see them when she came at dark to lead her mother in. I was all the way down the steps, going slow, hoping the dog wouldn't bark, when she spoke, "You don't know my Mr. Phil, does you?"

I walked back so she could hear me and said No, I didn't believe I

did. There was no use confusing her now and starting her to remembering my father and maybe crying. Nobody had told her when he died.

She felt for the tin can beside her chair and turned away from me
and spat her snuff into it. (She had said before that if she was going
sinning on to her grave after dips of snuff, it was her own business, but
she wasn't asking nobody else to watch her doing it.) Those few slow
moves as gentle and breakable as some long-necked waterfowl brought
her to life again, and when she had set her can down, I thought I ought
to say something so I got back onto how nice the weather was.

But she held her eyes shut, knowing maybe that if she had opened
them and hadn't been blind anyhow, she would have seen I wasn't who
she had expected all year long. "Yes sir, this here's the weather you all
wants for your dances, ain't it?"

I said, "Yes, it would be ideal for that."

"Well, is you been dancing much lately, Mr. Phil?"

She seemed to think she was talking to me so I said No, there wasn't
much of that going on these days.

"You a great one for the dancing, ain't you, Mr. Phil?" All I did was
laugh loud enough for her to hear me, but she wiped her mouth with
a small yellow rag, and I could see that—not meaning to, not meaning
to at all—I had started her.

She began with a short laugh of her own and drummed out a noiseless
tune on the arm of the chair and nodded her head and said, "You *is* a
case, Mr. Phil."

I asked her what did she mean because I couldn't leave now.

"I was just thinking about that evening you went off to some dance
with one of your missy-girls, you in your white trousers looking like
snow was on the way. And late that night I was out there on you all's
back porch, and it come up a rain, and directly you come strolling up
with not a thing on but your underwear and your feets in them white
shoes you was putting down like stove lids, and there was your white
trousers laid pretty as you please over your arm to keep from getting
them muddy. Does you remember that, Mr. Phil?"

I said there were right many things I didn't remember these days.

"The same with me," she said, "except every once in a while . . ."
A line of black children passed up the road. They every one of them
looked towards us and then towards the older tall yellow girl who led
the line and who had been silently deputized to wave and say, "How
you this evening, Miss Zimby?"—not looking for an answer surely, not
even looking to be heard, just in respect as when you speak to the sea.
". . . What put me to thinking about Mr. Phil is it's time for me some
new shoes."

And there I was with the shoes in my hands that I couldn't give her
now and wondering what I could do, and while I was wondering she
raised her own long foot and stamped the floor three times, and there
was considerable noise, as surprising as if that same bird she kept
reminding me of had beat the air with its foot and made thunder.
Before I could guess why she had done it, Vesta came to the front door
and said, "Lord, Mr. Ed, I didn't know you was out here. Me and
Lonnie was in yonder lying down, and I just figured it was Mama going
on to herself." Then she said louder to Aunt Zimby, "What you call
me for, Mama?"

It took her a little while to remember. "Vesta, when have Mr. Phil
been here? It ain't been long is it?"

Vesta looked at me for an answer but I was no help. "No Mama, it
ain't been so long."

"He ain't sick or nothing is he? Because it's getting time for me some
new shoes."

"It won't be long, Mama. Mr. Phil ain't never forgot you yet."

And that seemed to settle it for her. The little tune she had been
thumping out slowed down and stopped, and next her head began to
nod, all as quick as if she had worked the whole day out in the cotton
and come home and fixed everybody's supper and seen them to bed
and pressed a shirt for Uncle Ben who drove a taxi occasionally and
then fallen dead to sleep in the sounding dark with the others breathing
all round her.

Vesta and I stayed still by her till we could hear breathing, but when it began, small and slow, I handed Vesta the shoes. She knew and smiled and nodded, and I told her to go on in and let her mother sleep. I stood there those last few minutes, looking through sudden amazed tears at all that age and remembering my dead father.

Evening was coming on but the heat was everywhere still. I took the steps slowly down, and as I expected the old dog came up, and I waited while he decided what to do about me. Over the sounds of his smelling there came a crowd of high rushing nameless notes and her voice among them, low and quiet and firm on the air, "*You* can see them little birds can't you, Mr. Phil? I used to take a joy watching them little fellows playing before they went to sleep."

I knew it would be wrong to answer now, but I looked without a word to where her open eyes rested across the road to the darkening field and the two chimneys, and yes, they were there, going off against the evening like out of pistols, hard dark bullets that arched dark on the sky and curled and showered to the sturdy trees beneath.

THE ENORMOUS DOOR

T HE MONTH I was twelve, my family moved to a much smaller town than we'd lived in before. It was late in the Second World War; and in such a stable place, there were no vacant houses for the four of us. So we rented four rooms on the second floor of the small but rambling three-story hotel. My parents, my baby sister and I all slept in one bedroom; and though I'd long since discovered the pleasures waiting in my smooth body, at first I enjoyed their company. It reminded me of the ancient stories I'd grown up reading—everybody sleeping on the floor of a hut, even the animals (we had a beagle), and tasting each other's sighs in the night.

From the word *go*, I loved the air of mystery in the building. The stationery proudly and rightly proclaimed "Sixty clean rooms and a first-rate kitchen." Since my mother was a reluctant, though tasty, cook, we often ate in the tiled dining room. The good and copious country food was served by elderly black men, whose courtly air of self-respect and condescending wit would qualify them for any post today where bemused dignity is the trait desired. But my favorite part of our stay, from the first, was all those doors—sixty oak doors with brass knobs, locks and numerals, plus whatever secrets their tenants enacted in one-night stays or the thick walls' memories of lonely men inventing the ways to bear their lives.

When I had nothing better to do, I'd slowly patrol the carpeted halls.

20

I'd never quite stop to peer or listen; but if I heard a muffled voice behind a door, or even the scrape of a wire coathanger, I'd find a way to pause. I'd discover I needed to tie my shoes, or I'd lean to give my socks a good pull. Sometimes a claustrophobic man, or one so lonely he could stand it no longer, would leave his door cracked open to the hall; and then I'd make an extra pass, even slower than the first, to watch him open his pint of bourbon and take a long swallow, then frown at the taste.

Like many boys on the near edge of manhood, I had one constant flaming question—*What are grown men like, truly, in secret?* (I'd already given up on understanding women). I needed to study the make of men's bodies, chiefly the distribution of hair on faces, chests, armpits, groins, legs. I needed to know if any one of them but me had learned to use himself as I did, for the furious moment of self-ignition to which I was harnessed in joy and bafflement.

By the end of our second month there however, my hope of enlightenment was dying. The main cause was, I'd got no single useful look at a man's whole body, a man not too much older than me—say, fifteen or sixteen. Men that young didn't travel alone, and if they did they were sleeping in ditches. I doubt that my need, so early, was erotic. I'd have streaked for home like a shot dog if any human being, of any gender, had offered to touch me below the waist.

In one more laser-focused way, I was hot to find a truthful glimpse of the adult world—*the* glimpse (I knew the secret was simple) that would say I could leave the powerless trap of dumb childhood. But all I got in the first two months were a few cold glimpses of slack-gut Bible salesmen in their undershirts, scratching at themselves, and one old circuit-judge's bare feet as he sat exhausted on the edge of his bed and gazed my way in a smile I met with the pure revulsion that only a child in first adolescence can bear to sustain. If he could have known the force of my hate, he'd have vaporized in a puff of haze.

So maybe it was good luck in more ways than one that, about the time I was losing hope, my parents decided I needed a bedroom. They granted that four in a room was a crowd and I agreed. But I was still so locked in self-absorption that I thought they were being kind to me. It was years before I understood they were longing for privacy of their own. And before they told me, they had the solution. We'd rent the single room, without bath, across the hall from our main door. It did have a running-water sink and a bedside phone from which I could call them at the slightest need. Would I be afraid alone?

My relief and the thrill of a risk were so instant that I leaped at the chance. But after my father had seen me to bed on the first dark evening and shut my door—nobody locked doors in those safe days—I had second thoughts. Cold fears, to be honest. My fears at the time were all collected round the question I've stated. What hope on Earth did a boy like me have? I was slow at school, except for arithmetic. I was scaldingly shy with children my age, though a hit with adults, and a failure at every team sport I tried, though alone I could cut the air like a shaft; and speaking of which, I was also an archer, fast and true.

But when I lay dark that first night alone and faced a ceiling that might as well have been infinite space, for all I could see, my panic soon swelled for another round of the bitter certainty that I, of all the boys I knew, would stay a child. I'd wind up as one of those moon-men you see on the street, forty years old but with baby-soft skin and no trace of beard. Under my arms and across my groin, I'd be as hairless as a picked chicken. And every word that left my mouth would sound as if it barely escaped from a miniature can, that boxy and high. All the gates that boys pray to pass through—the tall gates opening inward on women and their hospitable good-smelling bodies—would stay as shut as they were tonight, though I'd see them above me everywhere I turned.

Half an hour of flinging in that direction, and I was ready to reach for the phone and yell for company. I knew better than to barge back in on my parents; they'd even moved my sister's crib to the kitchen when I left. My father was the finest man alive, but he had his limits. Beyond them, he never got mad or mean; he walked away slowly, looking very much like a would-be suicide bound for the bridge. If I called now, he'd come.

He'd check my closet, look under the bed and swear I was safe. He'd even lie down on the bed beside me and wait till I slept, if I asked that much. But since I'd never confessed my fear, and he'd volunteered no word of manly assurance, I couldn't speak now. He'd leave me at midnight, sadly confirmed in what I suspected was his new fear—this son had *stopped* and would not be strong enough to guard his old age, which he often laughed about as my duty.

But another ten minutes and I actually had the heavy old-time earpiece in my hand. Before the senile desk-clerk could answer, I heard a line of beautiful music, in a man's clear voice maybe six feet away. I knew two useful things at once—it was not my father, and it meant me no harm. I lay in a warming pool of calm and listened closely. I must have been nearer to sleep than I thought since, try as I did, I couldn't come up with a name for the voice, not to mention the tune. But that didn't scare me. Though the voice was a deep clear baritone, it went on carving the air between us in kindly shapes.

In maybe five minutes, I thought I could trust my legs enough to get up and try to find the man. On my bedside was a gooseneck lamp; but in my bravest choice so far, I didn't turn it on. I let my bare feet roam about to find where the voice was strongest or—whoa now!—the actual mouth that made it. The risky thrill had me glowing in the dark.

No luck though—nothing. I'd got as far over as the door to the hall, so I laid my ear against it. Maybe some young man was singing out there on the second-floor landing. In a dry town and county, there were still cheerful drunks; I'd seen more than one already in the lobby, mostly tired salesmen with sample cases. They'd mill around in the public space, praising the old-maid switchboard lady who quit at nine or calling me over to flip me a quarter for no better reason than that I might have parted my hair in the middle for comic effect or to give me a harmless pat on the butt and say something useless like "Be a finer person than me now, son."

When I heard nothing from the second-floor landing, I even silently cracked the door and looked across to the old leather chairs and the amber lamp—empty and sad. It was only when I'd shut myself in again and stood in place for my eyes to reopen that I saw the small light in the opposite door. By then the singing had stopped entirely. I've failed to mention an adjoining door between my room and the next room's bath. It was firmly locked of course from both sides; but now I discovered that somebody, sometime, had bored a hole low in the panel of the door.

The hole was no bigger than a robin's eye; it was about hip-level to me, and I was tall for twelve. Before I got down anywhere near it, I thought of how good an idea it would be. Young as I was, I well understood how one man could want to watch others in secret. I calculated, correctly I think, that the hole was drilled from my side inward—anyone looking from the other side into my room would have seen nothing more exciting than a door to the hall.

In the time it took me to work that far, the song recommenced with deeper swoops and sudden high lunges. At once I could feel its waves through the space. The young man was now in the bathroom beyond me. The lighted pinhole was aimed at him. The fact that the hole was still shining bright must mean that he was not looking through at me.

Still, crouching as I did and duck-walking three long steps to the hole was as reckless a deed as I'd put on permanent record till then. I started looking with my eye held back, five inches away. I could just see movement, something fast and white that flickered in the air. To close the gap and press my face to the actual wood was a further leap on the order of tasting a flaming sword. I closed the gap with chilling pride and waited for my eye to focus itself.

A man, buck-naked, was standing less than a yard away. I could see his body from the hipbone down. He was drying himself with a small white towel, and yes he was singing on and on. Now I could hear occasional words. Or a single word, over and over—*Darling* at several pitches and speeds, mostly deep and slow. Now there were also quiet stretches when his voice would soar in a wordless line that sounded the way the best birds look.

Those moments, I'd think of days I spent alone in deep woods, near our last town, times when I dreamed that people had vanished—painless but *gone*—and that now I was welcome to choose my life with nothing to see me but small wild beasts and the rare meat-eater, stronger than me but not as quick. In maybe three minutes, the man bent over to dry his feet. The hair of his head was thick, black and stiff as horsehair; but still his eyes and mouth were hid. Only enough of his arms were clear to show him, not just an agreeable singer but young and long-limbed, with firm tan skin.

There at my chink on a whole new world, I managed at least a quick thanksgiving to whatever power had answered this much of my need. Now all that was left was some deed or characteristic act which would prove that this partial masculine body was a preview of mine, a credible promise that I would also grow with the years.

But he only took one step in my direction, turned to face me and held rock-still. At first I was disappointed and hoped again that he'd *act*. Young as I was though, in an innocent time, I had no specific deed in mind, surely no blatant sex show. In fact, afflicted as I was by the mindless tumescence of a growing boy, there at the door that night, my parts were in unaccustomed abeyance. Not because I was scared—it was just my mind that burned with the sight. And in a few seconds, my mind understood the gift he was giving—for now at least, a warm anatomical model before me, almost in reach if the heat of my eye had widened the chink as it might have.

His penis was a good deal bigger than mine and also calm. The hair above it was black and wiry as African hair, though he had to be white. Like a great many boys (I've since discovered), my main anxiety resided in the hair. I knew I had a penis and balls that promised to grow; but would I eventually sprout this hair, in the true man's place? I tried to see how it differed from the texture of hair on my head. But aside from the curl and the wiry shortness, I got no closer to certainty.

The odd thing was, he didn't seem to know what a treasure he owned. He seemed to be drying the whole miraculous region absently, like an elbow or foot. But then he dropped his towel to the floor and spent the better part of a minute giving his parts a thorough inspection. I had no knowledge of syphilis then or even crab lice, so he may have been making a sanitary check. Whatever, he found no cause for alarm. His prying hands went back to his sides, and again he just stood frankly before me.

But was he standing here for me? Did he know I was near? Had he drilled the hole in the door himself, that afternoon? And who could he be? I'd seen no body this young and strong anywhere but the bathhouse at our swimming pool, and then I was always rushing to hide my own white skin. I suddenly thought of a possible answer. I could go to my phone, call down to the desk-clerk and quietly ask who was in 211. I stood up to go before I was balked by the child's steady fear, *He'll think I'm dumb and laugh and tell everybody.*

So next I told myself, "Go to sleep. You've got school tomorrow, and you'll be worn out." By then my mind seemed ready to be sensible; and I had actually touched my bed when the song recommenced, still nearer but somehow higher and milder. I had read a boy's version of *The Odyssey* and knew about the sirens' song. I even covered both my ears; but the voice came through, as piercing and magnetic as before. The light from the hole was a little dimmer but I knelt again.

What was in there now was entirely different. It stood where it was the moment I left. And the size and lines of its body were the same— a male human shape, larger than me but no great giant. The change was, it no longer showed tan skin. It had put out a stunning coat of plumage. The best I could see, his feathers grew in all kinds and sizes, from stiff wing-vanes to the softest down; and they all aimed upward on the body in colors that far outclassed any peacock I'd seen. I recalled a painting in *The National Geographic* of Montezuma and his noble lords, dressed in robes of the finest bird-feathers, whole tribes of birds killed off in the making.

This was no robe though; this was the actual skin of some creature unknown to science, not six feet from me. What had started as a strong but normal young man had just now changed his skin into this. Even the groin I studied was now all feathered in green and gold. And what had been a man's calm penis was a single winglike thing, flared up boldly toward a face I couldn't begin to imagine or hope to see. Yet strangely again, I felt no fear. And the human words it had sung before were now just notes in a seamless melody.

If this had happened six years ago, before I started school and tamed my mind, I'd have watched all night, or fallen asleep upright at the chink or died from prolonged exposure to the man-bird or flown with it some place better than this. But foolishly rational as I'd now become, I came to a common adolescent conclusion—*This is some kind of trick, intended to show the entire world, in garish red, what a fool I am.* I took a last look as the song went softer still and higher and the gorgeous fraud began to lean forward, on the absolute verge of showing its face. Then I got up again, went to my bed and hid myself to the ears in cover. Wildest of all, I'd seen so much that I even managed to sleep fairly soon, though the voice never quit while I was conscious.

In that town then, all twelve grades of school were housed in one building. I was in the seventh grade; but the next day at lunch, I heard the news that, over the weekend, the high-school math and physics teacher had suffered a stroke, was paralyzed and had been replaced by a man from Raleigh, named Simon Fentriss, just out of college. As soon as I knew, I began to hunt for him. Could he be my neighbor? But he wasn't on view at the teachers' lunch table. Nobody my age knew anything about him but his name; and only the wildest girl knew that much—Amantha Perry, with the premature breasts that everybody loved like a cause for pride that our class owned such a natural wonder.

I kept my previous night a secret; but the minute I got to the hotel that afternoon, I walked to the front desk with all my courage and asked if Mr. Fentriss was back?

The clerk said "I haven't seen him come in yet. He could've slipped past me though and be upstairs."

"In 211?"

"Right next to you, yes."

So the man I might take algebra from, two years ahead, was a curious trickster who practiced at home to fool more than me. I dropped in to let Mother know I was safe, then said I'd get right down to my homework in my new room. What I did though was actually lock my door, lie on the narrow bed and stroke my body to the ready relief it eagerly gave me. Then I fell straight to sleep, recovering what I'd lost in the night.

The room was nearly pitch-dark when I woke; my luminous watch said five-thirty. And through the adjoining door, I focused on the sound that had waked me—water filling a basin. I crept to the door and tried the hole. Two legs in dark-brown corduroy trousers and heavy brown shoes, the waist of a sweater and again the flash of a towel, drying hands. It all constituted a sight as normal as bread on a table, no song, no word.

But back in my room, the evening and night continued normal. He played his radio but kept it low, he made a short phone-call that I couldn't hear, he peed maybe twice. In everything, far as I could see, Mr. Fentriss moved like the model I'd asked for—a competent grown man, young enough to watch. And when he brushed his teeth at eleven, he was wearing light-blue boxer shorts on normal skin, though shaggier than mine.

After I heard him switch off his lamp, I also quit and climbed into bed. As I crouched up to sleep, I told myself to face the serious possibility that I might have dreamed the night before, might have put myself through fantastic hoops—a bird-man-neighbor—to celebrate my first chance to meet a whole dark night with no blood-kin in the sound of my voice.

*

The next few days passed similarly. I never saw him in the hall, the lobby or the dining room. But the bottom half of him, through the chink in the door, went on being so natural and tame that I quickly lost my taste for spying. And when Amantha rushed up on Friday, pointed across the lunchroom and whispered "Ain't he fine?" it took me a second to know who she meant. *Simon Fentriss*—I swear both names spoke out in my head as clear as gongs. And by the time my eyes set on him, he was facing me from ten yards' distance, past ten dozen children in the usual noontime barely contained riot. When our eyes met, I sheered off quickly and waited till old Mrs. Root spoke to him; then I got a long look.

The way some people can guess your weight to within three pounds, I've always been good at fixing ages. Only the richest plastic surgeon can hide you from me. And here I'm speaking of the 1940s, four long decades before such doctors had got this far off the beaten track. Simon Fentriss was twenty-four; he must have been in the war and finished college a few years late.

He had a strong face with the Indian skull I hoped to have—high cheekbones, a jaw you could make points with. The stiff black hair started high on his forehead; and though it was combed, it looked coarse and strong. In all, I thought he had the power to last for decades and work his will, both of which were my aim. Then his wide mouth opened on a long kind laugh. Nobody had laughed *with* old Mrs. Root in living memory, and she plainly liked it. After that, he didn't look my way again.

And I felt easier thinking he found my eyes by chance. But within five minutes, the way you do for the rest of your life, I picked Mr. Fentriss as my next magnet, the thing I'd try to grasp in secret and gain a man's power and knowledge from. You could call it *love* and be nearly right; I've loved only two people more than him in all the years since.

Yet I never met him, never shook his hand, though I did once brush his coat in the hall. I tried many times to draw his attention, in the lobby mainly; and he'd grin and nod as if I might have been a thriving houseplant or a Shetland pony, not the partner to the secret power of his manhood. Today boys twelve years old start babies on girls every minute, but back then we stood in shadows till they called us and asked our names. So I never spoke more words to him than "Hey"; and Mr. Fentriss never called me once, not by name as I hoped. I couldn't ask Mother to invite him to supper; and in two more months, Father found us a house and moved us out of the hotel for good. Before I was old enough for algebra, we left the whole town and moved to Kentucky. But one more night truly happened and it changed me.

Within a month of coming to town, Mr. Fentriss began having weekend dates. There were few unmarried women around, of his age and station; but he seemed to take them up one-by-one and give each a whirl. A whirl back then consisted of a trip twelve miles southwest to the next-larger town, a steak-supper there in the Glass House Restaurant, a movie maybe or (in summer) a dance in a big tobacco warehouse and whatever fun you could manage to take between then and driving her home at dawn.

Most Friday nights I had no more to do than any other night, so I'd stay close to my room and hear Mr. Fentriss dress for his date. It gave me ragged scraps of feeling what a man might feel with a whirl in prospect and nothing to stop him. I'd mostly lie on my bed and listen, having given up watching him, early on, since nothing had happened after that first night. And anyhow he hadn't sung one more note of audible music nor said a word, much less turned into whatever he was that first fine night. So listening to the sound of water was enough and the slap of his large bare feet on tile.

By that far along in his preparation, the simple sound of his moving feet would be enough to sling me far, on a golden thread way over the ground, where I could trace my whole life's path—a tall man making his dignified way, leading his wife and dependent children and earning respect. In flight, my body would stiffen and beg for the lightning moment my hand could give it, the finest drug on Earth and free. By the time Mr. Fentriss was ready to leave, I'd be serene as the Dalai Lama, gazing down on my homemade Himalayas of snow and dazzling white birds, riding the lustrous columns of air toward safe night and rest.

Then I'd join my family to play board games or three-handed bridge, with all of us tuned to the radio. By quarter-past eleven I'd always manage to say I was tired and head for my room. Each Friday I vowed I'd stay awake till Mr. Fentriss got back in and showed whatever he'd learned or won, in the hours of dark, from whatever girl or woman he'd found to bear his weight or spurn his touch.

But I almost always managed to sleep before he turned the key in his lock (more than once, when he was out, I tried his door handle). A time or two I woke to hear him brushing his teeth. My radiant watch might say three-thirty or, once, past five; and I'd lie awake as long as I could—a few stunned seconds—to check for music or any trace of song. I'd always hear water and sometimes the jingle of coins on his bureau. Once I thought I heard the beat of his iron bedstead as he lay down and used himself in whatever masterly way men employed. But even at the hint of that much news, I was too young to dredge myself upright from the bogs of sleep and rise to search what I could see of his legs and crotch for my own fate.

There was one last chance though, the weekend before we'd leave the hotel; and by various means I struggled to keep myself in the shallows and welcome him back in a secret alert. My father was an abject coffee-fiend and would always let me drink along with him whenever I asked. So with supper that Friday, I drank a good deal. And I stayed with the family till nine o'clock before bowing out. When I went to my room, I took a hidden tablespoon of dry ground coffee that I laid by the bed. I set my Big Ben alarm for midnight. Then I cut off the lamp and, high as I was, I managed to rest. It was not sleep exactly but a good kind of waiting, with snatches of dream in which again I was sure of my step as I led two sons that looked like me on a rocky path toward a broad clean river.

When the bell went off, I caught it at once. I said an earnest word of thanks to the god of sleep; then got up, washed my face at the basin and also peed. Any traveling man then, in the days of scarce toilets, understood that a basin with running water served nicely, provided you ran hot water once you finished. Then I fished my book from under the mattress, got back into bed, packed a big pinch of the coffee grounds into my lower lip and started to read, for the hundredth time, the most exciting words I knew.

The book was the only thing I'd stolen till then in my life. Two friends of my parents lived on the third floor, overhead. They had just got married the previous summer, and one of their wedding presents was a book called *Sacred Joy: The Marital Beacon*. I'd caught sight of its orange binding on visits upstairs, and a glimpse of its color and four-inch thickness was enough to thrill me dangerously. It was famous among the rare sex guides of those dark days for medical candor combined with a radical view of the "beauty" of sexual congress. Until moving here, I'd never seen a copy outside bookstores, much less run the risk of owning one. So hard temptation seized me; and one weekend when our friends left for Myrtle Beach, I walked in, seized it and hid it in my room. I figured they'd be bashful at owning a copy and wouldn't complain. So far I was right.

Whatever guilt I knew I should feel, it drowned the moment I cracked the pages. The paper was that old cream-colored stock I loved so well, fat and rough to the touch. I couldn't know then how fast it was on the way to dissolving in its silent acids (slower than me, come to think of it now); so all I felt was the almost terrifying blaze of discovery—sacred joy!—as I ate the pages in a first quick skim. Here were actual words I'd dreamed of hearing and guaranteed genuine drawings of parts that I'd seen nowhere but bathroom walls in brutal guesses by fools no better informed than me. The thought that I had it in my own hands, in a private room with a lock on the door was almost more than a twelve-year-old could handle back then.

I'd sometimes check five times a day to see if it still lurked under my bedding. And when I'd be with my parents and sister, I'd lapse into moments of shaking fear—the book would burst into sudden flame and gut the building, charring us all. Or worse, we'd hear footsteps on the stairs; and the sheriff would enter to chain me for larceny. But I never returned it; and strangely our friends never mentioned the theft, though I knew everybody was sure who did it.

Still that last night, I counted on it as my best insurance of staying awake for Mr. Fentriss. In the weeks I'd owned it, I ricocheted wildly through random sentences, too thrilled by my luck to read in sequence and pausing only to drain my pressure. Now I'd turn to page one and force myself to read straight on, with care not to sap my strength too soon. It was not a bit easy; the early chapters were about the virtues of youthful chastity and what unmappable joys await the virgin pair who meet at last on a blossom-strewn matrimonial couch. But I stumbled through the placing of "tapers" at safe yet strategic points round the bed, the moment of unison thanks to God, the exquisite patience required of you the groom, the tender use of your ample hand to coax her gates as wide apart as care can bring them, then your sadly noble conquering *thrust* and the hours of nurture incumbent on you as she learns to bear this lifelong breach that precedes your fertile life together in God's great family.

It got so anatomically vague that even I found myself half nodding; so I skipped to the third chapter, "Oral Tradition," and was back on form in very few moments. It was near two o'clock when the sound of a turning key alarmed me. Had I locked my door; was Father coming in? I hid the book and reached for my light before I realized the lock was not mine. Simon Fentriss was finally back. I seldom let myself say both his names; but in that charged moment, they sounded so clearly I feared I'd said them. I went on and killed my light anyhow. Darkness would make these last few seconds of wait more exciting. And I'd stay in bed till I heard his bathroom light switch on. He was one human being who never performed his toilet in the dark.

I never heard it. His entry to the bedroom had been nearly silent; and as I listened, the silence deepened. No old hotel, built mostly of wood, can keep quiet long. The more nights you stay, the better memory you get of each noise. Just in my short time alone, I'd learned the voice of every board in the two flights of stairs outside my door. You could have landed by silent helicopter on the twelfth step on the third-floor stairs, I'd have caught you blindfolded. And I knew not only the boards and tiles but the two kinds of carpet in Mr. Fentriss's rooms. I could tell, just by the sound of the soles of his feet, each time he forgot to lay down a bath mat. On my last night, there were no sounds at all. Not while I waited.

But lying in the dark was a big mistake. In that much empty black stillness, I slept. Any other boy, with a lipful of coffee and a brain aflame with imagined joy—rosy girls astride hard boys—would have waited it out. So all I know, thus all I can tell, is what I'm still convinced occurred, and not just in the chemical-dump of my brain that night. No vision from dreams, no handmade picture, has stayed with me the way every line and color has stayed, every move and smell of what was showed me at some real point on the clock before dawn.

What finally woke me was the voice again. By the time I knew I was conscious however, the pitch had risen till it seemed more like a separate flying thing, a small silver plane at a perilous height, than anything made by a human body. And it sounded farther away than before. I tested the air for any hint of danger. It felt well-intentioned so I got up, crept to the door and knelt.

What was there was the feathered man again, a grander thing than I remembered—no man at all now. It was on its own knees, facing away; but this time at least I could see the head, if only its back. It bore a thick crest of peacock green that was laid down now, though it twitched with a feverish life of its own and threatened to rise like a giant cockatoo's roused glory. The song was still in the air between us but was no more a song now than this thing was Simon Fentriss in feathers.

I was almost sure the thing was working—eating slowly or dancing in place. Its arms or wings were wrapped round something beyond it, but its torso hid whatever they held. In ten more seconds, it began to shiver in graceful waves that it seemed to control and that caused no pain. Till then I'd never seen a hummingbird stall in place yet spin its wings too fast to see. When I finally saw one, I thought back to this night and this thing's waves. As it went on trembling, I started wanting to see its face, if any such thing could have a face.

And in another moment, the voice quit. As if my hope had just now reached it, the great head turned with a glacial slowness and looked my way. There were eyes, to be sure—they had to be eyes—and an open mouth that gradually made what human smiles attempt to make, a warning sign of joy so strong it threatens to spill and flood you both. But all the skin was covered with feathers the size of dimes, set like gilded scales on a fish.

It was then I knew I was seeing an angel. Since it looked unlike anything I'd seen in pictures of angels, I must have been told somehow in the instant, some wordless way. Though I lacked the time and the words to think, I understand now that it was, past doubt, a being sent as a bridge to me from whatever god intended my life. Was it here to show or teach me things, or would those round eyes draw me now through the wood of the door and use me also?

In a whisper but clearly, I said the word "Please." I had no idea what I meant; but as scared a boy as I'd been for years, I now committed my first brave act. I gave in freely to what came next.

I think it made the slightest nod; and then it moved a few inches to the right, still watching me.

Both its arms were holding a woman, an actual woman of skin and hair. Whatever its mouth had done to her, it had not been harm, not where I could see. She was standing upright, aimed at my door; and I could see the whole midst of her body, from under her breasts to nearly her knees. She was young and firm and, while I knew she was as earthly as me, I also granted with wild delight that she was better than any girl I'd dreamed and loved when reading my book. The pyramid of curls in her groin was the same bright gold as the angel's face.

I never saw more of her body than that, for next the angel drew itself back against her. With occasional high recollections of song, the body resumed its waves that—for minutes longer—I went on understanding as joy. But soon in every plume and vane, it began to burn with light, not fire.

Again I suspected I ought to be scared but I wasn't. I held to my one fact—an angel was here, to give me this. If I burned away in sight of his dance, then at least I'd stayed like a man and borne it.

I well understand that veterans of the movies will yawn at this as a down-home version of *Star Wars*, with sex. But when it happened next-door to me, *Star Wars* was more than thirty years off; and sex in space had not been invented, though angels had. What I saw, I saw. And now it was ending. The waves became eventual shudders; and with the one high soaring voice, there was now a second in skewed but winning harmony.

I knew some destination was near. But the point it all was climbing toward was screened by light, no doubt with mercy to me. As the trembling angel and his real woman climbed, the light kept streaming from inside his body; the voices kept flying, till all I heard was one joined voice. And all I saw was a single great pulse at the core of the burn.

I thought of the still-live heart of a dog I once saw hit in the road, too hurt to live but struggling on. I bore that too. I may have even spoken again; what I felt anyhow was all grades of thanks. Something huge, far past any power I knew, had done this for me. Or near me at least. And had kept me brave enough to stand and learn it. By the time I said what little I said, the flare was cooling and I was tired.

But I stayed in place. No twelve-year-old I knew till then—even Jesus at the same age, preaching in the Temple—had been entrusted with this big a secret; if so, he kept it. I must see this finished. So over maybe the next three minutes, the light leaked off and my sight cleared. Then I could see what was left in the room, which was once again Mr. Fentriss's bath—him and the same young woman, both real, both naked as newts.

I wanted to know her name and face; I had a suspicion she might be the ninth-grade world-history teacher, Miss Watkins from Kansas (she'd washed up here as the war slowed down and let her out of the WACS at Fort Bragg). If so, Miss Watkins was as good to look at, by day, as here. Her face though far outshone her midriff, as I could attest to myself in private for the rest of the year.

Their bodies looked understandably tired, with a few sweat trails. And their visible muscles were slack from whatever work they'd been part of. Was it them after all? Had they, two average public school teachers, been converted to heat and light as a demonstration for one hot boy and then cooled back to safe blood-heat, all in maybe five minutes in a wood hotel that somehow survived?

Could be. Whatever the answer, they were there that night as sure as the angel. I knew when I stood up, went to my bed and switched on the lamp—the palms of my hands were bruised dark purple, though I'd felt no pain, where my fingernails gouged at the pitch of the act. And those eight cuts became my license to watch Mr. Fentriss the best I could. Like a starving hawk, I watched his movements every chance I got. The same with Miss Watkins but not so closely, since I couldn't swear to her having been there near me that night. The only times I managed to see them were moments in the lunchroom, near-passes in the halls. But I never brushed either of them again, and even at lunch they never so much as glanced my way from their chilling plates of macaroni-and-cheese with green beans. And of course I never looked again through this fine door that had shown me so much.

The coming Easter my parents planned to visit our friends in the Shenandoah Valley. I begged to stay home. I was thirteen by then, and what I dreamed of was taking ten dollars out of my savings and renting room 209 for a night and searching again. I had no expectation, or wish, to see a further round of wonder. They laughed in my face, and I drove off with them to watch chained bears at mountain gas-stations and a fat old Indian that charged to pose with you. But as long as we lived in that same town, it hurt my mind like a stove-in skull, how much I hoped to understand what the angel meant—I knew it *meant*, no question it didn't. And was that girl a messenger too but allowed to look human to brace my courage?

As I write this tale, I'm sixty years old—money in the bank and proud of my work that I pray to do till the night I die, a much-missed wife who died two years ago dreadfully of cancer, a son and daughter in driving distance with their own good children who bear my presence at Christmastime as if, in all they plan to do, their grandfather matters seriously.

I know I do. And now you know, having read this far. I'm the last man alive, so far as I've heard, to whom a god unquestionably came and showed the sacred joy that waits in any human body, if it has the wild courage to find its adjoining door and kneel to its chink or drill its own and wait there bravely—or scared to the bone—till at least one normal other body spreads its secret reckless beauty to taste and eat.

A TOLD SECRET

I DOUBT YOU KNOW how that hour ended, though it's in your mind through this long pause. After we'd choreographed our limbs through so much perfectly aimed free-flight, we understandably slid off to sleep. And while we were out, the sun that had been so fine all day worked round to the window and found our bodies. Half an hour before, we'd have overmatched its glamor and heat. But sleeping, I cooled; so the light was welcome down my bare side. I woke at the touch and for maybe ten seconds was simply thankful, a frozen child, for unblocked light. Another pause and it came to me, plain and incontestable, *Nothing will ever be better than this*—thirteen years on, it's true as it was.

Then I heard your breath and—though I was on my side, turned left—I knew you were still out. I generally took any chance to watch you truly asleep (your eyelids seemed the thinnest scrims on the last few secrets you maintained; I spent long stretches, hoping to read them). But that afternoon I dreaded to see you frowning or worse. I'd read, thrust up in banner type, the blatant claim that our meeting had counted less with you than me.

I even lay and punished myself the common way, inventing words for your shut mind and scrawling them on my own mockup of the back of your eyes—*He's crashed the last gate and ruined me. All I can do is beg for his death.*

39

I understand I'm more than half wrong. You're a free adult; you've let me cross a full continent to be here. You own the keys to this room, not me—they lie in reach of both your hands, beside your pillow. I dumbly multiply the proof—your sheets and quilt; even the mice behind the walls above our nights are your guests here: you could trap them out.

So maybe five minutes later, I turn, slow as the nearest glacier north. Ten inches apart from your face, I hold, hardly breathing but scenting at once the native health of your actual skin. Friends of Alexander the Great report that he gave off, day and night, the clean odor of mountain thyme—the natural gift of a generous soul, unknown on Earth till then except in the wake of a vanishing god. Twenty-two centuries, eight thousand miles west, I smell off you the same dry gift, a lure you're helpless not to spread.

Your still shut face defeats all fears—no frown, no smile: a peaceful, entirely unreadable calm. Behind this cabin, Mount Hokum above us, starved wildcats wait this instant for dark to scrounge our foulest rancid scrap. They'd tear and grind your peaceful hide to the final bone; but here you lie, serene as slate. And all my hawk-eyed apprehension can find no chink in such frank trust.

I risk your name a time or two—not whispered, not loud—but you stay gone. And I wait, peaceful now as you, in hopes of nothing but your next breath, the sight of your eyes when your mind decides to see a world not made by you.

A quarter-hour, twenty minutes, still gone, serene. My dry mouth starts to beg for water. Standing, walking, will surely rouse you. So I wait a last moment and know a last move. Entirely quiet, I rise to an elbow, reach and lift the old-gold hair from your right ear and say the best gift I ever gave. Silent, I say *Because of now, this perfect day— because of what you are and spend, believe one fact if all else fails: you'll live with me long past our separate crushing graves.*

*

Thirteen years on, I tell whoever reads these lines. Gone, unspeaking, still again, will you wake now, read and find the promise I planted then and say at last you know it's true?

WATCHING HER DIE

MY FATHER'S last aunt moved in with us when I was ten and she was a thousand. Eighty-three, to be truthful, and virgin pure but sadly broke down. She'd lived near us, in her family home, all her life and mine. Only when she tried to rise one morning, stepped through a wormy board by her bed and stayed there trapped till my father found her just before supper, did she even consider giving up the old house.

Pure as she was, she'd raised my father when his own mother died; but once he got her foot unstuck, even he had to put the truth to her plain. "Dear Lock, time's up. You've outlived your house. We offer you ours."

Aunt Lock knew *we* did no such thing. Not if *we* included my mother, which it had to. Mother had dreaded Lock's arrival from the moment my father proposed. She always said "He popped the question, then showed me the fly in his ointment—he was duty-bound to see Miss Lockie to the grave in kindness, assuming he or anybody outlived her." To explain that my mother was known, statewide, as loving to a fault and a martyr to kindness is a quick way to say what Lock was like by then anyhow, that far gone in time.

Her short legs were bowed as any hoop. She stammered every word; and she understood less than any two geese, though she didn't know it. She thought she specialized in God and healing. You'd run in the house with a bleeding hand; she'd seize your wrist and say "Lick it, son!" When your mother protested that spit might infect it, Lock would tell her "Child, watch the animal kingdom. They lick everything that hurts and it *heals*." She'd of course known several people who cured the last stage of cancer with timely licks from a warm wet tongue, preferably their own.

With all the facts Lock knew about God, she was oddly silent in public with adults. It was mainly with me that she let them slip, when my parents were absent. I had the standard childhood way of avoiding my parents when I felt unhappy. Like other children I'd walk off alone or seek out somebody neutral but kind—like a maiden aunt in the dim back-room of the busy house. I'd lie on the hooked rug Lock set by her bed and let her pour what dammed up in her when my parents wouldn't listen. It was frequently memories of my father's boyhood. I asked for them often, not understanding I was near the age when I'd start being a man myself and would need to know how another boy managed to grow and make his own son.

I doubt Lock comprehended that, having changed so little through the length of her span. But something would make her tell a brief story about Dad's mischief and then let a quick strange moral appear in the empty air like a quirky motto stitched on a sampler. She'd tell about the time he stripped the setting from the supper table, plates and all, hid them in the sideboard and ran for the woods while the family were coming from the porch to eat. Once she described the empty table and the ten baffled faces, she might draw a feeble breath and say "God showed him tricks like that every day."

She'd never explain but move back to telling how warts were cured by words alone, in new-moon light. I doubt she expected me to think for an instant about God's purpose in teaching Dad tricks, but of course I'd think of little else for the rest of that day. And the several times she let me know how "God has promised I will not die"—no explanation— I turned the promise over all ways from there on out, for her life and mine. I'd seen a child die on the street beside school, and I felt no need to share the fate.

Those words about death were almost the strangest, except for the time I confessed to torturing a boy with a withered arm at school—I twisted it hard and watched his face. Lock heard me tell the whole miserable act; and when I expected at least a scolding, she almost smiled, looked far out the window and said "Keep it up if you need to—worse, if you must. You're making him better than you by far." So altogether from the day she joined us, Lock became even more a part of my mind than the rest of my family (I've acknowledged my parents, plus I had two sisters older than me).

In addition, more than anyone else I knew, I could always find her. Her room was behind a dark brown door right off the kitchen; she was generally there in a green rocker or—on a dry day when her asthma let up—she'd be on a walk through the deep back yard that passed through carefully tended grass into thick ranks of scarlet sage and then into pines, far as any strong boy could hope to walk, much less an old woman on miserable legs.

It was such a day, I'm recalling now. Mid-October, a spotless sky and air as dry as a bona-fide desert, though pleasantly cool. Despite all that, I'd had a miserable day at school. Because of the strange way Lock responded to my old confession of cruelty, I'd left the crippled boy alone. He'd even started bringing me gifts of dried fruit from his father's store on the edge of town where white-trash houses shaded into black with no firm line except in blood when a trespass occurred. Peaches, apricots, pears and figs. I didn't care for them; but I didn't say so, just gnawed them at recess along with the boy and watched him grin.

Yet on that grand October day for no discernible human reason—a day for brave deeds—I suddenly saw my hand reach out, take that boy's arm and wrench it behind him till I heard a serious crack on the air. The boy said not a word of complaint, though silent tears rolled down his face; and his eyes never blinked. Then I watched him walk to the edge of the playground by himself and slowly test if his arm was broke.

His back was turned but, just by the slowness of how he moved I could guess the pain and the tears still rolling. His arm moved finally, straight out beside him like the school patrol; and then he just walked down the sideline and turned at the street and headed home, a quarter-past noon. As it turned out he stayed gone four more days.

By three forty-five on the guilty day, as I walked home, I knew I should climb to my white room, fall down on my back and beg the Lord, who'd memorized my meanness, to pardon me someway without demanding I find the boy and beg him first. His name was Zollicoffer Phipps, called Zollie. But since my path led through the back woods, I was deep in the cool shade, stroking through twigs and abusing my soul, when—Lord!—I heard my name out loud.

"Dalton Burke" in a high soft voice but keen as a sunbeam.

I stopped cold and tried to guess was it human. I'd had more than one communication from the unseen world, years before I was ten; so I had some grounds for judging the matter. But in five more seconds, I couldn't decide.

"Dal? Answer me." I'd also been asked to answer before by unseen voices that never spoke the question. But something made me guess it was a woman, even a girl—where the hell was she? (I'd started to cuss). I turned every way. Just thicker leaves and deeper shade on every side. All my life, what I can't see, I seldom address; so I held my tongue.

"D-*Dal*."

Aunt Lockie out this far alone?

Exactly that, though it took awhile to find her. Ten yards away in a neat clearing I'd never noticed, Lock sat on a huge uprooted oak. It looked freshly killed. The roots were still damp, but we'd had no wind or lightning for a month. Anyhow it had landed at the right height for Lock. She was firmly seated, holding a limb; and for once her small feet touched the ground—in chairs they tended to dangle useless. She was cool as the day and not even panting, so I figured she'd been back here a good while. That, and the distance she'd covered, made me think she'd wrangled with Mother, badly this time. So I moved on closer. "You waiting it out?"

Lock even smiled and refused the question. "I'm 'fust-rate,'" she said, one of her numerous old-time replies that gave me a fit when school friends were near, though many of them had similar antiques in their own back rooms. In general back then children knew many more old people than now. Living near them, having to kiss and greet them, we learned far more about the speed and goal of life than children today. But I honestly doubt it made us gladder to know them or kinder. Anyhow there was nothing Aunt Lock had done that was really first-rate—or so I thought then—except raising Dad, and that was behind her.

That opened a path for me to say "I'm worse off than I've been in living memory."

Mother would have laughed at the solemn phrase; but Lock took me as she'd taken my father, dead-earnest at all times, even when we teased her. So now she pointed to the dry ground below, and when I sat she said "What's your plight?"

I told the whole story in her own way. Lock couldn't just say "It happened one afternoon last week." She had to back and haul a good deal to establish the day, the hour and weather. Then she'd dress whatever rooms were involved and give you descriptions of everybody with such precision that years ahead you could pick them out from an angry mob. I told her every fact she didn't know since I left her at breakfast—the disappointment I'd had in reading class and all the other extenuators. Then I painted my crime in grim detail and said "I've mentioned excuses, Lock. They don't count, do they?" I hadn't looked straight at her eyes for a while; and even when she started, I couldn't look.

She said "Very much to the contrary, Dal, th-they all count against you." From then on she barely stammered again. She'd given me lengthy thumbnail sermons before on a lot more subjects than the powers of spit, but nothing had prepared me for what came next. She said two or three more sentences on the no-count nature of childhood meanness. Then she took a brief silent pause.

I risked a glance at her, but she was faced straight out beyond me at nothing but leaves, far as I could see.

Then still looking off she seemed to take a wide left-turn in her mind. She said "Now I'm asked to die for you, son."

She'd long since learned not to call me *son*; it riled my mother. So trying to grin, I said "I'm Dalton, your favorite great-nephew. And Dalton's asking for no such thing." Jokes from Lock were scarce as snow, but I thought somehow she was teasing me. Young as I was, I knew about Jesus dying for the entire human race; but I couldn't think Lock was meant to follow him. Bad as I felt about Zollie's arm, I didn't quite see myself in Hell. So I said "Lock, I've been died for, remember?"

At first she nodded. Then she thought awhile longer. By now she'd all but proved she was listening, so I watched her closely. She was not watching me; she still faced the woods. And with every second her face got paler and her skin got thinner. Soon a thousand hairline veins stood out in her spotty brow and down her throat. They turned dark purple as if her blood was desperate for oxygen, dying fast. In the space of two minutes, that seemed like a month, I had to believe my great-aunt was dying because she was asked.

She was somehow dying because of me and the cruel acts I couldn't stop doing, young as I was. Strangest of all, the change didn't scare me, though I finally said "Aunt Lock, hold back. You said God promised you'd never have to die." If she heard, it made no difference at all. So I finally made the painful offer I'd tried to shun. I said "I'm to blame." Still no good; she was past my reach.

By then her eyes had drifted shut, and soon they also started to die. The lids, that were always paper-thin, went nearly transparent till I could see the ghost of her pupils gazing through—thank God, not at me. And her lips, that had also thinned, drew up in a thorough smile of a sort I seldom saw on Lock unless my father bent to kiss her on Christmas morning or at the supper he always cooked for her birthday. More than once Mother said "Miss Lock's never known a whole happy day; and she means us to share her discontent." So while I estimated that her death was less than a minute ahead of us now, I asked "Are you happy?"

Any other time she'd have stammered badly at that big a question. And she did wait so long I thought she was gone. Then a voice, from farther out than she'd gone before, said plainly "Happy? No. But I'm honored, yes, and glad to serve." Another long wait while every cell of her skin went still as the dead oak she sat on.

I thought "Any second, she'll pitch over on me." And I braced to catch her.

But one more time that far voice spoke. "Shut your eyes now, son, and count to a hundred."

I not only shut my eyes; I bent way down and hid my face in my folded legs. I figured when she fell, I could roll her aside. Then I counted slowly. As always I got confused in the 60s and backtracked some; but from 95 on I spoke the last numbers. I thought if Lock was hearing me still, she'd say what next when I got to 100. But no word came, no sigh, no breath. Even the leaves all sounded dead. I shouldn't have been the least surprised since I almost never prayed anymore. I kept the decision a private fact; but at nine, I decided God had more work on his hands than my slim business. Still that October afternoon again I spoke out loud once more, "Sir, help me please." Then I looked.

I've said Lock never played tricks on us, but even the greatest actor on Earth couldn't have imitated death this well. I'd seen two old great-uncles dead and a friend of mine in the wreck of his bicycle near our school. Lock was dead all right; and I still wasn't scared or thinking ahead to what I'd tell my mother now, not to mention Dad when he got home. I put one finger out toward her, waited in midair to see if she'd flinch, then went the whole way and touched her wrist where it still gripped the limb.

Up till today she'd kept a steady heat, lukewarm and weird, like standing oatmeal; so I'd always shied off feeling her skin except when she absolutely required it. Now though she was cool and not weird at all, peaceful really. My finger stayed on her flesh so long, I felt her go maybe five degrees cooler with not a trace of pulse or twitch.

I stood up finally and stepped well back. No way on Earth I could get her home now with my schoolbooks and lunchbox. But I should stretch her out or she might fall—any breeze would tip her down in a heap. That's when I suddenly thought I should listen, listen at least as hard as Lock. Whatever voice had spoken to her might have some useful advice for me. Children this side of the early teens are still smart enough to know such things. I put both hands down calm at my sides, shut my own eyes and tried to slow my heart. It obeyed so soon that, for one cold instant I thought it was stopping too. But I stayed in place; and next I heard it thudding onward, slow but trusty.

Then a voice, the same old voice I'd heard in early years, said "Leave her here, boy. She's where I want her." I held on a good while, hoping it would offer some word on where I should go next, who I should hunt down and what I should say.

And eventually, once a crow had called, the voice said "Now you are free again; she saved your skin."

My mind was suddenly clean as a washed slate. I tried to think of my name but couldn't. I knew just one thing, *Haul your rusty ass out of here.* So young as I was, I hauled it home.

Mother was out, my sisters were on a field trip to Raleigh, the cook wouldn't be back till five o'clock. Dad, being a doctor, might come in early or not till past bedtime. For once I hated the house being empty, but I still wasn't what you could truly call scared. I believed the voice. I knew not to worry now about Zollie. He'd been repaid already by whoever ran the show, this peculiar day. Someway tomorrow or by Thanksgiving I'd make my amends. He and I would be friends for life; I'd be his protector.

In my own room though, my private belongings began to wake me. Familiar objects, like a Barlow knife and a silver dollar from the year I was born, stared back at me and saw my shame and my wild rescue.

An actual human being just now had volunteered to be my scapegoat and pay some debt I owed to justice. I had felt bad enough just on my own; but nothing had made me understand how hard the sky or the voice behind it viewed my cruelty and all such acts here and elsewhere always. Being not just young but normally human, I hoped the voice would let me lead my parents to Lock and say no more than that I'd discovered her, coming from school, dead there in the woods. And since the last place I'd said a prayer was in my bed, I lay down there, got still again and asked if I could take my father to the woods and not explain why Lock died on me.

I thought the voice was ready to speak, but no word came that I could hear.

I told myself the answer was *Yes.* I still think it was.

The cook came in a while later and worked on, singing so high she woke the local bats before sundown. Soon after five Mother was suddenly downstairs with her, laughing and saying "No, no, *no.*" I stayed in my room and finished my homework, praying that Dad would turn up shortly, then would climb up to take his evening leak and check on me. I honestly think, till the day he died, he thought I'd evaporate some unannounced morning between the time he left me at breakfast and touched me upstairs again at six. I'd known forever he prized me more than both my sisters, I understood my disappearance would ruin his life, I mattered that much in all his plans. But I wouldn't know why till I had one satisfactory child of my own, the green-eyed daughter who rewards me still.

When I heard Dad finish washing his hands, I was still on the bed. I rolled to the wall and balled myself up to look like sleep.

He came in anyhow, sat on the edge and tapped my hip. "Sarge, you sick?"

Just before I had to respond, I suddenly wondered if that was it. Was this whole afternoon some kind of sick dream? Was I laid up now in a hospital bed with a record fever, a puzzle to science? Was I the dead person and this was eternity? Had Zollie gone home and prayed for justice and all I was going through now was just my strange but fair deserts? I'd been saved though; I still trusted that. So I turned to face Dad and said "No, tired."

Dad studied me to test my honesty. Then he nodded. "*School*-tired." He had disliked school as much as me, and he always said how amazed he was that he spent thirty years on something that bitter. Whatever, it had made him a first-rate surgeon, widely sought. Next he sat on quietly, watching his hands. He had told me more than once lately how much he was hoping they'd last him out till he had to retire. He thought sometimes they'd begun to quiver.

So I whispered clearly "Stop looking; they're *still*." It made me think of Lock dead of course, but I kept my secret.

He searched my face again and then laughed. "You know too much."

I said to myself *He's righter than ever* but I laughed too.

"How's Lockie feeling?" That was nothing strange. He knew how Lock and I most afternoons listened to the radio from four to five— "The Lone Ranger," "Terry and the Pirates." Lock's favorite was "The Phantom," who knew "what evil lurks in the hearts of men." Every day without fail, Dad would see me first and ask about Lock—had we liked our programs? If I said yes and that Lock was normal, he could put off paying a before-supper visit to her back room and risking Mother's temper.

With him I always knew I could reach for the truth at once, no fooling around. I told him "You need to see something right now; but don't ask questions, not yet at least. Let's get downstairs, quiet as we can, and out to the woods."

The way he replied was the reason I'd loved him all my life and honor him still, long past his presence. He said "Then lead me."

Silent as braves we got outdoors, on through the yard and into the trees without so much as a yell from Mother, though she had to be watching at the kitchen window.

*

When we were a good ten yards into thicket, and our backs were hid, I stopped and faced Dad. I even asked him to step back a little. "I need to tell you something hard."

He'd after all had people die in his hands, his literal hands; so his face didn't frown, and he stepped well back.

When he pulled a red dogwood leaf to chew, I suddenly thought I'd spare him the mystery, Lock's awful merciful words before leaving. I said "Aunt Lockie has passed away. I found her body back deep in here when I came home from school. Her heart just stopped, no sign of blood. I couldn't lift her. She was peaceful and safe, so I didn't tell Mother but waited for you."

My father was strong on the order of iron, strong but ready to love what he loved. I'd seen him cry only once till then when a girl child died as he touched her heart to repair a valve. He climbed to my room that terrible evening, not stopping for Mother, and sat on my bed and said "This one finger *touched* her heart—for the first time, son, to give her the life she ought to have—and it stopped, stock-still." Here in the woods though, dusk coming down, he let my news pass into his eyes. Then he looked back awhile.

I thought he was hiding his grief this time—Lock was his mother to all intents—and I said "Don't mind. I won't tell a soul."

But he faced around and was smiling a little. He said "Have you told me the real truth, Sarge?"

I must have looked troubled.

"She's not been killed? You said no blood—"

I raised my hand in the standard boy's oath. "Sir, she's peaceful." That much was true.

Dad was no sunny-sider; he tended to frown. Till now I'd never heard him say any death was a blessing. I thought he meant Mother; it would finally lift the load of poor Lock off her mind and back. I nodded. "That's why I didn't tell Mother. I saved it for you."

Dad shook his head and waved me off; I'd misunderstood. What came next was the hardest thing he ever told me. "I've waited for this through long years now." He looked inward past me and stepped on forward to take the lead for maybe five yards. Then he recalled he didn't know where she'd be. I would need to guide him.

He'd never conceded that job to me, not till that moment; but I stepped forward proudly. As I passed him I touched his arm for an instant. "It's not bad, I told you—not one scratch or bruise."

As we went it suddenly dawned on me some dog might have found Lock and mauled her face. So I moved on faster than he usually walked, to get there soon enough and warn him back if her body was changed. For at least five years, I'd forged alone through these same trees, trying to imagine I was threatened by Indians and vicious beasts, all barely hid an arm's reach off. And I always tried to imagine *bravery*, how to walk toward what might be my death without the hair of my neck rising cold. Finally that dusk—with Dad behind me, trusting my knowledge—I was truly fearless. My blood ran warm and steady and smooth as an August river, and the hundred-yard trip seemed longer than Lewis and Clark's whole cross-country trek.

By the time I reached the edge of the clearing, the evening light could barely get through the circling pines. But right away I felt relief. Lock was still upright on the fallen tree, her eyes were still shut, one hand was holding the small limb for balance. I knew a single gust or a hard footstep might tip her forward in a heap on the ground, so I waited in place till Dad caught up.

Faced with a problem, he mostly reacted speedily. Now though he waited silent on my left.

I looked to his profile, and at first he wouldn't face me.

Then he relented and his gray eyes were calm. He all but whispered "Sarge, you're wrong."

I quickly tried to guess his meaning—what else was this old lady but frozen in *rigor mortis* by now? What had I misunderstood?

Dad reached across the gap between us, took my hand and slowly walked toward her.

In my eyes anyhow Lock seemed to quiver as fast as a hummingbird's wing, a visible blur. I figured the force of our gentle footsteps was reaching her body, but it hurt to see, and I must have pulled back on Dad's hand a little.

Anyhow he turned me loose and went on.

I stayed where I stopped, maybe ten feet back.

Dad slowed his pace but went right to her.

She was dead as ever, to my mind at least. Even the bird's-wing blur was still. For the first time I saw what you see on death masks—whatever fears and pains they knew, the dead faces of famous men, like Napoleon, are smooth as children. Maybe death is that easy. Or more likely maybe, before they can mix the plaster and make your mask, the pull of gravity eases the lines of fear and age, leaving you young and hopeful again. My great-aunt didn't look young or glad; but she did look tranquil, a whole new thing in the years I'd known her. I saw Dad's hand reach out toward her hand; and I thought *Lord God, she'll powder to dust*. I'd read about ancient maidens who powdered when their perfectly lovely corpses were touched. Nothing happened though that I could see. He'd only laid two light fingers on her, and soon I figured he was hunting a pulse.

The fingers rested gently on her wrist for a good long while. Then he seemed to shake his head in sadness. But next he drew back and almost whispered "Dear Lock, it's me."

I'd never heard him say *dear* till now. Mother told me once "He'd die for us both, but he won't say *darling* like everybody else." All I could think was *If he's glad she's gone, why's he trying to wake her?* I thought he was trying to pay his respects, to show he was there and honored her body. Then I knew we would have to call for help, strong men with a stretcher. I stepped on to Dad and quietly said "Before much later, we need to get help."

He waited a moment and said "We may have the help we need." With his hand still on her, he whispered "Dear Lock, now answer me." Then he said "Please. This moment."

And over what felt like the next ten years, Lock came on back. Almost no daylight was reaching us, but I thought I could see the color of blood creep back through her face. I knew I could hear the creak of her breath till finally her eyelids quivered fast, and then she was looking up at Dad.

He didn't speak but offered his other hand.

At first she didn't take it. Her eyes searched round till they located me. She didn't quite frown, she surely didn't smile, she gave a slight nod. Then she took Dad's other hand and gradually stood. He looked and acted like the olden beau she never had or the ideal son she claimed he'd been from the day he was born. They passed right by, touching me nowhere, and walked till they reached the thicket again. Lock stopped there and, facing just the woods, she spoke out plainly "Are you taking me home?"

Dad said "I am." They both moved on and I fell in behind them.

But I stayed close enough to hear that, every few yards, Lock would speak—short phrases about the leaves, the light, the weather. I'd never heard her say so much when she and I walked; her breath was too precious.

It seemed her breath was sufficient now, though she stammered some. We were all the way out the far edge of the woods with the house there before us—the kitchen lights—when Lock stopped once more and said a whole sentence. "It's bound to be time to eat and I'm hungry."

Till then I'd never heard Lock mention hunger; she ate a lot less than a hand-sized bird. So I stood in place and watched Dad lead her on to the house and up the back steps, slow as ever.

I was baffled beyond description of course. But I had the bare minimum of sense to wait and fix their picture deep in my mind—a son and his mother somehow alive and certainly changed. At the time I wasn't thinking I'd need the picture ever again. I didn't plan to store it buried in hopes it would bloom someday with news and hope. But here this instant I could take up a pen and draw them for you—Lock and my father—clear as I saw them, though full dark had very nearly fallen between us. All these years later I bring it up on the screen of my eyes more times than most memories.

Whatever happened, what changed in Lock from that night onward was seen by nobody else but me. All her worrisome traits stayed with her right on—the stammer, the ugly marks of age, the draining worship she paid my father were strong as ever. With all the strangeness of those dim hours in a single day, neither Dad nor Lock ever brought it up in conversation, public or private. It might just have been a long dream I had to punish myself for the vicious maddog kenneled inside me, hot to lunge. Did Lock really suffer some brand of death? I had no medical implements with me of course, but even now I'm ready to swear that she wasn't breathing when I left her upright that afternoon. Or was she merely fooling to curb a boyish tendency in me?

Was it all Lock's idea, or was she truly driven on by an unseen judge? If it was some brand of practical joke, it was the first and only such in a long solemn life. If death truly seized her, the way I saw it, then who brought her back—my dad with a touch and one loving word or the unseen judge maybe changing his mind? Dream or fact, it serves Lock's purpose of punishing me, to this minute now when I tell the story; and I've had maybe more occasions than most men to punish myself, again and again for common meanness, by simply calling back to mind the sight of a woman dying for me.

There is one fact I can still bring forward to prove that afternoon's story true, a chain of actions and deeds that happened to sane human creatures other than me. From that time forward, though she'd talk with me as before in public—at meals, in rooms with my parents or sisters—Lock never addressed me in private again, not so much as a *yes* or *no*. Even in public where she often addressed me as before, she never spoke my name, not once. I'd come home every day from school at four, turn on the radio and lie on the rug. Lock would hear the sound and come in from her room—slow and creaky, rolling on her bowlegs like some old sailor—to take her chair and hear our shows with no single word. She'd smile, laugh or frown in accord with the story. She'd meet my eyes as often as ever, always kindly. She'd darn any wornout sock I brought her; she'd still lean down and scratch my scalp as the plots tensed up in our radio shows.

But that was the only way we touched, from then till her second and last departure. I was never again compelled to kiss her powdery whiskers; never smelled her musty neck again, for all our laughter—and we laughed a lot. At first I thought of ways to scare her—to call the firetruck or claim my head had burst into pain like a gasoline fire and would split any instant and scald us both. I held back though and learned to respect her, the way you'd trust a St. Bernard that saved your life but was naturally mute.

That much of my great-aunt was dead to me, shut up and gone. It made me think of a thousand questions only she could answer. They all pertained to my father's youth, things he'd never tell me—what he was weak at, ways he failed before he got so strong and fearless. Finally though I had to believe Lock had told me the last hard thing to know. And she'd told it plainly in real daylight in actual woods the final day I was outright fierce. *You can somehow choose to pay the debts of a needy boy or other grown soul if you have that much to give and are willing.*

Lock died again, for what I assume was the final time, eight quick years later when I was away—my first year of college. Dad's letter said she went in her sleep, no trace of a struggle, ninety-one years old. At first I thought it was the worst kind of death; no living soul could truly mourn her. For years the thought seemed perfectly sound. But then I got my adult life and the ones I cherished, my daughter chiefly.

And the year I was fifty, a business trip took me back to my hometown for several days. The last evening, with time to spare, I found our house. We'd sold it fifteen years before when Mother died. Still it was in better shape than me, fresh-painted though empty—a weathered sign *For Rent* in the yard. I had the good sense not to look in the windows, but I found myself walking straight for the woods.

For whatever reason they were very much changed. Contrary to the general rule of memory, the trees were a good deal taller than before with serious girth way past my reach and a thickness above that shaded out the old thicket and briars and left a clean floor. My legs at least recalled the path; and dead though it seemed those forty years since, Lock's fallen oak was still where she left it the night Dad roused her. Some of the bark had peeled away, but the sturdy trunk was hard as ever. And the small limb that Lock's hand gripped was waiting still. I'm no great keeper of souvenirs; but suddenly there in the quickening dusk, I thought I'd snap off the limb and take it—my great-aunt's anchor in a world she surrendered. And I made two tries, but the limb refused and then I was glad.

Lock Burke blazed up there instantly before me—in my mind, understand—and the sight of her vanishing face and life repeated, clear as the long-gone voice that counseled me, a truth I hold ever close to my heart and mean to enact when my own chance comes.

I've doubted an awful list of things in my long life—the truth of my wife, my friends and God, even my all but flawless daughter. I've doubted that the Earth itself should last or my tragic race, all humankind. But since Aunt Lockie paid all for me—alone in dark woods with night coming down, that she couldn't navigate if we hadn't saved her—I've never since doubted my place in the world or my endless duty to find at last the needful heart for whom one day I lay my own life down and depart.

SERIOUS NEED

I WAS THIRTY-SIX years old, with all my original teeth in place, most of my hair and my best job yet—furniture sales on Oak Park Road, the rich-lady trade with occasional strays from the poor east end. Now that our girl Robin was twelve, Louise my wife had gone back to nursing at the county clinic. She worked the day shift; so that wasn't it, not my main reason, not lonely nights. And by Lou's lights, which are strong and fair, she was nothing less than a good woman my age that tried hard, wore time well and hoped for more.

I wasn't too badly destroyed myself, according to her and the mirrors I passed. So I didn't crawl out, wrecked and hungry, to chase fresh tail on the cheap side of town. But honest to Christ I saw my chance after three and a half of what suddenly felt like starved decades that had stalled on a dime. I knew it on sight—a maybe last chance to please my mind that had spent so long pleasing everybody else that was kin to me or that had two dollars for a sofa downpayment.

She came in the store one Saturday afternoon that spring with her mother—a heavyset woman and a tall girl. I thought I had a hazy notion of who they were, a low-rent family from up by the boxmill, most of them weasel-eyed and too mean to cross. The mother had one of those flat raw faces that looks like it's been hit broadside with a board this instant—none of which meant you'd want to fool with her; she had prizefighter arms and wrists.

Both of them stayed near the front door awhile, testing a rocker. Then they headed for me; and before I got my grin rigged up, I saw I was wrong and remembered their name. They were Vaughans; the mother was Irma Vaughan—she'd been in my same class at school, though she quit at fourteen. I remembered the day; she sobbed as she left, three months pregnant (the child was a boy and was now in prison, armed robbery of a laundry).

I said "Miss Irma, you look fresh as dew on a baby's hand." I had no idea what I meant; words just come to me.

Her face got worse and she stopped in her tracks. "Do I know you?"

"You chased me down one Valentine's Day, when the world was young, and kissed my ear."

For a second I thought she'd haul back and strike, but she hunted around my face and found me. "Jock? Jocky Pittman? I ought to knowed!"

After we laughed and shared a few memories, she said "Here, Jock, you've bettered yourself—good job like this, that old crooked smile. See what I done, my pride and joy." Big as she was, Irma skipped a step back and made a neat curtsey toward the girl. Then she said "Eileen, this is one smart man. He can do long division like a runaway car. You listen to him."

Eileen looked a lot like Ava Gardner in schoolgirl pictures (Ava grew up half an hour south of us). Like a female creature in serious need that you find back in the deepest woods on a bed of ivy—a head of black curls, dark doe eyes that lift at the ends and a mouth that can't help almost smiling, night and day. Almost, not quite, not yet anyhow.

I estimated she was near fifteen. So I held my hand out and said "Here, Irma, you're not old enough to have a girl eighteen."

Irma said "So right. She's sixteen and what?—" She turned to Eileen.

Eileen met my eyes straight-on and said "Sixteen and four months this Wednesday noon." She met my hand with her own soft skin; those eyes found mine and stayed right on me like I had something she roamed the world for and had nearly lost hope of.

With all my faults, I know my mind. Ask me the hardest question you got, I'll answer you true before you catch your next full breath. I met those steady hazy eyes, volt for volt; and told myself *Oh Jocky, you're home.* She felt that right, that custom-made, with two feet of cool air solid between us.

Not for long. Not cool, not two feet apart. That evening my wife and I were trying to watch some TV family story, as true to life but sad to see as a world-belt wrestling match in mud; and Lou said "Jock, you're dreaming upright. Go take you a nap. I'll make us some fudge."

Robin was off at a friend's for the weekend; the house was quiet enough for a snooze. But I said I was fine, just a touch dogeared.

Louise could sniff my mind through granite. She came up grinning, took my face in her hands, studied my eyes at point-blank range and said "I hope you're dreaming of me in there."

Both my eyes went on and shut of their own free will and stayed shut awhile. For a change Louise didn't start on one of her Interpol hunts for the secret locked in me, but just the feel of her firm hands stayed on my skin, and in two seconds I knew I'd find Eileen Vaughan someway before midnight, or I'd keep driving till the rainbow ended in a pot of lead washers.

She was on her porch in an old-time swing with one dim light bulb straight overhead; and she faced the road, though I guessed I was too dark to recognize. I didn't want to drive unusually slow; but I saw enough to know I was dead right, back in the store. A socket to hold this one girl here had been cut deep inside my heart before I was born and was waiting warm.

Her dress was the color of natural violets exposed to black light, that rich and curious anyhow. The rest of the house looked dark behind her (I vaguely knew there were no more children). Irma was likely playing bingo at her crazy church, the hollering kind. But I drove past to see who might be parked out back. Then I recalled Irma's husband had died some years ago. Like so many drunks, for some weird reason, he lay down to sleep on the train tracks at night.

And by the time I'd gone a ways onward, turned and pulled to the shoulder out front, I told myself *Eileen Vaughan's young enough to be your first daughter. You don't know who's got hooks in her or even who she's hoping for now. Go lay your feeble mind on the tracks. It'll be a lot quicker and will hurt just you.*

But what Eileen said when she saw me was "I guessed it would be you before you turned." Not said like she was the Earth's big magnet that drew me in but like the next nice fact of the evening—lightning bugs, the sweet crape myrtles and Jocky Pittman.

Dark as it was, her eyes got to me, even stronger now. I said "Miss Vaughan, my actual name is Jackson Pittman. Nobody yet ever called me that—will you be the first?" I reached from the ground up toward her swing and gave her the great ball of deep red myrtle I'd picked in the dark.

She disappeared down in it awhile. Then her eyes looked out. "Mr. Jackson, reach inside that door and switch off the light. Let's swing in the cool."

The fine and terrible thing is this. It is in the power of one young woman still in her teens to cooperate with your orphan mind; and inside a week, she can have you feeling like you're surrounded by kind ancestors, crown to toe, all waiting to do your smallest wish with tender hands. I've already said I had a good wife that tried the best she understood and a thoroughly satisfactory child. I hadn't exactly been beat by fate; but like a big part of the married men I knew in Nam, many nights of my life, and a good many days, I felt as hollow as a junked stovepipe. That is, till Eileen Vaughan took me that same mild night, saying she warmed the way I did, on sight at the store that same afternoon which felt like two lifetimes ago.

*

From there it went like a gasoline fire. If I could give you one snapshot of her face and mine, close together, you could spell it all out in however much detail you needed. We burned that high in every cell; we taught each other ways and means that even the angels barely know, though for six fast weeks we never moved a step past the three-mile limit from the midst of town. At first, to be sure, it was all at night on past her house in the heart of a thicket behind the mill.

But by the third week we were wild enough to meet by day, every chance we got. On three afternoons she babysat her brother's kids (his trash wife had skipped); but otherwise she'd get out of school and walk a straight line to the old cemetery where I'd be waiting by my paternal grandfather's plot—he lies among three exhausted wives and nine children, having outlived them all.

On weekdays nobody passed through there except black boys heading to swim in the creek; and they didn't know either me or her, though after a month, when boys passed too near the car more than once, Eileen sat up, buttoned her blouse and said "Mr. Jackson, if this is your best, I'll thank you and leave. Don't look for me here, not after today."

I asked what she meant, *If this was my best*. Turned out, she meant the swimming kids. She thought they might be seeing her skin. I'd lived long enough to estimate she had almost as fine a skin as God had produced; and while she was not conceited a bit, every move she made showed how steady she meant to treat herself with respect. "Nobody else has" she said that day.

I asked who she meant.

"Every goddamned man and boy in space." She was still half-smiling but I knew she was mad by the crouch in her eyes.

I laughed and said "I don't think Eaton's quite the same thing as space."

But she knew her mind like I knew my own. She said "So long and best of luck," then got out slowly and aimed through trees toward her mother's house a long mile off. When she vanished she looked like my last hope.

I let her leave though and said out loud in my thick skull *Thanks, kind Lord. You cleared my path.*

He hadn't of course. Or I strowed mess and blocked it again by that weekend—my old path here, a dependable worker, husband and father. Eileen had left the car on a Tuesday. By that Sunday evening, bright and dry, I was truly starved out. So I crept on toward her house again. It cost me almost all I had to climb those sagging steps and risk a knock. I felt like some untold crossbreed of the world's worst junkie and a child molester of the saddest stripe. The porchlight was on and burned my mind.

But knock I did, a single blow, and nobody answered. I waited a long time, in plain sight of slow cars passing behind me, knowing my name. Then I knocked once more and finally begged out plain through the wood, "Eileen, I'm pleading with you. See me." In another few seconds, I heard bare feet.

She'd been asleep. First time I saw her confused like that, a hurt child with a pale blank mouth. It cut me deep as anything yet; I felt like the cause. But then she surprised me.

She said "Big *stranger*" but she still hadn't smiled.

In twenty more minutes we were back in the cemetery, parked by my graves. Eileen wanted to talk about school—how it was nothing she could use in the future; how she planned to quit at the end of this year, then make enough money to own her own soul and go to a secretary school in Raleigh. She saw herself in a clean single room in a nice widow's house with a private door-key and kitchen privileges in case she wanted, every week or so, a softboiled egg or a slice of dry toast. Everything else good would follow from that.

I listened and nodded long as I could. But once she paused I politely asked her to leave the car with me—till then we'd stayed shut up inside.

She waited to think it carefully through but she finally nodded.

So I came round, opened her door, led her over to Grandad's plot and read her the tall old moldy stones.

To be sure, she was bored as any teenager faced with death; but she tried to listen. I think she guessed I was up to something entirely new; at first she let me run it my way, just listening and nodding. I told myself the night before that if I could take her that near my kin and still feel like I needed her bones beside me for good—her skin and bones—then I'd tell her plain and ask for her life.

I was reading my own grandmother's stone—*Her children rise and call her blessed*—when Eileen came up quiet behind me and played an age-old playground trick. She bumped the backs of my knees with hers, and I came near to kneeling on Gran. First I was shamed to be ambushed and act sacrilegious (I never knowingly walk on a grave), but all I could hear was high clear laughter.

I never heard Eileen laugh till then; we'd been so dead-down earnest and grim. But when I finally stood and turned and saw her leaning on a baby's stone, lost in her fun, I still had to wait. I was stunned again. Nothing I'd seen from here to Asia, awake or dreaming, offered what looked like that full an answer to every question my life could ask. Till then I'd known I lacked a good deal; but seeing her there in possible reach, I suddenly knew my two big hands were empty and had been all my life. I wondered why; excellent women had tried to fill them— my mother, Lou and even young Robin. I'd somehow declined every offer they made.

Now here was the fourth. I understood no offer was free, least of all from the hands of a girl with eyes like these dark eyes, that no Marine division could stem. If I reached out now and finally took, I estimated I'd feel and cause unmanageable pain. But before I thought another word, my mind made an actual sound like a tight boxlid that shuts with a click. I held my ground six yards away; and I said "Sweet child, run off with me."

I didn't think Eileen heard my words. Her laugh calmed though and she wiped her eyes. Then she leaned out slowly and set her lips on the family name, cut deep in the stone. When she faced me, even her smile was gone. She said "You got us a full tank of gas?"

I couldn't speak. But I nodded hard, she came on toward me; and my life bent like a thick iron bar way back in the forge.

THE COMPANY OF
THE DEAD

Eighty-some years ago when I was a boy, Simp Dockett and I were in modest demand as reliable and inexpensive all-night "setters." I'm talking of the early 1900s in a small country town; and when people died and the corpse came home from the mortuary, a member of the family was expected to "set up" all night by the coffin and keep the dead company. The coffin lid was open of course, though in hot weather there would be a veil of mosquito net to keep off moths and flies. I could always see what the flies were after, but the moths had me stumped. They barely eat so it can't be food; I eventually wondered if it might be light. Do some corpses give off actual light that we can't see but moths love and flock to? Later below, I will give my witness, for what it's worth.

By the time Simp and I had our truly wild night—the one I must tell before too late—we were good-sized boys, fifteen years old. But we started our business when we were still twelve. I'd like to think that the fact we lasted through our first job says something about what guts we had, but I know it only describes our greed. We made a small piece of money that night, and we wanted more; so from that point on, we guaranteed gentlemanly conduct and no dozing off in the loved one's presence. We even wore celluloid collars and silk ties. They made us look older and hurt so much they kept us awake.

What happened the first night is something my own children always loved to hear. The corpse in question was an elderly spinster who taught us in Sunday school, at age three or four, and later in grade school—Miss Georgie LaGrange. All times of the year, freeze or swelter, she brought a great bowl of warm apple float each Sunday and made us eat it in thin china bowls that had been her mother's. It was "good for our bowels," she'd promise in whispers. Simp and I had grown well out of her class when the elders finally had to retire her. She'd started weighing the children each week and recording the figures on a chart by the door. Nothing wrong with that, but then a few children told their mothers Miss Georgie would make them to peel to their step-ins before she weighed them. So the elders let a grace period lapse; then after six months they gently removed her.

Gentle to the elders; it killed Miss Georgie. Though well past seventy and too far-sighted to be helped by glasses, she advertised sketching and painting lessons—not a taker in town. So Jarvis, the yard man, found her cold at the wheel of her dead brother's Packard in the shed one Monday morning. Though she'd never driven a mile in her life, the coroner said she died of heart failure, no hint of suicide, and had been stone dead since at least Friday night. Knowing Miss Georgie's mind had softened, everybody believed it and I still do.

My father was the lawyer that drew her will. The yard man knew that and had nowhere else to turn. Miss Georgie's people were long since dead. Her only nephew was two states away; and everyone knew he was not in the will, given as he was to getting arrested in women's clothes. So all my family were well into smothered steak and biscuits that cool spring evening when the back door rattled; and there stood Jarvis with tears in his eyes, though we already knew he was Miss Georgie's heir.

The next evening Father went out again to be with Miss Georgie as they brought her body home. When he got back to us, we four children were doing our homework on the dining table by two oil lamps. I think this country might yet revive as a place where decent people dwell if the government turned off all the lights every evening at dark. At least it would force everybody back home, the ones who aren't already born-felons. And there, they'd gather in one or two rooms. It would be pressed on them by circumstance. Few people would have a great many oil lamps, and very few rooms in homes would be heated. All this mischief that's done now in basements—fathers and daughters, mothers and sons—could seldom occur. The crimes would be honest crimes of public passion, murders in the midst of family and friends, not faceless stranglings near the trash compactor at city landfills.

Anyhow Father stopped on the doorsill and called me—"Hubble."

I was his older son and worshiped his tracks. I still think he liked me, though he never confessed it. The sound of my name, even one odd as Hubble, was grand in his voice. I rose from my stool like mist from a pond and followed him out.

He didn't wait for me, didn't look or turn till he got to a standing water spigot far back in the yard. These dirty days, you'd need to go high in the Grand Teton range to see skies black as our sky was then, any moonless night. But the three million stars were beaming so clear, I could see my father waiting as I came. He stood a whole moment, staring straight up. I thought the starshine was burning his skin.

And seeming to confirm it, he looked down slowly, turned the spigot and waited. Then he washed his face in two hands of water.

By the time he looked up again, I was with him. I touched the flap of the left-side pocket in the coat to his suit.

He said "Hub, I've got you a grown man's job."

He asked me regularly, Sunday nights, what I planned to be. I'd always tell him some job he admired—a doctor or something to do with problems, like a civil engineer. So what he'd said wasn't all that strange. I just said "Good" and stood there to hear it. Many boys back then quit school at fourteen and trekked up the road to the nearest real town for a regular wage.

But then he veered, "How old are you, son?"

"Twelve and four months, sir."

His enormous hands must have still been wet; he wheeled them around in the air above me and finally said "Are you too young, you think?"

I should have said "For what?" but what boy would? I said "No sir."

He said "Then you and Simp can set up tonight with Miss Georgie's corpse."

I understood at once and it truly thrilled me. I'd already been to at least a dozen funerals, which meant that I'd also viewed the remains as they lay, banked with flowers, in a cool parlor or dining room. I'd always wanted to touch the skin—it looked so fragrantly powdered and needy, so ready to wake up and thank you for warmth—but there were always adults at hand, with forbidding eyes. Standing with Father outdoors in the dark, my next thought was that Simp and I would be the bosses, alone all night with a whole dead body to use our way. A friend of ours named Baxter Wade, just one year older, had worked last summer at the mortuary. And the stories he told nearly curled our hair.

He knew all about embalming fluid—how they pump it into a vein in your right arm and meanwhile drain out your blood on the left. The best news was, the fluid is green. So once the pickling replaces red blood, every inch of your skin is bright bottle-green. Then nothing is left but to make you up with flesh-colored paint and dusting powder. Every now and then, an embalmer slips and forgets a part. And family members have been known to fold on the parlor floor at the sight of a green earlobe on Mother. Baxter also said he knew one boy who claimed he fondled a pretty girl that died of the flu, and the boy didn't catch so much as a cold ("fondled" is my guess; Baxter claimed more). My next thought was, we could look at some hidden part of Miss Georgie, under the collar, to check for green. We weren't that sure we could take Baxter's word.

So I said "Yes sir. You can count on us." I knew Simp didn't have better plans; nobody we knew in those days had plans, for tonight or for life. Life was just forward motion, at the gentlest clip you could manage to take and still eat three meals a day and sleep dry.

Father told me to put on my black suit and his gray cravat; and as I bolted, he called me back. "Miss Georgie's estate will pay you, son—one dollar per boy."

The sum was handsome for those slim days, but I said "No *sir*." I'd have paid a good part of my savings for the chance.

He blared his eyes, the sign for *Get serious*. "You're a paid employee, this whole night, Hub. Miss Georgie's purchasing first-class care. Act according. Be respectful, no jokes; don't loosen your tie. You'll find some old biscuits in a bag by the stove, and I set out a jar of her fig preserves. Eat nothing else. Don't *touch* the coffin unless there's a fire, and don't shut an eye till I come by to spell you just after daybreak."

I said Simp and I would set right on as long as he needed; forget about school.

He smiled for the first time but said "There you're wrong." Then he motioned me onward to dress and find Simp.

By the time we got to Miss Georgie's porch, it must have been nearly nine o'clock. But a small group of mourners had already gathered. It turned out that Jarvis, the sudden heir, had barred the door till our arrival, telling the world that we were "the family" and would be here shortly. Meanwhile he stood in front of the door in his own black suit and a wine-colored tie. Neither Simp nor I shared a drop of blood with Miss Georgie, and the mourners knew it, but even Simp bucked up at Jarvis's claim, and we took on the role. We'd known everybody in sight all our lives; they were loyal members of our church or were some of the older teachers at school. Miss Georgie had taught the second grade, including me and Simp, from roughly the year they invented fire till five years ago. So the two of us climbed up toward them proudly. Young as I was, I already liked standing tall and big-eyed with shoulders squared, daring all comers.

At the top, Mr. Pepper—the drunkard school-principal—stepped over and personally shook our hands. Simp glanced at me and nodded to mean "You do the talking." So I said "Everybody step in. Miss

Georgie's ready." I don't know what I thought she was ready *for*; and as Simp and I led the way to the door, I suddenly prayed it wouldn't be locked. I had no key.

In immediate answer Jarvis trotted ahead and turned the brass knob. Then he stepped inside what seemed a dark house and pressed his back to the open door to see us in. I consulted Simp's eyes for an instant. When I saw they were scared, I took the first step of our manly job. And yes, she was ready.

By ten-fifteen every mourner had seen the new Miss Georgie. The undertaker had painted her thick, the face and hands, which added a century or so to her age; but everybody said what they always say, "She looks so natural, just like she's asleep." I of course didn't say what I thought at once. The real Miss Georgie had looked cold-dead since the day they made her quit teaching school. And the only place where the paint she now wore would look half natural was in a plush whorehouse for truly weird gents with serious cash.

Jarvis hung around in the back of the house for another short while. We guessed he was starting an inventory of his new possessions. In fact we were wrong—he'd had no warning whatever of his luck; and after the funeral when my father told him he'd inherited everything, he pole-axed over on the floor, unconscious, and had to be revived. By the time he was ready to leave that night though, Simp and I were searching the room for a deck of cards or a checkerboard. I was on my knees, rummaging a cabinet, when I heard footsteps. I looked up and Jarvis was tall in the door.

"What the hell you doing?" His voice was rusty but every word cut me.

I instantly knew it had to be the first curse word these walls had heard since Miss Georgie's brother died, so it struck me dumb, and I couldn't answer.

Simp said "He's just hunting some kind of game to keep us awake. She got any cards?"

Jarvis's face went awful in a hurry. "She ain't got *nothing* now, no more. And if there was something as sinful as cards under this roof tonight, you think I'd tell you?"

By then I was ready to say "No sir."

Simp faced me and frowned; you didn't call black men *sir* back then. So he took over and said "Look, Jarvis. We're nothing but boys; we like our sleep. But we can't sleep tonight. We need some help and you know where things are hid around here—"

Jarvis stayed as dark as before. "You can goddamn well believe I know every curl of dust in the furtherest corners. So don't touch nothing. Stay wide awake and watch Miss Georgie—don't shut a damn eye. I'll see you at daybreak." Then he vanished. I truly mean *vanished*. I'd still swear to God he just disappeared. If he did, however he brought it off, I knew from that instant how Jarvis was still there with us in spirit, his big black eyes in the chilly air.

Simp plainly agreed since he waited ten seconds and whispered to me "I bet his spirit will spy all night."

Both of us turned then, went to hard chairs and sat down firmly. I can't speak for Simp; but as for me, to stay awake, I thought the hardest thoughts I could manage. Both my parents and the sister I liked were being dragged naked through a field of barbed wire by slow blind mules at a steady rate. And that was years before barbed wire came into its own in the First World War. But awful as it was to see and hear, the thoughts eventually had me nodding in a chair as rigid as any steel strut.

I didn't know at first what woke me; my eyes flew open on the mantel clock. It was twelve-twenty and my first response was pride to have finally passed midnight, alive and conscious. In a town small as ours, children barely saw moonrise, much less midnight. Then I heard a sound I recognized; I knew at once it was what had woke me.

Simp was back in the corner by the open coffin. His right hand seemed to be reaching in; and two more times he whispered "Whoa, whoa."

I whispered "Hush and sit your butt down." I'd already thought about Jarvis again and how I knew he was somehow with us like the Holy Ghost. Simp had agreed just awhile before, but now he was acting the fool again. I said "This all belongs to Jarvis now. He'll burn us up."

Simp said "That nigger won't burn dry *cotton*." Don't think exceptionally hard of Simp; back then we were less than a generation from the Civil War, something as common and flat-incredible as chattel slavery; and we lived in a town that had been scoured over, like hot lye-water flung in your eyes, by Sherman's men not forty years past. We may have deserved it; but you don't forgive rape, not in under a thousand years.

All Simp did next was reach his left hand round behind him and beckon me on while he still said *"Whoa."*

I thought maybe something was wrong with Miss Georgie; so being half of her guard for the night, I had no choice but to come up behind Simp and face the facts.

There were two hard facts. Simp had unpinned the cameo from Miss Georgie's neck and opened three buttons. I might have paused to think it was doubtless the first time a man, or a boy at least, had touched her anywhere else but the hand. Yet the sight itself held me. Below the collar where the paint line quit, she was green as Ireland. Simp's index finger was touching the ridge of her collarbone; he seemed to be stuck, like your tongue on ice. That was not the worst. After all we'd halfway hoped to see green. The worst part shone as new as creation, a dread to behold.

Miss Georgie was blowing a sizable bubble. Few men or boys had ever seen her smile, though your mother might admit she'd caught her at it a time or two. And now her lips were still thin as paper, but the corners were plainly lifting in a grin, and between them an actual bubble was growing.

I fell back a step; it shook me that hard. Then I said "One of us has got to run, Simp, for reinforcements."

He didn't even face me. "The hell you say. I'm not leaving you, Hub; you can't leave me."

I understood him; the bubble had trapped us. As both of us stood there, it swelled on slowly to the size of a tangerine and more or less stopped. From that point forward it would sometimes grow a quarter-inch, then shrink back again. But it always stayed a little murky with a yellow hue, not the rainbow skin of a clean soap-bubble.

We had our work cut out for us then. Either it would keep on swelling and shrinking and keep us thinking Miss Georgie was somehow coming to life, green all over as we knew she was; or any second, it would burst and be done, a final gas attack from a lady who launched a number of memorable such. If the latter, then fine; we could sit back down and continue the night. The former didn't even bear thinking through. What would Jarvis say when he walked in at sunrise and found Miss Georgie frying our breakfast?

Neither thing happened. Simp and I stood there, give or take a step backward, an hour more. When nothing dramatic occurred either way, I reminded Simp it was he who must button her collar again and pin the cameo. He heard the news with bald-faced terror; but knowing his duty, he shut both eyes and managed someway. The bubble survived. So finally we sat down again in easier chairs and took turns shutting our eyes to rest. While the other snoozed, the one on guard would stay awake by hook or crook (I mostly sang hymns) and make sporadic checks on the bubble. I dreaded my turns and prayed between them that, next time, the thing would have dried and burst. Simp must have done the same—everytime he woke and went on duty, he'd say first thing, "Hub, tell me it's gone" and turn ashy pale when I shook my head.

Toward the end of my truly last watch, toward dawn, I made one more check, found the bubble intact and Miss Georgie no less dead than before. Then I sat back to wait and fell into sleep like an open well in strange woods at night. I didn't even wake at the sound of Jarvis's key in the back door, his feet in the kitchen. Thank God, Simp did and shook me hard. So we were upright, if not clear-eyed, when Jarvis came up the long hall to meet us.

His disgusted face showed he knew we'd shirked, but what he said was "Is she all right?"

Simp looked at me.

I didn't know what Jarvis had in mind; so I said "First-rate," which was what Father said if you asked how he felt on a sunny day.

Jarvis all but spit on the floor, then swallowed his bile and stepped to the coffin. If we had both shot him at point-blank range, he couldn't have jerked any harder than he did. When his body calmed he didn't turn to face us. He kept looking at her; but he said "What please, in the name of Jesus, have you fools done?"

We faced each other and together said "Nothing." But then we joined him at the coffin rail; and oh Lord God, the bubble had grown since my last check to the size of a healthy navel orange. The surface was still a jaundice yellow, but the cloudy air inside had darkened like a captive storm. And as we watched, before even Jarvis could reach with his handkerchief and wipe it away, the bubble burst and spread its remains across Miss Georgie from brow to chin.

We got our money all the same; and a few years ago, I heard my own wife's undertaker say that such things were not that rare in the inner sanctums of mortuaries, though they seldom happen now that the trade has learned its lesson and sews lips shut. The odd thing was, for a first experience, you might have thought it would balk Simp and me from further such jobs. Not a bit, or so I thought at first. Once word on the bubble got out in town, we were pitied and praised for our ordeal; and within three weeks, we were called to "set" with Brigadier General Matthew Husky's enormous remains. I thought we were both stronger boys for the test.

But that second night—as the house stilled down except for the

general's widow upstairs, snoring her way through thick plaster walls—
Simp said to me "Hub, did we learn our lesson?"

It was not his usual cast of mind; and while I'd always thought I was
smarter, I knew Simp was some months nearer to manhood, so I asked
what lesson he had in mind.

He was used to my being the wordsmith among us, and it took him
awhile to fix his reply; but when I'd nearly forgot my question, Simp
said "Well, you can't turn your back on the dead."

I said "If you're speaking of ghosts, forget it. Poor Miss Georgie didn't
blow that bubble; it was gas, a normal chemical event." My older
brother Tump was studying chemistry; the words were his. But the next
were mine, prepared in private to steel my resolve, "And it's unchristian
anyhow. God wouldn't let good souls hang back here to flummox boys
and scare old Negroes."

Simp said "I'm white and I'm scared to death. You've heard a lot
more from God than me. The Bible's got way more ghosts than good
women."

Simp was a Bible scholar; I knew he was right on the matter of
women, so I didn't risk faulting his count of the ghosts. I waited awhile
till Simp started nodding. By then I'd pulled my wisdom together. I
said "The lesson is nothing but this. Keep the corpse as cool as you
can, no more bugs than you can help, and don't go touching their
burial clothes."

Simp said "I beg to God you're right; but until further notice, my
eyes are peeled. One false move out of this old joker, and stand aside
or I'll stampede you down."

I knew when to humor him and shut down a quarrel. But through
that peaceful night by the general, I had more than one inspiration on
the subject of what we ought to have learned from the bubble and its,
after all, tempting hint at a prank by something *out there*, if not at a
frank demonic stab at scaring us dead. But despite the fact that it filled
the largest ready-made coffin like melted wax, General Husky's corpse

behaved with spotless dignity. The peace in fact was too great for me; and sad to report, I slept a good part of that second night.

Not Simp Dockett—he meant what he said; and for weeks to come, he would suddenly throw me a note in class with some new flash of purported memory from his sleepless watch: *The general sang two bars of "Dixie" at first sunrise.* I'd look back and laugh till the day I had to swallow one note (it bore the word *fart*) to keep Miss Miriam Bailey from seizing it—she taught us grammar and was martyred by flatulence. After that I made Simp keep his own so-called memories till recess.

But the time I started out to describe, and have yet to tell, was truly the last. We learned the lesson and it changed my life—I learned it anyhow and Simp was impressed at the very least. As we left the room on that bright morning after such a strange night, we eyed each other, white as paste. And both of us knew we'd silently retired. It had been that final, that wondrous and—worst—it has proved untellable in my life till now. I know Simp died with his half untold except to me; he confessed as much when I left his deathbed in 1939. Not one of his three chatterbox wives had prised a word about it from him, though each had tried.

Who died was a beautiful woman, a girl really. She was even a distant cousin of mine, Mariana Adams. She'd married at sixteen, three years before—an absolute scoundrel from up on the river, named Kennon Walters. The scoundrel part was owing to liquor; otherwise he was handsome as she was lovely, with his stiff black hair and eyes that could tell you a lie and make it stick like knives through your face. He was also at times a practicing lawyer, though honest to a fault in that respect. For all his regular quarterly drunks, nobody ever claimed Kennon was cruel. He was just so proud that once he was drinking, he'd ride away and hide his shame, till sanity returned, in an old fishing-camp his father had built ten miles from home on the Clannish River.

The last time Kennon rode off and left her, he stayed gone upward of two winter weeks. And finally Mariana lit out to find him. Her heart nor mind would let her wait longer; she had the news they'd both waited for. Kennon had always publicly said he would end his drinking the day his first child saw safe light, and now she was pregnant. Still she went on horseback alone in the cold. There was no other way to get there then, no passable road for a gentler conveyance. She'd ridden brilliantly all her life, and the horse was as tame as a thornless rose. But she hadn't told anybody she was leaving, and she left at sunup with just two saddlebags of provisions and a smallish lantern in case dark overtook her return—she truly hoped to return with Kennon but was wise enough to allow for failure.

Whether she got there or not is unsure. Late the next morning when the horse came home and the searchers beat the woods and found her, her frozen body lay crosswise in the track, aimed neither way. And though her stiff right hand was pointed as if to aim herself at a goal, the way she had fallen, nobody could guess which way she meant. Some said they found her provisions by Kennon where he lay in a stupor; some say no, he was in his own filth, no food in sight and no memory of her.

It seemed clear to me, though I barely knew her, that if Mariana had truly found him, she wouldn't have left with Kennon unconscious and in his own waste. But maybe he rallied and said something dreadful that cast her off, or maybe his mind was so far gone that he mistook her for some kind of threat and raised a hurtful hand against her. Her skin was not marked, except at the temple; and that was a bruise she sustained in falling from the horse, whenever, and striking a white flint rock in the ground.

Whatever—and God alone still knows—when half of the search party brought her home, Kennon's brother Phil pushed on and found him, told him the worst and brought him back too. It was not till the doctor searched Mariana's body that anybody knew what had sent her off on a risky mission in weather that cold. She was somewhere between three and four months pregnant. When they told poor Kennon, he first tried to kill himself, then the horse; then the doctor laid him out with morphine. Nobody thought he would wake for the funeral; but Simp and I could vow, though we didn't, that he saw her body one final time and that she saw him or knew he was there.

Because Mariana's wealthy father was long since dead, and her mother was too overcome by grief, again we were summoned to watch through the night. By then Simp and I were so well-seasoned that we had no trouble spelling each other in staying awake and dignified. And since our premier night with Miss Georgie, we'd had no untoward incident to spook us. But every white male in town, from twelve up, knew that Mariana Adams was a beauty surpassing mythical perfection; and men and women, white and black, had joined in ruing the day she flung her life away at the feet of Kennon Walters. So however hardened Simp and I were, when we entered that parlor and took our instructions from the weeping mother, we were thrilled to the sockets at the near prospect of a chance to guard this famous beauty as her body spent its last night above ground.

Mariana's mother only thanked us profusely, then asked us not to disturb the netting. Since it was winter, with insects asleep, we didn't know why she took the precaution; but we nodded agreement and, once she was gone, sat back to do our calculus lesson (we were both near failing). We hadn't exchanged a word on the subject of viewing the corpse and had worked at least an hour in silence when Simp rose, stretched, silently walked to the coffin rail and stood a long minute before he said "She's an angel by now; any fool could see—." Most Christians then as now believed that souls become bright angels in a flash at the moment of death, with harp and wings.

It was not their worst error; but it always disturbed me, even that young, and I told Simp the truth, "Right now her soul's in dreamless sleep and will stay that way till the trump of doom. Then God will shake her and decide where she goes." I was referring to Judgment Day; that far back, it was my favorite date. I expected it often and would search most sunsets for trumpet notes and the glint of wings. I felt that guilty, though I'd hurt nothing worse than bugs in the dirt beneath my shoes.

Simp didn't even turn. He gazed on at her and said "No fool but a blind man, with both hands missing, could say such a thing."

It made me mad and I stood up hot to see for myself.

She was every atom of what he said. Her mother had wanted her buried "as she lived," so the undertaker was not allowed to embalm and paint her. She lay before us in a white nightgown with her throat and shoulders bare. She'd always worn her black hair loose, not plaited or tucked; and it flared out beside her like a whole other creature, entirely alive. It was only her skin that assured us she was gone. Ever white, it was still paler now; and it all but quivered with a low phosphorescence that truly came from deep within her, a final remnant of the goodness she showed in every move. I thought through the moment in that way later, years later in fact; but even that night I felt no fear, no strange attraction—I was proud to be near her.

Nothing about her tempted me or Simp to lift the net and touch any part of that splendid a sight. I finally said "Simp, angels wish they looked good as this." And with no more words, we both went back to the calculus lesson, though more than once we rose up separately and stood to watch her.

I can't speak for Simp, but I know I was memorizing the sight and also teaching myself a hard truth—that this much beauty can still be stopped by a stumbling horse or a limb from a tree. Till then I'd nursed a boy's common notion that beauty counts in the eyes of Nature and will be protected by the ground itself, if not bright angels.

It was four in the morning, my turn to guard while Simp caught a nap, when I thought I heard footfalls on the porch. They seemed to climb the eight high steps and stop at the door, then a long silent wait. I still wasn't scared. If you were white, in that town then, the chances of meeting with harm from a human were practically nil. I guessed it might be Talcot Briley, an affable moron who seldom slept and made late harmless inspection tours of yards and houses.

But the front door creaked, slowly opened and shut.

And before I could move or call to Simp, a man strode past me and went to the coffin. I didn't so much see him as smell him, a strong good scent of leather and the night. It was then I said my single word; I think it was *"Please,"* some syllable that begged for mercy to Simp and me and for honor at least to dead Mariana.

He didn't look back but made a huge downward sweep with his hand that shut me up from five yards' distance and seated me fast. All I was good for after that was a silent reach to press Simp's knee. I wanted a witness.

Simp came to, saw my hushing finger and watched like me in frozen quiet from then on out.

I hadn't seen Kennon Walters for years, maybe not since my boyhood; but next I knew him. No man born around here since Kennon looks anything like as rank, wild and good. By *good* I only mean handsome, magnetic. You had to watch him and, as with Mariana, you worked to record his memory clearly as a future standard for strength and waste. Otherwise you knew he could take one hand and separate your leg from your hip; you also knew that he very well might.

By then he'd laid the netting back; and I almost thought Mariana's light, her peculiar shine, outlined his right profile that was toward me. He hadn't reached in and all he'd said so far was whispers that I couldn't catch. But finally, still not facing us, he said "Come here."

Simp and I stayed put, astonished.

So Kennon said "Come stand by me this instant, or I'll cut you both."

One way or the other, on liquid legs we both obeyed; and after what happened in the next long seconds, I've always guessed he meant us for witnesses, the way I'd wanted Simp with me. Kennon thought he could change the laws of Nature—he'd pretty well managed to do it till then—and he wanted us to judge. Whether he already knew the outcome, I still can't say. But he forced our hand; and hard as it's been to shut my lips on what I saw, I never once doubted I owed Kennon Walters at least that silence for the gift I got in sharing his deed.

Even that early in my long life, my sense of possibility could stretch. The fact that I did so badly in science, not to mention math, through all grades of school was my best early blessing. It kept me from stringing the barbed-wire fences that rational men put up against truth, the shapeless grandeur of what *may* be.

Next Kennon put both hands on the coffin and kept on watching Mariana's face for maybe a minute. If I'd been watched with half that force, I'd have burst into flame in under a minute. But nothing changed. So then he spoke to the body in a whisper that was clear in the room as any shout, "Come back long enough to say if I live."

I know he said exactly that; he spoke very slowly in a clear bass voice. I seized each word as it came through the air and pressed it hard on my mind that then was still uncrowded. I thought "He's planning to die if she fails him." I never wondered if he caused her death in direct fashion. That close to his shadow, his fine-smelling body, I knew he hadn't killed this Mariana, not against her will in any case.

Her eyes didn't open—Simp always agreed, the few times we ever mentioned it later. And for a good while she stayed dead still. Even the pulsing light from inside her withdrew and dimmed.

Kennon spoke again. This time I understood it was God he begged for help. He said "I need this word. Let her answer." Desperate as he sounded, he never said *please*; it was all commands.

Then something obeyed him—our Maker or a demon or Mariana her shining self, wherever she roamed. She went on waiting till I quit hoping and knew that even Kennon couldn't summon her back with all the fury of his parched soul. But then her pale lips worked to part in what I thought would be a slow smile. It proved to be sound, her earthly voice. I'd heard her say my name four times in earlier years and will know her tones in Heaven if I get there. What she said was "No."

By then I'd nearly forgot Kennon's question.

He had not. He issued a sob like nothing I'd heard on Earth till then or have met with since, and I've heard much grief. He said "Again," another order.

Her lips moved again and—this time I had no question at all—she made a smile so lovely it soothed my heart for years. But she said again "No." I remembered the question, *Should Kennon live?* No, twice No.

Simp and I looked at him.

We might have been air. Every lustrous hair on his head looked charged with newer force, and his wide dark eyes were fixed on her. Had they seen her the night she left home to find him? Had he repelled her and sent her out into freezing darkness? Or had she never reached him with her news of the child and perished, maybe lost and hunting the chance of safety at his crushing hands, wherever he lay—the father of what grew daily within her?

Now he laid a great broad hand on her mouth and pressed as though he'd press her through flooring, the ground, the mantling rock beneath our soil toward the world's red core of burning rock.

I took a step back in fear and dread. Would she fight; would bile press out of her gorge? Would God the Judge appear among us and burn Kennon down, maybe ruining me and Simp in the blaze?

Simp actually seized Kennon's bulky wrist and tried to tame it.

Kennon turned eyes on him that would swipe down a saint; and with one short swing of his weaker arm, he flung Simp off like water drops.

Simp landed by the settee and covered his head.

I crouched down by him in hopes of sparing myself worse damage.

When Kennon's steps crossed the front porch and left, I started to count. I told myself "If I get to a hundred and he's not back and fire hasn't struck us, I'll risk one more look out at the room." I truly counted to one hundred slowly—pure silence, still air. I took the look round. The room as before, no sign of strangeness. Simp was rousing too, not visibly bleeding. I said "Is he gone?"

Simp said "Hub, he's the least of our worries. He's bound to be dead." How Simp knew it, he didn't say. I thought of myself as the better detective, but of course he was right that one bad time.

They found Kennon Walters that morning at ten as Mariana's hearse drove up to her family plot with us all behind on ponies, in buggies. He had cut his throat and fallen in the hole that was meant for her grave.

I hadn't asked Simp that night, or ever, what the worst of our worries might be or become—maybe a thoroughly raised Mariana, bent on vengeance or a still deeper taste of the love she lacked and truly craved.

That at least was what I've kept from the night, my ultimate lesson. Love—this force commended by God and Christ his Son as the height of virtue—will freeze one life and char the next; no way to predict who lives or dies. No lover thrives or ends with flesh and mind intact, uncharred and smiling. In the long years since, I've kept that lesson hid well within me, a guiding secret like no known light in the mounting hours of age and loss. And through this generous hapless republic—where, all the length of the twentieth century, the one word *love* has stoked life and commerce, disease and health, swans and owls, child-killers and dolphins—I've struggled by the instant to keep my own heart dry inside me, not launched on the pointed stakes of love.

I'm ninety-two years old, writing this line, a man at peace with what he's done and what comes next. I leave this story, in both its parts, as my best gift to a world I've liked and thank, here now, but have never pressed for the black heart's blood of actual love.

GOOD AND BAD DREAMS

1. A Sign of Blood

SHE WENT OUT at eight, leaving him asleep. So he let her believe. He was only waiting behind shut eyes to have the room still and empty at last, his for the day—his first free solitary day in months; *years* it felt, by the weight that dissolved with each breath now. As he flung back the covers and stood, he thought "Chance." The word itself, clearly. Then, stripped and shuddering (she had not lit the heater), he smiled—chance for what? Well, nine free hours. The room his again. But *warm* first.

He scissored to the heater in three steps, squatted, inhaled, threw the gas jet. The breath was one that he always took—shallow and secret—before lighting the gas (fear of breathing fire; she had never noticed). But alone now, he also flinched at the puff. A minor luxury—with her he could not show a hint of fear.

Waiting in the warmth, he rocked farther forward to see the room upside down through his crotch. His dangling sex transfixed the unmade bed—stake in the heart of the vampire at the crossroads! He actually laughed, and caught the frail permanent scent of his groin—the room's ground-bass. He made, for the first time since adolescence, the lunge to kiss his sex. It needed the notice. But he fell on his tail and lay in the laughter like warming water.

*

A mirror. A long pierglass hung beside him. Flat on his back, he could not see himself—only windows opposite, still covered against light. So he stood, square before it, no longer smiling, chin firm and lifting, clenched hands at his sides—an archaic Apollo: *You must change your life*—even strode one solemn step forward toward his image. Unmoving, he studied his image by gaslight. The chest broad but flat (a pale hard tray); arms, legs thin and long, joint flowing easily into bone without display. "I am lovable," he said and kissed on the mirror all the mirror would permit—his lips. They could use the greeting at least. Then he went to the window to open the curtains.

Light. His day. He could open them safely, naked as he was, since the room faced backward, the high thick garden, no other house there. Only at the sight did he think of the storm. In the night he had waked to hear wind and rain; she had spoken—what? a word about the roof; would it hold through this? he had said "Live in hope" and fallen off again.

The roof had clearly held. The yard showed torn limbs and leaves but no shingles. He could work on that awhile, clearing trash—the day was not bright but neither was it freezing. No, he would read, draw, listen to music. First, to bathe and dress. The garden could wait. Let the trash be compost.

But, turning from the window, his eye snagged at one dark spot in the ground—a cap? a glove? Something soaked and wadded on bare dirt by the door. Tan or gray? He strained to see which, and consciously wondered *why?*—why linger on this? He was twenty yards away and above it; and he stared till he knew it was tan—or a richer brown, russet. Fur. A drowned mole?—it was larger than a mouse. He could not find limbs or eyes in its mass. Whatever, it was still. Dead. More rubbish.

Yet when he had turned and moved toward the bath, he felt the day begin to leak from his grip, like all the others. He knew what sapped them, every day for years—his promise to her—but this threat was new, with a taste of its own, a dry density. Oh a nag, not a threat. He stopped by the bed, still yards from the bath, and smelled himself. He was clean enough.

He was back at the window. The small corpse was there, still resisting knowledge, crouched on its precious death. Or was it only a scrap of a corpse?—rabbit, squirrel fur? No sign of blood, not from here at least.

He dressed in two minutes, was down and standing directly above it, and still did not know. He knelt and bent till his face was no more than a foot away. Lice, in the fur. They had ridden out the storm and were still hustling blood that was jelly by now. Then he noticed wings— the hooked tips of leather wings intricately folded. A bat.

Of course he stood. He had never seen a bat. Maybe in a zoo or occasionally swooping round a distant street lamp. But never this close. *Unprotected.* He felt instantly stripped again and vulnerable, precisely in his eyes and throat. He blinked and stepped back but knew it was dead and forced his fear down. He must move it though. How? Nudge it along with his foot toward the trashpile. Rabies—no. There had been rabid bats—two, three summers ago. Children had been bit. These lice were alive and stuffed with its blood. He must bury it deeper than dogs could smell.

When he found the shovel, he returned and stood again. Its back seemed shrunk, as though essence were leeching into dirt already. It was toy-sized, a winged mouse whacked down by wind. He would bury it in soft ground beyond the garbage. He slid the spade toward it gently—a funeral!—neatly, respectfully under it.

It convulsed—flung itself to its back on the spade, stretched its wings full-out, bared baby-pink gums, white needle teeth and—surely— screamed.

He knew it would rush at his face—his eyes—and he dropped the shovel to run; ran three steps. Then he stopped to see, remembering her—as though she were there in the window above him, his panic slamming at her.

Already it was calming—had flopped again to its belly on the ground and was folding its joints slowly inward again.

He knew it was dying, maybe of rabies; and though he had read of explorers infected with rabies by drizzling bat piss in caves, he knew he was safe so far—his skin unbroken, dry. Let it die there in its own good time, where it chose to fall, arranged as it wished. Only the shovel, abandoned beside it, disordered the scene. That could also wait. He turned to the house again, his day recovered. It was only eight-thirty; only this square yard of ground was off-limits. The other world was his.

Yet an hour later—fed, bathed, shaved, dressed again—he could do nothing more than stand at the window and watch the bat. It was still condensed too tautly for death. However it perceived its struggle, it struggled. "So would any virus"—he mocked his own thoughts as the bat threw them up. Why is a bat, the size of your hand, a source of terror when a horse, say, is not or even a frog? Childhood icons?— Halloween, vampires? Or older even, archetypal?—built into our genes since cave men fought them back with brands? A brush of wet fur across the lips in sleep, leather-coated struts of bone clasped to baby's throat?

When he'd dealt with all the clichés, he was left with its win. It had hogged his day—or two hours of his morning. If for no older reasons, then, an enemy. Kill and bury it. Broadside with the shovel. It must anyhow be gone when she returned.

Why? Why could she not be trusted, at her age, with the entire equipment of the created world? Why fence off this or that? Let her grow her own rind or shrink from sight. God knew he'd grown *his*.

So he went for himself. Slowly, sanely down again. "My race has agreed to hold bats repulsive. I'm man enough then to object to a sick bat dying in the yard." That served as reason through the quick kill and burying. It had been nearly gone—no more Dracula feints, just a quick relaxing as the spade slapped once. It had even had the grace not to bleed a drop. A tidy bat.

He buried it whole, on its belly as it chose—like everything dead, two sizes smaller; ludicrously defused—and not till he'd climbed to the room again, lighter, having won, and had bent to make their bed (the sheets as unused as invalids') did he know why the thing had destroyed his day and demanded brutality and—four ounces of leather, lice, fur— would change his life (something he and Apollo had never managed). It was messenger, sign.

No. Absurd. From whom? And how cheap—the celestial joker's usual taste.

She will kill herself.

2. Rapid Eye Movements

BUT WHO believes signs? Who can know what he knows till his knowledge is useless, beached by event? In a day, he'd forgot his sense of omen; and the afternoon of the second day (a Sunday, both at home), he was on her again, employing her facilities—or the single one he needed, in the late clear light.

She permitted him. He also knew that, but would not think of it— that she endured his poking in silent still puzzlement, as though he belonged to another species with analogous parts but incomprehensible needs or as though she were a faith (and the faith's central shrine) and he were the priest of a heresy who entered to perform his rite on her altar—in her presence and hearing but in language and gesture and, finally, reward that were sealed from her.

He'd have thought it out in some such language—and been eased by the image—if she'd given him time. But once he'd finished and paused for breath, he started again, entirely for her, slow deep strokes to offer her the coup.

She did not say Yes or No, her hands still lay—neither urgent nor repelled—in the small of his back. She only breathed deeply at the pit of each stroke—her breaths rock-steady, no quickening.

He slowed and raised to see her face.

Her eyes were shut; the muscles of her mouth and throat were still. She was nearly asleep.

"Later?" he asked. He thought she nodded; her chin dipped once. He rolled gently off her. Her body adhered for a half-turn toward him; so he lay and watched her slide into sleep, intending to think his way out now, her sighing head an aid to contemplation.

She gave him ten seconds to think of her warmth—in the room where he was rapidly cooling, she sent a firm heat across the gap between them (they were not touching, ten inches apart)—then her eyes began to move. Behind the thin lids, a quick frail jittering at first.

Rapid Eye Movements. The sign of a dream. He moved his own face closer to hers, slowly, not to wake her; and strained to see the story she saw. Soon the random movements slowed a little and settled into steadier horizontal sweeps—the balls of both eyes rolling left and then right, as though following a lazy tennis game. Then the slow sweeps would be broken by lurches—upwards or sideways. Then tennis again.

Or her battling parents. Yes. She had told him an hour before—the first time—of a night in her childhood out of Dickens or Zola—her father drunk and beating her mother. Her mother would run to a corner, crouch for more; her father would follow; and she, age five, had waked and come and flown between them, a shuttlecock, screaming for quiet. Surely that was what her shut eyes saw now. And would see till he stopped her. The circular past, she its willing victim. He called her name twice.

She shook; her eyes opened. She did not smile. "I was dreaming," she said.

"I know," he said and laid a hand on her, below her right breast.

What he does not know, what she will not tell him, is that her dream was not of her parents but plainly of themselves, not past but future— her need to stop their life. Need and plan. To wake her is not to end it.

3. Twice

SHE IS still right-handed. She holds the razor-blade—new, firm, single-edged—with that calm hand and extends the left arm.

The white, blue-strung antecubital space; the bend of that arm. She cuts with the chicken-flesh grain at the bend, three-quarters of an inch deep, two inches long. Her hand has not paused, the line is straight. The brachial artery and vein lurch, astonished; then pump on, but now in the air of the room. The arm clasps to her side. She has planned in advance to rush her death by assisting the artery—clenching and opening her left hand in rhythm. What she has not known is that, choosing this spot, she has cut (no choice) the median nerve. Her left hand and wrist are paralyzed. Useless, though wet. Her left thigh and calf, left foot, are wet; the white tile cubes of the floor are wet over eighty square inches.

Yet she still feels *herself*. She is still herself—what she's been all her life, less this much blood. Continuity.

She cuts again, as slowly and deeply, an inch above the previous cut, in clear flesh. The line is straight again. She severs the same vein, artery, nerve and tendons a second time. There is still pain enough to shake a house. "Supererogation"—she thinks that and smiles.

4. Washed Feet

H E H A S slept this soundly since four in the morning because when he came back, his mind was clear. It knew only one thing—the doctor's words on leaving her ward, "She can live if she wants; we've done that much." (They had, the doctor and his nameless team, had worked four hours repairing her try, patiently ligating all she'd severed—the brachial artery and vein—anastomosing tendons, pumping in the mandatory blood that would be at least no stranger to her than the pints she'd carefully drained tonight; then had wheeled her still unconscious to a lighted ward and watched her like a bomb.) The words had instantly swelled in his head, a polished plug molded to crowd his skull and exclude all else, every atom of air. And had perfectly succeeded. He had come here—a half-hour walk, a taxi—had lit the gas-fire (no other light), then stripped and slept. No question of why or who was at fault— "The woman with whom I have lived six years has tried to kill herself. A serious try—no skittish theatrics. I found her; they saved her; she can live if she wants." No question of how.

Two hours of dreamless sleep. It is six, but still winter dark; only the low red burn of the gas—he is sleeping his own way, in warmth.

This happens. A man is in the room, standing darkly in a corner. In his sleep, he sees the man and does not feel fear or curiosity; only watches till he knows what's required of him—that he thrust with his bare feet till they've cleared sheets and blankets and lie exposed. That is the necessary sign. The man moves forward to the end of the bed; stands waiting, still dark. No question of seeing his face or dress. He is dark. No need to know—only lie there flat on your back and wait. Now the man is looking round the room—he is needing something. Lie still, he will find it. And the man goes on looking, even moves a few steps in various directions. Is his face distraught?—lie still, don't wonder, he can fill his own needs. In calm desperation, the man returns to his place at the end of the bed; kneels suddenly. He silently spits in the palms of both hands and washes the bare feet propped before him. The gestures are gentle but the palms are rough.

He is scrubbed awake. He lies on his back, his feet are uncovered, they sweat though the room is hardly warm. He raises his head to see the room. Empty of all but red gas light and the customary stuffing, their stifling freight. He knows he was dreaming. No man is here. No one but himself.

Yet he also knows (he falls back for this) another new thing, more filling than the last—that from now (this night, this momentary dream) he must walk in his life as though a man had been here—one who had come precisely here by choice and, desperate to forgive, had searched for water, then knelt and washed his feet (till then unjudged) with the agent available—His spit, that wishes to clean but scalds.

5. Sleeping and Waking

AT THE end of his dream he fell or flew. Fall or flight, free or pursued, he could not say which, only that he hurtled or was sucked through space; but in his dream he knew he must know (as he must know awake), and he questioned his sleeping body. The legs, arms, head of his dream were calm; and his heart stroked on calm of fear or dread (his actual heart, the heart in his dream), flushing through him the news that he would be spared, that he would rush on, then a cord would rein him, arms or nets stretch to bear him, stop him in time. And he was stopped at last but not by arms, by one word said in an unknown voice—"Lucas" his name—trapped in terror, the voice a mouth on his helpless chest, dull-toothed, draining. He must wake or die and, asleep, he began to flail—at first with his will, then with actual arms against hot dark till he woke on his numb left side, in bed, his right hand fallen on her hip he had struck, in what light there was.

It was night, would be night for hours (he sensed it through blinds, saw it above in the well of the ceiling); but the room was red from the low gas fire that had burned on beside their sleep—another threat that had spared them, done only the duties of fire. The air was stifling and both their bodies though dim were clear. That had been her purpose. When they had stripped and were ready, she had said, "Let it burn. I can see you plainly." But sleep after eight weeks smothered his force, and soon they had turned into separate chaos. Now he saw. Maybe this was her purpose—not the sight of love but that he see her, separately drowned, raw to whatever might strike or seize.

So he saw—knowing he was safe, knowing from her breath, her tamed smell, that she slept, that his dream was his own, his hand unfelt. She slept on her right side toward him, and up from his hand she was mainly dark for the fire was beyond her. Only the crest of her side was lit—jack-knifed legs, the hip he pressed, sunken waist, the left arm splayed behind her—but he forced his eyes to her face. Then from six years' memory he remade it slowly—in stiff black hair a white heart of skin (smooth still but taut) cut by tiers of what now seemed wings— her upward brows, shut eyes, lashes (all wings to leave), a long top lip crouched even in sleep like the edge of an unstitched wound, a full bottom lip almost Negro brown, color of the first real scar beneath in the boneless pit of her neck where twenty years before in child's pneumonia a silver pipe had saved her life, color of the rounds of her breasts raised now, stretched by the backward cast of her arm, lighter only in color than all her hair, than her folded center a hand's breadth below his hand.

His eyes stopped there. For a while it seemed a resting place—dark core of a dark room, harbor, home, socket of his life. From which his life was wrenched eight weeks before, by her, for her own blind reasons which she had not told, would not, maybe could not.

The question was why? and he did not know, had still after eight weeks failed to ask, not knowing whether he had the right, whether six years gave him the final right to save her life, fight off the death she had tried to choose, might choose again when she woke. But she slept on beside him, beneath his hand; and seeing, he thought of sleepwalkers, oracles—answerers. And because he was free in this brief safety, he said to himself that if she would sleep, lie dim and drowned, he would rise to her ear and ask for her reasons, ask who was innocent? guilty? why?—force her answer, know before she woke.

She moved. Before he could ask or smile at himself, she turned away, crushing her left arm beneath her, sliding dry beneath his hand till she stopped nearly flat, his hand on her core. He let it rest, straining with eyes—jaws, even—to hold it calm, not to move or demand what time after time he had silently demanded, got. Then she seemed to flicker in that one place as animals choose one muscle from thousands to twitch beneath a fly—or a wanted hand. He thought she had waked, was conscious and waiting for his demand, demanding his need.

He would not, not demand, not ask for this so simply offered when he could not ask for his desperate need—her reasons, the blame. He took his hand to his own hard flank which, shielded by her, was colder—but was his, to count on. And free from his weight, she moved again, flatter, face to the ceiling, eyes and lips shut. He saw that—her face—heard her doubtful breath begin again. She had not waked. So he raised himself on his elbow above her, lowered his face till her frail breath touched him.

She frowned—the way his mother had frowned at the rise of death, from her belly a wave of dead blood flung blue toward her throat, thrusting chin, locked teeth, pressed eyes. Helpless, he only watched it rise, take not only her face but whatever mind worked on under sleep, telling himself it would leave as it came. But it held her, her face a mask, mirror—simply—of the only death he had watched, his mother's. Yet it was a mask, not death itself. Her lungs sighed on. He must wake her though, spare her this ordeal whatever it was. He could do that—but slowly, gently. He laid his face to her breast and, rocking his jaw, kneaded the flesh above her heart, the shielding bones, with the stumps of his beard—and forced a word, one sound, from her dream. It was a dream. He knew that now and whatever her dread, old or new, he would let her bear it, riding above her, one ear to her heart, one cocked for another word, her answer. "Whatever she says, if she speaks again, let it be the answer." He said that clearly though silently. "I will take what she says as her reason, her blame, and use it to save her, if she will speak."

She said his name—"Lucas"—aloud but in nothing like her daily voice, in the voice that had come at the end of his dream to break his fall.

He could break hers—and would. The question was why? but the answer was who. She had answered "Lucas" which gave him the blame but also the right and duty to save her. He rose from her chest to his knees above her, turned to face her, straddled her body at the parted calves, then bent, extended her hid left arm and kissed the two scars parallel as rails where she had slashed her veins eight weeks before. He felt her waking rise beneath his lips. For the final moment in all his life, he was safe, alone, free. Now he must look, take her open eyes (her answer his secret)—must and would. Then he could start his pitiful humping amends.

6. Morning Places

AT FOUR in the morning, having ceased to hope, he flings himself onto shallow sleep, random beside her—no rest but a flailing, oaring dumbness that leads him in terror, total dark, to the pitch of abyss where he wakes, fingers clawed against fall, heart seized. But attentive, attending, in every pore, straining to name this room, bed, woman beside him. Her slow breath crosses the air between them, chills his side but places him—"Home, our bed, my wife beside me." Saying that seems a form of stripped prayer, the core of surrender, "Your will. Yours." Then sleep is allowed him. He falls back from her and sinks for an hour, thoughtless, mute, gladly drowned. Then at five—the room still black, no sign of day—he bares this dream to himself in his clear mind's voice as carefully, slowly, as if it were new, were made this moment at whosever will to strengthen his rest, were never true.

"I lie asleep in my home, our bed, my place beside her—her at my left eight inches away but separate from me in all her length. I lie on my back as now, eyes shut; yet I have other eyes that lift through dark and witness from above, with no wish, will, fear or strength. So I see her waken, her eyes click open, all pupil for the dark but also fearless— yet willing and strong and looking only up, not to my still body. Her first move is speech. Her lips make five words but I cannot hear, only witness her readiness. She gathers her arms (winged above her head), her scattered legs—touching me no more than if I were fire—sliding left from me and, to spare me, rises as though she were weightless, jarring nothing as she goes—white gown, bare feet, bare arms, hands at her sides, fingers calmly spread. Past our door, she has left my actual body—all that might have saved her—but the eyes of my dream are allowed to stand in that door and watch her go twelve counted steps, stop, raise her hand to a light, a mirror—I see her ready face and cannot move, do not wish to act—a cabinet, a blade. Then that blade lowered to the bend of her left arm—bare, no bone between her life and her. She opens a line and before the astonished blood can start, opens a second, parallel above it as though it were ruled. She stretches the arm at her side, pumps her fist. Her feet, the floor are wet with her life. Then she turns toward me—the eyes of my dream, my hidden body—and takes the first steps, her arm now bowed at her chest, blood blooming suddenly as if from her breasts, heart, belly, core; red blade still in her red right hand. I see that and only count her nearing steps. On the fifth she begins to become something new—on her face at first which is not the face she carried away nor the face we have made in these six years but her early face and for two steps armed with that face like a sword. Then she bears a sword. The blade enlarges upward in her hand, its blood now fire—all her blood streaming fire, her arms sucked up into metalled wings, feet shod, heart shielded, riveted, only her early face unchanged. Having only eyes, I cannot fear; but at her last steps, I lose those eyes and am only my sleeping self in dark till I wake on my back in scalding heat. Stood above me, straddled my knees, scalding my face, bare chest, covered heart, is what she became in the last few steps, what I have known since a child as an angel and—by its face no longer hers, neither man nor woman's, its black eyes steady discs through the heat, its red mouth sealed to question or plea—a final angel, judge and killer. Yet its sword is upward, clamped in gloved fists; and its eyes though set are not on me but over my head, beyond through paper, plaster, lathing, stone. By that I am strengthened to ask its will. I say 'What is your name?' No answer, waver, flicker of notice. I say, 'Am I the man you have come to find?' It moves at that, forward both legs till between its ankles it presses my unguarded flanks. 'Why have you come here?' and knowing its mission, still, 'What do you need from me?' Its lips have vanished. Beneath its nose it is smooth to the chin. 'Take what you need.' I lie fully back, lift my chin to bare my throat, extend the tender pit of my arm. And it takes my offer, bows to its need. Its fists untwine, the sword of its own weight sinks toward me. These eyes are blinded but I wait for its stroke, lips sealed against cry. It is on my mouth—the stroke—and my lips part behind it like edges of a wound; but what I issue is speech not blood, one word 'Pardon' as the sword lifts. The stroke has forced me to say it once and, sparing me, compelled me to say it always—'Pardon,' that flatly, both plea and gift. My blindness continues but the heat recedes; and then I am seeing again—the ceiling. Still flat, I jerk my eyes round the room. There in the far corner, cooling and clearing, stands she again, her simple self, a younger she, unarmed, clothed in her early beauty (sword enough) yet bleeding in reach now and beckoning to me with her whole wrecked arm. Her force sucks at me like a need to fall. I lurch to rise, to rush to save her; but my heart refuses, inhales its blood, jells it within me. I may not go, not save her life; but with all my force I reach my knees, free my voice, tell her 'Pardon,' saying to myself, 'I must say it always. But she must listen, must separately witness my plea for pardon, gift of pardon, our constant death. We both are victim, judge, killer, witness, our simple selves.' "

   She has witnessed at least the end of his dream—or heard it, waked at its sound. For the word was actual, spoken aloud. But asleep, she heard the sound not the word; and awake to receive it, she strains to retrieve whatever he has offered, demanded. There is only quiet, the sough of their opposite breaths; but she sees at the window (through blinds, curtains) the signs of day, the world taking hold, the pieces of this room taking their morning places after chaos—chest, chair, table, bed, he flat beside her sounding asleep. She lifts to her right elbow to see; but his black eyes are open, steady, upward. He does not try to meet or avoid her. She thinks he has waked and struggles for his dream.

She tells him "You spoke." He nods once slowly. "What did you say? What did you dream?" No nod, waver, flicker of notice. Only his eyelids clamp on themselves as if force would thrust him again into rest. She says, "Go to sleep. We have two hours yet." She falls to her back, turns on her belly, lays on his bare chest her bare left arm. The scars in the hinge of her arm feed there.

MICHAEL EGERTON

HE WAS the first boy I met at camp. He had got there before me, and he and a man were taking things out of a suitcase when I walked into the cabin. He came over and started talking right away without even knowing me. He even shook hands. I don't think I had ever shaken hands with anyone my own age before. Not that I minded. I was just surprised and had to find a place to put my duffel bag before I could give him my hand. His name was Michael, Michael Egerton. He was taller than I was, and although it was only June, he already had the sort of suntan that would leave his hair white all summer. I knew he couldn't be more than twelve. I wouldn't be twelve until February. If you were twelve you usually had to go to one of the senior cabins across the hill. But his face was old because of the bones under his eyes that showed through the skin.

He introduced me to the man. It was his father but they didn't look alike. His father was a newspaperman and the suitcase they were unpacking had stickers on it that said Rome and Paris, London and Bombay. His father said he would be going back to Europe soon to report about the Army and that Michael would be settled here in camp for a while. I was to keep an eye on Mike, he said, and if he got to France in time, he would try to send us something. He said he could tell that Mike and I were going to be great friends and that I might want to go with Mike to his aunt's when camp was over. I might like to see where Old Mike would be living from now on. It was a beautiful place, he said. I could tell he was getting ready to leave. He had seen Michael make up his bed and fill the locker with clothes, and he was beginning to talk the way everybody does when they are leaving somewhere— loud and with a lot of laughing.

He took Michael over to a corner, and I started unpacking my bag. I could see them though and he gave Michael some money, and they talked about how much Michael was going to enjoy the summer and how much bigger he would be when his father got back and how he was to think of his aunt just like a mother. Then Michael reached up and kissed his father. He didn't seem at all embarrassed to do it. They walked back towards me and in a voice louder than before, Mr. Egerton told me again to keep an eye on Old Mike—not that he would need it but it wouldn't hurt. That was a little funny since Michael was so much bigger than I was, but anyway I said I would because that was what I was supposed to say. And then he left. He said there wouldn't be any need for Mike to walk with him to the car, but Michael wanted to so I watched them walk down the hill together. They stood by the car for a minute, and then Michael kissed him again right in front of all those boys and parents and counselors. Michael stood there until his father's car had passed through the camp gate. He waved once. Then he came on back up the hill.

All eight of the boys in our cabin went to the dining hall together that night, but afterward at campfire Michael and I sat a little way off from the others and talked softly while they sang. He talked some about his father and how he was one of the best war correspondents in the business. It wasn't like bragging because he asked me about my father and what my mother was like. I started to ask him about his mother, but I remembered that he hadn't said anything about her, and I thought she might be dead. But in a while he said very matter-of-factly that his mother didn't live with him and his father, hadn't lived with them for almost a year. That was all. He hadn't seen his mother for a year. He didn't say whether she was sick or what, and I wasn't going to ask.

For a long time after that we didn't say anything. We were sitting on a mound at the foot of a tree just high enough to look down on the other boys around the fire. They were all red in the light, and those furthest from the blaze huddled together and drew their heads down because the nights in the mountains were cold, even in June. They had started singing a song that I didn't know. It was called "Green Grow the Rushes." But Michael knew it and sang and I listened to him. It was almost like church with one person singing against a large soft choir. At the end the camp director stood up and made a speech about this was going to be the best season in the history of Redwood which was the finest camp in the land as it was bound to be with as fine a group of boys and counselors as he had sitting right here in front of him. He said it would be a perfect summer if everybody would practice the Golden Rule twenty-four hours a day and treat everybody like we wanted to be treated—like real men.

When we got back to the cabin, the other boys were already running around in the lantern light naked and slapping each other's behinds with wet towels. But soon the counselor blew the light out, and we got in bed in the dark. Michael was in the bunk over me. We had sentence prayers. Michael asked God to bless his father when he got to France. One boy named Robin Mickle who was a Catholic said a Hail Mary. It surprised most of the others. Some of them even laughed as if he was telling a joke. Everything quieted down though and we were half asleep when somebody started blowing Taps on a bugle. It woke us all up and we waited in the dark for it to stop so we could sleep.

Michael turned out to be my best friend. Every morning after breakfast everybody was supposed to lie on their beds quietly for Thought Time and think about the Bible, but Michael and I would sit on my bed and talk. I told Michael a lot of things I had never told anyone else. I don't know why I told him. I just wanted him to know everything there was to know about me. It was a long time before I realized that I didn't know much about Michael except what I could see—that he didn't live with his mother and his father was a great war correspondent who was probably back in France now. He just wasn't the kind to tell you a lot. He would listen to everything you had to say as if he wanted to hear it and was glad you wanted to tell him. But then he would change the subject and start talking about baseball or something. He was a very good baseball player, the best on the junior cabin team. Every boy in our cabin was on the team, and it looked as if with Michael pitching we might take the junior title for the Colossians. That was the name of our team. All the athletic teams in camp were named for one of the letters that St. Paul wrote. We practiced every afternoon after rest period, but first we went to the Main Lodge for mail. I got a letter almost every day, and Michael had got two or three from his aunt, but it wasn't until almost three weeks passed that he got the airmail letter from France. There weren't any pictures or souvenirs in it, but I don't suppose Mr. Egerton had too much time for that. He did mention me though I could tell by the way he wrote that he didn't remember my name. Still it was very nice to be thought of by a famous war correspondent. Michael said we could write him a letter together soon and that he would ask his father for a picture.

We wrote him twice but four weeks passed and nothing else came, not from France. I had any number of letters myself and the legal limit of boxes (which was one a week) that I wanted to share with just Michael but had to share with everybody, Robin Mickle included. Worse than the sharing, I dreaded my boxes because I kept thinking they would make me homesick, but with Michael and all the things to do, they never bothered me, and before I expected it, there was only a week of camp left and we would go home. That was why we were playing the semifinals that day—so the winners could be recognized at the Farewell Banquet on the last night of camp. The Colossians were going to play the Ephesians after rest period. We were all in the cabin trying to rest, but everybody was too excited, everybody except Michael who was almost asleep when the camp director walked in and said that Michael Egerton was to go down to the Lodge porch right away as he had visitors. Michael got up and combed his hair, and just before he left he told everybody he would see them at the game and that we were going to win.

The Lodge wasn't too far from our cabin, and I could see him walking down there. A car was parked by the porch. Michael got pretty close to it. Then he stopped. I thought he had forgotten something and was coming back to the cabin, but the car doors opened and a man and a woman got out. I knew it was his mother. He couldn't have looked any more like her. She bent over and kissed him. Then she must have introduced him to the man. She said something and the man stepped up and shook Michael's hand. They started talking. I couldn't hear them and since they weren't doing anything I lay back down and read for a while. Rest period was almost over when I looked again. The car was gone and there was no one in front of the Lodge. It was time for the semifinals, and Michael hadn't showed up. Robin, who was in charge of the Colossians, told me to get Michael wherever he was, and I looked all over camp. He just wasn't there. I didn't have time to go up in the woods behind the cabins, but I yelled and there was no answer. So I had to give up because the game was waiting. Michael never came. A little fat boy named Billy Joe Moffitt took his place and we lost. Everybody wondered what had happened to Michael. I was sure he hadn't left camp with his mother because he would have told somebody first so after the game I ran back ahead of the others. Michael wasn't on his bed. I walked through the hall and opened the bathroom door. He was standing at the window with his back to me.
"Mike, why in the world didn't you play?"
He didn't even turn around.
"We lost, Mike."
He just stood there tying little knots in the shade cord. When the

others came in from the game, I met them at the door. I told them Michael was sick.

But he went to the campfire with me that night. He didn't say much and I didn't know what to ask him. "Was that your mother this afternoon?"

"Yes."

"What was she doing up here?"

"On a vacation or something."

I don't guess I should have asked him but I did. "Who was that with her?"

"Some man. I don't know. Just some man."

It was like every night. We were sitting in our place by the tree. The others were singing and we were listening. Then he started talking very fast.

"My mother said, 'Michael, this is your new father. How do you like having two fathers?' "

Before I could think what to say, he said he was cold and got up and walked back to the cabin. I didn't follow him. I didn't even ask him if he was feeling all right. When I got to the cabin, he was in bed pretending to be asleep, but long after Taps I could hear him turning. I tried to stay awake until he went to sleep. Once I sat up and started to reach out and touch him but I didn't. I was very tired.

All that was a week before the end of camp. The boys in our cabin started talking about him. He had stopped playing ball. He wouldn't swim in the camp meet. He didn't even go on the Sunday hike up to Johnson's Knob. He sat on his bed with his clothes on most of the time. They never did anything nice for him. They were always doing things like tying his shoelaces together. It was no use trying to stop them. All they knew was that Michael Egerton had screwed their chance to be camp baseball champions. They didn't want to know the reason, not even the counselor. And I wasn't going to tell them. They even poured water on his mattress one night and laughed the whole next day about Michael wetting the bed.

The day before we left camp, the counselors voted on a Camp Spirit Cabin. They had kept some sort of record of our activities and athletic events. The cabin with the most Good Camper points usually won. We didn't win. Robin and the others told Michael that he made us lose because he never did anything. They told everybody that Michael Egerton made our cabin lose.

That night we were bathing and getting dressed for the Farewell Banquet. Nobody had expected Michael to go, but without saying anything he started getting dressed. Someone noticed him and said something about Mr. Michael honoring us with his presence at dinner. He had finished dressing when four of the boys took him and tied him between two bunks with his arms stretched out. He didn't fight. He let them treat him like some animal, and he looked as if he was crucified. Then they went to the banquet and left him tied there. I went with them but while they were laughing about hamstringing that damned Michael, I slipped away and went back to untie him. When I got there he had already got loose. I knew he was in the bathroom. I could hear him. I walked to the door and whispered "Mike, it's me." I don't think he heard me. I started to open the door but I didn't. I walked back out and down the hill to the dining hall. They even had the porch lights on, and they had already started singing.

THE LAST NEWS

Andrew,

Long as it's been since you left me here, I wonder if you recall the last thing you said to me. I was strapped, hand and foot, to that rusty gurney. And you said "Pa, live long enough to pardon this"—I knew you meant committing me, against my will, to a drunk-tank worse than Hell's cesspool. Before I found the words I wanted, the black man rolled me through those doors. So you didn't hear what I tried to say. It was some hot version of "Damn your soul for evermore." Anyhow I said it and even now I mean it, more than once per day.

But against my will, they've brought me onward to where anyhow I know what I've done and mainly who to. And one of the things I'm told to do is make my peace with who I hurt. You know, well as me, it's too late now to make amends to the one I hurt the actual worst. I've tried to beg your mother's pardon in prayers every night, but no answer comes and I'm giving up. You know prayer never meant much to me. Deep down, I doubt that Whoever set this world to spinning gives a plugged copper dime for my little errands—He, She, It or Whatever's there has sure-to-God kept itself scarce around me.

But here you are and while I can, I'm saying, Drew, excuse me. Is *Excuse* too weak? Is it more like *forgive*? Maybe I'm asking you more than a man can ask another man.

*

I stopped there, son, to let the night pass and a good part of daybreak. I needed to think, could I push on with this mean homework I'm told to do? There are women I strongly suspect are living all down the road from Raleigh to Nags Head, waiting for me to say I'm sorry. There's a child you don't even know exists, that's your half-brother, on the outskirts of Clinton, a good mechanic. He knows my name but not much else. I owe him the world. Or so my mind reminds me in dreams, black as he is. But after your dead mother, you come first—the oldest blood-child I helped to cause. So if I can make this terrible deal work out with you—Christ, I might have cut me a one-lane track anyhow out of here, not the same mean rut I'm circling in.

You're a sweet-natured man, Drew, have always been. I know you've already wiped your eyes and said "I forgive." And Christ, I'm grateful but this old Hell goes deeper than that. A whole lot deeper than you still know. I stretched last night on that hard cot and asked myself and the dark air around me if—any way on God's green Earth—I could keep my worst trespass still a secret.

I bet myself, and am betting this morning, that you don't even know what I mean. You were nineteen months old, I know that still. You were walking strong, could look at your mother like water in a drought. You even could call my full name plain and did so, any night I got home conscious before she shut the door to your room. If it's not known to you now, then why must I tell it? Why poison the well for the rest of your life?

They say I got to, if that's an excuse. They say it'll keep on eating its way from out of my heart; and I'll keep trying to drown it down, if I don't reach in here today and tear it loose and hand it to you. For you to recognize and then bury, if you're that strong. With all the mess you *know* you've seen, I tell myself you've got a cup full, your cup runneth over and I should die dumb. But after last night, I'm betting they're right. And here's this news.

*

Andrew Henderson, I your human father forced your mother to grovel cold-naked beside your bed and do my body every sick brand of pleasure my mind could picture, for the worst part of one whole deep night hour—October the 19th, 1963. You were wide awake. You stayed on your side but turned toward us, and you watched every move. There were times her head got so close to you, you reached through the rails and touched her hair.

That just made it worse. Made me run wilder and punish her more. I knew I was doing it to ruin her for you. You loved her too much, she loved you ways she never loved me and never could now. And why she followed my will that night, every order I gave, was—I was holding my loaded pistol the whole sad time.

She ought to just grabbed it and finished me. I was most likely too drunk to fight if she went for my hand. She never said a word, not one low moan. She was protecting you, I guess. I *know*, if I know any one fact still.

So I won't call you *son* again. I won't even say so much as your name, from here on till you say I should. If you want to kill me once I'm out of here, be my guest. I'll lay this head on the rock of your choice in the back of that cave in the farthest woods, you drill my brain and walk on out, and I'll have a letter inside my pocket saying "I, Paul Henderson, paid this pittance on my big debt to the living and dead and am proud to be quit."

The mail still works. I'm waiting to know your answer, sir.

THE ANNIVERSARY

ALL THAT WEEK every time Miss Lillian Belle got still and cool, she knew she was waiting for something, the way little leathery country boys wait on their porches in the evening, not knowing what for, their work done, holding their knees and looking out towards darkness and the road. But it didn't worry her. It would come in a little (something she had forgot that was already gone or something that was coming), and if she never remembered, well, she was seventy-two years old, and she couldn't get herself upset every time her memory failed, and anyhow she had work to do—her Brother's meals to cook. Betty their cook was out of the kitchen for the fifth straight day, grieving for Henry her husband, holding him out of the ground that whole rainy week to bury him right, in sunshine, and everybody knew Lillian Belle Carraway couldn't make a thing but mints. Still, she did her best. She forced herself through the suffocating heat, and all that happened to remind her of what was forgotten didn't remind her at all, not even the dove mourning by night in the silvered eaves of the house or Brother's dogs with all their barking at the moon or Pretty Billy's mustache cup she had dusted twice already that week without seeing any more than if she hadn't painted them there herself, forty-five years ago, the plain gold flowers and the words she had chosen then with such shy care, "Forget Me Not, Forget Me Never." And it might have gone on that way another week or longer—those pieces of the past riding by her no more noticed than old cars on the public road—if Brother hadn't said at dinner, "How are you holding up under this heat?" (His voice was cool and faraway as a medical doctor's.)

She told him, "Brother, I am not as strong as I look." And she wasn't, though sitting there under those grand cheekbones, round, high and pure white as china doorknobs, and her thick hair black as night still, she looked for all the world firm and impassable as a good privet hedge. ("The Indian blood," Papa used to tell her and laugh—"Very little, to be sure, and what there is from Pocahontas.") But strong or weak, how could she say what she had thought all morning?—that she had no business at Henry Twitty's funeral in the heat—when everybody knew she and Brother still owed Henry that great debt of thanks which dying didn't cancel for being the Negro of all they knew who offered to chauffeur their father in the very last days when his blood rose higher than science could record and all that would cool him off was to send for Henry, day or night, and say, "Take Papa to ride" and watch them sail off into the wind at sixty miles an hour, glasses rolled down and Papa like a statue on the seat till he felt relief and when that came, saying, "Much obliged, Henry. I'm much obliged"? Facing such a debt, how could she say "I'm staying home"? Letting Henry down, even now, would be like letting Papa down, and she couldn't do that of her own free will.

So Brother did it for her. He laid down his knife and fork and said, "You stay at home. Every Negro on the place will be there and every Elk from Warrenton." He took out the silver toothpick, and they were both quiet a minute. (He was right about the Elks. Henry was something big in the Elks and died dead-drunk on his own front porch. He had often told Betty never to let him lie down drunk or else his heart would float, but she didn't get home that evening till late and it had floated.) Then Brother stood and said, "Betty won't miss you in the crowd."

"That's a lie," she said. "You know there's a pew waiting empty for nothing but two Carraways."

He said, "I'm one Carraway and that's what they'll get today. You stay home and rest." He stepped to the porch and sat awhile, and she went back to the kitchen to finish there. When it came time to go, Brother walked through the hall and said "Goodbye" and went to the funeral, not letting her speak a word. She watched him awhile out the open kitchen window, pulling at her fingers, drawing the blood, slow and violet, back into them, standing that way till the dust of his truck had settled. Then she turned towards the parlor for the first time in months as it would be cool in there.

She sat and thought about fixing Brother's supper, rocking on Mama's green velvet carpet easy as if Mama herself was there in the door, looking long and saying, "Lillian Belle, would you tell me what you think this is? Sunday? You'll cut through to China in less than an hour that way." (One time she had answered, "Mama, me and Brother will just move to the Thorntons'. They let you rock till you're blue in the face and slam doors!") The air of the parlor felt her all over like the coolest kind of hand, and when she caught her head bobbing foolish as a hen's, she said out loud, "If I'm going to sleep I might as well give up now and go to the bed and stretch out." She stood and walked to the mantel where her glasses were. She always laid them there when she rocked. Rocking in her glasses made her dizzy. She put them on and looked up to get them adjusted. And there it was, hanging a little too high and almost out of her sight now but familiar and stinging still. Remembrance took her from her head down to every part the way a breeze will take itself straight down the hall of a house when you had almost given up hope for it, cooling every room as it goes.

Not moved once and barely dusted since Papa had it made for her up in Petersburg and it came down through the mail without even breaking the glass. A splendid likeness of Pretty Billy—eyes faded a little but still so deep in his head it seemed you could never come near them, not if you set out this minute and walked in that direction towards him, not eating or drinking till you dropped. And who in the world, was the first thing she always wondered when she saw it, had ever kept him still that long? And wasn't it funny after all? (though she never thought that till Papa died)—Pretty Billy Williams set there in a border of black with doves in gentle flight around him, thin white streamers in their crossed pink mouths falling over his head after so much time, curling in and out of the poem.

> *Death our dearest ties can sever,*
> *Take our loved ones from our side,*
> *Bear them from our homes forever*
> *O'er the dark cold river's tide.*
>
> *In that happy land we'll meet them,*
> *With those loved and gone before,*
> *And again with joy we'll greet them*
> *There where parting is no more.*

"All the time," she said, "that was what it was." And she would have touched the frame to straighten it if it hadn't stained itself in that one place Papa gave it all those years ago.

She came out on the back porch and shaded her eyes and tried to see down that way. She had missed getting the proper eyes, the Carraway eyes to go with the face, and the ones she had, narrow and dun, could only make out the large things now that hung on the sky flat and swaying as clothes on a line—the perfectly round oak tree people still drove miles to look at and where Aunt Dorcas Simpson's place had gone, leaving its chimney alone and old already as Aunt Dorcas was at death and getting older, and Liney Twitty's place huddled to the ground, cowed-looking and yet, you knew, as strong as a hound dog when you call his name and make him come. All the other things that belonged there were gone. At least to her eyes, and from here.

She took down her yard hat and put it on—lacquered black straw with plaster fruit like bullets on the brim—and in her right hand were flowers from the vase in the hall. She went down the steps to the yard, taking each step careful as some altogether new place, and began her walking by a fence that traveled in curves far as anyone could see, walking her age gently but worriedly the way an old mother dog must walk straddling gray and swollen dugs, and the white dirt powdered under her feet and sifted away in the occasional breeze. (It was dry already from the rain.) Then she came to where the dirt was hard and packed. That was Liney Twitty's yard, swept by brush brooms till it shone like Liney's own ivory hand. Any other day she would have gone in and sat awhile with Liney who was her own age, but Liney to be sure had a front seat at the funeral. She slacked up to rest just the same, and what had looked like a black fence post turned into General Washington standing by a chinaberry tree, breaking waxy berries with a dusty toe. He was Liney's grandchild who lived with her.

Miss Lillian Belle said, "Good afternoon, Wash. What in the world are you doing in the broiling sun—frying your brains?"

"Nothing," he said, "but waiting till the funeral lets out."

"Well, come on then and help me do what I've got to do."

"What you got to do, Miss Lillian Belle?"

"I've got to go to the graves. Three days ago was Mr. Pretty Billy's anniversary and I forgot."

Going to the graves they passed where the first house had been, the one Mr. Idle Carraway her grandfather had built and called Antaeus Hill (because its earth sustained him) till his wife changed it to Roman Hill (because nobody but Idle, she said, had ever heard of Antaeus before). Miss Lillian Belle told people who asked that she never saw Old Roman Hill "in person" because it burned from lightning while Mr. Idle was in Mississippi with his wife and children, selling race horses which all the Carraways raised back then. Somebody sent him the news and right away he telegraphed a poem to the Raleigh paper, and they printed it on Easter Monday. Every Carraway since got to know the poem by heart, including children, as Mr. Idle sent it in to the paper every anniversary of the fire until he died, and Miss Lillian

Belle and Brother and all kinds of little Negroes used to climb in the old black bones of the house, dodging flaming clusters of cow itch and screaming their grandfather's poem so loud that lizards broke off their tails in fright and scattered for the dark.

> March 12, 18—
> *The Hand of God did cloud the day*
> *To chasten Idle Carraway,*
> *For out the Blue a sizzling blast*
> *Hath laid to waste a Proud Man's past*
> *And all his hope to build on land*
> *A mansion that would ever stand*
> *To give sweet witness to his name*
> *And send through Carolin' his fame . . .*

They passed on by it in no time now, even walking slow as Miss Lillian Belle did with Wash spinning and flinging himself like a limber dishrag. He went by without looking once—just turned up to Miss Lillian Belle and said, "Big Mama have seen right smart dead peoples over there," and because she hadn't been there in over a year and because she had to stop to catch her breath, Miss Lillian Belle looked to where a few bricks and a beam or two were wrapped in yards of honeysuckle, and what she thought of was the nine upright beams that stood there through her childhood—to yell the poem to—till the Negroes commenced cutting at them by night for kindling, cutting at the base of each beam till all nine stood like pencils somebody was trimming patiently year by year. After that they fell too and were dragged away by whoever wanted them and used for things Mr. Idle Carraway, who was a strong man, would have wept to see.

She turned back to say to Wash, "I expect she has, Wash. I expect she has," but she said it to herself—Wash had flung to the end of the path and opened the wrought-iron gate. She couldn't see him but his high voice came to her through the heavy air, "Here he, Miss Lillian Belle. Here he be."

*

There were eighteen graves, seventeen of them Carraways who had died—the biggest number in bed back in the house—knowing this was where they would come. (One or two had been shipped in—one boy from Shiloh and one they knew very little about, a distant cousin from Walkerton that just turned up one day, boxed, in the Express Office.) And inside the fence there was periwinkle crawling everywhere to set the place off from the field all around and the rows of tobacco that came to the fence in order and stopped. With all that greenery you couldn't say where one grave stopped and the next one began, but they were there—all of them—the way they knew they would be, together. Miss Lillian Belle's Papa had lived long enough to plan it right, long enough to see that Lillian Belle and Brother were the last, and when their mother took the next-to-last place in the old plot and Brother suggested maybe they could buy a little piece for him and Lillian Belle in the church cemetery, Papa opened the fence and took in a few more yards of field and said, "I had just as soon you were buried upright in the State Museum as in a public graveyard where the ones that cut the grass over your head don't know any more about you than what can be got on a tombstone" which in Papa's case was

J. B. CARRAWAY

A BAPTIST   A DEMOCRAT

But Wash stood on another grave, square and still for the first time on the one place that wasn't a Carraway, with his feet hid deep in the vine and his legs growing up like narrow black trees to the mouth that kept singing, "Here Mr. Pretty Billy, here he, Miss Lillian Belle!" to the dry little tune he patted with his hand on the stone that said in small letters, WILLIAM WILLIAMS—A FRIEND.

The place was in full sun so under her broad-brimmed hat, Miss Lillian Belle stood in the gate while her head and her eyes finished swimming, and to stop Wash's singing she said, "What do you know about him?"

"Big Mama tell me things about him," he said.

Then she saw things plainer and went towards the grave. There was one fruit jar by the stone, half-full of rusty-looking rainwater. She bent over and put in the flowers, and the white skin of her breast fell down on itself in a host of involved wrinkles like a handful of crepe myrtle laid in there, and Wash said, "They won't last ten minutes in that."

She straightened up and studied them. "No, I don't reckon they will."

But Wash was back to the question she asked. "I know about them dogs," he said, "and him getting his neck broke." Then he danced off the grave and fell down in the periwinkle and said to himself, "I'm the onliest Nigger I know who ain't scared of snakes."

Miss Lillian Belle had given up trying to follow him with her eyes. She said, "You didn't ever see him did you?"—and laughed at her own foolishness.

Wash didn't answer right away but in a little he said, "Did he have red hair?"

"No, black as ink."

"I ain't seen him then." And again he waited—what he was thinking was his own business, but what he finally said was, "How old he now, Miss Lillian Belle?"

"That would take more figuring than I care to do," she said. There was a long minute while she looked round to confirm she was there at last before she took her seat sideways and slow on Pretty Billy's stone. "All I can say right off is I was twenty-six when he came down here for the first time to Mary Jane McNeill's wedding. Her name was just Mary. I was the one added on the Jane. And that made me the last one of my friends to be single. Papa was beginning to fidget about it, had been for several years so when this very fine-looking young man turned up the week before the wedding to be Best Man, Papa sat up and took notice right away. He was introduced to all as Mr. William Williams from Hamlet who was a telegrapher with the Seaboard Railroad, but Mary Jane and I called him by the name he offered us and then blushed—Pretty Billy. No need to blush. He *was* the prettiest-looking boy I think I ever saw—because that's what he was, a boy. When your Big Mama took her first look at him, Wash, she said, 'That gentleman must be a policeman to look all *that* fine in his something-to-wear.' (Don't ask me where she had seen a policeman before.) The wedding week was a right active one—the McNeills had money if nothing else— and Mary Jane paired me and Pretty Billy off together for several of the functions. At the candy pull he tried to teach me some of the Morse code. I could see right away that it required speed which I have never had, but I let him go on all evening because of the way he kept taking my finger in his hand—he had a surgeon's hands, that fine and narrow with nothing but a plain gold ring. Well, he kept taking my finger and saying, 'Guess what this means' and tapping out a message on the table and when I asked him what it was he had made me say, just smiling back behind his eyes and not telling me. The wedding was a big success, and Pretty Billy and I carried Mary Jane and her husband to Norlina to take the train for the wedding trip to Washington. I know it was the coldest night of the fall—it was November—and I believe I still had on my Maid of Honor dress (though all I can really remember is I wore a hat with ragged robins on it) so with the wind whipping through the curtains of the car, I was frozen to a polka dot in five minutes and sat there with every pore of my skin standing on end like flagpoles. Pretty Billy and I didn't speak a word till we got to the station and barely spoke one on the way home till I said, 'I have always said, just let me get in an automobile and the wind starts blowing' and he laughed. That finished the wedding and there wasn't anything else to hold him in Macon so he headed back to Hamlet the next day, and I never thought or even hoped, I guess, that I would lay eyes on him again. When Papa asked me what I thought of him, and I said I guessed he was right pleasant, you could see Papa's feathers fall a mile. I don't think I could have cared less. I just went back to my duties—teaching Sunday school and painting china and singing here and there—and every now and then I would go visit Norah Fitts who everybody *knew* was already an old maid. We used to sleep in this high bed of hers and tie our toes together in hopes one of us would forget and get up in the night and drag the other one out on her head. (I have done a number of silly things, but I have generally managed to laugh at myself before others laughed at me.) Then out of a clear sky comes this postal card from Hamlet with a picture of the jail on it—some of Pretty Billy's foolishness—which struck me as being a little forward at the time as he asked me to exchange greetings with him, but anyway the next trip I took into Warrenton, I bought a supply of cards and sent him one. That went on for weeks. Papa met every mail train, it looked like to me, and I had gotten to anticipating them myself. So when summer came Norah and I went down to Augusta for a month to visit the Bridges sisters, and I got a card nearly every day I was gone. (Norah said he must be manufacturing the things.) By the time we started home, I had so many I almost had to pay Excess Baggage on them. When I got back I pulled out all the cards, and of course Papa had a fit and so did Mama, and they bought me an album to keep them in with mother of pearl all over the cover. I hadn't been home any time when Pretty Billy wrote a letter at last. (By that time I had several views of everything in Hamlet. It's a small place.) He asked me to meet him in Raleigh at the State Fair. Somebody must have told him I hadn't ever missed a fair in my life— they just couldn't have one without me—so I wrote and said Yes, I could meet him, and Mama nearly had a stroke. 'The idea,' she said, 'of you Lillian Belle traipsing off sixty miles to Raleigh to meet a very-nearly rank stranger!' As if she didn't know for a fact he was Mary Jane McNeill's husband's bosom friend and from good folks in Moore County though his father and mother were not living. Well, Mama had put her foot down, and I was almost resigned when Cousin Florence Russell heard about it the way she heard about everything—right out of the empty air—and upped and volunteered to act as chaperone. (Cousin Florence was every bit as fond of fairs as I was and had been attending a whole lot longer.) I was humiliated. She looked like a tomato and belched at the drop of a hat, but she satisfied Mama so that was that, and we took the morning excursion train to Raleigh. It was held up I don't know how long waiting for some Negroes—none of ours—who had reserved a car to themselves and then at the last minute didn't turn up because they couldn't raise the money. I died a thousand deaths the whole way to Raleigh. I had wired Pretty Billy when I would meet him, and here we were going to be hours late, and he would more than likely give me out and leave, and there I would be with Cousin Florence laughing, because that's exactly what she would have done, and going back home to tell for the rest of her life how Lillian Belle and her beau hadn't made connections. Before long though it was clear we were going to pull into Raleigh almost on time after all. The engineer was handling the train like it was an express wagon, and in no time both of us were dizzy as guinea hens—Cousin Florence a good deal dizzier than me however, so much so that she suddenly took down the box of dinner we had brought and said we wouldn't be needing *that* and handed it to a little big-eyed boy who had anyhow been looking up at it ever since he boarded the train like he expected any minute for the lid to fly off and reveal—pistols! So I sat the rest of the way in hunger and misery, worrying that I might not even recognize Pretty Billy, but when we stepped off the train in this huge burst of steam that wilted me something awful and just made Cousin Florence redder, there he was on the platform with a little derby hat sitting on his ears and grinning like a possum. There wasn't any question about not knowing him on sight. And oh, we had the grandest time at the fair— took in everything right down to the pigs and managed to lose Cousin Florence in the prize oil paintings. (She waited happy for hours in front of 'The Alps Mountains Under Snow' because it cooled her off.)"

Wash said, "Big Mama say I can go to the Littleton Fair this year, Miss Lillian Belle, if there be anybody will take me." He was nearly out of sight in the vine, but you knew he was listening—he was so still a butterfly had lit on his shining forehead and moved there softly like breathing.

"Well, I hope you can get there," Miss Lillian Belle said, "but I won't fool you. It can't *touch* the State Fair with a forty-foot pole. In particular the fireworks. Pretty Billy wanted me to stay over for the grandstand fireworks display at midnight, but I had promised Mama I would be on the eleven o'clock train—and even that was daring enough to curl half the hair in Sixpound Township—and of course Cousin Florence had collapsed long since and was sitting by the fountain eating peanuts (of all things to come to the State Fair and eat when she had a bushel of them right on her own back porch). So he saw us to the train, and I cried off and on all the way to Macon for what Cousin Florence described as 'an unknown reason.' But it wasn't so unknown to me or to Papa either who met us at the train. One look—by lantern light—was all Papa needed. He knew me like a book. So what happened after that wasn't much surprise to any of the family (though it took right many outsiders off guard, and Cousin Florence went around telling everybody, 'Lillian Belle's got a beau from "off." ' I don't know where she thought Hamlet was—Europe?). There commenced a grand exchange of sealed letters between Pretty Billy and me, and Papa talked Mama (without much trouble) into asking him to spend Christmas with us. He accepted post-haste, not having any other place to go, and Mama and old Aunt Dorcas your great-grandmother and Liney turned the house wrongside-out, washing curtains that froze on the line and generally stirring up dust until they had sent Brother to bed nearly dead with asthma. I took it all right calmly—a lot calmer than Papa liked— and sat in the parlor making a whole series of Christmas presents for Pretty Billy, most of which Mama decided were too intimate. I spent half my time ripping W. W. monograms off of things Mama said just wouldn't do. Finally Papa told me to give him a mustache cup and that's what I did, but I didn't paint the sentiment on it for the longest kind of time after that. It didn't take much imagining to know that being naturally nervous, he would arrive on the wrong train—at least two trains earlier than he had said and so early in fact that he almost caught Mama in her shimmy which you would practically have to get up before day to do. Every once in a while I remember that Christmas as the brightest time we ever had. Pretty Billy couldn't stand the dark so Mama kept enough lamps going to light the Governor's Mansion, and he stayed with us nearly a week. Of course he had presents for every soul on the place. Mine was a gold cross and chain. Aunt Dorcas took one look at it and said, 'That man means business.' Even at Christmas it was quiet here, though nothing like now. Everybody I knew was married and had stopped having parties, and there wasn't much to offer him in the way of entertainment (and there's always been a limit to the time *I* can sit and talk to one person) so he and Papa went off hunting a lot— neither one of them could hunt worth ten cents—and I sat at home mortified for fear Papa was going to force his hand but he didn't. And when all of us saw him off on the train back to Hamlet, him waving and smiling out from under that little mustache, my youngest brother Doc, who died, asked him, 'Are you Lillian Belle's sweetheart?' And he said, 'I hope I am.' And by that time he was, I guess."

"I been asking Big Mama if it ain't time I'm getting *me* some sweethearts," Wash said. His butterfly was gone now.

Miss Lillian Belle gave a little laugh.

"Well, I'm nine years old and, Miss Lillian Belle, when am I going to get any bigger?"

"Time will tell," she said, and because he had rolled on his stomach and laid his face in the periwinkle and started whistling, she asked, "Are you hearing what I'm telling you, Wash?"

"Yes'm," he said without looking up, "you going on about Mr. Pretty Billy, and you say time will tell."

"It will too. It will. There were some claimed I had seen the last of him when he left after Christmas just because he spent so much time hunting and because I didn't fall all over him with love and care. But that's not my nature, never was, and he knew it and honored me for it though he *was* inclined to want to touch people all the time in spite of everything I said. Still he wrote as regular as clockwork, and his letters were just like his talk. You would read them, sitting right by yourself on the porch, and laugh like a nitwit. I suppose my replies encouraged him, and in February he wrote and wanted to know if he could ask Papa for my hand. It certainly wasn't a *new* idea to me, but coming from Pretty Billy towards the end of one of his foolish letters, I nearly had an attack. I slept on it several days and took out his picture and studied it a good many times before I answered to tell him he could. His letter to Papa came in about a week, and if Papa could have run all the way to Hamlet to say Yes, he would have. You would have thought I was a hundred years old. I was just pushing twenty-eight. So it all went very smoothly. Most of our plans were made by mail—setting the date, I mean, and arranging about the honeymoon at Old Point Comfort and deciding where to live in Hamlet (he suggested we stay at the Seaboard Hotel till I got adjusted)—and I only saw him one more time before the wedding week, and that was when he came down for three days at Easter and spent most of his time riding out alone because horses gave Brother asthma and Papa was having his spring rheumatism. I had no intentions of turning it into a tremendous wedding. I was never the bride type anyway so we were going to keep it small—small as Papa would let us with him charging around telling everybody in sight, white or black, and inviting them. We had decided on September the fifteenth in hopes it might be cooler by then and we could decorate the church with the last of the roses and leaves. The ceremony was to have been in the evening. I've always loved the dark. It's so sad. Pretty Billy arrived a week in advance. Papa and Brother met his train and brought him to the house. That was the only time he ever kissed me, saying it was about time for that now, didn't I reckon? There wasn't much entertaining for us and that suited me fine. I had miles of sewing left to do. After breakfast every morning I would step in the parlor and start to work, and Pretty Billy would come trailing after me. It never seemed to dawn on him that I might not want him watching me make my own step-ins and all but I never mentioned it. (He was the nervous type—always had to be poking up the fire or fiddling with something in his hand. Early in our acquaintance he broke the lacework skirt off of a china ballet dancer

Mama valued because it was sent to her from some capital, and when I looked up at him holding out the pieces in his hand and making no attempt to hide them, he said, 'See here, Lillian Belle, what I've done, just fiddling with it,' and I said—and laughed—'It seems to me if you are so much of a fiddler, you had better invest in a fiddle before you cause real trouble.') But he never bothered me long, and from the second day after he arrived, he was riding off every morning to hunt by himself. Most of Papa's dogs would follow after him. Mama would pack him some dinner, and we wouldn't see him again until late evening just before supper. I thought I would be seeing enough of him in the future so I never asked him not to go. He never brought any game or anything back with him except some lovely leaves to decorate the church, and once I asked him, 'Pretty Billy, what is it you are after out there all day long?' and he laughed and said, 'Most anything I can scare up.' (Lord knows what he was hunting at that time of year unless it was a breeze or a cool place to lay his head.) Before I could catch my breath good, it was Thursday morning—Saturday was the wedding—and I was getting more fidgety by the minute. I would jump out of my skin if you halfway looked at me, but Pretty Billy rode off that morning before I even got downstairs. Mama had taken over the sewing because I was so trembly, and I spent the entire day making mints on a marble-top washstand— one of the few things I do well. I looked for Pretty Billy to come in for dinner since it was Thursday and folks were beginning to call but he didn't. And he didn't show up at three o'clock either when Preacher Burton came to discuss details so I had all that to handle alone, and I have never been any sort of manager. It was a cool afternoon and bright, and I decided to sit on the back steps and wait for him, but he didn't appear and dark was fast coming on and the chill so I went in, but I couldn't eat a mouthful of supper. Papa and Brother were worried too though they made out like they weren't. 'He's a splendid rider,' Papa would say every few minutes. 'He must have met up with a friend.' Well, of course he was a great talker, but *who*, was what I wanted to know, did he know out there in the middle of nowhere?"

"Big Mama know if you want to ask her," Wash said—but only to the hot air around. Miss Lillian Belle had gone on to tell it before she forgot.

"When he hadn't come by bedtime, I was all to pieces and nobody could begin to think of sleeping. We all sat there and waited and tried to find little tasks to do, little quiet things that wouldn't jar the air, till the only noise left was Mama's needles knitting Pretty Billy a going-away scarf for his long neck, when out of the pitch dark came this high sad voice that was one hound barking at the moon. And off in the woods the others commenced to answer, and they sounded half the world away. Papa rose up and said 'It's my dogs'—like it might have been dragons. All of us knew enough about those dogs' voices to know they hadn't just now wandered in at Pretty Billy's heels. Papa and Brother went out but they couldn't quiet them down. They stayed out there till I thought I would scream, and when they came in it was to get their coats and lanterns and their guns to ride off looking, taking Uncle Smooth with them—your great-granddaddy—on a mule, and all those crying dogs. I sat by the window with a light till way past midnight. Then Mama made me take off my shoes and rest till we heard some news. That wasn't before nearly seven when Uncle Smooth rode up in the yard on Papa's horse and told Mama that Papa said Miss Lillian Belle was to come to where he was right away. I asked him if they had located Mr. Pretty Billy. All he said was 'Yes'm, they did.' I put on my coat and climbed on the horse behind him (we only kept three riding horses then) and didn't say a word till we got to where we were going. I just prayed to myself and Uncle Smooth took us crashing off through the woods. Where we finally stopped was at the Pitchfords'. You don't know them, Wash."

"Yes'm, Big Mama use their name sometime in stories."

"Well, the Pitchfords I'm talking about were farming a piece of Papa's poorest cotton land over beyond the creek bottom. There are some of them back there right now—the sort of folks you will have to knock in the head on Judgment Day. They had a little house very much like

Liney's except darker and dirty, and when Uncle Smooth and I flew up in the yard there was nothing in sight but eight or ten peaked-looking children standing in stairsteps by the door staring at me. Papa said many times afterwards that if there had been any way in the world to spare me the shock of walking in like that, he would have done it. But as it was, they had had to lay Pretty Billy out on a bed pushed close up to the fireplace, and he was the first thing I laid eyes on when I walked in that house. It didn't help one bit either that after I had stood in the door a long time, he rolled his eyes over towards me as far as he could and tried to smile and said, 'Look here, Lilly, I've messed up your shirt.' He had just recently been calling me Lilly, and the shirt was one I had made for him. Papa was there and what seemed like a hundred of those Pitchfords creeping around and looking at me out of their big squirrel eyes and saying 'Howdy-do, lady.' Brother had gone on the other horse to get a doctor. I didn't ask but Papa volunteered they had found Pretty Billy thrown down beside the creek a little way from the Pitchfords'. After a while old Mrs. Pitchford came up to Papa and said, 'Major Carraway, it's his neck, ain't it?' and Papa said 'I know that.' They offered me a chair by the fire, and I sat there for the rest of the time about four yards from Pretty Billy's head as I reckoned it. I never went a step closer, and when he died he died just that far from me. Brother and the doctor didn't come and didn't come, and nobody knew anything to do for him except Nettie Pitchford—she was their oldest girl, about seventeen— and she stood there by him and mopped off his forehead with cool water and fanned him whenever the flies settled. He looked at her most of the time and nowhere else. Papa said he couldn't turn his head. It looked like we might be there a long time, and Mrs. Pitchford came over and asked me if I wouldn't take a glass of her tomato wine. I said I didn't believe that was what I needed, and it was then that Pretty Billy called for Papa. Papa leaned over him and Pretty Billy tried to whisper, but in that room there wasn't such a thing as whispering. What he said was, 'Give her something she wants.' He was looking at Nettie and smiling."

A thin useless cloud passed over the sun, splotching the graves with

shade, and a little breeze commenced waving round in the tobacco—
nothing to get your hopes up about—but in the brief dark and under
the brim of her hat, Miss Lillian Belle's eyes went on getting brighter.
"I've always known Pretty Billy meant for Papa to reward that girl for
hanging over him faithful like she did with water. Then a fly landed
on his nose. He laughed and a thin stream of blood ran out of the
corner of his mouth, and he gave this little last sound twice—not a
word, but like a dove makes, round and alone, and I couldn't listen to
a dove for the longest kind of time after that. I ought to have cried right
then before it was too late. If somebody had laughed at me or said,
'Lillian Belle, I'm sorry' or 'Lillian Belle, you will never be asked to
bear a heavier load than this' then I might have broken down like any
woman should. But I didn't see it that way. The only person that said
anything was Papa, and all he said was, 'Lillian Belle, don't let me
down.' It just seemed like he was counting on me to hold up. It was
the first time I had ever been counted on for anything so I held up. His
brother came that same afternoon, short and scared-looking. Nobody
had given him a thought. He had come to be Best Man. Papa asked
him what was his wish about burying Pretty Billy, and he said he
thought it would be the sensible thing to bury him in Macon. That
was what Papa had hoped for so he offered Pretty Billy this space here
and did every bit of the bathing and shaving and dressing himself, using
my one photograph to locate the part in all that damp black hair. When
he had finished the laying out, he led me in to say goodbye or whatever
I wanted to say. The casket hadn't come yet and Pretty Billy was lying
on the bed he generally slept in with one pillow under his head so the
edge of his nose and lips and chin and his eyelids were raised up into
the light from the window and seemed to be shining from inside. Papa
had shaved off part of his mustache by mistake, and what was left wasn't
too much like Pretty Billy. The only thing I could think to do was
touch his hand once and then leave. But when I stepped forward to do
it, I saw how the fingers of his right hand had curled inwards to make
a cup like a sea shell waiting for water, and I didn't want to disturb that.

So I turned to Papa and said 'I'm ready' and he took me away. It was to have been a small wedding, and it was a small burial. Papa stopped our Virginia cousins by wire, and there was just Mama and Papa and Brother and Doc, and the preacher, and Mr. Williams' wife joined him for the service, and little Loyce Rodwell and I, and Nettie Pitchford and her folks turned up but kept their distance. Liney and Aunt Dorcas and Uncle Smooth and some of the others watched from the porch. It was a nice afternoon. Papa had turned the goats loose in the front yard to eat down the tallest weeds, and some little Negro boys had spent that whole morning rolling down all that was left with great big logs. Aunt Dorcas went out a dozen times, I know, and told them to hush up their laughing. Mama had asked Liney to sing a song, and she sang 'Precious Lord, Take My Hand' with no piano or anything, just that clear voice she used to have that carried to the road. Then the men put him on the wagon and brought him down here for the commitment. Loyce Rodwell, who was to have strewn rose petals at the wedding, sprinkled some in over the casket, and Mama and I walked back up to the house. Papa stayed behind, and Brother, to see that the rest was done. Everybody did their best and with time and a mild winter, things had pieced back together nearly when one evening Aunt Dorcas looked out of the kitchen window and said, 'Here come that Pitchford child.' Papa went out to meet her, remembering Pretty Billy's last words that I hadn't ever forgotten. She had walked all that way—four or five miles easily—to ask Papa if as her present she couldn't have that little gold finger ring of Mr. Pretty Billy's. Papa told her it was buried with him, which it was, so she said, 'Well, there ain't nothing else I don't guess' and turned and set off to walk back home in the night."

She had stopped and she sat on the stone, picking at any spot on her dress as was her habit. In a little Wash raised up from his greenery— "That's all you remember, Miss Lillian Belle?"

She nodded. "I'm a mighty good forgetter."

Wash took a small rock and scraped at the moss on the modest stone

Major Carraway had felt compelled to buy for that Walkerton cousin. Miss Lillian Belle stood and looked round her again. It had once been her wish to see the graves from the air because Dorman Spivey had passed over in a plane on his way to war and reported that the Carraway cemetery was the one thing he recognized in all Warren County. Then she said, "Wash, I'll need your hand back up the path," and as if he had been doing it forever, he took her arm and a good part of her weight on his shoulder, and they started—the old woman looking towards where she knew the house was and the little boy studying the ground and leaning into his work with his pink tongue just showing between the dark purple lips.

Soon they would be close enough, and the house would swim into plain view through the heat. Miss Lillian Belle said, "Hold up a minute, Wash, and let me catch my breath," and from there she looked up, but all she could see of it was the silver paint streaking over the eaves and down the east side where Buxton Bragg, a jack-leg roof painter, had spilled it early in the spring. Brother should have seen to that long ago. "I'll speak to him about that this evening," she said, "if I don't forget." Wash was still beside her, plowing little furrows on the dust with his toe and humming. "I'm all right now, Wash. You run on home. Liney and the rest of them will be there directly, and they can tell you about Henry's funeral."

"Yes'm. Then you want me to come tell you, Miss Lillian Belle?"

"Thank you, no, Wash. Brother will be telling me all I can say grace over."

So he said he would be seeing her tomorrow if the Lord was willing and he didn't die, and she moved on towards the house, towards what she could see—the light, that was all, the sun on the spilled paint, the sudden flashing reaching out to her even down here, shining like Christmas all those years ago or like her own old eyes as bright now in remembering as some proud mountain yielding the sun its flanks of snow or some white bird settling its slender wings with the softest cry into dying light.

INVITATION

for Jessie Rehder   *1908–1967*

T HE GIFTS that you gave me (*presents,* not *love* nor entire *loyalty*; they were daily issue) were few and small (we all laughed— you hardest—at your chinchery)—from your Caribbean Christmas, a dishtowel-map of the West Indies; from your California summer, a butcher's apron; from my last sight of you, a white hyacinth. (My thirty-fourth birthday. You'd called me to your house, too low to visit me; and when I'd gone, climbed your yard—littered now—and found you hunched at the living-room table, stroking accurate as a rhino at a paint-by-number canvas of yellow roses, and when you'd stood to show the pounds you'd lost since your little heart spell—slacks and jersey flapped round you, an idle tent—when you'd shown me your face bound for death like a ship, then you said "Many more!" and gave me my present—a hyacinth blooming in a cardboard pot. Did you see?— as I did at once—the petals were browning, the odor a furious final exhaling? Yet it outlasted you by a week of warm days; and its dry leaves are out my kitchen window now, bulb committed to my hard starved garden.)

But the two emblems of you which I possess (which, barring fire, will outlast me though their meaning may not) were not gifts but begged—I pestered you for them. Two photographs. The first of you at about twenty-three (say, 1930; three years before my birth). We came across it in your crammed scrapbooks one hot night last summer on your plastic sofa (after cold crab salad and peach ice-cream which, since we survived, surely showed us immortal). I was shocked by its sudden still loveliness among all your decades of prank-shots, gags (you a Viking chief in your senior play, you in rhinestones and tank-suit on the Riviera, you at ninety-five pounds after your breakdown, in a ballet pose—a camera was your signal for self-vandalism); and I said with our usual tactlessness, "You were lovely, Jessie," then bit my tongue.— "*That* day," you said. "It was Aunt Mary's fault. She had found me a husband, a millionaire widower. He'd never seen me and this picture was meant to be his first look. Aunt Mary worked on my wardrobe for days, would dress me like a doll, then strip me, try again—new coat, hat, scarf; best photographer in town, shot through foggy lenses, all haze and glow. Then I saw the proofs and stopped her there, wouldn't let her contact her rich prospect."—"But why?" I said. You studied the face—"She had covered me up." She had—silk scarf to your chin; soft Garbo hat shading all your high forehead, half your huge right eye. You peer from a cave and, shyly but firmly and permanently, you issue your message and invitation—*I will come, for the asking to your generous heart; be your laughing servant as long as I live.* No takers, not one. And the last day I saw you, you knew that at last. Your terrible offer was down; gate had crashed. Now we talked through a grill, you unlikeliest of cloistered nuns; I what?—parent, friend, lover, gently abandoned? Both of us free *and* sentenced now—you to your death in less than two days, propped reading in bed, the maid five steps away unwarned (autopsy found no cause—blood, lungs, veins entirely clear; heart simply reneged) and I to what?

—To, among unknowns of time and face, the other picture I begged from you, other message you grudged me. A blurred Kodachrome from your summer in France two years ago; from a Norman church, a peeling mural, four figures from a medieval Dance of Death—two elegant skeletons, wasp-waisted, prancing; between them two persons. A tall stout lady entirely in red—red cloak to the throat, red wide-

brimmed hat, red veil round her face (an abbess? in red?) and a gray
young man; face, cap, doublet, hose one shade of gray. Each is attended
by a skeleton, is gripped at the wrist by an icy bone. Each gestures with
the free hand, palm upraised—not a frantic "No" but a calm "Not
yet." In vain. The forward rhythm is set. Their feet are performing
what their hands refuse. You had had this enlarged for your living-
room wall. I asked for a print. You firmly said "No." The request had
been idle, my answer unthinking—"Tightwad," I said, "I'll gladly
pay."—"Not that," you said,"Ask for anything else—take the leopard
skin." So, baffled now and mildly peeved, I dropped the request. But
a few days later you brought me my print, much smaller than yours
(half-a-dollar saved!), laid it on my sofa with no comment. I thanked
you but asked "Why so reluctant?"—"Look at it," you said, "You have
not really looked." I had not, for all my famed eagle-eye. The lady in
red was a likeness of you—swathed, all but smothered, in her bright
tent of clothes—beseeching time from her only companion, loyal,
smiling, ready death. I said, "Never mind—just art not life" and you
went off fishing.

Jessie, answer me this—if you saw yourself as the lady enthralled
(danced buxom away), why did you hang it by your own front door,
your last sight on leaving the house each day before heaving yourself
into one more failure; and who did you see in the ashen young man,
eyes down, in need of a haircut, as he yields more slowly to his partner
in the dance?

Never mind, again. All messages delivered. But till then at least, I
work on here, issuing my own invitations (your message: *invitation
unacceptable*)—house stocked with food (even crab, peach ice-cream),
leaves broadening round me already, mid-April, a cave of green; pond
boiling with fish now swollen with roe you could never catch though
you tried countless hours; field cluttered with cows (your only phobia)—
and when nights are sleepless and I slouch after work, facing my black
window, the black woods beyond (the white-faced sniper we suspected

there), the sight I want most often is you—a ghost in slacks!—to stretch by me here on my Navajo rugs (your bleak warning given and acted upon) and tell me the joke of the ape in love, so bad we could groan again in delight; and bare your heart (smooth, glistening now), face mine again (though younger, ruining).

Come at will, dear hulk, slimmed a little perhaps from your final fright but needless at last, free, no longer tired, and laughing to be homeless.

LATE WARNINGS

My Parents, Winter 1926

MY PARENTS—not yet my parents—stand on a crude plank bridge. The sky behind them is bleak, trees bare—November, December 1926. (My mother's left hand proves the year no later. She casually hides it—no wedding ring yet. They will marry soon, deeper into winter, January.) But they wear no more than their Sunday suits (his black or blue, hers tan or gray); no overcoats, scarves, boots or gloves. My father's hat is in his hand. My mother's shoes are baby-doll slippers. Her spit-curl rests on her forehead, no wind. Yet the day is clearly cold—the air, the light. Late afternoon, by its slant.

They are unprotected. They do not feel cold. They lounge, unshuddering, loose in their clothes; stock-still for the camera.

Or perhaps they do not care but only yearn—to touch entirely. They have not, will come to their wedding as virgins (so my father believed). Then how can they stand so calmly at ease and smile so slightly at their cameraman? (Does he offer some threat?) My father's eyes smile inward only (his goal in sight, his five years' courtship now promised reward); my mother's only smiling is expressed in her stance—she cants herself confident against my father's shoulder, down his whole left side.

They must care, must quickly protect themselves. Take shelter in time.

*

They will not—did not, perhaps by then could not. And shelter from what?

Where, for instance, is my father's left leg? Why does their shadow not resemble them?

The Knowledge of My Mother's Coming Death

Saturday

OUR meetings now are allegorical. Each week I haul my soiled clothes thirty miles—my house to hers. Each week she brings them clean—her house to mine. This afternoon in May we meet at mine. She sits before my window in my new chair—its saddle-brown obscured by her blue dress, her gray hair streaked by green light off my trees. I face her from the sofa, near enough—she sees me best at three-yards distance now. We talk of daily things—her car, my leaking roof—as one man's hands might speak to one another, thirty-two years of mutual life between them or like cooled lovers, joined but satisfied. I even roam her face, discovering beauty—the dark gold eyes, the open smiling mouth (spread wings but resting)—all as familiar as if I had made it. I partly have. All but the neat scar railing down her forehead, one inch behind which beat two aneurysms, bared two years ago but covered at once, untouched and lethal. Her time-bomb, she calls it—who knows the time? But not today. Not now it seems. We are spared again. The sun is in the window now, behind her. She is bright. She turns from me an instant. The line of her features transmits warm light. Her face has assumed the translucence of age—youth and age—and I think inside my own sound head, "I have loved you all your life," then remember she lived twenty-seven years before starting me. Still I do not feel I have lied or blubbed. She says "Four-thirty" and faces me. She must start home before the evening rush; so I end on money, as I mostly do—but offering not asking. Proud as a camel (her bank account under twenty dollars) she smiles, "Not now. Save till I'm needy."—

140

"But you'll let me know?" —"I'll let you know. When I need anything I'll call on you." We walk to her car. She says, "I'll see you when your clothes are dirty." I offer again what I've offered before—to take the clothes to a laundry here, spare her the chore. I intend both kindness and separation. She recognizes both, accepts the first, laughs, "And put a fat blind sixty-year-old widow out of work?" —"No," I say. She says, "You hate this. I know you do." I look up rebuked but she means her car—its color, milk-green. I do, I forgot. "I forgive it," I say. — "Thank you," she says, smiles, we kiss, she starts. Her car snaps smartly down my drive. She does not look back. I watch her dust as she reaches the road, is consumed by leaves; think, "The best woman driver in history"; then suddenly know, not coldly nor in fear but know for the first time without the least doubt—"That is the last sight I have of her."

Sunday

I KNOW it is day but I still lie dreaming, the frail quick thread that races morning—scraps of rhyme, clever retorts, problems dispatched. Then I calm, fall awhile; fall slower, slower till in stillness I endure this knowledge: my mother and I move in her car (whose color I no longer hate) through the heart of a city. She drives as always effortlessly, the visible sign of her inner grace. I sit on her right in a passenger's daze. She stops for a light and another car stops on her side, close beside her. The passenger in that car is a girl age twenty. She could easily touch my mother's face, its left profile; but instead she stares and I watch her stare. It slowly becomes a crouch, a frown, then a silent scream. The light goes green. My mother shifts gear, moves forward first, proceeds through the junction, continues her way. Yet terror is stuck in my chest, a stob. I study what half of her face I can see—the right profile, unchanged, at work. I know what waits on the left side though—the girl's frown has only confirmed my knowledge. I say "Mother" calmly—"Look here at me." Half-smiling she looks full-face a moment—the time she can spare from the road—and I see my oldest fear enacted. The artery beneath her left profile presses forward—a tree. A bare purple tree, rocks forward, peels downward silently. I think, "She is dying. I must take the wheel." But she faces the road, still efficient though dead, bearing me forward—her urgent task.

I wake, the stifling weight of dread. At breakfast I down the impulse to phone her; but by noon when I still have not thrown the dream, I drive ten miles to visit a friend, then do not tell him, sit gray and quiet in his room a bombsite, he whole at its center laughing on. At last he says, "What has ruined your day?" I say, "I have dreamt my mother's death." He takes an unseen world for granted (battles it daily), says "That would ruin it."

Monday

THAT friend is with me at my house now. He sits in the new chair and I sit opposite. The doors are open to the loud spring night. We laugh against it, then are suddenly silent—a natural pause. But the night has paused with us, entirely still; and in that silence (two seconds at most) a tide turns against us, against the house. The night lunges brute at every opening, every dark pane. We two seem under crushing assault, hopeless, surrendered. I look to him, look first to his hands— broad, knob-knuckles; they are gripped to the sides of the chair, blood gone. His face looks to me from the pitch of a shudder. He is bearing the brunt. Then the surge subsides; first from me, more slowly from him. We sit a moment exhausted, grateful. Then I half-laugh, say toward him "What happened?" —"Nothing," he says. I have not guessed but I know he lies. And now I cannot accept a lie. I say, "But it did—and to you. What happened." He does not—cannot? will not?—face me. "Not *happened*," he says. "It has not happened yet."

Not yet but will. I am sure now of waiting.

Tuesday

I HAVE eaten my supper, stacked the three dishes. In an hour I must drive ten miles, a meeting. The trip takes less than twenty minutes; but I start to go now, pulled out of the house by my ancient fear of missing things—trains, friends, the smallest chance. I wrench on a tie, rush into my coat, take a single step from closet to door. The phone rings. Now. Do I know? Have I learned? No. The instant of fright, leap of response are my constant reactions to telephone bells—that all news is bad. I stop its ring, pause before Hello, embracing the silence. A strange woman's voice, "Is this Mr. Price?"—"Yes," I say. She does not name herself—"I am here at your mother's . . ."

I have not learned from the three past days but now I know. I silently recite in unison with her—"Something has happened to your mother." —"I know." —"You know? It only just happened." —"I mean that I know what has happened," I say. "Where is she now?" — "The ambulance has just left for Wake Hospital." —"Thank you," I say, "I will go straight there." I lower the phone, hear her speak against extinction, raise it again, take the explanation this stranger must give. She inhales deeply—"Reynolds" (awards me my first-name, consolation), "she was talking on the telephone, sitting in this chair where I am now. I was across from her, saw it all. She stopped herself in the midst of a sentence, put her right hand to her forehead slowly, looked at me and said, 'I have a terrible pain in my head.' Then she dropped the phone and looked at her lap and began to pick at the nap of her skirt as if it was stain. Then she slumped on herself so I went to her. You don't know me but I . . ."

I thank her, say I am on my way. Then in cold efficiency (a gift from my dream) I call the hospital emergency room. A woman answers. I give my name, say, "My mother is on her way to you now. She cannot talk, will be unconscious and I want to warn you what to expect. She has had two cerebral aneurysms for some years now. They are on either side of the optic chiasma. One was ligatured two years ago with a Crutchfield clamp. The other has burst." —"All right," she says, "we'll be looking for her." I say, "I am coming there now myself." "All right," she says—then, "Are you a doctor?" —"No," I say. —"You sound like a doctor." —"No," I say. —"You know so much I thought you must be." She intends it as compliment, has time to talk on—"How do you know so much?" she says. I tell her, "I keep my eyes very clean," then am seized in a scalding strangling shudder, set the phone in its cradle, say aloud to the room, "What do I know, what will anyone know who cannot, will not read plain warnings; who if I could read, could still not save my love from death?—save her skull slowly filling itself, a bowl of blood?"

Life for Life

SIFTING the debris of my mother's death—Death Mother of Trash (old bank books, canceled checks)—my numb hands find an emblem of her life, a stack of records (brittle 78s) which I have not played through in twenty years, island planted by her in her death, pleasant garbage to relieve my chore. I rock back on numb haunches, smile, suck breath (hot July breath), then lift the records to a cooler room, unlid the old Victrola, throw its switch. Like every other thing here now she's dead, it leaps to duty; eager, accurate spins. I pile on half the stack, fall heavily into my father's chair still dark with his head oil, he dead ten years, surrender to the waiting random order—hoot of Emmy Destinn as Mignon, Lucrezia Bori's lean *Vedrai carino*; then suddenly as bombs within the room, the forties: Spike Jones' *Chloe*, crash of kitchens (through laughter, crash of Warsaw, London, Frankfurt); then Franklin Roosevelt, 1941, the 8th December, "I ask the Congress to declare . . ." At thirteen on my own I sent for this, from N.B.C., a birthday gift for Father. Half-pained, half-peeved, I rise, reject it harshly. Still covered by one more, the next disc falls, clatter of changer, roar of needle, voice—"Good morning, Mrs. Jones. My name is Price. I've come to show . . ."

My father's voice. Forgotten. Lost. Now round me in his room. Slow, calm—the only music he could make. Twenty-one years of daily hearing it; but ten years gone, I could no more have heard it in my head than Lincoln's voice—have often tried at night to dredge it back, send it looping through some favorite joke, some mimic, even to bear again its last few words (nonsense fierce as flail across my eyes, gargled from cancerous lungs through silver tube). But here again I have him and remember. A demonstration record made by him in 1940 when he had sold more toasters, fans, lamps, stoves than any other salesman in the state and as reward was asked to speak his pitch in lasting wax (*reward* when he was locked in blank torment—downing his thirst to drink, drown finally, and baffled to find ten simple dollar bills to meet this month's new howling creditor).

I down my own new need to stop him. I grant him the rest of his respite, reward.

". . . Mrs. Jones, do you know that many children" (*chirren* he says) "will suffer poor eyes in years to come just because of the light they study by?" (His *just* is *jest*.)

I had even lost that!—the *jest* that littered his life, every speech of the thousands he for years unreeled on the stoops of strangers, incurious, ungrateful—merely and rightly bored, whole lives being daily laid at their feet, reeled out from twitching guts like garden hose, the past shames, present needs of grinning beggars. Postman, parents, lovers, mirrored selves.

"Now Mrs. Jones, if you will say the word, I'll bring you on approval our new floor lamp. No obligation on your part at all . . ."

I say the word she never can, calm No, and end his endless bottled plea for hope. Next record plays, bald irony, black jest, Anderson sings *Komm Süsser Tod* of Bach.

So Father, sweet death I have given you, mere silence, rest; vowed not to force you through your pitch again. To seal the vow I look up to your picture on the wall. Deep walnut frame, deep window on your face. 1918, you eighteen yourself, the worst of wars hung bleeding overhead (your brother Edward's lungs already gassed; your own Guard button in your left lapel, an eagle spread above a waiting world; you will be called-for weeks from now yourself but saved in port by Armistice) and still your gaze though high is clear, undoubting; a surety that even now seems firm, not boyish foolishness, seems well-informed as though you saw sure detailed happy futures, a life like water (clear, needed, useful, permanent, free), spared all you will so soon acquire (drink, wife, sons, labor, thirty-six more years). I touch the glass above your silent mouth, say silently—

Dear boy (dear gray eyes, broad nose, curling lip), locked on your browning cracking paper card, I offer you my life—look, it will serve. Cancel all plan of me, let me not be, so you may have free time, move always sure, accept with smooth hands what your eyes still see, elude brute ambush of your gurgling death.

Design for a Tomb

AMONG the things modern sons are spared are parental tombs—the bother, the crippling expense, the *arrangements* to find space, an artist; then choose a design that will honor the dead with a minimum of gas, guard their alarmingly indestructible bones and yield to any thoughtful stranger some sense of the lives discontinued within.

The job now is simple as buying a dog—a burial plot 18' × 12' at the cost of Manhattan real estate; a tasteful stone with the names blown in by compressed air through rubber stencils, as ruthless in placement as neon light.

I've bought you that. Mother bought it, in fact, at Father's death, ruinous as a pyramid—$600, consuming what insurance the cancer had spared—but I chose the design, remembering his wish of nine years before to have a gravestone like FDR's. Not quite the tonnage Hyde Park could bear but the principle, at least—two marble slabs, unveined Vermont white, one flat, one standing, PRICE the one interruption of the perfect planes since fouled by birds and blundering mowers yet broad enough to straddle the four of us.

But suppose I had not and the choice was now mine, to cover you both with whatever was due—unlimited funds and artists at hand. (I recall Father laughing two dozen times that when Mother died, he'd set over her "a Coca-Cola and a pack of BCs in Georgia granite." She'd rally, "I'll pile a little hill on you; name it Worry Wart.")

An allegory—*Grief?* (which I no longer feel); my own bust weeping, my brother grim beside me? *Generosity?*—a pair of hands, open? An eternal flame?—in Carolina summers? with Father fire-phobic?

—Your faces of course. The Greeks, again—faces are what we succeed in making (barring burns, cuts, pox, enemies with blades); triumph or mess, our one *personal* product. Therefore tombs should be portraits—smooth runner or bride taken young, gravely vapid; wife, husband, parent. The unique face, the hair often mantled—in prospect of journey—an arm almost always crooked toward the shoulder, palm toward the eyes. "Farewell"? or "Follow me"?

I'd set over you your faces—coarse stone, veined, soluble in time— your bodies to the waist; arms down however (you have not beckoned me, or have only begun).

But your faces when?

—Not in grace of youth (which I never saw) nor as stunned by your endings but as, say, six weeks before your deaths you met your days (work, sons, selves) filled, runnelled, pouched with all you'd learned— self-steerage, laughing charity, as yet unappalled by your readiness to die.

ENDLESS MOUNTAINS

THE SHOT went through the white inside of my right thigh on Wednesday near noon. I lay in a little sweetgum thicket to the west of the battlefield the rest of that day and the sweltering night. Men worse off than me were dying all round me, telling their Jesus they could barely see him but were coming anyhow, or calling out long menus to the air for their mothers to cook, who were worlds away. I may have lain on, a very long time. Anyhow I remember the one night passed; and next it seemed like late afternoon with long light the color of brown clover-honey before the redhead scavenger found me, rummaged my pockets, read my papers, balled them up and threw them aside, saying "Well now, Trump, it's your goddamned birthday."

Weak as I was, I said I could drink to the *goddamned* part.

But he just said "And it looks like your last, son"; then he bent towards me. That had to make it September fourteenth unless he was lying, which I doubt he was. Tall as I am, he picked me up like a back-broke doll, kissed my forehead and strode on towards the bloody tent I'd nightmared about since the day I left home.

It must have been that night or the next, I managed to get upright on my feet. They held up under me long enough for my arms to feel out slow in the dark—empty around me. Had I dreamed there were other boys moaning near me, packed close as a flock of starlings in the snow? Maybe—I was dreaming from the morphia, steady. All my hands found now though was air, hot empty air; and both my legs still bore my weight. I reached down far enough to find my thigh and the crusty hole, size of an onion and hotter than all the rest of me; and then I thought I recalled a man's voice, maybe the surgeon's, saying I'd get two choices next dawn—I could give him that leg or take it to God myself by dark.

It was already dark. Was I already dead? If so, time had left me two long legs—one of them pierced deep (what I call *time*, most people call *God*). All right, I'd trust I was meant to use them. I took five short steps into the night, expecting something to stop me each instant; but no, and then my face seemed to cool—I was maybe outdoors again. The air was dry and a light breeze moved to call me on. For the first hundred yards, I barely hurt. Then a fire blazed up where my right leg hinged onto my body—the leg wouldn't take real steps from there on. Ten yards later the pain had plugged my head so full, I stopped and thought "Fall here in your tracks; and if you're still alive at dawn, let them cut you into however many pieces it takes to stop this pain." My eyes were likewise failing fast.

But something told me I had to go, I was meant to *leave* (not to save just a limb but the rest of my life); so my left leg took a long step on its own, dragging the right. Then it took three more—by now I could see the coals of small fires and occasional tents not twenty yards off—and I let it pull on down a slope till it dragged me into full dark again where I could smell what had to be water, the first clean water I'd smelled after drinking hot slop for days. Upright I groped before me with my hands, knowing that—close to water so clean—I might just slide into enemy arms or hoist myself onto some warm bayonet waiting to end me. *Christ, please let it.*

But no, I was next at what I could feel was the verge of the stream. I wondered if I could manage to kneel—the pain by then was like continuous lightning through me. It was more like falling. Still I got to the ground; and when I'd scrabbled forward on my fists, I found I could take one long reach down into moving water, cold as the night (we were near the mountains). Just the feel of its kindness—unspoiled water, the fact that it bore my touch without shrinking—gave my mind the first firm thought I'd had since my wound. Deep in me, it said *They mean you to last. You find out how.* It didn't tell me who *they* was that meant my life to go on ahead, though I someway knew it was not my people back at home, not the waiting women; and it never said where it would lead nor when the actual end would come.

But I chose to believe them, step by step, though next I slid into thick black coma and lay there bathing that one hand till a cloudless first-day cracked my eyes. I rushed to crawl upright on my feet before some boy less mangled than me could spot me and drill my head clean through or some of my own boys could haul my ruins on back uphill and into that reeking flyblown tent where I'd be stunned like a beef in the stall, quartered with a blue-iron handforged cleaver, then parceled out for all I knew to waiting cripples hungry as me. I was dreaming half-awake by then—long scary visions of children that looked like offspring of mine, whom I'd never known till now they were caught in an attic fire that would eat everything they'd loved or trusted. They anyhow blanked the actual pain of the world I was in.

I must have walked that whole bright day, using only my own two legs and the dogwood stick I found by the path, a handy crutch. I think I remember speaking to several women I passed as they stood at stone gates holding their children or leading a horse no taller than me and scared nearly dead by the thunder beyond us—it was fresh killing surely but not for me, not now, no more. One of the young girls with no baby yet must have fed me something and found clean water that I could drink—I kept the strength to creep on forward—but who it was and what she might have asked from me, all that's gone completely now. What I remember is the ground beneath me. A whole lot smoother than I'd expected and always *up*, a gradual rise that even my bad leg managed to drag itself along.

*

It was night again with a hair of a moon—and the hole in my thigh scalded hotter than any outcry—when it dawned on me I was past all reach and truly alone. When that thought came down back of my eyes, I'd got to a ledge near the foot of what was all but a mountain. For a long time I'd strained not to rest, and I seldom stopped—rising and starting were still straight agony. But that new idea of being thoroughly on my own with nobody else in the whole world with me, that new idea sat me down hard on a cold flat rock; and it left me happy in tall waves of joy that rushed up through my legs and chest. It felt like I was the last live soul on a planet swept of the human race except for me, a lone man normal as milk in a bucket but the lord of all—nobody to owe, nobody to fail.

I may have sat there awake till day, a long time anyhow. And what I thought as the night died out was how the eyes I'd left might look if they were still living—my young wife and both our daughters, my pale strong mother and the brother I'd left to keep her alive through war and bone-deep deprivation (my father had been dead numerous years). Other eyes and faces flickered past me—some of them calling their full three names, some of them too far back to see or never glimpsed except in darkness and secret rooms—but of course my family's stayed with me longest. They were, every one of them, good to watch from this far off. They'd been good to know, give or take some hot silence and then cruel lies and the meanness they triggered (way over half the meanness was mine). But someway I knew my people were gone. And towards daybreak I knew their absence caused my joy—that sense I was *new* now, however near dead. Someway the entire Earth was mine to make from scratch in the time I had, which might be minutes.

At the first sight of the actual sun, I managed to stand and brace my knees. Right in the cold hard teeth of the light, I said my own name clear to the day and vowed my purpose. "Trump Ferrell," I said, "this time, get it true." Then by some means on a near-gone leg that steadily blanked my eyes in pain, I climbed on higher. Anybody could do it if the need arose as it had for me.

It was well past noon when I got to the ridge, and I'd lain down and dozed awhile in another bleak dream before I really looked at the place and saw it was more like an endless green table than a peak. I recalled several places I'd seen on maps that were called Table Mountain or maybe Flat Dome—western Virginia came to mind and down in the Smokies nearer my birthplace. But the fact was, I had no clear notion where I'd got to. I asked myself if I even cared whether this was ours or enemy country. Any cause for war I might have felt in my own mind—that had been fading for long months and seemed to have run out completely now right through my wound. So you might have guessed I'd be begging to die.

The cut of the light on these trees though and the dry ground deep in pinestraw beneath them—someway it threw me a thin thread of hope that I managed to catch. Holding just that much in my hand, I lay on through a chain of new dreams; and each dream had a lighted window in it—something to flee through to my new world or something to wait by till time showed a path. I thought I'd wait. I hadn't tried my leg again, and now I couldn't bear to see it. I stayed where I was in a pinestraw ditch in the ground in full glare and waited for what the sky intended.

The next I knew, and it may have been hours, I was moving steadily over ground—in the air, I mean, suspended someway. This time I truly took it for death and shut my eyes. The air felt cooler and smelled like far-off honeysuckle, and the pain was easing as I went. It seemed a long way. Then things got darker. Through my shut lids I understood the light was fading. It crossed my mind to wonder if my destination was up or down, Heaven or Hell, bright or black (I'm no churchgoer but no big fool; I believe in justice and I'd earned its toll). I even guessed that some tall man was bearing me in ample arms for his own purpose to a good dry place or a slaughter pen. But again slaughter seemed like a thing I'd gone through more than once and come out whole.

So I calmly figured that my fate anyhow was out of my hands. Whatever held me now would know wherever it needed to take my remains and how it would use me once we were there. The last clear thought I had for hours was *He knows it's me anyhow, knows it's Trump.* Some curious way I knew it was a *he* that bore me forward—likely because I'd been in the war and was just barely freed from its long mannish dream of glory, though I passed out again in the moving air and knew flat nothing for what turned out to be several more days.

Far as I know, the next human being that touched me was a woman. Whatever day of the year it was, it was late afternoon—the shine that fell in on me from a window was slanted and gold as a fall-in of old coins across my body. I seemed to be laid on my back on a table, long and narrow, with something comfortable under my head that felt like a folded sheet or sack. No fear, not even when my eyes first opened. The thing that said I was safe was the light, pure ripe late light. I'd slept a long time and was still myself, whatever good that was to the world. Next I felt down both my sides to see how much of my body was left. And that was when I heard the first certifiable voice I'd heard in what seemed weeks—a human voice, most likely a woman's.

It said from somewhere back of my head "Sir, you're in one piece anyhow. I can tell you that much, but this leg stinks and the other one's angry as any shot bull."

It had to be a woman, by the pitch and feel of how she cared. I shut my eyes in a flush of thanks.

And before I could speak or try to rise, she spoke again. "I'm praying you live though. Autry—he's gone now to make you the salve." I could almost hear her pointing towards Autry, marking the air where he'd last stood. She said "Old Autry's a healing soul. Hang on for him."

I understood her to mean my right leg was gangrened now and spreading to the other and death was close. By then it seemed just the next piece of news—the state of the weather, the casualty rate. My head must have nodded to urge her on.

But she said "No, you hang on here. Autry's planning to save you and he seldom fails."

I nodded again in courtesy.

Then I saw her face bend close—a pretty young face, sixteen or seventeen, perfectly heart-shaped with hazel eyes and chestnut hair. A face that in my former life I'd have risked at least one whole leg for. Her full lips were set in a hard line though; and while she tried to gentle her brow and steel my patience, she held up a stick of fresh fatwood and said "Chew down on this for the pain." She pulled my chin down and put in the stick.

I managed to say I wasn't in pain. I wasn't—it had gone past pain long since.

She said "You will be when I lance this pus."

I carefully spat the stick from my mouth. "You got any kind of license for this?" I had no idea what I meant.

But it set her back. She took a deep breath, then renewed her purpose. "I can't ask you to see this leg; but if you did, you'd know I'm bound by God to cut."

I raised my head and saw the bright razor she held like a torch. She brought it onward then—somewhere on the lower half of what had been my body for thirty-two years, the half that had given me plentiful fun far back as I knew, whoever it harmed or disobeyed.

With the use I'd made of women's bodies, I might have seen this as fair revenge. But weak as I was and addled with pain, I had one instant of seeing her hand as tame and welcome. All my grown life the sight of a woman's willing hand aimed towards that lower half of me had been the sight I'd struggled time and again to get, my permanent aim. And while I told myself as the razor met my skin, *This can't hurt worse than what I've known*, it hurt, Christ yes. A white-hot ramrod seared through my heart on into my mind, over and over for endless minutes. I'd long since gnawed the stick in two before the fire began to shrink, and then the girl was standing near me—younger still—laying a strong hand under my skull and lifting my head to help me drink from a shallow bowl. It was something cool, which was all I tasted; and in a few seconds I knew it had to be a powerful calmer.

Still I never felt a moment's fear, though I thought a drink as welcome as this might be merciful poison. And only when it had me addled and ready for sleep did I look round at the room I was in. A low small space walled with pine boards, no trace of whitewash; by the high rock fireplace, an eating table with two tin plates, a small stove, a clean wide bed, a pitcher and bowl with fuming water—all someway looking airless and untried as tombs in the hearts of granite hills waiting for God on Judgment Day with a firm chair ready to bear His weight and a cot for His rest.

The girl leaned on nearer down. "You got any message you want me to know?"

I tried to laugh but was too content. I said "No ma'm, I'm no kind of prophet."

She actually laughed then, clear as rung glass. It left her face as beautiful as any dawn I'd known (I'd risen at dawn since before the war). She said "I mean, you got any last instructions in case you pass on soon?"

I tried to tell her my wife's full name and where we'd lived. I know I managed my first daughter's name, which was Stella Dene.

The woman said "Look, I can't write a word; but I can remember— I've already memorized your keen eyes—so I'll tell Autry. He'll tell the world whatever you say, even if you pass before he's back. But you won't pass on from me, now will you?"

It felt like I was aimed right there, at restful death. Still I think I told her I'd enjoyed my stay, and I know that meant my entire life up till that time (give or take some hours when I got caught red-fisted in wrong). Anyhow by then it felt like I'd enjoyed every instant, though what I should have recollected was how much pain I'd leave behind in every head and heart that knew me, from my hard mother right on through every woman I'd touched and my smart daughters. But then I sank—no word, not a dream.

Then it was dark outside in the world; the windows and farthest walls of the room were nearly black. Around me though was a warm shine that clung tight to me, so close it was nearly hot to feel. I could smell lamp oil; but when I craned up to hunt for lamps or company near me, what I saw was the same sparse room surrendered to night. In my weak state and after so long with nothing to eat but that one drink, I took what came without strong question, not to speak of complaint. I even wondered calmly again if this didn't have to be the deep hereafter. If so, in my case it seemed to consist of lying still on a long pine table (I could smell it by now)—I'm more than six foot.

The next thing told me I was close to right. My hands went slowly down again and found I was naked below the waist, far as I could reach at least. I hadn't thought of it when the girl worked on me, but now my warm hands found my privates all in place and safe to the touch like birds in a nest. Recalling how Jesus bore his wounds past resurrection, I didn't let myself hunt for mine—I someway trusted the girl had drained me and left my tenderest skin a lot cleaner. I still wore my old canvas shirt though.

Would saved souls lie around in Paradise hid to the waist but stark naked downward? Would that be all we learn in bliss—that, against our teaching, the belly and chest is our shameful half, where black hearts beat and the offal steams? Apparently I laughed at the thought—I heard a sound resembling a chuckle—and then my mind decided I was live. If this was late September though and I was in the lower mountains, why wasn't I cold?—I could just make out that the fireplace was dark too, no sign of a blaze. My mind made the words *Thank Christ I'm dead.* I'm nearly certain I didn't say them aloud in the room. But an answer came.

A low voice said "You feeling the chill?"

My head stayed down. "No sir, I'm not."

He said "You got to lie this way."

I knew I hadn't really tried to rise, not since I got here (and was he the one that brought me?); but I gave it my best and rose to my elbows. There was no big outcry from anywhere in me, no pain worse than before my leg putrefied. Still it wasn't my leg I tried to find. However strange I felt up here in this new world, what I yearned for was company; and it seemed a fair bet that this voice now belonged to a man, not a demon at least. My eyes settled on him, and I asked for his name.

He took a long wait and then didn't speak; and he wasn't a man— a boy maybe fifteen, to tell by his eyes, but taller than me. In the light that cupped us, he had black eyes set slant in his head like a wild bobcat's that met me, not shying. His hair was nearly the girl's fine color, darkest auburn (the warm light came from a glass lamp beside him on the lid of a keg—no razor, no knife, no bandage in view). His eyes were mainly what told me that he and the girl were closer kin than married. Brother or sister, father and child. No, they had to be too young for that—even too young to marry anywhere but back in these hills, lawless and hid.

I asked him if his name wasn't Autry.

His white face made a try to smile, but his heart wasn't in it. "She tells people that."

"Told me, for one."

By then my eyes had opened enough to see he was dressed in parts of my uniform—the black wool pants that were clean of my blood and what was left of a black hunter's coat I'd brought from home. In the dark they blanked out his whole body but the burning face.

That was set on me, not wild-eyed but earnest. And then his hands moved into the shine. They were brown from work with fingers long as bamboo canes, knobbed at the knuckles from toil or age. *But he looked so young just now, just a boy.* He finally said "I got to ask you to lie back down and trust my work."

I recalled the salve the girl had mentioned—if this boy had any salve or balm, it was not in sight. And then I took the first look at my leg. It had not been washed since three hot days before the wound when I dipped up water from a muddy spring at the edge of a burnt-out wheel-wright's shop and washed myself the best I could. Where the girl had cut across my wound, a thin pale track of the razor showed (was it already healed?). Round the bullet hole my skin was flooded with vicious blood and puckered to a near-black purple. Worse still, red streaks ran up past my crotch and belly—the poison reaching towards my heart. And across my privates the same thick color was spreading over to my left leg. I've seldom been a praying man, not for my lone self; but at that sight I said what must have sounded like prayer—*God spare me* or something equally weak.

Whatever the words, they made the boy smile, full at last on firm white teeth, and it left him looking like a son any father would gladly welcome (I had no sons and had given up hoping). He said "I'm not nobody's God, Captain; but if you trust me, I'll do my best."

I was nobody's captain either, never would be; and I figured he was either ignorant or crazy. But I was in no state of mind to shy from help, even here at the hands of a boy who—if he was truly a human and not some useless child of my fever—could scarcely do more than wash me clean and lay me into a deep enough grave by dawn or whenever the sure end came. I lay back flat and waited through what felt like a year, lifting my head by two or three inches every week or so to test his progress. It felt that slow.

To strain for memory, I figure his hands stayed on me, holding, till towards daybreak—well over an hour—him still as a shaft of upright rock with his old-man fingers round my ankles and sometimes sliding as high as my knees but, far as I know, never touching the wound, pressing hard but always steady. So I never felt he'd slacked or was gone. It seemed he was certain that honest pressure by one careful soul could turn death back from another live body far gone as me and friendless to boot. His eyes stayed shut a good part of the time, though his dry lips moved every now and then in what I tried to read as words, whole sentences—were they prayers or spells? But I never recognized one whole syllable and never felt like I was in danger or even in the wasteful hands of a fool.

I just stayed wide awake every minute and again took the chance to bring up the eyes I'd known and left—the usual family members, my girls, my staunch friend Ray that fell beside me (drilled through the eye) the day before I took my bullet and a few of the bodies I'd loved in darkness, moaning my name. All moved past me, bright as I'd ever seen them in life or dark and twisting; and they all nearly smiled. Still for the first time since I left, not one of them spoke to call me back. They each looked satisfied where they were and gave no sign of needing or hoping to see me again.

And when the first sun made its slow cold way through the window and reached us both, I felt so free from my old moorings that again I thought I was borne through the air well off the ground and onward through the mountain dawn like some kind of messenger skimming the Earth to do good will for no other master than God on high. That finally tired me; and the last I saw before my eyes shut down on the light was Autry easing up on my legs, then laying a heavy quilt across me and slowly moving away with his lamp. And what I figured I knew was a sentence that ran, like a big child's alphabet, behind my eyes— *These people are saving your flesh to eat.* Wild as it sounds, that dawn it left me calmer yet and eased me into a sleep so deep that all I knew for days to come was fitful dreams of war and blood, real as my life but harmless to watch.

Turned out the girl and boy had failed. Her lancing razor and the drink she gave me, his praying hands—they'd poured right into my sucking wound, a precious food it brewed and spread like perfect poison through my body. I was scarcely a rack of skin-tarred bones that were hot enough to cauterize a field hospital of bleeding men, but I stank with maggoty meat and the readable news of death. By the time I plunged to the pit of those fears in shuddering fever, I couldn't have kept but a slim two thirds of my old size (which was near two hundred).

All I took for nourishment was warm and cold drinks brought by the girl and, night after night, the boy's close hands and his dry lips moving through whatever code he used to whatever god.

I lay on, locked in further hard visions far past the point either one of my keepers thought I'd draw the next safe breath. They told me later they gave me up more times than one. And in every vision, staring again, stood a person I'd failed in the world—the old place everybody said was peaceful before the war but still the world I made my mess in, my sins of faithless greed I forced on any woman that would grin my way and let my starving mind inside her final secret to gorge itself.

It would be long months before I was safe enough to know how far into death I went, and then I only knew what they told me. They claimed I'd sleep through stretches of days, then wake up clawing at whatever came near. They said I'd make them promise me death with the white-hot blade (they swore I always called it that) or how other times I'd beg them to put their promise in writing and sign it plain before my eyes—that they'd keep me the rest of my days and alter my story so no one from my old life could find me.

And nobody found me; but down I went on rushing towards death till one cold midnight I howled for the boy to take some gouge—one big enough to serve—and dig my stinking leg off at last at the deep hip-socket and burn it before it killed us all. By then I knew it had poisoned the air. I have a memory I think I can trust of howling the dreadful words in his face and then of seeing him go for a cleaver and bring it right to the edge of my side (I'd long since lain in an ample bed, the clean bed I'd noticed at first). I didn't feel a trace of fear; and I know my actual voice calmed down to confident peace as I said "Come *on*. Oh Autry, *help* me or fry in Hell."

He thought that through for a stunned minute, and I saw his eyes go darker still as the plan came on him like a dense bright veil that would have scalded any soul not chosen to do time's will. He gave one nod, accepting his duty. Then he laid the cleaver flat by his feet and quickly shucked his entire clothes, every layer of his and mine that had hid him. He stood there naked a long minute more, then turned the single quilt back off me and laid his clean length down my bones and the thin dry flesh that clung to me yet.

At first touch I thought he was on some private errand of his own that I couldn't help; but as he began to move and work, I guessed it might be purely a last hope of saving me. Far gone as I was, I saw the picture in my mother's Bible—Jacob wrestling a whole black night with the Angel of God and winning at daybreak.

And however long he truly stayed stretched on me there, however gone and weak I was, it felt till the end like a desperate fight between at least one human creature and something else like the will of God or even the evil face that lurks in the heart of a world run by any two sets of men as bent on havoc as the men I'd fought with, likewise the man I'd been till now. Wildest of all, at no one moment did I ever think it was strange or killing—what we did. It always felt like a *deed* we were doing. It felt like something planned for us (whoever he was) since time got started, and I always bet I'd end alive.

So in memory I guess there was new light near us, to show me we were still indoors with a roof above and a live world beyond us. The light could have come from the oil lamp or, Christ knows, maybe some shine from our struggle. It had the nature of fire in water, from old sea timbers, or far in the woods from slow decay. It played along my arms, his sides, his vise-grip legs, my straddled bones, his arms that were strong as any blacksmith's and what rode hot from the pit of his belly— his tall man's root that seemed as much a part of his work, whatever he meant, as the toiling face and open eyes that moved above me, dark and near, and never left my own dazed sight. I recall I only thought two words that I kept silent—*Hurry, son,* by which I meant I guessed he was killing or healing or maybe just hoping to warm my chill; so end it fast—I sure-God felt he was using me up, though all he said was (time and again) "Captain, Captain, this is nothing but *help.*"

I knew if he worked on many more minutes, he'd be alone in the bed by day—there'd be no sign of me left but the stain of my last sweat, and that would be mist on the chill of morning. It must have been then I faded again for God knows how long—a long fit of dreams or actual life too strange to recall. It did seem though that Autry—or whatever Autry turned into—was back on me for a black string of nights and that I never doubted, every time we struggled, how he was bent on curing me finally just with the force of his own body, on driving death back with nothing but skin and the hot intention of a boy as fevered as I'd ever been (and far more desperate, for his own reasons and the orders he'd got from whatever power).

So time and again I still believe he lay down on me, burning to pass his young health to me or—failing that—to grind my pitiful scraps of bone to an ashy powder he could strow to the wind and then move on with his warm girl to a life they'd won through kindness to me. Over and over anyhow I'd sleep through baking fits of heat where dreams were nothing but coals banked on me, and then I'd wake soaked through to the bone with cold salt sweat from broken fever—proof his help was somehow working.

Her name was Ruth and when I finally swam towards light, it was her again that met me first—her face above me backed by a flood of shine from the window. She said "It's snowing. You ever seen snow?"

Close as my family lived to the coast, there'd only been one snow that lasted long enough to mark my mind. I'd been a young boy myself, sixteen; and the night before the weather turned, I'd joined another human body for the first full time, close and deep into joy. It had been with the girl I later married, made two daughters on and left in tears. She was a younger distant cousin who came to us when her own people died of the red consumption that awful year when so many fell right where they stood—in fields, on horseback—foaming blood at their smiling lips (they mostly died smiling, strangest of all).

Anyhow when she'd been living with us for three long months—my distant cousin—she came to the loft where I slept one March night and dredged me up from a happy dream and asked without a single word for whatever comfort I could give her loss. Being my age then all I could think was to roll down on her and raise her shift the gentlest I could and visit her deep in the quick of her sorrow.

It did seem to help—her sleeping face was all but smiling when daylight woke me, blazing white at the frozen pane. At first I thought it was Judgment Day from the strength of the glare; still that didn't scare me or turn me against what she and I'd done. I calmly shook her arm to wake her and said "Something's new; look out here with me."

Together we crawled on our knees to the window; and all downhill from my old home, the better part of a mile towards the road, was untouched snow as pure as the hope we shared by then. I said to her "See, I knew we did right."

But bathed in the shine, she couldn't do more than say "Please, please." I understood she'd either spoken to the snow or me. She was telling the splendid sight to let up, it was too fine to watch; or she might have said it mainly to me, "Please keep me near you for good, here on."

I never could ask her to say more though, in explanation; and when she told me four months later she was toting my child in painful secret, I hitched a pony to Mother's green cart and drove us hard to a Baptist church six miles from home and married her legal, young as we were. Snow had done that to us, I always knew—the glare and the sheen like fire off the seraphim as they meet you, bent on either declaring pardon or haling your soul to postponed justice.

It was that bright anyhow when I came to with young Ruth near me in that same room I'd suffered in. So I managed to tell her that yes I'd seen one genuine snow.

She said "You feel like sitting up then? If you do I'll call him."

Him? By then I barely recalled my strong night visitor's name, but I said "Where is he?"

She pointed to the window. "Out melting snow. See, our spring's nearly two miles off; but Autry's out there now with a big fire, melting enough snow to warm you in if you mean to bathe."

If Ruth had said they were souls of the damned sent here to scorch me back to my home, I couldn't have felt any stranger than now. It was strangeness too that made me lie. I said "My name is Cullen, Cullen Duffy" (I'd someway remembered the redhaired man on the battlefield taking my papers; I'd come here nameless).

She was over by the fireplace poking logs. She said "I was hoping you'd live to tell us," and she threw a broad smile that reached me clear as the window shine.

I said "So I lived?"

"Sit up, man, and *look*." She came halfway back towards me on the bed.

I told myself not to reach down and feel, just try to get to my elbows and see what was left of my body. Weak as a drowned cat, I managed it slowly. The same quilt was on me, dark green and red; and beneath it there seemed to be two legs and feet. Then I noticed I was in a thick nightshirt, coarse as linen and clean as a shroud; and when I smelled my hands, they were sweet with maybe pine tar.

Ruth came the rest of the distance towards me and reached for the quilt. "You're way too feeble but let me show you."

The quilt spread back on her full arms, and there still on me were both my legs. The left leg was cloudy still near the thigh but normal size for a man that had starved through maybe long months. The right leg had shrunk to the size of an arm, and the wound hole was ugly but plainly closing with tender flesh. I knew I ought to be relieved; I figured I ought to burst into praise and gratitude. But what I found the strength to say was more a question than anything else, "This means I'm alive?"

She said "Either that or I'm in Heaven."

I mean to tell, I studied her slow and careful then. She looked as good as what I still guess Heaven contains if it's there at all. So I reached my right hand out and found her—just her wrist that was small but wiry as cable. I said "Sweet child, accept my thanks."

It seemed to shock her. She took a step back and looked behind as if for help or a quick retreat. Then she said "Oh we do." A frown crossed her brow, and it finally made her change her meaning. "It was Autry that saved you, Captain. Thank Autry."

I said "Your brother?" and when she looked puzzled, I mentioned how much they favored each other.

That nearly helped her to smile—not quite.

So I went further. "You might be twins."

She said "No, sir. We're not no kin on Earth to my knowledge."

"Husband and wife?"

Her whole face colored and again she looked towards the brilliant window. We could hear somebody outside chopping wood, and her eyes got urgent as she pointed that way. "We're trash. Just orphans scared of the killing."

By now I'd got enough strength back to prop myself on the high headboard. The room looked bigger than I recalled, still as clean as any picked bone, with no real signs of habitation but the coals of fire and her and my breathing eight feet apart. It was someway the emptiest place I'd been—there might not have been a roof and walls; the air was that vacant.

She caught my train of thought. "We don't stay here—" Her hand waved round; she meant the room.

"Who does?"

"Just you since the day Autry found you."

"But this is your home—"

"Oh no indeed. We stumbled on it when we'd been running so long we had to stop or die."

I said "You're saying you don't live here?" I meant I'd never seen them sleeping or eating in here, just working on me.

"No sir, when Autry found your body, we moved out yonder to give you air." She pointed again.

"But near, close by?"

She finally smiled and nodded behind her out the window. "In sound of your voice. Autry would hear you howling at night and run to help you."

Before I could say my thanks for that, the single door swung open on us; and there stood Autry taller maybe than I recalled but in my black clothes and finer across the brow and eyes than any son I'd dreamed of spawning and teaching the little I'd learned and could give. In his arms he strained to hold a copper tub that smoked like a cooking pit; but he stalled in place—facing me, not speaking.

I said "Son, if that's warm water bring it on."

Not looking at the girl, he said "It is" and brought it towards me, three feet from the bed. Then still watching me, he called her on— "Ruth, step here and help me show this man we saved his hide."

She said "I told him."

But he said "Step here."

As Ruth moved forward I thought better of it and said "Son, maybe I'm too weak for this."

Then he smiled too; his teeth were strong and white as a bear's. "If I'm your son, like you keep saying, then I'm the one you got to trust. Do what I tell you."

What could I do in painful joy but let those two afflicted souls wash my new body in clean hot snow?

That was in December—I'd crazed around and rested that long. And I stayed feeble the better part of three weeks, mostly up and dressed in my old clothes (that Autry surrendered without my asking). But I stayed low beside the fire, thinking of what time planned for me next. Or I'd lie hours across the bed, hoping to see some sign of a life to live in whatever world I joined if I left here. I already knew the war still lasted; the sky would light up most every night with phosphorus bombs from ten miles off and the burning spirits of men hurt worse than me or dead like mist down near the ground. I knew I was spending too much time alone for the good of my mind. My strength was coming back enough to start me thinking of things my fingers hadn't touched or my lips brushed for way too long (any number of which were in reach anytime Ruth was near me). I fought the hungers but they kept rising, and many times I begged young Autry to move himself and the girl back with me—I'd sleep on the hearth.

They'd nod and refuse and go on bringing me nourishment—dove, rabbit, squirrel and various colors of rank hot tea they'd brew from roots. Sparse as the fare was, Ruth cooked it tasty; it filled my shrunk belly day by day till slowly I got back faith enough in both my legs to offer to work. I'd once been a hunter, so I offered to hunt the table meat. Autry could spend more time cutting firewood for my room and theirs as winter bore down.

They lived in a shed at the edge of the clearing. I'd never gone in, never been asked (the whole place, Autry claimed one evening, had stood here empty the day they came, worn from fleeing their own burned home—mother killed, father lost somewhere at war: I doubted his word after what Ruth had said). From the hour I got here, I'd never so much as shared a meal with them nor had any human conversation beyond the barest needs of life. And while I was bad off, the silence sufficed. But once I was stronger and played a useful part by luring and trapping the game (we had no rifles)—I figured I'd try to feed my hunger for simple company as the nights still came down early and freezing.

On what I'd almost surely figured was New Year's Eve, I went to Autry where he was chopping and said I thought it might be the New Year—did he know for sure, and couldn't we cook whatever I'd caught and mark the evening with food at least?

He shook his head—"That's some days from now"—but he stopped his work.

I said "In that case let's say it is—New Year's Eve—in case our luck runs out and they find us between now and then."

Autry looked like he'd never heard years could start or that luck was invented.

So I said "My family cooked a big spread for New Year's Eve—ham, chicken and duck."

He barely faced me. "You got any people left down there?" When he gave a point behind to the valley, I recalled he'd never yet asked one fact about me or what I'd been before I was shot.

And what I told him was less than the truth. "My mother passed on some months back; my only brother's working the farm—he lacks one eye and can't fight a flea."

"You think I'm a coward?" It came out of Autry so low and fast, it tore his face. He might have been watching a wolf in the woods, blood on its teeth, not pale weak me.

I had to say "No and I didn't say you were."

He nodded. "I am."

So I said "Son, you rescued me when I was dead. And however dazed and childish I've been, I understand it was you that cured me." I'd told myself I understood it, which God knew I didn't—and don't today—but deep as my heart went, I knew this lanky boy had saved me by whatever means of skin or prayer, body or soul. And in my eyes that made him stronger than any six generals.

He leaned his axe against the block and finally met my face straight on. "I loved you," he said. "You were all we had."

If, that instant, killing light had poured from his eyes and blinded me, I couldn't have been any more amazed or scared any colder. I'd never leaned on the word *love* till now, not to stand for devotion of his size and kind. So I'd barely said it to my own kin, though I'd whispered it some to very-near strangers; and I hadn't heard the word used in the war, not in a decent way you could honor. I felt my tight chest wanting to laugh, in pure surprise and maybe true pleasure of a brand I'd lacked since my boyhood alone in trees with eagles at hand. But Autry's eyes were solemn still, waiting for me to take or turn back whatever offer he thought he'd made.

I said "I love *you*," having no real idea what I meant but someway knowing it ought to be true. Then I said the word *Thanks*—"I can thank you both." And when he nodded a calm acceptance—he knew what I owed, and he saw I'd paid—I rushed on further than I planned to go. "I can stay and help you two dig in. There's deep winter yet to come up here." I was thinking how much I'd need clean time and a big lost place to heal my mind and choose the path I'd take downhill.

He said "I mean you to stay for good."

I heard no threatful edge in his voice, and more than ever he looked like a son I'd have changed my life for. But now I knew not to make a binding promise. I just said what felt true again—they'd saved my life, especially him in his wild way, a way I still wasn't sure I'd fathom this side of the grave.

Autry took up his axe and said "You're welcome the rest of your life."

Four other people had offered as much to me in my time—my mother, my wife and both my daughters whenever they laughed—and I'd refused them, needing more of the world than they could give (or so I believed). Now I stood my ground in the cold and said "All right." Since he'd called me Captain more than once, I saluted him fully; I could feel I was smiling.

And Autry joined me the nearest he could; I'd never seen his lips grin wider. And as I stepped on towards the woods to check my rabbit gum, he said "You trust me now with your name?" His grin spread wider—he knew I'd lied to Ruth awhile back.

I gave a dry laugh and asked if I could hold off a week. I told myself I was waiting in secret for time's new plan (I craved a plan). I thought it was nonsense, to cover my shame.

Autry said "Take the time you want. But it's Trump something, ain't it?"

That not only stunned me like his claim of love; it proved he had the magic of that contending angel I'd dreamt he was and may have been.

But he said "You kept calling *Trump* in your fever. I figured it was pity for yourself or your son."

I nodded. "It's me—Trump Ferrell. I lied to Ruth."

"How come?"

"I was scared."

"What of?"

"Both of you—I was crazy with fever."

He said "From all you raved about, I estimate you were crazy for years." It seemed plain fact; he was sober-eyed.

I said "I had too much to give," then bit my tongue.

He nodded. "You were strong."

"Strong and bad."

"We tried to be good to you," he said.

It sounded pure as a child's first speech, but it felt as true as the Ten Commandments, and it broke the last weak dam in my heart. I said "I'm in a whole new life, son. Whether you meant to or not, you caused it. I can't go back and live where I did. I burnt that down with nothing but greed."

He waited, then looked to the ground between us. "We'll call you any name you want, long as you stay."

I'd meant to check my traps before dark, so I said "Call me Trap." It seemed like a name from *Pilgrim's Progress* or some boy's book, but I let it stand.

Autry said "Yes, Captain" and turned back to work. He could split heartwood the width of my waist with a single stroke like the firmest apple.

My lures turned out to be empty that evening; and though we had enough laid by to feed us for two days yet, Autry was nowhere in sight when I got back. A little baffled I went to my own place. It felt different now—soon I knew I was waiting for company, not hands necessarily on my hide but open faces that didn't need words or permanent pledges. No word came from Autry or Ruth though, not even the usual light at their window; so I ate cold squirrel and slept on the floor to brace myself for what I understood I must do. They'd welcomed me here but left me alone, a healed stranger they'd never take in to their hid core, whatever it was. My course was set then; it opened before me straight as rails when I offered my presence and met just silence and a black windowpane that shut me off from the last two humans I'd knowingly trusted with my bare skin and the quick of my life. Time spoke it out in the frozen room above my head, *Strike out of here. You've paid your due.* It was something I'd never paid elsewhere, so that much anyhow was new ground gained.

And new ground was what lay all before me, though surely the war still straddled most paths I'd take out of here. I couldn't risk seeing another dead boy, the mouth of a gun or a mad-eyed horse (not to speak of how they'd treat a deserter with two fit legs). I'd doze a few hours on the hard floor then and strike on inward—higher and deeper—before first day.

But whatever hand was moving me, sank me in a sleep so thick and dreamless that I didn't crack my eyelids once till warm sun slatted across my hands and took my face. It was well into morning; I'd missed one chance. *All right, catch Autry and Ruth some game and leave tonight. It's part of your plan.* I rose and broke the ice in my bowl to wash myself, then entered the clearing.

The usual thin smoke came from the stovepipe in their roof, and I walked on round the shed past the woodpile to check my traps. No sign of Autry chopping kindling, which he did most mornings—no fresh foot track. In a war most men lose half their hearing; mine someway improved. I stood in place in the empty clearing in full sunshine and listened hard—that way I could generally catch Ruth clinking a pan indoors or Autry yawning. Silence deep as any gorge. To my knowledge I'd never heard pure silence from them. If one of them went to the woods for something, the other one stayed in sight at least. Something hard in me said *They're gone; they've run again and it's from you, Trump.*

It actually shocked me and I felt a loss I'd never have guessed. *All right. It's yours. Leave clean or stay.* I stood a long moment, listening still. There was nothing for a while and then a high breath like the end of a laugh or a pitiful sigh. I went to the door and knocked one time. No answer. I tried it, a rusty latch but it opened.

It was one cold room that felt as low and round as a bowl tipped over and dark with just the square shaft of light from the window on a handsized piece of the swept dirt floor. A table made from the sawed-off stump of a sizable oak, a single white plate, two battered cups; then back in the shadows, a narrow pallet made out of croker sacks, a bolster stuffed with clean wood chips that spilled at one end—could it sleep two people? By now my eyes had widened to the dimness. Pegs on the walls bore a set and a half of faded clothes—two dresses, a man's shirt, a pair of trousers bigger than Autry and me together, remnants they'd snatched on their run or found here.

On the east wall alone hung one small picture, a tintype boxed in a walnut frame carved by hand with flat round roses. Before I got to it, the face burned towards me as strong as a thrust—a beautiful woman not twenty years old with dark hair glossy as horsetail pinned down tight at her ears and topped with a comb. Her eyes were plainly kin to Autry's and maybe Ruth's. Someway I knew I should make peace with her, the whole still presence of a woman clearly long-since dead; I took the last steps and kissed the glass lightly at her forehead.

Then the high breath sounded again from behind me, the sigh I'd heard in the clearing through walls. It froze me where I stood in midair bent towards the picture. I didn't look round but my empty hands rose up beside me to show I was harmless.

Nobody spoke though, no other noise.

And slowly my fright thawed sufficiently to turn me. At first my eyes saw nothing new. But just in the minutes I'd been indoors, the patch of light had moved towards the west wall another two inches and set up an odd white glow in that corner, a gentle shine like the memory of your best deed or dusk on the summer river, floating slow. Another pallet lay there, narrow; another pile of sacks for cover and one old quilt. Had they kept a dog or a pet wild creature that I'd never seen and was gone with them now? Or was it some secret final protection they'd kept and abandoned? For no sane cause I thought of great snakes I'd seen in books, Tasmanian Devils and wolverines, and I actually laughed.

A child sat up from under the quilt. No nightmare jackal would have shied me worse. I lurched well back, both hands at my face, before my mind could recognize the gold brown hair and gray-green eyes, the skin so young you could read the blood that ran beneath like a confident promise of life to come with fair rewards. A girl all but surely, startled from sleep and unafraid. Maybe six years old with a tall clear forehead, the sign of calm.

I said "I'm Trump—you heard of me?" Something about her had kept me from lying.

Her lips stayed shut but she nearly nodded.

"I work for your folks—I catch the game."

She was in a tan nightshirt square as a box, and she didn't look cold.

"Let me build you a better fire." The low tin stove was barely warm though wood lay beside it.

All the child did was take both hands and work at her hair, laying it straight. The more she smoothed it, the grander she looked. Then while I worked she stayed there kneeling but looked round the room as slowly as if for the world's last crumb.

It made me think *They've left this child someway for good. She's mine to tend.* With my history of shirking plain duties, any such fact should have scared me worse than leaving for the world and its various wars; but for all the next long minutes we spent in silence together, it made me feel entirely in place for the first time in years—maybe since that snowy morning far back, my first day's love. And once the stove was cracking with heat, I rummaged in the corners further and turned up more things than I'd have dreamed after our recent fare. A big tin box with two pounds of raisins dry as stones but sweet to suck, a small keg of meal that the mice hadn't breeched, three jars of honey and a glass quart of figs in clear syrup.

The child by now, when I looked again, seemed older still—maybe seven or eight. Surely she couldn't be Ruth and Autry's—weren't they too young? But with that hair like the tintype lady's, she could be their sister—their cousin or something they snatched from the house fire and brought here to leave. *They've gone and she's mine.* Now it made me happy to think so or warm at least. I said it out loud, "It may just be you and me here, darling. So tell me your name."

Her lips moved open and she raised a finger into the light, but where I expected words it was singing—some old-time tune I'd heard as a boy, too sad to carry onward through life. Just the first ten notes; then her hand came down. Silent again her eyes stayed on me.

So I went towards her.

And she never flinched. Whoever she was, wherever she belonged, you could tell nobody had treated her bad. Her spirit was in one close strong piece.

I stopped a yard this side of her pallet and went to my knees. I wanted her to see my face and eyes—the best parts of me, on the old Earth anyhow, that people thought they could trust right off.

She studied my eyes; then rummaged behind her deep in the sacks and held out her hand. A fancy comb carved in amber with mother of pearl inlay at the edge. It had been on the crown of the tintype lady's abundant hair, and now this child had clung to it through whatever she'd suffered. When I didn't move, she held it farther towards me.

One long moment later I was combing her hair, and she was accepting me naturally as kin or a friend. By the time I had it parted straight and was sorting the tangles, I felt the weight of this plain occasion. I'd touched no female creature in care for more than a year, and my hands trembled some at the pleasure. Whole tracts of my skin that hadn't known they were famished till now were all but weeping in silent thanks. I told myself *Trump, here's your chance—hell, you're in the midst of recompensing every woman you've harmed. Go gentle and use everything you've learned in waste and shame.* So when my temples threatened to split, I spoke again. I leaned back on my haunches to see her. "If you don't have a name you remember, let me call you Joyce." It had been the name of the bravest girl I ever knew, that I'd seen once in my early manhood and then she'd died with her eyes full on me (one girl at least I'd honored and spared).

I thought the child was on the verge of gladly agreeing—her mouth came open—but from well behind me, a voice said "No, she's Margaret Jane."

It stalled me again but when I looked, it was Autry filling the whole door frame. From his right hand the axe hung ready.

Ruth was behind him with an armload of holly, long thick branches of spiky leaves and plentiful berries.

I said "I heard somebody, see—breathing through the walls—and I knew you were gone; so I came in thinking it might be a stranger."

Autry stood on silent.

But Ruth said "We've known her long years."

Then Autry reached back and, out of Ruth's hands, took a whole branch of holly which he held towards the child. He said "Look, Margaret. This here's your New Year."

The child didn't speak but nobody's eyes—no bride's or mother's—were ever so bright.

It made me nearly that glad to see her, knowing well I hadn't scared or harmed her. It also let me know again, and in far harder terms than before, that my path surely led out of here—soon, soon—and might never end.

Turned out, none of us really knew if this was New Year's Eve or not; we'd lost any count of actual time. But that didn't hinder the bountiful goodness that flowed from then till late in the night. Neither Ruth nor Autry asked any more about why I was in their curious room; and I didn't so much as glance at the fact of the beautiful child—her sudden mystery here among us, hid so close. It had come over me that they hadn't found this place on the run—they'd been here all their lives at least, and the three of them someway constituted a merciful clan hid back up here to serve the world if more of the desperate world than me should ever need drastic help again.

This child was the visible guarantee, not just that I'd live to finish my time but that life in the vicious world would eventually settle and tame. If not in my day surely in hers. For all we said about Margaret's breathing presence though—a natural-acting child whose beauty was marked by silence—she might have been a soul from bliss that nobody saw but me, Trump Ferrell, saved from death by the strength pumped out of this room through Ruth and Autry's hearts and skin, from Margaret's soul and into me.

For the present anyhow we stood together in the warming shed and acted as if we'd known each other most of our days and trusted our backs to each other's mercy. Nothing more was said about New Year; but once the child and Ruth had hung big clumps of holly along the walls, I thought again of how I'd failed to bring in food for the past two days. I stood in place a last still instant tasting my luck, and then I said I'd better get going and hunt us a meal.

Autry said they'd be much obliged.

I spent the better part of the day back deep in the woods, calming my thoughts and studying various ways downhill. There was one real trail, nearly vertical and edged with boulders, and several rough scrambles through sharper flint and huge evergreens. I even showed myself to the sky at two or three points overlooking the valley, trying to see where troops were camped or the smoke of a skirmish. But what was there that one cold noon was nothing but a million trees (stripped for winter to their firm bones) and what must have been the stream I drank from the night I ran—not a human house or a creature in motion. Still every nerve in my new skin said *Don't go back there. Push on up;* and when I looked behind me, the line of the ridge ran steep and naked, blue slate and granite on into the mist that shielded the sun. I'd climb farther on then when my time came, though I had to guess that meant a whole world empty of all but me and my dreams.

The time wasn't yet. I felt I had new debts to pay at the clearing to my benefactors, however they'd saved me. I didn't want to see them too soon and be tempted to mention my aim to leave. So I found a bright cove beside three hemlocks and lay down there to rest awhile (by then my body was so hardened to cold, I could sleep on ice). I managed it easy and when I woke in the low slant light, I jumped up strong and went to my traps. They'd had good luck. I'd caught a fat rabbit and a covey of bobwhites tame as pups nested down beneath an old crate I'd baited with corn and propped on a twig.

When Autry and I had cleaned the game, Ruth came outside and cooked it right on the coals we'd nurtured. I went on back to my place to wait; but when I looked out the window towards dusk, I saw that Margaret had come outdoors and stood by the fire, still not speaking but looking glad. Her skin in the late sun was whiter still; but it didn't look sick, only fine-grained and sheltered. I'd pretty well answered the questions about her to my satisfaction—at the least she was near kin to Autry and Ruth. For their own reasons which may have been wise, they'd kept her hid; yet once I found her, they hadn't blamed me but told me her name and borne our nearness a few calm minutes. Who was I with my blotched record to dig on deeper and meaner than that into whatever mysteries these three held among them here? They'd saved my skin and maybe my soul—if I had one, which remained to be seen.

By then anyhow I'd searched my room for any small thing I'd left on the shelves and wanted to keep for my departure—the tailfeather fan of a grouse cock, the single picture I owned from my past life—a round tintype of my first daughter in her young mother's arms. I pocketed a blood-red rock I'd found in the woods that might be a ruby; and I kept the Indian black axe-head I'd carried with me since I left home right through my battles (small but deadly, I'd yet to use it). My daughters' picture I slid between the head of the bed and its side rails. I'd remember their faces long as I needed; and I'd thank them this far by leaving their likeness here on the spot where death and I struggled—or I and an angel or just a kind boy, desperate as I. It was after all where I learned I must free my kin for better lives without my greed to drain their strength and harrow their peace.

Then a knock at my door, the first I'd heard (before now Autry and Ruth just walked in, sure I was ready for company). It scared me, knowing somebody stood there with a long-due bill for all my forfeits—a kinsman, my colonel, any one of the women I'd tried to use up. I couldn't answer.

Autry's voice spoke through the wood, "Trump, I told you it's New Year's Eve. Eat beside us."

Skittish as my old loyalty was, I'd always liked big family feasts. So this new invitation from Autry ought to have shook my heart in its moorings—I owed him that much; they were still good to watch. But still I was balked.

So he tried the door. It opened on me, upright square in the midst of the room. He studied my eyes in lantern shine. Then he said "She wants you to follow me."

I told him to thank Ruth and say I was tired.

"It ain't Ruth, Captain; it's Margaret Jane."

No coffin hinge was ever colder than I that instant—the old world of people was swarming back: kin, friends, children, mates of my body, every one of them empty-handed and staring at me like the fountain of grace. But then my mind someway heard a sentence; a silent voice said *Do this last thing. We'll set you loose.* I still couldn't talk but I nodded to Autry.

He led me onward.

It was no big feast, but it filled our craws. We sat on the floor around the small table and just had the meat and a mush Ruth made from cornmeal and dried corn, the last they'd have till way into summer. I'd already forgot the things I saw in the corners that morning; and it came as a sweet surprise when Ruth and Margaret Jane slid back into darkness, laughing, and then returned with a jar of honey and the quart of figs. Each one of us ate with fingers scrubbed on a clean rag first—Ruth was clean as a bird. I'd eaten three figs and thought I was done when Margaret came forward to me with the honey. I thanked her and said I was way past full.

But she said "No"—I heard it clearly—and a smile spread on her to pick any lock on Heaven's gate.

The smile was so welcome, I barely noticed she'd said the first word, not to mention it was *No*; and all I wanted was to keep her talking. It seemed like something fairly enormous depended on that—her life or mine, the real world's future. I said "You'll have to say my name."

She held her ground, stone-silent again, with the honey held out.

Autry said "Captain, she's deaf and dumb."

I knew for a fact I'd heard her *No*; so my hand went out in the air towards her, clenched like a claw that could tear her skin. I think I was trying to tear something off her, some throttling fist that choked her throat or a plugged obstruction in her mind. I thought if a strange man scared her some she might break free (I'd thought that way too many times and trapped too many kindly girls).

It didn't faze Margaret. Or she didn't show it. Her right hand reached inside the jar, her white forefinger scooped down deep and brought up honey in neat cells of wax, then she brought it to me like gold I'd earned.

I knelt to meet her hand straight on and ate the warm wild sweetness off her that smelled like summer before the war, red clover and big old drowsy bees.

Next—swear to Christ—she said "Now rest." I'd never heard a child say *rest*.

I looked to Autry to see if he heard, but he'd moved away to the dark far corner. I could just make out that Ruth had already stretched out there on one of the pallets; it looked like Autry was ready to join her. And when I turned to Margaret again, she'd stepped back—still facing me—to her old quilt and was nesting there. I knew I hadn't obeyed a child since that first dawn I saw real snow, but I felt like pleasing this girl now. I said to the room "Would anybody care if I rest awhile?"

Nobody spoke, though the tin stove creaked on under our silence.

So I laid myself back full on the ground—the packed cold floor—as near to the midst of the room as I could.

Then we all rested, in proper places. Whoever Autry and Ruth might be to one another, they were fast asleep in a very few minutes with their work clothes on, ready to run or face daybreak. Margaret stayed busy a short while moving her hands in cold starlight to make horse heads on the wall beside her—mule heads, rabbits and almost surely a unicorn, though how she made it with just ten fingers I couldn't see. It felt like I was wide awake; and likely I was more than blessed to be lying here in the core of something that, far as I knew, was entirely well-meant.

I thought I might be able to whisper and someway coax the child to talk. Maybe she had fresh orders for me, some sure destination entrusted to her in her barred throat but meant for me who'd got words from her when no one had. I know I whispered my love her way and felt I meant it.

But by the time those few words left me, her breath had slowed to a rate I heard as tranquil sleep, the daily trip of a simple human child into worlds beyond her power to change or fight.

I tried to recall some fitting single verse from the past—a psalm of praise requesting strength—but my mind lay as blank as the snow I'd likely find when I left this warmth. And then I fell into my trance too. If any dream walked through those hours, it left no fear or further instructions; and if any sleeping heart ever longed to stay where it was and grow tap roots forever more, it was mine right then—that near the midst of one world that plainly worked for its creatures.

Whatever woke me came as a word, but in my head, not the freezing room. I swam up knowing I'd heard a voice addressed to me and saying one word. Quick as it came it woke me fully, and I lay on long enough for the message. Nothing more sounded anywhere near me except the living trust and calm of the same three souls I'd lain down with, their healthy sighs on the ocean floor of brief blind safety. At last I told myself it was *Now*; the word that woke me had to be *Now*. I checked the window—no trace of light but the last of the moon that silvered my hands which I held up before me. Dim as it was I could see they were clean, not just of the honest dirt of hunting but all my past.

Strike out of here now before they rise and hold or win you. I tried to think if I'd left anything in my old cabin. No, not a crumb. All I needed was on me—all and more. I put my silent hand down slowly into my pocket and found the rock that might be a ruby, that red anyhow and clear at the heart. My arm went out towards where it felt the force of Margaret's perfect eyes and mind, and I set the redness down where she'd see it as first-day woke her.

Then limber as any recent ghost, I stood to my feet. My shot leg tried to buckle once, but next it held and promised to bear me. I moved in uncanny quiet to the door, spread it open by quiet inches, slid my frame through and shut it behind me. Outside was barely colder than in, so my old summer coat would likely serve till sunup; I bound it round me and took a calm pause to listen again—nothing, just evergreens shifting in darkness, leading their ample harmless lives in one right place. Leftward the pitch of the sky burst open with white bomb light but still no sound.

So I turned right and crossed the clearing. In one more minute my feet were muffled in thick pinestraw; my legs could feel I was bound uphill and inward on these unplumbed mountains, aimed away from home and help except what my two hands could give. Endless mountains, utter freedom, lasting peace—a healed strong man now, done with war.

LONG NIGHT

In your rented Fiat, the size of a roller skate, you can drive south from the heart of Jerusalem and be in Bethlehem in fifteen minutes. It also makes an attractive walk—two gentle hours, no real climbing and the compact town strung out on its ridge as your visible goal through the clear desert day. That winter month, a dry December, I drove south a dozen times alone. Because I'm a licensed architect who veered into writing years ago, I was there to plan a commissioned piece on the Church of the Nativity, the town's great magnet. That big dim good-smelling warren of a place is the oldest continuously used church in Christendom and has a good deal to be said for it still as a showcase of Middle Eastern architecture from Constantine onward—a depressing good deal. The lines and pillars of the oldest church shame the Catholic and Greek Orthodox additions, a boatload of jimcrack pictures and lanterns—the eunuch Babe and his boneless Mother in cancer-causing pastel inks.

The beating heart of all that weight is a limestone cave. You walk toward the altar, then start down one of a pair of steep stairs. Twelve feet later, you're inside the cave. You look overhead, or steal a glance behind leather wall-hangings, to see the live stone. It's very much there despite two millennia of chiseling pilgrims. And trustworthy records that date to less than a century after Jesus' death say that here he was born, that simple a fact—a low space not as long as a schoolbus, which served as dry shelter for livestock and overflow guests from the nearby inn.

There's a silver star in a low corner niche that says "Here Jesus Christ was born of Virgin Mary." It was stolen early in the nineteenth century and caused the whole Crimean War before its return. Five yards away down three more steps is a trunk-sized niche where the manger stood, the feeding trough that served as a cradle on the night in question. When the emperor Constantine's mother came here in 339, she allegedly confiscated what was left and took it to Rome where it's still on view in St. Mary Major just under the altar, a few warped boards in a busy crystal-and-gold container.

Anyhow I was leaving for home the next day and had spent the morning in east Jerusalem, buying belated Christmas presents and a sidewalk lunch that either would or would not kill me. Then I napped for an hour on my narrow bed in the YMCA, an honorable hostel facing the famed King David Hotel with its high-rolling weird component of guests—American Jews and German civilians. I dreamed about a guided tour, where Jews walked Germans through Hebrew history, a long stage-pageant with actual blood. Though an Anglo-Saxon, since early boyhood in the 1930s I've dreamed I was Jewish and the prey of a hunting party of Germans who are blind but equipped with exquisite noses.

By the time I got my eyes full-open, the afternoon was more than half gone; and the sky had thinned to the good light-blue of your favorite work-shirt, a billion years old. Most of the weary cells of my mind longed to fall back and sleep again. But a sensible lobe, the size of a nickel, said "Haul yourself down there one last time."

As I crested the rise to Manger Square, Kamil, the parking manager, hailed me; and I suddenly thought I knew why I'd come. Lying on the occupied West Bank, Bethlehem has dapper Arab police in dark blue and white, plus anxious young Israeli soldiers with Uzis primed. They sometimes deign to help with traffic in the packed town-center. But

Kamil is strictly a free-will agent, a hometown boy who shepherds tourists to the scarce parking places with a hand ballet as good as any cop's in rush-hour Rome. He assisted me three or four times before I understood his problem. The boy is dumb—mute, unable to speak. He'll sound an occasional baritone note as he opens your door or shuts you in and waves you off with the small banknote you offer in thanks but not a word. Still his listening face is mostly as pleasant as his general mood, and he always sports a baseball cap in fire-truck red.

He loped toward me now, beckoning wildly with a barn-wide grin as he caught my face. I quickly knew I'd give him all my leftover shekels and not bother splurging at the airport tomorrow on the useless gewgaws of duty-free shops. I had about fifty dollars left; and Kamil had been my favorite Arab of the several dozen on this first visit who'd shown me the hawkeyed boundless kindness of their faith and tribe. And since he seemed to go home at dark, I'd give it to him now.

As I braked to park, he was at my window with the eager smile of a child actor; but I took a moment to see who was near us. A bus was loading German nuns a few yards away, all stout and grim. Their hard eyes blocked my immediate plan but I hatched another. I got out, locked up and shook young Kamil's eager hand. Then I risked a question, "Will you have coffee with me?"

The smile disappeared; he was painfully baffled. Had I somehow offended or was he deaf too? A local waiter had said he was mute; I'd forgot to ask about his hearing.

I pointed across the square to a restaurant, St. George's (he of dragon fame, the other local-boy-made-good, after David and Jesus—a fair enough record for a town you could lose in a block of Manhattan).

Kamil shook his head.

"Coffee? *Caffè?*" In the air, I drank from a nonexistent cup.

He finally got it. The smile beamed on and he took off his fingerless right-hand glove to shake my hand again, skin to skin.

The air was still warm; the outdoor tables were all but empty. So we sat outside and faced each other like players in a game. Musa, the waiter who'd also befriended me, showed no surprise. He met us with benign self-possession and eyes that could drill through armor plate, and may get the chance, but showed no hint of disdain for Kamil. Yet a dumb and grubby unofficial parker must have stood ten rungs down on the ladder from a spotless waiter.

And though I had a moment of panic—what would I say or do for these minutes?—once coffee came, the time went smoothly.

Kamil pocketed his cap, hand-combed his tan hair; and when he'd had his first long sip, he lapsed at once into what seemed a trance of meditative calm. The harried cords and lines of worry melted inward. In under ten seconds, he showed for the first time his actual age, maybe thirty-five.

Much older than I'd guessed. So I took his lead and also lapsed and was well away in thoughtless peace when Kamil bolted to his feet and waved at a bus that was struggling to park. I wanted to stop him, but he had his job so I nodded "Go."

He gave a quick but sweeping salaam like a movie sheik. Then the grin resumed and he jogged toward the bus that obligingly needed serious guidance. As ever, once the motor died, Kamil took his place by the door and met each tourist, dead in the eyes. He never appeared to expect a tip, and I never saw him get one. It seemed enough to search their faces—maybe news from where he'd never go.

I lapsed off again and watched the dance of some evening birds high over the church. They had the curved-wing shape of swallows but were twice the size of swallows at home. They went on tumbling with the fixed intent of carnivorous raptors. So as a further aid to calm, I chose the smallest bird and watched her weave through all the rest. Her rapid patterns calmed me too well. For actual minutes I never thought once of the son I'd lost five months ago, not to mention my present aim in a town that was known for births. And when the flock dissolved in space and I came to Earth, it was nearly dusk. The church would shut at the last trace of light. The square was empty of all but children. Kamil was nowhere in sight, surely gone. Another American charity foiled.

*

The church was open but the inside was dark and looked utterly empty. I'd walked a good halfway up the nave before I thought I might get locked in. By then I was reckless and pushed ahead. Any healthy person could do a lot worse than spend a night on the cold cave-floor. And the farther I went, the darker things got till, up near the altar, I was feeling the air itself for directions. I'd never longed for a Greek monk before, that surly breed, but I almost did. And then the precipitous stairs were at me—slick stone, no railing—and I almost fell.

The cave though was lighted, the usual candles and hanging oil lamps secreting a moist enfolding heat. Still no other human in sight. There are no chairs or benches, so you have two choices of respectful posture, standing or kneeling. I have a trick knee and in any case am not given to kneeling. I also have a nagging tendency to awe at the ancient sites of any faith that doesn't advocate a slaughter of the faithless, but prayer and prostration are matters I retired from in junior-high.

Still, there alone for maybe ten minutes, I came as near a physical bow as I'd come for decades. The thing my mind kept going back to was, some brand of touch. I'd bend my good knee and press my forehead—forehead, not lips—on the famous star. I told myself I could do the same at a few other places, like Keats's tombstone or the sill of a hut at the back of my grandfather's vegetable garden where an old black man, born a slave, had died after tending my childhood with well-meant patience. And I did step forward and start to crouch before I heard footsteps on the stairs. This would be the mad monk with beard aflame.

Instead it was Kamil—unsmiling, bareheaded again, even older. He came straight toward me and took my right hand; his gloves were gone.

He had never followed me before. I was glad of course and pressed his palm.

But his head shook hard. Then his face came down; and with lips so dry they scraped my skin, he kissed the heel of my hand by the thumb.

I thought that was more than a fair return on one cup of coffee; and next I laid my other hand on the crown of his bowed head, the kind of blessing you see in paintings of Abraham or Isaac and Jacob. I knew I would never do it elsewhere above ground in daylight, but here it felt apt.

When he stood back up, Kamil still hadn't smiled. He moaned a low note, no word but no grunt. And he turned to leave.

I may be a hack but I can be moved, every year or so. I called his name in two clear syllables, "Ka - mil."

He stopped in his tracks but didn't look round.

So I thought "He can hear." And I covered the ten feet of cave between us, pressed my gift in his hand and shut his fingers on it.

He looked down slowly, then carefully opened the dingy wad of shekels. On his fingers he counted meticulously. Then grinning wide, he folded them back and thrust the wad into my breast pocket.

I said "No. For you, my friend."

He kept on grinning but shook his head.

When I reached to my pocket and tried to insist, Kamil pointed to the star and raised a hushing finger to his lips. Many Arabs in Bethlehem are Maronite Christians, and Muslims honor Jesus as a prophet, so I understood him to mean "Pipe down." By then I had the money out again.

But his head shook hard; and when I said "Please" in a lower voice, his eyes went fierce and his dry right hand came up and covered my offensive mouth. Now he'd muted me, he still didn't smile. But a sudden idea lit in his eyes. The hand came down and he moved past me toward the end of the cave, waving me on like a smoking bus. By the time I joined him, he'd shouldered aside a leather curtain and pointed to a low door set in the rock.

It looked as old as the smoky stone. But closer by, I saw it was wood with an ancient iron latch and lock. Any instant a monk would howl down on us or burst through the door with a flashing blade.

Kamil paused to test the silence. We might as well have been on Neptune. Then he fished in his trousers and brought out a key, four inches long, as black as the door and older looking. It turned the lock, and the door crept open at its own slow rate on a blacker space than any I've seen in years of walking through nights in the mountains with no city lights for fifty miles.

But when Kamil took my elbow to guide me, I didn't resist and didn't feel strange. The cave itself was country as strange as the back of Tibet. In three short steps we were in the deep dark, and the door shut behind us. We stood there awhile.

Kamil kept a strong grip on my arm, but that and the wide-spaced sound of his breath was all that let me know he was with me. For a second I thought of movie theaters in childhood summers—how I'd enter from a sun-drenched street and be blind at the top of the aisle, groping my way and sometimes sitting on a lady's lap before I could see. But as long as we waited, maybe two minutes, my eyes never widened enough to find light.

Then Kamil nudged me forward again and brought my left hand down onto something. Dry wood apparently, the edge of something that felt manmade, some two feet long. I didn't want to go past the edge to explore. My hand must have stiffened; and still pitch-dark in a voice that resembled his parking grunts, Kamil said something. Some-way, this time, I thought it was a word. I said "Beg your pardon?"

He waited in place and again repeated what was surely a word, though I still failed to hear it. Then he turned my arm loose and fumbled in his clothes.

That was when I balked. What in God's name would come down next? I wouldn't stay to watch. I turned back toward what I thought was the door.

But a quick light flared. Kamil had struck a long kitchen-match and was holding it out. We were in a walled-off deeper niche of the same birth cave. It was ten feet long with raw stone walls and a random huddle of junk on the ground. I could make out oil lamps, a stack of icons and whatever thing I'd just now touched on a shelf at waist level. I walked back toward it.

It was coated with an even layer of dust except where Kamil and I had disturbed it. But at first I could only think of a boat. It looked like an antique child's canoe, roughly gouged from a straight tree-trunk and a good deal longer than my hand had guessed, maybe three feet long by two feet wide. Oddly I pictured the infant Moses afloat on the Nile in his bulrush boat.

The match burned down; Kamil lit a second.

In the moment of dark between them, I managed to guess this was some kind of manger, something the monks kept hid away for processions upstairs. I met Kamil's grin with a grateful nod—an average tourist seldom glimpses the family junkroom of Jesus' birthplace.

Again he took my hand and thrust it to the scooped-out bottom of the manger. I felt it and, this time, thought of my mother's old bread-kneading bowl, a fine smooth oak but sold at her death for under a dollar. I even paused to want it back. The second match was dead by then.

The voice that had made Kamil's dumb grunts now said a word.

I thought it was *real*. He had said the word *real*, and he somehow meant this wood trough here. We were back in absolute dark again; and the trough was still not glowing or pulsing, nothing my eyes could read as uncanny. But too much was coming at me too fast—this changing man and his awful place, the thick taste of dark and whatever wooden worn old thing my fingers touched. I only knew I must not ask Kamil to speak again. I must leave here now. I tried to slide my hand from his grip.

Strong as anyone I'd ever known, the man that held me rung my wrist with a huge warm hand and said again "*Real*"—the same one word, many times through the night.

A NEW STRETCH
OF WOODS

MY MOTHER was down for her afternoon nap, so I was taking my second aimless walk of the winter day. Then we lived way out in the country. Three sides of our house were flanked by woods—deep stands of pine, oak, poplar and hickory that you could walk beelines in for hours and meet nobody, no human being. But the ground teemed with foxes, raccoons, possums, squirrels, snakes, occasional skittish but kingly deer and frogs, salamanders and minnows in the narrow creek, not to speak of the birds who'd learned to trust me as if I could also fly and worry, which were their main gifts.

I was sure I'd formed an intricate union with each and all, even the snakes. I'd managed to touch one live wild bird. I'd handled three non-poisonous snakes. But even when they hid, I could sit by their haunts and talk my sorrows out by the minute; and childhood sorrow is bitterer than most, being bare of hope. As often as not, my mournful words would charm them. They'd edge into sight, then cock their heads and fevered eyes and wait till I finished. Often they'd stay on a long last moment, in silence that I could read as their answer, before disappearing. They generally managed to vanish like fog. Since I never scared them, they at least never ran.

But the strangest time began with the dog. My Boston bullterrier had died that fall; and with Mother pregnant, Father had told me to wait till the baby was settled in. As a man, I can see his practical wisdom—

Mother didn't need one more job now, a messy pup; and once a rival child arrived, I'd need a tangible private possession to share the trials of learning that I was no longer the fulcrum of household love. We had two housefuls of neighbors on the road and they had dogs, but the dog that found me that afternoon was not one of theirs.

It was an odd pale shade of gray with solid gray eyes that seemed to lack pupils, as if it saw without using light. Those traits today would make me think of a Weimaraner, but the dog then was half the size. It was also sleek as a greyhound or whippet; and though it never actually spoke, of the animals I was to meet that day, the dog came nearest and triggered the others. Those eyes alone plainly yearned to say what it knew so well but could not deliver.

And I know it was real, an actual thing with hair and bone, weight and heat. When it broke in on me at the Indian Round, I thought at once that it meant me well. I stooped to stroke it, then hefted it onto my lap for a moment. It bore those attentions with quiet ease; but it gave me none of the wild affection small dogs mostly give, the desperate kisses that put all human lovers to shame. So I set it back to the ground and watched. (I call the dog *it* since, that day, I never thought to look for its sex. But for years I told myself it was male—it came at a time when female friends mean little to a boy—but now I feel the need for precision.)

The Round was a secret name I'd given to a natural cleared ring in the woods where, for whatever reason, no trees or weeds grew. At once I felt that the Indians made it or found it countless ages before me. In any case I knew on sight that it had sacred power. I'd given very little close attention to God, but I knew when the ground gave off a force no human could name or overcome. And through the years we'd lived nearby, I brought any fine or mystic object I found back here and set it in the midst. A big white rock, three real arrowheads and the skull of what I guessed was a wolf with a crest of bone to which the mighty jaw and throat muscles had once been attached.

What I made, and was making, was more a museum than an altar or temple. I never prayed here or enacted rites. I recognized a fact.

This spot on the Earth was clearly magic; it gave off invisible force like a god and therefore deserved my childish tributes of care and beauty. The only private thing I did was sometimes to strip and lie on my back, staring at the hole of distant blue sky and telling myself all others were dead now, the whole world empty of all but me and the beasts I knew were watching me from secret lairs in reach of my voice and the smells of my body. I'd only begun to love my body late that summer, when I turned ten. So I already knew how dangerous my own loving hands could be, even then when I'd touched no body but mine and, rarely, the public parts of my parents.

But that first day, when I set the dog down, I suddenly knew that it came as a guide. And next it walked to the far north edge of the Indian Round where the woods began again, thicker still. At every few steps it would look back toward me and give a hook of its avid head, calling me on. Then it entered the thicket.

In my mind from then on, I called it Scout and thought of it as male. And I followed him close as the woods would let me, the briars and vines, the stinging limbs against my eyes. Scout stayed in sight, just glimpses and sounds, till we came to the stream. At first I thought it was my old creek, the one I explored in all kinds of weather, wading and probing under rocks with sticks or lying on the bank and going silent to watch its surface and deeps for long minutes as one by one the ghostly transparent crawfish or toads the size of your little-fingernail offered their private acts to my eyes, their brute and merciful transactions, finer and surer to last than ours.

But I quickly understood I was elsewhere. This was not the same creek I'd known before, no part I had seen. It was twice as wide and way too deep to see into. With a running start I just might jump it, but how would I get a running start in such dense undergrowth? And was that Scout's intention for me?

He was gone anyhow. I stood entirely still to listen. Even in winter no live stretch of woods is thoroughly silent. If nothing else, the drying hearts of the trees themselves will groan and crack. But now I was sunk in a well of stillness that was not only new to me but scary, though my favorite virtue was bravery. The trees and bushes were normal species, the water was wet and cold to the touch, only the air between us had changed. I doubt I'd heard of a vacuum, but I knew I was in peculiar space and that, all around me, the air was thinning in a quiet rush to leave me entirely unimpeded, more naked than ever, though I wore my leather jacket and aviator's cap.

Scout never returned. But in the new thin air around me, in my bald fear, his message sounded plainer than words, *Cross this water.* I retreated the few available steps, turned my fear into reckless strength and tried the leap—which I made, and to spare. I landed an easy yard past the water on ground I could feel was new to my feet. And before I was firm upright on my pins, I called myself brave.

Then came the bird, a perfectly normal golden eagle. The strangeness dawned only two days later when I learned that golden eagles were unheard of in the coastal plain of where we lived. It stood on a pine limb four yards above me and kept its head in rigid profile like something Egyptian fixed on me the way nothing can but meat-eating birds with the talons and beaks to do their will. For the better part of two or three minutes, it never so much as shut an eye.

I tried to freeze my body in respect; but after a while I needed to prove it was still alive, the ferocious bird. So I bent right over and touched the ground, just to make a move—I didn't plan to pick up a rock to throw.

Before I was back upright, it raised off its limb on wings the size of a black four-door new roadster.

If I'd been thinking clear and fast, I might have feared it was aimed at me and covered my eyes. But it went on skyward so straight and fast, with so much perfect power to burn, that I know I actually laughed a high note and followed with some such word as "Lord!"—I hadn't yet got to the harsher cries. Only when it had also vanished did I understand the words it left me, silent as the dog, *Stay still right here.*

I stayed till the sun was nearly gone, and an evening chill was taking my feet. I hadn't interpreted the eagle strictly. A few minutes after it disappeared, I went to a bent tree-trunk near the stream and waited there but facing the woods, the strange territory, not the way back home. Something had let me know all along that I wasn't lost, that home lay behind me the way I'd come. All I had to do was leap that stream a second time, while I still had daylight, and wind my old trail back up beneath me like a thread I'd laid behind me or crumbs.

The only question was, what would come next? And would it come before night fell and Father got home and started calling my name to the dark and scaring Mother, tender as she was these last weeks? For all I knew, Scout might come back and guide me in or onward to some whole other new life, elsewhere than here. I turned that last thought over awhile and knew I would go wherever he led, whoever wound up with a broken heart if I too vanished and no trace of me was found on Earth, no thread of my clothes. Most honest men will own to similar vengeful thoughts in late childhood.

Then the black snake streamed on out of the woods, crossed the narrow bank six feet beyond me, poured itself down the slope, swam most of the stream in a straight line across; then sank a few inches short of land and never surfaced, nowhere I could see. Like the eagle, it had all the normal traits of its kind. Only it was thick as a plump young python; and where I lived then, all snakes are deep asleep in winter and would no more enter an ice-cold stream than a raging fire.

But when I'd thought my way through that, I got the final news of the day. It stuck up mean in the quick of my mind like the snake itself, that strong and rank, *The baby your mother wants to make is a boy. It would be your brother, but it will not live.*

The news itself didn't hurt at first, but I wanted to stay for amplification. Had I caused the promise? Was it good or bad? Would I be blessed or punished next? Did it mean I must act thus or so from here on? And I did linger there on the tree till I knew I had five more minutes of light, then freezing dark with its own business that I couldn't yet face. I thought if anything, good or evil, was using me, it could follow me home and tell me there. I thought I'd say at least a short prayer for strength to make the leap again and bravery to see me back through the woods. But I found my mind would simply not pray; all I heard was the last news again, *It will not live.*

So I leaped and made it, though with no ground to spare. And each hedged step of the backward way was hard and cowardly. I somehow still couldn't pray for help, for me or my brother that had been so lively this afternoon when Mother told me to press her belly and feel his foot. Worse, I couldn't even pray for her—that whether he came out well or dead, she be spared pain, not to mention bloody death. She was three-fourths of all I'd known or loved, and she'd earned every calorie of all my heat.

But my arms and legs worked on as before; and by the time it was actual night, my hands alone could guess I was almost home by the touch of familiar trees, especially pines with the scaly bark I knew as well as my favorite skin. The last few yards took what seemed years, but the hands were right. At last home was there, bright before me in its own safe clearing.

Inside in Mother and Father's room, my mother's face was hid in their pillows. She was fully dressed but the tan wool skirt she'd worn all day was dark with blood, and I could count the wrenching cries that tore her heart. Around us three, the air had the hot iron smell of blood. It was so much my strongest sight till then that I can call it up whole this minute and be there again. I wanted of course to flee to the woods and learn a way to reverse the spell my trip had cast. But bravery showed me my kind-eyed father standing beside her, hands at his sides, unable to help. When he saw my face, he said "She lost your brother, son."

I saw his words had calmed her cries for the moment at least, which was all it took to brace myself for the sight of the eyes she turned on me next—her mouth like a razor wound in her face. I told her the only thing I knew, "I will be him too. You can love us more than ever."

Father shook his head and touched his lips for silence.

But slowly my mother rigged a smile and pressed it toward me before her head sank back to sleep.

THE LAST OF A LONG
CORRESPONDENCE

W HEN THE NURSE had turned Timson Larkin side to
side with gentle efficiency to make the bed under him, she lugged him
upright onto four pillows and rolled the tray table across his lap. "There
now—you set for the morning?" The coal-black skin of her face was
seamless, though she'd said more than once in his weeks here that she
was a few years older than he.

He said "Wilhelmina, call me Timson. Nobody else knows me well
enough now."

She checked the open door for faces—a momentarily empty hall.
"Timson, Mr. Larkin." She thought about laughing but touched the
dry back of her hand to his, a sensible meeting; then she stepped to the
window and tilted his blinds so he lay in the reach of strong fall sunlight.
He had what she thought of as "hospital ghost" skin, papery white and
drawn on his forehead; but he'd kept enough flesh to leave his smile
bearable, no corpse's grin.

Larkin lowered his voice and spoke through the smile. "If I had any
real money to leave, I'd give this place a marble statue of a black
trained-nurse—I'm that grateful to you."

Wilhelmina laughed. "They make black marble?"

"Streaky but black."

"No streaks on *me*. No, get you some tar, Timson—leave them a
sawed-off black tar-baby with a broad bohunkus. It'll cost you less and

they'll know it's me." By then her mind was in the next room with another lone man but one she dreaded, mean to the core and likely to live weeks longer than Timson, who was speeding now.

He saw her all the way through the door; then rocked his gray head back on the pillows, shut his eyes and sorted the people he still owed money or explanations. The vivid likeness of one young woman stood out from the rest, a tall redhead with wide blue eyes. He watched her stand there clear in his mind, a quiet minute, till he finally answered the question he'd postponed since his last surgery.

Of all the friends and kin he was leaving—and he had a fair number—it was she who counted most by a long reach, the one he bitterly hated to leave. Before he opened his eyes again, he knew that whatever fear he had of his coming death sprang fully from her—her perfect record in his life and his in hers; his hope to watch her and her two children through a little more time, which he'd never do now.

When his eyes came open, he saw his right hand on the table before him. The fingers worked anyhow, most mornings. So he worried the drawer of his table open; found the tablet of lined paper, the old pen, and set his mind to tell one story that was still inside him.

October 19, 1992

Dear Kit,

Your potted plant beat me here. It was by my bed when they wheeled me up from Offensive Care, minus what was left of that lung. It loves the shade and is already growing—the plant, not the lung (I very much hope). My best nurse says it's a century plant. In which case I count on knowing it better as we crawl toward my centennial, after all a mere four decades off. The plant's chances are better than mine but you know that. And I don't object. I honest to God don't mind the thought of easing on from here to Plan B or to Full-Tilt Hell in Barbecue Season, just so I either feel nothing whatever or recall your face.

I even know when I want to see you, in memory. It will be any one of the numerous ways you turned to me that bright weekend we spent when you were seven but looked a strong thirty, around your eyes. You seemed and acted, all those hours, like a full-fledged female guide with dangerous eyes but a heart that wanted me when others had quit. You were also funny—past any child movie star—and genuinely sweet at heart, not sappy. Memories of children seldom age well though, so I won't force you to cringe by harping on what made you adorable then. And I can't remember us ever discussing the time itself; so with your leave, I'll expatiate.

I don't even know if you recall the genuine trouble that hung right over us, fine as it was in the warm sun from Thursday evening on through that Sunday in late October 1962. The scare had started on the Monday night when young John Kennedy, hot as a fever, told the nation on grainy TV that Russia was mounting hydrogen bombs on long-range missiles in rural Cuba, ninety miles from downtown Key West. He announced that we were, at that moment, quarantining the island of Cuba from Russian ships with offensive weapons. Every missile in place must go, and any warhead launched from Cuba would be considered an assault by Russia and would call for the ultimate nuclear answer.

I was thirty years old, my whole boyhood had been World War II. I remembered the day Hiroshima vanished—I'd built a doghouse in our backyard. But that October night, watching alone, I knew we'd got to the worst place yet. Hitler could never have killed everybody. We could do that tomorrow, and so could the Russians. Seeing the glare in Kennedy's eye, and recalling Khrushchev's pudgy bluster, I knew the raw truth. It was more than likely the world would end this week or next, the human part.

It had been eight months since your dad's plane crashed with him and your mother; and I hadn't seen you since that night I left you by your grandmother's drive, pale and stunned from a double funeral and a houseful of cousins packed in behind you, feeding their faces on free deviled eggs and complimentary Jell-O. But when I'd taught my morning class on the Thursday after Kennedy's threat, I suddenly un-

derstood you were all I wanted to see, in the time that was left. That
morning had seen the first face-off between our blockade and a Russian
freighter bound for Havana. The news kept telling us every ten seconds
how far apart the vessels were, what instant they'd meet; and everybody
over six years old in the Western world knew that, if the Russians
refused our search, we'd sink them—and then?

I was fairly sane, even that far back; and I'd led a smart class through
the Treaty of Utrecht with a splendid day in progress outside as the two
ships met, but I was convinced they'd defy our orders. We'd scuttle
them and, in less than an hour, I and my twenty-odd rich sophomores
and every page of modern history, not to mention you, would be loose
atoms in a swarm of dust that could never settle. Years later I found
out Kennedy shared my bleak outlook; he sent his wife and children
into the Maryland hills to wait out the fire while he crouched in the
White House by the big red trigger.

By noon I'd stopped at home, packed a small bag, fed my two angel
fish and headed for you—a two-hour drive. The warm sunlight held
steady around me; and I reminded myself that wars start mostly in warm
dry weather, spring or fall, almost never in snow. And as I climbed
northwest in open country, it started seeming that everything knew an
end was bearing down; so even the dead things—rocks and dirt—were
showing their finer points to the light in a last display. At one spot ten
miles east of you, at the foot of House Mountain, a sizable cat that was
clearly wild—some brand of panther with tan hair and pale eyes—slid
out of a thicket and faced my car, completely unspooked. Later I
checked and found that panthers had vanished from there in the early
twenties, but I never doubted mine was real and was giving the Earth
a final chance to see her elegant eyes and body which killed just to eat.
She made me pick up speed toward you.

See, I thought you were mine. And most of what I want you to
know, once you read this, is why I believed it. It's easy to say with me
near gone, but I understand it may be hard for you to hear. I truly hope
not. I mean it to be true news you can bank on the rest of your life. It

can all be said in visible words—I'd loved your mother for so many years, we'd shared so much of each other so long, that when Connie chose your dad over me and you were born, I felt from the instant I saw your blue eyes that I'd helped make you.

Strictly speaking, and this is important for you to believe, I'd had no physical part in your birth. Connie and I had ceased to be lovers nearly six months before she met Walt; and in his bottomless confidence, he never asked if I'd done more than steer her elbow around most of Europe for nearly two years—she told me that much, the year she died. No, what I'm trying to set down here is the way a single human being who's never had a legal mate or his own blood children can, one day, know he's had a strong hand in somebody else's newborn child. I loved your mother that much from our childhood; and crazy or soft-brained as it sounds, I put so much into filling her mind and body with me—well, take it from there.

You loved me too, from the day we met when you were barely three weeks old. Walt had moved you and Connie to Charlotte. Though he and I had met and were civil, I'd never have made a special trip to barge back into Connie's life except for being invited down to speak at a men's historical banquet. Your mother read about it in the paper and wrote me to say, if I felt it was right, that she and Walt would thank me for standing as your godfather the Sunday morning after my speech. I doubt Connie understood how nearly I'd shucked off any belief I might have had that life was moving in a plan toward happy endings for all concerned (or even just the truly baptized). And I knew the priest would have me swearing to guard you from spiritual harm etc., but something more than memories of my years with Connie made me accept. So I saw you for the first time ever on steep church steps before we moved in to scrub your soul.

You were dozing in Walt's arms in blinding light; and you looked like a wretch in Satan's stewpot—red as any new rabbit, with hairline purple veins on your bald scalp. Of course I bore up manfully and lied about your native charms and your natural cool to be sleeping through this. The cool kept on right through the service, with you being held by the wheezy priest and plentifully soused. Your eyes were half-open, but you still looked raw and ready to yell. It was only when I had to answer the priest's first question that you looked up and met me finally.

I don't recall what I was promising—no doubt some inhuman guarantee—but my one answer, which had to be yes, did wonders for you. Your wonky neck firmed up for an instant, your eyes found mine and locked right on them, and your left hand came toward me slowly till it stopped in a bar of light from a window and held still there. Your fingers were less than ten inches from me; in the sun, I told myself I could see your actual bones, brittle as sticks. I told myself you were way too trusty to be near me that day, maybe ever—I somehow felt more unreliable than ever around you, but I didn't think why.

Still I put my hand out and let you feel my heat. Till then you'd fairly steadily smiled; but when you'd tested me a long moment, watching my eyes, your whole face cleared of the infant blankness and the plainness lifted. While the priest gunned through his benediction, you let me see deep into your mind that lay as calm behind your eyes as if you were ninety-five years old and had borne all sorrows known to the race before winning this peace. I had no doubt, that minute or now, that you were something I'd love from then out.

I pulled over after I saw the panther and phoned to let your grandmother know I was passing through and could I stop (I hadn't wanted to phone much ahead for fear of alarming her and you). She'd known me very nearly from birth, and I'd always called her Livia. She'd generally thought I was vague but firm as a family friend, and she left it at that. Your mother and I had most of our love, long miles from home when we worked abroad; so sure, why didn't I come for supper and visit with you? Even better than hearing her invitation was the fact she didn't allude to Cuba or the two men tensed in Moscow and Washington, dazed on testosterone and ready to lunge. Like my own mother, who was long gone, Livia was concentrating on questions that after all may have been more urgent than imminent death. *Would one baked hen feed the three of us?*

We were all three famished and it barely did. Afterward we sat on the old glassed-in back porch and watched full night sweep past the mountains beyond the valley and up the near side to take us too. It made me edgy, watching it creep; and you'd been unnaturally quiet all evening; so I was trying to ease my nerves by rattling on to you about school when Livia leaned and touched my hand.

She said "Tim, listen. Smooth that brow. It truly won't matter."

At first I thought she'd loosened a screw; and then I noticed you were facing her, nodding.

I said "I don't follow you."

Livia faced you as if for permission, then said to me "This dustup over a tropical island can't count for much."

I thought I should let it go at that; no use depressing the two of you with my timetable for planetary melt-down.

But then you laughed. "Want to show him the new paperdolls?" In another few seconds you were in a long giggle fit.

And Livia joined you, helpless with her corseted sides. Eventually she dried her tears and managed to speak. "We beg your pardon; we've been laughing all day."

Recall? You'd both spent the afternoon drawing what Livia called "celestial fashions" for paperdolls—planning your wardrobes and hair-dos for Heaven. Once I was laughing too, Livia brought out samples of both your designs; and we looked through them, making fancy additions. I especially enjoyed the fact that—not even knowing I was on the road—you'd made an angel getup for me, covered with stars and (over the breast of my floor-length robe) the planet Saturn with colored rings. You kept us at it through most of the evening, and then it was time for the late news. In the curt reports of a hunkered-down world, there was one glimpse of hope, the size of a pinhead. Kennedy and Khrushchev had told the U.N. that "each side strongly desired peaceful settlement," but neither man flinched from where he stood.

And by the time the weatherman promised another fine day, you'd dozed off on the sofa beside me.

Livia asked me to take you upstairs, and only then did I gauge your growth—you were solid as glove leather right the way through, though your face rolled back on your graceful neck, as limber as that first day I met you. Still you had enough energy to give me the first hard order all week. I knew at once it showed you were both a very young child and one that had some sense of the stakes outside in the world. You said "Don't let this happen to me."

I told you I'd do my very damndest, but even I won't claim it eased you. Your face looked ten years older since supper. You were bone-tired though and fell asleep fast, while I sat by.

For the first night since the crisis began, I also managed a few hours' rest. But just before daylight, I had a rough dream that saw me killing you and Livia in your beds. I slit your throats as easy as lemons, to spare you worse. It woke me up and, as day leaked in through the blinds, I lay in the grip of that and knew it wasn't the worst idea I'd had. Even groggy, I was sure we had no more than a few hours left till the first fireball rolled in across us.

Since I was near I could do no better than start right now to drive you farther into the mountains, hole up in some granite cave and watch each other starve or get shot by other fugitives, just for our canned goods or pocket money (I had less than fifty dollars on me and a handful of change). The more I thought, the more I felt that a quick end here on Livia's porch made better sense.

I heard a single tap at my door. When I went, it was Livia fully dressed and ready as ever to meet what came. She whispered for me to join her downstairs, so I pulled myself together fast and met her in the kitchen.

She had coffee on and was well into making a fieldhand breakfast like none I'd had for thirty years—eggs baked sunnyside-up on ham, link sausage and hominy, hot applesauce, corn muffins and biscuits with homemade jams. I saw right off she was cooking a wake, an old-fashioned feast to remember the dead or the soon-to-be; and suddenly knowing she took the Cuban news in earnest like you and me (she who'd laughed the most last night) scared me worse than Kennedy's eyes or the second splendid day unfolding along the ridge beyond the bay window. I drank half a cup of her strong coffee and tried to think clearly.

Even then I doubt I'd have tipped my hand, but Livia set a full plate before me and said "Eat without me."

I said "You've cooked enough for a tribe."

"I know I have but the tribe won't get it—I'm cleaning out the refrigerator." As she looked down on me, her face was bleak with the kind of certainty you dread to see.

Through the years I'd teased her about her prophecies. When Connie and I were hurting each other toward the end of our time, Livia would occasionally turn to us both and smile as if to warn she was joking but then say "*I* prophesy so and so"—we'd die before dawn if we didn't stop quarreling or we'd lose each other and live to regret it. The worst was when she turned on me once, "You're poisoning memories, Timson, fool. You'll grieve for this the rest of your years." That Friday morning in '62, I managed a chuckle. "You prophesying?"

She sat beside me. I noticed how young her long hands were—she'd thrust them out on the table top, and they barely showed a freckle of age. When she faced me again, she was smiling too. "You want to take Kit on out of here, don't you?"

"Sure, but where would we go?"

"Not we," she said. "Just the two of you—I packed her clothes."

"When?"

"Deep in the night; I hardly slept."

I could see she thought she wouldn't sleep again; she was that convinced. But her smile hung on as her fingers mocked at primping that lovely head of hair, still finer than any I've seen since. "I took a long bath and curled my wig. I'm ready as I'll ever be." She tugged at the roots to show it was hers, in case I doubted.

That trace of vanity was welcome in a morning where everything else had simplified to lines and graphs; and I noticed then how well she was dressed—a dark blue shirtwaist buttoned at the neck, a slim gray skirt and the gold rope-chain that you still wear. I thought *She knows*. But what I said was "I'm not going one foot without you."

She looked right at me. "This child's yours, Tim."

A direct hit from Cuba might have surprised me less. I think I just nodded, I may have thanked her, I know I said she had time to pack.

She glanced to the clock. "Old Dot will be here any minute. I can't scare her."

I thought by then that—old as Dot was, as many meals as she'd cooked in this room—she might be glad to find a locked door and one day's rest, not to mention eternity. But I knew Livia wouldn't see it that way. So I ate the whole breakfast while she woke you and got you dressed. We were in my car and rolling by eight.

And roll we did, that whole long day up through the valley. It never looked better and neither did we. I've still got the picture here beside me, the one the guide at the caverns took and mailed to me later. When I saw he had a camera, I'd given him five of my scarce dollars to take one of us and send it to me "if time permits." He'd laughed and said "You don't believe that Kennedy stud? He's not about to burn *his* money up."

But then the lights went out in the cavern, and who was the first voice to yell he was scared? Not you or me but the pimply guide. We could hear him scrambling back toward the sun, abandoning us, when you said calmly "I bet this is it." I remember thinking you sounded comically wise but right; then you pulled me down to sit on a rock bench carved from the wall.

Everything in me said you were wrong; a fuse had just blown. When we'd sat there quiet for two minutes though, I realized I'd forgot your face. I well remembered in principle that you'd been, for two years, the only beautiful child I'd seen—not charming or winsome but beautiful in the lasting way, still as a tall bird before she's observed. Blind as

I felt, I tasted cold panic. I'll be frank—it was fear for *me*. I barely thought of you or your safety for quite a while there, at least a minute.

Then you found my hand and began to tap on it. Those were the days when Morse code was something boys tried to learn, but I'd never known you to show an interest. Since I'd learned it back in the Scouts, I tried to read your taps as a message; and even when I came up with nonsense, I tried to think you were transmitting some new signal you'd learned. Honest to God, I was that impressed by what smelt like the crack of doom and the likelihood we were already posthumous.

Finally you said "Understand?" By then you were laughing, the way you could then, which always brought down the whole room with you—it came from that deep and was that good to hear.

I said "Sorry, I'm out of my depth."

You kept on laughing and tapped again.

Then a high voice yelled out "Rescue!"

I recall an instant of real disappointment. I'd truly believed you, *This was it*; and now you had a useful message that I'd never get. The next thing I saw was your face, grinning. The guide's flashlight was probing for us and had found you first. You beckoned him on and when he reached us, he said "I'm a walking zombie, I tell you. Haven't slept a wink since this past Monday, and now that old transformer blows. You think you two can crawl out if I lead you?"

We'd entered upright so why should we crawl? I was trying to think when you said "Sure."

So the guide asked you, "Your dad fit to move?"

You ignored his error and said "He's just a little nervous today." No movie nurse could have brought it off better.

Out we crawled—me still half-thinking we'd see a cloud on the near horizon, containing the world in separate pieces. For once I knew I wasn't crazy or a major coward. I don't know what you've read about the crisis, but everything I've come across says we got right up to the edge as I thought we did.

One more time the whole valley was laid out beyond us in every unfazed autumn color. And when I saw you again in daylight, you looked like an adequate reason to hope for reprieve, however brief. I asked the guide if he'd heard any news—it was well past noon.

He was eager to tell us. "My battery radio just now said we boarded a second Red ship bound for Cuba. No bombs on board so we let it go. We ought to just sink everything they got till they run out of boats or bombs, either one." He said *bomb* the old country way as *bum*, and he ended laughing.

You readily joined him. If you'd been even a little scared, you'd barely shown it and were easing up.

By then the guide was out of control in wild high shrieks. Finally he said "Like I told you inside, I'm a walking zombie. I know I got to get hold of myself—my mother's down in that pink house on the left by the creek, expecting me to save her. But guess her weight—two twenty-five, stripped." He giggled again and triggered you.

I thought *What the hell?* and joined you both. Then more than half teasing, I asked him his plans. "You staying close to the caves, just in case?"

He looked to you, then whispered as if he could somehow spare you. "I'd rather get burned to a greasy spot out here in the light than smother inside."

You actually nodded to his pasty face. By now you knew everything we could see was past taking shelter.

I reminded the guide to send me the photo if time permitted, then drove us on.

Can you fill in the rest of that Friday? Didn't we stop at a sad bear cage by a filling station and talk to a bear that looked absolutely like a man in a bear suit, old and trapped? And was that the time we found you the sapphire at Flip's Rock Shop where we paid a dollar each to sift through a big hill of dirt? I know there was nobody sifting beside us; but you let me see it for maybe three seconds before you hid it in my pocket and held up a finger to your lips for silence. Who did you think would stick us up, or did I dream the whole episode? I can see the stone anyhow, big as a pea.

I know for a fact we stopped that night up past Front Royal in a tourist court and phoned Livia with our whereabouts. I didn't mention the world situation; and neither did she, just wished us well and said she was fine last time she looked, "which was New Year's Day." And I know we lay back, tired as dogs on separate beds no wider than planks, and watched the evening news straight through with no talk between us.

The White House was claiming that work on the Cuban missile sites was rushing ahead with no sign of let-up. Even after the news went off and some awful slow-dance show began, we kept our silence. I think I may have napped a few minutes. When I came to, I felt I had a chance at least of getting us through the time that was left, which I still guessed was hours.

No thunder and lightning, no heat or cold, just a kind of ease I'd hardly known since my own preschool days at home, behind the house in that fern jungle down by the quarry, knowing I'd be a hero one day, a help to all. Without looking over I might feel you wide awake and waiting. I reminded myself of what might happen in the world outside. But even that couldn't touch the curious peace that was rising inside me. It began to feel like these cardboard walls could withstand whatever melted the Earth; but I couldn't think why, except to guess I was fooling myself the usual way, dreaming of hope. I was even hungry and realized we hadn't eaten since roadside sandwiches hours ago. We'd brush ourselves up and find a cafe.

But you were gone, in one of those childhood trances that start out seeming normal but go too deep.

I tried to wake you more than once; each time you were further off than before. So I lay on in the growing dark with the TV light on but none of the sound, and about nine-thirty I made a last try. I pulled you to the edge of the bed, aimed your legs at the floor and said "Kit, are you with us?"

Your eyes were glazed and your lips barely moved; but plain as a lawyer, you said "Who is *us*?"

I knew you were talking on automatic pilot. But it seemed such an adult question, I laughed and told my hunger to wait till breakfast. I got you out of your dress and shoes and put you under the blanket in your skivvies. Then when I lay back, fully dressed, to wait for more news, I likewise tumbled off into sleep that was deeper than I'd counted on. At one in the morning, "The Star-Spangled Banner" from the TV startled me—was it war or just the station sign-off? When I realized it had to be sign-off, I slipped out of my own pants and shirt and lay down under a cotton blanket, cool as it was in the mountain air.

Some time between then and daylight, you joined me. When I shifted to make room beside me, you said something that sounded almost disappointed like "Are we still here?"

Through the years, the times I stayed with you when Connie and Walt were on their trips, you'd often join me in the midst of the night— a welcome bundle, despite being always overheated as a hard-worked pony and about as demanding to lie beside—your prematurely long legs would stake out the space and leave me clinging to the mattress edge. So at first this visit seemed familiar; I thought you'd made a waking choice to find me. But when I laid my hand to your back, I could feel you were cold; and your skin was bare the whole way down. Maybe you'd slept too hard, wet your bed, then got up and stripped. But your butt felt nearly as dry and hard as if you'd frozen. I said "My darling, your *can* is cold. Are you all right?"

You were gone again that suddenly, back into your trance.

You'd waked me though for the rest of the night, maybe forty-five minutes. I have no idea what you recall of that dark stretch. I know I've never mentioned this part. Still I think you're strong enough in your own life now to hear the next fact; and I think you can use it—

I never spent a more complicated piece of time, before or since. No fault of yours. Just one more thoroughly normal gauntlet—scary as hell and risky as gunfire—that a grown man passed through, hauling a child as his main baggage, not knowing if he or she would make it.

See, through each of those minutes I held you, you seemed so nearly the same thing as Connie—something that Connie and I had made out of our best hours and that no one was left to treasure but me, at the world's end. Looking back now from another bed, I can also guess you felt to me like the world right then. I could hold you as one last sample of what I'd lose in the fire. And that said something new to my mind—I'd enjoyed my time on Earth more than anybody I'd run across, and now you'd confided all you owned into my scared hands to keep or ruin. In the next few minutes, every failure I'd known just liquefied and drifted off; and I was left with you in my hands, begging to live.

In that short while, your skin had warmed; the small of your back was hot as a lamp on the palm of my hand. And of course my own skin soon got feverish and ready for easing. I say *of course*; men generally have the morals of dogs, so few men will fail to recognize the weight I was under from my own need, which felt at the time like a wave of kind warmth. And that early morning young as you were—and sad as I was, with what I thought were huge odds against us—I ached to give myself to you, anywhere my need would fit. At first I drew my hands away; but then my mind said over and over *It'll be love, Timson, for her and her mother and all that Connie and you ever meant in the way of goodness.*

Maybe twenty percent of the people you see every day on the news, who've forced their daughters' or sons' young bodies, have started out with thoughts like mine. In some few cases, it may well feel like actual care, by their dark lights. I know anyhow I told myself you'd freely joined me. I knew I prized you and wanted to prove it to you and your mother (you can love a person in somebody else—and love them better than face to face while they're still with you). I also knew that if I tried to find Connie in you, it would kill your fearless trust in me and most of the world, assuming the world lasted awhile. And it almost surely would have burnt me down. But then a day has seldom passed in my grown life without me wanting to move some way that feels so right but might prove deadly to somebody near. All I did then on that hard bed, that Saturday morning, was lie beside you holding your shoulders and humming in every pore like voltage, till my eyes said I could call it day and wake you for breakfast.

We ate like a gang of riverboat sailors at that weird pancake house on the cliff by the shut gold mine. You had pecan pancakes with bacon; I had half the eggs in Virginia. And when we were finished, the mean-eyed waitress leaned over and whispered "You two walk out of here gentle please. Much as you ate, you could tear this place right off the moorings if you step too hard." She'd still never smiled.

You thought she was serious and walked accordingly.

I put one heavy foot down and said "We'd loosen it for you, but the Cuban missiles'll finish the job a lot neater than us."

She finally laughed. "Fat chance." When I looked puzzled, she said "Heard the news?"

"Not since last night." It was only then that I realized how drowned I'd been in your company and how it had eased me through till now.

She said "The Russians backed down in the night."

It was you that put your hands to your hips, frowned like the British ambassador and said "You can't be serious" (I'd seen Connie say it a billion times, with just that frown, and always at me).

The waitress nodded. "Serious as a kidney stone."

You turned back to me—"See, I promised"—and burst out laughing.

You hadn't promised me any such thing, not in actual words; but I didn't correct you—it was somehow true.

So we beamed at the waitress; she was only bearing the news we'd kept each other from hearing. The pancake house had a new long lease on the sheer cliff side. By the car radio it turned out Kennedy wouldn't formally take Russia's offer till Sunday, tomorrow; but the great black fog of doom that had spread all week was shrinking. And wasn't the finest news a secret from all but us? The world from here on would have us in it awhile at least, Timson and Kit, after all we'd shared and failed to share since Thursday night.

I anyhow would lean on that many times down the years as lesser offers came my way and begged me to settle for pocket change when I'd been flush one time at least. The last clear thing I remember, before we turned back to Livia's in glorious light, was standing a final moment above your breakfast plate and telling myself *You and Kit caused this.* I still think we did, and I want you to know it while I've got enough sense left to sign my name to this news that you may wish I'd borne to the grave and that I may not get the nerve to mail. It seems important, here while I can, to let you know how your trusting visit to me on a night I thought was the last—and the strength I found, just holding you clean—got me on through the years till I wait here, this near a real finish. I turned out not to need more than that, the pain we spared one another and the thought of your mother's presence in you.

Which is not to say I've leaned my body on just that memory for thirty years—I availed itself of occasional company, some of it helpful, all of it fun and most of it decent with willing adults. But after our days, I had a high flood-mark in my mind that nobody else could ever quite reach. Maybe now you'll have cause to think well of me on official occasions (my birthday, cemetery picnics, etc.)—maybe tell your children the story itself, of a strange full weekend, when their time comes for handling facts too hard to explain.

Let's lay it down there. If we meet next week, let's don't discuss it. I'm too much of a weeper to face it publicly with you in the room as you well know, I weep for gladness, never in pain; but it's still an affliction I like to avoid. If I slip off before you get here, tell yourself we cleared the deck. The deck and the hold and the captain's bridge.

We left each other thoroughly clean and open-eyed. It's been a rare privilege, old Kit. Thanks ever

And love from

Tim in his right mind.

When the last word dried, he folded the pages. No way he could read back through them, he was not disappointed with their feel in his hands, he estimated they'd serve the purpose. His script, as he finished the envelope, had never looked stronger—bold and upright like some world leader's on a global pact. His thin lips smiled to think he'd signed an almost surely more valuable document, useful for more than a season of peace or a fling at free trade. With the taste of the postage sweet on his tongue, he leaned back, ready again to leave.

DEEDS OF LIGHT

In the summer of 1942, no town in that whole end of the state was far from one of the big new camps, training soldiers for Europe and Asia. Tens of thousands of strong men, most of them boys, answered rollcall Saturday and were then cut loose till Monday dawn. Long on strength and curiosity, short on cash, they hitched in pairs to the nearest towns. And since that time and place were guileless, there were no saloons, few theaters and a grave shortage of dim dancehalls with willing girls. So the soldiers tended to take slow walks down leafy streets or lie in the sun on downtown benches and laugh with ladies that stopped to talk or vets from the First War with boring tales of body lice and mustard gas. At dark the boys might band into fours and rent a room in a widow's house and smuggle in some cards and beer, not to speak of occasional risky girls and the first stunned round of young war-widows.

But in the town we're watching now—that whole long summer of wondrous nights—boys would sleep by droves in the warm grass of Whitlow Park under ancient elms and clean black skies with amazing stars. Their chosen spot was a gentle hill above the lake, topped by a road. And full-moon nights, townspeople would sometimes drive past slowly to see that broad encampment sleeping or talking in clumps, all silvered and still. It was years before civilians used flashbulbs; or I'd have pictures to back my claim—a broad hill planted in shining ghosts, waiting to rise at the angel trump to tell their secret sins and hopes.

Sunday mornings my mother and I would drive to the park with friends from our church and furnish steamy urns of coffee, homemade biscuits, country butter and bacon—eggs were scarce. We'd go so early, the boys would wake up raw and stunned and wouldn't say much but "Yes" and "Fine." We were normal Methodists, not Holy Rollers; so we barely mentioned that our main service would be at eleven and they were invited. That hour was common for the entire Protestant country then; and numbers of the soldiers would turn up anyhow, wrinkled and grass-stained but shaved and, by then, wider awake than hunted creatures bayed in the woods.

Two weeks running I'd watched one boy above the rest. I'd somehow forgot the fact till lately when I ran across two pictures of him beside some older pictures of my father (Father had died when I was four, and pictures are mainly how I recall him); but comparing them now, I see how much the two men shared—clipped sandy hair, eyes so light blue that the pupils fade almost to dots when you step back and powerful jaws with wide mouths about to grin. They were like a matched pair of young lords packed with life and hope, unquestioned by any god or man; and they still are that, so long as I have working eyes and a mind to watch their fading traces.

Though I dream about my father still, I have to grant that the face on the boy Deke Patrick makes a stronger call on my grown mind, even now with what I finally watched Deke need and take. But after our first Sunday meeting in the park, I knew only one peculiar thing—Deke guessed my name on sight with no clue. He met my eyes dead-level, smiling, and said "Oh Marcus, wake a sad boy up."

I was too young to wonder why he was sad. I took his knowledge of me as a miracle—Marcus is not that common a name—and I blushed ferociously but managed the coffee and watched him butter two biscuits and leave.

He went twenty yards and sat on a swing that he kept still while he ate his first round. I thought he'd surely come back for more; they mostly did. Deke finished the last morsel though, wiped his mouth with the back of his hand and suddenly started to pump the swing till it flung him out parallel to the ground. From the highest peak he let it die, then rose and walked through a howling bunch of his fellow soldiers to the rim of the lake and stood a long time. Nothing strange happened—the ducks and lilies went about their business—but some stubborn mystery in the picture he cut, upright in weeds at the absolute verge of swimming or drowning, made me need to know him more than anything I remembered needing.

The other soldiers seemed to agree in a loud way. For several minutes they yelled and whistled to call him back—it was in their calls I learned his name—but Deke stood his ground. And when they started a football cheer on "Deekey, *Deke,*" he turned his back, rounded the lake and vanished in woods on the far side.

By then my brief acquaintance with his face may well have settled far enough down to find the buried face of my father. Whyever, I left the coffee urn and asked our pastor to estimate Deke's age and height (I'd seen him talk to Deke after me).

He said "Six foot, maybe twenty years old—a righteous face. Bet you a dime we'll see that boy in church this morning." He laughed but meant it.

I was already edgy around the word *righteous*; so I said "No sir, I won't bet against him."

I'd have won the dime. In church I sat near the door and watched. Ten identical soldiers walked in, thirty seconds before the sermon, but no sign of Deke. They sat on the front row, neat as if they'd slept at home—the park had a bathhouse with plentiful showers. Mother and I were twenty feet off, and I spent awhile not hearing the pastor but searching the necks for a usable substitute to Deke. Nothing—no instant burn of the kind I'd felt when he said my personal name and walked away like Adam naming the beasts in Eden but finding no mate.

As everybody rose for the last hymn, Mother asked if I'd like to invite a soldier home for dinner, as the midday meal was called back then. Around town lately the idea of bringing soldiers home for Sunday dinner was a growing fad, though we had yet to do our part on our slim budget and everything rationed.

So one more time I scanned the necks. To me, in the mercilessness of my age, they might have been dead meat. I faced Mother, shook my head and tore on into "Princely Blood, Our Sovereign Cure," all four verses and a low "Amen."

I was left for at least a week—maybe forever—to wonder how he knew my name when all the locals called me Snake because I could swim that fast and clean. Mainly though I wondered why so much of my mind went out to a stranger that I owed nothing but needed to watch, at close quarters soon and the rest of my days. I'd got to fourteen with no romances, no wolfish fix on another face; so this fresh hunger was hard to bear. And by the time I finally managed to sleep that Sunday, my mind had locked its teeth on a plan. It was new for me then but has stayed in use for the rest of my life and caused me tall waves of joy and pain, my kindest gifts and my devastations.

For me the plan amounted to one of those gleaming cries that humans die for—*Liberty or death!* or *God and my right!* My aim was too red-hot to think of failure—*Take what you need and hold on hard.* Young as I was and new to passion, I understood that if I saw Deke Patrick again—next Sunday or fifty years ahead—I'd find a way to learn him, know him, right to the quick of his adult soul. And if you don't think a fourteen-year-old can reason like that, then you don't know sufficient boys. Or you didn't know me.

And whatever else I did all week, I'd see that fervent demanding face that knew my name and a direct way to the place I kept my secret life. The face was what I focused on, the uncanny eyes; no other part of his ample body came back to call me, not that early. Despite the hot floods of puberty, I could sometimes float back and see the world with the cool unblinking eyes of pure childhood, that fair and true; and I knew my prey, this single boy that somehow shared my father's face (at supper later on in the week, even Mother remarked the likeness).

Next Sunday morning Deke's face was not in the biscuit line, and there was no sign of him down by the lake. I almost asked a red-haired boy where Deke might be. But that would have meant exposing my quick, and I was still green for a show of courage. All the next week though, I kept my inner eye fixed on Deke, drawing him toward me; and that third Sunday, there he stood awake near dawn and saying again "Oh Marcus, save me." I guessed he thought I could save him from hunger.

At one that afternoon, when Mother had got us seated for dinner, she asked Deke please to say the blessing. She and I shut our eyes and bowed, but a silence followed and stretched so long I had to look.

Deke was there, head up, watching the food. His eyes were dry and his lips were parted but still as wood. Finally his eyes came round to me.

I nodded hard and mouthed "Say 'Thank you.' "

He waited another few seconds, then gave a deep chuckle. Mother still hadn't looked, but I was watching and saw Deke spread both hands before him in the air palm-down above the food—he was still grinning wide. Then he just said *"Blessing"* and reached for his napkin.

For years it didn't occur to me that Deke may well not have come from a home where blessings were said and that he was merely balked in the gate. But then I knew he'd stumbled on the only appropriate way to bless, as those old Bible pictures with Abraham raising long arms up through the smoke of a burning lamb. I also took the moment as one more confirmation that Deke Patrick was what I hoped for, not for these past two bated weeks but all my life—a thorough man to learn and copy in every trait and skill I lacked.

By three that hot day, in our cool house at the round oak table, we'd eaten enough for a squad of boys—a brimming platter of Swiss steak, our own fresh vegetables and strawberry shortcake. Mother had quickly cleared the dishes and readied herself for the weekly drive to see her own mother, twenty miles off. Though she was my one live grand-mother, she gave me the fairly serious creeps with her white mustache and spidery hands; so Mother mostly let me use whatever excuses came to mind to spare the strain. Deke Patrick seemed my best excuse yet.

Even in that more tranquil time, few parents would drive off, leaving their only child in the hands of a stranger with training in the arts of death. So apparently Mother shared my sense of trust and expectation in this one soldier. She shook Deke's hand, gave him a standing invita-tion to be with us whenever he could—maybe spend a night this next weekend. She smoothed my hair, told me to show Deke some of my hobbies, then said she'd be back well before dark and left us clean as a streaking bird.

Since the clammy heat was stacking up in our dim rooms, I thought Deke might rather sit outside in the breezy shade or even borrow Mother's bicycle, ride with me to the city pool and swim awhile. I couldn't imagine he'd care to see a boy's collections of stamps and rocks or the model submarine I was building. An even stronger fact now was, I'd started feeling strange in his company. Not from fear—I thought his steady eyes were sane—but more because his private presence, in my home with no other people, was so near to being the perfect answer to years of hope that it spooked me mightily, waiting an arm's reach from him at the table.

I could feel a ringing charge in the air, but I couldn't tell if it drew me on or pushed me back. And since Deke kept on talking and laughing about the miseries of basic training, I couldn't tell if he understood how much force his body threw off in the normal room. I thought I could ask what time he'd leave and maybe break the spell that way. But then I knew I liked the mystery. Something crucial to my whole future might happen here, in a minute or never. So I tried to turn loose and take what came, though I braced myself by thinking *He's a lonesome human that'll leave here soon.* Then I said "We could bike ourselves to the pool; it opens at three."

Deke thought and said "We could also wash that world of dishes we just messed up."

It almost shocked me to think Deke had noticed the plates at all. I said "Mother says dishwashing calms her nerves."

Deke said "Same here. Then you got a bathing suit my size?"

The darkest shadow I'd ever known passed over my sight. I thought it came from a cloud outside. Now I can guess that it came from within me; whatever, it brought up a wave of gladness. *Everything's moving my way now.* I said "Sit tight," then trotted to find my father's trunks in the cedar chest.

The trunks were the old kind, burgundy wool with a white belt and a moth-hole or two. At first they seemed to cheer Deke up. He laughed and said all he needed now was to part his hair in the middle and grow a handlebar mustache. But once we'd parked our bikes at the pool and entered the bathhouse, he sat on a bench, unrolled his towel and shook the trunks in the air before us. Two boys a grade ahead of me nearly fell out laughing.

I suddenly thought I'd shamed Deke. So without meeting his eyes, I said "We don't really have to—"

He groaned a low note, then leapt to his feet and vanished through the restroom door.

I didn't know whether to put on my own trunks or wait to see what he'd do next. But I could feel the lingering charge of where he'd sat. Nothing he'd done yet, nothing he'd said, had stemmed my appetite for help. I'd brought us this far, there were too few hours till he had to leave, I'd take the next step till he said *Quit.* And before I tied my drawstring, Deke was back in the antique suit. At once I was glad, but then I felt wing-shot and falling. So far I hadn't realized how much I needed to see Deke's body, the secret zones; and his shyness had foiled me. I even said "You sure are modest."

He smiled but moved toward the sunny door. "I just don't like to terrify people."

I tried but couldn't begin to guess if he was joking about his size or somehow telling me he had a scar too bad to show.

We swam around in the deep end awhile. Deke swam a lot better than I expected from the coal-miner's son he said he was. When I told him that, at first I thought he'd taken offense.

He didn't smile but wiped the chlorine out of his eyes and said "We learned in the old mineshafts that flooded—pretty good swimming but dark and cold, and then sometimes you'd bump a dead miner they never rescued."

I nodded as if I truly believed him.

He shivered and said "Let's rent us some sun."

I said it was free and led him out. We spread our towels on sloping ground above the bathhouse, and Deke may have napped. He lay a good while with both eyes shut, his chest barely breathing and all of him roamed across by sun that was surely bad for skin light as mine. I ignored the risk since there unquestionably he was, a strong man condoning my nearness, my dumb requests for facts about his life and the world. I won't even try to repeat them here—they were so mundane: his favorite sport and movie actor, his shoe-size and weight. I only need to set down clearly the declaration that I'd have stayed beside Deke Patrick in broiling sun till nothing was left of Marcus Black but a handful of ashes.

I was that ready for big news to break. Meanwhile Deke lapsed out again; so I tried to match his power to rest in the yelling midst of children trying to drown each other. I'd nearly snoozed when a girl from the tough side of town walked up to Deke's head and fell to her knees. They cracked like shots.

Deke never looked.

And I pretended my eyes were clamped; but I studied her slyly (old as I was, I was waiting for girls to matter). As long as I watched her two-piece suit and her prominent parts, she seemed like a serious threat to the day.

But again Deke ignored her or was he asleep?

Finally she leaned halfway to his ear, snorted like a skittish mare and said "Aren't you in the 41st?"

No word or look.

She bent farther and breathed cigarette smoke over his eyes. "If you're Deke Patrick, my sister knows you."

His eyes stayed shut but he said "You've got the wrong man, lady. I'm Marcus Black and I was in Heaven till just this minute."

She didn't know me from Moses' dog, but she said a quick "Foo" and walked on off.

I thought Deke would look up and wink.

He didn't, not even a nod my way.

So grabbing the end of his lie to the girl—that he was Marc—I told myself Deke was maybe my father, back for this one afternoon to show me useful facts and secrets he'd failed to show when he left so young. I also told myself to wait and not so much as mention what I knew. I'd let his secret purpose pour toward me in its own time.

For now I only knew how he'd answered Mother's questions at the table—he was from Kentucky "more or less" and one of such a crowd of poor children that even his father "barely knew our names at noon, not to speak of midnight." But when half a quiet hour passed, and shadows were starting to cool the ground, I thought I'd better say something at least—Deke hadn't really moved again or talked. I stretched back flat, to look nonchalant, and faced the sky. Then I figured I knew the first question. "Will this war last till I can join?"

Deke took so long I almost thought he was back asleep, but then he rose to an elbow and faced me. His eyes were slow but they looked down my whole lean frame, that had never felt more childish than now. And whatever he thought, he said "Old Marc, you a god-fearing man?"

I said "Some nights."

"Then promise me, every night of your life, you'll ask Friend God to stop this mess before it kills me."

I saw he still hadn't mentioned my chances, but I somehow said "That's already settled" and found myself smiling.

That woke him fully. His eyes spread wide; he started to laugh but pulled up short. "You got some inside dope on me?"

What I wanted to say, I knew I shouldn't—*You mean you're scared?* I let the next sentence in line roll out. "You're the strongest soul I know on Earth." I even believed the outsized claim, and I shut my eyes to certify it—I was in calm charge here, I knew the future, my elders could rest.

Deke let me stay like that a whole minute, but then I heard him standing up. When I looked, he was halfway down the green hill in an excellent rolling chain of cartwheels till he hit water and backstroked a length of that long pool in what felt like world-record time.

He showered with his suit on and dressed in the men's restroom again. So when he came out, combing his hair, I was mad enough to say "You don't have to go with me home."

Deke said "You plan to ride two bikes at once?"

"I can ride mine and hold onto Mother's—done it plenty of times."

He thought about that. "It's a first-rate trick; but if you say Yes, I got my eyes on one last dish of those ripe strawberries."

I seldom ate even homemade desserts (I craved them too much and had sworn off a year ago), but I said "You're welcome to whatever's left. I got to get back to the model I'm building." The whole slow day, I'd kept myself from asking Deke a hard question, hard for me—when would he have to leave for camp? I guessed he'd start out trying to hitch sometime before dusk while cars were frequent. Now though with both of us dressed—and Deke not trusting me with even the sight of his body—I made myself say "You get yourself on back before night."

By then we were out by the cycle rack. Deke said "You forecasting harm if I don't?"

"No sir, I just—" It shocked me to see a grown man take any words of mine that earnestly; no other man had and few have since.

Deke said "Goddammit, son, don't call me *sir*. You're older than me."

That was crazy but it hit even harder; I stopped to look him square in the face. At one and the same time, everything on him looked young and easy to hurt as a child set down by his mother in an open field but also older than my grandfather who'd died last year, half-starved with pain. I said "Get on your bicycle please. We'll take the shortcut."

The shortcut ran through a railroad yard, and the ground was paved with broken glass from drunks' wine bottles. I rode on slowly to watch my path; but Deke overtook me, rearing up and lifting his front tire off the ground—that eager for something I couldn't see. Or so I figured; I also figured it had to be something involving a person older than me. Maybe a secret message had passed to the girl at the pool and she was waiting. Anyhow he never swerved or slowed till he was back in the shed at home.

I parked behind him and offered my hand to say goodbye.

Deke looked it over, then solemnly shook it. "You won't even spare me a cool drink of water?"

I halfway knew he meant me to laugh, but the other half (the look in his eyes) reminded me of numerous dreams where I had seen my hungry father locked outdoors in pouring night behind a window that I couldn't raise or even break. I said "Come on" and tried to hide what a nameless struggle—brand new to me and bigger than any I'd known till now—was waging itself inside my head each step of the way to the kitchen door.

Those were times when nobody thought to lock a house, when your neighbors helped themselves to sugar and left the shelves as neat as if they'd never walked in. So Deke and I had drunk two glasses of warm tap water before he spied a note on the counter and passed it to me. It was from Lennie Crumpler, the lady next door.

Marc, your mother just now phoned me and wants you to call her up

in Watson soon as you can. She sounded worried so call her, hear? Then
come tell me if she's all right.

Deke held out his hand and asked to read it.

Meanwhile I was breaking out ice for more water.

But Deke said "Haul yourself to the phone. Ma needs you bad."

I told him my mother could handle herself in a rattlers' den.

He shook his head. "Don't leave her hanging at the end of your
rope."

I'd never seen it that way before, so I went to the phone and placed
the first long-distance call of my career (back then children didn't just
phone Europe to see how their best friends felt that day).

Mother answered, first ring. "Oh Marcus, thank God."

This saying *Oh Marcus* was catching on; and it lifted my spirit to
hear her thanks—she was such a self-sufficient woman, kind but able
and hard to serve. I said "Are you O.K. or what?"

She said she was all right but that her mother was having a spell.
"You know the flashes she gets in her head?—an hour ago she and I
were wandering out in the garden; and she flopped down between the
tomatoes. Just buckled gently in the sandy dirt and waited there. I was
deep in the corn and didn't see her; but when I got back, she was still
on the ground."

I said "It's too hot. You ought not to—"

"Marc, I well know Mother's limits. She's better now but her left
hand is cold and that whole arm, almost to her elbow."

Grandmother's skin was always cold, but I didn't say it. I said "You
sure this isn't a stroke?"

There was such a long pause, I thought I'd lost her. Then she
whispered "She's calling me Sybil"—that was Grandmother's sister
who died far back. "I'm worried, Marc."

"You called the doctor?"

"You think I should?—it'll scare her badly."

"It'll scare her worse to die," I said. I don't know where such words
came from, but they chilled my teeth, and I waited for Mother to

shame me. She didn't but paused. And I understood that was why she'd called, hoping I'd tilt her up or down. She'd once been timid but since the evening my father died while dozing in his chair, Mother feared nothing but threats to me and her own mother's death. So I chose a kinder voice and said "I'll hang up now, you call Dr. Fritz, then call me back if you need me."

"You can't get here—"

I said "I can thumb a ride and be there quick." Then I knew I'd raised a worse chance for her than a stroke in the family—me killed by a drunk or kidnaped six states off by dawn and strangled in some mangy garage (however safe America was, the tragic fate of the Lindbergh baby a decade past was still a nightmare for thoughtful parents).

Mother said "You stay by the phone till I know more." Then she thought to ask when Deke had left.

I said "Maybe fifteen minutes after you." It gave me a pleasure I knew was wrong. And when Mother hung up, I looked toward the kitchen.

Deke was propped in the door, shaking his head at what he already knew was a lie.

I didn't beg pardon though and didn't wait by the phone one minute. Just in the time I talked to Mother, the sun had slipped down farther toward dusk; and whatever light was left in the house was almost gold. For the first time ever, some new thing in me lunged for what I knew I needed. I walked on straight to the hall closet, found the Kodak and faced Deke again. "Let's take a picture before it's too late."

He was still in the kitchen door, still somber. But when he finally spoke, he smiled. "You said it wouldn't get too late—for me anyhow."

I stepped closer to him and beckoned hard. He seemed to nod and I led us out in the last of the heat, which is why I have two pictures now and these old memories, fresh and true. In the picture I've thought about most through the years, Deke stands on the edge of our Victory garden with staked tomatoes tall behind him. He's cupping a great ripe

globe in his hand, but I always think he's facing me. And even now—
with hardly a clue to his fine eyes—I can stare on at him and know
again what a draw he was in that green place, that day of my life and
on through the night. I know, for instance, how he held the bright
tomato toward me; and as I clicked he plainly said "Son, never say I
never gave you nothing." To this day anyhow I've never said it.

By the time we were back indoors, I saw it was nearly six-thirty; and
I guessed Deke would leave in a minute. But before I could put the
Kodak away, the telephone rang. Deke was near it, took up the receiver;
and for a long moment, I thought he'd answer and then take over the
rest of my life. On the spot there, it was not a bad thought.

But he held the phone toward me.

I could hear Mother's voice as it passed from Deke's long hand to
mine—"Marcus? Where are you?"

I begged her pardon. "I dropped the phone."

"Marc, Dr. Fritz says you were right. She may have had a very slight
stroke. No reason to go to the clinic yet and scare her to death. But he
wants me to sleep down here tonight."

I understood, for the first time, that my last grandparent was leaving;
and even if I didn't like her that much, for a while I felt as tall and
unsurrounded as the last whole tree on a burned-out hill. I must not
have spoken.

So Mother said "You're not mad, are you—me staying here? Just
take your pajamas and your toothbrush to Lettie's and sleep in her new
attic. I'll see you well before supper tomorrow."

I said I would and sent my love to her and her mother, though what
I knew—all over my body—was *I'll stay here tonight, come what may.*
And when I'd hung up and looked toward Deke, I knew I'd lie to him
as well. I said "Things are fine. She'll eat supper there and head on
back." From here I can guess that, being a child, I was trying to make
the bitter axe fall, not hang on above me. The day had been sweet,

though my wild hopes had slid away in the trough of Deke's silence and inwardness. He had to leave here well before night; so sure, *Force him out, have the house to yourself.*

He rolled my false news over in his mind, then said "Don't lie to me. I *know* you." His eyes and jaw were fixed and blank as any threshing machine in grain.

I nodded, clutched my chest as if he'd shot me, moaned in pain and dropped to one knee.

Deke said "I'm a guard. I've been on guard. I'll see you through."

Fear and happiness both rushed on me. Was this man addled or a crook on the run? Or say he was just an average soldier, wouldn't he land himself in the stockade if he missed rollcall tomorrow dawn? In a few more seconds, the fear passed; only the stinging hope stayed in me. Somehow tonight I'd learn the big news I'd been starved of. I said "Please. And thank you, sir."

Deke said "I'm a private. Drop the *sir*."

By eleven o'clock we'd made and eaten waffles with syrup. We'd done my English and history homework, listened to the radio, checked the stars in the deep backyard (they seemed to multiply as we watched; and Deke knew more of their names than me, though now I suspect he made them up). We mixed lemonade and drank the whole pitcher, then finally climbed upstairs bone-tired—Deke laughing that we might both wet the bed with that much sour juice in our veins. At the top of the stairs was the guestroom door. Mother kept the bed in there made up, and I switched on the light to give Deke his chance at a private room.

He considered the offer, standing on the rug and turning round the whole white space till at last his eyes got back to me. "One ruffle too many. Where do you sleep?"

I pointed two doors down the hall. "Bunk beds in my room."

"Who you expecting?"

I told him the truth. When Mother was pregnant with me far back, my father had been so sure I was male—and so convinced they'd have a second male in short order—that he went out and bought bunk beds at a bankrupt furniture store for eight dollars. I slept in a baby bed of course for the first two years and no brother came. Then two more years and, with Father dead, I took the lower bunk and slept there ever since, except for ten idiotic nights at Boy Scout camp on the Cape Fear River. The top bunk was covered with a Pendleton blanket that had been my father's, a Navaho pattern; and even at fourteen I spent a fair number of afternoon hours lying up there, trawling space and the deeps of my mind in hopes of knowing whether I could make it on through life and be a sturdy reliable man, maybe even the father to my own child—boy or girl, whatever they sent me.

By the time I more or less told Deke that, he'd slid past me and entered my room. It burned me a little, his forging ahead with no permission, and I hung back.

But then he said one word, "Outstanding."

That drew me on. When I walked in, he was on the top bunk—legs under him, Indian-style. He was holding my submarine model.

It was far from finished. I'd already botched the tricky sanding along the hull that meant to be sleek, and now I despaired of coming near the snaky lines of the handsome picture on the box. The longer I watched Deke hold and stroke it, the worse it looked—one more thing I'd helplessly ruined. I said "I'm planning to burn it up."

Deke held it out with both hands before him. "I got another plan— you give it to me." He sounded earnest.

"Help yourself," I said. "Just don't tell anybody who ruined it."

He shut his eyes and rubbed the hull down the edge of his jaw, then held it toward me. "Finish it please by next weekend."

"What happens then?"

"My last furlough; they're moving us on. I'll take it next Sunday." He held the boat out further toward me; he meant what he said.

I took it and, Lord, it looked even worse. That far back I was one mad perfectionist—any flaw and a whole thing was lost. But here for the first time, somebody said he wanted something I'd halfway made. So finally I said "Help me then." Before the words could cross the narrow space between us, I knew I'd never asked a man for help till now—not a grown man who could crush my skull like a walnut shell and walk on free. A chill crept through me as Deke cleared his throat and moved to speak.

By midnight though—spelling each other with the finest sandpaper—we'd nearly repaired my blunders down one side of the hull. In all that time we talked very little, and nothing Deke said came near to sounding like a sermon or blame. I mean him no insult—in fact I mean it as genuine praise—to say that sitting at work with Deke was like the granting of one more postponed boyhood dream: living beside a majestic dog that understood my every need and could now and then speak a few clear words of patient advice.

And if I learned a useful thing in that late hour, it's bound up deep in the memory I have before me still—the lasting sight of a man's strong hand, polishing slowly with a touch so light it couldn't have marred a baby's skin but gradually mended most of my flaws. From here I know, Deke worked no magic. He was likely a sensible family boy who'd learned the right relation to time for any hand with a hard job to do—building a model or a ten-room house or carving a stately face in granite: *Assume you've got forever to finish, but start today and don't look up till it's truly done.*

At last Deke set the submarine at the back of my table and said "You knew how all along; you just got rushed. Take a whole slow week and finish by Sunday. Then I'll give you the seal of approval." He knocked the top of my head with a fist. "Old Marc, next thing—you need to sleep."

The job had waked us both up awhile; but now he was right. I also knew there were miles of questions I meant to ask. For instance, we hadn't even started on the mysteries of my new body, this astounding equipment that grew by the day and ached to drive me in opposite outlandish ways, all of them leading far from this house and the peaceful life I'd spent till now. But as I stood there watching my rescued submarine, I asked the only question that came. "Why in the world are you here?"

Again he didn't laugh and he finally said "I already told you—normal guard duty."

I nodded. "But this town's safe as a tub. I could sleep on the center line of the road and not get scratched."

Deke shook his head. "Not so. I know. Go brush your teeth."

I wanted to ask for more details—what danger, from whom?—but like a child in the midst of a party, I suddenly felt my strength run out. I might as easily have dropped in place and slept on the rug, but I took my pajamas to the bathroom and undressed there. When I got back Deke had switched on the desk lamp and was lost in reading *The Boy's King Arthur*, a book that had been my favorite for years. Any hour but then, I could have sat on the edge of my bunk and recited him entire pages of the story—finding the Grail in a blaze of light, shown only to men who were pure in heart.

That way I might have bolstered his courage, more anyhow than I'd yet managed with my dumb promise of a healthy return. He seemed so lost in reading though that all I could do was to tell him the upper bunk was clean. He hardly nodded so I said "Good night." I don't believe he even replied. In the final instant I silently said a one-line prayer—*Don't let either one of us hurt the other.* Before I could think how strange that was—how could I hurt Deke?—sleep drowned me out.

My whole life I'm a marathon dreamer, and a good many dreams stay in my mind when I wake up. I can replay dozens of detailed stories that have come to me at crucial times from the age of four or five till today. But hard as I've tried to think what story I told my sleeping self that night, I come up blank. What I'm sure of is what I saw with clear eyes when I woke up near three o'clock, though it feels to this day more like a dream than provable fact.

Understand this first—the lady who owned the house before us had put up mirrors everywhere. No room escaped; she was that concerned to meet the world with all curls screwed. And her daughter hauled most of them off when the lady died, but one was bolted to the outer face of my closet door, and with our permission she left it there directly opposite where my eyes would open each day. In early years it meant little to me. Every week or so I might try out a promising frown or grimace— wiggling my ears or raising my eyebrows curious ways in hopes of winning affectionate laughter from my classmates.

But lately with my fascinating body in progress, around and beneath me, I'd taken to that tall scabby glass as if it amounted to my first love, a living creature lonely as me. I'd started pressing my lips to the surface two years back; and months before I met Deke Patrick, if I got home in the afternoon and Mother was out, I might well wind up stripped before it, longing to press my warm self through that cold glass and meet the needy body beyond me—the body I half-believed was me, though I knew it was just a common deed committed by light.

So what I saw, as I woke up on the night in question, was a young man standing beyond my bunk, completely naked and serious-eyed. You'll have guessed that first I thought *My father is here.* For years I'd silently begged to see him, a long clear glimpse if nothing else; and everybody said that, sooner or later, prayers got answered Yes or No. Dazed as I was, it took me maybe ten seconds to see that—if this was the answer—then I couldn't say if the answer was Yes. What I faced was not exactly my own father but more like a changed Deke Patrick in the mirror, more of Deke than I'd bargained on.

Was Deke in some mysterious way a younger model of the man who'd helped to make my life and whom I needed more than ever, with time pell-melling down the road and dragging me breathless? Whatever else I might see later, the live Deke's back was turned toward me and was nearer yet. He was thoroughly still, both hands at his sides; and his eyes never blinked but watched the reflected man in the mirror.

For a long time then, I didn't wonder what this could mean to the man or what it meant to do to me and maybe the world. If it wasn't someway my lost father, it was anyhow a soul that banked on me to sleep in reach of whatever this new presence was. And like the average curious child, I rushed to study the news before me—the first bare grown man in this house in the ten years since my father died, standing frankly in my room, as still as a hunting heron or leopard.

I see the sight in my mind clear as then. No point in straining to show it here. Our language sadly lacks the meanings to summon a well-made human body, much less one as awesome as Deke's. The truest poets fail in the try to convey any part of the simple flesh that makes our first and final claim on the world's love and pity, its craving and rage, because no words can set such a gift before the reader, clean of shame or lure and threat. I'll only say that, fully awake, I looked for minutes at skin and hair, limbs and nails as finely made as any since. And all the while I thought a single furious thing, *Don't let this end. Let it teach me everything I need.*

But Deke moved. Both hands went up and rubbed his eyes. And then I was almost sure I saw the signs of tears. Next his right hand prowled his chest and belly like a careful doctor—probing, searching. What had he lost? From that point on I changed from famished watching to guessing—what again could this sight mean and who was it for? I understood that nobody else was witnessing this but Deke and I (had Deke seen my eyes open behind him?) and likely God.

What I decided at last was easy; and yet these many years on in life, I can say it was my first manly finding. *Deke is memorizing his bones in case he's wounded or loses a part or comes back home a frozen corpse or just a free invisible spirit, recalled by maybe his mother and me for our short lives.* I felt I had him printed deep in memory; but I went on watching, long as he stood there, to guarantee that my mind anyhow would hold his likeness—him at his best—let come what might. I even realized I was standing guard on him, the first of many nights I've guarded other burdened men and the good woman who bore our child, though none has meant an atom more than Deke that night, near as he was in time and place to my father's death and chiming with everything I'd lost, like a tuning fork that rings in perfect harmony with an unheard chord.

Maybe I dozed. For how long though?—when I looked, the window was maybe a whole shade lighter. But suddenly I looked again; and Deke was taking a step toward the mirror, a handspan off. Slowly he leaned and pressed his forehead high on the surface, both eyes shut. I thought *He's telling somebody goodbye,* whatever I meant. Then he came back upright and reached to the chair. From a neat pile he found his drawers and pulled them on. He took a long last stare at the glass and made what seemed a sign of the cross all down himself, from head to thigh. I'd seen movies with nuns and priests and was old enough to think how few Kentucky boys were Catholics; but maybe he just meant something else, some private bet on health and safety. Then he took two backward steps—I might have reached and touched his calves— and I took the chance to turn away silently, facing the wall.

Next I heard him move again. I felt my sheet lift back, and cool air struck my arms. I had the time to run or say No to whatever he planned, unless he held a knife or worse. But nothing in me was scared or mad. I stayed there toward the wall, eyes shut. And then I felt him lay himself down flat beside me, maybe a palm's breadth from my back. I guessed it was Deke—I still hadn't looked—but we lay on awhile, and the clean salt odor of his hair confirmed it. I was much amazed but still not scared.

I understood from other boys' jokes, and from camporees with weird troopleaders, that men could get as strange as women and reach for more than you could give. I also had a new hot sense of what two bodies could give each other or take by force. But I never feared Deke Patrick's hand, his mind or any other part. And now I can almost swear that, once he had the sheet back on us, he said one sentence in a calm voice—something about excusing him, could I pardon him please?

I'm sure I didn't speak at the time, and I'm well aware that it's late for regrets; but if pardon was something he truly needed, then I never gave it. I was lost in trying to understand, was he asking for help or trying to give it? At least I hope he knew I didn't blame him—far, far from it. And after a while I tried to signal my grateful trust by rolling back a little, still not touching, though both our bodies were in the range of each other's heat. Then I got my next manly thought. I stayed there, honored, and told myself *This boy is lonesome. Stay still now and let him rest.*

It was all I could feel that early in life, but I may have been right. In a minute longer anyhow, I heard the sound of regular breathing— Deke was plowing sleep like a narrow dugout slow through black marsh water in the dark. I took a minute to say my thanks to the bountiful night; and though I meant to stay on guard till first light showed, the weight of what I'd seen and learned began to press me. Soon enough I was also plowing the blackest sleep I'd ever known.

Morning, I woke alone again. Deke had slid out on me—when and how? I lay to listen for steps in the house; I almost prayed I'd hear him cooking, or I'd smell fresh coffee. But what I heard were empty rooms, the old walls shifting in early warmth; and all I smelled were our hedge roses in heavy bloom. Was I shocked or sad? I thought I'd soon be one or the other; but no, I waited and still felt calm. I finally said one fact aloud, *That was no dream.* Then I stood and rushed to dress in cooler air than I expected. It was Monday and Mother had made me promise to mow the lawn and paint the shed; then she'd be back (I knew if my grandmother had died, I'd have heard by now). I searched my table for some kind of note—nothing, no word.

But the submarine was there in the place where Deke had left it, rescued and waiting for my new skill. With summer on me, I told myself I had the time to finish it right by Sunday morning, if Deke ever showed. Then I told myself another thing—*Deke's long gone.* That seemed to mean that he and I had finished our business well before day, and neither one of us needed more or had more to give. But even before I went downstairs, I knew I'd have to ignore that chance, in the short run at least.

None of our neighbors had seen Deke leave, so Mother was flabbergasted to hear I stayed alone an entire night, but that passed off and all she did was call her mother and tell the news of Marc's big dare. The rest of the week, I worked in happiness, hours each day, patient as any carpenter bee but also hot to finish on time. Late Saturday night I set the final painted boat back where Deke had left it. I stood and watched it a long time till I knew I'd finished a thing I was almost proud of, my first fair job. I felt nearly sure that Deke would approve. And when I finally managed to sleep, I steadily watched Deke walking toward me from those same woods by the lake in the park, where he had vanished the day I met him.

But Sunday came and soon I knew that part of me had guessed correctly. I gave out the coffee and biscuits again but Deke never showed. As the line of boys passed my table, I dreaded one of them joking about me and Deke last week. I thought our day, not to mention the night, had been a thoroughly private truce; but what after all did I know about Deke and who he was in other places? If he could leave my room and house without a word, then couldn't he tell his friends any number of lies about us or even the truth?

But none of the hungry soldiers said so much as a word or faced me; they loaded their plates and walked away. I'd known right along that, if Deke didn't show, I'd never mention his name again. So when we got to the end of church, and still no sign, I told myself I had this much—*Since nobody knows the deal but me, I've got nobody but me to explain to.* With the calm I'd gained, I sat down late that Sunday night and made a list of the news I'd learned from knowing Deke.

The list, to be sure, is long since gone. But I know it said a lot about friendship—what two people can give each other. Since I've done better as a friend than a mate, those cooler bonds have been a lifelong study of mine; but my first lesson came from Deke and amounted to this. Friends can give you a guarantee that your poor body is a fit companion; they can teach you the dangerous duties you owe to neighbors and strangers. Friends lead each other across rope bridges with jagged valleys far below; and then they go their separate ways, though not forgetting the pure air and noble view at such tall heights. Friends, I thought—and time has proved—can show you sights like nothing your kin, your lovers, God or Nature herself will ever show: no purple canyon nor the boundless pardon in a saint's bright eyes.

For years I wondered, did Deke live or die? On in my forties, when Mother died three months ago and I went home to clear the house, I found his pictures—the only two—in *The Boy's King Arthur*; and the past rolled back as real as my hand. I vowed I'd write to the Pentagon and see if they had records on a boy named Deacon Patrick from east Kentucky (he mentioned his full name late in the night and made me spell it). But then I didn't. Some cowardice in me, or maybe good sense, made me think that any news I got would be grim—he'd been dead for years and buried in Europe or the South Pacific or he lived on now as a black-lunged miner on welfare and food stamps or many things worse.

I told myself I'd known Deke Patrick the single day that fate intended. Though I'm no staunch believer now, in fate or God, I tend to believe at least this much—*Things happen in their time.* Whether Deke knew it or not, he gave me what I needed then, that urgent summer, which was human hope—a halfway decent way to start the endless trek out of childhood. He showed me I was made to last a normal while in a world as loaded as any shotgun. I could do what I had to, storm or shine, like most men, women and—Lord God—children (Deke's war proved at least that much: children can last through hunger and torment worse than any man will take). Nothing ahead was truly fearsome but bodily harm; and even harm could pass you by and let you sleep beside rank strangers to end your life at age ninety-six with kind descendents round your bed.

I'm several decades short of ninety; but still my skin, give or take a few pounds, is the direct heir of the younger skin that a grown man trusted for the first time when I was a child on the last doorsill of a guarded life. As I stepped forward to the baffling world, other humans came at me with other big gifts and some with weapons; but nobody stayed much longer than Deke, not till now at least. I don't say that in hopes of pity or mountains of mail with outright offers of hearts and lives. I'm the only man I know today who claims and can prove—in the bitter face of heartbreak, pain and mortal wrong, all caused by me—that he meets most days with sensible hope; that he sleeps most nights, unpunished by blame, and is partly healed by silent dreams.

WALKING LESSONS

MY WIFE killed herself two weeks ago, her twenty-sixth birthday; and I, not anticipating Christmas at home, wrote to Blix Cunningham (a college friend in VISTA—Volunteers-in-Service-to-America—a med-school dropout, four months short of his degree; he calls it a *pause*) and volunteered to visit him at his post on the Navajo reservation. His reply seemed less eager than his letters eight months before—when he'd landed cold among hostile Indians and urged my wife and me to join him any time—but by then I was grasping any hand extended; so I flew to Albuquerque and rented a car and drove on to him. Dunder, Arizona; half an hour past Gallup off route 66.

Nothing, nothing—a truckstop, a trading post, shoebox post office, the abandoned 1930s tourist cabins in which Blix lives. VISTA volunteers try not to live better than their chosen unfortunates. Blix lives considerably worse than most Navajo (thereby approaching some ultimate in discomfort). Night before last in Albuquerque I stayed in the best motel I've ever seen—everything provided (for $16) but a happy life—and watched TV, the Ed Sullivan Christmas show; a mouse talked Italian and Leontyne Price sang *Vissi d'arte*. Then last night in Dunder in Blix's two rooms that make Beethoven's study look anal compulsive (old meals petrifying under symphonies, cold pots of piss on the pianolid). He sleeps in the inner room on an iron bed, no sheets but at least an electric blanket. I sleep in the outer room in Blix's sour sleeping bag laid on the springs of an army cot. The only hope of heat against the snow (14° last night) is a potbellied stove in which Blix burns old furniture—and from Dora.

Dora. Dora was there when I arrived. I walked through snow toward the only lighted windows in the ring of ruining cabins, knocked, a wait, then Blix opened on me, as unsurprised as ever—"You made it."

Inside was barely warmer than out and almost as dark. To show I was myself, I made an obscene remark or two on the temperature and decor, my eyes slowly opening to the debris of clothes, sausage cans, books, records (Leontyne Price again, *Porgy and Bess*), wood scraps for the stove, muddy boots, a cherry pie (uncut on the table)—and Dora unmentioned in a corner on a broken chair.

I smiled but didn't speak, suspecting maybe (from her obvious Indianhood) that she wouldn't know English (many Navajo don't). She was nineteen or twenty, lovely not beautiful, standard Indian equipment (enameled black hair and eyes, clearer skin than most, unpocked, a fierce beige).

Then she giggled in response (toward Blix not me) and showed bad teeth, nursed on Coke from the cradle, rotted in a dark perfect crescent in front.

I looked to Blix too and he said "That's Dora" and pointed quickly as though I'd smiled at something else—the cherry pie.

I was hungry, had driven for hours without stopping; so I said, "Dora, did you make the pie?"

She giggled some more till I felt I had landed in a geisha house— where was her red offended dignity?

Blix said, "No, my landlady did. It's for you. I told her."

Told her *what*, I didn't ask (nor who landladied this disaster-site), but to cut the ice, strode forward to the pie, cut a slice and ate it ravenously—for comic effect but also to cover my sudden suspicion (dread colder than the room) that Dora was here for the night, would stay, and that I must listen.

Two slices of pie were no charm. She stayed. An hour of tired talk between Blix and me—about nothing: jobs, my trip—then he stood and said, "Bedtime. You're sleeping on the cot. The bathroom's there."

Dora headed for the inner room and shut the cracked door.

Blix went on behind her but stopped once more and smiled for the first time, "Don't mention this in Washington"; then lower, in pig-French—"*Je t'expliquera matin. Elle est en trouble.*"

I worked at guessing what trouble she was in—through my trip to the bathroom (a cold-water tap and a john that didn't flush; I leaked out a broken window into the snow) and back in the dark and seizing cold, into my sleeping bag. The obvious reading was, she's pregnant. Who by? Our Volunteer-in-Service-to-America, who else? She'd worn no wedding ring but did any Navajo? What would Washington do?—send Blix home to Carolina, no doubt, with Sacajawea and her copper papoose.

The only sound—above the stove's dying—seemed confirmation. Not only was she pregnant, they were struggling to abort her. And they worked at it nearly an hour, no pause. I never moved an inch toward their closed cracked door; but I heard every flicker, could hear every impulse leap every synapse—from Blix's slow start, her dark dumb acceptance (they were straining at first for silence—why? sparing me *what?*), onward till they gained a fierce plateau which they held. *Held.* Every nail and joint in the two collapsing rooms was involved, dragooned into their effort.

And I. I did move. When it seemed Blix's gouging would never slacken, no end be reached—release *or* destruction—and that Dora's acceptance swelled more monstrous each moment, I sat upright in my sleeping bag and thought of two things. I could shout to them "Stop!" or, under the cover of their thrusting, I could leave—do my little packing, walk back to my car and, in less than a day, be back in my own house (more ruined than this one would ever be).

So I stayed—stayed in bed, upright, freezing in my underwear but listening. Feeding. Forcing my eyes through the dark, noise and cold; inserting my vision through their door and *among* them. Dipping and probing, diving and stroking and licking between them, around them, above them in their work—till I came to rest in Blix's clenched head and rode out there (battered but helpless to leave, not to share) the rest of the time till they'd reached their yipping yelping end.

—With nothing destroyed, aborted, stove-in. Not even me. I could in fact have killed them—rushed on them *in extremis* with my cherry-pie knife and ended them there (that after all being what they had struggled to offer one another—total vulnerability). One another, though, not me. So I stayed in place, *my* place which they'd assigned me; and silence was all that rushed in on their stillness. No wind outside, the stove cold and mute. I alone awake, upright and listening, my face and the front of my T-shirt wet with tears. (I come from a long line of weepers—never mind. I am going to survive.) Mouth open, still hungry, I fell back and slept.

And didn't wake or turn till, in faint morning light, I heard steps pass me and looked to the outside door to see Dora leaving. No sign of Blix behind her, no noise of a car. So I slept another hour, then woke for good, rose to pee and check on Blix. He was dead-asleep still beneath his hot blanket, coiled against the indoor temperature which must have been well under 20°. I called his name.

He moaned, coiled tighter.

So I went to dress and start a fire, knowing that nothing but a steady din had ever waked Blix. An unexpected transistor radio helped. I flipped it on top-volume and out came a song called "Navajo Sugar-time"—minutes and minutes of heavy tuneless droning by an ancient man in (I take it) Navajo, then a sudden switch to (still tuneless) English for his stunning refrain—

> *Sugar in the morning,*
> *Sugar in the evening,*
> *Sugar at suppertime.*

That routed Blix. He leapt from bed in a single loud stride, flew by me buck-naked with a shameless erection and shouted from the toilet, "They can't even *sing*."

Twenty minutes later we were warm in the truckstop a mile up the road, eating eggs and sausage beneath a machinemade tapestry of John F. Kennedy; and Blix was volunteering his news, half-whispering—the waitress and cook were Indians. "You're wondering about all that, I guess"—he waved with his hand as though the night were still near, parked just outside. "She's Dora Badonie. Twenty-two. Two kids under five. Their father—her husband, I guess; God knows—is now living with her mother. Maybe *married* to her mother. Sophocles himself would die of surfeit out here—everybody's everybody else's grand-mother and is humping her daily. Now she lives with her father in a shack up a wash. But they're better off than most—father works at the trading post and they have a pickup truck. She does nothing, I guess, but hang around me. I don't *know* that. I don't see all that much of her—that many hours a day. All these people live mysteries, weirder than snakes—what they're thinking or feeling, what they're doing even when they're out of your sight. But I've helped her a little. She was the first one that asked. You remember what I told you it was like at first? I got here ready to pay all debts—mine, the white man's, America's. They wouldn't look at me! Much less speak. It was six or eight weeks of wandering round daily before even the children would wave at me. So there I was in my lush tourist court, alone as a dry bone—and speaking of which, that was fairly desperate too; no help at all, long hours of self-service, pounding time to my five favorite records and 'Navajo Sugar-time.' Then Dora arrived on the doorstep one morning. I'd seen her at the trading post. She'd even smiled once—on those gorgeous teeth—but her father had seen it and called her down, or said *something* in Navajo. She never looked again. But here she was, that morning, at my door. Was I going to Gallup in the next day or so? 'Why?' I said. She said, 'There's a baby that's cut his foot.' I knew her father owned a truck and she'd waked me up; but of course I was weak-kneed with gratitude—I'd have driven her to Tulsa. So we hauled her youngest child to Indian hospital—nineteen stitches; he had dropped his Coke bottle—and after that she began turning up most every day. Just to sit, at first—she can barely do more in English than giggle—then to mend a sock or two. Then to start mending all my less tangible needs—at my invitation. I still don't know if it'd crossed her mind before I asked her. I still don't know if those first two babies weren't virgin births."

"But this one isn't?" I said.

Blix said "What does that mean?"

"You said she was in trouble when we turned in last night, and then you proceeded to do about an hour of demolition on her. I was stunned to see her able to walk this morning."

Blix pulled at his coffee. "She won't much longer."

"Won't what?"

"Walk."

"Meaning what?" I said.

"Her trouble is multiple sclerosis."

"Since when?" I said.

"Since yesterday. The doctor told her then—they'd been testing for weeks. She had stopped in to tell me just before you came."

"No wonder you met me like a sack of dead babies."

"Sorry," Blix said. "I'd hoped to cheer you up."

"It's incurable?"

"She knows that."

"What will she do now?"

"Stay here and die."

"How long will that take?"

"Years. Who knows?"

"What will you do?" I said.

"I don't know," he said. "Are you ready for the next thrill? I had to have a physical myself last week—I'm suspected of having a touch of TB." He gave a little Garbo cough, laughed a little.

But I reached out and stopped him, pressing his wrist. I begged him, "Stay with her." Tears instantly poured. "Don't leave her now."

Blix jerked his wrist free, stared wide-eyed at me as though I were lethal, had powers, could force him. Then he said—aloud at last: the waitress looked up—"Oh Jesus, *I'm* all but cured already!" Then he burst into laughter that seemed so nearly the last thing we shared, so necessary, that I joined him helpless.

The rest of this morning and the early afternoon, we did good deeds. Or tried to do them. Or tried to discover what deeds needed doing, then wheedle the numerous permissions to do them. Someone had told Blix the day before that an Indian named Atso had been sick in bed for over a week and needed food and firewood. Blix had waited till this morning, he said (I asked), for several reasons—he'd been told after dark and didn't want to risk getting snowbound with his truck (four-wheel drive though it is) three miles off the highway up a steep arroyo; this Atso was a drunk, that was his trouble (a weeklong drunk) and Blix was sick of running taxi service for hopeless winos. His aims had been higher. This morning the problem was sun—a thaw. The washes would be mud.

But we made it very slowly, up a ditch deep in mud between pink cliffs, all bare as the moon and so beautiful, profuse, as to be unnoticeable—an occasional plant neither of us could name, odd strips of barbed wire surrounding nothing and the standard-issue dead coyote (defrosting, collapsing inward on himself but grinning to the last). Then the Atsos—my first hogan. Round, of mud and logs, a domed roof cut by a stove pipe dissolving in rust, it seemed a low but immortal growth implored from the ground by protracted bellowings (hunching gyrations, gashings, blood) from the wretched of the earth—the only gift they would ever receive, except cur dogs (three groveled at the door) and their adamant faces. And government food—the yard was strewn with cans of white man's food they would only feed to dogs: string beans, dried milk. And our little grudging visit, mine and Blix's.

Blix went in, through the barking dogs, past the dwarf oblivious grandmother spreading quilts on a line (quilts *made* of dirt).

I waited in the truck. Blix had said it would be hard enough doing business without me along, a fresh white stranger. So to pass the time, I filled out a form for a Carte Blanche credit card (I mean—I'll *need*—to make a lot more trips). Then—no sign of Blix, just me and the dogs, the mud and the quilts, pinyon and snow and sandstone cliffs—I defaced the application by writing lines on the clean backside:

> *Ten yards to my left an Indian man—*
> *age 30, alcoholic, Navajo—*
> *lies locked in unknown illness, silence, calm.*
>
> *My friend—whose job it is—yearns patiently*
> *to comprehend, heal ancient various wounds;*
> *gives solemn smiles, shows new-grown neck-length curls.*
>
> *I stay outside beside the truck's strong heater,*
> *complete my application for* Carte Blanche—
> Income? *I write in* Thirty thousand dollars,
> *growl at the Indian's dog, begin this poem.*

I'm cheating, you'll say—"You were thinking then, alone there and idle." What was I thinking? Do I have human feelings?—his wife freshly dead and he two thousand miles from home at Christmas on an Indian reservation the size of West Virginia (and twice as miserable), his only two companions struck with maybe fatal diseases? If you've followed me this far, you'll be grumbling for such answers. And a good many more—*why did she do it?* Wait; please, wait. Remember, Tolstoy tells you only two or three facts about the life of Anna before the book's *present.* I'm struggling to tread the waters of the present. Tread with me or sink (or swim back out—simply shut the book). The present is my story. The rest is waiting.

In fact, at the time, I wasn't thinking. The manual labor (application, poem) took care of conscious thought—analysis, self-pity. In its own way, each gesture now is desperate, each step a kind of busy-work. The unconscious was whirring away, no doubt—because, by the end of the poem, I was *feeling*. The inside of my skin was rapidly furring (a sick child's tongue) with unfocused misery; and I was considering disobeying orders—entering the hogan. At least I'd have sights, new grist for the eyes.

But Blix appeared, fast and furious. He tore the door open, climbed in, gripped the steering wheel and shook it as though he were tetanizing. No glance at me, no word.

"All dead?" I asked.

Another siege of spasms, a long wait—"Yes, goddammit."

I was ready to think he had cut their throats. "Be serious."

He laughed. "No, but everybody's sick as dogs—*except* the dogs and that old woman. Atso's not drunk—sober as you—but he and three kids are baking with fever and nobody can—or will—speak two words of English. They don't trust me so there's no chance of hauling them all to Gallup. They want a medicine ceremony—they haven't got ten cents to buy dry beans—and I, being me, don't even own an aspirin. Dr. Cunningham." By then he had calmed. He was galvanized, on-stage, a clear duty at hand. He sat awhile longer, then said, "I'm sorry. We've got to do this—I'll go to Window Rock to get a tribal nurse. If I try to phone her, she'll never find the place. With the roads this muddy, that'll take four hours. But will you wait here?—at my place, I mean? I'm supposed to be visited sometime today by the thinly disguised regional spy from VISTA. You can tell him I'm at work, saving lives Hell for leather—you'll even have a share in this glorious work. Then, as reward, when I get back and we've stocked the Atsos' pantry, we can go in to Gallup for a gourmet meal—cold grease tacos—and an Ann-Margret movie."

"Click heels," I said and smiled; but as we drove off, I rushed into dread. Had I run all this way to turn now and make my stand among cold debris (half a cherry pie) in a 6′ × 8′ abandoned tourist court in the Arizona desert?

I had. Yes.

Blix barely stopped but handed me the key and, over the loud engine, said, "There's lots of books and records. If you'll clean house, you'll find them."

I cleaned as though they were the walls of my head—the two wrecked rooms—as though every misplaced letter, sock, can, were a clot of contagion that could kill if not forced into place at once. (*Kill* by a kind of sympathetic magic—by forcing my head to acknowledge its own mess. Seductive and true but avoidable.) Well, I fired the stove and then I forced it into place—the two rooms' freight of junk, every disordered atom. Half the battle was finding the places—Blix had no sense of any object's place—so I ruthlessly defined all his space as to *function*. All clothing, shoes, birthcontrol apparel in the inner room (where I made Blix's bed—no sheets; he had none—by smoothing the blanket on the mattress stiff with waste). All scrap wood and paper in the corner by the stove. All unopened cans, cereal boxes, two mugs in an opposite corner. All records, books, letters and magazines by the two usable chairs in the center of the room where I had slept. Then I scoured the wash basin, poured Clorox in the john. Then I swept all the floors (several pints of mouse turds). Then I thought of scrubbing. No wet mop or brush or bucket for water. (All the place had been scrubbed of was medical equipment—not an aspirin, as he'd said; no trace of his mammoth delicate training, his former purpose pursued with a force that drills bedrock, in which he'd paused.)

But by then—an hour—I was calmer, safer. When the VISTA spy came, he'd find sanity, space. I could take a little walk, still in sight of the road; but the sun shone on, only deepening the mud and I had no boots, only suede ankleshoes. I'd buy real boots tonight in Gallup. I was safe enough to sit now, hear music, rest and read. Leontyne Price again, lobbing great silver spinning frisbees into air, each note above A more curative than the last, but vanishing. And Kluckhohn and Leighton's book *The Navaho*. I skimmed the tragic history (all the Trails of Tears) and economics and settled more slowly into Chapter 5, "The Supernatural: Power and Danger." By the time I reached the subheading "Ghosts," I was reading—consuming—every word:

> *The Navahos seem to have no belief in a glorious immortality. Existence in the hereafter appears to be only a shadowy and uninviting thing. The afterworld is a place like this earth, located to the north and below the earth's surface. It is approached by a trail down a hill or cliff, and there is a sandpile at the bottom. Deceased kinfolk, who look as they did when last seen alive, come to guide the dying to the afterworld during a journey that takes four days. At the entrance to the afterworld, old guardians apply tests to see if death has really occurred.*
>
> *Death and everything connected with it are horrible to The People . . .*
>
> *Most of the dead may return as ghosts to plague the living. Only those who die of old age, the stillborn, and infants who do not live long enough to utter a cry or sound do not produce ghosts, and for them the four days of mourning after burial need not be observed, since they will not be injurious to the living. Otherwise, any dead person, no matter how friendly or affectionate his attitude while he was living, is a potential danger.*
>
> *A ghost is the malignant part of a dead person. It returns to avenge some neglect or offense . . .*

I broke off there, turned to the index—*Suicide*. Two references— the first unnourishing: a man had shot the witches who killed his children, then had killed himself. The second though was this:

Indeed, except for the (by no means universally accepted) view that witches and suicides live apart in the afterworld, there is no belief that the way one lives on earth has anything to do with his fate after death.

I am twenty-eight years old, a well-trained teacher of college English, a would-be poet and novelist who has not been to church (Episcopal) since age nineteen; but I said then—aloud, I'm sure aloud—"They do, they *should*." And I felt the need to know how *far* apart, in what kind of place, and how are they punished? Maybe the wretched Navajo have learned what *I* know, what all of Virgil, Aquinas and Florence couldn't teach Dante who discovers suicides in the Seventh Circle only (as brown, stooped and fruitless trees that exude poison, or blood if torn). The Ninth, the *Ninth* Circle! Sealed, up-ended in perpetual ice—as "Traitors to Their Kin," even gnashed forever in the triple mouths of Satan as "Traitors to Their Lords and Benefactors." Judas, Brutus, Cassius had the kindness at least to *kill* their lords, not leave them behind alive, abandoned, dumb with guilt and mystery, unable to answer the final indictment flung at the living by a suicide.

But I read every word on witches and ghosts and found nothing else to my need or purpose. Blix would not be back for maybe two hours. I fed the stove again, came back to the stack of tattered books I'd arranged, glanced through them again, then took up the only thing I wanted—the pack of letters which, oddly, Blix had kept together, neatly rubberbanded. His news from outside, proofs of another life, answers. I sorted them furtively. The top half-dozen were clearly Christmas cards, two letters from his mother, mine announcing the death and my arrival. I had not read a word yet, beyond the postmarks—not even my own (there were six or eight; I'm a good correspondent). If I'd read my most recent you'd have known the bare facts by now—so soon!—but I didn't, not because I was already shaping my day as a Work of Art—a Joan Crawford movie: Joan reads us a letter, voice-over, leaves blowing—but because I was sparing myself all I could. *Sparing!*—two-thirds through the stack, my wife's hand. The standard rotund upright hand of the 1940s American girl—but hers without a doubt, her heavy-weight blue paper, our postmark, November.

I set the other letters down (I'd yet to read one) and studied hers (the envelope, the *object*). Blix had opened it neatly, top-edge, with a knife; most others he'd torn open any crude way. And it had not been crushed, as most others had, by a full day's work in his Levi hip-pocket. It was fresh and clearly valued, like an invitation, a girl's souvenir. Personal property. I was calmer then than I'd been in days, maybe since the day. I'm sure I felt no trace of suspicion—that the letter contained secret news; she and Blix had hardly met. Nor of pity for her, myself—nor Blix, Dora, the sick Mr. Atso and his hungry children. Only anger, disgust—all as cold and contained as this room could make them; maybe 40°—and curiosity. How could they do it? Any one of them, not to mention the twos?

The music had stopped and I set her letter down, on top of the others, and began to stand. More music. Price again—"Summertime." (Hear it, if you haven't, in an unheated shack in late December; you'll have *heard* it at last.) But I knew I could neither return and read her letter nor replace it unread in Blix's little pack, not at the edge of the music. I sat back and read it.

> *Dear Blix,*
>
> *This is meant to bring light to your life. Your letter seemed so lost that I've thought of you all morning as our man on the moon, or in some satellite gone out of control and circling, perfect but irretrievable.*
>
> *You can come back if you want to, though. Life's a plane-ride away. Familiar life. If you want it, come back. But you left because you didn't. You're old enough to know. So am I. Don't think of it as quitting. Do what you need to do and if no one understands, so what? forever. I'll understand—and still so what?—*

That was her last whole sentence. I saw it had a close, a perfunctory "Love" and her name. I couldn't look at those, can't yet take her name but must treat it for now (for my own clear reasons) as my personal Tetragrammaton—the name of unspecified punishment, permanent damage; not love. I listened to the room, the road outside—not a sound; I'd raided Blix's mail in secret.

For what? Not a gram of revelation. A girl at the lip of suicide writes a letter that might have come from—Eleanor Roosevelt, sensible, bland, a little sententious. And yet, to my knowledge, the last page of writing she ever did, beyond grocery memos, checks. But no note—to me or the lethal world at large. What would I have wanted? If she'd asked me to draft a final message, from her to me, what would I have said?—*I'm as sorry as you need me to be. All debts canceled.* So what? she said to Blix. Can I say it to her? So what?—nothing adds up to a suicide, nothing leads down from it. Apart in the afterworld—Amen.

Someone knocked at the door. The VISTA spy. Good. Another *event*; he'd be good for half an hour. But I opened on Dora, ten yards away, already leaving.

At my sound, she stopped and turned and faced me broadside—a girl five-foot-two in a boy's thin poplin windbreaker, tan skirt, white sneakers, white socks, grave as the gymnasts her get-up resembled. And as tense and reluctant.

And powerful—I could not simply say Blix was gone and let her leave (she was on foot, in snow and mud, no sign of her truck). I called her by name and said "Come in."

She stood on awhile, serious as before, her sneakers blotting up dirty water. She was studying me.

"Remember me?" I said.

She nodded—no more giggling—as though she remembered more than she'd seen. My role in last night's loving.

"Then come in. It's dry at least."

She came and walked past me through the room now miraculously clean since morning and took a place, standing, at the far wall near the window. If she'd noticed the cleaning, she gave no sign.

I asked her to sit in the chair I'd just warmed, but she shook her head No. I thought we might be up against a taboo on women sitting while men still stood, so I sat in the broken chair and again said "Sit down." She refused again but this time she giggled and I felt we could talk. She had shown no curiosity whatever about Blix's whereabouts, had not glanced to right or left—maybe she could *smell* his absence—so I started with that. "Blix has gone to Window Rock to get a nurse for a man that's sick—Atso."

She said "I know that."

"Did you see him on the way?"—in which case, I wondered, why are you here with me?

"No. Atso's been sick."

"What's his trouble?" I said.

"Tokay wine," she said, serious again. Then she said—she was facing me—"I got trouble too."

I was trapped (by the word) into thinking she meant herself, her multiple sclerosis; and in a quick hail of amazement (that she, the Silent American, was telling it to me—after all though, we'd spent a fairly close night together)—and gratitude and because my own heart was so compressed inside me, I said "So do I."

She took a step forward—necessarily toward me—and said "You hungry?"

Every exit from my body was instantly clogged, not with tears this time but with more gratitude—a great rush of gratitude, like birds from a cave, toward this small girl who, dying, thought trouble was hunger. I stood and took a quick step toward her.

She held ground, neither inviting me onward nor repelling me. She seemed to have decided from the moment she entered that she was mine to use, whoever I was, whatever I might choose. Her face had the patience of landscape—rocks, trees. *This* landscape, of course.

Pausing, I knew she was right. It was well past noon. I was very hungry. Hunger was sculpting my face from inside; I felt dangerously lean. So I said "Yes, hungry."

"You like Vienna sausage?"

"Yes."

"He always eat sausage."

I thought she would move to fix me a meal but she stayed in place. She had made the diagnosis, suggested the cure. Now over to me. I found a small can of sausages—food-corner—opened them and extended the can to her, across the whole room.

She smiled, shook her head and went back to the window, to watch the road.

I sat and ate the sausages, then stood to get the cherry pie. She stood so still and expectantly—but for Blix, I thought—that I'd watched her whole minutes before recognizing a "situation," this hour's dilemma. Blix had said not to mention her "in Washington"; should I tell her now that the spy was expected and let her flee (leaving me alone again) to return at all-clear (tonight, for another jamboree) or should I let her stand on there to greet the spy and earn Blix his reprimand, maybe his walking papers? The abandonment of her.

I sat, with the pie, and said to myself, "If she gives some sign before I finish the pie, I'll help her—or warn her, whether that's help or not." I had no idea what a sign would be, and I'd got almost to the deadline— silence.

Then—not turning, still her back, still waiting for something—she said, "That's all you meant?—you hungry?"

I had meant a good deal more—ten minutes before, in mentioning trouble; but her very presence with me had dispersed that jam. My needs now were toward her. But the only help seemed *warning*, not a heart-to-heart cry. I said, "Dora, Blix asked me to wait here while he's gone. He's expecting a visit from a VISTA man. Any minute now."

She waited, not turning, but all her force seemed flowing toward the door, to leave, take cover. "*I* know that," she said—her *I* the first word she'd accented since I'd known her.

"Blix told you?" I asked.

She nodded Yes but kept her place.

So tables were turned. I was no longer driving, if I ever had—no

longer sparing lovers. That she knew and was staying, was the new
dilemma. Right. I'd also stay and watch—an independent citizen, let
Washington beware.

And I'd no more than eaten the last of the pie when Dora turned to
face me and said "He's coming."

"Blix?"

"The other man."

There seemed a quick note of alarm in her voice and, rising, I
thought, "What other man?—her father? husband? lover?" Was I lured
to the brink of my debut (or Act II?) in melodrama?—shot or stabbed
as a rival for the love of a girl with bad teeth and multiple sclerosis? So
what? Who would mind? A knock at the door. I looked back to Dora—
inscrutable—then advanced, really half expecting Fate.

A white man in an army surplus jacket, thirty-two maybe, already
balding. He was straining—in the face of a stranger: me—not to smile;
but with his face, as full, fed and deeply incurious as a baby's bottom,
formality was hopeless. I knew at once he'd go no farther than hurt
feelings, bafflement.

He said, "My name's Tim Neely. Is Blixford Cunningham still
registered here?" He surrendered then, tried to smile but laughed.

So I laughed along and said, "He's gone to Window Rock—an
emergency—to get a tribal nurse for a sick man here. He asked me to
stay here and meet you if you came."

"Good," he said. "Good."

I asked him in, not knowing whether Dora would have fled through
a window or be hiding under the bed.

She was where I had left her—where she'd been last night, when I
arrived; her receiving-post.

And like me last night, Neely didn't seem to see her though the lines
of vision were uncluttered now. Before I could try to introduce her, he
saw the finished pie plate—"Blix has gone in for baking, eh?"

I said, "Yeah, that's been our Christmas"; then I offered him instant
coffee.

He accepted and while I was warming the hot plate, I saw him see her. I could make a lot of cheap jokes at his expense—I've tried a few already, the itinerant do-gooder working through Christmas, breathless with *hope*—but now I was with him. Suddenly he was "on," all his resources summoned, every course he'd ever taken. I could see tact and patience, sweet deference, bubbling up in him like spring water through sand—had he met her before? did he know the whole story or any part? Was that why he was here today—boom-lowering?

There was no way to guess from Dora's face—she was doing her piece-of-nature stunt again. Or was her face already slightly sclerotic?

Neely turned back to me—the kettle knocked with heat—"It's sure been a cleanup campaign in here. Who do we have to thank?"

I took that as a straw flung kindly to the drowning. I nodded toward Dora—"Her. Thank her. That's Dora Badonie."

He exhaled visible relief—I was playing-up grand; why were fellows like me not Volunteers? He could now speak to Dora—"Well, thank you a lot. You been helping Blix out?"

No giggle. "I live here."

The rooms seemed instantly vacuumed, utterly empty. We all seemed about to be sucked against the walls at ferocious comic speeds.

Neely broke the lock—a little puff through his nose, his try at a chuckle. "Which Badonie are you? Who's your father round here?"

She was merciless. "No. Here." Then she smiled not giggled.

I wanted to harm her, lunge against her, strike her—above all, to *stop* her. Whatever she was launched on was harmful itself—at the worst, shipping Blix out of here in disgrace (worse still, her with him, paralyzing daily); at the least, embarrassing this well-intentioned man. It was in my mouth to say "She's lying."

But Neely spoke first, to Dora not me—"I know. I know a lot." Then he turned to me. "What are you in all this?"

His sudden attempt to switch the controls—from Friendly Equal to Steely Superior—drew it from me. "I'm a poor unfortunate cripple seeking help."

I'd kept a straight face so he had to pursue; I was in his field now. He looked me over for a gimp-leg or arm, then said "What help?"

"Are you married?" I said.

"Yes."

"Your wife nearby?"

"Back in Gallup with the kids." He actually pointed east.

"Then tell me please—you're older than me—what kind of help would you plan to need if you got home tonight—what time will that be?"

"Soon as I see Blix."

"—Well, five o'clock, say; it'll still be light. What help will you need at five o'clock today when you get home and find little what's-her-name stretched dead on the floor, drained dry as a kosher chicken?"

Neely licked his lips; I was baking him out! Then, helpless, he smiled—reflexes dying hard. "Hold on a minute, friend. There are laws against you; threats are frowned on by the law"—still smiling, a struggle to josh his way clear. "Anyhow, we're not Jewish."

"Sorry," I said. "You asked who I was."

He said, "OK, you told me." Then he walked toward the door, had his hand on the latch before stopping again. "I'm not waiting here. Tell Blix Cunningham to phone me collect, by noon tomorrow."

"Does he know your number?"

He had shed all his roles, was down to a core, could stand on its firmness. "He knows everything he needs to know. Even knows what's coming." He opened the door.

"Wait," I said. "Mr. Neely, I'm sorry if I've acted rudely. I *am* in trouble—"

He waited long enough for me to feel the second law of thermodynamics stage a demonstration round us—my scarce, nurtured heat rushing headlong through the door. Then he said, "You're one of millions, son" and obeyed the law himself.

His car had cranked and gone before I turned to Dora. She was pressed against the window to watch him go; but when my staring turned her, I said "What was that for?"

"What?"

"Your lie."

"No lie," she said. She walked to the open door of Blix's bedroom. "I sleep here every night before you came." Her voice had hardly altered—soft, uninflected—but a new hard vehemence thrust up in her stance, the words themselves. She paused for air and when I had not answered—assent or challenge—she half-turned and pointed to the bed behind her. "Come here. I'll show you."

I was locked down suddenly in the sense of enacting my old ended life, of facing a ghost—"*the malignant part of a dead person.*"

So—whoever she was—she said again "*Here.*"

I'm a human at least, not a Skinnerized dog. I said, "No, I made that bed; I've seen all you can show."

"Please come," she said—a change of words not tone.

I said, "I'll give evidence—eyewitness evidence—in any court you name that you've spent any number of hours right there, stretched flat of your back, hauling Blix's ashes."

She didn't understand; I was glad of that much. In a moment she could smile. "You're funny." Then a wait—"You're in trouble too, you tell him?"—she pointed after Neely.

"My wife—you know."

"You married?" she said.

"Well, no more," I said. I thought she was probing—not for news but to punish me.

"Where's your wife now?"

"In the Navajo afterworld—off to one side."

"I don't understand."

I saw that she didn't. "Blix hasn't told you?"

"He don't tell me nothing."

I said "My wife is dead," half hoping to leave it there.

"Oh," she said; her hands did one silent flap at her sides, as though

they were vestigial wings that had tried once more to fly. Then—
"Having a baby?"

I knew I was glad. I would get to tell her—some human at least (Blix had yet to mention it). That would be for me—pressure released—but what could and would it be for Dora?—terror? compulsion to shelter me, love me? or a crushing memento of her own creeping death? I said, "No. No babies; we never had babies. She didn't want babies. No, she killed herself."

It pulled her one step forward toward me—three steps between us now—and her small dark head made a twisting thrust, as though to bring nearer still her eyes, ears (lips? do they kiss? it's not in the book). Her face gave no signal of feeling or intention—I was nodding, helpless—then something deflected her. Something from me, or her, or elsewhere. She turned, as though I were The Road Not Taken, and went back to her window and looked out awhile.

Nothing passed, we were freezing, I must feed the stove.

Then she faced me again and asked—really *asked*, with misplaced inflection, but pressed by need—"*When* she killed herself?"

I'd planned to say *how*, but I gave what she wanted. "Two weeks ago. It's why I'm here with Blix"—here with frigid empty air!—"I thought he would've told you."

She was off Blix for now. "She was real old, your wife?"

"Twenty-six."

"Oh," she said. "She was real sick?"

"Yes."

"What kind?"

"Well, her head."

"What you mean?" Again she was pressed.

I couldn't think what phrase she'd know or, then, what would say at least part of what I meant without baffling or blinding her. So I said "Mentally ill."

"She don't know what she was doing to herself?"

Was that part, at all, of what I'd meant?—or felt or believed? I said,

"Maybe not. Maybe she thought it wouldn't work—not completely, not death; just enough to hurt and warn me. A pistol in the mouth."

Dora didn't understand, not even the words. Her face had made again that half-screw forward.

But I wouldn't stop now; this was not for Dora now—"She knew this much—what she was doing to *me*."

Dora said "I got to go," but she stayed in place.

"Don't," I said. "Please."

She nodded fiercely. "Yeah. I got to go."

I said "Come here. Please."

She said "I got to get Blix."

"He's gone—why?"

"He'll help me. I got trouble."

"*I* know that," I said. "He told me this morning."

"He don't know this morning. I don't know it then."

I'd given up understanding—interlingual misfires. I said "Well, wait. Come here."

She looked to see where I meant—I'd pointed nowhere. The army cot? sleeping bag? the clean-swept floor?

I didn't know either but I saw her, after what seemed a soundless subaqueous hour, begin oaring to me through the room's thick air.

Blix of course arrived then—the truck in the yard (by its clashing gears), the actual sound of his boots in the slush (through walls, our bones), his height and face in the doorway beside us.

Dora hadn't heard him. She was aimed on me—three more steps to take.

But Blix never noticed, locked as he was in the newest defeat—neither Dora nor the clean room nor however she and I stood, drawing one another. Face white, he said (to the room more than us), "Are you ready for this?—I drive to Window Rock and the nurse is at Chinle. She may can come tomorrow, if the roads dry a little—to bathe the corpse! Now I'll have to go to Atso's again—take food to those children, tell him to wait. But he's good at that." He was turning to leave again—follow if we wished. Had he yet seen Dora? Was she visibly there?

She said "Help *me*."

Blix stopped, looked a moment. "Help you do what?"

"I got trouble," she said.

"I know that," he said. "I told you No."

"This is new," she said and she looked to me.

I'd really never meant to cause Blix further worry, never needed or intended to slosh my own woe; so I braced for Dora's latest inscrutable lurch—denunciation? cry-rape? whatever.

She said, "My truck. My grandma took it up the Zuni road last night and my brother come down to tell me this morning—she got it stuck up there."

"That's the trouble?" Blix said. "That's all I've got to do?—feed a starving dying family, then drive fifty miles in foot-deep mud and unstick your truck? Two more days of sun, a little wind—you'll be able to drive it out on your own." He took another step, to go to Atso.

I moved to follow, having soloed and dueted enough for one day.

But before we could reach the door and pause for Dora, she said loudly "No."

We both looked—tears. They were pouring through our silence. I wanted to rush past Blix—bail-out.

But he blocked the way. He studied her a moment, then said gravely "No what?"

She said "Help me."

He broke, for the second time today, into total laughter; and relieved to see him that free (or desperate), I joined, loudly.

Dora stood on in tears, bathing her troubles.

But he helped her. (*Why?*) Of necessity, *we* helped her—I being determined not to spend another minute alone in those rooms today. We drove to the trading post (no sign of Dora's father), bought groceries

for Atso (Blix paid) and we left Dora—to look for more men to help us
with her truck. Then we wallowed back to Atso's—the tracks half-again
as deep in mud as this morning—and again I waited alone in the truck
for the minutes Blix took to leave the food and attempt to explain that
a nurse would come tomorrow, wait one more night.

I only had five minutes (Blix was rushing now—toward what? and
for whom?); but I worked at questions, nagged at them, dog-like—
neither Dora nor I had mentioned Neely's visit and Blix had not yet
asked. Should I wait till he asked or tell him now, in our last few
minutes alone today (describing Dora's gambit); or should I just say
"Neely says phone him"?

Not till I saw his face emerging from the hogan—firmed with purpose, locked into senseless duties, *happy* against his better wishes to
have fed a sick drunk for one more day and assured him of help in a
foreign tongue—did I know: say nothing. Wait. His life, not mine; he
must ask all the questions, invent his own threats, secrete his own
solutions, make his own errors freely. I, in any case, am safe—in this
one corner of my stunned life. Blix and Dora are separate; they are not
me.

He didn't ask (has he really forgot or does he not want to know?); but
to give him the chance, I rode in silence; and when he did speak, it
was now, at last, to include me in his purpose, his new grip on life,
his charity (I am not ironic; I'm seriously needy). He said my name—
which in itself startled me (he'd not said it before, I realized; eight
months with the Navajo and he had their fear of using any man's
name).

I faced him across the long empty space.

But he faced the road—or the track he was struggling to lay through
mire—and said, "Do you want me to ask you any questions?" (He only
possessed the barest facts, from my last letter to him.)

I said, "Ask. I'll answer some. Some I won't know. Some I'm not
up to tackling."

If he'd had questions ready, that threw him into silence. Or maybe it was only his struggle with the mud.

So I turned from him and tried to watch the famous scenery. Surely solace waited there for the lacerated spirit? Rainbow colors; stones, even plants, the shape of the light; God's imagination pressed by the local conditions (self-imposed in His case) to an effort, say, as total in its perverse triumph over limitations as Michelangelo's on the Sistine's architecture, Beethoven's over the human voice. (*Lesson*: I could do it too. *Question*: Why should I?)

Blix had found his tongue—ithyphallic in tension—"How *alone* do you feel?"

Long as I've known him, I wouldn't have given him credit for that much—to rock me off-balance with the Compassionate Unexpected, verbal Pentothal. I found of course that I welcomed the dose and without calculation, said, "Fairly completely. But I don't much mind. That's hardly recent."

Blix nodded. "No company?"

I said, "Aunts and uncles, a few colleagues, neighbors with casseroles"—then realized he was on detective duty: *was adultery at the bottom? catting round again?* So I said, "But no, less company than you've got here, by one precisely."

He smiled—on my side of his face at least—at the puncture of his tactic. Then he struck for the heart. "What was it about?"

My sources on suicide are not entirely limited to the Navajo overview. Masochistic as it's been, the books I left behind on the bedside table were Durkheim's *Suicide* and Menninger's *Man Against Himself.* So I gave the readiest answer—"She wanted to kill somebody, she chose herself, and—the key to her success was—she also wanted to *die*. Hence the pistol—rare for women."

He said "That's what you believe?"

I said "You know it's not."

"Had she warned you ever?"

"From the day I met her. She'd been issuing warnings since she learned to talk, since she learned to move (eyes, hands)—she never spoke them."

"Did she leave a note?" he said.

"Not to me. Not a word."

"To anybody else?"

"If so, they haven't told me."

He said "That's something."

"How?"

"What's not written is easier forgot."

I said "Think again."

He said "OK," which I took for kindness; but after the last few yards of mud, the highway regained, the grind of the four-wheel drive reduced, he said "What comes next?"

"In what?" I said—"this day, this conversation?"

"Your life," he said.

It issued, ruptured. I regretted every syllable that rushed my teeth— "Are you the man to ask that?—Mr. Ambition, Clear-Sight, Dr. Steady-Aim?"

He was quick but calm. "No, but you're here. You've always been aimed before; God knows, on-target far more times than me—"

"Block your metaphor," I said. "The target succumbed. But I know, Blix; I'm sorry. I'm just treading water—no signs in the sea."

"You'll make it," he said. As though it were a fact as dry and indisputable as a grain of rice.

Blix has such impeccable credentials as a man whose lips never touched a lie that I had to say "What makes you sure?"

For the moment, his tone (still loose in the truck), his unsmiling profile seemed to promise a chart, a followable plan which he now possessed and offered to give. But he said, "Because it's all you've wanted."

"What's *it*?" I asked.

"To be scraped, like you are, bare—owing nobody life, help or any piece of you. Did you ever *come* for her, ever donate that much?—a teaspoon as rich as Eagle-Brand milk of all your precious life-codes treading cream? Or is that secret too?—being saved for *who?*"

I said, "Who do you suggest? Name somebody—Dora?"

"Good as any," Blix said. "Take her—my blessing. She'll be ready when we round this curve right here. Look up on the left, any second now! Just say 'Dora, follow me' and she'll follow, forever. No wait— no going home to get the kids or say goodbye, no toothbrush to pack. And a taboo on suicide—of course, she's petrifying."

I said "Stop." I meant the truck—stop and let me out. I would walk to my car and head for home.

But Blix thought I meant his speech and did stop that, as we rounded his curve on Dora, ready.

I dreaded that he might pursue his urging in Dora's presence—be converted, by his own life and the nearness of mine, to monstrosity.

He stopped in the mud by the gas pump however and, as Dora came toward us, said quietly "Just a minute." He got down and said four words to her, then went to the back to pump his own gas.

Dora opened the driver's door and climbed up the high step to sit beside me—so close (already, with Blix not there to crowd us) that I had a quick thought of contagion—she'd infect me—and pressed against my door.

But she said "We got help" and pointed out the window at a knot of people advancing on the truck—four Indian men, all five-foot six, all in khaki pants, not a coat among them (white and blue shirtsleeves) and a single woman (more nearly a girl) in a Pendleton blanket, ma-chinemade, green, dirty and hideous. The men walked in mud as though it were pavement (or familiar at least, if miserable); the girl lurched.

I asked "Who are they?" and turned to look through the small rear window into the tarpaulined truck-bed where they hoisted and jerked and shunted one another.

Dora said "My brothers."

I could see the girl groping at a man's hip pocket for a bottle, and the bottle's label as she seized it, studied it a moment—LAIRD'S STRAIGHT APPLE BRANDY. "Who's the girl?" I asked.

Dora said "Somebody's wife."

I stared on backwards—which poor somebody? The girl had leaned against the rear of the cab and was sucking off a good inch of brandy, raw. She'd have emptied it—and still been unappeased; a face like a gully, that famished and demanding—if the man who seemed to own it hadn't wrenched it down from her. The bottle socked her teeth; I heard it through plate glass. The other three men laughed; the girl bawled and rocked in misery.

I asked, "What help are they going to be?"

Still not looking, Dora smiled. "They're strong. And they want to go home."

"Where's that?"

"Up where my truck was trying to go—my grandma's; there." She pointed rightward, across the highway toward the line of low hills in middle distance, pink where the sun had begun stripping snow.

"Why are they down here, then?"

"Looking round."

Blix opened his door, climbed in and sat. He cranked, then said— toward the glass but to Dora—"This is our help?"

"Yep." She smiled.

"The girl's pregnant—right?"

"I guess so—yep."

"God bless her," he said and shifted into gear.

"—Us," I said. I was looking across Blix and Dora toward the store.

A man had rushed out and was loping toward us—an Indian, tall, his white hair banded by a blue forehead rag in the old style, face all but bursting with barely held fury. Geronimo.

Blix seemed not to notice and engaged the clutch.

But Dora said "Wait; my daddy" and nodded.

Blix looked, depressed his foot and waited, straining for calm but betraying fear—when the man had stopped a foot from the truck, a foot from Blix's face, his windowglass was still tight shut.

So the man simply waited, staring down.

"Roll the glass," Dora said.

Blix rolled it down, took Badonie's first look and tried the Navajo greeting (one of his three phrases)—"*Yah-ta-hey.*"

Badonie said only "You going to Gallup?"

Blix said "Yes—passing through."

Badonie stepped nearer—the last step available before cold steel— but turned his back and looked toward the store—a long wood bench bearing five old Indians, three women, two men. One man wore the old high-crowned black hat and held a pint-bottle, half-full on his knee. Two of the women watched it—its guardians or threats? The third woman—separate—watched the air before her, past us, the south hills. Among pure misery, she condensed a purer brand—no mixture, no compound: Silent Pain. Badonie faced Blix again and pointed toward her. "That old woman yonder has been waiting two days to go in to town. She been sick and her son-in-law—he's a Navajo policeman— said he'd pick her up here and take her to the hospital. So she walked to here yesterday morning early—from way back that way, five or six miles—and he didn't never come. She waited all night and all day today. He hadn't never come."

It was offered as fact, with the veiled passivity of subject peoples. The Negroes of my childhood would come like that, to the backdoor at night, with some tale of woe—someone's shot, cut, dying; then would stop and stand silent. You would think they were waiting, confi- dent in the cunning of their desperation; but at bottom, they were not. They were calmly, utterly, hopeless. They had merely told the truth, had been impelled to come not so much in need or expectation of help as in the simple—simple!—wish to tell a story: *This is what's happen- ing; I want you to know.* Then if you acted—said "Climb in the car" or "I'll get the doctor"—your act was accepted with, again, calm grace, not as due response but as miracle (miracles were not infrequent), a blessing detached.

Badonie seemed now to stand like that—as the old woman sat— beyond hope or pride; and when Blix said "I'll take her," he said "OK" and, not going to her to help or explain, he called out to her in Navajo.

In maybe ten seconds—the time it took to reach her—she stood and started toward us.

Dora said, "Mae Clain. She just got rheumatism."

The woman was moving to the back of the truck; so Blix climbed down and said to Badonie, "Tell her to come up here."

He did and she came and—the two men standing back—she struggled up the step and onto the seat beside Dora, twelve inches from me. She at once faced forward—a face as text-book Indian as the Buffalo Nickel's, seamed as skirts on Egyptian statues, the oiled black hair scraped tightly back (not a white strand in it) yet impossible to date. Sixty-five? Eighty-five? either or neither. Her only sound was shallow breath, labored from her climb; her only admission of kinship with us (even with Dora who touched her) was the high scary odor that leeched from her rapidly as hemorrhaging blood. Made of metal like us but an older grade whose hardness shames.

Dora also didn't speak or look—some clan taboo?—and when Blix remounted, neither did he. (I glanced quickly back—our helpers were oblivious, tussling round their bottle.) He looked out at Dora's father still.

Badonie said, "OK. You going to town?" He had never acknowledged Dora. She lived with him.

"Now," Blix said.

"She got a daughter live in town somewhere"—he seemed to mean Mae Clain not Dora; but he gave no directions, again made no connection. He held up his hand to Blix's open window, a little package in it. I could read the label—SKOAL WINTERGREEN FLAVORED CHEWING TOBACCO.

Blix looked on a moment, then reached out, pinched a half-inch, stuffed it in his lower lip, said an awkward "Thank you" and we rolled away.

Dora giggled through the first hundred yards.

I had stopped guessing *why*—the source of the power of her unannounced swings from woe to mirth. Now that I knew she could not harm *me*—being worse off than I—I could witness her presence with nothing worse than boredom. But after ten or so silent miles—the heater working beautifully, Mae Clain's odor taming—I wondered what we *were*, what this truckload constituted in the eye of God (or a thoughtful onlooker, possessed of the facts)? A Ship of Fools? Blind Leading the Blind? Wise and Foolish Virgins? Try it another way— who would be the ideal painter to paint us? Goya? (does one of us possess the dignity, the unworked stillness, to bathe the others in his idiot light?). Brueghel, surely. We are all lean enough. But what would Brueghel call it, what would be his allegory?—four drunk Indian men, one pregnant drunk squaw (all huddled in cold wind on the springs of a truck—the passengers) and we up front, the steerers (two sick Indian women, both abandoned by men; Blix and I). Name us, name us!

We were in the hideous heart of Gallup (standard-American hideous—gas stations, burger stands, cat's-cradles of wires, slush in gutters; its one unique feature, on every corner as invariable furniture or like berserk Christmas decorations, a Navajo couple, drunk, in velveteen, gorgeous silver and turquoise, haranguing each other in the hoarse voice of hatred—wide mouths, clenched fists); and I still couldn't think what we were or where headed—*The Lame Entering First?* but entering what?

We had turned south by then—HOSPITAL ONE MILE—when the old woman jerked forward, slapped the dashboard and croaked in Navajo.

We were moving slowly—through small gray houses packed onto low hills—but Blix slowed more and asked Dora "What's wrong?"

"She say stop."

Blix pulled to the curb and stopped, looking forward.

The woman was struggling to rise now—clawing at Dora, the dashboard, the seat, to exit on my side.

Dora sat still, as though a cat were playing.

Blix said, "Do me a favor—see what in God's name's happening."

Still not moving, not touching the woman, Dora said a short sentence.

The woman let out a long ululation—a single syllable in the pit of her throat, surely no word—and again strained to stand.

Dora was silent.

Blix turned, laid one hand on the woman's shoulder and said through clenched teeth, "Help out, for Christ's sake."

Dora faced him and smiled. "What you need me for?"

"I can't turn her out here in the road. She'll die. What the Hell is she after?"

Dora said, "She say she got a daughter lives here. She's going there now."

"Where, here on this street?"

Dora said another sentence.

The woman groaned again.

Blix said "I'm helping *you*."

Dora said, "You can't stop her. She know what she wants."

I knew Dora was right and reached for my door-handle to climb down and help the woman leave.

Blix said to me "Sit still."

"She's old enough to vote," I said.

"Oh Jesus," Blix said.

He had worked, I noticed, through the names of deity in an interesting order, impersonal to personal—*God* to *Christ* to *Jesus*. He was in personal need.

He was looking now at me—first time in an hour—"Mr. Scorch," he said. "Everything scorches in your little wake."

"Or *stiffens*," I said.

"Or bleeds."

"This woman's got nothing but rheumatism; that's not mortal."

"Try to understand. I work here. I'm responsible. I told Dora's father I'd leave her with a doctor."

"Then do it," I said. "She won't jump out. Do it by all means if it's for old Cochise, your friend at last, your chewing-tobacco pal." I opened my door and slid down to the road.

The old woman crawled over Dora in an instant and, in two steps, joined me—or passed me, briskly, in her own direction.

Until then, I hadn't thought my way beyond freeing her; but the sight of her now—small and boned like a bird, consuming her freedom like a trail of suet laid suddenly before her—suggested again the simple solution: *Leave; there are things you can spare yourself, you owe him nothing.* I had turned her way, back away from the truck, and reached the tailgate (heading where? *away*) when Blix met me head-on, arriving from his side—and as two of the drunk men climbed out and strode off.

Blix halted among his collapsing duties and said "*Wait please*" toward the farthest gone, the woman and the drunks.

The two men stopped, faced round; but the woman never paused. (At the sight of Blix—dry-faced and pale—I'd been the first to wait.)

He watched the woman for a moment, then abandoned her—what did it cost him? with what could he pay and whom? pay *whom*? He said to the men, "Are you helping us or not?"

One of them took a few steps nearer. "We going to get my radio."

Blix said "I can't wait."

The man considered, nodded.

"How'll you get home?"

He pointed high, the way we were headed. "That ain't my home," he said and they left.

Blix looked then to me and slapped his flanks in desperation. "—Mine neither," he said and smiled.

The drunk pregnant girl had one leg out the tailgate, struggling down.

I pointed Blix to look and he took it by the ankle and firmly shoved her back—not a word. The skin of her thin leg had dried till it took his gesture like a slate—as she fell back howling, I could see he had written on her skin with his nail, a zagging white line, impossible to read. Blix scrubbed his hand.

I said "What's it mean?" and pointed to her marked leg, out of sight in the truck.

Blix had not seen it. "Look. I'm fighting," he said, "not explaining human life."

"Fighting what?"

"To draw breath one more hour and unstick a truck worth two hundred dollars that may not be *there* when we get there."

I *bonged* like a fight-bell, to start his next round.

He scrambled for the cab.

I followed, on my side—to keep the girl inside and on her way home (was it her home? was her husband one of those that had gone for the radio?); to preserve Blix's sense of donating help; changing lives; to avoid solitude. Those were reasons I gave myself anyhow as we drove on south toward Dora's truck and whosever home.

A mile from town, houses thinned, all but vanished for miles. We might have been rammed down some time funnel to Judaea, first century—sudden small hills, tan and gray, clumped with low growth (pinyon, sage, juniper), still scattered with snow that had lasted the day and a few lambs scrounging. If I'd seen on my right, in the gap between hills, thirteen shaggy men in dirty robes, wet sandals, with cold horny feet, trudging up with staves for an afternoon rest-and-homily, I'd have thought it only right—as natural, as naturally *produced* by the place, as the dark kids (Navajo? Mexican?) who'd begun appearing now, home from school, along the road, checking rusty mail boxes set a tenth of a mile before tarpaper shacks, occasional hogans. Two Indian boys, eight and nine, were being met as they walked up a gully toward their hogan by a brother, age four or five, grim as Polyneices with a plastic bow and arrow aimed at their hearts. All among *litter*. Now that dwellings had begun again, however sparsely, the hills showed litter wherever snow had melted. Nothing native or exotic, nothing blessedly organic that would silently rot but good immortal American litter—fuchsia hairspray cans, wine bottles, white plastic jugs that will outlast Mount Rushmore. All as clear in this light, as equally *near*, as in noon-drenched Di Chiricos or prisoners under question.

Odd, I thought—the sun was low now, coming from my side—four-thirty, five—and the light was thin and watery. Thin as the air—that would be it; the thinness yielded clarity. Objects hurtled freely toward me through the thinning air, their images at least. We were rapidly climbing. My lungs and my heart seemed suddenly to have new floors, half higher than usual. I'd try for deep breaths, the release of a yawn (I'd slept very little); but depths were not there. I was breathing all right—with Blix and Dora by me, still no sense of shortage—but I felt like a castaway, living on his muscle, no fat, no reserve, hands-on-ledge department. To comfort myself and to show I'd survived our confrontation, I asked Blix "What's our altitude?"

"No idea," he said.

"Do you?" I said to Dora.

She shook her head. "I don't live here."

Blix said "Your grandma does."

"Yep. I hadn't been up here since I was young."

Blix chose to make it some sort of last straw. Facing the road, he clenched his teeth and showed them; then he said "Why?"

Dora looked to him but didn't answer.

I wondered if, again, some taboo were involved (Navajo men mustn't see their mothers-in-law; may children see their grandmothers?) and I watched Dora closely.

She was neither tense nor smiling—no signal yet of outburst. Her face (the quarter I could clearly see) was an image of patient curiosity—*why ask that of me? why be who you are?* She couldn't turn Blix.

Still not looking, he said "You speak English?"

She nodded Yes.

"Then I asked you a question."

Patience again, but twitches of baffled apprehension now.

"How come you've never been up here to your grandma's but are making me go?"

"You're helping me," she said.

"—In strange territory, with mud waistdeep, that you've never seen before?"

"I never wanted to see it."

Blix considered, took nearly a minute. "Maybe you'll get your wish. Maybe we'll never get there. Or if we do, maybe you'll just see it this once."

Dora understood what I'd already refused to believe he meant. She said "You think I'm dying."

He'd had time for regret, hadn't meant her to read him so thoroughly. "You told me what the doctors said."

"And you think that's true? You think they know? They *don't* know—because I never did tell them."

Blix said "Tell them what?"—his pressure leaking.

"—What's wrong with me, the reason my arms go dead and I faint."

He said "Tell me."

"A snake. I touched it."

Blix and I smiled simultaneously.

She struck his shoulder with her clenched right hand. "You listen. It's the truth. When I went to school, about eight years ago, we had this teacher—a man named Simmons—and everybody say they're scared of snakes. So one day he come into school with a snake—live and moving—and all the other kids, they jump back scared. But he say, 'No, it won't hurt nobody but rats and prairie dogs'; and he say ain't nobody brave enough to touch him? So I say yes. All the other kids yelling at me—'Don't touch no snake!' But I been brave so I walk up and he hold it out between his hands, and I rub it one time. Then he say to me 'Hold it,' and he hand it to me, so I take it and hold it. It's so strong in my hands, I can feel it living but I never been scared. Everybody else real quiet now. It was real dry. Then I hand him back and I go sit down. Everybody tell me, coming home, that I'll get sick and I'm still not scared. But I got sick. You know how?—like now, fainting, falling down, my arms going dead. I was real bad sick and nobody knew why since I wouldn't tell them; but my mama get a man and he come and sing all night and all day and—you know what?—I don't tell him neither, but he pull a snake right out of my arm. That morning. And I was better. That's all that's wrong with me."

She had transformed, telling it—from her prior sealed silly petulant self to something not larger but harder, lighter, radiating faith in the simple lies that would not slow her death. She looked on at Blix's profile a silent moment, then faced the road.

He said, "Well, I'm glad. Glad you know." No irony, no pity.

He's abandoned her, was what I knew next. *He's left her to die*—her face ten inches from him, her thigh touching his; she's farther away than if he'd never come, never borrowed her narrow but deep resources. So I took her part—again, remember. My whole addled heart flowed across to her now. She was not of course looking. I saw her as the lady in Dickinson's poem—

> *Because I could not stop for Death—*
> *He kindly stopped for me—*

and merely to companion her, this moment on her trip, I said (aloud, calmly), "Here's all that's wrong with me."

Blix was first to turn—long enough to swerve the truck; I could hear our drunks tumbling.

Dora listened, not turning.

I knew she listened. I said it for her. "I am left alone because I wanted to be."

She still didn't turn. She had not understood.

Neither had Blix but he wouldn't rest in that. He said, "Did you really want it badly as that?"

Dora looked on at her own hands, flat on her flanks, and began to move her fingers as though playing some tune, some instrument. Random, atonal—her own "Sugar-time"?

The clear revelation, as though her hands made signals—that not only did she not follow me or Blix but was already bored and had lapsed into music not misery—came to me as comic, exhilarating. After years apart, after life-between-the-eyes, still we were talking like college roommates—or (better) like ladies in late-Henry James, hieratic, oracular, lethally threatening, playing slow holy tennis in their heavy silent skirts. And that quick vision produced another—or a feeling not a picture. The ballooning of pleasure in my belly, chest, throat— astounding (in *me*, after these weeks, months) as grace descending on me in the beak of a dove. No sense of its cause or source till I spoke— my answer to Blix produced as the crest of the rise reached my lips— "Yes, what I wanted." I had not known that. But finding it now and saying it aloud—in a snow-covered desert with dusk coming on, to a truckload of cripples—I looked again to Dora, in hopes that she still would not understand.

Her fingers played on, a little slower than before and her eyes watched them. If she'd followed a word of what was said or meant, it had done nothing to her. Surely she'd heard—seen!—every day speeches, acts, that would shrink my pleasure to tepid tameness.

It was Blix I had struck. I could see it in his side face—tight again, bluish—though the truck required his energy just then. Having come maybe twenty miles south of Gallup on the narrow paved road, he was turning right now—at Dora's signal—onto what seemed a ten-foot-wide dirt track, deeper in mud than the one to Atso's.

I thought at once of boyhood newsreels—the Second War, halftracks mired to the axles in French or German mud, bone-tired dogfaces sunk to the calves in its loud cold clasp.

Blix had turned too fast and, in the first few yards, had to jockey furiously to hold us in the road—the single set of ruts from the last mad truck that seemed our only hope of continuing. But when he'd saved us from ditching and slowed to a crawl and shifted into four-wheel drive, he could speak—he'd saved it for us through his little crisis—"What's wrong with me—why I'm in this fix, where I'm here today in mud thick as shit—is I can't believe there are people like you."

I said, "Is your pronoun singular or plural?"

He said "Meaning what?"

"—Meaning me alone, as a single monster, or Dora and me?"

He drove a little more—or his hands rode the wheel; the truck seemed safely locked in its ruts. Then he said "Plural."

"There are," I said. "Touch us and see." I held out my hand, palm down, across Dora. Rough as the ride was, it hung there steady.

He had the guts to do it—the stagey guts. He let me wait suspended as his free hand moved to Dora's arm (but cloth not skin); then he moved for mine and, watching the road, covered and pressed it with his own strong fingers as though really confirming.

He held for so long that I felt how much colder he was than I, felt my warmth passing toward him, and rolled from his grip. I said, "Careful, but I feel my power leave me."

"Jesus," he said and before I could wonder (was he joining my joke—one more rally in our match—or was he further appalled?), he had lost control (or obeyed the track and the Great Sky-Pilot) and sunk us in the ditch. We were listing heavily leftward, unsavable clearly; but he gunned the gas in a try to blast us free. The drunks were bobbling like empty hogsheads. Only when we'd plowed twenty yards up the ditch—deeper each yard—did he stop, kill the engine and sit a moment, silent.

Dora and I were also silent, as though at the shrine to a fallen hero. I thought one thing—"I didn't buy boots; I am in suede shoes."

Then Blix said "Beg my pardon."

I thought he'd slipped, had meant to beg ours so I said "Of course."

"No, do, please," he said. He lowered his head almost to the wheel.

Dora looked to me and nodded in confirmation—we were back on ground she could recognize.

"I am Prince of Darkness, then," I said. "Now you know. Don't hold it against me."

Blix shook his head. "I do."

But by then the drunks were bailing out in back; their girl was wailing.

I turned, before Blix, and could see the two men already on the ground, the girl starting down. "We're ditching our ballast anyhow," I said.

Blix didn't answer but opened his door and stood on the little ledge and said to the men "Just wait." Then he leapt far out, across the ditch to the low snowy shoulder and looked down from there at the truck, the buried wheels, not at me or Dora (now the least of his problems).

Dora turned to him though and slid into his place behind the wheel.

I said to the back of her head "What now?"

She looked back quickly and gave a short giggle, her first for hours. Then she slid across the seat to Blix's door and—with no hesitation, barely looking as she went—she jumped up toward him and landed in soft snow; her sneakers sank to the ankles at once.

My being the monster permitted me to hold my own inside, warm and dry anyhow, till word to abandon ship. I did lean across and say to Blix, "I'll drive if you'll push."

He took it calmly—someone would have to drive; someone had volunteered—and nodded, not looking. Then he said to Dora, "Whoever they are, tell the girl just to wait."

Dora said "She won't listen."

Blix said, "Tell her anyhow; then they can't blame me."

Dora shrugged and went.

Then one of the men, the smallest, came up, mud already to his knees, and said "You ain't going to move."

Blix took it as offered, as fact, delivered calmly, disaster number so-and-so; and he clearly believed it. But he said, "Yes I am. I got chains in back."

"How you going to put them on?"

Blix said, "On my hands and knees in the mud" and walked back to start.

I suddenly thought, "I am at their mercy. Again I have volunteered to be at the mercy of incompetents who can harm me, ruin me. Why? Blix asked me 'What next?' and has made me see the answer—to be free in my own life, free *not* to volunteer for work I neither need nor want, free not to yield again to Love the Great Occupation, Time-Passer, Killer. Free to say 'So what?' to everything but food and air. Yet now he has wrecked me in a desert mudhole with night coming down, the air cold and thin, my only hope for rescue three drunk Indians, one that's turning to stone and a social worker with his head up his ass about six light-years." I knew of course there was no real danger. We were hardly more than two miles off the highway. If we were firmly stuck, if worse came to worst, we could simply walk out and hitch a lift to Gallup and thence, by bus, to Dunder (and my rented car, and home)—providing the Indians stayed drunk and docile, didn't kill us for our cash. But what then? what next?—once home and free? At that, I felt as precious as uranium, *made* of energy, each cell an atom that could radiate, steady and generous, for years without visible exhaustion—the radiance of simple knowledge; of what I know, having had my life; the wasteless conversion of mass into power. Power for what?—further life and freedom. So I sat, a little huddled round myself as round a glow, while the truck rocked gently with shoulders from beneath and voices came to me in Navajo and English, exasperated, stripped of the upholstery of kindness—"Stand there, goddammit . . . Hold this, goddammit . . . Why dontcha put it here?" We were now, I thought, *The Drones and the Mate*—I the consort chosen (for *qualities*) and groomed for union, toward which I am borne through dangers and trials. Union with what?—that new life and work, my fresh rich chance, clear hope, ahead. If they rescue me now, award me survival.

Blix jumped to the shoulder again, at my left—a mudbaby, frowning.

I slid a little over and lowered the glass.

He said, "Please crank it now and drive it slowly out."

"Why don't you?" I said.

"You'll need me back here—need all three of us pushing."

I looked back at Dora and the one man in mud, then quickly through the window into the cab—the girl and the second man unconscious, flat-out. I'd need Blix there, as he'd said, so I nodded.

"Drive slow and straight," he said, "till the ditch goes shallow; then gun it out into the center ruts and keep moving slow. We'll have to jump on."

I cranked, shifted gear, waited till Blix yelled "OK" from the back, then released the clutch slowly. The wheels spun once; then the chains gripped somehow and—heaved by three shoulders—I moved straight forward at my leftward-listing angle for maybe ten yards till the ditch, instead of shallowing, deepened. Or the mud did. I still moved, but slower; the list was increasing with every yard, the left wheels sinking. I'd gone twenty yards and I wanted to stop—I was wrecking us deeper than we'd been before; an axle would break—and I did raise my foot from the gas an instant.

But Blix yelled "Go!"

So I floored it and went, wallowing grandly—the drunk girl, the girl!—and the truck saved itself. Or saved me maybe. The ditch never shallowed but, slowly, the wheels were grinding rightward; and I was borne out and up, across to the haven of the center ruts—Blix still close behind me, still yelling "Move!"

I moved a little faster, feeling the sudden need to *leave*—leave the three rescuers, filthy, in my wake and flounder ahead (with my two oblivious drunks). Toward what though? So I slowed and, seeing I had reached a short level stretch at the crest of a rise, I stopped and waited.

First to reach me was the man. Embarrassed by his speed, he looked back to Blix and laughed and said, "Him! You ought to hire him. He'll get us there." (I could hear Dora giggle.) Then he gave me a fumbling army salute, said "Pretty good all right!" and vanished toward the rear.

Blix appeared and stood two steps away, looking.

He of course said "Jesus." Then "Hand me that towel."

I was still at the wheel, giddy from success and vision and the height; but I looked to the floor and saw a wadded towel. "It's dirtier than you," I said.

"Most things are."

"I advise against it, Doc. Barely sterile," I said.

"Me neither," he said. "But *you'll* sterilize it. Just touch it once for me."

I took it up, held it a moment before me—Blix made a sizzling sound—then threw it out to him.

Dora had come up and waited separate from Blix, but watching him. My wheels had spun mud into her face and hair; but—unlike Blix whose hands hung isolated beside him, untouchable—she seemed not to mind. Her hands touched her skirt. And she was breathing as though the air were sufficient, calm and thick. As though she were home, despite her denials.

Blix scrubbed at his hands and wrists—his face was clean—then handed the towel to Dora and said to me "You did it."

"Black magic," I said. "It was nothing, just my Powers."

He stepped toward me, not looking back to Dora, and said, "My thanks. Now see can your Powers get us all the way there, wherever *there* is."

I didn't want to yield my grip on the wheel; but Blix had a foot on the running board already, scraping off mud. I hadn't moved. Dora came to her door and climbed and entered.

Blix said "You want to drive?"

I could not imagine riding a mile *between* them. I smiled and said "You trust me?"

"No," he said and smiled. "But I don't trust anybody else who's with us either."

"Not yourself?" I said.

"Oh, *me*, yes," he said. But by now he was lit with something like glee. Cold, wet and stiffening with mud, he looked up to me once more from the ground and said, "No, you do it. Magic, magic—" He flung out his arms in a wizard posture, his hands clawed downward, eyes blared, laughing.

"How far do we go?" I said.

"Ask Dora," he said.

She said "About two mile."

Blix held his fading pose—"You've never been here."

Dora said "I know."

Blix said, "Two miles may mean twenty but—magic! magic! We're charmed, we're saved." And before I could think—accept or decline— he'd trotted through sucking mud to the passenger side and taken my old seat.

So I drove us on—nothing else to do; I could not fold now—and after a hundred yards, I was glad. The steering demanded every quantum of my energy—time, eyes, mind. (The truck would hold the road calmly for yards, in the ruts as on rails; then—no warning—the wheel would lurch in my hands and I'd save us again. Blix and Dora understood and barely spoke.) And after all, I was piloting at last—not ideally, not alone (with all this breathing cargo) but at least at nobody's mercy but my own (and the engine's, the snow and mud's, the night's).

For instantly, it was night—the air too thin to hold light or color once the sun had sunk. In my concentration, I'd hardly noticed and pressed toward the glass to see the road.

Finally Blix said "Light has been invented."

I looked over to him for clarification and the truck slewed badly; I fought it into line.

"Your *headlights*," he said.

I said "I can see."

"It's my truck," he said.

"It's Uncle Sam's," I said, "*ergo* mine as much as yours." But I switched on the lights and wallowed ahead at an unsteady ten or so miles an hour. Through pure intensity of searching, I saw in my first slow mile a single house set far back on our right (not a hogan—logs?), no trace of light but the voices of dogs above our roar; then nothing again, then a '49 Buick abandoned, maroon (its lovely slave-bracelet hood-ornament intact!); then nearer the road on my left a sheepfold built carefully of wood (where was all this wood *found?*) but abandoned too, collapsing, not a sheep in sight. All this time the road was struggling to halt us, expel us, ditch us—short flat stretches of a hundred yards or so that (though the mud was deep) raised our hearts (all three; I could taste that in the air—hope! we'd *continue!*); then a sudden bucking of steep hills, deep drops. I thought, at the top of every hill (they were steeper and steeper), that we'd see Dora's truck; but half an hour later (five miles farther in) we were still moving on through emptiness. Not exactly desolation—the Dead Sea, Death Valley, are no doubt sparser—but this road, the few feet of shoulder we could see (barbed wire, short old-style power poles, then sage again and pinyon), was competing handsomely. I thought of Auden's stanza from "The Shield of Achilles"—

> *A plain without a feature, bare and brown,*
> *No blade of grass, no sign of neighbourhood,*
> *Nothing to eat and nowhere to sit down,*
> *Yet, congregated on its blankness, stood*
> *An unintelligible multitude.*
> *A million eyes, a million boots in line,*
> *Without expression, waiting for a sign.*

—Whose eyes? What boots? For it did seem inhabited, waiting, watching unintelligibly. No signs of people though, beyond my little cargo. We might have been voyagers bound for Arcturus. We had passed that single house at dark—nothing proved it a home except barking dogs— but nothing since, unless that Buick was inhabited (a genuine possibility). And not only no imaginable place to sit but, I suddenly knew, no place to turn around. Not a driveway, sideroad or wide turning space. I could circumnavigate the globe in these two ruts—a Flying Dutchman in search of rest. But the thought didn't faze me; cheered me slightly, in fact. I was on-course; could not choose *not* to be; to Hell with future bridges.

Blix said again "Jesus."

He had seen before me, being free to look farther than the ten nearest yards. Up the road—a level stretch—a white pickup truck, its tail toward us, immobile in our tracks. Dead-center of the road.

"Is it yours?" I asked Dora.

"Yep." She nodded, frowned.

We were twenty yards from it. Blix said, "Better stop here. If we can't get it out, we'll have to get round it."

I could see, even from there, that it wasn't stuck at all. The road, in this stretch, sloped to each side from a crest; and the crest was not mirey. The tires were resting in no more than two-inch mud. I thought, quite clearly, "Abandoned as ruined"; then I stopped and said to Dora, "No grandma in sight."

"She don't live here," she said.

Blix said "Good thinking" and opened his door.

The previously ambulatory Indian in back had climbed out already and was at the truck looking, hunkered up beneath the rear, before Blix touched ground. And as Blix moved toward him, the drunk looked up and, smiling broadly, said, "Broke! Half-in-two! Goddamn if she don't broke the damn axle!" He paused, lit with pride in Grandma's achievement.

Blix simply stood.

Dora, who'd stayed in by me, slid out; and again in back the other drunks were rousing, muttering, trying to climb down.

Again I stayed inside. I'd already, in my head, abandoned Dora's truck, and was rapidly computing. By my watch—past seven—we were eight miles in, off the Gallup-Zuni road. Where did this track lead— if we could pass the wreck somehow? To Grandma's hogan—how much farther was that? Would we be welcome there?—would Dora go at all? I'd kept the engine running for the sake of the lights; but I had my window open and, even without the sun, the air seemed not too cold, nothing scary, maybe 40°.

The drunk girl and the second man had come round now and were hauling one another toward the others in the light.

Free again. But trapped? No room now even for dream-escapes. I could not gun past them or race in reverse alone through eight miles of mud. But I was not responsible. The trap was not mine—not chosen by me, not self-deployed (except insofar as I'd meant this trip to be a change, relief, light-entertainment among the more seriously deprived than I)—and clearly I was safe. At the worst, a night in Grandma's hogan (a few fleas, chilly, the sounds of family-humping); at best, an exhilarating triumph over mud (a tricky turn-round, then the trip back out—surely faster now, three Indians lighter, the mud chilling and thickening).

Blix turned and came toward me, opened my door, climbed up.

I stayed in place, behind the wheel.

"Slip over," he said.

"You still don't trust me?"

"No."

I didn't move.

"Please," he said. "I have got to try and drive us around this wreck."

I moved, he sat, I said "What's beyond it?"

"Grandma's, I'm *assuming*. I'm assuming somehow we can stay there till morning or turn and come back."

"She won't have you," I said.

"You know her?"

"No. Do you?"

"Never saw her," he said. "Can't read her mind either." He shifted gear downwards.

"I can," I said. "She'll hate your sight."

He actually waited. He shifted into neutral, faced me and said "Why?"

I was looking ahead. No Indian-Bureau expert could have separated

Dora more effectively from her drunk—what? kin?—than our white headlights. In their glare, ahead, huddled at the wreck, she had crossed back over—to my eye at least—and hung there by the others (not *with* them though) as oblivious to us as a fetus to its mother. Not true exactly. They all were fetal now—pale, lunar in our light, but with simple needs only, which their element supplied (the thin air, the muck), not in need of us. Cruel to addict them. I answered Blix, "Because you've ruined Dora."

He nodded. "Check," still hung-fire, not moving.

"Leave then," I said.

"Now?"—his tone considered it as possible, not preposterous.

"The kind thing," I said.

"How?" Blix said.

"Is this a through road?"

"Who knows?" he said.

"—We won't till we try."

"What if it dead-ends at Grandma's hogan?"

"That'll be round," I said. "We can circle it."

"We'd meet her coming back—Dora, we'd meet."

"She'd have got the message by then," I said.

"What would it say?"

I thought. "It would say, 'It is a far far better thing—' "

"That would be from you," he said. "What would *my* message be?"

I said "Write it yourself then." I was tired of the game and thought for the first time since dark of the VISTA spy. I could play *him* now, an invincible trump.

But Blix said, "Oh I have. Many times in many tongues." He was of course looking ahead to where she stood, talked at by her kin, silent herself but not turning to us. Allowing us our choice now—why? Blix said, "What it would say—'I love you and you'll sit in my head till I die, but I'm leaving now because you need me too much; you are needing something from me that I have not got, not enough to give at least, that you won't even name. Don't wave when I pass.' "

" '—Don't groan when you die,' " I said.

Blix appeared to accept it, if he heard me at all. He began to reverse us, slowly, twenty yards. Then he moved slowly forward on Dora's truck, bearing gradually right.

The Indians moved left, out of our way, whatever we were doing.

Dora watched with grave attention but took no step to join us.

When we'd got twelve feet from the back of the wreck, the lights showed our only hope—a channel only slightly wider than our wheelbase, its right third composed of a shallow-looking ditch.

I said "Can we make it?"

Blix said "I'm trying."

I didn't say what I wondered—trying *what?* He'd left our sure ruts, entered virgin mud, was skirting Dora's truck. Even our engine was silent with tension; yet clearly it was working—we were moving, and forward. Blix and I had already flanked the front of Dora's truck; ten more seconds we'd be clear. They passed and we were; her wreck was behind us; our lights again shot ahead unblocked, open road.

Blix began to ease us left, back up toward the center; and our front end went, maybe half the way, before our tail slewed round and down toward the ditch. Blix pumped a little gas and we made a little distance more toward safety; then our tail slewed again and began to sink. Blix said once "No" and gunned, to blast us out. The wheel spun quietly in its wet relentless socket; the chains seized nothing.

So I said "Yes"—meaning nothing in particular, to break the silence.

And the helpful drunk appeared at Blix's window. "You stuck again. You better let *him* drive." He smiled toward me.

I nodded to take the compliment, then lowered my glass and tried to look back. The tail was in darkness thick as the mud; but what lay beneath my door seemed solid snow, trees a few yards beyond. The Indians were gathering on my side to watch; Blix was climbing down on his; so I opened my door and stood to see and then jumped to earth, the first touch in hours. I almost expected an Antaeus jolt of energy— I would love all this, I would sacrifice to serve it, *Everything we look upon is blest.* There was no real jolt; but I was at least in snow not mud, the drunks seemed gentled and sobered by this latest, only one wheel was stuck and it seemed within rescue; so in gratitude, I struck a little inward from the road to gather brush—traction for the wheel.

Blix was standing, staring, mute.

Dora still had not joined him but hung with her own. (It *was* her home.) They were talking rapidly, quietly, like diffident machines, without stress (passion or complaint) in a language claimed to be the most delicate of all, the most difficult to master. Four desperate souls— three drunk as loons—mired to their ankles in snow and mud, murmuring steadily (no trace of urgency) in the world's most sophisticated language. Chinese sages in a late Yeats poem. Helpless idiots.

Only Dora was silent but she listened.

There were clumps of stunted trees a few yards away. I went to them and took an armload of sticks. The four minutes' effort had me sweating lightly and breathing fast—I thought more of the warmth than the altitude: good, tonight would be warmer than last night at least; Grandma's might even be bearable. The sky showed the reason—low thick clouds, the day's warmth trapped on us; we were under a bell; pray it didn't lift.

When I got back to the truck—my shoes still barely damp—Blix was up in the cab. Dora, the girl and the happy drunk were bracing themselves to push from the rear. Only the other man—too dazed to push?— was standing aside.

He watched me coming with my load of brush, really studied me; then when I stopped near him, poised to hand it down to Dora (who was nearest the stuck wheel), he had reached his conclusion, drained my meaning. He even came to me—three or four steps—touched my loaded arms, shook his head No and said, "You ain't gonna start no fire with that."

Fire had been the furthest thing from my mind, but I had to ask "Why?" He'd threatened an irrational prohibition and I wasn't welcoming those.

His head shook on, a mime of negation—"We ain't got no matches."

I laughed but he didn't. He was in dead-earnest (and right, as it turned out—not a match among us; how did he know?). So for racial harmony, I tried to stop. I managed a solemn nod—still more loaded with sticks than anyone in Grimm—then surrendered to the spectacle of me marooned (maybe) with four redskins in snow and mud at roughly 7,000 feet and not one of us with the simple knowledge of how to nurse fire.

Before I'd decided to sacrifice my shoes and join the pushers, Blix made his first try at driving out, a forward-backward-forward struggle that left the four Indians stuccoed with mud—Dora in sneakers—and the wheel buried deeper, and sinking fast. In a moment of waiting, it settled six inches—was it in quicksand? or (far more likely, considering the day) in some small spot where the earth lacked a crust, some tunnel to the center? Entrance to the afterworld, a four-day journey.

Blix shouted something then from the cab, and I assumed he would make a second try and that pushing was more good to him than sticks; so I dropped my bundle and said to the drunk, "No, but come on; we can push." Then I stepped past him to jump for the ditch.

But the other drunk—the helpful one, pushing—said "No! Stay there."

I thought he meant his friend so I kept climbing down.

But he said again "No."

I stopped and said "Me?"—my feet still clean; only my hands were wet.

The man didn't answer but held out both arms toward me. It seemed the gesture of father to child—*Jump, I'll catch you*—and I took another downward step.

But a woman said "No."

I looked—Dora surely; she was facing me; the drunk girl was yards away, leaning on the far wheel (retching or pushing?).

"Yep, he means you stay there"—Dora; I saw her say it, with as much force as she'd yet mustered today.

"Why?"

"You better stay." She turned from me to brace for another push.

The helpful drunk waited—to see that she stayed?—and when I'd held still for four, five seconds, he tensed himself again, ready to push. But the engine died. They didn't relax but waited in place for Blix to recrank. The girl *was* retching—with a vehemence that threatened to produce her baby, from one or more orifices.

Blix's door opened, his feet hit mud; he showed at the back—stepped round the girl—and stared at the sunk wheel, then up at the hooded sky, then to Dora not me. He asked her "What now?"

She did not move to him but held her ground—or was held by it; her sneakers were buried. She shrugged once, unsmiling.

The two drunk men moved back toward Dora's truck (leaving the retching girl) and began to talk there.

Blix said, across six feet of space, to Dora, "Do you know where we are?"

She looked behind her—which was my way, but past me. Then she faced Blix and pointed back. "We walk through there to Dunder."

He asked "How far?"

"I don't know. Not far."

"It's not a road though."

"Nope," she said.

"Have you ever walked it?"

"Not since I was little."

I saw us scrambling down uncharted canyons in pitchdark snow, bodies on crags—but only that: I *saw* it not *feared* it.

"Where's your grandma's?" Blix said.

She waited, debating the admission of her lie; then yielded partly—"Up this road."

"How much farther?"

Another wait—longer; was she really figuring distance? She said "Pretty soon."

"Close?"

"Yep."

Then Blix looked up to me and said "You decide."

I was shocked by the burden, but at once I said "Grandma's." (*Why?* It seemed *help* but, better surely, it seemed a necessary test for Blix, an ordeal to face—Dora in her rank dark mysterious family, mute in their impenetrable language but condemnatory: *She is dying slowly, you are speeding her toward it, but you will not come with her.* I wanted to watch that, through cold, fleas, meanness.)

Dora said, as quickly, "No."

Blix touched his sunk truck. "It makes the most sense," he said.

She waited, looking down. She had not seen me for whole long minutes; and that was as I wished—to be transparent now, a witness clear as a pane of glass. But of whom *was* she thinking?—who waited at Grandma's? who were our drunks? was it all of her and Blix? some desperate dance-for-two she was planning? She said to Blix "Wait." Then she went, head bowed, toward her own truck, her kin. With her back to us, she began to speak at them.

"What's this about?" I asked.

Blix said "What are *you* about?"

"I asked first—what's the powwow?"

"Who knows? Just think of it as Mystery-of-the-Minute. There'll be millions more before day—and day may get here before they finish talking."

They did seem Biblical now or T. E. Lawrencian, no longer sage and calm—a small knot of shepherds locked in suddenly urgent hassle over some microscopically trivial issue, beneath the sky and the wheeling constellations.

After Dora's first statement, the helpful drunk talked most—with raucous lunges from the pregnant girl, now hoarse from retching.

Blix simply stood, showed no inclination to climb out of mud to the shoulder with me; so I said "Why this honor?"

"Meaning what?"

"—Letting me choose our fate—the stranger in your midst."

He hadn't thought but he said at once "I'm tired."

"I didn't sleep either—different reason, remember? And we clearly won't tonight, whatever she decides."

"No," he said.

"I could transport us psychokinetically to a motel in Gallup—hot showers, blankets; ready?" I extended wizard arms, as he had earlier.

"That's why," Blix said, "—why I told you to choose, not your magic games but your cool clear head. Frozen—Birdseye Brains."

"Meaning what please?"

"You know," he said, "—know I think you're a monster."

"What kind please?"

"There's only one—the killing kind."

"Her?"

"Yep. You know it."

"Not true," I said.

"Oh don't get me wrong; I admire you," he said, "—envy you your powers, all but worship you." He bowed, where he stood, deeply from the waist; his right hand touched the mud.

"Don't," I said.

"I'm just a man," he said.

And Dora started back toward us. She came to Blix, stopped four feet away and said "We better walk."

"On to your grandma's?"

"Back home," she said.

"Dunder?—that home?"

"Yep."

"Which way?"

"Back the way we come."

Blix said, "That's miles—eight, nine—just to the highway. By the time we get there, we'll never catch a ride—it's not Times Square."

"We can't walk that other way," she said and again pointed my way, but still not looking.

"Why?"

"Maybe too dark."

"Can't one of them lead us?—they walked it this morning."

"Nope," she said.

"He's sober by now." Blix meant the helpful drunk.

"No he ain't," she said.

I knew, whatever happened, I was in for mud and wet; so I scrambled down finally and walked up between them and asked Dora, "What about your grandma's then? Can't we stay there till morning and send for help?"

She answered to Blix—"No."

He actually touched her—reached out and took her wrist in sight of her kin—and said "Why not?"

She waited, then turned to me as if that were punishment (for her not me), then pointed and quietly said to Blix, "Him."

"He's my friend," Blix said. "He won't hurt *you*."

"I know that," she said. "I won't never let him but my brother and them other people say No."

"No *what?*" Blix said.

"They say they ain't sleeping nowhere he sleeps."

"—And they sleep at your grandma's?"

She said "I guess so," yielding one more lie.

Blix seemed prepared to leave it at that. He opened one hand and jingled his keys, then walked to the passenger door and opened it, then looked back to me and said, "You need anything out of here before I lock it?"

"No," I said. What I needed now of course—if we were abandoning, striking for the road—was reasons why the drunks had refused only me. I stepped back a little from Dora—not to press her—and said "What's wrong with me?"

"You know."

"I don't."

Blix had gone round to lock the other side.

"They think you some kind of witch or something."

I looked toward them.

With Blix's taillights off, they were now all dark, standing close and waiting silently—for Dora, I guessed; to receive their own, however damaged.

"Why would they think that?" I said.

She shrugged, know-nothing.

"You told them something?"

Blix had returned, stood back and watched us.

"Yep," she said.

"Then I want to know what please."

"—Your wife shoot herself." She took a step toward Blix; he gave no answering step or touch.

"And that makes me a witch?"

"They say so, yep."

Blix said as calmly as a Hollywood doctor, "They think you'll be followed by her ghost, at night."

I puffed out something midway between a laugh and an incredulous gasp. Then I said, "I am. That's between me and her though. She won't harm them—you either, I guess."

"Just him," Blix said to Dora.

She accepted that as true, nodded to us both.

Blix looked to me. "We'd better start for the road then."

"Toward Gallup?" I said.

"The way we came—we know that much."

I computed it again—eight miles of this mud (not a single way-station); then the Zuni-Gallup road by, say, midnight; rush-hour in the desert. The hope of hitching a ride to Gallup—twenty more miles. Then—what? by bus to Dunder? Well, adventure. "Pray for clouds," I said.

Blix looked up at our greenhouse-dome. "They'll break," he said. "With *me* along, they'll clear in no time and then—Labrador!"

"Do you know where we are?"

He pointed to the truck. "I checked a map. Are you ready?—Remnant Mesa, just south of Remnant Mesa. 'A remnant shall remain.' "

"*Who?*" I asked.

He turned to Dora. "Who are you going with?"

Had she decided? Was it automatic yet? She waited ten seconds, looking at the dark ground. "You and him," she said.

So I was included. Odd—why? To show she didn't fear me? didn't countenance my powers or my hauntedness? Or maybe that she *did*—ranked me with her snake as a cause of woe—but was tolerating me as a necessary adjunct to her time with Blix? One more landmine in the field she must walk. I asked what Blix wouldn't—"Do they know? Do they mind?"

She nodded to me. "I tell them." But she kept her place.

Blix at last said, "You'll *tell* them or you've *told* them already?"

"Yep," she said. "Already."

We both—Blix and I—looked toward them then.

They were still in the dark at the front of Dora's truck, twenty feet away, between us and the road. They stood close and silent; even the girl had recovered and stood straight and still, her blanket tight round her.

Blix said "Where are they going?"

"I don't know," she said. "They live round here."

Blix said "Why are they waiting?"

She only shrugged.

I laughed and said, "Do they ever kill witches?"

Dora said "Yep."

Blix said "At intervals." Then he asked Dora, "Anything else to tell them?"

"I ain't talking to them."

"We're off then," Blix said and took the first step.

The drunks stood in place.

"Blix. Wait," I said. Oddly, I'd thought of the trucks—no one else had seemed to.

He and Dora stopped, looked back.

"What about all this hardware?"

"It'll wait," Blix said. "There's a motorpool in Gallup. They'll tow mine in."

"Dora's?"

"It's OK," she said. They started again.

"We're blocking traffic," I said.

"Whiz, whiz," Blix said. "Walk-to-left-facing-traffic." His next three steps were a bobbing-weaving dance as he threaded Broadway.

The helpful drunk stepped forward from his group.

"You're fired," I said.

Blix didn't turn; Dora followed him.

"Blix, you were fired this afternoon. The VISTA spy turns out to have teeth."

That stopped him, turned him. He walked three steps back toward me, past Dora. "I forgot him."

"Yes, you did."

"He came by, did he?"

"—And got an eyeful. And left you a message."

"What was the eyeful?"

"Dora at her post—the bedroom door."

"What was the message?"

"Wait—he also got an earful."

"Who from?"

"Dora and me."

"What did *she* say?"

"That she lived there."

"You?"

"I sort of scared him—Leaves from My Life or The Bloody Wife."

We all were frozen still—Dora, the helpful drunk, the silent others.

Blix said "And the message?"

"To phone him collect by noon tomorrow."

"For what?"

"He said you'd know, said you'd know what's coming."

Dora had waited where she'd stopped, no nearer.

Blix looked back to her now—"Did he?"

"I guess so."

"He did," I said. "I don't tell real lies—not anymore. His name was Tim Neely—looked helpless, apparently isn't."

"No, he's not," Blix said. He stood a moment, facing me. Then he beckoned to me, with a kind of kitchen gesture (stirring soup)—"On to the nearest phone. Bitter pills." He turned and went.

Dora let him take the lead again, then fell in behind—four, five paces. In a second they had flanked, then passed, her kin—who did not look after them but stared on at me.

I knew no more delays; my lines to Blix and Dora were lengthening with each step; I was nearer her kin than she. They could not so much as start a fire though. So I followed.

And they let me pass in silence—no muttered imprecations to meet my powers in dark midair, no visible gestures to turn my gaze, no movement, breaths held.

Scared as I was, I longed to rush at them with some Halloween groan—*Arrgh! It's I!*—but I only said "Thank you" to the helpful drunk and never broke step.

No need to compel you through the first hour's walking. You'd have nothing to do but play drill sergeant, counting cadence at my heels— unless you're a fight fan, which I am not. Ordeal (the actions of ordeal, its present-time) is invariably unrevealing to a witness, except of his own fragility and blood-lust, no news to most adults—Harold Lloyd on a ledge, fingernails in mortar, or Jesus crucified or Jacob and the man who wrestled all night. What's revealing there is not the grunt and groan—what holds were used and why, the man's dirty move in crippling Jacob's hip—but what was said at dawn, the words between the battlers ("Your new name is Israel" —"What is *your* name?") which flood the night backwards with terror and joy, the dirty winner having been God of course. So you and I will know, only at the end—and in my words—if the trip was worth joining. Not that I had a choice; the choice was to die.

There were no sights to see—with the cloud-cover holding, thank God, no moon; and we walked in near blackness on the right-hand shoulder where the snow had not melted and the ground was mostly level. No acts to study, for character or motive (or grace or *eros*)—foot following foot, silent breath on breath. No talk to hear—not a syllable from Dora, only rare relaxed questions from me ("How fast are we walking?") and Blix's replies ("Not fast enough"). No thoughts to overhear.

Not from me at least. I didn't think—my brain a ball of cheese. Oh no doubt the ancient cellar lobes were grunting intermittently in their precious perpetual night; but mostly they were doing their oldest intended work—answering alarms, directing each nerve and muscle onward through snow toward warmth, dryness, food; and doing it with pathetic spaniel eagerness (being so seldom called upon, my life being largely safe as a stone).

Till now. Safe till now. And in that first hour I felt more than safe—exhilarated, simply triumphant. I had won, would win. Won what?—freedom, competence. Two hours ago, I'd felt fragile as a glass, rocked round in mud by the hands of drunk Indians. Now the sense of *fragility* had changed to *value* and *worthiness*, plus the new-proved power to protect that value. I remembered my father once saying of my mother, "She's fragile as a lamp-chimney but stand me behind her when the A-bombs fall." I felt that now—a fine lamp-chimney that's survived Hiroshima. Entirely undisturbed. Adamantine, in fact.

Felt it though, as I said, not *thought* it. I was near as I've been since, say, age eleven to a state of pure being—the mind of God. I speak for myself of course, not the others. They were moving like me (Blix leading, Dora between us); we were even in step three-fourths of that hour; but what they were thinking or feeling or suffering, I didn't guess or care. Not in the first hour.

But soon after that, the charm began to fade. No sudden vanishing, no emergency bells, no change of weather or scenery. But my lower brain, for its own slow reasons, began to suspect it knew more than my upper—that it wasn't merely chuffing me along through a lark, my first winter-carnival, but was straining to ram me through danger to safety (or ram itself through; I was mainly its luggage). After the hour of surprise that my lounge-lizard's get-up was perfect kit for a forced march through desert snow—I had walked warm and dry—I began to feel stripped. Not instantly but slowly, and from the ground up. My feet, in suede, were finally ice; my scrotum was coarsening, tightening at its base like draw-strung marble-bags in my childhood; and my heart, warm till now in its Harris-tweed jacket, lurched into fast-time to flush down warm blood. And in its new rhythm, the coded message any fool could read: *It is possible to die. Here. Soon.*

My first thought was defiance—"I refuse to die here, a foreign death, out of my element. I must fight to die *in place*, to die where I should (which is where? where?) not in some stray ditch, erroneous, muffled—Jesus in the sink of the Colosseum, not on high Golgotha; Cleopatra frigid in the mistletoe of Gaul; or the first man to die on Mars or Uranus. Will he have time to notice (or sufficient emotion?—will that have been trained-out?) that he suffocates in scenery which he cannot even use for metaphor, much less life? He won't know the name of the rock he falls on. My wife on the tiles—to spare the rugs, upholstery. Me near Remnant Mesa. The answer is No."

By now the road had begun to rise and fall—hard climbs, steep drops—and the warmth of day, despite clouds, was rising. No remnant would remain. The ground beneath the snow was colder, the snow was thickening—not ice yet but poised. My feet were the ice.

Look. This is not my line of work at all, not the tune to which my faculties march. I may have to die of boredom, embarrassment—one more failed scoutmaster, draped on the rocks. I'm capable of spelling it out for you, in every increasingly pressurized moment—finding stripped howling language to compel your company every step of my way toward agony, physical and mental desperation; but you've read Jack London, you've seen Yukon movies (Preston Foster, Bruce Cabot—eyelashes frosted). May I leave it to you?—Chinese-opera scenery? You have all the elements; build it around me—the night, the struggle. It had started well, was getting bad, would clearly get worse unless an Army tank—nothing else could make it—should have left Gallup, say, three hours ago intent on nothing but our personalized rescue. *How much worse?* of course. That is all no more than the gears of melodrama; do your work on the weather, the road conditions; leave me free to dissect the *action* for you.

After three or four hills and their drops, I was scared. Frost-bite, trench-foot, amputations, stumps. I called to Blix "Stop please."

He obeyed so quickly that Dora walked into him; and he not only stopped but, moving her gently aside, came toward me. He stood a moment, silent, a foot from my face.

I extended my left hand and gripped his shoulder (to steady myself to remove my left shoe and check for frost-bite).

He accepted, stood still but he said "What must I do?"

"You're doing it," I said. "Prop me up a minute while I saw off this foot."

He said, "No, I mean *me*. What must I do now?"

"Feel my foot and see if it's frozen yet."

"It's not," he said, not even looking down.

"Thanks, Doc," I said. "You learned a lot in four years."

"No, tell me," he said.

"*You're* the doctor," I said.

"*You're* the man that's made it—tell me what I must do. Now."

Massaging my wet foot—far warmer than my hand!—I tasted relief. I thought he meant *now*, our physical dilemma—how must he, our Volunteer-in-Service, serve us now? how dodge us past death? I was not alone then. So I said, half whispering to spare Dora (*what?*), "Go back up front and put right foot after left for another six miles and pray through your teeth for the clouds to hold and the highway to be there where we left it, bumper-to-bumper traffic, hot soup and warm baths and eiderdown beds."

"No." He waited, bearing my weight. "No. After that—" as though that plain miracle were guaranteed, a matter of form, just round the next bend. I *was* alone.

"Wait till then," I said. "You may have me to ship east for burial, stiff as a popsicle, twice as sweet. That'll keep you busy, take your mind off yourself." I was done with my feet, I'd released his shoulder. My heart was still racing—the altitude—my breaths, even standing still, were little yips, love-breaths, ecstasy. I needed to move.

But Blix held ground. In full voice, to spare nobody, he said "Help me."

"Why me?" I said. I could just see Dora's back. She was still faced forward, awaiting her leader, her sneakers well out of sight under snow.

"You're the only white man within twenty miles."

"Then hump your black ass, boy, and tote me *home*."

"You're my oldest friend."

I hummed three notes of "Hearts and Flowers," as though blowing a comb. "Not good enough," I said.

"You've made it," he said.

"Made what?"

"Your way out."

"Out to where?" I said, "—Remnant Mesa by night, on hoof through snow?"

"Tell me how," he said.

I decided he meant it, was really *asking*. The truth seemed simple— "Because I wanted to."

"Not good enough," he said.

"Blix, I'm freezing. Lead me out and I'll plan your whole future— an entirely happy life, money-back guarantee."

Dora came toward us three steps and waited, facing Blix's back.

Meaning what? I wondered. *Is she audience or client or investigator for the prosecution?* I spoke past Blix to her—"Dora, tell him what to do."

"Stay back," Blix said but did not turn to her.

She said "OK" and retracted a step.

I said to Blix, "You're asking about her?—or is she already settled?"

"—Her," he said.

"Let *her* say then."

"She won't do that." He had spoken full voice from the start, no concealment. I'd accepted his lead.

"Let me ask her," I said.

"For yourself or me?"

"Oh Jesus—for *you*. All *my* questions were answered two weeks ago. You are facing a man who is Fully Informed."

"Liar," Blix said.

"Shall I ask her? She'll answer. They answer me."

He turned and faced her.

I remembered his chronic myopia—how much could he see? He could strike a match and test her. But then—O, Tara!—clouds broke on the moon. We were instantly blanched, our shadows pitched silently forward in snow.

She was watching him—watching, not searching or consuming or extracting.

Blix broke and turned to me. "Now you're in trouble. Clouds lifting. You'll freeze."

We all looked up and, as in some old DeMille Bible film, the dome had cracked. Our warming clouds were rapidly yawning on a sky like a gullet, black and bottomless. Where there had been only muzz and moisture, there were now fierce stars by the tens of thousands that seemed (for the first time in my experience) set, not in one plane of uniform distance (a Ptolemaic globe) but at infinitely variable heights and depths. Desert clarity. We seemed—all three, staring up, bathed with light—under desperate treatment, chosen for some titanic ray-therapy as last resort and pinned here now under massive bombardment. Dora's sclerosis. Blix's bad lung. My what? Or was it therapy? Perhaps annihilation? We were withering as we stood.

Blix said "We'd better move" and took steps to go.

He was passing Dora when I said "No. Listen."

"To what?" he said.

"My Last Words to Man." I sniffed once to show that I thought I was joking. "You'll never walk alone—but you sure as Hell can *run*." I expected more would follow but my mouth hung empty.

Blix said "Is that my answer?"

"Yep."

"Warm thanks."

"Make 'em hot," I said and stamped my dead feet.

He turned and took the lead again; we all trudged on.

Another hour, worse with every step—and we never paused, never spoke a syllable (breath was too scarce). In the first twenty minutes of open sky, the snow had frozen stiff—so suddenly that in memory it seems to *clank* shut at the instant of rigidity. Our wet feet labored now to break its crust; and since in any case the shoulder was narrowing (the barbed wire on our right had snagged me now twice; my jacket was ruining, shoes long since ruined), Blix led us down into the road—a lesser evil. The mud was still soft, warmer than the snow though it couldn't hold for long at the present rate of chilling. All wind had dropped. Nothing whatever could return the fleeing warmth—unless, by *fiat*, there should be another day, a sunrise tomorrow. Eight hours at least. We were utterly flayed. So was the desert, this half of the earth. Lidless, stripped. Nothing between us and entropy. Three running-down lives in a running-down world.

Maybe it had *run* down, the world, there—we the last hold-outs, doomed but *here*. Another victory—I'd have made it unaided to the absolute end (unless I should drop now, before Blix and Dora) when she had bailed-out with so little time to go, two bearable weeks. I was thinking by now—or tasting, touching triumph. I was bare of regrets as a six-weeks baby. I could see the questions that would go unanswered as clearly as the moon. Why did I want it? Simply because I had ceased to need her? How had I come to that so soon? How does it happen to a human being?—that after ten million years of herd-life, pair-life, he wants pure freedom, the freedom of a child (not to yearn or lean), of a primal cell with no need to divide, no thought of conjugation, bathed in hot salt seas for the few days it has, few hours, minutes? Unanswered and, now, unanswerable. By me at least. *I will not care.* I would die unpuzzled, if nothing else. Not appeased, not pleased but not defiant either and, now, not puzzled. A youngish ox (who might have pulled his load) led lowing, not bellowing, to the slaughter.

Oh I knew the world was there, where we'd left it—the searchlight beacon from the Gallup airport showed clearly now that the sky had lifted, a rising-collapsing stroke of light on our left hand. Little Piper-Cubs could be puttering in every minute now, hauling what?—rich Indians to the Shalimar Motel? Steaks huge enough to gorge every mouth and doggy-bagsful for the wolves at the hogan, the children, Grandma; warm rooms, hot water, warm beds.

But the light's place was rigid. It would not recede, not fall behind us. When it first appeared—Blix pointed it out, not speaking—I had welcomed it as a buoy, a still point against which to judge our forward progress; but now, much later, it was where it had been. Was it following us, at precisely our speed? Or were we not moving at all but on a treadmill, the earth sliding beneath us, consuming our efforts? I would never arrive to claim my reward, to say what I'd learned—how I'd foiled her death, her punishment by the simple expedient of desiring it, *requiring* it. So by her own lights—motive and purpose—she has died in vain, her gunshot as silent as an ice-crack at the pole. *No one there to hear it.* Yet I did hear of course—not the shot itself (I'd been ten miles away) and not at once but now its fullest double meaning— her intent and mine; her accomplishment and mine. Now, could I ever tell it? To tell it is to beat her at her own hateful game. I called to Blix again—"Please stop!" My voice now was frail, the sound as scary and disembodied as though it had leaked from the power wire overhead that had been our companion every step of the way, silent till now.

Didn't he hear or did he refuse? He didn't stop.

I knew I'd made noise at least—Dora glanced back once but also kept moving.

I would overtake her, touch Blix direct. But I'd need that strength for later—for worse than this. I stopped in my tracks, let them gain a few steps; then I called from that distance—"Blix, I'll answer you."

He took another three steps before he spoke, still never stopping— "Too late. I know my own."

"Then tell me that."

They were twenty yards ahead now. "No use to you," he said.

"Let *me* decide that."

No word. They walked on.

I would not catch up now. I would soon be alone. "Wait, anyhow, please."

Blix said "We can't." His voice was unshaken by his stride, unfatigued. *He works here, he's at home.*

I knew that was his answer, reached since he'd asked me—that his *we* meant *them*, him and Dora. They would make it safely out, regardless of me, and pack their junk and leave tomorrow together, without her children, by bus from Gallup. Or stay and sink here, two more litter factories, their own home-industry, their lifetime's work—a mutual surrender: Blix to a simple need fillable elsewhere, under a roof at least, in a dry bed at least, where his own simpler language is understood and answered; Dora to a further more humiliating bondage than any laid on her by her people, their past life, her own short ugly life, her body gone mad now and crawling toward its death. Not crawling—striding. I needed to laugh but again gauged my breath and knew I must wait. What mattered was to catch them.

And in four minutes of agony, I did. (I'm speaking precisely; agony is accurate—the sense, with each step, of over-extension of every resource; my heart blundering wildly against chest and throat like a terrified child in a cell walled with paper from which air is draining; can the paper contain him as it crushes inward? can he tear through and breathe?) I reached out now and touched Dora not Blix. "Listen, please."

She stopped and turned and faced me, smiling.

My eyes, blurred and dancing, saw a moving light above her—a star, not falling but belting the sky, laterally, slowly. "Look there," I said.

It was not a tactic but it stopped Blix and held him. He followed my pointing finger, waited a moment. He was breathing calmly.

I said "What is it?"

Dora shook her head—did she see it at all? or a different sky entirely, wreathed with crippling reptiles picked out in light, or opening in tunnels on her new safer life that Blix had confirmed?

"A satellite," Blix said. "First one I've seen, even out here."

"—Watching *you*," I said. "Another VISTA spy."

"Good luck," he said up toward it.

Dora giggled and looked down to me. (The road sloped up; I was downhill from her, even three feet away.) "Watching you," she said.

"Why me?" I smiled too.

"You know," she said.

I did. It was what I had run to tell them. "I killed her."

Dora nodded, murder no doubt weekly news to her.

Blix stood in place, still watching the satellite, but said "What else is new?"

"I did," I said. "I'd know."

"You think you did," he said, "—like to think you did."

"I know—yes."

He looked down toward me then. (Was the satellite gone? I'd lost it anyhow.) "That's your answer," he said, "—that you stopped us for?"

"Yes."

"To what question please?"

I could not remember. I laughed and said "Help me."

"That was it," he said.

He had lost me entirely—fear of him stood up now with other fears: night, cold, exhaustion. Blix would be her avenger—she had written to him, Last Written Words. He bore her blessing to condemn, punish, abandon me here. It had been her plan; she had won after all. For the moment, I believed that—or it squatted on my chest and throat, a stifling weight, therefore surely a fact. But I said "I'm lost."

He stood in place, watching me, offering nothing.

"I don't understand you," I said, "—don't live here, don't speak the language, can barely breathe the air, what was the question?"

Dora took one step down toward me. "He asked you, awhile ago"— she pointed behind me to where we'd been—"to say what must he do."

I remembered. Right—weeks, years, miles back. And I'd offered banter, shirked a clear duty. I waited a moment to be entirely sure— that I knew a true answer, that I wanted to give it. I *knew* and not only wanted but needed to give it. My earlier joke about Last Words had hardened—a serious possibility. I was near some extreme. They seemed merely inconvenienced—Blix and Dora—delayed in their flight toward a smiling South. Oranges, cures, children rising around them. But I knew better. I gave it to her. "Kill you now."

She turned back to Blix as though he would obey me instantly and she must meet him, ready but calm.

He had heard me—I'd seen him flinch—but now he'd turned and started again. Four, five steps away.

She looked to me and said "How come?"

"Because you are dying this slowest death. Because he is planning to take you off from here, thinking he understands what you need and can use—when what's got him trapped is your warm hole on cold bedsprings. They grow on *trees*. More than half the world's got one— and yours is cooling." I knew—as I said it—that it meant no more to her than a Mozart aria and forgave myself before I'd even finished. I *knew* it was that—an aria of my own (well-built, self-pleased) that barely concerned her; a soliloquy of rage simply flung at her as the nearest ear. *I am not even cruel.*

But she stood and seemed to think. No more backward checks on Blix—I could barely see him beyond her. Then she said "How about me waiting?"

"—Waiting?"

"Just till I die." She thumbed behind her, again as to a place, a clear geographical destination, visible on maps, toward which we would move if we moved again.

"When will that be?"

"Pretty soon"—no shrug, no smile; she was dealing in facts.

"Who told you?"

She pointed, not looking—the Gallup light. "Hospital doctor."

"Sclerosis?"

She nodded.

"You may have years; it can take twenty years."

"I won't take 'em though."

"You'll stop it?" I said.

"Yep."

"When?"

She calculated. In the dark and with her so foreign, it was like— what?—witnessing an animal's decision. The stock analogies for primitive peoples—cats, panthers, cougars. Are they thinking at all or in a state of being as inviolate as bread?—that dense and pure. I thought of rushing on her, splitting skull in my hands to trap this thought she was boring through now, a mole in loam—children crush pet fish to see what they hold.

She said "Let me wait."

"Sure," I said. "OK by me. I was just giving answers, just aiming to please."

She waited again but with no hint of thought. Now she was searching—my face, eyes, hands. She said "Then you."

She had skipped several steps in a human argument. I said "Me what?"

"You go on—do it now."

I meant to laugh but didn't. "Kill you?"

"Yep."

"Why me?"

"You good at it."

I waited, then looked round me—tracked snow, barbed wire, scattered brush ten yards away. I remembered her kinsman—no matches, no fire. I finally could laugh. "I forgot my tools."

"What you need?" she said. "I'm making it easy."

She was—I saw. Nothing so obvious as chin-back, throat taut; but in her silent breathing, her short bird-bones, entirely destructible. She could not only have been easily killed here by hand with the little strength I had, but killed entirely—razed, no remains, all instantly dissolved to earth, thin air; or departed, bag and baggage, for her afterworld. I said "Wait; you can wait" and stepped to go.

She was in the path, not moving. "No. Now, you please."

I was ten inches from her. She was giving off cold, not body heat but cold more intense than the night's—waste from her burning. A *different animal*. I looked again for Blix. Nothing. Gone. Past the crest of the next hill. Two dogs began barking then. A quarter-mile ahead— or five or at hand? Dogs? Coyotes? Wolves? Navajo wolves? "Blix will do it," I said.

She nodded—"Slow."

"But you wanted that."

She waited. "Yep." Then she turned and led off. No waiting for me. No squaw's place in line.

We moved toward the howling. Wherever, whatever, it was strengthening, nearing. I thought of Blix, already torn and consumed and of us straining now in every fiber to add the remains of ourselves to the feast—as eaters or eaten? Cold suppers indeed.

She spoke as she moved—no pause, no looking back, her breath completely adequate. "You think you winning."

I heard it as a question, though her voice never rose, and I quickly said "Yes."

"You ain't," she said.

It had been a stated fact—what I'd taken as question. The first fact she'd stated since the cause of her illness, the snake touched in school. All the rest had been shifting—lies, questions, half-jokes, trashy speculations. (Who was she? Who was her father? Where was her mother, her two alleged children? Who were all those drunks and where had they vanished to? Whose truck had that been? Was her name what she claimed?—or what Blix had told me; she'd never said her own name, certainly not mine.) I said "Dora?"

She didn't turn.

"Dora?"—again, louder. The howling could have drowned me. Or the wires overhead. They were humming now steadily with an idiot force—feeding power to whom? to start what engines? Or bearing what voices, planning what? in what language?

No turn. But no quickening either, no fear or flight. This girl, whoever, was holding ground—only the ground was snow and was sliding beneath her as she pumped on toward survival, effortlessly. (*She* should be telling this—a calm winter's tale, cool pastoral, a day in the hills by purling streams, ample breath, warming blood, obedient limbs.)

Speech was difficult again, simple breath. But I said "I've won."

After three steps—"What?"

"—That I'm free now in my life, have what I need."

"Need what?"

"*Room.*"

"You ain't got room?"

"—To live my life, work."

"What you mean by work?"

"I'm a writer, I write."

"What sort of writing?"

"Stories."

"What you going to tell them?"

"What I know—how I've won."

Another set of steps—"That's what you won?"

"All I tried to win."

She laughed—a soft luxurious laugh, unjogged by her steps. "And you think you'll get it home?"

"With you helping," I said.

"I'm helping."

"How?"

"—Leading," she said.

She was. Toward what? "What's howling?" I said.

"Dogs."

"You sure?"

"Yep," she said.

"Whose?"

"Bekis," she said.

A name? A word? "You know him?"

Silence.

"He kin to you?"

Silence.

They are not dogs. She is leading me to them—as I sent Blix to them. But I didn't feel more fear. Feeling had quit. "Where is Blix?" I said.

"Who?"

"Blix," I said. "Blix, your friend."

Silence. But her head shook, clearly, side to side.

What—and in what language—does she mean? Where is Blix—and on whose side? Who are we now? What do we become? "OK. Lead," I said—as though she had stopped or was losing heart, when she moved like an engine, the perfect machine of my punishment, fed by power that leaked from the wires now roaring above us. For I was in punishment—I saw—to the eyes. What would constitute the end?—death, release, maiming? We were climbing a hill now, the first for a mile. Surely it was the last screen between the dogs and us—me. I dropped a little behind her, not from choice or fear but necessity—something was failing. Or trying to fail—every three or four steps, with a clear metal *tick* a spot on my brain, on the left frontal lobe (I could have found it with a needle, gouged it into action), attempted to refuse, to halt me here. A soft fall in snow warmer than I, sleep till they woke me. *They?*

The top of the hill. Moonlight flattened the foreground beneath us. At our left—a quarter-mile—the single dark house I had seen at dusk, one sizable tree, a parked truck, silvered. The dogs' home—Bekis's? Was Blix there now? Intending what? With Dora's drunk kin?—their drunk wife as leader?

No. She said "Wait."

I took the order, stopped, sucked loudly for air.

But she hadn't meant me. Her own steps continued. Her right hand extended quickly before her and she said again "Wait." She was calling to a distant, approaching figure—a man two hundred yards beyond her.

Though she had not raised her voice, he obeyed. Stopped, facing us. *Us?*—maybe only her. Or me.

I waited. Passive suffering. No ordeal at all nor the charged aftermath but a death dumbly welcomed—not even welcomed, *borne.* A guy with his frozen balls strangulated, his penis retracted to a bloodless little tit, takes death without a peep—from him or the sky. Sorry; I waited.

But she went on; her meeting-place was *there*, ahead, plotted where the man had been stopped and stood. No question of *her* waiting now.

I was the waiter and scrambled toward her will.

Blix—having gone where, for what, since he left us? Her last letter to him—*light to your life.* He seemed baked there by light—moonlight, monstrous cold cookery; unable to move or save himself, *willing* in fact to accept this death so he might obey orders. Punish me. Light to *my* life. There are things the dead forbid, have *died* to forbid and—even dead—have ample means to enforce.

She was six steps ahead now—I'd counted them off. She cast a shadow. I used her own call—"Wait." Mine was plea not command.

But she stopped, again signaled Blix to stay; then she came back to me. She waited a step away, downhill from me now.

It's her. The malignant part. No, the *just* part, at last. Whatever other senses and functions were failing, I saw that clearly. Registered. I opened my mouth (I had caught a second wind in my moments of rest and was nose-breathing quietly); thin frozen air rammed in. Something still fought to stop me. But I won and said "Pardon"—and intended it chiefly as question not gift.

She shook her head slowly, then giggled, stamped her sneakers.

She didn't know the word.

"I'm sorry," I said.

"OK" she said. She still was baffled. But not by my second word— simply by newness. She was twenty-two years old. No one had ever yet asked her forgiveness. Or offered it.

I thought I was dying—simply failing in my tracks—but I said "OK what?"

"OK we got to move." She pointed to the hogan—"Or he be mad."

He was. He tried to kill us—mad or afraid? I could understand anger—that Blix stood in moonlight on the road before his house (a hundred yards before) and waited for us or for Dora as she'd asked; that this world was not big enough for him, his dogs and us—but as his first shot fired, I consciously thought, "No fear, no fear. I'm not followed now—actually alone; what I've meant to be."

The bullet struck the snow six feet ahead of Dora. She was twenty yards from Blix.

I walked on in silence but I studied her for advice—my own reflex, exhausted as I was, was to hit the deck, proceed by crawling or sleep here and die. I thought, "The first shot ever fired at me." Then remembered—"The second. Will there be a third? Will that one land?" I tried to care but couldn't.

Dora strode on as calmly as on Miami Beach; and the dogs at least had quieted, gun-shy, in terror.

So I tried to mimic her and managed at least *continuance*. I wondered only one thing and asked her as we moved through the trough of that shot—"You know him you said?"

She nodded, a silent "Yep."

Another shot. Still just ahead of Dora and a little beyond, only this much more conclusive than the last—that if he had a target, the bullseye was Dora or else he was wild and striking out blind. I remembered how tender, how *at-mercy* I'd felt last night, earlier today, and wondered why not now—with a crazed redskin pumping hot lead my way and I under moonlight brighter than some noons? But again I didn't, couldn't—no certainty of safety, no clear death-wish, but no reluctance to die—and when we reached Blix—Dora stopped three steps from him—he must have seen me smiling. I was too cold to know or to alter a muscle.

He looked past her to me and smiled—first since when?—and said "How are you now?"

"Dying happy," I said—I'd read my own state backward from his grin.

"Why happy?" he said, not denying I was dying.

No answer came to me—not to that; I couldn't think. Yet happy I was, if being past fear and with all debts paid is a brand of happiness. I stepped up toward him, leaving Dora behind us.

Another shot, in my old tracks behind her.

"What's his problem?" I said.

"This is his," Blix said.

"She knows him," I said.

He had not looked to Dora since our present meeting but said to me quietly, "She may say she does."

The links in Blix's thought and speech were weak now as mine—like tramps in Beckett, all connectives dissolved by acid fatigue; or like Jesus and Mary, Jesus and Judas, all courtesy, all human ritual abandoned—for pure discourse, *intercourse* (intention, comprehension). One dog cranked up again—his master back asleep? his master dead, vanished? or waiting to draw an infallible bead? I stepped between Blix and him, as best I could figure. Did I think I was a shield?—and if so, shielding what? Blix's simple head and heart? For what?—a future of nursing Dora? stuffing bedpans to a paralyzing Indian for ten, twenty years in a filthy room? Too tired to know. I had simply moved, acted, abandoned myself again to accident—or plan. To die together maybe, one bullet for both, Dora our survivor. What would Dora do? Stand a moment and look, then leave us to stiffen six miles from her truck (was it hers at all?) and walk straight forward in her socks and sneakers to Bekis's house (was Bekis a person?), join him there in the dark. Warmth, giggle, hump, sleep, warmth. The wires overhead had quieted, were silent—a safety blackout or mission accomplished?

Blix renewed his smile. "Why happy?" he said.

"I know," I said. "There are people like me."

"So what," he said—no question at the end. "There are more like me."

"Should I go on smiling then? Or bellow? Or die? Doc—prescribe! prescribe!"

"Just hush and breathe gently. You're getting *air*. There's air to go round. Uncle Sam provides it for all us white folks, even out here—just a small service charge; we'll bill you in April. Colored don't use it." He smiled again, breathed deeply, a demonstration—that this air, a frigid blade thin enough to pare cells, was the warmest stoutest drink at a good day's end.

I was better. I nodded "Look. You left us," I said. "Why were you headed back?—just now when we saw you, the top of that hill."

"I can hear the road. I was coming to tell you." His arms stayed down, too tired to point; but his head ducked backward.

So he could. So could I. Above the dogs, the still-silent wires and despite the fact that the airport light still searched *there* beyond us, unpassed, uncaptured—the wheels of cars. There was another world. This one. Ours joined it. Waiting, reachable, if not engaged in rescue. I asked Blix still—"Why did you come back?"

"To tell you to hurry."

"I can't."

"You'll have to. Basketball traffic's what you're hearing now, two miles ahead. Game over in Zuni. When the last fan's passed on his way to Gallup—forget it; road closed; we'd have to walk till dawn. Twenty more miles."

Dora took three steps—obedience—then stopped beyond Blix and looked back, waiting.

The dogs were asleep or dead or had got her family scent.

Blix moved in on me, took my elbow, pulled me toward him—the direction of safety.

Oh Jesus I'm safe. "I can't," I said. (I had been safe here; why depart for the world?)

He still was smiling—so now was Dora. "We can't tote you."

"I don't ask that," I said.

"Then why are you smiling?"

I felt that I knew, that if they would wait—postpone their precious lives, say, twenty seconds till I organized my heart, lungs, freed my dry tongue—I could say it for them here in a line so lucid, so instantly permanently usable as to constitute recompense for all my family's damage, hers and mine—paid in full now to Blix Cunningham and the girl he'd chosen (whatever her name), to Atso and Neely, Mae Clain, the apple-brandied drunks, and paid where I'd won it: on a lethal little sideroad near Remnant Mesa under Navajo guns, an unfiltered moon, seven thousand feet in the air above my home. But it gobbed my throat (just the words, short breath; no hand at my larynx now, spectral or human). So when Blix pulled again—on my wrist now, still holding me, my pulse warming under him—I moved off beside him;

and when I could speak (knew it all, controlled my means), the paved road stretched there clearly before us (taillights, heaters—*my* goal) and Blix had run ahead again to flag salvation; so I said to myself (which is to say, to you) since Dora lacked the English words to hear me, even— "You know every answer now, or all you need. What we are—we three, the name of our spectacle: *Happy Though Breathing*. And beyond this night—how I caused it, how I didn't. Why she did it, why I'll never know. Why I'm glad and smiling. *Glad* despite my begging pardon, two miles back, under force but not from guns—because, look, she has *given* it, an act of oblivion. I am both free and working. I have forced you this far. You know this story, know all I know once I've told you this last—she is dead and dumb. Hammer-dead. Her name was Beth."

HIS FINAL MOTHER

CRAWFORD LANGLEY was twelve years old and still a child; but the first traits of manhood were on him—tall for his age, no baby fat, no pointless smiles, a broad forehead and steady gray eyes that gave his head a claim on the dignified notice of adults. So it was early in that crucial year when he took what he saw as his first grown step. He managed to stamp out his old nickname. It was nothing more obnoxious than *Ford*, but he calmly told his friends not to use it.

A few children laughed and tried to taunt him—*Fordie* or even *Model-T*. He smiled but then refused to know them; and since he was anyhow the main child to know in his town and school—the funniest surely, the most open-handed—they all came round in a matter of days, even his teachers and the baseball coach; even his mother, who privately called him *Strut* and *Dub*. All but his father. Crawford's father stuck with *Ford* since that had been his own father's name. Crawford liked and trusted his father enough to humor him, and causes for that came thick and fast once his mother was gone.

She left in an instant—no warning or pain, so far as they knew. She was in the backyard, hanging an ancient quilt on a clothes line and then she knelt. Crawford and his father had left for the day, but the cook had watched it clearly from the porch. She said "Miss Adele went

to her knees like somebody needing to pray, *hard*. Then it look like she
needed to rest her head—she went right on down slow to her side and
smoothed the grass and stroked her hair. She was cool as a window by
the time I touched her."

The cook phoned school and Crawford was home on his bike in ten
minutes (his father was an hour away, taking an Irish setter pup to his
lonely aunt). By then the ambulance men were there; her body was
covered in the dim front hall. Young as he was, Crawford walked
straight to her, lifted the sheet and leaned in a slow curve to kiss the
forehead. *Cold as glass*—he thought it before the cook could warn
him. And though he loved his mother deeply, they'd all understood
her racing heart would take her soon.

He expected tears and when none came, he told himself his natural
feelings were in shock now. But before he took his hand off her arm,
a tall new thing stood up in his mind. It was not a thought or even a
feeling. It was more like watching his hands grow strong in a slow
instant. He hoped it was one more sign of manhood. It calmed him at
least and dried his eyes.

He told the ambulance men where to go, Bond's funeral home.
Then he tested the newborn strength again—it poured right through
him like iron in his blood. So he thanked the cook and asked her to
wait till his father was back. She nodded and went to fix normal supper.
Then Crawford thought he had to go pray. The word surprised him—
Pray for what? But when the cook had shut the kitchen door, he obeyed
himself and climbed to his room.

There he stood in the midst of the rug and waited to see if any word
came, any message from him for God or man. But again his mind was
still and firm. He thought he'd taken another grown step, no need to
lean on others or the sky. He could handle this trial with his own strong
body and his new brave mind—bravery was still his main ambition.
He went to his shelf and found the old copy of *Robinson Crusoe*, his

pick among books in recent months. Then he stretched on his bed and turned to page one.

Crusoe was sunk in waste and shame, and hellbound for shipwreck, before Crawford thought of himself again or the world below his silent room. What brought him back was his father's car door, slamming in the drive. Crawford said one sentence aloud to his ceiling, "This'll kill Dad too and I'll be gone." He knew it was hardly courageous thinking, but he didn't wait to understand the solemn further questions he raised—*Gone where and why?* He sped downstairs to tell the sizable news before his father could step indoors and call "Adele?" and find her vanished. One of the main things Crawford knew was strong in his mind as he faced the father he'd long since tried to shield from harm— *This boy is a whole lot shakier than me.*

Later that night when their friends were gone, Crawford's father said they better take a walk before bedtime if they meant to sleep. They hadn't gone walking at night for years—since the time they had to admit in silence that they had nothing better to talk about than baseball or school—and tonight anyhow Crawford wanted to keep on reading *Crusoe.* But his father stood, so the boy said "Yes sir." And they went right out through a kitchen that now was broad and empty as the plains of Gobi.

After a speechless fifteen minutes, they left strong moonlight and entered the woods. His father was leading and, though they were taking their same old path, the whole idea of a walk was strange. So Crawford asked himself *What will we be when all this settles?* He was still not asking *Where are we going, here tonight?* In any case no answer showed. He guessed he was safe though and tried to keep step, but his father stumbled a time or two, and then Crawford brushed his enormous back which seemed too hot for the time and place.

The woods stopped sooner than either one expected, and their feet were on the verge of the river before their eyes had opened enough to see the sudden end of the path. Crawford laughed a little at the near escape.

But his father said "It might have been better."

"Sir?"

"Drowning tonight, not waiting around—I mean me, Ford. Not you, not yet."

Crawford knew his father was an excellent swimmer; so he thought the words were no cause for worry, just some kind of smoke from the hot pain in him. The boy moved on into reaching distance; but his father stayed still—no touch, no look. Then fear, like a tickling feather in sleep, flicked Crawford's mind. This man could do his will on a boy—*Has he lost his mind? Does he blame me?* So the boy chose his latest version of a grown man's voice and told his father "Sir, she's fine now. You just need to wait."

"For what?" His father's voice was changing, darker and deep.

Crawford said "You mostly tell me time's the big doctor."

"I've told you some lies."

The fear struck now in Crawford's throat and begged him to run, but the boy knew he had to keep talking. "What I really meant—she's waiting for you. In Heaven, all well."

The man's throat rasped at itself to spit, and his new voice said "You don't believe that."

Crawford was suddenly shivering cold, though the night was warm. He told himself the man was wrong. With his mother's encouragement for years the boy had thought of her long-dead pitiful father as safe in Heaven, literally hunting and a far better shot than ever on Earth. And since Crawford's own father prayed every night and often commended the habit to him, the boy now felt a huge trapdoor fall open in the ground nearby—if he took three steps in any direction, he'd surely drop through an endless hole. In an almost final hope of rescue, the boy said "Sir, I don't feel right about any of this."

The man said "Then you must be growing."

"Sir?"

"Nothing's right and won't ever be again. Get that through your head."

It was already there; Crawford felt it as a hot ball stuck far back in the quick of his mind. So he said "I need you to calm down now."

The man's big hand shot out and seized Crawford's neck.

The fingers were colder even than the boy, though he thought he recognized the scrape of his father's thick palm. Crawford said "I'm still not strong as you." The man's grip eased. Then suddenly he seemed to be gone, that strange and quick. Crawford waited for a clue and finally spoke as strong as he could, "Am I out here alone?"

From what seemed a far distance, the man said "You always were."

The boy had roamed these woods his whole life and was all but sure he knew the way home, even in dark this heavy and close. But he thought that if he moved, any way, he might crash into his father's body or whatever changed man waited out here. So he tried again to say a prayer, *"Our Father . . . Lord, please—"* Crawford knew the words—they gleamed in his head as hard as signs—but some new way the world around him, the actual air, refused to let words out of his lips. He'd read of men abandoned by God—young Crusoe himself for his worldly wrongs. Still what had *he* done, Crawford Langley, to pay like this? Had he someway caused his mother pain in broad daylight, alone in the yard? At the thought an arm of the night rushed the boy's cold face and choked his words.

What felt like half his lifetime passed, though a real forty minutes; and then Crawford broke through the maze of dark woods. There set in a space that looked familiar was a house he guessed was his own old house, dark in every window and door. In all his years he'd never seen it completely dark. Hadn't he and his father left it well-lit? The boy was past a child's automatic fears—of falls and darkness—but it came to him now that, in this house, the man who left him alone by the river was hid and ready.

Crawford also knew there was nowhere else. He had school friends and their parents liked him; but he couldn't turn back and run to them with such a wild story, not this late. All he could think was to set his face and volunteer for the rest of what was stored up for him, life or death.

He recognized the dent in the doorknob as he entered the kitchen; but from there on through, the dark was so thick he might have been walking on the far side of Venus. After four steps Crawford saw in his mind, as clear as fact, that his father was hid right now in his path. He saw a butcher knife in the hand that had never once punished him, so much as a slap. He saw the gray eyes wide as a wolf's, fixed on a boy and perfectly aimed.

Still the boy put out both arms before him to grope his way toward the foot of the stairs. If he got that far and his heart still worked, he knew he must try to find his own room and wait on his bed for a key to the meaning of this fresh news. Like all sane children with baffling, even murderous parents, he understood that something he himself had done—some unintended but last-straw fault—had brought this fate down on him, and rightly.

Each individual stair creaked out; but once Crawford stood intact at the top, he paused to test the air for warnings. Never in all his life in this house had it been so absolutely silent. He held in place till he heard his mind want one of two sounds—either the final slash of his father's vengeful knife or Crawford's own voice promising, *Dad, I'm sorry for my whole life. I swear I'll be anything you say.*

But still the boy was in one piece. So he crept on past his father's door (no crack of light), found his own empty bed and stretched on his back. This time he never tried to pray. What he tried was a thorough backward search of his recent life. His mind was clear, and a thousand details marched past his eyes. But no fault showed, nothing worth much more than a "Goddamnit, Ford" from his tired patient father.

So the boy kept coming round to the fact that, as lately as two or three Sundays ago, he and his father had walked an hour out into the fields. There'd been a hard rain the night before; and that was always a lucky time for the hobby they shared—arrowheads, shot or lost by the Tuscarora ages past (no Tuscarora left in the state for two hundred years).

And when Crawford dug out a clear quartz knife, white as glass—a priestly knife they'd only dreamed of—he trotted to his father, held out his shut hands as in a child's game and said "Pick one." At once his father tapped the left hand. Crawford grinned, cried out "It's Father's Day!" and opened his palm on the stupendous find. Father's Day was months ahead, but his father took it with a look that deeply underlined what he mostly showed and had said more than once—he prized this boy. Surely this moment the sacred point was on his father's desk downstairs with the only other treasures he kept—a bullet dug from an ancestor's leg and, locked in a tiny glass box, one curl of his father's sister's hair (she died at two weeks).

For a moment Crawford wanted to find the crystal knife. What else now under this strange new roof might bring him luck or help defend him? But then he thought in some terrible way it might be used in the night against his heart. He remembered how Aztec priests had cut the beating hearts from men with just such points to feed their gods. At the chance—almost the certainty—of that, Crawford spread his arms wide and shut his eyes. Still facing up now he only waited—balked as any mind can be but likewise ready, he told himself, though soon he slid into scrappy dreams, then exhausted sleep.

Crawford knew it was day, well before he woke. His last dream told him he'd lasted the night and that now he was fully a man but alone. His eyes came open—no, still night. Then as he lay in the ongoing quiet, he knew that yes a light was growing but not at the window. In another minute he saw a glow was actually blooming, a great slow flower of morning light till his ceiling was patterned with numerous leaves in shades of cream and gold like nothing he'd ever seen or heard of. He wondered if he'd already died and this was his next home, high or low. But the same old lighting fixture hung there and, on a short string, the one plane model he'd ever finished. Whatever then, the mild colors and gradual speed of the bloom were saying he was past the threat in the heart of the night.

He rose on his elbows and looked to the door. He'd left it half-open, and now he saw where the light came from. It streamed from the hall in a narrow shaft, then spread in these strange shapes through his room. In a long stretch from the bed, he could reach and carefully test the beam with his hand. It was not only fine to see but the same temperature as his skin. So he had to be safe. He'd get up and make his way to what caused it.

The time it took to walk up the hall through the streaming glow seemed longer even than the moment when he touched his mother this afternoon and knew he was somehow as changed as she. For the first full time, in his mind Crawford saw her welcome face and heard her voice that had been the better part of what he loved for his first six years. He thought the day was bound to come when he'd miss her bitterly—not yet tonight. This hunt he was on, through what still seemed his father's house, was all his mind could manage now.

By now he stood at his parents' door. Never before had he seen it closed (his father's only dread was of traps). But the stream of light was coming from there, around the edges of the door and beneath it. The boy bent slowly and laid his ear on the wood to listen. At first he thought he could hear a whole crowd of friendly voices, but he couldn't hear words. He waited till his ears adjusted. It was just two voices, a man and a woman—more likely a girl, that young and bright (he'd only begun to lean toward girls). Soon he knew the man was his father but younger too; the girl stayed strange. The boy never understood a word, though he knew from their tone and slowness they were peaceful.

A thing he'd always respected was privacy, even more now as his own body grew its secrets. But here this late on this big day, his heart had got so huge in his chest that he knew he had no other hope than to turn this knob and take what came at his eyes or mind.

After maybe two minutes his pupils narrowed enough to see, in the core of the glare, his father seated at the foot of his bed. His father wore his regular pajamas, cool sky-blue and neatly pressed. That much was normal. He sat like that each night of his life for five or ten minutes with both eyes shut, saying his prayers in a deep silence (his painful kneecaps kept him from kneeling). Now though his head was tilted up, and his eyes were halfway open in the blaze. His lips were moving as if he went on saying whatever he'd said while Crawford listened outside at the door, but if words came they were swept away. Crawford thought his own body might also drown or burn past hope; but in his new bravery, he knew not to leave.

In another minute the boy's reward began to rush him. Either she somehow came from above or had been there right along, too bright to see. Whatever, suddenly a girl stood clear and tall by his father: the single sight both boy and man could watch from then on. It took Crawford another slow wait to see her face and know it was someway kin to the face that hung in a frame by his father's bed—Crawford's mother before her wedding, lovely and strong as he still could see her in occasional dreams from his cradle days. The picture showed no more than her head, a graceful neck and the top of a yellow dress. But the girl here now wore the same dress which seemed to fall right down to the floor, though it drowned in light; and her dark eyes were surely the same.

The boy thought he was brave enough to say her name; at least he felt the powerful need. Let her hear his voice and then just laugh and call him *Dub* or *Strut* a last time. But before he stoked his courage for that, her face turned gradually in his direction and all but smiled before she faced his father again, closed his eyes with two long hands; and (like the mother she once had been), she helped him lie in place on the pillow before she was somehow gone again; and his father was covered with the old dark quilt, plainly asleep and harmless as any new pine in the woods.

The light continued long enough to see Crawford back to his own bed, then faded quickly. He sat at the foot and knew his father had surely prayed her back to life to tame him down and save her son. Then the boy slowly asked himself if he wanted to beg for a similar visit—now, he knew, was the only chance. But didn't that girl's face belong to his father, the girl he picked when he was not much older than Crawford tonight? The boy's oldest memories rose—himself in his mother's arms in a chair by the sunny window, consulting each other's eyes for secrets, then laughing together at what they found. It was still the face the boy loved most; it would be that all his life on Earth. And though it was gone from his daily world, it was maybe changeless and better in dreams.

Next he thought he could steal downstairs, find the quartz knife and bury it deep in a moonless corner. That would keep it safe, and him and his father, and leave it ready as food again for the hungry gods, if they were there still watching man. But no, he was tired and knew he was rescued. He gave one thought to how his mother had looked this morning, cheerful and firm but calling him back from the edge of the yard, giving him one last kiss on the brow, thumping his skull with a healthy finger and saying "Strut, *fly!* or you'll be late" when she was the one who'd flown in time.

So the tired boy stood, shucked his clothes (the room was still warm) and then for the first time entered his sheets as naked as he left her lovely body long ago in pain and blood. As his head lay back, he felt—again and for the last time—the hardness of that long black first trip to reach daylight. But the pain subsided and, through the rest of that short night, he slept like some boy thoroughly safe whose days hereafter will each be brave, whose nights will bring him—whenever he calls—the face and voice he understands are utterly gone: his only mother, lost forever, young and free for good and all.

THIS WAIT

THE FIRST few minutes after I died were the healing part. I'm fairly vague on what must have killed me, but I think I died in my own bed in my room at home and nobody with me—all upstairs asleep, my son and his boy, my one grandchild. I think that was it. I'd slept very soundly on a merciful drug, and I seem to recall waking up to die. I think my eyes came open in the dark, and I think a pleasant baritone voice said "Things are ready. Come on here now." I think I understood that I had a choice. I could say yes or no for a few years more, not forever to be sure.

I took a whole minute to calculate. I think I was some years short of fifty, but I probably knew I'd used my time. I knew I was sick. The word *radiation* is one old remnant that's clear in my new mind like luggage from a trip I'll never repeat. And I must have weighed my will to stay and what I thought it would do to my few kin, my handful of friends that would see me through. I think I decided they'd had all of me they could fruitfully use, that more of me now would be far harder than they ought to bear. I know for certain I answered aloud. I said "I'm ready as you. Take over." My last old thought was a single question—Who was *you*? Who had spoken? Who was I yielding to?

*

Till now, however much time has lapsed, I still lack answers but am calm in the wait. I won't describe the life I have, since no one living possesses the terms to gauge, much less to understand, the goodness I feel here now alone. I can say this much, *I'm entirely glad, though perfectly alone.* And I was a man, I seem to know, who thought I needed people near me most hours of the day and all of each night— one person at least and I seldom went begging.

What more I can say is, I wait so calmly because I remember those first few minutes I mentioned above. One moment I was flat on my bed in the night, saying "You take over." The next, I was sitting in tall green grass near a great beech tree with names that seemed familiar but weren't, carved into the bark in careful handsome Roman letters— *Anna, Walter, Sybil, Marc.* My mind was entirely at ease in my head; my hands were hands I knew on sight, though my old wedding band was gone. Somehow I raised my long right fingers in the general direction of the tree and beckoned. I know I wondered if birds would sing or a kindly child step toward me with food. Food was my one wish; I seemed to be hungry. And fairly soon a girl looked out from behind the beech. I knew I had one more choice to make and I beckoned again.

So she came into full view and walked toward me. I was steeply downhill; she moved down slowly on bare tender feet—a tall girl, dark hair and brows and a constant smile in the shape of a long symmetrical almond below brown eyes that seldom wavered. I know I recall her long soft dress, which was summer blue. I know that, before she was three steps from me, I thought I'd never seen anything to match—not in girls, not this well-made and kind. I was thoroughly wrong. Her next few moves were more unlikely than endless love, but I know they happened and only for me.

She walked till the fronts of both her ankles touched my knees which were folded before me, and she met my eyes.

I chose again, *Please.*

That freed her to kneel and open her dress. The breasts were young as she, high and lifting, more welcome again than any past sight—a scarcely grown girl in need of me. But then she slowly pressed on toward me till she brushed my lips.

And warm milk bathed my needy mouth. Well before I drank my fill, I knew she was my young mother returned, the girl that built me from one merged cell and met my eyes the instant I left her dim safe harbor for the lighted world. I also knew I could wait forever for answers to who had called me here—why and what for and would this end too?

Any hand that took my agonized mother, who died enraged with her reason gone, and made her new and sent her to greet me, surely means me well at the absolute least, though once she'd filled my hunger and pressed me down to sleep, she left again and has not been seen, for all the ease and thanks I feel and long to show.

FOOL'S EDUCATION

1. The Happiness of Others

THEY KILLED two hours of the twenty remaining over lunch at the Lamb, chewing each bite as long and mercilessly as though their stomachs held ravenous babies, open-mouthed to suck in the stream of tepid pap. The work of eating also saved them from talk, that and their pretense of fervent eavesdropping on the two other guests as late as they (an apoplectic retired colonel and his, what? daughter? wife?— a colorless moony horse in flowers whose only words when the old man asked "Are you happy?" were "Thank you").

Then when even the colonel had yielded to the waitress's glare of perfect hate—it was half-past two; her life awaited—they finished their coffee and entered the sun, the day like a baby dumped on their doorstep, gorgeous but unwanted, condemning as an angel. And gilding—it made Sara's body seem gold, warm and workable. Even the black hair transmuting quickly, through bronze to gold. They stood a moment—Charles Tamplin seeing that, she knowing he saw it, both knowing its deceit.

She reached for his wrist. He gave her his hand. But she did not take it—"I was looking for the time," she said. He extended his watch. She studied it carefully, returned it to his side, gave him the sum, "Eighteen hours till I rest on the bosom of the deep." They both gave the brief statutory grin—they spoke of her sailing, their permanent parting, in jokes: "The Noble Experiment Ended Smiling"—then stood again, loose. "Where now?" she said.

"The church?" he said.

She nodded, stepped to go. "You can say me the poem. A final performance."

He smiled, bowed slightly, double-stepped to take the lead; and they walked down the High Street, as separate as sisters, to the old stone bridge, short and narrow, at the bottom. She looked right to where the spire stood, tan and clear. But he pointed to the crossroads beyond the bridge, right to Shipton-under-Wychwood, left to Stow-on-the-Wold; vital junction still guarded from Nazis by a pillbox smothered in roses now, its black slot empty, unarmed, unused, shielding only village lovers seized here by urgency or tramps in the rain. They had once crawled into it themselves, been amazed by its neatness—no garbage or excrement but well-pressed earth and a few penciled names.

She smiled, said "Ah-dew," the word she had chosen all week for last views. Then she ran up the loud Windrush to the church.

He gave her the lead, loped behind in her tracks.

They had been through the church three or four times together; he more often, alone, or with college friends. But they trailed through its dark chill now as if discovering—the Lady chapel defaced by Round-heads, the lead font scratched with the name of a prisoner shot by Cromwell next morning in the yard, the tomb of the barber to Henry VIII; then the small painted bust of Lucius Cary (beside his wife's with her breasts displayed), killed at Newbury, age thirty-three, Viscount Falkland, Lord of Great Tew, friend to Ben Jonson and mourned by him.

Sara touched the bust, its pink features fresh and vapid as a baby's. Then she said with more force than the stillness required, "Any man of thirty with a face bare as this, deserves to die."

"It's the sculptor," he said. "Don't blame poor Cary."

"But I do," she said. "If he'd been half a man, left behind a man's memory, his wife or whoever would have never paid for *this*—" She thumped the smooth forehead; it thudded, all but grunted. "Say his poem anyhow."

Charles Tamplin obeyed, for one line, in a whisper—"*It is not growing like a tree*—" Then refused, clamped shut. *Deserve*, she had said. She did not deserve this. One waste he could spare himself.

In his pause, she prompted; completed the sentence (all she knew of the poem)—"*In bulk, doth make man better be.*" Then she watched him and waited.

He did not face her but he shook his head. She accepted, walked on, so he stood alone and said to himself, slowly and clearly to the walls of his skull, Jonson's ten perfect lines to the memory of Cary—

> *It is not growing like a tree*
> *In bulk, doth make man better be*
> *Or standing long an oak, three hundred year,*
> *To fall a log at last, dry, bald and sear.*
> *A lily of a day*
> *Is fairer far in May*
> *Although it fall and die that night;*
> *It was the plant and flower of light.*
> *In small proportions, we just beauty see;*
> *And in short measures, life may perfect be.*

He felt as though a green leaf uncoiled on his lips. A kindness to himself, the first for weeks. As though he might yet survive the scorch, live to tell the tale. What tale? His and Sara's, the one he knew, only tale there was. Name another than theirs. Nothing so grand as betrayal or treason; only the oldest story of all—the simple entire failure to meet, to serve one another and delight in the work. Imagine a life of telling that—stories, poems for another fifty years. Well, he could and must, beginning tomorrow, in eighteen hours. His own small proportion, just beauty, alone.

*

When—stronger for the moment of solitude used—he had wandered toward Sara, past altar and choir, he found her not in tears nor with her pallor-of-victim but with head back, eyes wide and fixed on a spot high above on the crowded wall, the skin of her forehead and jaw taut with triumph.

"Do you know that?" She said. Not facing him, she pointed to a marble plaque—*Bartholomew*.

He knew of a house by that name in the village, but this he had missed—a long inscription. He shook his head, No, and began to read silently.

"I found it," she said and forced him to listen—

> "Lo, Huddled up together lie
> Gray age, green youth, white infancy.
> If death doth nature's laws dispense
> And reconciles all difference,
> Tis fit one flesh one house should have,
> One tomb, one epitaph, one grave;
> And they that lived and lovèd either
> Should die and lie and sleep together.
> Go, reader. Whether go or stay,
> Thou must not hence be long away."

He heard her to the end, eyes on her not the poem. Then he left, half-ran to the south door, the yard; and had run through half the ruining tombs there (of wool merchants, stone wool-sacks on each) before he knew he was fleeing again. He stopped in the light and, though he did not turn, knew she had not followed, was still inside. Could he leave her there now; go his own way at last, unexplained, free?—give her all the time she needed to copy, memorize, digest her newest triumph; then find her own way to Southampton, her ship? No. He turned.

She stepped through the south door herself, into sun; walked briskly to him. "It's better," she said. "It's a truer poem. It could change whole lives."

He shrugged in a quick gust of wind—still not spring. "We'll drive toward Shipton," he said. "They had snow."

So they had—a late flurry, two days before, of which rare patches clung on in the sun, at the roots of trees, the lee of walls. As he drove them slowly upward through the long empty hills, it was all they had to fasten on—a hunt for snow, like a child's hunt for lucky white horses to stamp. He would see a white patch, point it silently to her; she would crane, nod silently, then find one herself. Time unreeled behind them, an exhausted ribbon. Then they reached a crest and rode for a while on its bare bright ridge—not a flake of snow, not a house, a tree. For half a mile, Charles Tamplin continued searching, the rising taste of panic plating his teeth. At last, again, they were locked alone together. And all his doing, a simple ride to kill a day as painlessly as possible; and now the whole world, in conspiracy, had slunk into hiding, leaving him and her, her *on* him, no escape, no choice, only needs to face, their airless symbiosis to swallow, their sentence to accept.

But she did not speak, continued searching too; so the panic leeched away and he felt alone, not with her but with her story, hers and his— this very day a well-shaped story itself. Their neutral lunch, his victory over her at Cary's bust, her excited discovery of a mass-epitaph, his moment of flight and now this ride which would last on till dusk, bring them down silently from the hills into Woodstock—a walk by the darkening lake at Blenheim (the lake sliding through a whole gallery of painters with each moment's change of light—Corot, Monet, Manet, Courbet), supper at The Bear, then Oxford, separate sleep; in the morning a calm end. He drove now mechanically, no longer looking, seeing only the shape of that story, lean, rounded. A small sad proportion, short measure, but beautiful. He was smiling slightly. He was healing. Safe.

"*Look,*" she said.

He looked, straight ahead, hit the brake, barely stopped them. A flock of tan sheep filled the road, buffed his fender.

"My god," she said. "You nearly killed us."

He winced, invisibly, at her automatic *us* (women had invented the first-person-plural: when *we* got our doctorate; when *we* were in the army); but the whole offered sight was compensation. The stalled car straddled a narrow road. The road was the spine of the highest hill. Sides sloped away quickly onto milder hills, green and gold prospects hung like flats, "effects" in a nineteenth-century play—villages, towers, warrens of life. Sheep filled the road before him and were aiming rightward through a breeched stone wall down the sinking slope. Grass seemed no greener there than where they had left, browner in fact; and a squat bare fruit tree was all the shade. But that seemed their aim— why? "To see the other side"?

They crossed on another half-minute or so, rising from the left, eyeing skittishly the car, but bent all the same on their profitless choice, as though south Ireland lay yards away, sweet green to their knees. Then a black dog shot up, a harassed sergeant, smartening his line, butting, nosing in furious silence—or was it? The car-glass excluded all noise, all sense but vision.

Charles Tamplin felt himself suspended, space and time. This might as easily be Galilee as Oxfordshire, before Christ, before green hills burnt to sand.

And with the last sheep—mostly new slow lambs—a shepherd rose. Young himself and slow—maybe fourteen, red-haired, a credible David, a stick in his right hand which hung loose, languid, oblivious to his flock. As he hopped the shallow ditch, stepped into the road, he might have been awakened that instant by warmth, drawn from sleep under leaves by sun, the melted snow. His eyes squinted sleepily; his face, hands, clothes seemed fresh with dirt of a hibernation. He took less notice of the car than his sheep, passed an arm's reach from it, never flickered a glance. Only—at the last moment of his profile—he faltered a step, cocked his chin as though listening but to something ahead, in his own slow path. Another sound Charles Tamplin strained to hear, balked by glass. Yet though the road was clear now, he did not move, to crank the car or speak; for the shepherd had reached the bare fruit tree and—his sheep gone on—bent now and reached to the ground at its roots where a patch of snow no larger than a plate had survived both sun and the trampling flock. Now he stood, faced round, ate a handful of snow, rubbed the rest on his eyes, smiled—awake now and quick—quite clearly to Sara, said a word to her, waved. His lips had said "Sorry."

Sara smiled in return, nodding pardon to him happily.

He took it, waved again, then ran with his dog out of sight down the slope.

Charles Tamplin looked to Sara—the back of her head. She still watched the boy—or the space where he'd stood and staged his grace as natural as breath. She was gone now, a foot away, still here beside him but gone for good. There were other doors. She had seen that at last. Had opened one at least—and shut another. The crown of her black hair stood now against him, the thickest gate, barred, guarded, perilous. He cranked the engine, shifted gear quietly. She still faced the bare tree, the uneaten snow; so Charles Tamplin thought they could move on now toward the end of the day, tired and calm. But the wheels had not rolled one turn before he knew—clearly and from her, as though her hidden eyes had flung it backward, a vise for his heart— that the day, the story, ended here, not before or later; ended with the happy boy's word, with Sara's smile; an end but a door blown fiercely open on a world, older, simpler, deeper than he'd known. A family huddled together in death, a handful of snow in early spring light, a "Sorry" through glass, a smiling pardon. Small proportion?—gigantic perhaps, crushing, stifling but just and most beautiful, a possible tale, a possible *life*, secret extended to all but him. Yet *tale, life, secret* which it now must be his duty to describe, celebrate, adore at a distance. The happiness of others. He adored them through tears.

But Blenheim now, dinner, sleepless night, their final day.

2. A Dog's Death

I HAD WATCHED the ship leave—and among waving hundreds, one still passenger—at ten that morning, prompt and smooth as a Swiss railway. And it did seem to slide on rails not water—unpitted, firm, two-way, returnable—though it moved toward the winter Atlantic on a trip which would never return to me at least. Then I had driven home dangerously, courting a sharper permanent pain, my conscious destination being bed, drowned sleep. Home was one rented room in the house of a childless working couple—brown walls—and I reached it by noon, fell fully clothed on my narrow bed, flung myself onto sleep like a bale. Sleep took me—as it always kindly has—held me dreamless, careless, alone but not lonely till knocking reached me wherever I lay. I have always waked as quickly as slept, and as desperately—each nerve instantly flayed and clanging—so I was on my feet and moving before I knew what the noise was or where.

Only the knuckles of a hand on my door, a voice—"Mr. Tamplin?"

My landlady—home. Why home at this hour? I glanced to the window, the sky—gray of course but not late, not evening. "Coming," I said and opened on her face; said "Oh," helpless, at what she had become since breakfast—her skin ribbed and thin as cigarette paper, whiter even; hennaed curls collapsed and clinging to her skull, a monstrous child; her eyes red; lips drawn; long neck corded by the effort to speak.

She said, "I am sorry. You were sleeping, I know, on troubles of your own but help me ple—" Her throat refused her.

I waited till she had control again; but when her lips moved they were silent, only flapped—a rain-soaked flag. So I said "Oh I'll live" to her opening apology, smiled, went on—"What's the trouble, Bett?"

340

She began and found she could manage, but slowly. "Mr. Tamplin, I meant not to worry you, knowing you have your own heartache. I told Buck this morning when he said you'd help. 'Buck, he's low himself. We won't tell *him* till it's over and done and the flowers planted. We must face it ourselves.'" She stopped, looked over the stairwell rail. "But she's down there now and we can't face it. Not after twelve years."

I honestly did not understand. "Face who? Face what?"

"Her," she said. She stabbed with a finger down again. "The lady vet. She's come for old Peter."

"What's happened to Peter?"

Again she was silenced, stared struggling at me. (Peter was their dog, a low white Sealyham; had been theirs all his life—twelve years—was half-blind now but still, I thought, as strong as a trap. Not a week before, I had entered the front door late at night—on Peter in the hall, lurching on stump legs but galvanized by my sound and smell. He had charged, bare teeth that could pierce a boot. I had dodged, he had lunged—a small rhino—missed me, struck the wall, fallen. I had made it safely to the dark front lounge, another joke on Peter, Bett laughing behind me as she came to retrieve him.)

But she won at last and said, "Tumors. All over. He's chocked with tumors. I found the first one four days ago when he wouldn't eat. I was feeling his soft throat"—she felt her own—"when I found this bird's egg in there, slipping out of my touch. Then I felt him all over. They had beat me to him—everywhere, little sliding eggs. For three days I didn't say a word to Buck nor you—I knew you faced your own separations—but I fed Peter what he would eat, sweet chocolate. Still he's failed every day. Wouldn't move this morning so Buck went to pet him and felt for himself. They had grown half-again as big in that time. He went to the vet, paid her extra money to come to the house. She's just now looked and says it's hopeless, nothing but pain. We must put him down, the only kind thing—she must; *we* can't."

I said, "I'll miss not having him to dodge."

"That's it," she said. "He didn't take to you. Nothing personal though. Never took to anyone but me and Buck. He'd have torn that vet's hand off by now if he wasn't so weak. What I'm asking is, why I've waked you is—since you and him never got along, would you go now and be with him when she puts him down?"

I had said "Yes" before I thought of a reason—it would wrench my mind off me awhile, a chance to begin a life again.

She went down two of the steps, called "Buck." Out of sight, he opened their parlor door. She said, "You come here with me. He's coming."

Buck said "All right" and I went down past her, pressing to the wall not to touch her body—any part of her, clothing, hair—pressed past Buck also as he climbed toward her, paused, said to me, "It'll only be a moment. Quite painless, she says. But you're very kind."

I nodded but did not say a word. No word, no touch. This new chance had its own rules, cold as glass.

Peter lay in his circle of wicker basket on a bed-pillow covered with a clean white case. His upward eye was open, black, on guard toward the woman, the vet on a hassock beside him; it flicked to me as I entered and said my name; and with recognition he rose in front on two legs, but silently.

I waited, hand on door, for his verdict—enemy breaching his citadel or final friend.

He only looked downward—no other move, no growl, no teeth.

"Come in," she said firmly—a large woman in her late forties, bobbed hair—then softer, "Did you shut the door tightly?"

I nodded Yes, still pressed against it.

"There is really no use your being here—nothing for you to do, that is. Simplest job I ever perform—simplest in the world—but they wanted a witness. Of my kindness perhaps. I *am* kind," she said and raised (not flourished) her large right hand which poised in the air, an elaborate claw composed of her fingers and a hypodermic—middle-sized, plunger drawn on a column of air.

I nodded comprehension.

But she had her own rite to perform, her defense to build—before only me though she spoke it to Peter as she kneaded his chest with her empty hand. "The kindness is not what I do but when—not whether to kill; *when* to kill, you see."

The last had not been put as a question; but again I nodded, as sanction now of her motive and act.

The claw moved swiftly toward its job.

I said "No."

She looked to me stunned, her fine hand balked three inches from Peter. Her lips said "*No?*" in genuine fear. I had questioned her life, defied her defense. "He is not yours," she said. "I have orders from them."

Before her fear became anger, I said, "I must do my part." My part, I saw, was to stand nearer in. I took the steps, stood a foot from Peter—he was still half-risen, watching his feet. I said "All right."

The claw flew toward a taut space she had stretched with two free fingers in Peter's chest. The needle popped as it tore the rind. Her thumb pumped downward for three steady seconds, every atom of air.

Peter buckled on his legs, fell forward on his pillow. He had never looked up, shown surprise or coughed.

She breathed and began to stroke his ear. "Beautiful," she said.

He seemed now to me—had always seemed—a pile of soiled feathers. "Peter? Beautiful?"

"That death," she said.

I knelt and touched the ear myself—the rules allowed that, now he was dead—brushed her own still finger, thought of a ship on the black Atlantic, in its white heart my love borne smiling away from me kneeling here, my throat crammed with knowledge that now was the time, that the time was past, to murder that love but powerless to serve myself, unkind.

3. Scars

SAPPED BY a bath, Charles Tamplin slept on his back entirely naked but alone, unthreatened, leaned on only by afternoon sun, the light a quiet unneedful companion—as was the room. He had propped the room slowly round himself in the weeks since his first love failed and left; and though it was forming like a reef, with no plan, it seemed already (sparse as it was, awaiting funds) a sufficient fort against all but death. And portable—nothing his car couldn't haul wherever his future, his new self-sufficient life, would steer. "Companion and guard," he meant it to be; and the chief guards mounted watch now on his sleep—his books in shelves; on the desk a draft of half his thesis and notes for his novel; beside them a six-inch Japanese ivory (two men, a lady and a baboon dancing, tight in a ring, calligraphy all down the baboon's kimono); above on the wall two large dark etchings, one a perfect old German Rembrandt fake, the Hundred Guilder print, Christ ganged about by most of His life (disciples, Pharisees, the sick in carts, children for blessing); the other, genuine (bought with the savings of his recent solitude), Picasso's naked minotaur by a sleeping woman, his huge left arm lifting her cover, right arm extended—extending?— toward her, both urgent and static; she naked and plain, bleached in moonlight, oblivious but troubled.

His own sleep—a nap before cold supper, work—was as soothed and restorative as a child's, neither hectic nor drowned. His dream told him that—hardly a dream, a simple sense of walking alone, of seeing through clear eyes an entire world less free than himself, hostages given by all but him.

Yet the moment a hand touched the door of his room, turned the knob to enter, he leapt the two long steps to the opening door and reached for his wet towel hung on the knob. A strong woman's hand had reached round before him and, gripping the towel, pulled it slowly outwards into the hall. He said "No!", seized an end and tugged toward himself. The other hand fought for a moment, viciously; then slackened, yielded but not before the door was open on his instant of nakedness, two women's staring grins. In his panic they both seemed strangers, threats.

But when he was covered, the near woman moved in on him, still laughing, said, "Laid out for love, eh? Then why so shy?" His landlady Bett. But the other was strange, no one he had seen though she laughed like his oldest acquaintance, shared his secrets. When he backed away from Bett, the stranger followed to the center of his room—larger than Bett, younger (maybe forty), handsome, almost grand like a high leather chair, ample, tawny, all surface, hard. Bett spoke first—"We're going to the laundry. Give us your towel." She poked his ribs. No word of who the stranger was though he watched only her, her knowing eyes.

Bett had moved behind him so he spoke backwards to her. "I'm using it. You startled me. Step outside and you're welcome to it. I was sleeping. You startled me."

The stranger said, "—Frightened you. You're pale all over."

Bett said, "You seen more of him than me then. Let's have a look." She lunged from behind to strip off his towel.

He laughed for the first time, twisted his shoulders to throw her off and held the towel round him with two clenched hands, easily winning.

But the stranger rushed on him when their gaze had broken and, with only her hands, pressed his wrists to his sides—her hands inhuman, a hot machine.

At once his mouth was brassy with fear; and in one convulsion he threw Bett backwards, freed a hand, hit the stranger hard across the mouth—he felt the silent wet of her inner lips, her brittle teeth.

Bett stayed giggling where he'd flung her—by his cupboard.

The strange woman stood, one hand across her mouth, concealing his stroke, eyes smiling no longer, tight with rage. Then her hand dropped and he saw from her mouth jagging down to her chin a purplish scar, old but burning—as though he had struck her days ago and she'd stood here badly healing in his presence.

The time that followed had the quality of time (pressure, weight)— three seconds, maybe four, in which he was locked with this woman he'd offended, the last two alive, only two ever alive and eternal; he brute, she victim. Time and a sudden silent act which were both his familiar home and his prison. He saw of course his mother's face, Sara his love's, in the stranger's, half-hidden but judging, waiting, two feet away.

They were rescued, freed, by a ripe banana which Bett extended across his shoulder, saying loudly and laughing, "Here Mary, take this home to Ron."

The woman looked toward the banana, took it, laughed to Bett— "Right!"—weighed it plump on her palm, dandled it three times, then looked back to him—"May I have it please?"

He could not hear at first, still held by her scar—his scar for a moment, made and borne by him—so Bett moved beside him, poked him again. "Let her have it. Sure. Cost you—what?—all of four pence. Her need is greater than thine by far."

Mary studied it again as though it mattered. "I don't think I've had one since oh before the war. Never got back in the habit of buying them."

Bett said, "Don't give us that. You had them all during the war. I *know*. Lovely young chaps, dances every night—"

Mary asked him again, "May I have it please?"

"Mary *who?*" he said. "We haven't met."

"Blimey O'Reilly!—old Mary," Bett said. "Mr. Tamplin, *you* know. You've heard me recounting her escapades half the mornings you're here, remember?"

He remembered and smiled. "My name's Charles Tamplin."

Mary said, "I know. Know lots about you."

"Oh?" he said and pointed to the fruit (intended for his supper), "Yes, take it. Gladly. Glad to be of service." He grinned—"Put it to good use, I trust."

"None better," Bett said. "No needier cause. Her poor Ron's a candle in August, ain't he, Mar—"

"Hush," Mary said. "I make do, don't I?"

He saw she had said it to him—not leering—but he had no answer, joking or serious; indeed, felt nothing but a mild unease at their being here at all in the midst of his nap, he stranded in a towel.

Bett answered. "You make do, all right. Watch you don't do somebody in—somebody like yourself."

Mary said—still to him, "I watch. I watch. You *believe*, I watch. But I take every chance too. Know every path, above-ground and under. I'm *having* my life."

"Have on," Bett said, "but have it on your own time please, not mine. I'm washing clothes before Buck's tea—that's flat." She passed them both and stood in the door. "Come on, Mary, get yourself out so old Modesty can hand us his fig-leaf."

"I'm noticing his things," Mary said and moved deeper inward, stood against his desk, her broad thighs pressed hard into the edge. She quickly looked at the etchings above. Then she looked down and touched his straight rows of work and plans, lightly with her one free hand—manuscripts, note-books, ink-bottles, pens—as though she were blind and they each might be one word of a message, or as though she had grace and were blessing them. She looked back to him—"How on earth do you do it?"

He noticed for the first time her pleasing voice—calm, without Bett's highs-and-lows and one firm rung up the accent-ladder from Bett's proud harshness. "Do what?" he said, uneasier still.

"Sit here day in, day out; do your work?"

"Oh because I *know* my work," he said. "Know the life I want and am going for it, here." He pointed to the desk.

So she looked down again and saw his small ivory. "Can I touch it?" she said.

"If you're careful," he said.

"Care's my middle name."

"—Like Hell," Bett said from a distance, collecting more wash from the bath, a room away.

But she already held it, with both hands gently, having laid the absurd banana down. "Is it real?" she said.

"*Real?*" he said—as though the lady, men and baboon moved in her hands and perpetually, in their smiling ring. What answer did she want? What answer did he need to give?

She meant the simplest. "Is it all handmade, I mean?"

"Oh yes," he said. "It's ivory. Carved two, maybe three, centuries ago."

"What's it say?" she said. She was stroking the text on the baboon's robe.

"Wish I knew," he said. "I showed it to a Japanese friend at college but he couldn't decide. It's an ancient script. I'll have to find a scholar. I think it's a poem—hope so, at least."

"I'll tell you," she said.

He smiled. "You know ancient Japanese?"

"No," she said, "but I know what all this means"—she held out the dancers, still carefully grasped, and waved her other hand back to the pictures. "Shall I make it a poem? I was good at poems, as a girl, in school."

"Yes," he said, sensing dread like a stir in the still, cooling air.

She studied it a moment, glanced again at the pictures, shut her eyes, creased her forehead, raised her chin, lips apart—all the standard signs of creation. Then she lowered her face, eye-level to him, looked at him, moved her lips silently at first, then said "Hold-Me-Not . . ." and stood another long moment silently, lips moving still.

"That's your poem?" he said.

"Maybe not," she said. "Does it seem like a poem to you? It's what came to me. A motto then. Say it's my motto."

"Mine too," he said.

"I know," she said.

"Know what?"

"Know it's yours. Look at this—" She shook the dancers precariously, waved back at the pictures—"And you, standing there. No one's touching anyone in any of this. Hands off. No holding." She had started the sentence calmly, smiling; but the last four words seemed said by her scar—he watched it redden, move like a louder stronger mouth.

He shuddered once, passed it off as a shiver by hugging his shoulders.

"You're cold," she said. "Here I'm growling on and you're catching your death"; and again from the bottom of the stairs, Bett called. Mary set the ivory in its exact place, tapped the banana (now browning and fragrant), said, "Thanks for the offer, Mr. Tamplin—you're a gentleman—but I'll take my chances in the cruel world." She laughed once and quickly moved past him to the door, meaning to say nothing else, it seemed.

But he ducked a little bow, still hugging himself, and said to detain her, "The next time you come, I'll be better dressed."

"You're dressed," she said—he flushed. "I've not even *seen* you, you're dressed so thick. Well, my hat's off to you, sweet love—good luck!" Before the heat eased in his head, she was gone, down the stairs, out the door, Bett mumbling behind her.

After all, they had left him his chilling towel. He unwound it, spread it on the ledge to dry and dressed for work, no further thought or hope of sleep. But when he was ready and went to the desk, the light from the window was too dim now; so he switched on his lamp, which lit the pictures he had meant to ignore (since Mary's poem), made the dancers gleam, warm though hard. He surrendered to her lethal discovery, fed on his treasures, now related and bared—no one touched in any of them. The dancers brushed one another's robes but no flesh met; only the baboon touched himself. The minotaur's arm withheld its intent (Picasso had said of it to Françoise Gillot, "It's hard to say what he wants—kill her or wake her"). And Rembrandt's Christ—he tried for the first time to count the figures: forty-five people (counting hats of the concealed), a camel, ass and dog, all in say sixteen-inches-by-eleven. Not one of them touched. Christ's hand extended toward a baby, two cripples' toward Him, a boy's toward his mother but none succeeded. Not one. Even mothers holding babies were touching only *cloth*. Space prevailed. Miracle, blessing, forever delayed though they waited in dusk—no light but His—and must always wait.

Early next morning at his table for breakfast, Charles Tamplin asked Bett as she huffed in with food (eggs, bacon, bread marooned in grease), "How old is your Mary?"

"How come?" she said; then stood before him, serious in her cooking smock—"Get your mind off Mary right now, Mr. Tamplin. She's in dirty trouble. In a mess, she is."

"My mind isn't on her. I only asked her age."

"I don't know that," she said. "Younger than me. But a damned sight too old to be mucking about with young chaps, I know."

He continued chewing through his own mild defense—"Oh she didn't bother me. I can take a joke. I was only startled, still half-asleep."

"Not you, fool," Bett said. "I know you're safe—Christ, padlocked and all now, ain't you? How's it feel?"

"Fine, Bett; feels fine—free air again." She was dusting now with the hem of her smock. "Then *who?*" he said.

"Mind your own business," she said, still dusting.

"Bett, you were the one shoved her into my bedroom on me, strip-naked. I don't send out engraved invitations to my afternoon naps. Not any more."

Bett did not beg pardon—the house was hers. She worked on awhile, plumping pillows, moving chairs (he had made his own bed); then began to talk on the move, as to herself—and from the beginning, her accustomed start. "The war must've done it. No, long before then she was wild as a cat. She grew up down the road from my Mum's. Being older, I'd left; was already married, but naturally I heard it all, *saw* a good slab of it when Mary went after Bill my youngest brother. But Bill had her beat from the start, he did—had more girls tucked away waiting on him than Samson had hairs. Which reminds me of the end of their la-de-da." Bett stopped and laughed. "Bill had give her the jilt one Saturday night, took some other girl to the dance, I reckon; and Mary dressed herself up and went down on the bus and walked in on them. She didn't raise Hell then-and-there for a change—found chaps to dance with and danced all night—but next morning, first post, Bill had a letter from her, careful, in ink. It said, 'Mr. Barnes, you have broke my heart and soon as my lovely new perm wears out, I'm drowning myself in the barge canal!' "

Bett stopped and acknowledged Charles Tamplin's presence—"Do you get her meaning, about her new perm? She meant *Piss off!* but she did say it clever, I'll grant her that. And she kept up a laugh through another year or so of slouching about. Her job (at a butcher's) was all that kept her from being a proper tramp—her time was limited. Her job and her Dad. Her Dad's all she ever loved, to this very day, for all her mess. And he caused half of it. He raised her, you see; let her have her way from the time she was twelve, when her mother died; just laughed when she told him her escapades though he's never known a tenth of the Hell she raised; and now he's old and can barely see, she don't even have to bother to lie. Still, she's good to him; pets him like a china doll—his heart's bad too. I've always said to Buck when he talked Mary down, told me not to see her, 'Buck, she's good as gold to her Dad.' '*Dad*, Hell,' Buck says. 'She's married to Ron and she treats Ron like dirt!' Buck's right and all. She always did. Ron's eat pecks of her dirt right from the start. Her teasing him on unmercifully, in her spare time from others, till she had him worshiping, buying her things arse-over-tip with every farthing from his scrap of a job—lovely sweaters, fur-lined boots, things to protect her (she'd rush stark-naked, arms open, into a storm if its name was Fun). He was older than her by five or six years, so he should have known better; but somehow he got her in the family way—she *said* it was Ron. Why I'll never know, if she hated his sight like she says she does, unless it *was* his baby or unless the other chaps involved had ducked out. Anyhow of all things, she told her Dad; and he went to Ron, blue-faced with rage, to say Ron must marry her. *Must!* He'd have married her smiling if she'd been stuffed full of a dozen babies, black as pitch.

"Well, married they were and the baby came—a girl, nothing special. But Ron worshiped her too and Mary settled in a bit and minded her duties. That's when I made pals with her. Her and Ron and the baby lived just down there then, near us; and me knowing her since she was a girl, she came up most afternoons for a chin-wag. I took to her right from the start. Buck hated her. But I like a laugh—Christ, I've had a few—and she'd come and put the baby in the corner to sleep and then tell me all of her past escapades—what lengths chaps had gone to even touch her wrist; how she'd drive them up the wall night after night; then, quick, give them a chance and they'd pop like crackers, half-weep with joy! She kept me in laughs for months; I'm still grateful. I'd always shove her off before Buck was home. He could smell if she'd been there but he's never run *me*. Then the baby died before anyone had really noticed it—anyone but Ron, as I said. He was crushed. Oh I don't mean to say Mary laughed at the funeral. Of course she didn't. Her feelings are keen as a blade to this day—I'd no more mention that child to her than I'd spit in her face. But she healed, don't you know— quick, her old self again.

"The war had just started—I guess that was it—and everything was soldiers everywhere. Not Yanks—the Yanks didn't come for years, dirty dogs they was when they got here too—but good English boys, young as pups and scared stiff. Everything was 'doing your bit for the troops'; and as I've never knitted so much as a cap, I did my bit going to dances. Dances every night at the Assembly Rooms. Buck went along at first to help with the food (his shocking hernia kept him out)—keep an eye on me was his main intent. *I* was safe though, young as I was—oh I love to tease a sweet young chap; I'd get them so het-up they'd glow like grates but teasing was all. I'd dance like a dervish till five-to-eleven, then I'd dash for the last bus. Often I was chased but never caught! So Buck stopped going and I don't know who brought it up, me or her; but Mary went with me every night from then on—nights when I didn't go; dancing's not my *life*; I've had cares to attend to since I was a girl.

"When her and me went, she always came home with me. We'd get off the bus and there would be Ron, waiting to walk her home, the streets being black as pitch of course, blackout and all. It seemed to set her teeth on edge—Ron waiting. She'd give him a look like an open grave, then stump along home without a word, barely 'Goodnight' to me. It got worse and worse—her resenting him there till one night she told him off with me looking on, words to make even me shiver, and I tried to leave; but she said, 'Wait, Bett, wait. Let's *all* wait here at the public bus-stop till James Ronald Campbell stiffens into a man.' Then she went up to him—it was a warm night, September, bright moon; he hadn't a coat on, only his jacket—and began pawing at him, stroking him up, saying, 'Now then, Cock, the Army won't have you. Let's see if *I* will. Let's see if you pass my test, old Cock.' He stood there and bore it too—as long as I watched. I broke away soon—and didn't seek her company for weeks after that. We met at the dances and she'd sit by me on the bus coming home; but she knew I was still sick from watching her show and she laid low awhile, where I was concerned—with Ron, too, it seemed. He had given up meeting her at the bus, and she never mentioned him no more than dust. *I* certainly didn't. He had my pity but not my respect—not after that night; for a while anyhow. I'd have knocked her flat—Buck would've killed me, soft-hearted as he is. What I couldn't understand was why he *stayed*—or let her stay, for she got far worse.

"Ron went on a night shift at the Works; and Mary started bringing chaps home, that's all. One night when I was still cool towards her, she climbed on the bus with this soldier, younger than her—she's always picked youth, except old Ron—and ginger-haired. Well, she set him by me on the long seat, you know, and made introductions polite as a party. You know I'm not nosey—I've got my own life to lead, which takes my time—but I reckon I all but amputated my tongue with my teeth on that ride. I nodded to her not him, and sat still. I was cold as marble and when the bus stopped I said to Mary, 'After you. Very far after you.' She said 'Righto!' and smiled and stepped off, her chap in hand. We went that way for weeks after too—Mary in front with some new soldier (seldom one twice) and me behind. A time or two she tried to speak, turn and ask me questions—how was Buck and the dog? I'd ask her how was Ron and she'd say something cheeky— 'Keeping busy' or 'Away a good bit'—but she stopped soon enough. She'd stopped coming round from the first awful night, and God knows I didn't set foot in their door. I didn't know what I might walk in on— some chap in his pants or old Ron hacking Mary down with a knife. The awful part is, I don't think he knew. I'd see the chaps leave her gate about dawn—she took *that* care—and Ron might have gone on in the dark till this day but that one night they had a power failure at the Works and Ron got home long before the dance ended.

"It was dead-winter, cold and pouring with rain; and when Ron come in, he must have found her boots in the hall. She'd left them; the rain hadn't started till late, so he took it in his head to meet her at the bus and have her boots ready for her so she wouldn't spoil her shoes no worse than they already were. The first sad thing was, the bus was late—maybe five or ten minutes—and Ron himself was soaked to the skin, just standing in the open, no shelter or nothing. I had stepped onto the platform early; ahead of Mary and this night's chap—I'd had enough of tailing her, like spying from behind—so I saw Ron first as the bus rolled past him; he had a little torch which of course was illegal. Christ, what could I do? Well, nothing. No time to gather my wits— and none of my business. I stepped down and shunned him—he didn't see me, wasn't *looking* for me. I tried to walk on but I had to look. I went a few yards, then turned and saw it by his dim little light. She leapt off the bus nimble as a cat, the chap on her heels—not so young this one and big, far bigger than Ron. She took a few strides—head down in the rain, her chap a bit behind—before she saw Ron. She stopped of course but she never lost breath—why fear him *now*, was her thought, I guess—and she said, 'What the Hell are you up to, moping in the rain?' I could see him side-face. He saw the soldier. Then he took a step to Mary. He held out her boots and he tried to explain. He really did. But he flung them in her face. He had bought them; he figured they were his to use. They were good boots, peacetime, fur-lined with brass buckles. One of the buckles cut into her mouth. Which was when I left—the sight of Mary all blood from the mouth down, her soldier standing there dumfounded in the rain, old Ron's mouth working still trying to explain. Well, I left them to it—not from fear, understand; more like disgust. My life is too short to stand by watching others ruin theirs; I've got my *own* fight. And to this very day I'm in total darkness about what happened after that—who went with who, what awful things were said. I didn't lay an eye on Mary or Ron for weeks after that, more like months. For all I knew they were dead, murdered, hanged. Well, they weren't. They had moved. To Mary's father's. He had had a fall shortly after that night, was crippled-up bad; so they moved in with him, and there they've been ever since—what? fifteen years."

"That's her scar," Charles Tamplin said. It was not a question. He had finished his breakfast and, with his right hand, traced the exact path of Mary's scar down his face.

Bett said, "You noticed that. Don't miss a trick, do you? Well, to be fair with you, I couldn't swear to it. I didn't have her face memorized, you know; and after that night it was so many months till I saw her again that I didn't notice it right off. Buck did, at once. We met her in a shop in town one morning—just greeted one another—and the moment she left, Buck said 'Well, she got it.' '—Got what?' I said. '—What she's been begging for. Someone knocked Hell out of her mouth.' And I hadn't said a word to Buck about the boots. Then I remembered—she'd held up her hand when she spoke to us, like someone with new teeth, shielding her mouth; but there had been a scar. So I guess it was Ron. He'd marked her at last. And from what I knew in years after that, Buck was right again—the Hell *had* been knocked right out of her. Not that she sprouted wings of course; but between her sick Dad and whatever Ron had done, she kept home at night for the rest of the war—long after the war. I say 'kept home.' What I mean is, I didn't see her down at the Assembly Rooms for years; and if she'd been dancing between here and London, old Bett would have seen her—*I* didn't stop but then I'd kept my head and all, hadn't I?"

"Yes," Charles Tamplin said.

"Like you," Bett said.

He said "Thank you," smiled quickly—"But you see her now. She's your friend again."

Bett said, "Never. Not my friend. I don't have friends—no, I really don't. I've never felt the need. I've had Buck of course all these years and Peter while he lived and my old Mum; but the rest are just faces I natter with, wave to as I go about my own business. Mary, least of all—"

"But you see Mary. What about yesterday?"

"That's only her. The past few years she's begun dropping in. I give her a laugh—a little time-off from her old Dad and Ron. But it's got to stop—I must make it stop. She's dangerous, she is. Oh not to me— and not to you either; I was only joking a minute ago. It's herself she'll ruin of course—again. Herself and her poor Dad and Ron, though if you ask me, they'd be damned lucky if she took her lad and flew off to China."

"What lad?" he said.

"Don't ask me that. I know—know his name and his job (a chauffeur); but not *him*, thank God—and I'm sorry I know. She told me before I could stop her, bragged it to me—how he's put new life in her. If that's life, Christ! Deliver me. 'Life and hope,' she said. Hope for what?—a slit throat. He's a bad one, he is—this new one she's got. He'll throw knives not boots, you mark my words."

Bett had finished, he knew. That was often her exit—"Mark my words," a justified sibyl, generally right. She scratched at her hair, glanced toward his clock—"Crumbs! Half-past nine, and all *my* work! You can make me talk worse than anyone—and what about? Pure rubbish, I reckon. Your mind's meant to be on higher things. I thought that was your latest plan anyhow." She was sweeping his dishes onto a tray.

He did not answer.

"Eh?" she said and laughed and pointed to Picasso's naked woman, asleep while love or death poised above her—"Higher things such as that lady's bare bum, eh? You don't fool me."

"I *do*," he said. "I've fooled you completely" and moved to his desk. But he said it to the walls. Bett was gone; hurled into her day, he thought, her desperate useless day.

And surely he had, for he spent the whole morning in his quiet room in the silent house and, ignoring lunch, on into the afternoon, not moving from his desk—beneath the lady's bum, Christ's hand (untouched, untouching), beside the dancers—writing into his notes, with sustained exhilaration of loathing, Bett's ragged wasteful gamy tale in Bett's own words of Mary entirely surrendered; and with—toward the end, as time reached the present, this warm afternoon—the thrill of power, to have gripped in his own hands this proper mess, this shoal of rubbish, and made it part of his own hard understanding of what, in the world, he could stride across; his own needs harnessed, tense but obedient. Then he read through the pages and wrote at the bottom these questions they raised—

—*The name of the story?—Scars perhaps.*
—*Why should Bett tell this story at all? Why is she so clearly fascinated by Mary that she tolerates her here against Buck's orders, after all this past and whatever is present and threatens now? Why tell it to me?*

Who am I—must she think—to need this news? (I am all she has—her Wedding Guest. She cannot speak of it to Buck or her mother, cannot even mention the past to Mary.)

—What is Mary's demon? Simple sexual famine? "Appreciation"? What is her vision of the life she insisted to me she was having? What has Ron withheld all these years—or lacked? Why—as Bett asks—has he not thrown her out or at least struck (or scarred) again? Why— knowing what he knew—did he follow Mary to her father's house?

—And who is her father in all of this? What does he know of her? need from her? fear? Why is he her one apparent pole?

—Why should she be anyone's pole, center?—least of all, three men's: her old Dad's, Ron's, her lethal lad's?

—Surrendered *to what?*

Then he clamped the pages neatly into his folder—the latest in all that awaited him there, his past and others', subdued but unfinished, requiring him. Then he was tired—as exhausted as from love—so again he lay on his bed, clothed fully, leaned on only by yellow light, alone in the house.

He had slept an hour when the doorbell woke him gently (a bell that worked on a wind-up spring always unwound so that callers announced themselves timidly, like broken toys). He lay a moment waiting for Bett's footsteps—silence—so he stepped to his window and, hid by the curtain, looked to the street. A clean black Austin stood at the curb and a driver waited—or sat, staring forward, not noticing the house: a man maybe twenty, large head, black hair, hunched shoulders in black, huge hands on the wheel. Was it he who rang? No—the bell gave a final spent wheeze, a hand rapped. He did not want to go and did not know why till a voice called "Bett?"—Mary's voice, out of sight. He would not go, had not made a sound, crouched in on himself behind the curtain, then crept to his bed, lay silently down and waited for Mary's footsteps departing. But the sound was the unlocked front door opening, Mary entering. Once more "Bett?", then "Mr. Tamplin?", then her steps climbing quickly toward his door.

He flung himself backward into feigned dead-sleep so deep that when she knocked at last, he heard as in paralyzed terror of dream, could not reply. But she knocked again, then opened his door. He did not look, lay still on his back, eyes clamped, unflickering—so that while he had known the voice as Mary's, he could not see her face (see *any* face yet) nor chart her progress across his floor as her steps moved slowly toward his bed. Her steps?—was it she? Was it Mary at all? Why? Come for what? And was his sleep sham? Was he locked in actual nightmare now or was someone, something, here by his bed, above his vulnerable body, poised unseen for an unknown purpose? He wished to scream. Scream what?—*Help* or *Leave?* And scream to whom? He saw faces now. The old faces rose as they had yesterday and would always rise; each, judge and victim. He fought them off, fought back a scream by clenching his jaws again and again.

"You kept your promise." She spoke above him.

He opened slowly on Mary's face, her scar smoothed off by the tension of a smile, her black coat open, touching his bed. "What promise?" he said. He remembered none.

"—To carry me away to America and happiness."

He was genuinely dazed from his sham sleep, his terror. "When did I promise that?"

"You don't remember? *Shame,*" she said. "I suppose you promise that to every girl. You Yanks *are* rotten." But her smile hung on.

"I'm sorry," he said. "My promises now are all to myself."

"No," she said. "Sweet love, don't fear. I'll survive somehow." Then she laughed (her scar returned)—"What a face! Don't weep. *I've* made arrangements. No, I meant you had promised to be better dressed when we met again."

He studied his body a moment, relieved. "So I am," he said. He smiled, sat up. "Bett's out, of course."

"Out where?" Mary said, suddenly efficient.

"Her mother's, I guess."

"When's she due back here?"

"God knows," he said. He stood, took the steps to reach his open door, took his post there to see her out.

"Where's Buck?" she said.

"At work, I'm sure. Bett's always home before Buck, making tea."

"Then we'll wait," she said.

"For what?"

"Not *us*, sweet love—not you and me. My friend in the car—" Mary pointed to the street. "We'll wait in Bett's sitting room. I'll call him in." She moved toward the door, one step from Charles Tamplin.

He shut the door, shut them both in his room. "Bett's is locked," he said, speaking rapidly. "She always locks their part of the house whenever she leaves. Got in the habit when the dog was alive—Peter being so ferocious, would push doors open and lunge after me if I made a sound. No it's locked, I know—"

Mary smiled again slowly. "Up here," she said. "There's rooms up here. The stairs aren't locked. No way to lock them. *I'm* here, look."

He thought a moment, leaned against his shut door. "Buck," he said. "Buck may come any time. He's often early."

"Let him come," Mary said. Her smile was set now. "Let him join the party."

"I'm leaving too," he said. "I must run into town." His door stayed shut.

"Can we stay here then?" She gestured behind her, meaning his room.

He looked past her, followed her pointing hand. The room—walls, bed, desk, papers, pictures—seemed blotched and stinking as though her hand had blindly sown stain, as though he must scrape it all, scour it with acid before he could rest again, work again here. He faced her— "Please. No." It was begging—he the beggar.

"You know what I'm asking for?"

He nodded.

"Only this much space—" In the air she measured off the width of two bodies.

He nodded, shut his eyes.

"You know what I've been through in my so-called life?—Bett's told you of course—and you won't help me into this new chance I've found?"

He would have to look. He looked. She seemed young—taut with her hunger—but he shook his head, no.

"That's final?" she said.

He nodded, yes.

"Let me out," she said.

Then he saw that he blocked her, still leaned on his door. He opened it slowly, took a step aside; and she left through the narrow space, not touching him at all—no further word or look. But he shuddered in the chill air that moiled behind her; and though he heard the click of the gate, the black car leaving, old safety of silence, it heaved in his throat, slapped his teeth like nausea—suspicion that his room, his life in this house was ruined, fouled at least; infected by exposure to virulent dependence, the lethal illusion of contingency, the sight of lives propped together like cards, humped down like dominoes, a fallen row. Could a room recover, serve him again?

He stood in his open door facing downward—the yellow hall; unable to take one backward step or look. He touched his pockets—car keys, wallet. He could walk straight forward, door open, no message; abandon all this as tainted burden; go like Bunyan's Christian, stripped for the journey. Journey to where? He was three thousand miles from America his home. Cornwall perhaps?—Tintagel, grand shattered bone barnacled by tearooms. The Scilly Islands?—a bland Indies. Or Brighton?— the home of his nearest friend, acquaintance really, a fellow student now teaching there, sharing rooms with his mother high back on the chalk in sight of a sea flat as gray ditch water.

Nonsense. Weak nonsense. His work was his journey; work his home—in the midst of whatever. And thinking of Brighton, he recalled unfinished work, notes he must make on a recent trip there, a scene to store, both eye and shield. He turned, faced his room—already cleansed—walked quickly to his desk and began to write, from flawless memory—a title first, *Seeds*. Then

David Caldwell invited me to Brighton for Easter—two weeks in advance, by letter, promising sun. I had meant to refuse and work on here; but early one morning I dreamt his death, in the form of a story my mother tells of her brother in France in the First World War—how he and a boyhood friend from home sat playing cards with others in a trench, took a direct hit from a German shell, and how my uncle looked round (in what light?), saw the others dead and his friend prone beside him. But his friend's heart beat (he swore that always), an artery pumped live blood from a shoulder; so my uncle took him up, bore the friend in his arms like a child—how far? Say a hundred yards to a small aid station, told the man on duty (another friend), "He's alive, work fast," then laid his friend down and looked in full light. His friend lacked a head. The blood that had pumped from the stump of his neck was already drying. I dreamt that of David—I my uncle, he my friend; the identical story except that I bore David miles not yards through a no-man's land white and rough as the moon—and woke so depressed that I stumbled through the morning unable to work, resisted the urge to phone and confirm he was still alive. We are not close friends.

But at noon I did write and accept his invitation, still not wanting to go but curious now to crack my dream. So on Friday I spent three maddening hours on the Brighton road, reached the Caldwells' at five and was met by the mother—David out with his girl. The mother (Nell Caldwell) is fiftyish, small, steady on thick legs. Beneath brown hair fine and thin as a baby's, her round face smiles perpetually, from the nose downward. Her eyes, cheeks, forehead are lined, gathered, never relaxed. Is she worried, fearful, on guard?—against what? She has only one fear left—her own death (or David's, I suppose, though they move so separately of one another, more like bees in a hive—considerate but busy—*than mother and only child, that I doubt his death would break her stride). She has weathered all the rest—the death of her father when she was eleven; the need then for her to stop school, nurse three brothers; her early marriage in the deepest Depression to a boy from Kent, named Jack, who sold shoes and lived above the shop in two rooms where she joined him, to wait out the worst of those years—they hoped—before having a son, in '38. Then the war, the raids—she was caught in London the first day of bombing, waited in the Tube beneath Victoria Station till the trains recommenced, not knowing what ruins Brighton might be in, nor Jack nor David—"They were well," she says, "Jack had worried over me, when I'd told him before, 'I'm a born hedgehog—duck under danger'; but there I'd seen them in my mind all day at the top of those stairs, David naked in the air, less than two years old, just tiles between them and whatever chose to fall. But they were well—Jack and David—and laughing, I felt I could kill them after all my worry."*

Jack was dead in six months—*called into the Army, sent to train in Kent near his father's home and killed when a lorry overturned on his cycle (he a motorcycle messenger). Nell had told me that much on two previous visits, at times when David was out or sleeping—she does not recall the past in his presence. Why? But this day, this gray Good Friday, she finished the tale—how she and a friend had taken young David by bus to Worthing (a Sunday outing) and were sitting there near the front with him—he was playing on some public child's equipment, still open for use despite the threats. "It was near tea-time," she told me, straight at me. She never looks down, always holds to your eyes as though they were straps but without that starved intensity of unhappy women. We were seated in the parlor before a small fire—"and I'd said to Kay my friend that we must go. David looked really frozen though he still played on—even then, still not three, he played like a Turk, hands white with pressure as he seized iron bars on the swing or whatever. Kay looked at her watch and said, 'A bus is just due'; so I ran for David who began to cry at the sight of me; and odd as it seems—though I knew he cried not to leave his game—I said to myself in my head as I ran,*

'Oh what does he know? Why cry? Why cry?' Then Kay said, 'Don't run. What luck! Look here.' I had not reached David but I stopped and looked—he bawling louder, three steps away. I did not go for him; for what Kay had seen was Fred my brother in his scrap of a car, stopping by Kay. Fred was younger than me but the Army wouldn't have him—spotty lungs like our father. I took a few steps on towards Fred, quite baffled—why on earth was he here, mid-afternoon? I remember mostly feeling anger—strange. So angry I forgot David crying behind me. Perhaps he had stopped, gone back to play—yes, he must have done. What I did was stand quite a distance from Fred—still in his car—and call to him harshly, 'You should be at work' (as though the little work he could manage, at a stationer's, would hold off Hitler, win the war). Then he came towards me—passed Kay as silent as a cloud of smoke—and as David had with me, I knew at once. Though I didn't cry. To this day, I haven't cried—not for Jack." She stopped and rose and poked the fire but not from emotion; her eyes were dry—the fire was low, it needed attention; so she worked with it patiently.

Not wishing to speak, least of all to question, I looked to a table where a picture was propped in a yellow wood frame—Jack, I knew; she had told me before. I'd have known anyhow. The head, face, shoulders are an outline of David's, an exact silhouette. The face is older—not in actual years (it was made when Jack was about David's age, 22, 23) but in form, evolved form. It is still the face of a Kentish farmer, each feature rounded as by ages of water or scoured by ice. David's face is finer, newer, unworked, unworn—a memory of his father's but also a correction.

Perhaps she saw me looking and dreaded a question; so she said, "I'm afraid I must leave you now—shocking David, still gone! I must run to my mother's, warm her meal"—(her mother, past eighty, lives alone down the hill, refuses to leave though her mind is gone; sees herself in a mirror and tells Nell a woman is trapped behind glass, leaves plates of chilled food by the mirror to feed her)—"You'll read here, won't you? David's due any moment." I said "Of course" and then in the front door

*we heard a key turn—David finally. Yet we both stood and waited as
though uncertain, for a total stranger, purpose undeclared.*

*Four unseen strides and he stood in the open door, facing us—David
of course though he did not speak. He grinned to me but greeted his
mother—in an odd slow bow, deep from the waist, made entirely for
Nell, face unsmiling, extended right hand barely grazing the rug, left
hand clenched at the small of his back; then slowly rising till he faced
her solemnly and suddenly grinned, still to her, all for her. That was
what puzzled me—the degree of attention; why? was he tipsy?—but I
laughed as he rose and, it being Good Friday, said, "Lo, he is risen—
and two days early!"*

*His mother's eyes brimmed tears, had surely produced them before my
tasteless joke. Now we all stood baffled till Nell could speak (her tears
never fell, drained back as quickly as they came)—"Tell me where you
learned that?" —"Learned what?" David said. —"That bow for
me . . ." He began it again—he was slightly high—"In my own sweet
heart, I have made it for you," completed it poorly, then dashed for the
toilet.*

*Nell turned to me, said with startling vehemence, "His father's bow,
Jack's greeting to me after every parting. David never saw that, can't
remember that, less than two years old when Jack last left." Then she
asked me to judge—"Is it memory, you think?" I had not thought it
out; but I said what she needed, "Memory, surely. It must be memory";
yet before she had cleared the doorsill, leaving, I said to myself, "It was
surely a seed, buried in his conception, to flower now."*

That was all, he thought—more poem than story, only the crushing
metaphor of David's bow—and glancing back, he thought it was finished, solved, as his record of Bett's long tale was not. He knew no
questions to ask of this—except, metaphor of what? and why the bow
should have surfaced when it did, why not years before, years later,
why to Nell? What could it tell her? What use could it be now but pain
renewed? So, calmed, his sense of control firmer now, he stood and

thought he would rest awhile—not sleep or escape but a short reward, a drive in the country, supper in Burford.

He was in his coat and down in the hall, when he saw, through the opaque front-door glass, a large close shape. He stood quiet, waited— Bett? Buck? surely not Mary again? The door was not locked but the dead bell rustled a half-turn, stopped. He checked his watch. It could not be Mary—too near Buck's tea-time—so he moved forward quickly and opened on a tall man, thin, mid-forties, cloth cap held in twitching hands.

The man's eyes hunted Charles Tamplin's face for a silent moment. Then he withdrew a step and studied the house-number screwed to the wall, looked backward to his bicycle propped by the gate. The right house, yes. His face tightened, filled from within as from pressure, fury, sudden youth; but his hands still twitched. "Betty?" he said.

Charles Tamplin said, "Bett? She's out, I'm sorry."

"Oh," the man said, turned his hat half round in his kneading hands, found his next request—"Will you give her a message? I'd be most grateful."

"I'm sorry, I'm just going out myself. You could leave a note."

The man nodded slowly and shut his eyes, stood in place but rocking.

Charles Tamplin turned inward. "I'll get some paper—"

The man gave a sound—a croak, a grunt.

Charles Tamplin looked. The man's face was white, tears poured down his cheeks, fell on his topcoat, his thin lips worked—open, shut, silently. Charles Tamplin stood where he was, in the hall, three steps from the man. "Are you all right?" he said.

The man shook his head but did not go. So they both stood like challengers, unthinking but adamant. Then the man found his voice— "Let me in for a moment please. Betty's a friend."

"Her rooms are locked." Charles Tamplin pointed behind him, simple proof.

"I'll stand in the passage." The man pointed also—beggary, the second time today.

Charles Tamplin said "Yes" and, not wanting to open his own room now, searched in the drawer of the hall table. He found a used envelope, took his own pen and gave them to the man now standing inside.

The man said "Thank you," stubbed the corners of his eyes with a thumb and wrote his message slowly but fluently, well-prepared, bearing hard on the uncovered surface of the table as though permanently gouging whatever he must say.

Charles Tamplin waited till the man stood, finished, eyes red but drying. "If you leave it there, they'll see it, I'm sure." Then he buttoned the last few buttons of his coat to remind the man.

The man understood, squared the envelope neatly dead-center on the table, returned the pen. Half-turned to go, he caught his own face in the small dull mirror, shook his head at himself but without expression, neither smile nor frown. He went to the door, said to Charles Tamplin, pausing but not looking back, "I'm very grateful." Then he left.

When the shadow had faded beyond the glass, Charles Tamplin read the note—not lifting, not touching it; from two feet away, its round script as legible as epitaph—

Dear Betty and Buck:—Mary left a note sometime today to say she is gone for good at last. I do not know to where or who with if anyone but her Dad found the news before I was home and had a bad spell with his heart, worst yet. I found him half-dead on arrival from work. He is going to hospital now, by ambulance. It looks like the end. If you meet Mary anywhere, tell her this. She will want to know.

Many thanks,
Ron Campbell

His first clear thought was "Grateful for what?" Ron's final thanks flung shame in his face, for coldness, impatience, and worse—for waste, the wasted chance for answers to questions Bett's story had raised; Mary's life had raised, her father's dependence, Ron's vacant abandoned spectacle. Why had any sane man collapsed in the hole of Mary's departure?—small vacuum surely, welcome relief. But then he wondered "When did she go?" and his own neutrality was breached. Suppose that today, this afternoon, Mary's own intent had been no worse than to bring her man to Bett's, use him here somehow in Buck's certain absence (maybe only show him off) and that by Bett's absence and his own refusal to play the dingy game, he had fanned her fury, burnt her bridges for her, unknown to himself, sent her home to leave her final note. Suppose what else?—that she left her note, abandoned her life and came here to bend above his fake nap and joke with him? The hall was cooling though not yet cold; but Charles Tamplin shook against his will—a shudder at first as though rousing himself, then a long moment, violent (neck rigid, eyes shut, hands clenched beside him) as he faced his probable part in the day, his choice of amends.

No choice in fact; one distant chance—find Mary, take her to her father in time. Find Mary where? Her man had waited at the curb in a car. They could be forty miles away by now, on the edge of London, total escape. His only hope was Bett, that Bett knew more than she'd told and would help. Again he checked his watch. It was time for her here, Buck's tea-time shortly. But she often missed that if her mother was low, left Buck to himself and came much later.

He would go to her mother's on the far side of town, beyond the station. (He knew the house, had driven Bett there through snow one day—a row house, grimy stripe of brick.) He had reached the door before he thought of the note—the note was not his but if Buck came first, found the news before Bett, she would have Hell to pay, days of justifying; or Buck might destroy it, never tell Bett a word.

He stepped back, took the note, folded it once, held it in his right hand—no hint of concealment—and went out the door.

He drove slowly over Bett's usual route, searching each cyclist's exhausted face as he flanked it, passed. No sign of Bett. She still waited safely at her mother's, surely. He felt that, trusted that, as strongly as if Bett were a magnet concealed in the town, pulling him effortless, powerless to her, her battered simple self his urgent goal—rest, forgiveness, sanction for his course. The road ahead—to the next long curve—was clear of riders now. Free for a moment and elated, he gained speed; but round the curve was the city coach station (a paved square packed with red and green buses). The stretch past that seemed a thicket to him. He slowed, threaded carefully through cyclists, children, old ladies on foot; then was stopped by a light, surrounded by a surge of homebound workers. His eyes flicked rapidly across each face—no Bett. Then the light went yellow. A final couple crossed, taking infinite time as though pavement were bog. The light was green but he could not move. They were passing his front bumper, looking ahead to a cranking coach—LONDON. Mary and her man, unsmiling in black coats, their hands entirely empty. They broke into a trot—the coach door was closing.

Charles Tamplin rammed through the intersection, stopped by the far curb and ran back loudly—the coach door was closed, smoke chuffed from the rear. He reached it midway along its length, struck the green side with both hands open. The motor calmed, door opened for him. But he stood where he was, looked up to the windows and saw Mary's face two feet above him, knowing but grave, locked behind thick glass, her man dim beyond. "Your father is ill," Charles Tamplin said.

She could not hear, pressed nearer the pane.

He spoke slowly, mouthing a visible message—"Your father's near death. His heart. Wants you."

She heard, nodded once—message delivered, then looked away, not to him or her lad but forward, the driver's neck, the road; her profile expectant, lifting, like a girl's.

The door shut and though Charles Tamplin struck again, the coach left him gagging in blue exhaust, encased in haze, a harmless ghost.

But he *saw*, with new clarity, Mary's gift—ten yards away his abandoned car, a tall policeman tagging it grimly (NO WAITING of course); in clots, the stalled white faces of passers, stopped by his scene (as outraged by noise as baffled by his purpose), intent on finding a way to ignore him, hopeful only that his little racket would not demand help, not keep them from home ten seconds longer, not change their lives.

He would not—he saw—maybe could not change another life, surely *had* not ever. He only, in the jostling world, safe alone; for he also saw that the name of all stories was Scars not Seeds—all stories but his. Scars made and sought, gladly begged, grinningly killingly *rightly* pursued—by Mary, her lad, weak Ron, her father; by Bett, Buck, David, Nell, Sara his own chance he'd stripped from himself, his uncle bearing a headless friend; by the minotaur, the woman (whether death or embrace), Christ's impatient hands yearning for nails, the dancers launched smiling into hot exhaustion. All surrendered but him. He envied them all. For this moment, he worshiped their wasteful courage, ruinous choices, contingency. The name of his story was, what?—Flight, surely. Would always be. His car was free now, policeman gone, faces dispersed. He took its roof as a still point, a guide, that might welcome him. Then he jogged toward it, speaking his love's name silently, lips gaping slowly with each hard step, a fish in air, a hostile element.

4. Waiting at Dachau

THE CAMP ITSELF—its active life—only lasted twelve years ('33–45). Twelve years after that, we parked by its gates. Now, twelve years after that, I still don't know; the question has gathered force with every year's distance—why did you balk and refuse to enter Dachau, letting me, forcing me to go in alone? I need to know several things— my version, your version, then the truth.

Is the answer simple?—you were sick or tired or fed-up with sights after six-weeks' traveling? Or were you miffed about the night before, or—being a little younger—you may not have seen my urgent need, as a radio-and-newsreel child of the Forties, to test my memories against the source? (Dachau and I are almost exact contemporaries; I'm one month older than it and still running.) For months in advance, I'd braced for the prospect. Me at the Abyss—*us*, don't you see?—the heart of darkness head-on, between the eyes. (What did I expect?—to stagger? vomit? No, I knew all wounds would be internal, all effects delayed.) Or maybe you understood quite well—you and your Imagination of Disaster—and were only invoking your famous policy of kindness-to-self. Surely, though, your chances of bearing-up were as good as mine—we'd been told the camp was hip-deep in flowers! Couldn't you have entered as a simple gift to me?

Well, you didn't. You waited. The last time you waited—for me, at least—and I still wonder why.

My version is this: we'd planned it from the first. Christmas vac. of my first Oxford winter you'd flown from Paris and we'd stretched on the frigid floor of my digs, maps and budgets around us, and plotted the summer (should it ever come: your nosedrops had frozen on my bureau Christmas Eve!)—a slowly warming arc. You would join me again in mid-July. We would ship my new Volkswagen—Newcastle to Bergen. Then we'd push slowly on—a week each for Oslo, Stockholm, Copenhagen; then a non-stop plunge through Germany to Munich. Dachau.

Why Dachau at all? We passed within twenty miles of Belsen, Nordhausen, Dora, Buchenwald, Ohrdruf, Flossenburg. Dachau was never a major death camp. Only a third of its inmates died. Yet I never considered another camp. Three reasons, I think: I knew it was there (most others were razed); the name itself was the perfect emblem, as it was for the Germans themselves, it seems—anyone who disappeared was assumed "to be in *Dachau.*" (Something inheres in the name, the sound—pronounced correctly it contains an unstopped *howl.* So does *Auschwitz* but Auschwitz could be—for Americans born after 1950— a brand of beer; *Buchenwald* could be a national park; *Belsen* a chocolate factory. *Dachau* seemed to me then—and seems now—only a terminus; last-stop, as Auden knew in '38—

> . . . *the map can point to places*
> *Which are really evil now—*
> *Nanking. Dachau.*)

And then nearby was Salzburg, as antidote—*Figaro* with Schwarzkopf, Fischer-Dieskau, Seefried, Karl Böhm. Then we could slowly climb the Rhine to Cologne (still without a whole building), the Hague and Vermeer, Amsterdam and Rembrandt; then (healed by now, stronger for the burns), we would ship back to Oxford, take a look at our gains, our chances, maybe marry. You'd pack up your chaste tight paintings in Paris (adjectives yours—triangles, oblate spheroids, cubes, all aching with loneliness in empty space) and join me for a last Oxford year on my thesis; then we'd sail home to all the books I'd write (my dreams of extracting love from my past, the boneyard of my childhood)—having already, well before we were thirty, faced the worst that life had ever offered any human pair, the final solution.

We made it to Munich precisely on schedule, only slightly in the red and apparently in love after four weeks of cold-water hosteling, cold roadside meals—canned potato salad, canned corned beef; we had bought a case of each and would only need bread every day at noon. I keep a photograph of one of those lunches—even without it, I'd have it in my head. We have stopped for lunch by a lake somewhere between Geilo and Oslo. Clear sky, the light a lemon yellow. You sit on a large stone, ten yards from the water, surrounded by smaller stones round and large as baseballs. The sounds are: our feet in those stones, water stroking, your opening of cans. I squat watching you warmed to fragrance in the light, adding to my luck only one more sound—in my head, the voice of Flagstad. She is still alive, a hundred-odd miles from here in retirement, playing solitaire and knitting—and that voice like a new lion in a zoo, *intact!* If she'd sing now we'd hear it cross valleys, through pines! (she will of course return to make those last recordings which calmly eliminate all future need for Wagnerian sopranos). You speak—"Sir, your lunch." You are holding out your hand with a plate of food but you have not risen. I must come to you. Halfway is halfway. I rise and go. *The happiest day in all my life*—I say that silently, moving toward you. Now, twelve years later, it is still unassailed. There hasn't been a happier. Yet, how do I have this photograph of it, in which your hand and the plate of food are blurred, moving toward me? Did I force you to offer it again for the camera or had I waited, shutter cocked, for the moment? Why did you let me complicate your simple service—you smile in the picture but you have at least the grace to refuse to meet my eyes. Your refusal has begun; your heels are digging in. I am drowned, though, in what tastes to me like good fortune; so I fail to notice for weeks, days or nights.

In the days I could see you—walking gravely past acres of Norwegian painting (every painting since the war in shades of pink and yellow) to smile and say at last "A nation of fairies!" Or sitting in a Stockholm park, eavesdropping on a Swedish girl and her compact rapidly heating French boyfriend (the girl so liberated that I all but expected a taut diaphragm to pop out and roll to rest at our feet when she uncrossed her legs), you said, "Knock her up and she'll wail like Queen Victoria!" Or stopping in the midst of tons of bland Thorwaldsen marbles in Copenhagen (all like variations on the head of Mendelssohn)—"Well, I like the *Danes*. They're crooks." Setting those down makes you sound studied, tough; a big reader of Salinger and Mary McCarthy. But I *saw* you. You were then, every minute of those long summer days, the perfect customized answer to all my optical needs. You seemed—you threatened!—to lack outer boundaries, integument; to vibrate within only vaguely held limits which, each night, permitted—welcomed!— me in to form a perfect compound.

Was I wrong, self-deceived, about that as well? I could even see you then—by the Midnight Sun; the birds never slept. Were you merely drumming time through all my happy hours of artful plunging? (the years spent studying van de Velde, Eustace Chesser)? It's accurate, I know, to say you never turned to *me*. I was the one to initiate action. But once I had laid a hand on your hip, you would rock over toward me and open like—gates! Very earnest, weighty gates that not every man could move. And you'd smile and *thank me!* Always at the end— and you almost always made it or threw Oscar-winning acts—you would say (not whisper; have you still never whispered a word in your life?) *"Thank you"* as though I had zipped the back of your dress or made you a small expensive gift (when there stood my donor capped with high-smelling rubber, Reservoir Tipped to *block* small expensive gifts). And that in the Fifties before the Revolution, when ninety–eight percent of the girls I'd had still shuddered at the end and asked forgiveness—asked me, Count Vronsky! I would lie some nights for hours, too grateful to sleep. You'd be gone in ten seconds.

Was I really wrong? Wasn't the only bad night the one in Munich?

Where did we sleep there?—some station hotel or with one of our specialty, war widows with lace-curtained bedrooms to rent and permanent frozen killing smiles propped round government-issue teeth? I can't see the room but I heard the silence—that I took you, really *had* you, against your will for the first time ever. You were tireder than I; but even then you laughed when I'd hacked to my reward, all huffs and puffs, and questioned your stillness. You said—*said!* surely our *Witwe* heard you—"Riding shotgun in a Volkswagen daily leaves a body badly tuckered." Well, pardon me, Sara—twelve years too late, if you even remember. Hadn't all the other sex till then though been mutual? Wasn't it *love?* We had known each other for ten years exactly, grown up together. We knew all the ways—more than half of them hidden—to protect each other; and any damage was a slip, inadvertent. We could have lived together as easily as dogs; and I'd thought—till that day at Dachau—we meant to. If we didn't love each other, who ever has?

—The de Wieks anyhow, if nobody else. You won't have heard of them. I hadn't till two years after we parted—in Ernst Schnabel's book on Anne Frank. A Dutch Jewish husband and wife flushed from hiding in 1943 and shipped to Auschwitz, where the husband died and the wife survived to remember Anne Frank's death. But this is the thing I want you to know—Mrs. de Wiek's memory fifteen years later of a moment on the packed train threading toward Auschwitz:

> *I sat beside my husband on a small box. The box swayed every time the wheels jolted against the tracks. When the third day came and we had not arrived, my husband took my hand and suddenly said: "I want to thank you for the wonderful life we have had together."*
>
> *I snatched my hand away from him, crying: "What are you thinking of? It's not over!"*
>
> *But he calmly reached for my hand again, and took it, and*

repeated several times: "I thank you. Thank you for the life we have had."

Then I left my hand in his and did not try to draw it away . . .

There is no photograph in the book of him or her; but they've walked, since I read that, as clearly in my head, as in *Daniel* three just Jews walk safe through the flames of Nebuchadnezzar's furnace. Shadrach, Meshach, Abednego—and a fourth, their angel. The de Wieks walk alone, two stripped Dutch Jews, dark-eyed, grinning, safe in my head; to Hell with *my* head, safe through all time should *no* one know of them, sealed in the only knowledge that turns fire—to have loved one another through to the last available instant, to have *known* and then had the grace to say thanks.

Were you just not that good—that strong and pure—or did you choose not to be that good *for me?*

I see them in their flames (or you by your lake) much more clearly than I see Dachau. My world-famous total recall deserts me. Or does it? Can it have been the way I remember? (I've never gone again.) The latest *Britannica* gives this much—that Dachau is a town eleven miles northwest of Munich, population ('61) 29,086, first mentioned as a market village 805 AD and continued as a village till 1917 when an ammunition factory was built there—the site in March 1933 of the first Nazi concentration camp; that the town stands on a hill at the summit of which is the castle of the Wittelsbacher and that the other sight is a parish church (1625).

What *I* remember is driving through sunny fields of potatoes and grain, you watching for road signs and calling the turns (German roads then were still under heavy reconstruction; and one of your frequent bursts of song was "*Umleitung*—there's a muddy road ahead!"). Wasn't my right hand holding your thigh, except when a farmer waved from a yard? Wasn't the town still a village after all, merely houses (no business street that I remember)?—low white houses with small sandy yards, green gardens in front? Don't I remember screened porches, green rockers, dusty ferns in cans, geraniums in boxes? A gray frame railway depot and platform? Don't I ask to stop and walk awhile or to drive slow and aimless (we had hours till the camp closed) through the loose grid of streets that seemed home at last (were they really unpaved, ankle-deep in white dust)? But you led us on—"Turn right; here, here." Your unfailing sense of where we were, where we must go. I was ready to wait, stop short of the camp. The village itself, your warm proximity, had eased my urgency for confrontation. What we had—there and then—seemed tested enough by time and chance, to require no further *pro forma* buffeting. It was you—I'm sure of this—who forced us on. An Ariadne who—calm in her beauty, perfectly aware of the course she's set—calmly leads dumb Theseus back into the lethal heart of the maze, its small tidy utterly efficient death chamber, the patient minotaur who has only played possum and waits now, famished.

From the parking lot (!) on—in my memory—it does seem a room, not ample but sufficient and sturdily enclosed. The new small gates (where are the old ones?—*Arbeit Macht Frei*), the cyclone fence thickly threaded with vines, the no-nonsense sign (*Maintained by the Corps of Engineers, U.S. Army*), the clear sky, the light—seemed interior, roofed, sheltered, shrunk or a model scaled precisely to a larger form. Is that why I didn't lock the car?—after weeks of paranoia, left our luggage available to any passer? Or had I started guessing you would stay behind?—guessing and hoping?

You had got yourself out ("Chivalry ends here," you had told me in Stockholm) and stood in sun that suddenly had the weight of sun at home, that seemed each second to be loading you with burdens. Also the color—you were bleaching as I watched. Yet you took off your sunglasses and stood by your shut door, hands at your sides, squinting straight at me.

I came round to you and extended my hand. You accepted. I took a step onward and engaged your weight, gently.

You said "No." You were planted. Your hand stayed in mine but your face refused.

I said "No, *what?*" and laughed.

"Not going," you said.

I didn't ask why but said what my father always said when I balked— "Are you sick?"

"No," you said.

"Then you promised," I said.

You had not; you should have laughed. But you shook your head.

"If I ordered you?" I said.

"You wouldn't."

"If I did?"

"I wouldn't go."

I said "*Wouldn't* or *couldn't?*"

"Wouldn't," you said.

We had not smiled once!

You took back your hand.

I said "Will you wait?"

You nodded yes.

"Where?"

"I'll *wait*," you said. You half-waved behind you, a cluster of trees, shady grass beneath.

So I moved again to go—to leave in fact—not looking back, and entered the camp. Dachau. Left you waiting, as you chose. Are you waiting still?

You have never seen it and, as I've said, my otherwise sharp pictorial memory is dim on Dachau; so to write this, I've spent three days trailing information through volumes of war-crimes trials, memoirs, histories of the S.S., photographs (forty Jewish women—nude, mostly pot-bellied, three of them holding children—queue up for a massacre in some Polish ditch: two of them are smiling toward the camera). Guess what a good three days I've had—to learn very little more than this (the memoirs on Dachau specifically are in Polish and German, shut to me): Dachau was opened in March 1933, a pet project of Goering and Himmler. The site, a mile square, was equipped for 8,000 inmates. At its liberation in April '45, it contained 33,000—90% civilians, 10% war prisoners. The civilians, from the first, fell into four groups— political opponents, "inferior races" (Jews and Gypsies), criminals, "asocial elements" (vagrants, pimps, alcoholics etc). Further divisions were recognized by the colored patches on prison clothing (selected with a grinning irony)—black for "shiftless elements," yellow for Jews, pink for homosexuals, purple for Jehovah's Witnesses. Though the oldest camp and the popular symbol for all, it was classified in the S.S. scale as a class-I camp—the mildest rating (Auschwitz was III). Only 70,000-odd inmates are estimated to have died there (4,000,000 at Auschwitz). The existing gas chamber was used only experimentally. Indeed, experiment was among the camp's functions—the famous experiments of Dr. Sigmund Rascher in chilling prisoners to 19°C., then attempting to thaw them with live whores stretched on their bodies (Himmler regretted that the chosen whores were Aryan). Or locking prisoners in mock altitude chambers to observe when they'd die of oxygen starvation. Or the study of asepsis by inducing infections which were left to gangrene.

—You know most of that. Everybody over thirty does (though to anyone not there, as prisoner or liberator, it has never seemed credible). What I'd like to tell you is what I saw, twelve years after its liberation. I have the four photographs I took that day. I can build it round them.

The gates were unguarded. I walked through them onto a central road wide enough for trucks but closed now to all but lookers like me— there were maybe a dozen in the hour I was there. To my left, one compound (the only one or the only one saved?)—a four-acre piece of flat tan dirt enclosed by stretches of concrete wall (seven-feet high, electrified on top), relays of barbed wire and, in each corner, an all-weather guardhouse (twenty feet high, all empty now). No trace of barracks, no sign of shelter. Where were the famous "dog cells" in which prisoners could only lie on their sides and were forced to bark to earn their food? Razed apparently (on a partial diagram I count thirty barracks). A few weeds grow and, in my picture of a stretch of wall and guardhouse, a leafy branch decks the upper right sky. (Good composition. But how old is the tree?) No entrance there, no gate in the wire. To the right, though, free access—trees, grass, flowers, buildings.

All the people were there. I remember them as old and all of them women; but my photographs show one man (late forties, his suit and tie American—was he a prisoner here?) and two children under ten (a boy in *lederhosen*, a girl hid behind him)—otherwise, old women in long cheap summer dresses, stout shoes. All in clusters of two or three, simply standing akimbo or reading, their lips moving drily at the effort. There are no talking guides, no sign of a staff to question, only scattered plaques and inscriptions in German—the single attempt at a monument, modest, dignified, undistinguished, a ¾ths-lifesize gaunt bronze prisoner gazing across the road to the compound, head shaved, hands in his scarecrow overcoat, feet in wooden shoes, on his marble base DEN TOTEN ZUR EHR, DEN LEBENDEN ZUR MAHNUNG ("To Honor the Dead, To Warn the Living") and an urn of red geraniums. Granite markers maybe twelve inches square set in beds of geraniums—GRAB HUNDERTEN NAMENLOSEN (that's from memory—"Grave of Hundreds, Nameless"; was it *hundreds* or *thousands*?). Then twenty feet onwards— it is all so small—six or eight women wait beside a building. It is one-story, cheap brick, green tile roof, straight as a box car and only twice as long. At the pitch of the roof there are turret windows; in the end near me, one large brick chimney eighteen feet tall. Along the side, frequent windows and doors. The only sign was a single black arrow aimed toward the far end (the end farthest from the compound and hidden). I followed, past a post-war willow tree, and found at the end a door—normal size, no wider than the door to my own bedroom.

From here I am on my own—no pictures. I think I remember the logic of progression, each small room labeled in German and English, giving into the next like a railroad apartment—*Disrobing Room, Disin-*

fecting Room (roughly ten feet by twelve, nine foot ceilings, unpainted plaster walls scratched now with the names and hometowns of GI's). Then another normal-sized wooden door opening into a larger room— maybe fifteen by twenty, shower spigots, soap dishes, floor drains, a ceiling window.

—I've built that effect outrageously—I'm sorry—to the oldest surprise of the twentieth century. The shower was gas, Zyklon B; the window was a deathwatch; the drains were for hosing down the products of surprise and suffocation. The next room was small again—*Storage Room.* The walls were printed from floor to ceiling with dirty bare feet, all turned neatly up. Corpses stacked like cord wood for the ovens. Next room, the ovens. The largest room and last, *Crematorium.* Four or five brick ovens spaced six feet apart, their iron doors open on seven-foot grill racks. The walls bore sets of black iron tools—tongs, prods, pokers, shovels. Behind the ovens, in the wall, were little doors—ash chutes to outside, for the *Namenlosen.*

End of tour. No more sights—oh an old woman kneeling by the farthest oven, clicking off her rosary. Otherwise nothing else to linger for but sunlight, geraniums. Or to make you wait awhile. I thought you were still waiting; and I thought, retracing my way toward you, that I was returning.

You could easily have stood it—have I made you see that? It lacked— now I understand the vagueness of my memories—the mystery of place. There are places, objects, quite literally impasted with the force of past event; places in which one is pulled up short by the pressure of actual atoms of the past. Almost never in America—our shrines being ruthlessly scalded and scoured if not bulldozed—and almost always in sites of suffering or wickedness. The Borgia apartments in the Vatican still are oiled with the presence of Rodrigo Borgia's rotting body; electrons that witnessed, sustained, his life still spin in the plaster, the stones underfoot, can be gouged (brown and rank) with a quick fingernail; unaltered atoms of hydrogen and oxygen that occupied his holy dissolving lungs in 1495 rush over one's lips and teeth with each breath. Or the Domus Aurea of Nero, subterranean now and leaking, where I rounded a dark corner on an elderly English gentleman masturbating (English by his clothes). Or the dungeon beneath the Capitol in which Caesar strangled Vercingetorix—45 BC. Or—another thing entirely— the crystal reliquary in Santa Maria Maggiore which one Christmas Eve mass was borne toward me, immobile in the crowd, its scraps of wormy wood, whether hoax or not (the remains of the Manger), as immanent with promise and threat to my life as a gram of radium bombarding my eyes. Dachau is one month younger than I. It saw— caused—the agonizing unwilling death of tens of thousands while I was still paying half-fare at the movies; yet its huddled remains bore me less of a threat, less pressure of the past than Williamsburg, than any plastic Hilton lobby.

—Why? That's *my* question. Why was I unshaken, unmoved? Anger with you? Tourist fatigue? (I who could weep years later in Chillon at the pillar to which Byron's Prisoner was chained?—and that after ten days hiking in the Alps.) What had I expected?—a Piranesi prison with eighty-foot ceilings, thick brown air, torture wheels staffed by malignant dwarfs? No doubt that would have helped. The physical remains of Dachau are so mindlessly disproportioned to the volume of suffering they were asked to contain, the literal volume of agonized breath ex- pelled in that square mile in those twelve years. The slaves who died building pyramids are at least survived by pyramids, not tar-paper shacks and geraniums.

But no—don't you see?—I'd expected *home.* It's taken me these twelve years to understand that even—my curious memory (dead-wrong surely) of the town itself as a scene from my childhood (porches, ferns, dust!—eastern North Carolina) and my readiness to dawdle there with you, my near-panic at the camp gates when you refused. I had secretly thought through all those months of planning that this would be our home, that if we could enter Dachau together, face and comprehend its threat and still walk out together, then we'd be confirmed—a love not soluble in time or death. *Home* in the sense of birthplace; we'd have been born there, our actual marriage, a perfect weld-job in the ultimate crucible.

Nonsense, you're thinking. Were you thinking it then? Is it why you refused?—you would not be a party to soft-brained theatrics?

But surely you're wrong. Sappy as my whole secret plan may have been—so sappy it was even secret to me; a Fiery Consummation!—it was not a fool's plan, not built on lover's lies. I wrote of "comprehending the threat of Dachau"—hadn't I done that already, in advance, by insisting on this visit? Its final horror—and that of all the camps, class I–III—was not the naked fulfillment by a few thousand gangsters of their fear and hatred on impotent objects (that, after all, is everyone's dream) but precisely the threat to human attachment, loyalty. The ghastliest experiment of all was not one of Dr. Rascher's mad-scientist pranks but the high voice that pulsed out its desperate need like a hypertensive vein—and at first uncertain of its power to enforce!—"Let me set you apart. Mothers here, children there. Husbands left, wives right." And millions obeyed, even the de Wieks—the most successful human experiment in history.

No, the horror is not that the camps did not revolt, that Treblinka stood alone—the horror was accomplished, ineradicable, the moment any one man entered Dachau—but that no husbands, wives, parents, children *stood*—by their radios or sofas or milking stools—and said, "No, kill us here in our tracks together." Oh maybe some did—then why are they unknown? Why aren't their statues in every city center, our new saints of love?—so far surpassing Tristan or Abelard or Antony as to burn like constellations over fuming brush fires. We are only left with endless processions of pairs who *agreed*—to abandonment, to separation by other human beings (not death or time). You know that there were mothers who hid from their children on arriving at Auschwitz—buried their own heads in coats or crawled through knees—to escape immediate death? Can they be forgiven that?

Every American over thirty has his favorite obsessive Holocaust story which he's read or, rarely, heard and retails ever after as his version of

Hell. An entire sub-study might be done of these stories and their relevance to the teller. I *heard* mine, and after we parted. A colleague of mine—age 38—is a west-Polish Jew. His mother died of TB early in the war. There were no other children and he lived with his father, a practicing dentist. When the roundup came in '42, my friend was eleven. In warm July weather he rode with his father in the packed train to Sobibor—two days, I think, stopping and starting—and once they were there and unloaded on the siding and a doctor came round to eliminate the sick, my friend's father said that his son was consumptive. It was news to my friend; but being a child, he only thought, "Of course he's right; they kept it from me." But his father never touched him and my friend was led off, presumably for gassing or a lethal injection. Some balls-up ensued, his death was delayed; he never coughed once, chest sound as a stone. But he never saw his father. He was strong enough to work, my friend—farm the camp potatoes—so he managed to live through two more years and a transfer to Auschwitz. Then one day—age thirteen—he was standing in a compound when a line of new men passed. One man fell out for a moment and came toward him. My friend said, "He thought he was running; he was creeping" (too weak to run). Of course, it was his father. They both knew that. But they didn't speak and, again, didn't touch; and a guard beat his father into line—fifteen seconds. Never met again.

Well, in the immortal words of King Lear—"*Howl.*" My friend thinks the question in his story is *why?*—why his father did that. I'd never tell him but the question is *how?* There are degrees of offense at which motive is irrelevant. Can he ever be forgiven?—that father (out of Dante) stumbling on his appallingly vital son whom he'd lied to kill? Can any of the millions ever be forgiven?

Can you, Sara, ever? And not just by me. It was you who refused. Only you were not killed. You could have walked into that tamed camp with me; you could have had the guts to settle it *inside*—to have seen it all with me, to have armed it with the threat which without you it lacked and then (if you needed so desperately) have said to me, "No, I will not live for you." Instead, for your own no doubt clear reasons, you lurked outside on the shady rim, half-sadist, half-coward—unwilling to choose, thinking you could wait and that I, having waited for half an hour beyond a wire fence among debris as meaningless as M.G.M. sets, would presently return.

I did and didn't. When I came back through the gates, I didn't look for you but went to the car and sat in its oven-heat. I already knew that I was not waiting and had not returned, not to you at least; but— stopped short of panic or the courage to act my feeling—I was not prepared to abandon you physically, to leave your bags on the empty parking space and drive off for Salzburg with your twenty-dollar *Figaro* ticket in my wallet. So I thought in the heat, "I may go-under but I won't go looking."

In three or four minutes you walked up slowly, got in and sat, facing forward. How did I feel to you? What vibrations, what aura? Or were you receiving? Had you ever been?

What I felt was hatred. What's *hatred*, you ask?—the wish that you were absent from my sight, my life, absent from my memory. I had put my hands on the wheel for steadiness, and I thought my hatred was shaking the car. Then I saw, in my head, a Volkswagen jittering-away in the sunkist parking lot at Dachau; so I cranked up and moved.

You said "Where are you going?"

I did not want to stop now and look at you—I must keep my hands busy. I said "I? To Salzburg."

"Am I coming?" you said.

"Unless you jump," I said.

I think you took that to mean you were forgiven. You behaved as though you were. Slowly through our drive to Salzburg you loosened, slowly became the girl I'd thought I needed—smiles at my profile and, then when we'd got in sight of hills, you sang the whole final scene of *Figaro* (from "*Gente, gente, all'armi, all'armi*"), taking all the parts, chorus included. Your text was letter-perfect, your Italian B+; only your baritone plunges failed. Yet I knew your motive far better than you. It had nothing to do with the coming evening. It all bloomed out of your need and wish to sing five lines—

THE COUNT:

> Contessa, perdono.   [*Countess, your pardon.*

THE COUNTESS:

> Più docile io sono e   —*I'm gentler now and I'll*
> dico di sì.   *say yes.*

ALL:

> Ah! Tutti contenti   —*Ah! Everybody's happy*
> saremo così.   *with that.*]

That, I think, was the climax though the day (and this piece) had a good while to run. I took that to mean you were pardoning *me*—for not having cheerfully granted your independence back at Dachau, for not having bought the metaphor your refusal offered (we'd be hitched to one load but in separate yokes). So I thought I would launch a spot of unforgivability. When you'd sung through the orchestral *tutti* to the curtain, you faced forward resolutely—no bow in my direction. That meant I should applaud—right? Well, I drove a good mile before making a sound; and then I said "One question."

"What?"

"Why in all your extensive *reconciliation* repertoire"—can you still do Cordelia, Marina, Fidelio?—"is it always the *lady* dispensing largess?"

You'd have bit off your tongue before admitting you hadn't noticed. You said, in an instant, "It's the way the world's built."

"Many thanks," I said and by then we were threading the fringes of Salzburg, its castle as stunned by the day as I.

I said that this would be my version, what I remember and understand. The rest of the day—what I thought was the day—is necessary;

then tell me yours; I genuinely need it. Yet, again, my memory of *places* is vague, my grip on surfaces. You've greased my hands, greased every wall; or is it only some new lubricant from myself, manufactured now in me—suddenly—in response to your refusal, to ease me away? Anyhow, it's still produced. Some days it pours.

Mozart's *Geburtshaus*—we saw that together but what do I recall? Two or three pokey rooms, white walls, dark brown woodwork, an early piano on which (the guide told us) Harry Truman had just played. Was there even a *birth*-room? Were they sure of which room? I couldn't say. It seemed more like the birthplace of some dry chip—say, Metternich—than the Sublime Foul Mouth. And didn't you recognize that? When we'd made our separate rounds and I passed the guest-book on my way downstairs, I saw you'd signed with your comic alter-ego— *Veronica F. Pertle and traveling companion*. We were already lethal, in under three hours—we'd agreed to be a team of cut-rate Midases, transmuting all we touched to chalk.

I slept through a good deal of *Figaro*—all that endless nocturnal business at the start of Act III, the confused identities. I've slept through greater performances than that—Melchior's Lohengrin, Welitsch's Salome—though always before from travel fatigue, biting off more grandeur than I could chew, but here I wasn't tired. I'd slept eight hours the night before, driven ten miles to walk maybe five hundred paces round a concentration camp, then eighty miles farther on a good wide road. No, I was retreating. The great death wish, Sleep Mother of Peace—if I couldn't lose you, I could lose myself. You woke me toward the end with a firm elbow—"Don't miss the forgiveness." So I can still hear that (Schwarzkopf's perfect frailty, a bulldozer disguised as a powderpuff); thanks for the elbow—the trip was not in vain.

What I think I remember—as clear as the Norwegian day, your offered food—is the rest of the night. Correct me on this—

We had late coffee in some hotel lobby which seems, in memory, entirely upholstered in 1938 Pontiac fabric, and were spared conversation by a pair of purple-haired American ladies drinking *Liebfraumilch* six feet away. They had also heard the opera and debated the performance. One defended it stoutly but the doubter trumped her in the end—remember?—"Lena, all I know is, when I hear great singing something in me swells up. Tonight it didn't swell."

—"Mine neither," you said and stood and we left, heading toward Munich still hungry (no supper). Yet you didn't mention food, barely spoke at all; and what did I feel?—that really I was racing, to end this night, the trip, what we'd had and you'd failed, that I could go without food and sleep for days, an emergency encystment for however long it took to deliver you to whatever door you chose.

Then on the edge of Munich you said, "I'll never sleep without some food."

It was pushing two a.m. So I had to hunt awhile; but we found a place open somewhere in Schwabing, down a flight of stairs thickly cushioned with dirt.

"More dikes than Holland," you said going in; but in what light there was, they seem more like gypsies to me on hindsight.

You wanted fondue but we settled for something merciful and a good deal of wine; and with all the eating, surely we hadn't said fifty words when the two men entered with the lion before them. If they weren't gypsies I'll surrender my license—they laid down about them that heavy metal air of offense and threat I've known all my life (they still roamed the South when I was a boy, telling fortunes and offering odd skilled services no one would accept, though by then in trailers not painted wagons; and their squat swart women with the Carmen earrings and their men whose hard faces all wore livid scars are high in my childhood pantheon of menace).

They picked you at once. Do you still think I signaled them? I *saw* them see you the moment they entered, even the lion.

He was straining toward you on his red dog-leash—maybe six months old?—and no one held him back though I swear the rear man—the one with hands free—passed the huge lady-owner a small piece of money in their rush to you. Were they illegal, bribing their way? The lion was smelling your foot before you saw; and of course you didn't flinch—a male lion cub in a Bavarian dive at the end of a day comprising Dachau and Mozart: oh.

They were photographers—take your picture with a lion; best American Polaroid, instant result. I told them No—didn't I? I'm almost sure I did—but the contact man (the one with the leash) held the lion up and said "See, he *begs*." With his free hand he clasped the cub's front paws together in a mockery of prayer (its high tight testicles were pink as salmon, utterly vulnerable). The man's English seemed more Italian than German but maybe just basic PX English— "He begs you to warm him; four dollars for picture, give to your husband. He lose his mother, he lonely here." The cub's eyes were shut, so lonely he was dozing.

You continued eating but you asked him "Did you kill her?"

That seemed the terror-button. Surely these two oily small-time spivs had not been poaching in Kenya; yet at your question, they both threw grimaces at once another, and the talker said, "Look. No charge for you." He extended the lion, eyes still shut—"He need your help."

"He's asleep," you said.

The man jogged him hard; he looked out, groggily.

"No," you said.

But I said "Do it" and produced my wallet. I wanted you to do it and I wanted to pay.

Looking at the lion not me, you said "Why?"

"I want the picture."

I extended twenty marks to the man and you stood.

"You sit," the man said, "then we take you both."

"I'll stand," you said. "It's me he wants." You stood and reached out. You were in the black dress with narrow shoulder straps—much white skin showed.

He moved close against you and hung the lion on your shoulder like a child. The photographer—the silent man—backed off and raised his camera; the talker said "Big smile."

You smiled sideways, no teeth. The other diners paused, awaiting the flash. It came. In its light, blood streamed down your arm.

The lady-owner bellowed, came waddling forward. The two men leapt toward you. The lion was clamped into the meat of your shoulder.

I was still in my chair.

"Stay back," you said.

They understood and stopped a foot from the table.

"What's his name?" you said.

The talker said "Bob."

The lady-owner babbled coldly in German. They must get him out, get out themselves, *die Polizei!*

You were stroking the back of Bob's locked-on neck, simply saying his name again and again—the two of us the only calm people in the room, only still ones at least. Us and the lion—he was motionless, teeth deep in you. What nourishment was he taking?—what pleasure, fulfillment? What did he think you were?

—A lion-tamer, anyhow. You stroked him free; he looked round at his owners. You had never smiled, talked baby-talk to him, given the odor of fear or asked for help; you had saved your day. You handed Bob over to the trembling talker.

He slapped him once across the nose, laid my money by my plate; and they left at a trot—the owner behind them, maledicting.

(*I don't have the picture.* Have you thought of that? Did we ever mention that? Of course, I didn't pay but a picture was taken, at the instant of the bite. Does it still exist in some gypsy's pocket?—an image of a bad night, another close call, image of his *life*, assault and impotence, the helpless witness of another's competence to solve hurtful puzzles? I would give a lot for it. What is on your face?—still, after twelve years? What did I miss in the moment of flash, your moment of sudden unexpected pain? Whom were you blaming? I need that picture badly.)

Before I could stand up to check the damage, you had asked a bystander, "*Wo ist die Damen?*" and loped off to that.

So I sat again and was wondering what next when the owner pounded back with a rusty first-aid kit and stopped at me, aghast.

"*Wo ist ihre Gattin?*"

I said that the *Fraulein* was in the cabinet, washing.

She considered attempting to wither me for negligence but no doubt remembered that in her situation *die Polizei* was a two-edged blade; so she said, "*Nicht toll, nicht toll. Er ist nicht tollwütig*" *(not rabid)* and headed for the *Damen* to disinfect you.

I ate on and in five minutes she returned to say you were all right, would be back soon and would we, in recompense, have a free dessert? I thought that seemed uniquely German—for a lion-bite, dessert—but I accepted and she quickly produced two enormous wedges of obscenely moist chocolate whipped-cream cake. I thanked her, she assured me again "*Nicht toll*" and that you were fine. Then she left.

I waited awhile—thinking what? Most likely, nothing. (I can sit for whole half-hours, thinking nothing, my consciousness a bowl of thick soup, cooling. You'd never accept that; so often, on the road, when we'd ridden in silence, you'd say "What are you thinking?" and when I'd say "Nothing," you'd clearly disbelieve me. *Why?* What mutterings filled *your* silence? It is how I understand the life of objects. Keats said that he could inhabit a sparrow and peck in the gravel. I can inhabit, say, a walnut log or the white blind heart of a loaf of bread.) Maybe though I thought a few calm sad thoughts on our imminent split—*past* split, in fact; it was hours old. But I know I wasn't yet asking *why?* I was now an engine geared for one purpose—the expulsion of waste parts, self-starting restored. And when, in five minutes, you hadn't come, I began my cake and called for coffee. In ten more, I'd finished; you were still absent; and the owner walked past me—no word or look—to check you again.

She returned and I managed to understand through her fury that now you had the outer door locked and had spoken to her but would not open.

I couldn't think of how to say "Give her time"; so I must have stared blankly till the owner said in English in a python-hiss (discovering *Ssss* in two s-free words)—"Go. *You* go!" She'd have punched me in the breast bone with her short fat finger, but I leaned back and stood and went to the *Damen*.

I knocked and called your name.

You must have been against the door—no sound of steps—but you took a few beats before turning the lock.

When I opened, you were standing three feet away, by a grimy wash basin, your back to me, your head down but silent.

I said "Are you hurt?"

You turned to show me. Your face was splotched from crying; but you weren't using that—no mercy pleas. You pointed to your shoulder. One single strip of bandage, one inch by two.

I looked from where I was—I'd entered entirely but the door was cracked open (for needy *Damen*). It didn't occur to me to take another step, touch you gently, peel the bandage back and check—was that all my fault? Weren't you throwing off a field of volts that I'd never have pierced, however determined?

"One tooth," you said, "one canine puncture."

"Good," I said. (I knew you'd had tetanus shots and, now from the owner, that Bob was not rabid.)

You said it to my eyes (I grant you that), "*Good?* Well, I guess"— another three beats, no shifting of gaze—"Yes, *marvelous.* Something *in* me finally. And a permanent mark." You pressed the bandage. "I'll carry a little white scar to my grave, the size of a navy bean—a real lion, my summer in Europe. I can show my children." You reached for your purse and, as you came toward me, said "Chocolate on your teeth" (was I grinning by then?). Then you said, "I need air. Please wash your mouth and I'll meet you at the car." You went out past me, half-closing the door again.

So since the room was empty I went to the basin. In the mirror I seemed unaltered though my teeth were socketed in chocolate. I was

flushing my mouth when (i never told you) I saw your little message—
to the side of the mirror and in small printed letters but quite clearly
your hand (the only graffito, your color of ink, of course in English).
Before I could read it, I knew it was not for me. You'd had no way to
know I'd enter the *Damen*—or had you? did you wait to force me to
come and see the two lines? Is it why you wouldn't let the owner in?
How could she have minded? She'd have never understood. Who on
God's earth would?—

> *Jesus, will you help me now?*
> *I will. I have.*

I thought at once of Salinger's *Franny*—mystical union in the Ladies
Room—but I knew that, even if you'd read the story you'd have thought
it unforgivably corny to mimic its action, like quoting Edgar Guest at
a family funeral. In any case, Franny only squeezed her little book,
The Way of the Pilgrim; you addressed Jesus straight and claimed a
straight answer. You were surely not drunk, surely not joking. I dreaded
facing you. What help had you got? What new fierce power? How
much farther could you thrust me?

But I went, paid the bill, thanked the owner for her help and the
chocolate cake—she smiled but despised me—and climbed to the street.

The car was parked five steps away—no sign of you. I looked toward
both dark ends of the street—nothing, empty. I stood yearning to run—
to enter the car silently, crank and drive away. You had your passport
and traveler's checks. And I'd taken a step—would I have done it?—
when you rounded the nearest corner, stopped in the cone of light. I
waited for you to come on to me.

But you pointed behind you down the hidden street and held your
place.

So I went to you, more curious now than dreading. You were back
in darkness before I reached you—I was both spared and deprived full
sight of your face. "You're all right?" I said.

You didn't answer that. You pointed again toward the end of the street—what seemed a small park, a knot of trees.

I said, "Do you want to walk?"

You said, "No, I've got something to show you."

I walked beside you but you were leading.

The park was two concentric rings of sycamores that all but filled the dark space above with limbs, leaves. Only a piece of sky twenty feet square, say, was visible; but despite the glow of Munich and the few park lights, there were stars—oh a dozen. You took us to the center.

I looked round—alone; all benches empty.

Then you said "Straight up!"

I looked, half-thinking you had lost a screw; even one-tenth wondering if you'd stab my unprotected gut (you who trapped spiders in my Oxford rooms and conveyed them, live, outside to grass).

Again you were pointing. "See those two stars there?"

"Yes."

"Now shift to the right and down an inch or so."

I did.

"See that blur?"

I waited, straining not to blink; then I saw it—a faint smear, an old chalk fingerprint. "Yes."

You moved closer on me and, there as I was, hands loose at my sides, head back, throat stretched taut, I considered again that you might have plans and means to kill me—a sacrifice to what? Your Jesus-of-the-*Damen?* Some Eastern star god?—Ishtar, Ahura Mazda? For that moment, it seemed an acceptable fate—or not to over-dignify it, *acceptable next act,* Tosca and Scarpia, *finalmente mia!* (Is it from this whole full day that my total fearlessness emerges? Death would startle me, granted, but roughly as much as an air-filled bag popped behind my ear. I face all prospects quite nicely, thank you; let Nothing mishear me though and apply misfortunes.)

But you only spoke. "Do you know what it is?"

I said "Do you?"

"NGC 224."

"Is that a space ship?" I said (no satellites yet, though the Russians were cranking up, a little to our right).

"No, the great spiral galaxy in Andromeda."

I had vague recollections of boyhood astronomy, photographs in *My Weekly Reader* from Mount Palomar; but I certainly made no leap of awe.

You said, "Do you know how far away it is?"

"No."

"One million, five hundred thousand light-years. And what its apparent diameter is?"

"No," I said.

"Sixty thousand light-years." Your hand was still up, no longer quite pointing but in a sort of arrested Boy Scout salute; and your lips were parted—you were just beginning.

Yet my dread, such as it was, was ebbing. The worst possibility now seemed clearly nothing more than a Thornton Wilder sermon on Justus and the Stars—you *were* drunk, I thought; this was way below standard.

You dropped your hand but continued silently looking up.

So I felt I had to speak. "What am I supposed to do?"

"Forgive me," you said.

That was meant to be worse than a sacrificial knife. It was. I must have wobbled. At some point I said "For what?" I was facing you now— or your dim profile; you would not look downwards.

"You know," you said.

"For waiting back today at Dachau?"

"More than that," you said.

"Say what then, please."

"For not thinking you were safe to follow."

"Into poor Dachau? It's a national park. There are not even bears."

"Don't joke. *You* know."

I didn't know but I didn't ask—because, just then, I didn't want to know and, after the whole day, couldn't care much. Simple as fatigue.

You apparently knew—had thought through your balking and, in asking for pardon, were asking your way back into my life. I was safe, after all, to follow?—was that it? Or safe as you guessed you could hope to find? Or maybe you'd realized after all that you'd led, not followed, all those years in any case?

I wasn't standing there, in silence, asking questions—again I was locked in simple fatigue.

Then you looked at me and said "You haven't answered."

"What?" I said.

You said again "Forgive me?"

I should have said Yes. It was surely the instinct, the reflex of my feeling; but with Yes in my mouth, I balked and thought, "I must wait till tomorrow. It would be my tiredness talking, and the wine." It would—I know now—have been my heart but wait I did. I said "Give me time."

You nodded, gave it and went to the car only slightly before me.

But in two further weeks on the road, I never answered. (Not that I forgot; it was all I thought of—a glaze of scum which I laid across all those Rembrandts and Vermeers that might have saved us if they'd cared enough to fight. They survived it though, my self-surrendered vandalism. You and I didn't, no masterworks.) And you never asked again. You should have. Why not? You had led so much of the way. Your silence and patience only fueled my flight, stoked a natural warmth of sadism in me which let me ride beside—*lie* beside you— for weeks more and still wish that you would vanish, speaking civilly but coolly, touching you only by accident. (If you were awake—and I did wait until you were breathing like sleep—I beg your pardon now that twice in those last weeks I lay beside you, not ten inches away, and took what pleasure my head demanded from my own dry self with my own dry hand: dry to keep the slapping down. Fun, fun.)

Why? You never asked that even. Why, after years of assuming I required you—daily sight of you, daily touch—after gladly embracing the prospect of *life* with you, your one false move in the parking lot at Dachau thrust me from you in a helpless irresistible rush? Worse than helpless, *grinning.* I was glad, I thought, to go. Blessed clear space at hand—empty, free—toward which I flew at stunning speeds like your galaxy.

Well—Jesus—we've uncovered the secret of Dachau, of all the camps, every act of submission, why no one refused, even the de Wieks—they were glad to go! In secret glee, which they could not have borne to face or seek themselves, millions like us were permitted to abandon all human contracts, bonds—*duties!*—to shed all *others* like last year's skin and to stand, if only for a few hours, free; breathing free air (unshared by wives or children) till the air became gas. There were two women smiling in that photograph, remember? holding their children for the last heavy moment before pitching forward, dead in a ditch, but alive maybe one moment longer than the child. After such knowledge, what forgiveness? We should never have acquired it, by chance or intent. Yet you forced it on us—by your simple refusal twelve years ago at Dachau.

I'm back where I started, Sara—why did you refuse?

Never mind. I won't care now. But one more thing—your astronomy lecture, so unheralded that night in the Munich park, when I thought you'd gone nuts if not homicidal (messages from Jesus and NGC 224)? I've been working on that lately—what you might have intended, short of an open-air homily on the need for love in the drowned depths of space. I've read up on your pet galaxy Andromeda—Fred Hoyle, the *Larousse Astronomie,* even old Sir James Jeans' *Mysterious Universe* with its chilling, exhilarating, unanswerable conclusion—

We discover that the universe shows evidence of a designing or controlling power that has something in common with our own individual minds—not, so far as we have discovered, emotion, morality, or aesthetic appreciation, but the tendency to think in the way which, for want of a better word, we describe as mathematical. And while much in it may be hostile to the material appendages of life, much also is akin to the fundamental activities of life; we are not so much strangers or intruders in the universe as we at first thought. Those inert atoms in the primaeval slime which first began to foreshadow the attributes of life were putting themselves more, and not less, in accord with the fundamental nature of the universe.

Were you making one last try, that night, to accord us with the universe?

I've bought its picture—your galaxy's. After years of wondering and stumbling across it, badly printed and dingy, in various books, I ordered its photograph from Mount Palomar. For two weeks now it's hung above my desk—only just below Jesus, your other messenger (Rembrandt's Hundred Guilder print, in a first-class fake). So it watches me this minute (as it watches perpetually, day-sky or night). The picture (through the 48″ Schmidt telescope) is in color—the great spiral itself in white, rose and lilac on a matte brown sky pierced by single stars. If I didn't know, it could be several things—a Miami lady-decorator's dream of the ultimate ballroom chandelier. Or—for me most pleasing—the loveliest toy ever made. It could be that (sixty thousand light-years across)—a cooling circular platter of light that whirls round its billowing center in utter silence, having no final rim but diminishing slowly into thinner clouds of stars and finally night; my dream of a mobile to hang in my bedroom to wake to at night; or the sort of gift that God the Father might have willed for the Infant Christ (trumping the Magi) in a Milton ode (what if Milton could have seen it?)—

> *And for a sign of My delight in Thee,*
> *I hang this tilted wheel above Thy bed,*

> *Attended at the rim by Hosts who smile*
> *And, smiling, face the axle drowned in light*
> *Whence My eternal love for Thee streams fire.*

Did we really see it that August night? Was that smudge above Munich really it? Or were you lying? Or did you not know? I haven't yet found in any of my reading whether or not the Andromeda galaxy is visible ever to the naked eye—and if so, was it visible in Munich that particular night (or early morning)?

Look. I'm going to assume that you really thought you saw it and that—calling me and pointing up and reeling off those almanac-facts as prelude to asking forgiveness—what you meant to say was something like this, another effort at the poem you were always aching to write (your poem, not mine; mine would be better but that's my job, right?)—

There it hangs, a million and a half light-years away, sixty thousand visible light-years across, composed of billions of separate stars all drowned in isolation yet all wheeling round a common center at something like a half million miles per hour, a stroke of radiance on your retina dimmer than the luminous dial of your watch. Or there it hung a million years ago, for the instant it took to launch this present light in its unimaginable outward flight toward the curved walls of space. Flight from what though?—the Big Bang? Maybe. But maybe flight from us, simply you and me, the two repellent objects at the core of space from which all other matter hurtles at speeds increasing till they pass the speed of light (and hurtled for millions of years before us in anticipation of this one day). Or a little less narcissistically—in flight from the blue planet, home of men. For elsewhere, all creatures desire perfect union— desire not require—and each one's desire is silently achieved. Parallels meet. It is how the world is made. Andromeda—the millions of other universes, the billions of planets—is swarmed with pairs who serve each other. Or, barring that, is empty; has the grace to be empty. We will not be forgiven for forcing their flight. Turn. Return.

I'd add only this—it is all no doubt grander, funnier than that. God only watches comedies, can only smile. Waterloo, Dachau. The end is planned. There are no options.

Sara, come back.

THE GOLDEN CHILD

I F S H E W E R E alive she'd be sixty-seven. But she died at nine, in agony. And so while she lives in a few minds still, she lives by the name she was always called in family stories—Little Frances. The stories were few and remarkably sketchy, as if my endlessly tale-telling kin knew they must use her but could hardly bear to portray her fate on the bolt of wearable goods they wove from the lives of all our blood and neighbors.

We knew she was "both her parents' eyeballs," a local expression which meant "their all." Her father was "Stooks" Rodwell, my mother's youngest brother. Her mother was "Toots," from Portsmouth, Virginia; and all their married life, the two lived there. By the time I knew them, Frances was dead; and they showed how badly scarred they were. Stooks was roughshod and raucous, the family cynic. Toots was acid and managerial, though both craved fun and were as loyal in trouble as good sheepdogs.

Before I was five I knew nearly all I'd ever know about Frances. She was blond and fine to see. She fell while skating on the concrete sidewalk and scraped a leg. The scrape got infected but seemed to heal. Then a few weeks later she ran a high fever that wouldn't break. The doctor diagnosed it as osteomyelitis, a deep bone infection. In 1931 there were literally no effective internal antibiotics. The only treatment was to scrape or saw out the affected bone, crippling the patient.

But with Frances' fever, surgery was impossible. Infection roared through her. The relentless fever triggered convulsions. My mother told me more than once how "Little Frances' head would bend right back and touch her heels—she spasmed that hard." The child suffered torture for several days. Her lips dried crusty, her voice went hoarse, but she still pled for mercy. Everybody hovered and prayed; nothing helped in the slightest but death. It came at last, though nobody left alive was the same ever again, not at the thought or mention of Frances—Little Frances, welcome as daylight, tortured to death as a lovable child.

When I was born two years later, it was touch-and-go from Mother's slow labor well on into my third year. Inexplicable convulsions would seize me, a long spell of whooping cough, skin eruptions that left me bloody. No infant had died in either of my parents' families in forty years. But the recent fact of Frances must have appalled them night after night as they watched me suffer too, helpless and pleading. From the year I retain my first strong memories, between three and four, I can call back vivid pictures of her still. Mother had a hand-colored picture of her, framed on the bedroom dresser.

It's a bright warm day. Little Frances stands outdoors in a pale dress, four feet tall and half turned away. But someone holding the camera calls her name; and she turns to look, turns forever in fact. Her blond curls reach almost to her neck and are blurred by the move. Her eyes are crouched against the sun, so I have no sense of their color or size. But her lips split open on a smile so strange that, even then, I guessed the smile was a clue to some big secret she kept. This girl, my tortured cousin, knew something big and kept it hid.

In a few more years when I'd seen two or three old kinsmen's bodies, dead and still and cold as dressed chickens, I thought I'd caught the heart of Frances' secret. *She knows she'll never get old like this, this cold and smelling like celluloid. She'll stay there smiling in a handmade picture*. But I took little comfort in my discovery. I still had most of childhood to travel before penicillin and sulfa drugs were widely sold; and Little Frances would be brought to me, again and again in Mother's voice, at any chance of physical harm.

Touch football, running, sledding in snow, my first roller skates—as I left for every innocent game, Mother was liable to cloud and mutter "Little Frances would be here, strong today, if she hadn't fallen and scraped her shin." And I just now recall that, since Frances came from Mother's family, her name was absent from my even more direful father's warnings. With no such terror in his bloodline—and though a staunch Democrat—Father resorted to President Coolidge's son, who blistered a heel at tennis and died of infection swiftly thereafter.

Yet for all the use of my dead first cousin as a somber omen, I never came to resent her name or to gloat in private on the early end of a family saint. I can no longer hope to explain my logic; but somewhere long before puberty, I told myself I loved my cousin Marcia so much I would marry her down the road. I also guessed there was something skewed in the plan, some kink. I'd do my research in cool disguise, concealing my hope for Marcia under a different name. So one after-noon—age seven and back in the kitchen with Mother—I chose my best absentminded voice and said "If Little Frances was living, and we loved each other, could we get married?"

Mother said "No."

"Why?"

"She'd be your first cousin."

"What's wrong with that?"

"Son, it's against all kinds of laws. You might have two-headed babies or morons."

"Why?"

"You just might. It works that way." (We lived in medieval oblivion to sane genetics. Years after, when Mother was bearing my brother, a neighbor stopped by with a live lobster somebody had shipped him, on ice, from Maine. Lobsters were as rare in the South in the thirties as antibiotics; and when he was gone, my mother said "I hope this baby won't come here wearing feelers and claws"—she was only half-joking.)

First cousins were out then, unless we eloped and deceived the Law. But there might be hope—Marcia and I were first cousins once-removed. I'd try that next. I started to say "What about once-removed?"

Mother's eyes had filled though. She said "I think Little Frances loved me more than anybody else before you. I used to take her horseback riding when she came down with Toots on the train."

I'd never quite heard that before, how I had overtaken Frances in strength of love for someone as easy to love as my mother. It thrilled me right at the roots of my scalp because I loved her with a depth so dark it hurt more than not.

But before I could think of envy or pride or ask more questions, Mother painted one of her oldest pictures. "Little Frances walked down the aisle at my wedding ahead of me and scattered rose petals to guide my path. Toots had made her a dress with Belgian lace; and when I walked toward that altar behind her, I prayed to have a child that fine— she was five years old, smart and sweet as the day. I can see her hair right now in candlelight."

I said "Did you get it?"

"Get what?"

"A child," I said, "that fine and smart."

But though Mother often said God chose wisely in sending her a boy (she was half a boy herself many ways), at that strange moment her tears poured free; and she left the room.

Her unpredictable bondage to the past, always a grim past, was one of the few sad facts about her—her parents had died long before she was grown, and she marked their birth- and death-days yearly with a taut brow and full eyes. But that one time stuck in my mind as the worst of all, the day she chose Little Frances over me. It became the day I began to cross the wide threshold that waits for us all; I began to see my own death ahead.

At the moment I didn't think to follow my mother and ask more questions, on Frances or me or the aim of life. Like most young children I had mostly assumed the world was one enormous breast, full and generally trusty. Its purpose was feeding and caring for me. How had this terrible door swung open—a good child wrenched into burning hoops, then dragged out of sight in screams forever? I almost certainly went to my room and played with my soothing menagerie of toys— elephants mostly, friends to man, but also a pride of treacherous cats.

And before many nights I started the dream that rode my sleep for years to come. In the past I'd occasionally waked up scared from a nightmare and run to Mother and Father's bed, my safest harbor. Hard as this new dream was however, I kept it secret and paid the tolls it took on my peace. It sometimes changed the setting and lights, but it always told the same cruel story. *I'm lying in bed or maybe outdoors in my new tent. Sometimes Marcia sleeps beside me; sometimes my black friend, John Arthur Bobbitt. But whoever's with me, they sleep on peaceful through my trial. What happens next is I wake up suddenly in the dark and find I can't move—not a muscle, a cell. I can't even blink my open eyes. All I can do is somehow draw light shallow breaths. I tell myself I'm dead like Little Frances; and though I am scared and hate my stillness, I also think 'Well, at least it didn't hurt.' Soon after that my backbone twitches, then spasms gently, then hard* hard. *My head and heels draw backward slowly toward each other. Then pain like nothing I've known or dreamed jolts through me like current. I understand that I'm not dead yet, but I cannot speak to ask for help or even for company. My partner, Marcia or black John Arthur, has not cared enough to wake and watch. This may not end. I wonder if Frances is trapped like this, or has she gone on somewhere free?*

The dream came back maybe two dozen times throughout my childhood till I left home for college and the world. Then I thought it stopped. And I thought I knew why. My mother had died; nobody was left above ground, near me, who'd known my pitiful cousin and could bring her pain back toward me in words. Bad as it was I went on keeping it secret from others because it gave me a serious *size* in my own mind. I would someday stop. Something was loose in the world or inside me that watched my moves and sooner or later would seize my legs and lay me down forever. From knowing of Frances Rodwell's fate, I understood that much before I even started thinking of eternal life, much less hoping for it.

I was so lonely and my life was so calm, till I was near grown, that such a grim prospect was not unwelcome. It dramatized my days and nights, all the risks I took in playing alone. It illuminated the faces of friends I made at school. Each year I'd fix on some boy or girl as if he or she were the light I needed to move and grow. But at some unpredictable point in my passion, the picture of Frances would stand beside them as an actual threat when I studied their eyes or the strength of their arms and envied their laughing ease, their power. Overnight they could be clawed down in pain and die with no rescue.

For instance in the fourth grade I knew a chubby and very shy girl who would talk to no other boy but me. She was never a target of my adoration; but the spring we were ten, she suddenly died of diabetes. She got home from school one afternoon while her parents were still at the hosiery mill; she lay down to take her usual rest on the living-room couch before putting on the potatoes for supper. But by the time her father walked in at half past four and called her name, she had drifted off—so gently, he said, that "not one hair of her head was wrinkled."

Mother and I went to pay our respects; and there she was—her name was Hallie—laid out in a short white coffin, dressed in white with a white carnation in her bloodless hand. No star in all the movies I'd seen held my eyes like Hallie. She seemed both stiller than any rock mountain and also trembling like a dangerous substance, pouring out rays. I understood that her luck was awful; but I also envied the pale allure that drew us toward her and would keep this final sight of her face as clear as a stab in our minds forever. I knew better than to say it to Mother. But standing there and later at the funeral, I more than half-planned a rival attraction—my own death soon.

And I almost got it. That same summer my family and I made a weekend trip to mine and Mother's birthplace, the Rodwell home. Little Frances' parents were there on a visit; and with all the joy my mother took in each of her kin, there was no way not to drive up there and see Stooks and Toots. Already I'd secretly turned against them. Stooks was loud and a mean joker. Toots was gentler but would still ask scalding questions in public such as "Don't those knickers smell a lot like pee?" And the two together, once Frances was gone, had fallen deep in love with Marcia, my first cousin once-removed and Stooks' great-niece. At the age I was, I could see no reason for their favoritism except that Marcia was a light-haired girl and was born nine months after Frances died (the fact that I too loved Marcia only raised the pitch of the tension I felt).

The first night there, the house was full of siblings, aunts, uncles and cousins. Marcia and Pat, her younger sister, and I had been shouldered out of the living room and were playing cards in the long dim hall. Our skills were limited so the game must have been either fish, slapjack or maybe old maid. Anyhow I recall I was cheating to win. Marcia and Pat were loudly complaining, though with no great rancor; they'd soon have curbed me back into line.

But Stooks, in the living room, heard the debate and came out to check. He was always trying to barge in on us with rough dumb jokes to make us like him, when I understood that his principal aim was guarding Marcia from worldly harm. That night once he learned I'd cheated at cards, he lit into me with what I remember as unearned meanness—*Who did I think I was, some prince? Didn't I know a cheat was the lowest scoundrel on Earth? Who would ever love me? I'd better get myself honest, right now.*

With the passion for justice and fine proportion that all children share, I knew he was way out of line and hateful. I also knew he was Mother's brother, however unfair, and would get away with it. So I said not a word but fought back tears long enough to stand and retreat, by the dark back way, to the west bedroom where we would be sleeping and where I was born. For once I took a reckless course and shut the door behind me. I was truly alone now. That would show them.

Then in savage misery I fell face down on my narrow birthbed and actively wished hard luck on Stooks. I waited long minutes for Mother to come and ease the pain, for anyone out of that crowd of laughers to take my side and stand for the right—it had just been a *game*. When nobody showed up and laughter continued elsewhere without me, I pulled my mind back into my skull and relied on me, my only friend. In fairly short order I found two facts I'd ignored till then—that Frances died to punish her father and that I was glad. The truth was no more mysterious than that. And I said it over time and again with a merciless smile in the thick black air till I finally dozed.

What woke me, whenever, was a dry *tap tap*, hard and inhuman. I was not much braver than the average child, but at first I lay still and tested the sound. It was not the shut door, no knocking hand. It came from the far west side of the room, entirely dark. I'd already read *Treasure Island* and stored the news and sight of Blind Pew, tapping on the road with his walking stick and bent on vengeance. So at once I guessed this was no kind gift aimed toward me in recompense for my mistreatment. Then it tapped again, harder still.

I propped myself on both elbows and looked toward the farthest tall window, moonlit. In the lower right corner, the size of a bucket, was a long black head with upcurved horns. The Devil, who else? *For me*, why else? He had heard Stooks blame me and was here to gloat, if not to haul me off to Hell. Like most boys then I had a general notion of Hell, useful in sorting through life's million choices and oddly appealing, as a balance for Heaven, to a child's ruthless hunger for symmetry.

Tap tap again. His horns were knocking the glass to break it. In another minute he'd be in on me, choking or pressing me down to death. Upright in bed then, I set up a howl. The tapping went on and nobody came. I didn't think that, with the door shut and an empty room between us, nobody could hear me. With every second I grew more desperate; but addled by sleep, I never thought to stand and run toward light and my family. Maybe my anger and shame also stalled me.

Whyever, I stayed there staked to the bed, crying in terror and the worst self-pity I'd yet indulged. I thought hours passed and it helped not at all that eventually the tapping stopped and the head disappeared. It was surely lurking just out of sight for my next false move. The bitterest word of all I thought in the eye of that storm was *abandonment* (or whatever form of the word I knew). I never felt a trace of guilt for cheating at cards—what were cards but a *game?*—and before much longer I passed the black point at which I expected rescue or even life itself.

Then rescue. The shut door opened quickly, grown bodies poured in; and one of them strode to the midst of the room, found the hanging cord and switched on a light. It was my parents with Stooks beside them. Later I learned that the next-door neighbors had heard my cries and alerted my parents. I'd never been gladder to see anybody; the concern on their faces was almost enough. The thing that muddied the rescue of course was Stooks there, grinning and saying "You're *fine*, nothing wrong with you."

I raced to tell of the Devil's head and the butting horns. My father especially heard the news grimly. He believed in the Devil and God more than most.

Mother said something like "Whoever you saw, he's far-gone now."

Stooks had to wade in with a quick line of jokes, "The old Scratch loves little tender white meat" (*Scratch* was the Devil's local nickname).

When he kept on laughing, I'm sorry to say I told him I knew why Little Frances left. I hesitate to guess my actual words, but right now I know they meant to be satanic.

I wonder still if Stooks really heard me. My memory is dim on the aftermath, but I think he said "Well—" or some such lifeless baffled word. I know his face fell in on itself; and though he kept standing there, he said no more.

I can't believe my mother didn't hear; but then or later, she never responded. With her adherence to the laws of family love, I know she'd have made me beg Stooks' pardon. But next she told the men to leave us. Then she went to the pitcher and bowl on the dresser (there was no bathroom). She wet a cloth with cool water and, old as I was, she washed my face and finally asked for details on the Devil.

I pitched in, telling it all again and scaring myself almost as bad as the moment I saw him.

Then the door reopened and Father was back. I've said that I saw, right off, he believed me. Far more than anybody else we knew, he saw the powers of Good and Evil as utterly real and always ready at the tips of our fingers, the crack of our lips. He said "Son, that was a cow you saw—Buck Thompson's cow. I went out there with Ida's flashlight. There's a pile of manure and some deep hoofprints. Buck's out there right now, tying her up."

I let them think that news relieved me, but I also knew it would cause much laughter in the living room (what Reynolds' overheated mind had made from a cow). But then and now half a century later, I have long spells of knowing I saw the pure condensation of evil that night—no comic Scratch but the cause of all hate toward children and beasts, the personal manager of Frances' torture who reached toward me in the stifling night and helped me strike my uncle Stooks Rodwell a cruel blow.

Stooks lived on another ten years. I know he was back home many more times, but I've kept no memory of his face or voice after that bad night. Maybe my mind was too ashamed of what I'd thought and said in meanness to store later pictures of his final years (I know he never taunted me again). I also have no recollection of Mother mentioning Frances after that in the twenty-four more years she lived. The obliterating mercy of time is widely praised; but Mother was not the woman to bury thoughts of a loved one—surely no child that died in innocence, gnashing her teeth.

Yet when Mother died and I winnowed the tons of paper she left, I found no trace of the old framed picture of Frances Rodwell with the close-held smile on death's doorsill. And so I lived for nineteen years past Mother's death, four decades past the Devil's visit. Then merciful time, in one of its notable lightning-changes, donned a monster face and struck me with a spinal wound that consumed four surgeries and 4,000 rads of blistering X-ray.

By then Little Frances was gone more than fifty years; every member of our family who had known or seen her was also gone. And I'd thought of her only when passing a friend who limps a little from childhood osteomyelitis in the 1930s. So it came as a shock to meet her once more but a shock that calmed into one of the actual helps I gave myself, or was given, in my own bad times.

In the first night after my third long surgery, which spent nine hours inside a foot-long stretch of my spinal cord with lasers and knives, I was on morphine; but it helped very little. My previous times on strong doses had all been dreamy womblike days of absolute safety and dreamless nights of deep brown rest. Only when the drug was withdrawn after three or four days would I dream again, mostly nightmares as though my mind must suddenly splurge on terror after its long pause. But this third time the opiate flew on through me helpless as fruit-juice to touch my pain. And all that night I woke fairly often and told my tape recorder the dream I just had. Most were stories.

Listening now to the halting tape, I can still be held by two of the dreams, both thoroughly pleasant. The first was a poem about a piece of music that, more than once, had helped me survive.

> *One of the palpable reproducible pleasures of the race—*
> *To lie in a dark room and hear Bach's third orchestral suite*

Build and destroy, assail and regale its golden pavilions
In the air of one's ears:
                              The healing light of utter power,
Utter content, actual promise.

In the second dream my mind took the urinary problems of a bedridden paraplegic and wove them into a full-dress imitation Bible story. On his deathbed an aged patriarch bade farewell to his grieving sons by explaining the useful symbolism of the shape of a large pee stain on the sheet. The name of the stain, he said, was *Djibouti*; and somehow to me that seemed good news, worth storing at least.

But then as the pain continued to mount, sometime near dawn I underwent my old boyhood dream of total paralysis. I noticed two big differences at once—*I'm now a grown man on a hospital bed, not a boy in a tent; and at first I seem entirely alone. The fear of my body's total stall is as high as ever though. I don't give a thought to Little Frances; she left my mind too long ago. Yet when I fail to wake myself, my frozen eyes begin to catch a rising light on the bed to my left. I do my best to watch it, and what I finally manage to glimpse is a woman my age in a standard-issue hospital gown—blond hair but streaked with gray. Her eyes are clamped shut; can it be my cousin Marcia?*

But then as I watch, her whole body gives a terrible shake as though an awful fist has struck her. Next her fine head jerks back hard; and still not opening her eyes or turning, whatever afflicts her draws her whole shape up from the bed till she makes an awful hoop in the air. I hear the sickening crack of bones as her head and heels meet beneath her. Then she turns one slow revolution above me till her face meets mine. Her eyes split open and of course it's Frances—grown, even older and worse off than me.

I try to think of a way to thank her, to beg her pardon for using her name to punish Stooks—his face sweeps past me for the first time in years, falling in on itself as it did when I hurt him. No way I can reach

out and bring him back. I only think that maybe here in my own
ordeal—if I bear it more bravely—I can somehow reach back and lighten
Frances' own long crucifixion. Someway I can suffer, here and now, to
lighten her pain all those years past.

But when I find that my lips can open, my tongue can move, Frances
starts to fade above me. Not before she speaks two words. Just as she's
almost gone from the room, her parched lips move; and she says "Stay
here." I understand she's heard my offer, silent as it was, to suffer for
her. So I stay as she goes; and then I try to draw my mind back down
inside me and wait in dignified calm, if not peace.

In general I'm readier than most of my friends to share the ancient
human belief that some dreams may well come from outside us, as
warnings or omens or practical aids from whatever made us and watches
our lives. So even now I'm not prepared to swear that Frances didn't
really arrive in my mind that night on a useful mission. Likewise I stay
openminded on what her two words meant. *"Stay here"*—stay where?
In a hospital bed in driving pain? Or stay on Earth till she comes back
and leads me again? But where to and how? Is part of the trouble I've
recently known intended to do what I guessed in that dream—to give
some backward help to Frances; some sharing and thinning of her
ordeal, her dreadful knowledge?

Whatever it meant and goes on meaning, I obeyed her. I stayed, that
night and till now. When I woke at daylight after she'd gone, the upper
half of my body could move. My legs were still frozen, useless as logs
screwed onto my hips. But three years later my hands still work and
have told this story. When Marcia and I and all our generation are
gone, at least this picture of one good child's burning death will stay
behind us.

No one could help Frances Rodwell back then, even there at her
bedside with cool compresses. How much less can I reach her now, a
boy cousin not even born when she died. But strangely now I can hope

to save her simple name a few years longer by fixing her fierce ordeal in words that may or may not move a few readers to look her way in their own short spans—a golden child clawed down by the dark but ready to live again any year in a patient mind that pauses a moment and gives her room.

TRUTH AND LIES

GUESSING THE SIGNAL Sarah Wilson flashed the car lights once. Nothing came or moved, only a rabbit close to the car, tan and quick in momentary light, eye congealed in terror. So she signaled again. Then dark and alone she said, "I will not break down. If she comes, if she's who I think she is, I will not give her that satisfaction." She shut her eyes to test her strength, to probe again the hole at the core of her chest. Then she hung her hands on the wheel, gripped till her ring ground loud on the grinding of crickets outside, and spoke again, "Don't let me break down now." That much was prayer to whatever might help—offered up through clear August night or ahead through glass to weeds of the railroad bank ten yards away where a girl had risen and stood now giant on the tracks and, seeing the second light, ran toward it. The crickets stopped as she split the weeds (safe down the bank from nights of practice), and her face stayed hid (a smile surely curled in the rims of her mouth). But she shrank as she came. That much made her bearable and when she crossed the last few feet and opened the door and lit the light, she reached her natural size; and Sarah Wilson could look and say, "Ella. I hoped it would not be you."

There had been no smile. There was none at their recognition. "Yes ma'm. It's Ella."

"And it's been you all this time."

Ella straightened into the dark, then leaned again. "I don't know how much time you mean, Mrs. Wilson."

"Oh I mean since before you were born, I guess."

"I am eighteen, Mrs. Wilson. It has been me since last December twentieth. Whoever was before me, I don't know her name."

That was true and saying it, hearing it, drained what was left of Ella's smile, Sarah Wilson's starting courage. So they hung in dull creamy light, picking each other's familiar faces for something to hate or forgive. But nothing was there, not yet, nothing they had not known and seen hundreds of times the past four years—Ella Scott's that had narrowed and paled beneath darkening hair to the sudden hot papery looks that all her sisters wore from the time they slouched through Sarah Wilson's class into a mill to watch loud machines make ladies' hose till the day they won boys who set them working on babies and the looks dried in as the skin drew yellow to their bones. And Sarah Wilson's that had never won praise even twenty years ago when she came here from college, had only won Nathan Wilson and then watched his life with no sign of cracking, yielding, except on her lips that did not close, that stretched back always to speak (speech being something that held back conclusions).

Sarah Wilson said, "*I* know. Sooner or later I know every name. But I didn't know yours till he came in at seven, drunk, and fell on the bed asleep and I undressed him and found this note." She took up a folded note from the seat, opened, studied it again—*I have got something to tell you and will be on the tracks tonight at nine o'clock.* No name. Then she looked to the girl. "Well, your writing has improved." Then "Ella, if you don't mean to run *now* and never come back, never see Mr. Wilson or me again, will you get in here and talk to me? You know I don't mean you harm."

"I know that, Mrs. Wilson." Ella still leaned in the open door, a hand on the seat-back. "I don't think I mean you no harm either; so if you need to talk—yes ma'm, I can listen."

Sarah Wilson's throat closed at that. Then she could say against her will, "I don't need anything you've got to give"; but she smoothed the cloth of the empty seat and Ella slid in. "Shut the door please. We have got to ride. We'll burn up here."

Ella nodded—ahead at the glass. "Yes ma'm. But I got to be home by ten o'clock. My daddy's home tonight and he wants me back."

"Whoever you're with?"

"Daddy knows who I'm with, who I come to meet anyhow."

"And he didn't stop you or warn you?"

"Mrs. Wilson, you know I have paid my way since I was sixteen." The engine ignited, the lights struck dust, weeds, the crest of the bank. "I have stood in that dimestore thousands of hours ringing up Negro quarters for some plastic nothing that lasts as far as the door. Daddy just owns the lock on the house—or rents it. He don't own me, if he ever did. Looks like nobody owns me now." She faced Sarah Wilson and managed a smile.

But Sarah Wilson missed it. She had taken the wheel and turned them slowly toward the road; and they went two miles in silence— flanking the tracks at first and, beyond, the huddle of mill-owned huts where Ella would sleep; then across on a road that narrowed soon to a damp dirt swath through tobacco, cotton, black pine. They did not look beyond open windows. It was all their home, their daily lives. Ella stared forward. Sarah Wilson drove and felt the questions stack in her forehead; but the air swept cooler over them, bearing the cold sound of crickets again, and when they had passed a final house (its single light well back from the road) and nothing lay ahead but eight miles of burnt field, wild woods, Sarah Wilson started. "Ella, I think you have told me the truth so far and I'm grateful; but I'm asking you to answer some things I need to ask. You may say it's none of my business—"

"—It's your business, yes ma'm. And I come on this ride of my own will, so you got a right to ask anything; but I got a right not to answer what hurts."

Sarah Wilson set that against what questions were waiting, said to herself, "She is nothing but an ignorant child Nathan tinkered with. I knew her, taught her before she had power to hurt a flea much less break my life. Don't let me hurt her now." She waited a minute to strengthen that purpose. Then she started from the edge. "You say it's been you since December twentieth. That was the Christmas program."

"Yes ma'm. After Mr. Wilson carried you home, he come back to check on us and close the auditorium. Everybody was feeling good and it took awhile to clean up the stage, and by then it had started sleeting. None of the others were headed for the mill so Mr. Wilson took me."

"—And started his Christmas drunk."

"No ma'm. Mr. Wilson don't drink where I am. I never have seen him take a drink. I have smelt it on him and known what it was—I have got brothers—but he has been nice about that with me."

"Well, he started it after he left you then and brought it to me next morning for Christmas. The drinking is something he saves for me."

"Yes ma'm. I noticed that was it. Marvin is that way—Aleen's husband. He'll be gone whole days at a time, but let him get tight and he heads for home and hands Aleen a drunk like his pay." It had come to her naturally—Aleen's trouble. But once it was out, she guessed it might slow Mrs. Wilson, win her a rest; so she faced the open window.

And it worked. Aleen was the first Scott girl, Ella's senior by nine or ten years. Once a student left Sarah Wilson's class, she lost count of dates, age, their work. But she often retained the thought of their faces. Years later they would rise when she saw in the paper their weddings, children, by now even deaths (faces full for that year with premature life knocking beneath still formless noses, jaws); and Aleen's came to her now as it had a month before when she read *Mrs. Marvin Maynard has returned to her home after two weeks in Baptist Hospital*. So slowing a little she said to Ella, "I saw Aleen was sick again. Same trouble?"

"Yes ma'm. Third time. They fixed her though so she couldn't go through it again—her heart's affected. This one lived four days but they said he wouldn't never be right. Then he died, which I guess was a blessing."

"Poor Aleen. Tell her I sent my sympathies to her."

"Yes ma'm. Aleen has not had a easy life. I thought it would work this time. She took things easy, wanted it so bad. To calm things down, she said."

The hole fell open in Sarah Wilson's chest. Her foot weighed down on the gas; and she said, "You slept with Mr. Wilson that first night, didn't you?"

"Yes ma'm."

"And you've gone on sleeping with him—eight months nearly?"

"Yes ma'm, I have."

"And you don't think that's a sin?"

"Yes ma'm, I do."

"Then why didn't you stop? Just stop?"

"I don't know. Because Mr. Wilson was nice to me, I guess. I don't mean to say he gave me things. He didn't—oh a Pepsi now and then, and we drove twenty miles for that so nobody wouldn't recognize him— but he talked to me. He told me once he needed me to listen. So I just listened."

"To what?"

"You know it already—the times he had when he was a boy and being in the Army and coming here to teach and jokes his classes play on him—"

"—And marrying me."

"No ma'm. He don't speak of you. The one time I mentioned your name, he said 'Stop.' I was just saying how good you had been when you were my teacher, talking me into finishing high school and helping me get that job."

"So you could hang around four more years to sleep with my hus- band." She held back because they had come to a junction, then stopped, thought, turned to the left. Then, "Was he the first man you slept with, Ella?"

The road they were on was paved again, concrete joints thudding under the wheels at a regular count of three; and shortly they met a car. Its light struck Ella's turned face and its horn tore loudly past them.

Ella swung toward it and watched it away—four ducking heads, two laughing girls, two boys. Then facing backwards she started, flat and sudden, turning as she went, "I ain't *slept* anywhere near your husband. All him and me has had is a dozen or so twenty-minute spells on this dirty seat." She slung her thumb toward the dark back seat, looked to confirm the vacant place, rushed on—"No ma'm, he was not the first. He was just the nicest. Still is. He is the only person in my whole life who asks me what I want to do—and waits for me to decide. What we have done is what I wanted to do; and look what it's been so far"—her thumb stabbed again—"a lot of quick dirt. But I'm not turning loose. Not now. Not with the little I've got. No ma'm." Still half backwards she laid her head on the top of the seat, her eyes toward Sarah Wilson but shut, dry.

Sarah Wilson managed to drive through that; and when Ella finished they were on the outskirts of Kinley, Sarah Wilson's birthplace, hardly a town. She drove through it slowly, the car lights dully slapping two strips of wooden buildings that lined the road, three general stores, post office, gas pump; then, set back, the squatty houses that held what was left of the dozen white families who owned the stores, the farms, still owned the best part of whoever lived in the broken ring that lay in the dark, farther out behind this road (tenants, field hands, nurses, cooks). Beyond that far ring was Sarah Wilson's home, the place she dreaded. She was numb to the rest of Kinley; and she passed it thinking only, "I have gone too far. I will turn at the station and carry her home and ask her to quit."

The station was at the end of town. Only two trains a day came now, except for the freights that gathered pulpwood; and the evening train was surely gone, so the station should have been dark. But when she turned in, a last light showed in the passenger office, then vanished. She swung the car round on a cushion of pine bark; and just as she straightened to pull away, a man appeared in the station door and came down the steps, old and careful, not seeing till he reached the bottom. But then he waved and hurried toward them. It was Mr. Whitlow, the station master; and though he had been here always, Sarah Wilson had not seen him in the twenty-five years since he sold her the tickets that took her from Kinley to teacher's college. So she waited now and he came to Ella's side and said, "Train's left. Nothing on it but Negroes. Were you looking for somebody?"

Ella said "No" and looked to Sarah Wilson.

Sarah Wilson said, "It's Sarah Shaw, Mr. Whitlow—Sarah *Wilson*. I haven't seen you in twenty-five years."

He stared across and said, "Sarah Shaw. Has it been that long? Why don't you come to see us sometime?"

She said, "I keep busy. I do come down every once in a while to see Holt, but since Aunt Alice died I don't come much. She was the last I had down here."

He said, "I know it. I saw Holt today, walking past here. Straight as a rail and about as hard. Too mean to die. Is anybody out there with him now?"

"Not a soul and he says that's how he wants it. The others are gone—dead or in Richmond."

"Just Holt and the devil." He touched Ella's shoulder. "Sarah, is this your girl?"

"No sir. We don't have children. This is Ella Scott. She was my student four years ago."

"Was she a good one?"

"Good enough to finish. She finished this spring and is leaving for Raleigh, to business school."

He said "Good for her," looking past Ella to Sarah Wilson.

But Ella said, "I am thinking about it."

He studied her and said, "Go. If you've got good sense you'll get out of here. Your teacher yonder had the sense to leave. If she had stayed here she'd have died in misery twenty years ago. Trouble was, she came more than halfway back. *Love*, won't it, Sarah?"

"I don't remember that far. Maybe it was. How is your sister?"

He leaned farther in. "Sarah, I didn't mean you harm. Sister's alive—old like me. Not old enough to shut up though, not yet." He held his arm across Ella, his hand palm down; and Sarah Wilson took it a moment. "You did what you had to, Sarah. I hope you have got satisfaction in life. God knows you deserved it."

She thanked him and he withdrew his hand, touched Ella again and took four steps. Then before they moved he turned and said, "I never did ask could I help you tonight?"

Sarah Wilson said "No. Thank you, sir."

He said, "Well, I guess you know what you're looking for" and went across the road toward his home and his sister, using the beam of Sarah Wilson's lights as path.

She noticed that—that he walked in her lights—so she waited and watched him, then realized the lights were dimmed and pressed with her foot to raise them; but he was gone, sooner than she'd counted on. She thought, "That is somebody else I will never see again"; and the new way was suddenly there—what to do, how to fight, maybe win, maybe save their lives. She looked to the clock, then to Ella. "We have got forty minutes. We might as well see this through."

Ella said, "I have said all I mean to say, Mrs. Wilson. Don't ask me no more questions tonight." She stared at her lap.

"I'm not. I'm not. What I know already will keep me sick long enough. But you say you have listened to Nathan so much. Now sit there and listen to me, to what you don't know, what Nathan wouldn't tell you if he talked ten years."

Ella stared on downwards, rocking the heel of one hand in her groin. She had said her say. Forty minutes was left and she could not walk eight miles tonight. She said, "I'm listening."

Beyond the station a dirt road cut back into the dark. It was one way—the old way—to Ogburn. It was also the way to Sarah Wilson's chance. She aimed them there and at once they were in total night, loud weeds pressing from the ditches, low pines choked with kudzu pressing above, boxing their lights. They sped through that till the sides opened out and the lights fell flat on fields of gapped dry corn that in nine hours would take the sucking sun again. The corn, the land were Holt Ferguson's, would be his for the next quarter-mile—and the dark oak grove, the house set back which they came to slowly on Ella's side. It was blacker than the sky behind it and so stood clear—a long low house hunched against the road.

Sarah Wilson stopped, not pulling to the edge, and leaned toward Ella to look. Then she drew back and made a small sign with her hand to the house. She hung that hand on the wheel and began, meaning it to be her life, the truth, that would speak for itself. "You can't see it now. There's no reason why you ever should; but when I was your age, I would sit in my room and press my head for relief, and what would come was the fact that I had this house, that if somebody would have *me*, we could come here and make as good a life as my parents had had. I thought this house was as surely mine as the soles of my feet. But I didn't even own the bed I was born in—a white iron bed behind that far big window on the right."

She pointed again, no hope of Ella seeing. "The house belonged to my father then—built for his marriage on land his father left—and that was their bedroom, his and my mother's. They slept there six years before I came. There was one boy before me who died, but I lived easily and I was the last. I never knew why. I used to ask Mother for brothers, company; and she would say, 'Sarah, I thought we were happy. Why aren't you satisfied?' I would think and decide I was. We were not rich—Father made eighty-five dollars a month as station agent plus half-shares on his farm—but we had what we needed, we valued each other, never stopped talking except from fatigue.

"Then when I was twelve they did try again on another child and that killed Mother. She lived four months after losing the child, but it poisoned her heart and she died one morning by the front porch swing. I had fallen at school and torn my skirt, and the teacher had sent me home to change. It was early November and warm, and she was out in the swing in her robe. Jane Phipps, her nurse, was sitting on the steps and Jane saw me first. I must have looked bad—dirty and torn—so

Jane yelled, 'Sarah, what have you done?' and Mother stood up. I ran toward her to show I was safe, and she dropped at my feet. Thirty years ago and I know every second, could draw it if I could draw. Nobody told me. I saw it.

"I saw the next three years too, but I barely remember them. They were the happiest—after the shock, when Father and I were here alone. I've thought about that—not remembering those years—and I know it's *because* we were happy. I have never forgotten one painful thing. So we had three years. I say *we*. I was happy and I thought Father was. I thought we were sufficient to one another and would go on being; but when I was fifteen one June morning, I was sweeping the yard and a Negro boy ran up and said, 'Yonder—they are rolling your father home.' I ran for the road and met them on that last curve. They had him on a two-wheeled mail cart—black Ben Mitchell and Mr. Whitlow who was Father's help. They stopped when they saw me, and Ben waited in the shafts while I looked. Father couldn't speak. He had had a stroke, forty-eight years old.

"It didn't kill him, not more than half. But that was when Holt saw his chance—Holt Ferguson, Aunt Alice's husband. She was Father's half-sister—his mother's child older than him—so the Shaw land was Father's; and he let it out on halves to tenants. Well, when Father could sit up and halfway talk, Holt came and said he and Alice would move here and keep house and farm as long as they could be of service. I was in the room. Father thought ten seconds; then he turned to me and said 'Sarah, how about it?' It killed me to think he would welcome them when we had done so well alone; so I said the house and land were his, that he could ask in gypsies or Negroes, that I would be gone in two more years. He caught at his breath but he managed to tell me to calm myself; then he turned to Holt and said, 'Come ahead. We need you. I thank you and so will Sarah when she understands.'

"But I never understood—only that the Fergusons came and went to work, on the farm and on Father; and from that day I recall every waking minute till now. I have slept very little. Father and I had the right side of the house, but we crept around and cleaned up after ourselves like cats. So did Holt and Aunt Alice—I give them that. She never did an unkind deed in her life, and Holt was working till late most nights. It was the boys I minded. They were younger than me and the house was their home in fifteen minutes, every rock in the yard. I grieved myself to sleep every night, but I never spoke another word to Father about asking them here. I got through the worst by telling myself, 'This place is Father's and will someday be mine.' And when Father was working—he limped around part-time—I fought for my own, thinking I knew what was my own.

"But I didn't, not till Father died. He lived till I was seventeen. Then the second stroke came and took him at the station on the *floor*, with no time to tell me what he had done. What I knew was what Aunt Alice told me after the funeral—that no plans were changed, that Father had arranged it with Holt, I was going to college and should think of this as home. So I lived through that last summer, sleeping in the bed I was born in, thinking I would go and come back and teach and marry—I was not in love; I had friends but no one I needed—and give the Fergusons the old Shaw place and start my life. September came and Tim, Holt's oldest boy, drove me to the station. I bought a round trip ticket from Mr. Whitlow; and when we could hear the train in the rails, I said to Tim, 'I will see you Christmas.' He said, 'I'll meet you. You might not know the house.' I said 'Why?' and he said, 'After we put on that new kitchen.' I said it was odd that Holt hadn't told me; and over the whistling train Tim said, 'I guess since it's his, he didn't think to tell you.' That was the first I knew, first *hint*. There was nothing to do but ride the train and wait for a letter.

"It came a week later—from Aunt Alice begging my pardon, saying Holt and the boys thought I knew, that she was supposed to tell me but failed. Father had sold Holt everything. He had seen he was dying, he must have remembered me saying those things, and he saw only one way to get me to college. Holt had got it—house and land—for the price of college and his word to give me a home if I needed one. I didn't then. I redeemed what was left of that roundtrip ticket. Then I went four years without seeing Kinley. In the summers I stayed at school and worked to pay for my clothes. I make it sound bad. It did seem the worst of all my luck, but once I got breath I was not that unhappy. God knows I wasn't happy, but I had work to do and friends to visit in my few vacations. One was Martha Hawkins in Ogburn.

"I went to her on Christmas night of my last year in college. I had spent three days in Kinley, here. Aunt Alice asked me, saying I had broken her heart, so I came. I had had four years to show my feelings and I made up my mind to do my share of healing wounds. So had they. We grinned through a lot of food and presents, and she put me in Mother and Father's room; but I thanked God hourly that I had arranged to leave Christmas day for Martha's. When I left, Aunt Alice said they hoped I would come here to live and teach. I thanked her and said I would take the best offer wherever that was. Then again Tim drove me away, to Ogburn. That time he hardly spoke so I rode alone with what I had after those three days, twenty-one *years*—a suitcase of clothes, three Christmas gifts, three-fourths of a college diploma. Not one other thing and I knew it.

"Well, I took the first offer, not the best. It came from Nathan Wilson. Martha was giving a party that night; and when I walked in, he was the first thing I saw—Nathan—and within an hour I was telling him this same story. *Because he was drunk.* I don't make a policy of sharing trouble; but drunk as he was, he read my face and when we were half alone, he said, 'Who knocked the props from under you?' and I told him, whispering so no other human would hear. He said, 'She was right. You must come here and live and make peace or you'll die on the run.' I had seen from the first that he was running—drunk two states north of his home—but I asked him what he was running from and he told me. Himself of course and what he had done to people that loved him—his dead mother and the first girl that offered him her life. But you know all that if you've listened like you say. I listened then—listen now if he asks me to—and when we were done,

I had offered him my life too. Not that night, not openly, though before I slept I could feel he had stuck himself in my mind like a nail, being like me—running from wrecks, needing someone to halt him, plug up his chest.

"The next afternoon he came back to Martha's and begged my pardon for anything out of the way he had done—*out of the way* when he was already what I needed. We took a ride that afternoon and he said there was something he *had* meant—that I must come here to teach—and he offered me a job. He had come to Ogburn as principal three years before. Being what he was, he made me think he was right; and I accepted, already back in my mind, making peace. Then he drove me to Kinley to tell Aunt Alice. She said to Nathan, 'If you are the reason, I am grateful to you.' I laughed but he *was* and I was so grateful I married him. He had come to see me most weekends; and by May when he asked me, I knew everything I would ever know—that his past was people he had let down and left—but I needed him and I thought he needed me. He never said so but he acted like need, still does— coming to me tonight like a child, not even trying to hide your note. So I said Yes, eyes open, and we married in June, here.

"Holt gave me away which was not easy, but we said it was part of our new beginning. *Beginning* when in two years it had died on my hands—Aunt Alice dead and Holt alone going harder and harder; Nathan and I crammed in rooms in Ogburn teaching all week, then taking long dark Saturday rides to buy his liquor, watching him pour it down secret from everyone but me, watching him tear on past me in this race I can't stop, can't slow, taking the best part of me with him through his hot quick dirt as you call it. But not killing it—the need I have to gouge out the drinking and women and calm him. The women anyhow. They started six years after our marriage when we finally knew we could not have children. It wasn't me that wanted them—things going so badly—but during those years I would sometimes say, 'Nathan, when will you stop?' and he would say, 'When I have a child to hide from.' He had never had to hide a thing from me. Then we found it was him at fault. There was one more hole through the middle of him. He was really no *good*—"

Ella said "Stop." She had heard every word looking down, not moving, giving Sarah Wilson that chance; but she pointed now to the lighted clock—the dim lights were on. "I have got twenty minutes. What are you trying to tell me please?" Then she faced Sarah Wilson.

It took her awhile to know. "I have just now told you. Nathan Wilson is no good to you, no good on earth to anyone but me. What do you want out of half a man, young as you are?—when the half has been mine twenty-one years, is grown to me and must never tear loose. *Will* not."

"I was not *tearing* nothing—I wish I had been. I do not love your pitiful husband. What I said tonight—about not turning loose—I said it wild. You made me say it, digging so ugly. Mr. Wilson is yours and I thank God for it. But I need to see him one more time."

"No Ella, please. Just end it now."

"You are too late, Mrs. Wilson. Two days too late. I have turned loose already, *torn* loose. I have ended the little we had, myself." She took up the note from the seat beside her, held it between them. "But I told him here I had something to say."

"Then say it to me. I'll see that he knows."

"He knows, he knows. Oh—" Ella shut her eyes, clamped her teeth, said, "Say to Nathan, to Mr. Wilson, that Ella has done what she promised to—" Breath and force refused, sucked back into her, grated her throat. Her hand wadded in on the note; her head faced the black grove, the house. Then noise came in chunks from the pit of her neck.

That saved Sarah Wilson, gave her strength to crank the car, turn it, aim for Kinley, the highway, the quick way to Ogburn—thinking she had won and numb from winning, from not breaking down. Past Kinley she steered on quickly through fields darker now, insects thicker and dazed by the heat, no other car in sight and only one man in the eight fast miles—a Negro stalled, beside his old truck in open white shirt, one hand on a fender, the other flapped once like a wing as they passed, signing for help he did not expect (as if she could help an angel of light after this night's work, could speak again, even think, before morning). Yet they were nearly back and soon she would have to speak—whatever awful last thing to Ella, to calm her, thank her, find the end of her message to Nathan. Sarah Wilson slowed to plan her speech but too late—her lights had nudged the first ranks of mill huts coiled so dense they would flash in a trail if one spark dropped, dark in the windows but each throwing naked hall-light into dwarf dirt yards through open doors. She checked the time. Five more minutes and Ella's father would wait in one door, ready to lock. Not wanting to know which house was Ella's, she took the tracks; and when Ella looked up puzzled, she said, "I will put you out where I met you—here." They were there again at the foot of the bank and Sarah Wilson stopped.

Before they were still Ella reached for the door.

Sarah Wilson touched her, her cool bare arm. That was the thanks. Then she said, "Ella, wait. I did not mean to press you to tears. What I meant to do was tell you my life and let that speak as a warning to you. But I went too far, telling that secret. That is *our* grief, mine and Nathan's. I had no right to give it to you. I beg your pardon and, bad as what you have done may be, I thank you for promising to leave him now. I'll hold you to it. So give me your message and go on home where your father is."

Ella opened the door, slid from beneath Sarah Wilson's hand, then leaning in as she had at the first—but her hair caved down on her bloated eyes—she said clearly, "I have not promised you nothing, Mrs. Wilson. I won't need to see your husband again, but that's not because of a promise to you or because of what you thought up tonight. The promise I made was to Nathan Wilson; and I went to Raleigh this week and kept it—went on the *bus* and ditched a baby in a nigger kitchen for two hundred dollars. Tell him that and tell him I said I will pay him back my half when I can work." She said that three feet from

Sarah Wilson's face. Then she turned and walked toward the tracks, leaving the car door open. She went slowly purposely to show she was free; that whatever her debts, she owned herself.

Yet slow as she was, she reached weeds and bank before her meaning reached Sarah Wilson's mind, entered through still open mouth, spread through palate, skull. Her head had turned forward while Ella spoke; and it stayed there rigid, seeing Ella walk, then quicken in the weeds and take the bank running, stumbling on top to her hands and knees but rising at once, sinking on the far side slowly again. Sarah Wilson shut her eyes, struggled to shut her mouth; but it hung apart—taut not slack as if it would speak of its own will, free and pure. Yet no words came, only the strength to move the car, give it signals to take her home—at least to where Nathan slept (if he slept, if he was not gone), breathing aloud on the bed they shared.

The car obeyed and turned beneath her toward Ogburn. There would be one mile of air to breathe before the town streets exhaling day, the houses she knew, that knew her, knew all but this night and would soon know this—if it was true, had been and would last beyond morning. That hope, simply, sent her on—that it *all* was lie, would end when Nathan woke and eased her. But the car reached Ogburn. It did not slow. It mounted the hump where paving began and threw light left on the first open yard, scalding a rabbit with sudden discovery. Tan and quick it was sucked toward Sarah Wilson, beneath her wheel. In the bones of her hand—her fine bones gripped to swerve—she felt its brittle death. Too late she braked, slewed in the street, halted. Then her mouth spoke freely its waiting threat. "How could I, why should I tell the truth when I thought I could save what was left of our life— that had *stopped*." Her lips sealed down. Grunts like steam rammed her heart, her teeth.

BREATH

S<small>ON</small>,

You ask me to help you see where we come from and how I could use you the way I did through all those early years of your life when you got almost nothing from me in the way of mercy, not to speak of love. Of course there's no way left on Earth for me to tell you—it's so long gone from my mind anyhow, dazed as I am and drunk as I was every time I laid a hand on you or your dead mother—which Christ truly knows is no excuse but a fact more shameful than most cold killings.

I thought about us many hard nights before you asked me—long years before—and all I can halfway come up with is this, no answer. Still if I could someway haul you down through time again and take you through my entire life from all the way back to my own dad and the blood he beat out of me many times, then you might see I was more your older beat-down brother than your actual dad—a beat-down brother years older than you that got his nerve lines badly crossed and wound up trying to turn your life into what *he'd* had, with no improvement at all for the years that ought to have healed him.

My dad, see, was raised by a mother that died before I was old enough to know her—which may have been my main piece of luck, considering what I heard about her when I was old enough to hear what men at the plant were saying about her years after my dad found her strangled on the kitchen floor and no one suspect. They were *all* suspects was what I heard—she'd been the county whore all her life or since she was old enough to count cash money, lie down and not be smothered by a grown man gouging her crotch or face. My dad was the only kid she kept and while I figure he saw enough to freeze most minds, well before he learned how to run—her bringing six men home per night on weekends—the fact was, he claimed to worship her memory.

He'd sure God tell me how sweet she'd been every time he made me sit beside him at the kitchen table and wait till he'd drunk himself half blind and then decided I needed my weekly beating to tame her share in me—he'd truly say that. "You've got her blood all in you, Sim; and I'm draining it *off*." I'll swear to you now he came as close as a man can come and stop short of murder till I got strong enough to tell him one night "You lay one finger on me again—not to mention Mama— and I'll see you to a painful grave in a New York minute if I have to spend the rest of my life in solitary."

Considering that my pitiful mother never tried to shield me from him, not with more than a tear, I'd *been* in solitary fifteen years. It's nothing but the truth that from the time I was four years old till the night I stopped him in his tracks, I never cut my bed light out without expecting to be torn out of my sheets by dawn and smashed or screamed at at the least and at the worse be forced to watch him do sick things to Mama—her body and mind, neither one of which were tough enough for the normal world, whatever that was, not to mention this nightly savage we had where other families had cats or dogs.

So there—you won't know that much, I guess, unless your mother told you more than I think she'd dare to, little as she ever tried to change me or fought for you. She was not a bad woman—I never said so—but I do say she laid down in the floor time after time or sobbed in the basement when just her face or a kind word from her might have stopped my arm from slamming on you to numb my brain like you were the brother too late to help me and were punished for that.

I don't expect this to help you see your way ahead, not by one inch. It's what you can hear all hours of the day from TV talkers who blame every watt of their clear-eyed meanness on somebody standing years behind them or cold in the ground. I only claim I've told you the truth in these few lines as far as it goes. It ruined me before I could shave and for some lame reason I let that be my entire life, that fifteen years. I'm fifty-four years old tonight; but you'd be right if you said my life stopped cold on a dime when I was four, maybe nine at the most. A stronger human—with a useful mother or a God that noticed—would have brushed his clothes off, stepped on into the permanent present and shut the awful past door behind him.

You may not yet be old enough to know how very few humans manage that, simple as it sounds—just closing a door and throwing the bolt. I'll have to say I've known a few men and women who did it. But they've been rare as my good nights. As you know I've spent the rest of my days hunched back in the corner like the boy I was—that is until you were strong enough to walk and laugh around the place, and I roared out of my miserable crouch and made you pay for all I'd eaten from a hateful man. I've prayed to your mother's soul in Heaven and have seen her gray eyes fixed right on me, but she hasn't said a word till now—not pardon or pity or even a nod.

You may still have a soul deep in you. I tried to kill it, but I hope it's there. If so you might try to climb out far enough from where I flung you to face me anyhow and damn my life to Hell forever; or say you'll try to sit beside me long enough—in some safe place—and let me beg as much of a pardon as you can give so both of us stand a chance at time, a few quick years when we could breathe in the same clean room.

You know my address,
Your actual father

TOWARD HOME

1

THE WAITRESS had worked two straight shifts in the Christmas rush and was numb on her feet at past midnight; but this child had almost saved her day—she'd seldom seen a natural creature this good to watch. Maybe nine years old with chestnut hair below her shoulders, straight as a rail, and eyes so green you could swan-dive in. "What's your name, heartbreaker?"

The man beside the child said "Lee."

"Well, Lee, you saved a tired girl's life. I was ready to cut my throat till you showed."

Lee nodded, in serious thanks for the praise. She was less conceited than an April day; the praise was just a familiar fact—people liked to watch her. Still she looked up into the woman's eyes and launched a smile.

The woman turned to the man. "Granddaughter?"

Hart lied—"No ma'm but thanks for the compliment."

She cleared their soup bowls and still was intrigued. So she dried her hand and gently tested a strand of Lee's hair as if it might tarnish. "Say something, hon. Let me hear those *tones*."

The man said politely "She just speaks German, she's being adopted, I'm taking her on to a new home now."

434

The part about German and being adopted was also a lie. But the claim that he was taking her home, or somehow finding home at last, was Hart's true hope and had been now for nearly a month.

He and the child met such questions more than daily. And the foreign language was the child's idea. In early years she lived in Germany—her father was stationed there, a fighter pilot (Hart's son, Alton). And the night that she and her grandfather ran, Lee taught him phrases in pidgin German. They hid behind those, at least when they saw no Germans near. So here with the waitress still beside them, Lee met Hart's nervous grin and said *"Was ist los in das gasthaus, Tonto?"*

Deadpan, Hart said *"Nix, Kemo-sabe."*

The waitress said "They got the Lone Ranger in Germany too?"

Lee slipped and said *"Ja."*

They backed out fast and, bushed as they were, drove another hour north to Indiana in case the waitress called the law. Lee fell asleep on the seat fairly soon, though she moaned more than once and finally said her dead father's whole name—"Alton Wright."

At three in the morning, just into Illinois, Hart found a room in a widow's house (her sign was still lit). And Lee roused long enough to stumble in, be civil to the widow, choose the narrow white bed, peel to her cotton underwear and brave the cold sheets.

Hart followed soon, in the wide oak bed, but was too worn out for instant sleep. He lay on his back and struggled hard to fend off both the sheet of blood that lately hung above his eyes, aching to fall, and the perfect memory of his son's last words *Please sir, no.*

2

LEE'S ninth birthday was February 8th. By then they were calling her Nan in public; she'd cut her own hair boyish-short and rolled it up each night in ringlets. They celebrated in a motel room in Iowa—lit one candle on a green cupcake and sang "Happy Birthday" (Nan sang too). Then she opened his sensible gifts—corduroy overalls, flannel shirt, stout brogans and leather gloves with rabbit-fur lining.

She prized the feel of the blue-gray fur; and having it warm against her skin, she guessed what next. To Hart on the opposite bed, she said "We going on into the mountains then?"

3

HART was crouched behind the woodpile, grubbing in the last of the snow, when Nan called his name. At first he tried to hunch down lower, but then he thought *Why not? We're leaving.* So he raised a long arm—"Here, old buddy"—and then went back to serious digging with the spade. She came so softly he didn't hear a step; and once her shadow fell on his hands and stretched well past him—a ten-foot ghost—he thought for the first time *She's too old for this; she's bound to know.* But he smiled up at her.

Nan held out one wild crocus, deep purple and flecked with ice. But what she said was "I bet we're leaving."

Hart took the flower, smelled its neutral heart and returned it. "I think we better, with the road thawing fast—how did you guess?"

"You digging up the money."

It startled him—he'd hid their money at night two months ago—and he sank both fists in the ground beside him to keep from falling.

But Nan laughed. "Right after we got here, you went to Durango early; and when I got up, I looked out and saw that crook-tailed squirrel digging here. I thought he smelled the world's best nut; he just wouldn't stop. But after my coffee when I came out, I saw the lid of your jar and the cash. I packed the dirt back."

Hart couldn't face her. He said "Just step in the cabin a minute."

"I'm *with* you, Grand. I want to be."

He nodded but once more waved her off.

She held there a moment, then gave a child's extravagant sigh and slowly turned. But before she moved too far to hear, she said "I'm counting on some place warm."

From where Hart knelt, near eight hundred dollars in a buried jam jar, he watched her leave as the finest thing he'd got in a stingy life— taller by the day and, hid in all that admirable hair (exactly the shade of his own lost mother's) was the mind he was living this nightmare for, to rescue her for actual life: the rest of her childhood anyhow. One long instant he begged in silence *Go. Be safely gone when I get there.* But well before Nan shut the door, Hart clenched his eyes and canceled the thought—*Please,* no. *Grand's all you got and he'll save you yet.*

Even as he counted the frozen money and knew they could leave and move on west, he felt no relief but only a rush of threat from the blood, that patient tide of blood he'd stalled just out of sight. Through the short walk back—with red-tailed hawks in the trees above him, calculating that his flesh and eyes might see them through till the ground unlocked its mice and snakes—Hart begged again and again in a whisper *Keep her please from asking. Let her just thank me and not ask why.*

4

MEMORIAL DAY, they were in a dry hut near Gold Beach, Oregon playing cards (Hart dealt blackjack at a local saloon and had the night off). After a week of steady gray, they'd hoped for a glimpse of the sun but not yet; and it was past noon. Nan was now called Martha and had made a picnic when she woke early. So they broke it out—a can of salmon, saltines, cream cheese—and ate it while they played out their hands.

When Martha saw she was bound to lose, she told herself *You can dedicate this losing now and ask for the sun to shine awhile* (in Germany she went to Catholic school; the nuns had taught her such useful facts). So she made that silent acceptance of loss; and almost before Hart could say "I won," the sun fell in through a seaside window and lit them both like parched bonfires. Martha got up and said "Let's walk."

Hart shuffled the cards for one more hand. "I got to give you a last chance to beat me." But when he saw the flare in her eyes, much finer than the day, he stood and found the stick he carried on their rare walks. It was stout as a club.

They'd gone no more than a hundred yards toward the high brown boulders when courage rushed on Martha like wings. She turned and waited for Hart to catch up. And when he was still four steps away, she put out her right hand—an open palm.

He took it as if that were natural for them (when he'd barely touched her since the night they ran); and he thought they'd fall in together like always, in step, counting.

But Martha pulled back and when Hart faced her puzzled, she said "Grand, tell me. Did we do it or not?"

In two hard seconds, he understood; but he still said "What?"

"Kill him." Her face was clear as the whole sudden day. Since she felt no actual pain at the thought, her eyes were swept of dread or blame.

Nothing in Hart's life—fifty-eight years—had stood in reach as fine and awful as this child now. Young as she was, she'd earned at least some part of the truth; so he said "Not *we*, my darling. Surely not *you*."

"But it happened, I think. I saw it again two nights ago—a dream, I guess, but I recognized it."

The blood poured finally, all Hart could see through a long wait. He thought *She'll vanish. She'll burn on off in this new light and leave me for good.* He also thought that would be the just thing. But he met her face and told the truth "I did it for you."

"To spare me, right?"

Hart shut his eyes and nodded.

Martha—Nan—Lee took awhile; in her mind, she wondered *Do I run?* But she also knew her age and weakness. So she finally said "We could go back and make a new lunch and bring it out here."

5

BY THEN she'd missed more than half a school year, with slim regret. But in late June with children skating past their windows, Martha began to miss the regular job of lessons and homework, dumb kids and laughing. So when Hart came in from work at six, she said "Grand, I'm *ignorant*"—she'd misread the label on a box of rice and had cooked enough for a Chinese family.

He leaned to kiss the ends of her hair that was growing again. It was the nearest he'd come to speaking his love in all her life. Her hand came up, made a short ponytail; then she pranced three steps with a grace no horse on Earth possessed. So Hart laughed once. "You want to start back to school next fall?"

To hear him say it was like quick dawn (she'd seen a good many). "In Yakima, here? We'll be here then?"

Hart said "I thought I told you we stopped."

"And you aren't scared?"

"I think I stopped that too. They've let us be." He looked to the window above the sink. The single maple in healthy leaf and the clear straight edge of the white garage were part of a place he could hope to rest in, slim as hope was. Till here this minute, he hadn't felt that in the whole long run. He very much feared he might break now and let her see how dark it was.

But Martha was hard at work by the stove. She could barely reach the bottom of the pot; still she was stirring her ton of rice.

At last he could say "And you're all right?"

She froze in place but didn't turn. Then when she'd thought, she plainly told the room itself "I'm the child in this. I may well make it."

"Take a step more—can you say you're fine?" More than ever, even faced away, she looked worth anything, pain or death.

Martha waited and still didn't turn; but she said "I'm cooking this big supper, O.K.?—for us, not the pitiful children abroad. You do your part."

He said "Say *please*."

But she'd said her piece. She set down her spoon and clamped both ears.

So once Hart thoroughly washed his hands, he slowly set two spotless plates and real cloth napkins on the old cardtable.

THE NAMES AND
FACES OF HEROES

${\rm A}$FTER AN HOUR I believe it and think, "We are people in love. We flee through hard winter night. What our enemies want is to separate us. Will we end together? Will we end alive?" And my lips part to ask him, but seeing his face in dashboard light (his gray eyes set on the road and the dark), I muffle my question and know the reason— "We have not broke silence for an hour by the clock. We must flee on silent. Maybe if we speak even close as we are, we will speak separate tongues after so long a time." I shut my eyes, press hard with the lids till my mind's eye opens, then balloon it light through roof through steel, set it high and cold in January night, staring down to see us whole. First we are one black car on a slim strip of road laid white through pines, drawn slowly west by the hoop of light we cast ahead— the one light burning for fifty miles, it being past eleven, all farms and houses crouched into sleep, all riders but us. Then my eye falls downward, hovers on the roof in the wind we make, pierces steel, sees us close—huddled on the worn mohair of a 1939 Pontiac, he slumped huge at the wheel, I the thin fork of flesh thrust out of his groin on the seat beside him, my dark head the burden in his lap his only hollow that flushes beneath me with rhythm I predict to force blood against my weight through nodes of tissue, squabs of muscle that made me ten years ago, made half anyhow, he being my father and I being nine, we heading towards home not fleeing, silent as I say, my real eyes shut, his eyes on nothing but road. So we are not lovers nor spies nor thieves and speaking for me, my foes are inward not there in the night. My mind's eye enters me calm again, and I brace to look, to say "How much further?" but he drops a hand which stalls me, testing my flannel pajamas for warmth, ringing my ankle and shin and ticklish knee (in earnest, tight not gentle), slipping between two buttons of the coat to brush one breast then out again and down to rest on my hip. His thumb and fingers ride the high saddle bone, the fat of his hand in the hollow *I* have, heavy but still on the dry knots of boyish equipment waiting for life to start. I roll back on my head to see him again, to meet his eyes. He looks on forward so I go blind again and slide my right hand to his, probing with a finger till I find his only wound—a round yellow socket beneath his thumb where he shot himself when he was eight, by surprise, showing off his father's pistol to friends (the one fool thing I know he has done). My finger rests there and we last that way maybe two or three miles while the road is straight. Then a curve begins. He says "Excuse me, Preacher" in his natural voice and takes his hand. My eyes stay blind and I think what I know, "I love you tonight more than all my life before"—think it in *my* natural voice. But I do not say it, and I do not say I excuse him though I do. I open my eyes on his face in dashboard light.

I search it for a hero. For the first time. I have searched nearly every other face since last July, the final Sunday at camp when a minister told us, "The short cut to being a man is finding your hero, somebody who is what you are not but need to be. What I mean is this. Examine yourself. When you find what your main lack is, seek that in some great man. Say your trouble is fear—you are scared of the dark, scared of that bully in your grade at school, scared of striking out when you come up to bat. Take some great brave, some warrior—Douglas MacArthur, Enos Slaughter. Say your trouble is worse. Say it's telling lies. Take George Washington—personal heroes don't need to be living just so they lived once. Read a book about him. Study his picture. (You may think he looks a little stiff. That is because his teeth were carved out of cypress. A man makes his face and making a good one is as hard a job as laying road through solid rock, and Washington made himself as fine a face as any man since Jesus—and He was not a man.) Then imitate him. Chin yourself on his example and you will be a man before you need a razor." I need to be a man hard as anybody so riding home from camp and that sermon, I sat among lanyards I plaited and whistles I carved and searched my life for the one great lack my foe. He had mentioned lacking courage—that minister. I lack it. I will not try to do what I think I cannot do well such as make friends or play games where somebody hands you a ball and bat and asks the world of you, asks you to launch without thinking some act on the air with natural grace easy as laughing. He had mentioned lying. I lie every day—telling my mother for instance that the weeks at camp were happy when what I did was by day whittle all that trashy equipment, climb through snakes in July sun with brogans grating my heels, swim in ice water with boys that would just as soon drown you as smile and by night pray for three large things—that I not wet the bed, that I choke the homesickness one more day, that these five weeks vanish and leave no sign no memory. But they were only two on a string of lacks which unreeled behind me that Sunday riding home from camp (unseen beyond glass the hateful tan rock turning to round pine hills where Randolph is and home), and on the string were selfishness to Marcia my cousin who is my main friend and gives me whatever she has, envy of my brother who is one year old and whose arms I purposely threw out of joint three months ago, envy of people my age who do so easily things I will not and thus lock together in tangles of friendship, pride in the things I can do which they cannot (but half pride at worst as the things I can do, they do not want to do—drawing, carving, solo singing. I am Randolph's leading boy soprano and was ashamed to be till a Saturday night last August when I sang to a room of sweating soldiers at the U.S.O. I was asked by the hostess for something patriotic, but I thought they would not need that on their weekend off any more than they needed me in Buster Brown collar and white short pants so I sang

Brahms' *Lullaby* which you can hum if you forget, and if it was a mistake, they never let on. I do not mean anybody cried. They kept on swallowing Coca-Colas and their boots kept smelling, but they shut up talking and clapped at the end, and as I left the platform and aimed for the door blistered with shame, one long soldier gave me the blue and gold enamel shield off his cap, saying "Here you are"), and far graver things—wishing death nightly on two boys I know, breaking God's law about honoring parents by failing to do simple things they ask such as look at people when I talk, by doubting they can care for me daily (when my mother thinks of little else and Father would no more sleep without kissing me goodnight than he would strike me), sometimes doubting I am theirs at all but just some orphan they took in kindness. I made that list without trying seven months ago, and it has grown since then. Whenever I speak or move these days new faults stare out of my heart. The trouble though is I still do not know my greatest lack, my *mortal* foe. Any one if I stare back long enough seems bound to sink me. So I seek a hero grand enough to take on all my lacks, but for seven months now I have looked—looked hard—and am nowhere near him. Who *is* there these days, who has there ever been broad enough, grand enough to stand day and night and ward off all my foes? Nobody, I begin to think. I have looked everywhere I know to look, first in books I had or bought for the purpose—*Little People Who Became Great* (Abraham Lincoln, Helen Keller, Andrew Carnegie), *Minute Lives of Great Men and Women* (a page and a picture for everybody including Stephen Foster) and a set called *Living Biographies of Great Composers, Philosophers, Prophets, Poets and Statesmen*. I have not read books that do not show faces because I study a man's face first. Then if that calls me on, I read his deeds. I read for three months and taking deeds and faces together, I settled on Caesar Augustus and Alexander the Great as final candidates. They were already great when they were young, and they both wore faces like hard silver medals awarded for lasting— I got that much from *Minute Lives*—so I thought they were safe and that I would read further and then choose one. But as I read they fell in before me—Alexander crushing that boy's head who brought bad news and when they were lost in a desert and famished and his men found one drink of water and gladly brought it to him in a helmet, him pouring it out in the sand to waste, and Augustus leading the wives of his friends into private rooms during public banquets, making them do what they could not refuse. All the dead have failed me. That is why I study my father tonight. He is the last living man I know or can think of that I have not considered, which is no slight to him—you do not seek heroes at home. No, when the dead played out, I turned to my autographs and started there. I have written to famous men for over a year since the war began. I write on Boy Scout stationery (I am not a Scout), give my age and ask for their names in ink. I have got answers from several generals on the battlefield (MacArthur who sent good luck from the Philippines, Mark Clark who typed a note from secret headquarters, Eisenhower who said in his wide leaning hand, "I do not think it would be possible for me to refuse a nine-year-old American anything I could do for him"), from most of Roosevelt's cabinet (but not from him though I have three notes from Miss Grace Tully to say he does not have time and neither does his wife), from Toscanini and a picture of Johnny Weissmuller on a limb crouched with his bare knife to leap, saying "Hello from Tarzan your friend." But studying them I saw I could not know enough to decide. They are surely famous but I cannot see them or watch them move, and until they die and their secrets appear, how can I know they are genuine heroes?—that they do not have yawning holes of their own which they hide? So from them I have turned to men I can watch and hear, and since I seldom travel this means the men I am kin to. I will not think against my blood, but of all my uncles and cousins (my grandfathers died before I was born), the two I love and that seem to love me—that listen when I speak—and that have dark happy faces are the ones who are liable at any time to start drinking and disappear spending money hand over fist in Richmond or Washington until they are broke and wire for my father who drives up and finds them in a bar with a new suit on and a rosebud and some temporary friends and brings them home to their wives. My father has one brother who fought in France in the First World War and was playing cards in a hole one night when a bomb landed, and when he came to, he picked up his best friend who was quiet at his side and crawled with him half a mile before he saw that the friend lacked a head, but later he was gassed and retired from battle so that now, sitting or standing, he slumps round a hole in his chest and scrapes up blood every hour or two even summer nights visiting on our porch from Tennessee his home. My other male kin live even farther away or do not notice me or are fat which is why as I say I have come to my father tonight—my head rolled back on his lap, my ears sunk in his shifting kernels so I cannot hear only see, my eyes strained up through his arms to his face.

It is round as a watch when he does not smile which he does not now, and even in warm yellow light of speedometer-amp meter-oil pressure gauges, it is red as if he was cold, as if there was no plate glass to hold off the wind we make rushing home. It is always red and reddest I know, though I cannot see, under his collar on the back of his neck where the hair leaves off. There is not much hair anywhere on his head. It has vanished two inches back on his forehead, and where it starts it is dark but seems no color or the color of shadows in old photographs. Above his ears it is already white (he is forty-two and the white is real, but five years ago when it was not, I was singing in bed one night "When I Grow Too Old To Dream," and he heard me and went to the toilet and powdered his hair and came and stood in the door ghostly, old with the hall light behind him and said, "I am too old to dream, Preacher." I sang on a minute, looking, and then cried "Stop. Stop" and wept which of course he did not intend), and each morning he wets it and brushes every strand at least five minutes till it lies on his skull like paint and stays all day. It is one of his things you cannot touch. His glasses are another. He treats them kindly as if they were delicate people—unrimmed octagons hooked to gold wires that ride the start of his firm long nose and loop back over his large flat ears—and in return they do not hide his eyes which are gray and wide and which even in the dark draw light to them so he generally seems to be thinking of fun when he may be thinking we have lost our house (we have just done that) or his heart is failing (he thinks his heart stood still last Christmas when he was on a ladder swapping lights in our tree, and whenever I look he is taking his pulse). And with all his worries it mostly *is* fun he thinks because when he opens his mouth, if people are there they generally laugh—with him or at him, he does not mind which. I know a string of his jokes as long as the string of my personal lacks, and he adds on new ones most days he feels well enough. A lot of his jokes of course I do not understand but I no longer ask. I used to ask and he would say, "Wait a little, Preacher. Your day will come" so I hold them mysterious in my skull till the day they burst into meaning. But most of his fun is open to view, to anybody's eyes that will look because what he mainly loves is turning himself into other people before your eyes. Whenever in the evenings we visit our friends, everybody will talk awhile including my father, and then he may go silent and stare into space, pecking his teeth with a fingernail till his eyes come back from where they have been and his long lips stretch straight which is how he smiles, and then whoever we are visiting—if he has been watching my father—will know to say, "Mock somebody for us, Jeff." ("Mocking" is what most people call it. My father calls it "taking people off.") He will look sheepish a minute, then lean forward in his chair—and I sitting on the rug, my heart will rise for I know he has something to give us now—and looking at the floor say, "Remember how Dr. Tucker pulled teeth?" Everybody will grin Yes but somebody (sometimes me) will say "How?" and he will start becoming Dr. Tucker, not lying, just seriously turning himself into that old dentist— greeting his patient at the door, bowing him over to the chair (this is when he shrinks eight inches, dries, goes balder still, hikes his voice up half a scale), talking every step to soothe the patient, sneaking behind him, rinsing his rusty pullers at the tap, cooing "Open your mouth, sweet *thing*," leaping on the mouth like a boa constrictor, holding up the tooth victorious, smiling *"There* he is and you didn't even feel it, did you, darling?" Then he will be Jeff McCraw again, hitching up his trousers with the sides of his wrists, leading us into the laughter. When it starts to die somebody will say, "Jeff, you beat all. You missed your calling. You ought to be in the movies," and if he is not worried that night he may move on through one or two more transformations— Miss Georgie Ballard singing in church with her head like an owl swivelling, Mrs. V. L. Womble on her velvet pillow, President Roosevelt in a "My friends" speech, or on request little pieces of people— Mr. Jim Bender's walk, Miss Amma Godwin's hand on her stomach. But it suits me more when he stops after one. That way I can laugh and take pride in his gifts, but if he continues I may take fright at him spinning on through crowds of old people, dead people, people I do not know as if his own life—his life with us—is not enough. One such night when he was happy and everybody was egging him on I cried to him "Stop" before it was too late and ran from the room. I am not known as a problem so people notice when I cry. My mother came behind me at once and sitting in a cold stairwell, calmed me while I made up a reason for what I had done. She said, "Let your father have a little fun. He does not have much." I remembered how she often warned me against crossing my eyes at school to make children laugh, saying they might get stuck, so I told her he might stick and then we would carry him home as Dr. Tucker or Mrs. Womble or Miss Lula Fleming at the Baptist organ. That was a lie but it was all I knew, all I could offer on such short notice to justify terror, and telling it made us laugh, calmed me, stopped me thinking of reasons. And I did not worry or think of my terror again till several months later when he came in disguise. It was not the first time he had worn disguise (half the stories about him are about his disguises), but he did not wear it often, and though I was seven I had never seen him that way before. Maybe it is why he came that night, thinking I was old enough and would like the joke since I loved his other fun. Anyhow the joke was not for me but for Uncle Hawk, an old colored man who lived with

us. I was just the one who answered the door. It was night of course.
I had finished my supper and leaving the others, had gone to the living
room and was on the floor by the radio. After a while there came a
knock on the panes of the door. I said, "I will get it" to the empty room,
thinking they were all in the kitchen, turned on the porch light and
opened the door on a tall man heavy-set with white hair, a black derby
hat, a black overcoat to his ankles, gray kid gloves, a briefcase, a long
white face coiled back under pinch-nose glasses looking down. It was
nobody I knew, nobody I had seen and what could he sell at this time
of night? My heart seized like a fist and I thought, "He has come for
me" (as I say, it is my darkest fear that I am not the blood child of Jeff
and Rhew McCraw, that I was adopted at birth, that someday a strange
man will come and rightfully claim me). But still looking down he
said, "Does an old colored man named Hawk work here?" and I tore
to the kitchen for Uncle Hawk who was scraping dishes while my
mother cleared table. They were silent a moment. Then my mother
said, "Who in the world could it be, Uncle Hawk?" and he said "I
wonder myself." I said, "Well, hurry. It is a stranger and the screen
door is not even locked." He did not hurry. My mother and I stood
and watched him get ready—washing with the Castile soap he keeps
for his fine long hands tough as shark hide, adjusting suspenders, the
garters on his sleeves, inspecting his shoes. Towards the end I looked
at my mother in anxiety. She winked at me and said, "Go on, Uncle
Hawk. It certainly is not Jesus *yet.*" Not smiling he said, "I wish it was"
and went. Again I looked to my mother and again she winked and
beckoned me behind her into the hall where we could watch the door
and the meeting. Uncle Hawk said "Good evening" but did not bow,
and the man said, "Are you Hawk Reid?" Then he mumbled something
about life insurance—did Uncle Hawk have enough life, fire, burial
insurance? Uncle Hawk said, "My life is not worth paying on every
week. I do not have nothing to insure for fire but a pocket knife and it
is iron, and Mr. Jeff McCraw is burying me." The man mumbled some
more. Uncle Hawk said, "No" and the man reached for the handle to

the screen that separated them. Uncle Hawk reached to lock the screen but too slow, and there was the man on us, two feet from Hawk, fifteen from my mother and me. Hawk said, "Nobody asked you to come in here" and drew back his arm (nearly eighty years old) to strike. My mother and I had not made a sound, and I had mostly watched her not the door as she was grinning but then she laughed. Uncle Hawk turned on her, his arm still coiled, then back to the man who was looking up now not moving, and then Hawk laughed, doubled over helpless. The man walked in right past him slowly and stopped six feet from me, holding out his hand to take—he and I the two in the room not laughing. So I knew he had come for me, that I was his and would have to go. His hand stayed out in the glove towards me. There were three lines of careful black stitching down the back of the pale gray leather, the kind of gloves I wanted that are not made for boys. Still I could not take his hand just then, and not for terror. I was really not afraid but suddenly sorry to leave people who had been good to me, the house which I knew. That was what locked me there. I must have stood half a minute that way, and I must have looked worse and worse because my mother said, "Look at his eyes" and pointed me towards the man's face. I looked and at once they were what they had been all along—Jeff McCraw's eyes, the size and color of used nickels, gentle beyond disguising. I said to him then fast and high, "I thought you were my real father and had come to get me." He took off his derby and the old glasses and said, "I *am*, Preacher. I *have*, Preacher," and I ran to circle his thighs with my arms, to hide my tears in the hollow beneath the black overcoat. And I did hide them. When I looked up, everybody thought I had loved the joke like them. But I had not. I had loved my father found at the end with his hand stretched out. But I hoped not to find him again that way under glasses and powder, mumbling, so when he came into my bedroom to kiss me that night, I asked would he do me a favor. He said "What?" and I said, "Please warn me before you dress up ever again." He said he would and then my mother walked in and hearing us said, "You will not need warning. Just stare at his eyes first thing. He cannot hide those." But he always warns me as he promised he would—except at Christmas when he comes in a cheap flannel suit and rayon beard that any baby could see is false— and even though I know in advance that on a certain evening he will arrive as a tramp to scare my Aunt Lola or as a tax collector or a man from the farm office to tell my Uncle Paul he has planted illegal tobacco and must plow it under or suffer, still I fasten on his eyes and hold to them till somebody laughs and he finds time to wink at me.

As I fasten on them now heading home. He travels of course as himself tonight in a brown vested suit and a solid green tie so I see him plain—what is clear in dashboard light—and though I love him, though I rest in his hollow lap now happier than any other place, I know he cannot be my hero. And I list the reasons to myself. Heroes are generally made by war. My father was born in 1900 so the nearest he got to the First World War was the National Guard and in October 1918 an Army camp near Morehead City, N.C. where he spent six weeks in a very wrinkled uniform (my mother has his picture) till peace arrived, so desperately homesick that he saved through the whole six weeks the bones of a chicken lunch his mother gave him on leaving home. And when I woke him a year ago from his Sunday nap to ask what was Pearl Harbor that the radio was suddenly full of, he was well and young enough to sign for the Draft and be nervous but too old to serve. He does own two guns—for protection an Army .45 that his brother brought him from France, never wanting to see it again, and for hunting a double-barreled shotgun with cracked stock—but far as I know he has never shot anything but himself (that time he was a boy) and two or three dozen wharf rats, rabbits and squirrels. Nor is he even in his quiet life what heroes generally must be—physically brave. Not that chances often arise for that class of bravery. I had not seen him face any ordeal worse than a flat tire till a while ago when we had our first mock air raid in Randolph. He took an armband, helmet, blackjack and me, and we drove slowly to the power station which was his post and sat in the cold car thinking it would end soon, but it did not and

I began to wonder was it real, were the Germans just beyond hearing, heading toward us? Then he opened his door and we slid out and stood on the hill with great power batteries singing behind us and looked down at the smothered town. I said, "What will we do if the Germans really come?" Not waiting he pointed towards what I guessed was Sunset Avenue (his sense of direction being good) and said, "We would high-tail it there to where your mother is liable to burn down the house any minute with all those candles." He did not laugh but the siren went and lights began and we headed home—the house stinking tallow on through the night and I awake in bed wondering should I tell him, "If you feel that way you ought to resign as warden"? deciding "No, if Hitler comes let him have the power. What could we do anyhow, Father with a blackjack, me with nothing?—hold off steel with our pitiful hands?" (the hand he touches me with again now, his wounded hand but the wrist so whole so full, under its curls so ropey I cannot ring it, trying now I cannot capture it in my hand so I trace one finger through its curls, tracing my name into him as older boys gouge names, gouge love into trees, into posts—gouge proudly). But with all the love I mentioned before, I do not trace proudly. I know him too well, know too many lacks, and my finger stops in the rut where his pulse would be if I could ever find it (I have tried, I cannot find it, maybe could not stand it if I did). I shut my eyes not to see his face for fear he will smile, and continue to name his lacks to myself. He makes people wait—meaning me and my mother. He is a salesman and travels, and sometimes when school is out, I travel with him, hoping each time things will go differently. They start well always (riding and looking though never much talking) till we come to the house where he hopes to sell a stove or refrigerator. We will stop in the yard. He will sit a minute, looking for dangerous dogs, then reach for his briefcase, open his door and say, "Wait here, Preacher. I will be straight back" I will say "All right" and he will turn back to me, "You do not mind that, do you, darling?"—"Not if you remember I am out here and do not spend the day." He of course says he will remember and goes, but before he has gone ten yards I can see that memory rise through his straw hat like steam, and by the time a woman says, "Step in the house," I am out of his mind as if I was part of the car that welcomed this chance to cool and rest. Nothing cool about it (being always summer when I travel with him), and I sit and sweat, shooing out flies and freezing if a yellowjacket comes, and when twenty minutes has gone by the clock, I begin to think, "If this was all the time he meant to give me, why did he bring me along?" And that rushes on into, "Why did he get me, why did he want me at all if he meant to treat me the way he does, giving me as much time each day as it takes to kiss me goodbye when I go to school and again at night in case we die in each other's absence?" And soon I am rushing through ways he neglects me daily. He will not for instance *teach* me. Last fall I ordered an axe from Sears and Roebuck with my own money, asking nobody's permission, and when it came—so beautiful—he acted as if I had ordered mustard gas and finally said I could keep it if I promised not to use it till he showed me the right way. I promised—and kept my promise—and until this day that axe has done nothing but wait on my wall, being taken down every night, having its lovely handle stroked, its dulling edge felt fearfully. And baseball. He has told me how he played baseball when he was my age, making it sound the happiest he ever was, but he cannot make me catch a fly-ball. I have asked him for help, and he went so far as to buy me a glove and spend half an hour in the yard throwing at me, saying "Like this, Preacher" when I threw at him, but when I failed to stop ball after ball, he finally stopped trying and went in the house, not angry or even impatient but never again offering to teach me what he loved when he was my age, what had won him friends. Maybe he thought he was being kind. Maybe he thought he had shamed me, letting me show him my failure. He had, he had. But if he knew how furious I pray when I am the outfield at school recess (pray that flies go any way but mine), how struck, how shrunk, how abandoned I feel when prayer fails and a ball splits hot through my hopeless hand to lie daring me to take it and throw it right while some loud boy no bigger than I, no better made, trots a free homerun—he would try again, do nothing but try. Or maybe there just come stretches when he does not care, when he does not love me or want me in his mind much less his sight—scrambling on the ground like a hungry fice for a white leather ball any third-grade girl could catch, sucking his life, his time, his fun for the food I need, the silly clothes, sucking the joy out of what few hopes he may have seen when his eyes were shut ten years ago, when he and my mother made me late in the night. That is the stuff he makes me think when he goes and leaves me stuck in the car, stuck for an hour many times so that finally sunk in desperation I begin to know he is sick in there—that his heart has seized as he knows it will or that strange woman is wild and has killed him silent with a knife, with poison, or that he has sold his stove and said goodbye and gone out the back in secret across a field into pines to leave us forever, to change his life. And I will say to myself, "You have got to move—run to the road and flag a car and go for the sheriff," but the house door will open and he will be there alive still grinning, then calming his face in the walk through the yard, wiping his forehead, smiling when he sees me again, when he recollects he has a son and I am it (am one anyhow, the one old enough to follow him places and wait). Before I can swallow what has jammed my throat, my heart in the previous hour, he will have us rolling—the cool breeze started and shortly his amends, my reward for waiting. It is always the same, his amends. It is stories about him being my age, especially about his father—Charles McCraw, "Cupe" McCraw who was clerk to the Copeland Register of Deeds, raised six children which were what he left (and a house, a wife, several dozen jokes) when he died sometime before I was born—and he needs no crutch to enter his stories such as "Have I told you this?" He knows he has told me, knows I want it again every time he can spare. He will light a cigarette with a safety match (he threw away the car's lighter long ago out the window down an embankment, thinking *it* was a match) and then say, "No sir. If I live to be ninety, I never want to swallow another cigarette." That is the first of the story about him at my age being sent outdoors by his father to shut off the water when a hard freeze threatened. The valve was sunk in the ground behind the house, and he was squatting over it cursing because it was stiff and pulling on the cigarette he had lit to warm him—when he looked in the frozen grass by his hand and there were black shoes and the ends of trousers. He did not need to look further. It was his father so while he gave one last great turn to the valve, he flipped his lower lip out and up (and here at age forty-two he imitates the flip, swift but credible) and swallowed the cigarette, fire included. Then he may say, "How is your bladder holding out, Preacher? Do you want to run yonder into those bushes?" I will say "No" since I cannot leak in open air, and he will say, "Father had a colored boy named Peter who worked round the house. *Peee-ter*, Peter called it. The first day we had a telephone connected, Father called home from the courthouse to test it. I was home from school—supposed to be sick—and I answered. He did not catch my voice so he said 'Who is this?' I said '*Peee-ter*,' and he thought he would joke a little. He said 'Peter *who?*' I said 'Mr. *McCraw's* Peee-ter,' and he said, 'Hang up, fool, and don't ever answer that thing again!' I waited for him to come home that evening, and he finally came with a box of Grapenuts for me, but he did not mention Peter or the telephone so I didn't either, never mentioned it till the day he died. He died at night . . ."

But *tonight*. This hard winter night in 1942 and he is silent—my father—his eyes on darkness and road to get me safely home as if I was cherished, while I rush on behind shut eyes through all that last—his size, his lacks, his distances—still threading my finger through curls of his wrist, a grander wrist than he needs or deserves. I find his pulse. It rises sudden to my winnowing finger, waylays, appalls, *traps* it. I ride his life with the pad of flesh on my middle finger, and it heaves against me steady and calm as if it did not know I ruled its flow, that poor as I am at games and play, I could press in now, press lightly first so he would not notice, then in and in till his foot would slack on the gas, his head sink heavy to his chest, his eyes shut on me (on what I cause),

the car roll still and I be left with what I have made—his permanent
death. Towards that picture, that chance, my own pulse rises untouched, unwanted—grunting aloud in the damp stripes under my
groins, the tender sides of my windpipe, sides of my heels, the pad of
my sinking finger. My finger coils to my side, my whole hand clenches,
my eyes clamp tighter, but—innocent surely—he speaks for the first
time since begging my pardon. "Am I dying, Preacher?"

I look up at him. "No sir. What do you mean?"

"I mean you left my pulse like a bat out of Hell. I wondered did you
feel bad news?"

"No sir, it is going fine. I just never felt it before, and it gave me
chills." He smiles at the road and we slide on a mile or more till I say,
"Are you *scared* of dying?"

He keeps me waiting so I look past him through glass to the sky for
a distant point to anchor on—the moon, a planet, Betelgeuse. Nothing
is there. All is drowned under cloud but I narrow my eyes and strain
to pierce the screen. Then when I am no longer waiting, he says, "It
is the main thing I am scared of."

I come back to him. "Everybody is going to die."

"So they tell me. So they tell me. But that is one crowd I would
miss if I could. Gladly."

I am not really thinking. "What do people mean when they say
somebody is their personal hero?"

It comes sooner than I expect. "Your hero is what you need to be."

"Then is Jesus your hero?"

"Why do you think that?"

"You say you are scared of dying. Jesus is the one that did not die."

He does not take it as funny which is right, and being no Bible
scholar he does not name me the others that live on—Enoch, Elijah.
I name them to myself but not to him. I have seen my chance. I am
aiming now at discovery, and I strike inwards like Balboa mean and
brave, not knowing where I go or will end or if I can live with what I

find. But the next move is his. He must see me off. And he does. He
tells me, "I think your hero has to be a man. Was Jesus a man?"

"No sir. He was God disguised."

"Well, that is it, you see. You would not stand a chance of being
God—need to or not—so you pick somebody you have got half a
chance of measuring up to."

In all my seeking I have not asked him. I ask him now. "Have you
got a hero?"

Again he makes me wait and I *wait*. I look nowhere but at him. I
do not think. Then he says, "Yes, I guess I do. But I never called it
that to myself."

"What did you call it?"

"I didn't call it nothing. I was too busy trying to get through alive."

"Sir?"

"—Get through some trouble I had. I *had* some troubles and when
I did there was generally a person I could visit and talk to till I eased.
Then when I left him and the trouble came back, I would press down
on *him* in my mind—something he told me or how he shook my hand
goodbye. Sometimes that tided me over. Sometimes."

He has still not offered a name. To help him I hold out the first one
at hand. "Is it Dr. Truett?" (That is where we are coming from now
tonight—a sermon in Raleigh by George W. Truett from Texas.)

The offer is good enough to make him think. (I know how much he
admires Dr. Truett. He has one of his books and a sermon on records—
"The Need for Encouragement"—that he plays two or three nights a
year, standing in the midst of the room, giving what wide curved
gestures seem right when Dr. Truett says for instance, " 'Yet now be
strong, O Zerubbabel, saith the Lord; and be strong O Joshua, son of
Josedech, the high priest; and be strong, all ye people of the land, saith
the Lord, and work: for I am with you, saith the Lord of hosts: according
to the word that I covenanted with you when ye came out of Egypt, so
my spirit remaineth among you: fear ye not.' " And here we have come

this long way to see him in January with snow due to fall by morning.)
But he says—my father, "No, not really. Still you are close." Then a
wait—"You are warm."

"Does that mean it is a preacher?"

"Yes."

"Mr. Barden?"

"I guess he is it."

I knew he was—or would have known if I had thought—but I do
not know why. He is nothing but the Baptist minister in Copeland, my
father's home—half a head shorter than Father, twenty years older,
light and dry as kindling with flat bands of gray hair, white skin the day
shines through if he stands by windows, Chinese eyes, bird ankles, a
long voice for saying things such as "Jeff, I am happy to slide my legs
under the same table with yours" and poor digestion (he said that last
the one day he ate with us; my mother had cooked all morning, and
he ate a cup of warm milk)—but he is one of the people my father
loves, one my mother is jealous of, and whenever we visit Copeland
(we left there when I was two), there will come a point after dinner on
Sunday when my father will stand and without speaking start for the
car. If it is winter he may get away unseen, but in summer everybody
will be on the porch, and Junie will say, "Jeff is headed to save Brother
Barden's soul." My mother will laugh. My father will smile and nod
but go and be gone till evening and feel no need to explain when he
returns, only grin and agree to people's jokes.

But *tonight*, has he not just offered to explain? and to me who have
never asked? So I ask, "Mr. Barden is so skinny. What has he got that
you need to be?"

"Before you were born he used to be a lot of things. Still is."

All this time he has not needed his hand on the wheel. It has stayed
heavy on me. I slip my hand towards it. I test with my finger, tapping.
He turns his palm and takes me, gives me the right to say "Name some
things." I fear if he looks at me, we will go back silent (he has not
looked down since we started with his pulse), and I roll my face deep

into his side, not to take his eyes. But they do not come. He does not look. He does not press my hand in his, and the load of his wrist even lightens. I think it will leave but it lifts a little and settles further on like a folded shield over where I am warmest, takes up guard, and then he is talking the way he must, the best he can, to everything but me— the glass, the hood, the hoop of light we push towards home.

"I have done things you would not believe—and will not believe when you get old enough to do them yourself. I have come home at night where your mother was waiting and said things to her that were worse than a beating, then gone again and left her still waiting till morning, till sometimes night again. And did them knowing I would not do them to a dog. Did them drunk and wild, knowing she loved me and would not leave me even though her sisters said, 'Leave him. He won't change now,' would not even raise her voice. O Preacher, it was Hell. We were both in Hell with the lid screwed down, not a dollar between us except what I borrowed—from Negroes sometimes when friends ran out—to buy my liquor to keep me wild. You were not born yet, were not thought of, God knows not wanted the way I was going. It was 1930. I was thirty years old and my life looked over, and I didn't know why or whether I wanted it different, but here came Mr. Barden skinny as you say, just sitting by me when I could sit still, talking when I could listen, saying 'Hold up, Jeff. Promise God something before you *die.*' But Preacher, I didn't. I drank up two more years, driving thousands of miles on mirey roads in a Model-A Ford to sell little scraps of life insurance to wiped-out farmers that did not have a pot to pee in, giving your mother a dollar or so to buy liver with on a Saturday or a pound of hominy I could not swallow. And then that spring when the bottom looked close, I slipped and started you on the way. When I knew you were coming—Preacher, for days I was out of what mind I had left myself. I do not know what I did but I *did* things, and finally when I had run some sort of course, your mother sent for Mr. Barden and they got me still. He said, 'Jeff, I cherish you, mean as you are. But what can I do if you go on murdering yourself, tormenting your wife?' I told him, 'You can ask the Lord to stop that baby.' I told him that. But you came on every day *every day* like a tumor till late January and she hollered to me you were nearly here. But you were not. You held back twenty-four hours as if you knew who was waiting outside, and Dr. Haskins told me—after he had struggled with your mother all day, all night—'Jeff, one of your family is going to die but I don't know which.' I said, 'Let it be me' and he said he wished he could. I went outdoors to Paul's woodshed and told Jesus, 'If You take Rhew or take that baby, then take me too. But if You can, save her and save that baby, and I make You this promise—I will change my life.' I asked Him, 'Change my life.' So He saved you two and I started trying to change my life, am trying right now God knows. Well, Mr. Barden has helped me out every once in a while—talking to me or just sitting calm, showing me his good heart. Which, Preacher, I need."

I can tell by his voice he is not through, but he stops, leaving raw quiet like a hole beneath us. I feel that because I have stayed awake, and my finger slips to the trough of his wrist where the pulse was before. It is there again awful. I take it, count it long as I can and say, "It feels all right to me, sir" (not knowing of course how right would feel). He says he is glad which frees me to see Mr. Barden again. I call up his face and pick it for anything new. At first it is very much the same— bloodless, old—but I settle on the faded stripes of his lips and strain to picture them years ago saying the things that were just now reported. They move, speak and for a moment I manage to see his face as a wedge—but aimed elsewhere, making no offer to split me clean from my lacks *my* foes. So I let it die and I say to my father, "I still think Jesus is your real hero."

Glad for his rest, he is ready again. "Maybe so. Maybe so. But Mr. Barden was what I could *see.*"

"Who has seen Jesus?"

"Since He died, you mean?"

"Yes sir."

"Several, I guess. Dr. Truett for one."

I know the story—it is why I have come this far to hear an old man tremble for an hour—but I request it again.

"Well, as I understand it, years ago when he was young, he asked a friend to come hunting with him. He came and they went in the woods together, and after a while he shot his friend. By accident but that didn't make him feel any better. He knew some people would always say he killed the man on purpose."

"Maybe he did."

"No he didn't. Hold on."

"How do you know?"

"The same way *he* knew—because after he sweated drops of blood in misery, Jesus came to him one evening in a dream and said not to grieve any more but to live his life and do what he could."

"Does that mean he really saw Jesus?—seeing Him in his sleep?"

"How else could you see Him since He is dead so long?"

I tell him the chance that is one of my hopes, my terrors—"He could walk in your house in daylight. Then you could step around Him. You could put out your hand and He would be there. But in just a dream how would you know? What would keep Him from being a trick?"

"The way He would look. His face, His hands."

"The scars, you mean?"

"They would help. But no—" This is hard for him. He stops and thinks for fully a mile. "I mean whether or not He had the face to say things such as 'Be ye perfect as God is perfect'—not even say '*try* to be,' just '*be*'—a face that could change people's lives."

"People do not *know* what He looks like, Father. That is half the trouble." We are now on one of our oldest subjects. We started three years ago when I first went to vacation Bible school. At the end of that two weeks after we had made our flour-paste model of a Hebrew water hole, they gave us diplomas that were folded leaflets with our name inside and a golden star but on the cover their idea of Jesus—set by a palm under light such as comes after storms (blurred, with piece of a rainbow) and huddled around Him, one each of the earth's children in native dress, two or three inside His arms but all aiming smiles at His face (jellied eyes, tan silk beard, clean silk hair, pink lips that could not call a dog to heel much less children or say to His mother, "Who is my mother?" and call her "Woman" from the bitter cross). I took the picture but at home that night I handed it to my father and asked if he thought that face was possible? He looked and said it was one man's guess, not to worry about it, but I did and later after I had studied picture Bibles and *Christ and the Fine Arts* by Cynthia Pearl Maus full of hairy Jesuses by Germans mostly—Clementz, Deitrich, Hofmann, Lang, Plockhorst, Von Uhde, Wehle—I asked him if in all the guessers, there was one who knew? any Jesus to count on? He said he thought there was but in Student's Bibles, the ones they give to boys studying ministry. I said had he seen one? He had not and I asked if he could buy me one or borrow Mr. Barden's for me to trace? He said he did not think so, that Student's Bibles were confidential, secrets for good men.

So tonight I ask him, "Then how did He look in your mind when I was being born and Mother was dying?"

"He didn't look nohow *that* day. I was not seeing faces. I was doing business. If I saw anything it was rocks underfoot, those smooth little rocks Paul hauled from the creek to spread in his yard."

"I think it is awful."

"What?"

"Him not appearing. Why did Dr. Truett see Him and you could not?"

"Maybe he needed to worse than me. He had killed a man, killed somebody else. I was just killing me, making others watch me do it."

"That is no reason."

"Preacher, if I was as good a man as George W. Truett—half the man—I would be seeing Jesus every day or so, be *fishing* with Him."

"I am not joking, Father. It is awful, I think—Him not helping you better than that."

"Preacher, I didn't mind"—which even with this night's new information is more or less where we always end. It does not worry my father that he is not privileged to see the secret. But it scalds, torments any day of mine in which I think that the face with power to change my life is hid from me and reserved for men who have won their fight (when He Himself claimed He sought the lost), will always be hid, leaving me to work dark. As my father has done, does, must do—not minding, just turning on himself his foe with nothing for hero but Mr. Barden when it could have been Jesus if He had appeared, His gouged hands, His real face, the one He deserved that changes men.

We are quiet again, so quiet I notice the sound of the engine. I have not heard it tonight before. It bores through the floor, crowds my ears, and turning my eyes I take the mileage—sixty-three thousand to round it off. My father travels in his work as I say, and this Pontiac has borne him three times around the earth—the equal of that nearly. It will get us home together, alive, and since in a heavy rush I am tired, I sleep where I am, in his heat, in his hollow. Of course I do not think I am sleeping. I dream I am awake, that I stand on the near side of sleep and yearn, but it *is* a dream and as sudden again I wake—my head laid flat on the mohair seat, blood gathered hot in my eyes that stare up at nothing. My head lifts a little (stiff on my neck), my eyes jerk round collecting terror—the motor runs gentle, the knob of the heater burns red, burns warm, but the car is still and my father is gone. Where he was the dashboard light strikes empty nothing. My head falls back and still half dreaming I think, "They have won at last. They have caught us, come between us. We have ended apart." I say that last aloud and it wakes me fully so I lie on (my head where his loaded lap should be) and think what seems nearer truth—"He has left as I always knew he would to take up his life in secret." Then I plunge towards the heart of my fear—"He knew just now what I thought when I pressed his pulse, and he could not bear my sight any more." Then deeper towards the heart—"God has taken him from me as punishment for causing his death just now in my mind. But why did He not take me?" Still He did not. I am left. So I rise and strain to see out the glass, to know my purpose for being here, what trials lie between me and morning, what vengeance. The first is snow. The headlights shine and in their outward upward hoop there is only flat gobs of snow that saunter into frozen grass and survive. The grass of the shoulder is all but smothered, the weeds of the bank already bent, meaning I have slept long enough for my life to wreck beyond hope—my father vanished and I sealed in a black Pontiac with stiff death held back only long as the draining battery lasts and now too late, no hero to turn to. My forehead presses into the dark windshield. For all the heater's work, the cold crawls in through glass, through flesh, through skull to my blood, my brain.

So I pray. My eyes clamped now, still pressed to the glass, knowing I have not prayed for many weeks past (with things going well), I swallow my shame and naked in fear ask, "Send me my father. Send me help. If You help me now, if You save my life, I will change—be brave, be free with my gifts. Send somebody good." My eyes click open on answered prayer—coming slow from the far edge of light a tall man hunched, his face to the ground hid, head wrapped in black, a black robe bound close about him, his arms inside, bearing towards me borne on the snow as if on water leaving no tracks, his shadow crouched on the snow like a following bird, giant, black (killing? kind?). I stay at the glass, further prayer locked in my throat, waiting only for the sign of my fate. Then the robe spreads open. The man's broad hands are clasped on his heart, turned inward, dark. It is Jesus I see, Jesus I shall touch moments from now—shall lift His face, probe His wounds, kiss His eyes. He is five steps away. I slip from the glass, fall back on my haunches, turn to the driver's door where He already stands, say silent, "If Father could not see Your face, why must I?"—say to the opening door "Thank You, Sir," close my lips to take His unknown kiss.

He says, "Excuse me leaving you asleep," and it is my father come back disguised. "I had to go pee—down that hill in the snow." (He points down the road as if he had covered miles not feet.) "I thought you were dead to the world."

I say, "I *was*"—I laugh—"and I thought you were Jesus, that you had been taken and I was left and Jesus was coming to claim me. I was about to *see* Him."

Standing outside, the warm air rushing towards him, he shrugs the coat from his shoulders, lifts the scarf from his head, lays them in back, slides onto the seat. Shrinking from cold I have crawled almost to the opposite door, but kneeling towards him. He faces me and says, "I am sorry to disappoint you, Preacher."

I say "Yes sir" and notice he smiles very slow, very deep from his eyes—but ahead at the road. Then he says I had better lie down. I crawl the two steps and lie as before, and we move on so I have no chance to return his smile, to show I share his pleasure. Still I root my head deep in his lap and hope for a chance before sleep returns. The chance never comes. Snow occupies his eyes, his hands. He cannot face me again or test for warmth. Even his mind is surely on nothing but safety. Yet his face is new. Some scraps of the beauty I planned for Jesus hang there—on the corners of his mouth serious now, beneath his glasses in eyes that are no longer simply kind and gray but have darkened and burn new power far back and steady (the power to stop in his tracks and *turn*), on his ears still purple with cold but flared against danger like perfect ugly shells of blind sea life, on his wrists I cannot ring with my hand, stretched from white cuffs at peace on the wheel but shifting with strength beyond soldier's, beyond slave's—and I think, "I will look till I know my father, till all this new disguise falls away leaving him clear as before." I look but his face shows no sign of retreat, and still as he is and distant, it is hard to stare, painful then numbing. I feel sleep rise from my feet like blood. When it reaches my head I shut my eyes to flush it back, but it surges again and I know I have lost. My own hands are free—he has not touched me, cannot—so my right hand slips to the gap in my pants, cups itself warm on warmer trinkets long since asleep, soft with blood like new birds nested drowsy. I follow them into darkness, thinking on the threshold, "Now I have lost all hope of knowing my father's life," cupping closer, warmer this hand as I sink.

First in my dream I am only this hand yet have eyes to see—but only this hand and a circle of light around it. It is larger by half than tonight, and black stubble has sprung to shade its back, its new thick veins, its gristly cords showing plain because this hand is cupped too, round like a mold, hiding what it makes. It lifts. What it has molded are the kernels, the knobs of a man still twice the size of mine I held before I slept, but cold, shrunk and shrinking as my hand lifts—their little life pouring out blue through veins gorged like sewers that tunnel and vanish under short lank hairs, grizzled. Then I have ears. I hear the blood rustle like silk as it leaves, retreats, *abandons,* and my hand shuts down, clamps on the blood to turn its race, to warm again, fill again what I hold. But the rustle continues not muffled, and my hand presses harder, squeezes the kernels. Through my fingers green piss streams cold, corrosive. But my hand is locked. It cannot move. I am bound to what I have made, have caused, and seeing only this terror, I find a voice to say, "If I cannot leave may I see what I do?" The light swells in a hoop from my hand filling dimly a room and in that room my whole body standing by a bed—the body I will have as a man— my hand at the core of a man's stripped body laid yellow on the narrow bed. Yet with this new light my original eyes have stayed where they started—on my crushing hand and beneath it. I tear them left to see the rest. So I start at his feet raised parallel now but the soles pressed flat by years of weight, the rims of the heels and the crowded toes guarded by clear callus, the veins of the insteps branching towards shins like blades of antique war polished deadly, marred by sparse hair, the knees like grips to the blades, the thighs ditched inward to what I crush—his hollow his core that streams on thin with no native force but sure as if drained by magnets in the earth. Then his hands at his sides clenched but the little fingers separate, crouched, gathering ridges in the sheet. Then his firm belly drilled deep by the navel, his chest like the hull of a stranded boat, shaved raw, violet paps sunk and from under his left armpit a line traced carefully down his side, curved under his ribs, climbing to the midst of his breast—the letter J perfect, black, cut into him hopeless to dredge out a lung, laced with gut stiff as wire. Then under a tent of soft wrinkled glass his face which of course is my father's—the face he will have when I am this man—turned from me, eyes shut, lips shut, locked in the monstrous stillness of his rest. So he does not watch me, shows no sign of the pain I must cause. Yet I try again to lift my fingers, to set him free, but rocking the heel of my hand, I see our skin has joined maybe past parting. I struggle though— gentle to spare his rest. I step back slowly, hoping this natural movement will peel us clean, but what I have pressed comes with me as if I had given love not pain. I speak again silent to whoever gave me light just now, say, "Set him free. Let me leave him whole in peace." But that prayer fails and turning my eyes I pull against him, ready to wound us both if I must. Our joint holds fast but the rustle beneath my hand swells to scraping, to high short grunts. "Jesus," I say—I speak aloud— "Come again. Come now. I do not ask to see Your face but come in *some* shape now." A shudder begins beneath my hand in his core our core that floods through his belly, his breast to his throat, bearing with it the noise that dims as it enters the tent. I stare through the glass. His head rolls towards me, his yellow lips split to release the noise, his eyes slide open on a quarter-inch of white. The noise scrapes on but behind the tent it is not words—is it rage or pain or wish, is it meant for me? With my free left hand I reach for the tent to throw it back, saying, "Stop. Stop," but I cannot reach so "Father," I say, "I beg your pardon. Pardon me this, I will change my life—will turn in my tracks on myself my foe with you as shield." But he yields no signal. The eyes shut again, the lips shut down on the noise, the shudder runs out as it came, to our core. What my free hand can reach it touches—his wrist. What pulse was there is stopped, and cold succeeds it till with both hands I press hard ice, final as any trapped in the Pole. I can see clearer now, my terror calmed by his grander terror, the peace of his wounds, and facing his abandoned face I say again (to the place, the dream), "Pardon me this, I will change my life. I make this . . ." But pardon comes to stop my speech. My cold hands lift from his hollow, his wrist. My own hot life pours back to claim them. Then those hands fail, those eyes, my dream. A shift of my headrest lifts me from sleep.

I face my live father's present body—my present eyes on his belly but *him, tonight*, above me, around me, shifting beneath me. My lips are still open, a trail of spit snails down my cheek, my throat still holds the end of my dream, "I make this promise." So my first thought is fear. Have I spoken aloud what I watched in my dream? Have I warned my father of his waiting death? offered my promise, my life too early? I roll away from his belt to see—and see I am safe. He is what he has been before tonight, been all my life, unchanged by my awful news, my knowledge, undisguised—his ears, his cheeks flushed with healthy blood that also throbs in the broad undersides of his wrists on the wheel, in the wounded fat of his hand, his hollow, even in his eyes which are still ahead on the road for safety, able, unblinking but calm and light as if through snow he watched boys playing skillful games with natural grace.

His legs shift often under me now—braking, turning, accelerating— and we move forward slowly past regular street lamps that soar through the rim of my sight, gold at the ends of green arms. We are in some town. From its lamps, its wires, its hidden sky, I cannot say which— but not home yet I trust, I hope. I am not prepared for home and my mother, the rooms that surround my swelling lacks, direct sight of my doomed father. I need silent time to hoard my secret out of my face deep into my mind, granting my father twelve years fearless to work at his promise, freeing myself to gather in private the strength I will need for my own promise the night he dies, my own first turn on what giant foes I will have as a man. And clamping my eyes I seize my dream and thrust it inward, watching it suck down a blackening funnel, longing to follow it. But his legs shift again, his arms swing left, our wheels strike gravel, stop. Beyond the glass in our stationary light are bare maple limbs accepting snow, limbs of the one tree I climb with ease. Too sudden we are home and my father expels in a seamless shudder the care, the attention that bound him these last three hours. His legs tense once, gather to spring from beneath my weight, then subside, soften. I ride the final surge, then face him—smiling as if just startled from sleep.

He takes my smile, stores it as a gift. "Did you sleep well, Preacher?"

I hunch my shoulders, say "Thank you, sir," and behind my lie floods sudden need—to rise, board him, cherish with my hands, my arms while there still is time this huge gentle body I know like my own, which made my own (made half anyhow) and has hurt nobody since the day I was born.

But he says, "Lift up. Look yonder at the door."

I roll to my knees. Through glass and snow, behind small panes, white curtains, in the center of the house no longer ours stands my mother in a flannel robe, hand raised in welcome the shape of fire. "She waited," I say.

"She waited," he says and reaches for his scarf, his coat, beckons me to him, drapes them around me, steps to the white ground and turning, offers me open arms. Kneeling I ask him, "What do you mean?"

"I mean to save your life, to carry you over this snow."

"Heavy as I am?—you and *your* heart?"

But he says no more. His mind is made, his trip is ended. He is nearly home, facing rest, accepting snow like the trees while I stall. Then he claps his palms one time, and I go on my knees out of dry car heat through momentary snow into arms that circle, enfold me, lift me, bear me these last steps home over ice—my legs hung bare down his cooling side, face to his heart, eyes blind again, mind folding in me for years to come his literal death and my own swelling foes, lips against rough brown wool saying to myself as we rise to the porch, to my waiting mother (silent, in the voice I will have as a man), "They did not separate us tonight. We finished alive, together, whole. This one more time."

NINE HOURS ALONE

Saturday morning when her daughter Leah left for country day-camp and Davis her husband went in to finish a budget request for the trustees' meeting, she washed every spotted object in the kitchen, dried each gently and laid it in place with a loathing indistinguishable from fondness. She made a full list of what they'd need from the grocery store before day ended. She set each item in the order in which they'd come across it if they took a cart and worked the aisles from left to right—Leah would know. She had bathed herself as she did every day on rising at dawn. So once she hung a clean hand-towel on the oven handle, rinsed her hands and face at the sink, gave the white azalea a grateful look and went to the bedroom, the rest flowed freely.

She sat at the rickety lady's desk that had been her mother's and wrote two letters. The first was to her husband,

> *Dear Davis,*
>
> *You are absolutely not to blame for what I do. You have tried in every way you know to guide me free, but I cannot go. I have squandered all I promised you, at God's white altar sixteen years ago; and I will not stay any longer to watch you take the meager scraps I offer now in lieu of the bountiful thanks I owe.*
>
> *I leave in utter shame and regret. I cannot even think of the world*

I leave for you and Leah to walk. And the heart of our tragic fate is this, the person for whom I ruined our lives is still too young to weigh or judge the love I tried to take from you and load on him.

If you see him again, I trust your forbearance. He has never touched more than the palm of my hand, and he will be as baffled as we at where these two years have ended.

I understand that, with your faith, you will think I now forfeit salvation and the chance to meet you two again and comprehend how strong you are to urge, as you have, that I remain. I hope you are wrong. I hope we all will sleep forever, no glimpse of dream.

Thank you,
Frances

The second letter was to the person on whose account she would ruin four lives.

Tom,

This will not reach you before the news. Like everything that happened around us, it was my idea, the only way I can now imagine to clear the room for you to walk forward into your man's life and for my husband and daughter to last.

Teachers have hung their lives on students since time began, I know, and called it love; so at least my crime is old and familiar, if bitterly comic. Knowing clearly that today I harm a patient husband and a valiant child, still I only regret—in all the world—that you had less to give than I dreamed and, though you are three long years from manhood, will never have more.

That does not stop me wishing you now a useful life, with courage to take what you turned back from me, the harmless gifts that your face earns.

Frances Barnes

She propped her husband's letter on his pillow; Tom's she sealed, stamped and left on the desk. Then she crossed an enormous stretch of floor to the dim tile bath. There she opened the bottle of sleeping pills that were hid in the deepest back of the closet. She rinsed the toothpaste stains off her glass and dried it hard on a clean towel. Then she ran tap water to the count of sixty—cold and fresh. She counted out twenty capsules and drank them in half a minute. The only words in her mind were numbers—*sixteen, seventeen*. She smoothed her hair. In her final sight of the face she'd worn for thirty-eight years, she was smiling mildly.

She turned aside and moved to their bed. As she scuffed her shoes, lay back and covered herself with the afghan, she knew that she had nine hours alone before either Leah or Davis was due. It was ample time. The weight of the melting drug in her stomach was welcome like Leah's first shrug in her womb. She held to that thought till her mind forgot it. As her eyes shut down, the muscles along her lean jaw pulled again at her lips, reclaiming the smile from light-years back.

NIGHT AND SILENCE

FORTY YEARS later I'm still astonished at the luck we had and managed to hold—to meet at the excellent pitch of youth and give each other our entire best: unadulterated coupling, the fullest courtesy and never less than the plan to last together somehow all our lives, no grudge or stint. What's that but the rarest bird in the woods? I was twenty-two at the start, you twenty-one; and a hundred snapshots make a case for the primary fact—we were both the heirs of strong-faced kin; and even that early we were good to see (you with gold hair that sprang at the touch and hooded eyes the color of your old Viking genes).

Three years on, we'd passed that peak; and our bodies slowly spent those legacies, turning in time to normal skin. But while that rank power lasted, we saw each other clearly and shared our unearned gifts, openhanded as children. And though I hope to last years more, lately I've felt a pressing duty to note at least the better days so others we know or strangers unborn have one gauge anyhow for states like flat-out pleasure and trustworthy peace, the bounds of magnanimity through long lives.

The week before Easter we flew as far as student funds let us—misty London to misty Geneva—then plunged south through the smug white Alps, the stifling dark of the Simplon Tunnel and a break-out onto full sun pounding the station at Domodossola where Italy starts. We

473

stretched our legs on the snowy platform, bolted down salt ham on bread and gave our passports to a customs guard no older than we. Despite his underpowered mustache he still had the right to bar our entry on the mildest whim; but he barely glanced at the aim already condensing between us, our imminent threat to the laws of man; and he smiled to himself as he stamped us in, *"Benvenuto"—Well - come* then: two sworn conspirators breach the frontier. I all but shook in the hope he somehow knew our future and grinned at the prospect, but even to you I mimicked freezing and blew out a cold white cloud on the air. Your face had been so much my target these past five months— the face and all that lay beneath it—I could barely watch you; but I guessed all of it was mine for the asking, though till then I'd never asked for more than your sight in a room.

Milan by dusk in stinging rain and on by tram to the central square. No reservations, not even the name of a likely hotel and maybe thirty dollars between us. You'd said if we stood on the steps of the duomo and merely waited, a reliable tout would step from the crowd, offer us a warm dry room at negotiable rates and lug our bags to the hotel door. (It often happened, those better days before the world was gorged with tourists. Even somewhat farther south than this, you could leave your bag on a station platform and go eat a meal, with beggars on all sides; and your bag would be in place when you finished.)

But we stood on till the rain had soaked us; and no one broke from the evening mob to take us in, though there was one madman endlessly boxing the square at a trot and shouting numbers as he turned each corner. When I finally heard him cry "Ninety nine!" I offered to pay two-thirds of the bill for just tonight at the too-deluxe hotel there beyond us, a shining rescue launch in high seas.

Past midnight, after two hours standing in the roof at La Scala as Karajan hauled a wrecked soprano through *Salome*, we'd fed ourselves at a trattoria and were back in our exorbitant space. You'd refused my offer of most of the rent and paid your half; so we had a big room, a thick mahogany brassbound door, twin beds stiff with actual linen and pillows bulky as dirigibles.

I've lost the link to what came next, five of the crucial minutes I've lived through, the bridge across a laughing short friendship to the next steep plateau—strange as floating Tenochtitlán with Moctezuma hid in its heart and found by me, uncovered in all its buried veins of untold profit by my right hand, reckless as Cortez. But rising tired before sunup and crossing the lap of Europe all day, we must have thought we were dead with exhaustion. When we'd laughed though at a memory or two and turned our separate ways to sleep, the tide of the night—in its own rhythm—reversed in thorough mountainous silence and towed us in through the strong rip-current.

In all that speechless strain to breathe, I must have told myself we were safe as we'd ever be. I know by then your back looked ready; and before the final light was out, I was by your bare side, bare myself and eager to serve as you rolled flat and lay full-length to offer all the eye could see and all the other senses seize, stupendous goods laid freely out in your and my lives' first frank meeting—four stories high over nearly a million sleeping workers tossed like damned souls between our dare and the city limits as late dawn sifted in through blinds and Leonardo's ruined *Last Supper*, a few blocks over, entered its four hundred fifty-ninth year of crumbling off its soggy wall, awaiting our visit if morning came.

Good Friday in a black drowned Venice, fording the floods on wobbly duckboards; then a melodrama of parting skies and pale sun for the rush in a packed express toward Rome on Easter night, reaching our hostel to find I'd slipped and booked a room for thirty days hence (they showed us my plainly mistyped letter). So there we hung—dog-eared, dirty and barred from touch by the fish eyes of groggy pilgrims on the holiest day of the Christian year.

Your turn to solve a quandary—back to the station at one A.M., the door of a pokey office you'd seen as we arrived: *League for Protecting Catholic Youth*. When we crossed the sill, you gave me an earnest backward look and said—full voice in 100-proof blarney—"We're Dublin *Irish*." And once we'd waited till the nun in charge arranged a ticket to Malta for a knocked-up girl fierce-eyed as a panther, you told the nun an honest tale, far as you went. We were victims of our own foolishness and needed a bed—*un letto*, singular.

She took you, face value; and as we stood, she also rose and bowed your way. "Buon Pasqua, signore. Christo è risuscitato." I'd never heard your views on Christ, live or dead, still haven't today; but I know you bowed to her then, unsmiling, and said "Ah, *sì*."

By two A.M. we were warm in a cell in a private school for Catholic boys decamped for Easter—two stern cots, a crucifix, a pitcher and bowl with midget towels, doll-sized soap and, down the hall, a cavernous toilet that always sported at least one monk on the porcelain throne of a covered stall, moaning in terminal constipation or some clandestine ecstasy of soul or body.

Chaste as the schoolboys—likely chaster, and I at least as famished as sand—for two long wandering days and nights (Capitol, Forum, Rostrum, Palatine, Mamertine, Sistine, the intact Pantheon grand as the sky). Then our hostel emptied of bankrupt pilgrims; and we were back in secular walls: a narrow room of bone-white plaster, two narrow beds and the landlord's radio on through the night (soccer from the walls of space). Yet there in all but total dark through ten more nights, time and again you climbed like a phosphorescent vine through every plane and entry of my willing skin, grappling every secret I'd kept till you said "Now," then freely yielded.

And long before we paid and left, I'd many times consumed the codes of your warm gist and made them silent units of me, the means of comprehending what you'd need or dread right down your life, while down our block some fifty yards the Field of Mars still rocked in the

dark to three millennia anyhow of soldiers' feet—wide-eyed delicate
bird-voiced Etruscans, sun-kilned Roman legionnaires, the shaggy
Goths (drunk on clear light) and us this past slow afternoon: polo-
shirted, maps in hand, you as frankly splendid as Cleopatra's son by
Caesar, gold doomed Caesarion borne in triumph by desert slaves
blinded to spare his face their eyes.

A Sunday drive with Roman friends our age but rich, in all but our
news, and plumed like pheasants for a country visit—a village an hour
south of town, lived in from the Old Stone Age through the eighteenth
century, then ghosted out by a plague of fever. One churchtower,
roofless huts, a hundred miles of hungry ivy, a billion shards of brick
and limestone, silence broken only by our plumed friends' cries of
baldfaced wonder at the peace those years had made from silence.

And finally you, somehow safe, high in the cracked belltower and
the best these ghosts had seen in centuries. You set your head in the
empty socket of the old town clock; and your voice struck the hour,
five P.M., mimicking the lost bell. Bass notes passed our startled ears
and lazed off down the broad campagna to a hairline river, bright as
mercury (the source, no doubt, of the leveling plague).

You'd ended the day and, though our speeding host's Fiat struck a
child in the edge of the road by a tenement (and we poured out, sick with
fear to check her limbs from crown to toe as a mean mob gathered—she
was scarcely bruised and left the scene in her father's arms with a fistful
of cash), you and I were back in our poor-boy quarters less than a
minute before your voice—the day's curfew—said "Rest now please."

Hard as we worked in the swarming dark, it amounted to rest.

Our pensione lacked tub or shower; so when our sponge baths began
to lose ground against the spring heat, the landlord sent us back to the
station—public baths beneath the concourse: clean private white-tiled
rooms with showers, liquid soap, a scrubbed-down bench, no windows

and a lockable door. In such dream cubicles, Jack the Ripper could have flayed a whore with impunity, not to mention the lavish conditions for love.

We only washed. And even now I can wonder why, with no regret. I have that lucid sight of you as you dried yourself with the patient care of an invalid, though you burned with an unselfconscious force umatched by all the marble hulks we'd seen—the ruins of the Emperor Domitian's baths adjoined the station, museumed now and chocked with gods and paramours. Not all the tangled crests that rode their canted groins could match the burnished wiry shrub that, on your drying body there, threatened to speak God's private present name— "I Am."

Florence (the English Italy, all indoors and muted but with David's oddly untrimmed cock for mascot); then back through Geneva on our way north toward college again for a summer term that drowned in torpid afternoons, stuffed with cakes, by the pond at Blenheim; on the broad brown river or country rides in my new Morris down Cotswold roads past Iron Age forts and the inexplicable megalithic leavings of a people older than the Celts.

Near as we were in the red-trimmed car, we never left its low-slung roof to bare our hides to the English sky—was it weird respect for your native ground or a caution learned from the older faces and limbs we passed, cycling slow up hedge-bound lanes at the end of light with profiles dull as hatchet blades, their worked-out bodies lost past finding in thornproof wool? Still no technician or artisan since known to me has neared your mastery of the gawky room of a compact car; in seconds, up a hawthorn track, you'd have mine rhapsodizing like Liszt.

July though and all of August, we'd ferried the car from Tynemouth to Bergen and eased our way through dirt-road Norway, warm as new bread, and immaculate Sweden, chill as a scallop. We sat on the porch of an elderly widow outside Stockholm, followed her pointing hand to the road and heard her say "I sat in this chair and watched the Nazis march, with our blessing, across my fields toward Norway ten hot summer days and cursed my country's treachery" (all night in her blond-wood guest room we worked at a new fidelity).

Then we split the still-numb heart of Germany—*Hitler!* still scrawled red on walls—to redeem Bavaria and the west end of Austria, pausing in Mozart's Salzburg birthhouse, clean as a modern delivery room, buffing the sides of his boyhood spinet with our cotton jackets and grooming our vagabond beards in its mirror; riding out midsummer nights as luminous as the dawn we watched past each other's brow in Munich the week they freed Admiral Dönitz, Führer for less than a week after Adolf burned to cinders in flat Berlin.

Laying the curse on a thousand rooms in which the S.S. racked and murdered, we only ever joined in rooms; and our invisible joy and knowledge multiplied along the road back up the Rhine through sacked Cologne and Holland where we risked our bond in the blasting radiance of almost endless rooms of Rembrandt, Hals, Vermeer, Van Gogh. It held unfazed and for relief we walked the beach at Scheveningen where Vincent aired his foaming brain, sketching the grass and lapdog waves like answers to prayer as his self-hatred flung out strangling intrinsic roots.

And dozens more complete concords as fine and healing but in our hideous Cowley digs under framed chromos of waltzing dogs. They all persist in my eyes still as early now-proved guarantors of what's ensued—these parallel lives that confound physics and manage to meet through five decades past the claims of others and with no hard word between us in all that nearness, not one bitter day.

Stranger still—never, once we'd slept and waked, did we speak an actual audible word about our invention: total meeting, a secret fail-proof hanging garden of staggering opulence that wanted only night and quiet to float its full renewable gift toward us again till a Cunard liner hauled you down a pier at Southampton and out to lay an ocean between us.

Young as I was through that first absence, I was either watching your latest picture (your eyes invariably met the camera) or mutely howling round the clock and scrawling poems of damp self-pity till twelve months later we dug our way through granite and water and joined again a final stretch of American years before, one summer night, we stood—replete now, thoroughly fed—and walked to opposite ends of the Earth with other aims in other arms.

Still the thought of our transaction mends a surprising lot of current pain—the fact we've never ceased to meet, as aging friends increasingly hid in gray and girth; the fact I've stood at christening fonts and vowed to guard your elder son from the snares of Satan and all his works till they can meet him, eye to eye.

No other human lives I've watched at pointblank range, and I'm a watcher, have yet disclosed a rival brand of usable reward and rest. Others can read this dense brief now, take fire from our enormous luck and simon-pure audacity, reaching as we once did to find their private food at will and eat its bloody fuel.

A final sight—damp morning, Venice, near San Marco, we round a corner and crash against the fuming grandiose parade to Easter mass beneath the dome. We lurch back, wait and suddenly—alone in a globe of hollow space—the Patriarch of Venice walks, no palanquin or fanning guards: old bald Angelo Roncalli, round as a melon and cardinal-capped. His eyes the size of walnut shells look light years gone; but flanking us an arm's reach off, he meets our monster heretic gaze and—not quite smiling but plainly focused and knowing all—his huge

brown peasant hand lifts toward us and blesses the clean rejoicing air
we then breathe in.

Two years on, elected Pope, he'll take the name John XXIII—as apt
a pontiff as any since Peter.

I never thought his gift was random; it scalds me still.

SUMMER GAMES

OUTSIDE, in our childhood summers—the war. The summers of 1939 to '45. I was six and finally twelve; and the war was three thousand miles to the right where London, Warsaw, Cologne crouched huge, immortal under nights of bombs or, farther, to the left where our men (among them three cousins of mine) crawled over dead friends from foxhole to foxhole toward Tokyo or, terribly, where there were children (our age, our size) starving, fleeing, trapped, stripped, abandoned.

Far off as it was, still we dreaded each waking hour that the war might arrive on us. A shot would ring in the midst of our play, freezing us in the knowledge that here at last were the first Storm Troopers till we thought and looked—Mrs. Hightower's Ford. And any plane passing overhead after dark seemed pregnant with black chutes ready to blossom. There were hints that war was nearer than it seemed—swastikaed subs off Hatteras or the German sailor's tattered corpse washed up at Virginia Beach with a Norfolk movie ticket in his pocket.

But of course we were safe. Our elders said that daily. Our deadly threats were polio, being hit by a car, drowning in pure chlorine if we swam after eating. No shot was fired for a hundred miles. (Fort Bragg— a hundred miles.) We had excess food to shame us at every meal, excess clothes to fling about us in the heat of play. So, secure, guilty, savage, we invoked war to us by games which were rites.

All our games ended desperately. Hiding, Prisoner's Base, Sling-Statue, Snake in Gutter, Giant Step, Kick the Can. We would start them all as friends, cool, gentle enough; but as we flung on under monstrous heat, sealed in sweat and dirt, hearts thudding, there would come a moment of pitch when someone would shout "Now *war!*" and it would be war—we separating, fleeing for cover, advancing in stealth on one another in terror, inflicting terror, mock death, surrender, till evening came and the hand of the day relaxed above us and cool rose from the grass and we sank drained into calm again, a last game of Hide in the dusk among bitter-smelling lightning bugs, ghost stories on the dark porch steps; then bath, bed, prayers for forgiveness and long life, sleep.

Only once did we draw real blood in our games; and I was the cause, the instrument at least. One August afternoon we had gone from, say, Tag into War. It was me, my cousins Marcia and Pat, and a Negro boy named Walter (who played with us for a quarter a week) against older, rougher boys. They massed on the opposite side of the creek that split the field behind our house. We had gathered magnolia seed pods for hand grenades; but as the charge began and swept toward us, as Madison Cranford leapt the creek and came screaming at me, he ceased being Madison (a preacher's son), the game ceased, the day rose in me, I dropped my fake grenade, stooped, blindly found a stone (pointed flint) and before retreating, flung it. My flight was halted by sudden silence behind me. I turned and by the creek on the ground in a huddle of boys was Madison, flat, still, eyes shut, blood streaming from the part in his sweaty hair, from a perfect circle in the skin which I had made. Walter, black and dry and powdered with dust, knelt by the head and the blood and looking through the day and the distance, said to me, "What ails you, boy? You have killed *this* child."

I had not, of course. He lived, never went to bed though a doctor did see him and pass on to us the warning that, young as we were, we were already deadly. My rock an inch farther down in Madison's temple would have done the work of a bullet—death. Death was ours to give, mine.

The warning was passed through my mother that night when she came from the Cranfords', having begged their pardon, and climbed to my room where I feigned sleep in a walnut bed under photographs of stars. I "woke" with a struggle, oaring myself from fake drowned depths, lay flat as she spread covers round me and heard her question launched, tense but gentle. "Why on earth did you throw a rock when everyone else was playing harmless?" What I suddenly knew I held back from her—that the others were not playing harmless, were as bent on ruin as I but were cowards, had only not yet been touched hard enough by hate. So I blamed the summer. "It was so hot I didn't know I *had* a rock. I was wild, for a minute. I will try not to do it again next summer." She said "*Ever* again" and left me to sleep which, tired as I was, did not come at once.

I lay in half dark (my sacred familiar objects crouched in horror from me against my walls) and thought through the lie I had told to save my mother—that summer was to blame. Then I said aloud as a promise (to my room, to myself), "I will tame *myself*. When the war is over and I am a man, it will all be peace, be cool. And when it is not, when summer comes, we will go to the water—my children and I—and play quiet games in the cool of the day. In the heat we will rest, separate on cots, not touching but smiling, watching the hair grow back on our legs."

Then sleep came unsought, untroubled to seal that further lie I had told to hide from myself what I knew even then—that I was not wrong to blame the summer, not wholly wrong; that wherever summer strikes (its scalding color), even in years of relative peace, something thrusts from the earth, presses from the air, compresses that in us which sets us wild against ourselves, in work, in games, in worst of all our love. Summer is the time wars live, thrive, on.

A CHAIN OF LOVE

T HEY HAD observed Papa's birthday with a freezer of cream even if it was the dead of winter, and they had given him a Morris chair that was not brand-new but was what he had always wanted. The next morning he was sick, and nobody could figure the connection between such nice hand-turned cream that Rato almost froze to death making and a tired heart which was what he had according to Dr. Sledge. Papa said "Tired of what?" and refused to go to any hospital. He said he would die at home if it was his time, but the family saw it different so they took him to Raleigh in Milo's car—pulled out the back seat that hadn't been out since Milo married the Abbott girl and spread a pallet and laid him there on pillows with his head resting on the hand-painted one off the settee, the gray felt pillow from Natural Bridge, Virginia that he brought Pauline his wife six years before she died, off that two-day excursion he took with the County Agent to the model peanut farms around Suffolk.

Much as she wanted to, Mama couldn't stay with Papa then. (Mama was his daughter-in-law.) She made him a half a gallon of boiled custard as he asked her to, to take along, and she rode down to Raleigh with them, but she had to come back with Milo in the evening. It worried her not being able to stay when staying was her duty, but they were having a Children's Day at the church that coming Sunday—mainly because the Christmas pageant had fallen through when John Arthur

485

Bobbitt passed around German measles like a dish of cool figs at the first rehearsal—and since she had organized the Sunbeams single-handed, she couldn't leave them then right on the verge of public performance. So they took Rosacoke and Rato along to sit for the first days till Mama could come back herself. Dr. Sledge said there was no need to take on a full-time nurse with two strong grandchildren dying to sit with him anyhow.

And there wasn't. From the minute Papa had his attack, there was never a question of Rosacoke going if Papa had to go—no question of *wanting* to go—and in fact she almost liked the idea. There was just one thing made her think twice about it, which was missing one Saturday night with Wesley. Wesley Beavers was Rosacoke's boyfriend even if Mama didn't like the idea of her riding in to town with a boy two years older every Saturday night to the show and sitting with him afterwards in his car—Rato there on the porch in the pitch dark looking—and telling him goodbye without a word. That was the best part of any week, telling Wesley goodbye the way she did when he pulled his Pontiac up in the yard under the pecan tree, and if it was fall, nuts would hit the car every now and then like enemy bullets to make them laugh or if it was spring, all those little rain frogs would be singing-out over behind the creek and then for a minute calming as if they had all died together or had just stopped to catch their breath. But Wesley would be there when she got back, and anyhow going to the hospital would give her a chance to lay out of school for a week, and it would give her extra time with Papa that she liked to be with. Rosacoke's Papa was her grandfather. Her own father was dead, run over by a green pick-up truck one Saturday evening late a long time ago, almost before she could remember.

But Rato could remember. Rato had seen a lot of things die. He was named for their father—Horatio Junior Mustian—and he was the next-to-oldest boy, nearly eighteen. He didn't mind staying with Papa either. He didn't go to school, hadn't gone in four years, so he didn't have the pleasure of laying out the way Rosacoke did, but seeing all the people would be enough for Rato. Not that he liked people so much. You could hardly get him to speak to anybody, but if you left him alone he would take what pleasure he needed, just standing there taller than anybody else and thinner and watching them.

Dr. Sledge had called on ahead, and they didn't have any trouble getting Papa in the hospital. He even had the refusal of a big corner room with a private bath, but it cost twelve dollars a day. Papa said there was no use trying the good will of Blue Cross Hospital Insurance so he took a ten-dollar room standing empty across the hall, and they wheeled him in on a rolling table pushed by a Negro who said he was Snowball Mason and turned out to be from Warren County too, up around Sixpound, which made Papa feel at home right away and limber enough to flip easy onto the bed in all the clothes he insisted on riding in. But before he could get his breath good, in came a nurse who slid around the bed on her stumpy legs as smooth and speedy as if she was on roller skates with dyed black hair screwed up and bouncing around her ears. She called Papa "darling" as if she had known him all her life and struggled to get him in one of those little night shirts the hospital furnished free without showing everything he had to the whole group. Everybody laughed except Rosacoke who had undressed Papa before and could do it in the dark. She gritted her teeth and finally the nurse got him fixed and stepped back to look as if she had just made him out of thin air. Milo said, "Papa, if you have somebody that peppy around you all the time, you won't be tired long." The nurse smiled and told Papa she would be seeing lots of him in the daytime and then left. Milo laughed at the "lots" and said, "That's what I'm afraid of, Papa—you getting out of hand down here," but Rosacoke said she could manage fine and wasn't exactly a moper herself and Papa agreed to that.

Soon as the nurse got out—after coming back once to get a hairpin she dropped on the bed—they began inspecting the room. There was a good big sink where Rosacoke could rinse out her underwear that she hadn't brought much of and Rato's socks. (Anywhere Rato went he just took the clothes on his back.) And Mama liked the view out the window right over the ambulance entrance where you could see every soul that came in sick. She called Rato's attention to it, and the two of them looked out awhile, but it was getting on towards four o'clock, and much as she wanted to stay and see what Snowball was serving for supper, she told Milo they would have to go. She couldn't stand to ride at night.

Practically before the others left the building, Rosacoke and Rato and Papa had made their sleeping arrangements and were settled. There was one easy chair Rosacoke could sleep in, and since Rato couldn't see stretching out on the floor with his bones, he shoved in another chair out of the parlor down the hall. That dyed-haired nurse saw him do it. She gave him a look that would have dropped anybody but Rato dead in his tracks and said, "You camping out or something, Big Boy?" Rato said, "No'm. Setting with my Papa." Then he went off roaming and the first thing Rosacoke did was open her grip and spread out her toilet articles all over the glass-top bureau. They were all she had brought except for two dresses and a copy of *Hit Parade Tunes and Lyrics* so she could get in some good singing if there was a radio and there was—over Papa's bed, two stations. And at the last minute Mama had stuck in what was left of the saltwater taffy Aunt Oma sent from Virginia Beach that summer. It seemed like a good idea—nurses hung around a patient who had his own candy like Grant around Richmond, Mama said—so she took a piece and gave one to Papa and began to paint her face, trying it out. Papa gummed his candy and watched in the mirror. Mama would have jerked a knot in her if she could have seen the sight Rosacoke was making of herself but Papa smiled. He had always said Rosacoke looked like an actor, and since the only picture show he ever saw was *Birth of a Nation*—and that was forty years ago in the old Warrenton Opera House with a four-piece band in accompaniment—then it must have been Lillian Gish he thought Rosacoke looked like. And she did a little that winter—not as small but thin all the same though beginning to grow, with a heart-shaped face and long yellow hair and blue eyes. That was what Rosacoke liked the best about her face, the eyes. They were big and it was hard to say where the blues left off and the whites began because everything there was more or less blue, and out the far corner of her left eye came this little vein close under the skin that always seemed to Rosacoke to be emptying off some of all that blue, carrying it down to her pale cheek.

But she couldn't stand there staring at herself all the time—she wasn't that good looking and she knew it already—so after the doctors began to ease up with the visits on the second day, Rosacoke got a little tired. That is, till the Volunteer Worker from the Ladies' Guild came in in a pink smock and asked if maybe they wouldn't want some magazines or a deck of cards maybe? She had a pushcart with her full of razor blades and magazines and things, and all Rosacoke had to do was look at Papa, and he—so happy with a lady visitor—pointed to his black leather purse on the table. The best thing she bought was a deck of Bicycle Playing Cards, and Mama would have jerked another knot if she could have seen Rosacoke right in Papa's bed, teaching him to play Honeymoon Bridge and Fish which she had learned awhile back from town girls on rainy days at little recess. But she never mentioned Slap Jack, her favorite game. She knew in advance Papa would get excited waiting for a Jack to turn up and maybe have a stroke or something so they stuck to quiet games which Papa took to easily, and you could have knocked Rosacoke off the bed with a feather when *he* started teaching her and Rato to play Setback, playing the extra hand himself.

They could count on the cards keeping them busy till Sunday, but they would have to do something with them then. Mama had said she would come down on Sunday to sit her turn with Papa. Milo would bring her after Children's Day. Milo was her oldest boy and he pretty well ran the farm alone with what help Rato could give him. He would probably have to bring Sissie along for the ride even if Papa couldn't stand her. Sissie was Milo's new wife. Just try leaving Sissie anywhere.

*

The doctors didn't tell Papa what was wrong with him, and he didn't tell them but one thing either which was that he wanted to die at home. He told them they had been mighty nice to him and he appreciated it, but he couldn't think of anything worse than dying away from home. They said they would take care of that and for him to rest till they told him to stop and they would send Dr. Sledge a full report. And Papa didn't worry. He had left it in their hands, and if a doctor had walked in one morning and said he had come to saw his head off, Papa would have just laid his neck out on the pillow where the doctor could get at it. But the doctors didn't bother him for much of his time, and taking them at their word, he slept the best part of every day. That was when Rato would roam the halls, never saying "p-turkey" to anybody, just looking around. And when Rosacoke could see Papa was asleep good, she would tip over and listen to his chest to make sure his heart was beating regular before she would walk across the hall to the corner room, the one they had offered Papa. It was still empty. The door stayed open all the time, and she didn't see any reason for not going in. There was reason *for* going—the view out the window of that room, a white statue of Jesus standing beside the hospital, holding his head bowed down and spreading his hands by his side. His chest was bare and a cloth was hanging over his right shoulder. Rosacoke couldn't see his face too well, but she knew it, clear, from the day they brought Papa in. It was the kindest face she had ever seen. She was sure of that. And she went to that empty room more than once to look out at him and recollect his face the way she knew it was.

But that didn't go on long because on the third day Rato came in from sitting in the hall all morning and said they had just now put some fellow in that empty room. Rosacoke was sorry to hear it. It meant she wouldn't get to go over there in the afternoon any more but she didn't say that. She would rather have died than tell Rato how much time she spent there, looking out a window. Papa wanted to know who it was that could take a twelve-dollar room, and Rato said it was a big man. Papa was disappointed too. He had got it figured there was something wrong with that room, lying empty three days or more. Rato said the man's wife and boy were with him—"I expect it was his boy. Looked like he was anyhow. The man hisself didn't look a bit sick. Walked in on his own steam, talking and laughing." Rosacoke wanted to know if they were rich, but Rato couldn't say, said he didn't know. You couldn't ever tell about Rato though, how much he knew. He wasn't anybody's fool. He just liked the idea of not telling all he knew. Keeping a few secrets was everything Rato had. So Rosacoke said, "Well, he's getting a beautiful room" and then walked over and buttoned Papa's night shirt. She made him stay buttoned square up to the neck all the time because she couldn't stand to look at his old chest. Papa said he was hot as a mink in Africa and that his chest had been that hairy ever since he shaved it to be Maid of Honor in the womanless wedding Delight Church put on when he was seventeen years old.

The night before, when the lights were out but they were still awake, Papa asked Rato to name the best thing he had seen since arriving, and Rato said, "That old lady with all the cards in the big ward down the hall." Rosacoke said, "What sort of cards?" "Every sort there is— Mother's Day, Valentine, Birthday, Christmas . . ." Papa said, "Get-Well cards?" "She ain't going to get well. She's too old." Rosacoke said "How old?" and Rato said, "What's the oldest thing you know?" She thought and said "God." "Well, she's something similar to that." Rosacoke and Papa laughed but Rato said, "I'm telling the truth. Go take a look if you get the chance. She sleeps all the time." Then they went to sleep but Rosacoke knew he was telling the truth, and anyhow he spoke of his doings so seldom she thought she would take his advice. So the afternoon the man took the twelve-dollar room, she went down while Papa was nodding, and at first it looked the way Rato promised. There was a lady older than God in the bed by the door (saving her a walk past nine other beds), covered to the chin and flat as a plank with no pillow under her head, just steel-colored hair laid wild on the sheets.

Rosacoke stepped close enough to see her eyes were shut, and thinking the lady was asleep, she looked up towards a sunburst of greeting cards fanned on the wall over the bed, but she hadn't looked fifteen seconds when the lady shot bolt-upright and spoke in a voice like a fingernail scraping down a dry blackboard—"Praise my Jesus." Rosacoke said "Yes'm" and the lady smiled and said, "Step here, honey, and take a seat and I'll tell you how I got saved at age eighty-one in the midst of a meeting of two hundred people. Then I'll show you my cards—sent by my Sunday school class and my many friends"—and commenced scratching her hair. But Rosacoke said, "No thank you, ma'm" and walked out quicker than she came. She went a few feet outside the door and stopped and thought, "I ought to be ashamed, getting her hopes up. I ought to go back and let her talk." Then she heard the lady's voice scraping on to the empty air so she said to herself, "If I went for five minutes, I'd be there all afternoon, hearing about her cards. Papa is *my* duty." And anyhow she didn't like the lady. It was fine for your friends to send you cards, but that was no reason to organize a show as if you were the only person in the hospital with that many friends and all of them with nothing in the world to do but sit down and write you cards all day. She thought that out and then headed for Papa.

She was walking down the mile-long hall when she saw him—not right at first. At first she was too busy looking at people laid back with their doors open. She didn't know a one of them, not even their faces the way Rato did. The only thing she knew was Snowball Mason in one room, talking to some old man that looked so small in his little outing pajamas with his legs hanging off the bed no more than an inch from the floor like thin dry tan gourds swinging in a wind on somebody's back porch somewhere. Snowball saw her and remembered her as being from Warren County and bowed. She stopped to talk but she happened to look towards the left, and there he was—Wesley—sitting way down across from Papa's door, dressed to the ears and watching the floor the way he always did, not studying people. Still he had come sixty miles to see her so she whispered to Snowball she had to go and went to meet Wesley, holding back from running and trying not to look as if she had seen a ghost which was close to what she had seen, considering this was the last hope she had. He hadn't seen her yet and she could surprise him. She hadn't really missed him so much till now, but when she got nearer she knew how sorry she would be to miss this Saturday with him, and she speeded her steps but kept them quiet. She was almost on him and he put his hands across his eyes—it would be Wesley all over to go to sleep waiting for her—so she came up to him and smiled and said, "Good afternoon, Mr. Beavers, is there something I can do for you?"

But it wasn't Wesley at all. It was somebody she hadn't ever seen before, somebody who didn't really look very much like Wesley when she thought about it. It took whoever it was a little while to realize she was speaking to him, and when he looked up he looked sad and nearly as young as Rosacoke. He looked a little blank too, the way everybody does when you have called them by the wrong name and they don't want you to know it. In a minute he said, "Oh no ma'm, thank you." "No ma'm"—as if Rosacoke was some kind of nurse.

It just about killed her to have done that like some big hussy. The only thing left to say was "Excuse me," and she almost didn't get that out before shutting Papa's door behind her, the hot blood knocking in her ears. Papa was still asleep but Rato was standing by the window, having some Nabs and a Pepsi for dinner, and when she could speak she said would he please peep out and see who that was sitting in the hall. As if Rato had ever peeped in his life. He had done plenty of looking but no peeping so he just pulled open the door as if he was headed for dinner and gave the boy a look. Before he got the door closed good, he said, "Nobody but that man's boy from across the hall. That man they moved in today." Rosacoke said "Thank you" and later on that afternoon she wondered if since he looked like Wesley, that boy could say goodbye like Wesley could.

*

If they didn't do anything else, those people across the hall at least gave Papa something to think about. They kept their door shut all the time except when somebody was going or coming, and even then they were usually too quick for Rato to get a good enough look to report anything. Something was bound to be wrong though because of all the nurses and doctors hanging around and the way that boy looked whenever he walked out in the hall for a few minutes. Rato reported he saw the man's wife once. He said she was real pretty and looked like she was toting the burden of the world on her shoulders. Even Rato could tell that. So Papa couldn't help asking Snowball the next time he got a chance what was wrong with that man. Snowball said he didn't know and if he did he wouldn't be allowed to say and that made Papa mad. He knew Snowball spent about two-thirds of his time in the man's room, taking bedpans in and out, and he told Snowball at the top of his voice, "That white coat you got on has gone to your head." Rosacoke could have crawled under the bed, but there was no stopping Papa once he got started. You just pretended hadn't a thing happened and he would quiet down. She could tell it got Snowball's goat though and she was sorry. He walked out of Papa's room with his ice-cream coat hanging off him as if somebody had unstarched it.

But that evening when it was time for him to go home, Snowball came back in. He didn't have his white coat on, and that meant he was off duty. He had on his sheepish grin, trying to show he had come on a little social call to see how Papa was making out, but Rosacoke knew right off he had come to apologize to Papa who was taking a nap so she shook Papa and said Snowball wanted to speak to him. Papa raised up blinking and said "Good evening, Snow," and Rosacoke couldn't help smiling at how Snowball turned into a snake doctor, dipping up and down around Papa. He said he just wondered how Mr. Mustian was coming on this afternoon, and did they have any old newspapers he could take home to start fires with? Papa said he was tolerable and hadn't looked at a newspaper since the jimsonweeds took over the

Government. What he meant was the Republicans, and he said, "The bad thing about jimsonweeds, Snow, is they reseeds theyselves."

Snowball hadn't come in on his own time to hear that though, and it didn't take him long to work his way to Papa's bed and lean over a lot closer than Papa liked for anybody to get to him and say it the same way he would have told a secret. "Mr. Mustian, they fixing to take out that gentleman's lung."

"What you talking about?"

"That Mr. Ledwell yonder in the room across the hall. He got a eating-cancer. That's what I hear his nurse say. But don't tell nobody. I just thought you might want to know so soons I found out . . ."

"A eating-cancer? That's what it is?"

"They don't seem to be no doubt about it. I done already shaved his chest for surgery. He taking his operation in the morning at eight."

Papa wanted to know, "Is he going to live, Snowball?"

"Can't say, Mr. Mustian. He spit the first blood today, and alls I know is they ain't many lives past that. They ain't many. And if they lives you almost wish they hadn't. That's how bad they gets before it's over."

And Papa remembered that was the way it was with Mr. Jack Rooker who swelled up to twice his natural size and smelled a long time before he died. "I can recollect sitting on the porch in the evening and hearing Jack Rooker screaming clean across two tobacco fields, screaming for his oldest boys to just let him rest because there won't nothing nobody could do for him, not nothing. And I'd say to Pauline, 'Pauline, it don't look like Jack Rooker is ever going to die, does it?' " But that was a long time ago when Papa was a lot younger and a lot farther away from dying himself. That was why he could feel so for Jack Rooker back then. It had just seemed as if Jack Rooker was going through something wouldn't anybody else ever have to go through again.

Snowball was nodding his head up and down, saying, "I know. Yes sir, I know," but Rosacoke could tell he had made his peace with Papa and was ready to leave so she stopped Papa from running on about Jack

Rooker and told him it was time for Snowball to go home. Papa thanked Snowball for coming in, as if he had never been mad a minute, and said he would count on him keeping them posted on all that happened to that fellow across the hall.

Rosacoke followed Snowball out. "Snowball, what's that man's name again?"

"Mr. Ledwell."

"Is he really going to die, you think?"

"Yes'm, I believe he is. But Miss Rosacoke, you don't have to worry yourself none about that. You ain't going to see him."

"I know that. I just wondered though. I didn't even remember his name."

Snowball said he would be stepping along and would see her in the morning. But Rosacoke didn't hear from him till way in the next afternoon. Papa was taking his nap and she was almost asleep herself when Snowball peeped in and seeing Papa was asleep, whispered that the gentleman across the hall was back from his operation.

"How did it come out, Snow?"

"They tell me he doing right well, Miss Rosacoke."

"Has he waked up yet?"

"No'm, he lying in yonder under his oxygen tent, running on about all sorts of foolishness like a baby. He be in some pain when he do come to though."

"Are his people doing all right?"

"They holding up right well. That's his two sisters with his wife and his boy. They setting there looking at him and waiting to see."

She thanked Snowball for letting them know and said she would tell Papa when he woke up. After Snowball left she stepped into the hall herself. The door over there was closed, and for the first time it said "No visitors." She wanted to wait until somebody opened it. Then she could at least hear the man breathing, if he was still breathing. But there wasn't a sound coming through that oak door thick as her fist, and she wasn't going to be caught snooping like Rato so she went back in to where Papa was awake, spreading a game of Solitaire which that dyed-haired nurse had taught him to play. That was *all* she had done for him.

Since they were away from home, they went to bed around ten o'clock. That is they cut out the lights, and Rosacoke would step in the closet and undress with the door half shut. The first evening she had shut it all the way, and Papa told her there was no use to be so worried about him seeing her as he had seen her stripstrod naked two or three hundred times before she was old enough to walk, but she kept up the practice, and when she was in her nightgown, she would step out and kiss Papa and tell Rato "Sleep tight" and settle in her easy chair under a blanket. Then they would talk a little about the day and home till the talk ran down of its own accord though Papa was liable to go on another hour in the dark about things he remembered. But it would all be quiet soon enough, and Rato would be the first to sleep. After Rosacoke's eyes had opened full to the dark, she could look over and see her brother stretched sideways in his chair, still dressed, with his long hands caught between his drawn-up knees and his head rolled back on his great thin neck and his mouth fallen open. Most people seemed to be somebody else when they were asleep. But not Rato. Rato went to sleep the way you expected he would, like himself who had stopped looking for a while. Then Papa would fall off, sometimes right in the middle of what he was remembering, and Rosacoke could see him too, but he was different—sweeter and with white hair that seemed in the night to be growing into the white pillow his dark leather head rested on, holding him there forever.

After Papa slept Rosacoke was supposed to but she couldn't this night. She kept thinking about it, the man and his boy. Papa had forgotten all about Mr. Ledwell. She hadn't told him anything about the operation, and she had asked Snowball not to tell him either. She didn't want Papa to start back thinking and talking about that poor man and asking questions and sending Rato out to see what he could. She had it all to herself now. Snowball had told her Mr. Ledwell's boy was staying there with him through the nights. Mr. Ledwell had made the boy promise him that before he would go to the operating room, and the boy would be over there now, awake maybe with his father that was dying and she here on her chair trying to sleep with her Papa and Rato, her Papa turned into something else in the night.

Still she might have gone on to sleep if she hadn't thought of Wesley. If she was at home she could go to sleep knowing she would see Wesley at seven-thirty in the morning. He drove the schoolbus and went nearly four miles out of his way on the state's gas to pick her up first so they could talk alone a few minutes before they looked up and saw all those Gupton children in the road, knocking together in the cold and piling on the bus not saying a word with purple splotches like thick cobwebs down their legs that came from standing by an open fire, Mama said, and in winter afternoons Wesley would put her out last into the cold white yard that would be nearly dark by five, and she would walk on towards the light that was coming already from the kitchen windows, steamed on the inside like panes of ice stretched thin on frames. And huddled there she thought how Wesley had said they would go to Warrenton this coming Saturday for a traveling show sponsored by the Lions Club—an exact copy of the Florida State Electric Chair with some poor dummy strapped in it, waiting for the end. Wesley was interested in anything mechanical, and she would have gone with him (no charge for admission the paper said, just a chance to help the Club's Blind Fund) if that was how he wanted to pass time—striking up friends with the owner of the chair whoever it was and talking till time to head back home. But that would have been all right with Rosacoke. She would have waited and been glad if she had got the chance, but she wouldn't now and like as not Wesley would take Willie Duke Aycock which was what Willie Duke had waited for all her life. That was just Wesley. Let her miss school even two days at hog killing and he practically forgot her.

It was thinking all this that kept Rosacoke from going on to sleep.

She tried once or twice to empty her head the way she could sometimes at home by closing her eyes and thinking way out in front of her, but she couldn't manage that tonight so she listened till she heard slow breathing from Rato and Papa. Then she got up in her bare feet and felt for the closet door and took down her robe from a hook and put it on. It was peach-colored chenille. She had made it herself and it had been honorable mention at the 4-H Fall Dress Revue in the Warren County Armory. She took her shoes in her hand and opened the door. The hall was empty and the only light was the one at the nurses' desk, and that was so white, shining into both ends of the long hall and against the white charts hanging in tiers. The two night nurses were gone or she could have talked to them. She hadn't ever talked to them, but they seemed nice enough not to mind if she did want to talk. She guessed they were out giving sleeping pills so she walked towards the big ward to pass time.

It was dark down there and all these sounds came out to meet her a long time before she got to the door like some kind of Hell she was hearing from a long way away—a little moan strained out through old dry lips and the grating of each private snore as it tore its way up the throats of the ones who were already asleep. Rosacoke stopped in the open door. The nurses were not there. Nobody seemed to be walking in the dark anyhow. All she could really see was, close to the door, an old woman set up in bed, bent all over on herself and scratching at her hair real slow. But she knew the others were there, and she knew there ought to be something you could do for such people, something you could say even in the dark that would make them know why you were standing there looking—not because you were well yourself and just trying to walk yourself to sleep but because you felt for them, because you hadn't ever been that sick or that old or that alone before in all your life and because you wished they hadn't been either. You couldn't stand there and say to the whole room out loud, "Could I bring you all some ice water or something?" because they probably wouldn't want that anyhow, and even if they did the first ones would be thirsty again and pitching in their hot sheets before you could make it around the room. You would be there all night, and it would be like trying to fill up No-Bottom Pond if it was ever to get empty. So she turned in the open door and saw one nurse back at the desk and walked in that direction, stopping to look at the flowers waiting outside the room of an old man who said they breathed up too much good air at night.

She was some way off when she saw the man's boy. There was no doubt about it being him this time and she was not surprised. The boy walked fast towards the desk, his shirt open down the front, the white tails sweeping behind him in the light of the one lamp and his chest deep brown almost as if he had worked in the field but you knew he hadn't. When he got to the nurse he shut his eyes and said, "My father's nurse says please call Dr. Davis and tell him to come now. It's serious." His voice was low and fast but Rosacoke heard him. The nurse took her time staring at a list of numbers under the glass on her desk before she called. She told whoever she talked to that Mr. Ledwell had taken a turn for the worse. Then she stood and walked to his room. The boy went close behind her so she stopped at the door and said "Wait out here." When she shut the door it stirred enough breeze to lift his shirttail again. He was that close and without stepping back he stood awhile looking. Then he sat by the door where Rosacoke had seen him that first awful time.

She looked on at it from the dark end of the hall (she was not walking by him in her robe even if it had won honorable mention), but she saw him plain because a table was by his chair and he had switched on a small study lamp that lighted his tired face. His chin hung on his hand like dead weight on delicate scales and his eyes were shut. Rosacoke knew if he looked towards the dark he might see her—at least her face—and she pressed to the blackest wall and watched from there. For a long time he was still. No noise came through his father's door. Then clear as day a woman's voice spoke in the open ward, "I have asked and asked for salt on my dinner"—spoke it twice, not changing a word. Some other voice said "Hush" and the boy faced right and looked.

Rosacoke didn't know if he saw her or not (maybe he was just seeing dark) but she saw him—his eyes, far off as she was, and they were the saddest eyes in the world to Rosacoke, that pulled hard at her and called on her or just on the dark to do something soon. But she didn't. She couldn't after the mistake of that first time. She shuddered in the hard waves that flushed over her whole body and locked her there in the shadow. Once she put out her hand and her foot and took one small step towards the boy whose head had dropped onto his folded arms, but the bleached light struck her robe, and she dropped back the way one of those rain snails does that is feeling its path, damp and tender, across the long grass till you touch its gentle horns, and it draws itself back, hurt and afraid, into a tight piece you would never guess could think or move or feel, even.

She couldn't have said how long she stood there, getting so tired she knew how it felt to be dead, before the doctor they called came in. He didn't have a tie on, and sleep was in his eyes. He saw the boy and touched him and said something, and they both walked into the room. Before they shut the door a sound like a mad child catching at his breath after crying ran out behind them to where Rosacoke was. She didn't know what was happening, but the boy's father might be dying. She knew that much. She felt almost sure that if the man died they would make some kind of public announcement. But he didn't die and she had waited so long she was nearly asleep. The hall she had to walk through back to Papa's was as quiet now as a winter night in an attic room when you could look out the window and see a sky, cold and hard as a worn plow point shining with the moon. All those people in the ward were asleep or maybe they had given up trying and waited. It seemed as if when you waited at night for something—maybe you didn't know what—the only thing happened was, time made noise in a clock somewhere way off.

It was the next morning that Rosacoke made up her mind. If Mr. Ledwell had lived through the night, she was going to call on him and his family. It was the only thing to do, the only Christian thing to do—to go over there and introduce yourself and ask if there was anything you could do to help such as setting up at night. The way she felt she might have gone over that morning if the room hadn't been so quiet. She hadn't seen a soul come or go since she woke up. She didn't know how Mr. Ledwell was getting along after everything that happened the night before. She didn't know if he had lived out the night. All she could do was wait for Snowball to tell her. She wasn't going to ask Rato to do any more looking for her after the last time.

Snowball was late coming by that morning, but he got there finally and called her out in the hall to talk. He said Mr. Ledwell had a relapse the night before, and they thought he was passing away, but he pulled through unexpectedly. "He not going to last though, Miss Rosacoke. The day nurse tell me he full of the cancer. It's a matter of days, they say, and he know that hisself so all of us try to keep his spirits up. He ain't a old man. I old enough to be his Daddy. He resting right easy this morning, but he was bad sick last night. In fact he was dead for a few minutes before the doctor come and brought him around. They does that right often now you know."

That made Rosacoke think of the day the Phelps boy fell off the dam at Fleming's Mill backwards into twenty feet of water, and three men who were fishing dived in in all their clothes and found his body facedown on the bottom and dragged it out, the mouth hanging open in one corner as if a finger was pulling it down. He had stayed under water four or five minutes, and his chest and wrists were still. They said he was dead as a hammer for half an hour till one man pumped air in him and he belched black mud and began to moan through his teeth. But what Rosacoke always wondered was, where did they go if they died for a while—Mr. Ledwell and the drowned Phelps boy—and if you were to ask them, could they tell you where they had been and what it was like there or had they just been to sleep? She had heard that somebody asked the Phelps boy when he got well enough to go back to school what dying was like, and he said he couldn't tell because it was a secret between him and his Jesus. Mama had said that was all you could expect out of a Phelps anyhow—that she wouldn't ask him if you paid her cash money and that you couldn't just suppose he had gone to Heaven and if he hadn't, you could be sure he wouldn't admit going elsewhere. (She had smiled but she meant it. She had never had a kind word for that branch of Phelpses since they bootlegged their way to big money some years before.) But not everybody felt the way Mama did. A church of Foot-Washing Baptists up towards South Hill heard about it and invited the boy up to testify but he wouldn't go. And from then on Rosacoke had watched him as if he was something not quite natural that had maybe seen Hell with his own eyes and had lived to tell the tale—or not tell it—and she had followed after him at little recess, hiding where he couldn't notice her so she could watch his face close up and see if his wonderful experience had made him any different. As it turned out it had. He was the quietest thing you could imagine, and his eyes danced all the time as if he was remembering and you couldn't ever know what, not ever.

By the time Rosacoke thought that, Snowball had to leave, but before he went she asked what he thought about her going over to see Mr. Ledwell and his family.

"It couldn't do no harm I can think of, Miss Rosacoke, if you don't stay but a little while. He can't talk much with his one lung, but he be happy to have a visitor. You wait though till he get a little of his strength back from last night."

She nodded Yes but she hadn't planned to pay her visit that morning anyhow. She had made up her mind not to go over there till she could take something with her. She might be from Afton, N.C., but she knew better than to go butting into some man's sickroom, to a man on his deathbed, without an expression of her sympathy. And it had to be flowers. There was that much she could do for Mr. Ledwell because he didn't have friends. He and his family had moved to Raleigh less than six months ago. Snowball had found out the Ledwells were from Baltimore. But of course there wasn't a flower for sale anywhere in the hospital, and anyhow it wasn't cut flowers Rosacoke had in mind. She got a dime from Papa by saying it was time she sent Mama word as to how they were getting along. Then she hunted down one of the Volunteers and bought two cards with the Capitol on them. She wrote one to Mama.

> Dear Mama,
>
> We like it here alot. I hope you and Baby Sister, Milo and Sissie are all O.K. Papa and I are getting plenty rest. Rato is the one taking exercise. When you come down here would you bring some of your altheas if they have bloomed yet?
>
> > Yours truly
> > Rosacoke Mustian

She wrote the other one to Wesley Beavers.

> Dear Wesley,
>
> How are you getting along? I am fine but miss you alot. Do you miss me? When you go to see the Florida Electric Chair think of how much I would like to be there. If you see Willie Duke Aycock tell her I said hello. I hope to see you Monday early.
>
> > Your friend,
> > Rosacoke

Then she mailed them and waited and hoped the altheas had bloomed. Mama had got an idea out of *Life* magazine that you could force things to flower in winter, and she had dug up an althea bush and set it in a tub and put it in the kitchen by the stove and dared it not to bloom. If it had she would gladly pick a handful of oily purple flowers that bruised if you touched them and hold them in her big lap the whole way to Raleigh on Sunday.

And Sunday came before Rosacoke was ready. She woke up early enough (Rato saw to that—he could wake the dead just tying his shoes), but she took her time getting washed and dressed, straightening the room and hiding things away. She didn't expect the family till after dinner so it was nearly noon before she set Papa up and lathered his face and started to shave him. She had finished one side without a nick, singing as she worked—the radio was on to the final hymn at Tabernacle Baptist Church—when the door burst open, and there was Baby Sister and Mama close behind her with flowers. Baby Sister said "Here I am." Rosacoke got her breath and said, "Blow me down. We sure didn't look for you early as this. Mama, I thought you had Children's Day to get behind you before you could leave."

Mama kissed her and touched Papa's wrist. "I did. I did. But once I pulled the Sunbeams through 'Come and Sing Some Happy Happy Song,' I felt like I could leave so we didn't stay to hear Bracey Overby end it with Taps. I know he did all right though. I hope he did—he practiced till he was pale anyhow. Then after leaving church like Indians in the middle of everything to get here early of course some Negroes drove up at the house just as we was starting—some of those curious Marmaduke Negroes with red hair. Well, they had heard about Baby Sister, and they had this skinny baby and wanted her to blow down his throat." (Negroes were always doing that. A child who had never seen its father could cure sore throat by breathing on it.) "It's a awful thing but Baby Sister enjoys it—don't you?—and I can't deny her any powers she may have, especially on Sunday." (Nobody had denied Baby Sister—six years old and big for the name—anything she wanted since she was born six months to the day after her father died. Even the nurses didn't try. Mama marched her in past a dozen signs that plainly said *No Children Under 12* and Baby Sister in Sweetheart Pink and nobody uttered a sound.) All through her story Mama looked around, and when she was done she said "Where is Rato?"

Rosacoke said, "Patrolling, I guess. He'll show up for dinner," and before she could wonder where were Milo and Sissie, they strolled in from parking the car. Milo kissed Rosacoke and said, "Wesley sent you that." Mama said, "No he didn't. We haven't seen Wesley." Then he laughed and kissed Papa—"Miss Betty Upchurch sent you that, but I don't tickle as good as her." (Miss Betty was a crazy old widow with whiskers that he teased Papa about.) Everybody laughed except Sissie. When they quieted down Sissie said "Good morning" and showed her teeth and settled back to looking as if a Mack truck had hit her head-on so Milo explained it to Papa. "Sissie will be off the air today. She's mad—woke up mad but didn't find reasons till we were leaving home. Then she found two good ones. One was she had to shell butter beans all the way up here because Mama didn't read the directions and froze her damn beans in the shell. The other thing was she had to sit on the back seat to do it because Mama and Baby Sister had spoke to sit up front with me and the heater. Well, she sat back there shelling, and when she finished—it took her a hour and we were on the outskirts of Raleigh—she lowered the glass on her side, intending to empty out the hulls, but Baby Sister said, 'Shut that pneumonia hole,' and Sissie got flustered and threw out the beans instead. Mama capped the climax by laughing, and Sissie ain't spoke a word since except just now." He turned to Sissie who was already staring out the window—"Say some-thing, Doll Baby. Turn over a new leaf." She wouldn't even look so Milo laughed and that did seal her. It was a good thing. Nobody could make Papa madder than Sissie when she started running her mouth.

Mama frowned at Milo and said, "Everybody calm down. We got half a day to get through in this matchbox." She meant Papa's room that was ten by twelve. Then she went to the bureau and while Rosacoke scraped chairs around, she took off her hat and her white ear bobs and combed her hair and put on a hair net and slipped off her shoes. She went to the chair where Rato slept—in her stocking feet—and said, "Rosacoke, get me my bed shoes out of my grip." Rosacoke got them. Then Mama settled back and blew one time with relief. She had come to stay and she had brought three things with her—dinner for seven in a cardboard suit box, her grip, and enough altheas to fill a zinc tub. She made it plain right away that Rosacoke would go on home with Milo and Sissie and Baby Sister but Rato would stay on to help her with Papa. Milo said he planned on leaving between eight and nine o'clock. (What he had in mind was to pacify Sissie by taking her to supper at the Chinese café she liked so much and then going on to a Sunday picture. But he didn't tell Mama that.) And Rosacoke couldn't object to leaving. In some ways she would be glad to get home, and Milo's plans would give her time to pay her visit to Mr. Ledwell, time to do all she wanted to do, all she thought she could do—to step over when she had seen her family and pay her respects and give them the flowers that would say better than she could how much she felt for Mr. Ledwell, dying in this strange place away from his friends and his home, and for his people who were waiting.

So she had that day with her family (Rato appeared long enough for dinner), and the day went fine except for three things. One thing was Sissie but nobody ever looked for Sissie to act decent. Another thing was, after they had eaten the dinner Mama packed, Papa reached over to his bedside table and pulled out the playing cards. Rosacoke had taken pains to hide them way back in the drawer, but Papa pulled them out in full view and set up a game of Solitaire and looked at Mama and grinned. She made a short remark about it appeared to her Papa was learning fancy tricks in his old age. Papa said couldn't he teach her a few games, and she drew up in her chair and said she had gone nearly fifty years—seven of them as a deaconess in Delight Baptist Church— without knowing one playing card from the other, and she guessed she could live on in ignorance the rest of the time. But she didn't stop Papa. He just stopped offering to teach her and lay there the rest of the afternoon, dealing out hands of Solitaire till he was blue in the face. He played right on through the nap everybody took after dinner. You couldn't have stopped him with dynamite. The third thing was after their naps. When they all woke up it was nearly three-thirty and the natural light was dim. Rosacoke stood up to switch on the bulb, but Milo said "No don't," and even closed the blinds. Then he went to Papa and pointed at his necktie and said, "Watch this. Pretty soon it'll start lighting up." It was something he had got that week by mail, and he claimed it would say "Kiss Me In The Dark!" when the room got dim enough, but they waited and the only thing the tie did was shine pale green all over. Rosacoke was glad he didn't get it working but Papa was disappointed. He asked Milo to leave the tie with him so he could test it in total darkness and show it around to the nurses, but Milo said he was intending to wear it to some crop-dusting movies at the high school that coming Thursday.

In a few more minutes it was five o'clock, and Milo started his plans by saying he and Sissie were going for a little ride and for Rosacoke to be packed for home by nine. Then he got Sissie up and into her coat and they left. Whenever Milo left a place things always quieted down. Papa went back to his Solitaire, and Mama crocheted on a tablecloth that she said would be Rosacoke's wedding present if the thread didn't rot beforehand. Even Baby Sister, who had pestered all afternoon to make up for Sissie being on strike, was worn out and sat still, sucking her thumb, so in the quiet room Rosacoke took down her grip and packed in almost everything. But she kept out her only clean dress and took it down to the nurses' utility closet and pressed it and put it on. She had washed it in the hall bathtub the night before. When she came back to the room, nobody paid her any mind. They thought she was just getting ready to go home. She washed her hands and face and stood in front of the mirror, combing her hair and working up her nerve. She turned her back to Mama and put on a little lipstick and rouge to keep from looking so pale. Then she took the altheas up out of the water Mama set them in and dried the stems with a clean towel and wrapped tissue paper around them. Mama said, "You are dressing too soon," and Rosacoke said, "I reckon I am," but before anybody had seen her good, she slipped out the door in her yellow dress, holding the flowers. She had tied a white card to them. Snowball had got it for her the day before. It said "From a Friend Across the Hall."

She took three steps and stopped and stood in front of the oak door, taller than she would ever be, that said "Ledwell." Behind it was where Mr. Ledwell was and his people that she didn't know, where he had laid down that first day Rato saw him talking and laughing, where he had gone out from to take his operation, and where it was not his home. Rosacoke was nervous but she told herself she looked as good as she could, and she had the altheas in her hands to hide the shaking. She knocked on the door and she must have knocked too soft because nobody came. She knocked again and put her ear to the wood. There were dim sounds coming from the other side so she pushed the door open a little, but the room was dark and quiet as an open field at night with only the sky, and she was drawing back to leave when the moving light of candles caught her, streaming from a part of the room she couldn't see into, drawing her on. So she went inside and pressed the door silent behind her and stood up against it, waiting till her eyes had opened enough to halfway see. There were five or six people in the room. Mr. Ledwell was a ridge on the bed that the sheets rose and fell over in gullies like after a rain, and his boy was by his head, holding one of the candles. In the yellow light the boy looked a way Wesley Beavers might never look, and the same light fell through a clear tent that covered his father's head and chest. A little of it fell on three ladies off in a corner, kneeling on the hard floor, and on a man standing near the bed by a table with two candles on it. He was all in black and falling from his neck was a narrow band of purple cloth with fine gold crosses at the ends. He was talking in words Rosacoke didn't know, almost singing in a voice that was low and far away because he was old with white hair and was looking down, but finally he looked up at Mr. Ledwell's boy, and the two of them pulled the tent back off him. Rosacoke knew he was alive. She could hear the air sucking into his throat, and his eyes were open on the boy and on the yellow candle.

The old man in black moved his hands in the air three times carefully, wide and long over Mr. Ledwell. Then he took a piece of cotton and waited for Mr. Ledwell to shut his eyes. He wiped the cotton over the lids, and they were shining for a second, wet and slick under the light before Mr. Ledwell opened them again and turned them back to the boy. The boy rolled his father's head to one side and then to the other while the old man touched the cotton to the ears that looked cold, and all the time Mr. Ledwell was trying not to take his eyes off the boy as if that sad face in the soft light that came and went was what kept him from dying. and except for that same soft light, the walls of the room would have disappeared and the ceiling, and Rosacoke could have walked out through where the window had been that she used to stand by. It seemed to be time for her to leave anyhow. She didn't know how long this would go on. She didn't know what it was. She only knew they were getting Mr. Ledwell ready to die in their own way, and she had taken the first step to leave when the boy's face turned and saw her through all that dark. His face changed for a minute, and you might have thought he smiled if you hadn't known that couldn't have happened now, not on his face. That was why Rosacoke didn't leave. He had looked at her as if he knew why she was there, almost as if he would have needed her if there had been time. But the old man touched Mr. Ledwell's lips, and Mr. Ledwell strained his head off the pillow and sucked at the cotton before the old man could pull it back. He thought they were giving him something to drink. And it went on that way over his hand that had to be pulled out from under the cover and his feet that seemed to be tallow you could gouge a line in with your fingernail. When they finished with his head, they put the tent back over him, and Rosacoke couldn't hear his breathing quite so loud. From his feet the old man walked back to his head. He put a black wood cross that had Jesus, white and small, nailed on it into Mr. Ledwell's hand. Then he shook a fine mist of water over him and made the sign again, and Rosacoke heard words she could understand. The old man told Mr. Ledwell to say, "Thy will be done." Mr. Ledwell nodded his head and his eyes opened. He took his hand and tapped on the inside of the clear tent. When his boy looked at him, his voice came up in pieces—but Rosacoke heard him plain—"Don't forget to give Jack Rowan one of those puppies." The boy said he wouldn't forget. Mr. Ledwell looked easier and when the old man reached under the tent to take the cross and Jesus away from him, he nodded his head over and over as he turned the cross loose.

The old man went over to speak to the lady who must have been Mr. Ledwell's wife. She was still on her knees, and she never took her face out of her hands. That was when Rosacoke left. They might switch on the light, and there she would be looking on at this dying which was the most private thing in the world. She had stayed that long because the boy had looked at her, but he might have forgotten by now. He had never looked again. A chair was by the door. She laid her flowers there. In the light somebody might see them and be glad that whoever it was stepped over to bring them, stepped over without saying a word.

She waited in the hall for the sound of his dying because he had seemed so ready, but it didn't come—nobody came or went but a colored girl, pushing a cartload of supper towards the ward—so she had to walk back into Papa's room, dreading questions. The room was dim though and still with only the light over Papa's bed that shined on his hair and the cards spread out on his knees. But he was just turning them over now, not really playing, and when Rosacoke shut the door, he looked and put one finger to his mouth and pointed towards Baby Sister, asleep at last in Mama's lap, and Mama nodding. Rosacoke thought she was safe and halfway smiled and leaned on the door, waiting for breath. But Papa stared at her and then tried to whisper— "You are leaving me, ain't you?"—and Mama jerked awake. It took her a while to get her bearings, but finally she said, "Where in the world have you been with Papa's flowers?" Rosacoke said, "To see a friend." Papa said, "I didn't want no flowers. Who is your friend?" She said "Mr. Ledwell" but Papa didn't show recollection. Mr. Ledwell hadn't crossed his mind since the operation, but just to say something he asked was the man coming on all right? Rosacoke said, "He ain't doing so good, Papa" and to Mama who had never had a secret, never wanted one, "Mama, please don't ask me who that is because I don't know."

Then she went to her grip and turned her back on the room and began packing in the things she had left till last. She was almost done when Rato walked in. Nobody had seen Rato since dinner. He walked in and said it the way he might walk in the kitchen and drop a load of wood in the box—"That man over yonder is dead. Ain't been five minutes." Mama said she was always sorry to hear of any death, and Rato said if they left the door cracked open they could see the man because a nurse had already called the undertaker to come after the body. But Rosacoke faced him and said "No" and said it so Rato wouldn't dare to crack the door one inch. He just left fast and slammed it behind him. But Baby Sister slept through it all, and Mama didn't speak for fear of disturbing her so the room was still again. To keep her hands busy Rosacoke rearranged the few little things in her grip, but she stood sideways to look at Papa and have him to fill her mind. Papa had his cards that he went back to, but he dealt them slow because he was thinking. He was so old himself you couldn't expect him to be too sad. Lately he always said he knew so many more dead men than live ones that there wasn't a soul left who could call him by his first name. And that was the truth. That was what took the edge off death for Papa—grieving over so many people, so many of his friends, burying so much love with each one of them till he had buried them all (everybody he had nearly) and pretty nearly all his love, and death didn't hold fear for him any more. It wasn't as if he didn't know where he was going or what it would be like when he got there. He just trusted and he hoped for one thing, he tried to see to one last thing—for a minute he stopped his card playing and asked Mama could he die at home, and Mama told him he could.

That was what made Rosacoke think so long about Mr. Ledwell who had died in that dark room. She wouldn't be able to go to his funeral, wouldn't even be asked. But that wasn't so bad. She had done what she could, being away from home, hadn't she, and didn't she know his name at least and hadn't he died not cut up or shot or run over but almost in his sleep with his wife and his boy there, and with all that beautiful dying song, hadn't he surely died sanctified? If he had to die wasn't that as good a way as any, leaving his living picture back here in that boy? But she hadn't ever seen him alive really. She hadn't ever told him or any of his kind—out loud—that she felt for them. She hadn't ever said it so loud she could hear her own voice—that Rosacoke Mustian was sorry to see it happen. That was why she spoke at last. She had been quiet so long, and now her slow lean voice cut through all the dark in the room. "It don't seem right," she said. "It just don't seem right. It seem like I had got to know him real well." And her words hung in the room for a long time—longer than it took Papa to pick the cards up off the bed and lay them without a sound in the drawer, longer even than it would have taken Rosacoke to say goodbye to Wesley if it had been Saturday night and she had been at home.

TWO USEFUL VISITS

Bᴀᴄᴋ ᴛʜᴇɴ your kin could lean down on you with the weight of the world and still not quite say "Get yourself up here to see Mary Greet; she's dying fast, and it's your plain duty." So in mid-February of 1960, on the floor of my own despair, I got a postcard from my cousin Anna Palmer. It said "Aunt Mary is sinking fast and speaks of you." I changed my plans for the next Sunday and made the two-hour drive to see her through clear warm weather that lifted a corner at least of my spirits.

When I'd seen her last in August '58, Mary claimed to be "somewhere way past my eighties." And though she'd picked sixty pounds of cotton the day before—a great deal of cotton—the pictures of her I took on that visit show a balding head, eyes opalescent with the film of age and the fixed stance of an ancient sibyl, senior to God. So if she was, say, more than ninety in the pictures, then she might very well have been born a slave. Even in those years of frank segregation, I'd never been able to ask her the truth. My older kin never mentioned slavery, as if it were some much-cherished dead loved one, too painful to summon. And I'd hesitated with Mary Greet from a vague, maybe misplaced courtesy—you seldom ask men if they've been in prison. The time had come though. I had a need now, to understand pain, that licensed the probe. I'd ask her today.

*

When I pulled up by her match-box house, she was out in the yard in a straight-backed chair, apparently searching an old hound for ticks. I knew she couldn't see me till I got much closer; so I stood by the car and raised my voice, "Aunt Mary, dogs don't have ticks in the winter."

She didn't look up and I thought "Now she's deaf." But then she spoke to the dog clearly, "White man claiming it's winter, Saul." And when I walked closer, there in her lap was a rusty can with fat ticks swimming in kerosene. I said "Can you tell who I am?"

Still picking at Saul, Mary said "You who you been every day I knowed you."

I admired her skill at staving me off, but I had to keep teasing. "Am I Sam House?" Sam was my younger brother, then twenty-six.

She finally turned her long face toward me and shaded her eyes, "Fool, you used to be Hilman. Sit down." That far, she was right—the summer loss of my wife and daughter had reamed me out at thirty-four; but could her eyes really see that well? She pointed to the sandy ground beneath us. It was good enough for Saul; who was I to decline on a warm dry day?

I sat and, since she'd called me a fool, I thought "All right, I'll ask her right off." When Saul's next tick hit the bottom of the can, I said "Aunt Mary, were you born a slave?" For the next still minute, I thought I'd struck her.

But next she let out a dry chuckle. She lifted Saul's droopy right ear and leaned down, "Tell him, Saul. *You* know." She faced me again and said "Hilman, you feeling good as you look?"

I said "No *ma'm*" but I felt some ease; and for nearly two hours, we sat in the last of that midwinter spring and asked each other aimless questions about our safe past, both dodging the traps of here and now.

This much came clear, from her answers and my memory. Mary cooked for my mother's parents from the week they settled here in 1882. And though she retired before I was born, she was in and out of my grandmother's house all through my childhood. She took the rights accorded her age and always came in through the front door—no knock, just a statement, "It's nothing but *me*." Then she'd head for the kitchen and sit by the sink, a new addition since her days there. Most of my kin ignored her politely. They thought they knew all she had to tell. But early she won my affectionate awe. She treated me like the full-grown man I meant to be, that tart and dead-level, that unforgiving whenever I failed.

One morning when I was maybe ten, she asked me a thing no black person had, "Hil, what you meaning to *be*, down the road?"

I said "Aunt Mary, I'm busy right now" and pounded off to start some game.

She said "Here, *sir!*" Then in sight of my mother, she said "You turn your back on this old a soul, and you'll see a heap of backs turned on you."

Mother nodded and I stayed in place to say I planned to be a doctor; by then it was already my great goal.

She said "No sir, you waited too late."

Mother smiled behind her and we mutely agreed—Mary was cracked. But of course she was right; and many more times when she sounded wild to other bystanders, she thrust straight fingers deep into my quick.

Even this afternoon in 1960, as I stood to leave, having said nothing about my loss, Mary finally said "When you setting up house and making *your* young uns?"

I said "I'm trying to learn from you—you thriving out here with nothing but a hound and doing grand." I'd yet to see any sign of poor health.

Saul had loped off an hour ago, but Mary looked for him as though he mattered. Then she found my face again and tried to smile, but her eyes wouldn't light. "Us mean old women, we free-standing trees—don't need no trellis to help us climb. I estimate you ain't that free." She tried again at the smile and it worked. There were four good teeth.

I gave her five dollars and drove back home, thinking she'd likely be standing free when I'd thinned down from loneliness and vanished.

But late the next August, Anna Palmer phoned me. Calls from Anna were rare as blizzards; and before she finished expressing her delicate worries for me—I was known, in the family, to be still "blue"—I thought "Mary's dead." Strictly speaking, I was wrong. Anna said Aunt Mary was on her deathbed and refused to rise. I thought "By the time I drive up there, she'll rise and be out pulling more cotton."

No, Mary was in the same one-room shack she inhabited alone long before I knew her. All the windows were covered with old cardboard, but there'd never been a lock on the door, so I'd tapped loudly and then stepped into punishing heat. You could have baked bricks in the palms of your hands, but you couldn't have seen an inch ahead till you stood in the heat and let your eyes open. The one oil lamp was full but not lit. And as ever in all my visits here, there was no human with her. Today there was even no trace of Saul. She was in the far corner on a narrow cot, under three wool blankets; and she seemed asleep or already dead. But as I stepped toward her, her head tried to find me.

Anna had said that she cooked Aunt Mary two meals a day and spoon-fed them to her and that Roy, Mary's great-great-nephew, turned up to watch her every few nights and give her milk; she craved buttermilk. So maybe she weighed a scant eighty pounds, but her scalp was bald as any old man's. And when her mouth gapped open to breathe, I could see that the last four teeth had dissolved. I drew up the chair, "Aunt Mary, it's Hilman." She didn't look up so I said "Hilman House. You resting easy?"

Then the huge eyes ransacked my face and found nothing. But she found the strength to say a fierce "No."

I thought she meant she didn't recognize me; so I said "—Rosella Hilman's son, that you used to like."

She said "Not so" and waved a spider hand as if to cancel my presence.

I leaned back. But the hand came on, took the edge of my coat and pulled me down, eight inches from her face.

She whispered "They working me to death, Mr. Phipps."

I thought she said Phipps, though later I recalled a long-dead kinsman named Brownlee Fitts. But I said "No, I'm Hilman."

If she'd had her old power, she'd have snapped my neck. But she only nagged at my coat again, "You hear what I say and *help* me, else I be laid out dead at your feet by dark today."

So I said "Mary, where would you rather be?"

She was eager as any child to tell me, "Lord Jesus, in bed. I'm *tired*, man. This last piece of work bout broke my mind—my back broke sometime yesterday." Both hands were out of the cover now, busy with the work old doctors called "picking," a reflex act of failing nerves.

I drew off the blankets, smoothed her bunched nightgown, settled her flat. She was light to move as a locust shell, though the only woman I'd touched in months. I smoothed her pillow, a cast-off towel of Anna's but clean in a linen case. Then I bent and said "Is that any help at all?"

She thought a long time and said "No" again but not as hard. And when I'd sat another half hour, trying to think of anything under the sun but me and the two I'd lost, I gradually saw that Mary Greet had also gone, from this nearby, with no further plea, command or moan. No one alive had made me the gift of so much trust, though I knew she'd left both me and the world as a girl again, in pain more hopeless than any of mine.

A FINAL ACCOUNT

D~AVID,~

Once you left this evening, the sun broke out and lasted well past normal dusk. Even as I try to write this at seven, what looks like three new goldfinches are still in the airshaft, roadhogging each other's final snack. I trust you also benefited from the extra light and got home safe by dinnertime. I likewise trust you've given my best to Jean and the boys; and I need to underline one thing—I truly mean you to tell your mother I'm leaving this life with unchanged thanks and hope for her, whatever that's worth at this late date. You'll know when she can bear to hear that. You'll likewise know it's a solemn duty I've laid on you that cannot be shunned. Though I walked off from her, half her life ago, she matters that much still in my mind—the soul of decent fairness. Tell her she'll count that highly with me until this plague consumes whatever mind is left in my ruined body that you just now took in your arms and brought indoors from the first real feel of sky I've had in six weeks flat on a narrow bed.

Son, you count the most to me of anybody left alive. I knew if I said that straight to your face, near blind as I am, I'd just seize up. I was also scared you'd somehow say you didn't believe me. God knows, you've got every reason for doubt; and you asked enough questions that

I couldn't answer with you nearby. So while I've got this last strength left, I'll try at least to tell the truth that got us to here and is killing me.

I knew, far back as I remember—well before I started school—that what was deeply magic for me was the simple presence of certain men near me in a room or in my head. The first such presence was my young father. If you'd known him in his early prime, you'd have seen he earned all I tried to pay him. Though I loved my mother like food and air, it was always just my helpless dad that I felt I owed some kind of worship—praise for how he looked there, tall in clean white trousers beside my cot in the summer night, hearing my prayers or promising me he'd stay nearby the rest of my life if his luck held out, which of course it couldn't, not with all his hungers.

By the time he was gone, I was in high school; and the similar pull I felt from a few tall boys my age was homing me in on their new bodies that had just filled out with the normal powers of the human race, normal but worthy of more than respect. I already knew that the sudden power in those boys was nothing more or less uncanny than the strength to do a grown man's part in making life go on, with a wife and children in a safe clean house. I'd kept pace with them where growth was concerned; my body was manly. But I didn't want that main life they were leaning toward. I wanted to go on finding a way to honor and thank the strength that hid in the eyes and bodies of a few men, young as me and better to watch.

The clearest thing I can say this late to help you understand my decision is maybe this—I had no choice, from the day I knew there were others on Earth and that my part of all those others was men. Try thinking your way to the time a girl first dawned on you, the time you couldn't help needing to ease your skin and reward your mind with all of her, or all she'd give. You almost surely felt that much by twelve or thirteen, when a certain girl who'd been near you for most of your life just started reeling you slowly in like a willing catch on a taut line toward her fine eyes and secret body. Surely you wanted to know that secret and know it steadily, years to come. What way was there but reaching to touch her, then sinking yourself as far as love and kindness allowed in her sweet deeps?

My whole adult life, as I said, I felt that way for a short line of men, most of them worthy, and their lean bodies. In college though, I also felt the same for your mother. I honestly did. Nobody I'd met or watched till then was better to see and know than her, in her slow laughter with those green eyes to spike her meaning. I saw no reason to think I wouldn't need her all my life and hers—need and want her, to use and thank.

You came out of that, the natural result and a great satisfaction for her and me. Right from the time I first saw you in her tired arms the night you were born, I thought I'd never share in making a finer thing. Here at the end, I know I was right. For the whole nine years I lived beside you, you never gave me serious cause to change my mind—you were that calm to be with, that smart and watchful of the world around you. Right from the start, your main trait was *welcome*—you welcomed more or less whatever came, though I felt you specially welcomed me till you were maybe eight when other children took the lion's part of your time and all your thoughts.

Then I left you with no goodbye, not that you heard; and you need to know why. I have to admit, when you asked me today, it gave me the first taste of hope I've had in these two years of flat despair—the news that you can still demand an explanation of that cold scar after long years.

A sentence can say all I know about it. One gray noon a man walked into a room where I was and asked for my life, a careful man with a clear tenor voice and no big needs that I couldn't meet, as time would tell. I'd worked beside him for several months and known I liked him but had never let myself suspect how he saw me. He looked like God on God's best day, far back in His youth. Still I thought he was bound to be crazy—Ferrell Lee—or joking at least. I bolted halfway to the moon before I stopped and let my mind think through his offer and try to picture his face down the years, in reach of my hand. More and more in the next six months, I needed him so steadily that I shied off the rest of my duties. But I never touched him once, not once, till that last night I told your mother I had to leave.

She heard me out and then she stood, no question or blame. We were in the kitchen; I thought she'd walk toward you at least—you were long asleep. But she met my eyes as strong as ever and said "You wake our son up then and let him know this is your idea; and if you go, then do us the kindness not to turn back, not to hurt us by looking in when you feel like it." Small as she was, she was that near perfect—I mean it as praise—and I sat there wishing to God I could stay. But no, I stood and went toward you. She followed me to be sure I did it, but at your room I drew a last line. I stepped through the door and shut myself in with you asleep. She left us alone and I knelt by your hot damp head and felt your breath till I knew the size and risk of my choice—it might well break you, where you couldn't mend. But I kissed your neck as light as I could to spare your dream—your eyelids jerked in some fast tale your mind was telling.

Light as I was, you looked out at me, clear as dawn. Then you said "What you bring me?" and laughed a little. It was our old joke now you were nine—when you were a baby I'd bring you something every evening, if only a dry dandelion from the yard.

For maybe ten seconds I thought "All right. I'm here for good." But something stronger than you spoke out inside my brain. It said "These people are better without you." *People*—I know I thought the word *people* instead of your names. So I told you "I'm taking myself away."

You watched me what seemed like a slow year, then said "So *long*" and slid back under the same deep dream.

You were right; it was so long—twenty-four years till your Aunt Margaret saw my name on a hospital door and had the goodness to push it open and take my hand and, five days later, write to you with the news that I was fully alone on Earth and dying, with strangers, of this new curse that eats grown bodies faster than children and has no name but four initials, an idiot pun.

You came straight to me—endless thanks—and now we've had these three meetings that, whatever they will mean to you in years to be, mean this much now to your blood father. I know I've met my young self again, the one that loved your mother and you; and I've gripped his hand. One circle anyhow is closed.

That's not repentance or scared remorse or a plea for pardon from you, your mother or God on high. I understand that the major part of humankind sees my brand of choice as ludicrous, pitiful, evil or worse. They're welcome to whatever pygmy judgment they make on millions of useful humankind that they've never troubled to comprehend. No, what I truly regret tonight is not the natural course I took and stayed for two decades, nor losing your mother's goodness and you—you grew without me, finer than me—but two facts are pressing me down so hard I pray for my skull to crush. First, I may have killed the man I prized above all. He was true to me as any good dog—who passed him the virus if not starved me, more goat than dog? And second, I lost so much of my eyesight before you surfaced and came to me here.

So I die not knowing your grown man's face the way I'd hoped. I'm past the point of asking to feel the planes of your head; but in my mind you're the boy I left, still wise and realistic as pain. That memory will hold me till you come back or I fade out. You understand that nothing stands in my fast track but your one face in my skewed mind. You offering me the right to know you again is better than any actual cure.

I won't attempt to read this over; I doubt I could. I only hope you can read this scrawl and find the start of answers at least to what you've asked me—they feel true to me, however hard. Your father lived the natural life that opened before him as he moved on. When he moved past you, at first he honored your mother's wish that he vanish entirely—it wasn't that hard; he was that relieved. And since neither she nor you ever let him know if the wish had changed, he went on living the way he had to. He knows that caused considerable pain to the only two people that had blocked his way, but he can't regret the needs he fed by moving on. By his strong lights, he had a good life. It was all he needed and more than he looked for. He thanks you though here, thoroughly, for the unearned mercy you've found to give.

Till our next meeting, if that's my luck.

Honestly now, son,
Newton Brooks

UNCLE GRANT

Supposing he could know I have thought of him all this week. Supposing I was not three thousand miles from northeast North Carolina and supposing he had not been dead six years and I could find him and say, "I have thought of you all this week"—then he would be happy. Supposing though he was alive and I was still here in England—in Oxford whose light and color and trees and even grass would be strange to him as the moon (as they are to me)—and supposing he heard I had thought of him. It would go more or less like this. He would be in my aunt's kitchen in a straight black chair near the stove, having finished his breakfast. My aunt would have finished before he started and by then would be spreading beds or sweeping the porch, in her nightdress still. So he would be alone—his natural way, the way he had spent, say, sixty per cent of his life, counting sleep. His back would be straight as the chair, but his body would lean to the left, resting. The way he rested was to feel out the table beside him with his left elbow (an apple-green table with red oilcloth for a cover) and finding a spot, press down and then lay his head, his *face*, in his hand. His long right arm would lie on his hollow flank, the fingers hinged on the knee, and his legs would be clasped, uncrossed not to wrinkle the starched khaki trousers and ending in high-top shoes that, winter or summer, would be slashed into airy patterns, clean as the day they were bought, just ventilated with a razor blade. His white suspenders would rise from his waist to his shoulders, crossing the starched gray shirt (never with a tie but always buttoned at the neck and when he was dressed, pinned with a dull gold bar), but his face would be covered, his eyes. Only the shape of his skull would be clear—narrow and long, pointed at the chin, domed at the top—and the color of the skin that covered it, unbroken by a single hair except sparse brows, the color of a penny polished down by years of thumbs till Lincoln's face is a featureless shadow but with red life running beneath. That way he would be resting—not waiting, just resting as if he had worked when all he had done was wake at six and reach to his radio and lie on till seven, hearing music and thinking, then shaving and dressing and spreading his bed and stepping through the yard to the kitchen to eat what my aunt cooked (after she fired the stove if it was winter)—and he would rest till half-past eight when the cook would come and say towards him "Mr. Grant" (they were not good friends) and towards my aunt down the hall, "Miss Ida, here's you a letter," having stopped at the post office on her way. My aunt would come and stand by the stove and read with lips moving silent and then say, "Look, Uncle Grant. Here's a letter from Reynolds." He would look up squinting while she read out something like, " 'Tell Uncle Grant I am thinking about him this week,' " but before she could read any more, he would slap his flank and spring to his feet, rocking in his lacework shoes, opening and shutting his five-foot-ten like a bellows, and flicking at his ears—"Great God A-mighty! Where *is* Reynolds?" When she said "England" he would say, "Over yonder with them Hitalians and he been thinking about Grant? Great God A-mighty!" and then trail off into laughing and then for a long time to come into smiling. He would be happy that whole day and it is a fact—there is no one alive or dead I could have made happier with eight or ten words.

But he is dead and the reason I have thought of him these few days is strange—not because I remembered some joke on him and certainly not from seeing his likeness in the blue-black Negroes of the Oxford streets but because I went in a store to buy postcards and saw a card from the Berlin Museum—on a black background an Egyptian head, the tall narrow skull rocked back on the stalky neck, the chin offered out like a flickering tongue, the waving lips set in above (separate as if they were carved by a better man), the ears with their heavy lobes pinned close to the skull, and the black-rimmed sockets holding no eyes at all. I looked on, not knowing why, and turned the card over. The head was Amenhotep IV, pharaoh of Egypt in the eighteenth dynasty who canceled the worship of bestial gods and changed his name to Akhnaton, "it pleases Aton," the one true god, the streaming disc, the sun. I bought the card and left the shop and walked ten yards and said to myself in the street what I suddenly knew, "It's the one picture left of Uncle Grant."

His full name as far as we knew was Grant Terry, and he said he was born near Chatham, Virginia which is some hundred miles to the left of Richmond. (There are still white Terrys near there from whom his family would have taken its name.) He never knew his age but in 1940 when he heard of Old Age Assistance and wanted it (you had to show proof you were sixty-five), my father took him to our doctor who said, "I'll certify him—sure—but if those Welfare Workers took a look at his eyes, they wouldn't need *my* guarantee. He's well past seventy." So assuming he was seventy-five in 1940, that would make him born around 1865—maybe born into freedom and named for a general his parents heard of who set them free—but we didn't know about his youth, what he did to live when he was growing in the years after the war. There was nothing much he could have done but farm for somebody—chopping or picking cotton or ginning cotton or sawing pine timber or at best tending somebody's yard. We did know he had a wife named Ruth who gave him a son named Felix. It is the one thing I recall him telling me from his past (and he told me more than once, never with tears and sometimes with laughing at the end as if it was just his best true story)—"When I left my home in Virginia to come down here, I said to Ruth and my boy, 'I'll see you in Heaven if I don't come back.'" And he never went back.

He came south eighty miles to North Carolina. He told my father he came in a road gang hired by a white contractor to pave the Raleigh streets, but he never said when he came—not to me anyhow, not to anybody still alive. He never said why he came to Macon either. (The streets of Macon are still not paved.) Maybe he had done his Raleigh work and meant to head back to Ruth and Felix but never got farther than sixty miles, stopping in Macon, population two hundred, in Warren County which touches the Virginia line. Or maybe he came to Macon with a railroad gang. (That seems a fair guess. He always called Macon a "seaport town." It was more than a hundred miles from the sea. What he meant was Seaboard Railway—the Norfolk-to-Raleigh tracks split Macon.) Anyhow, he was there by the time I was born in 1933 though he wasn't attached to us, and his work by then—whatever it had been before—was growing things. He planted people's flowers and hoed them, raked dead leaves and burned them, and tended lawns—what lawns there were in Macon where oak-tree shade and white sand soil discouraged grass—and then he began tending me.

Not that I needed much tending. My mother was always there and my aunt down the road, and a Negro girl named Millie Mae looked after me in the morning. But sometimes in the evening my parents went visiting or to a picture show (not often, it being the deep Depression), and then Uncle Grant would sit by me while I slept. I don't know why they selected him, *trusted* him, when my aunt could have kept me or Millie Mae. Maybe they thought he could make me grow. (When he first came to Macon and asked for work and somebody said, "What can you do?" he said, "I can make things grow" so they gave him a chance, and he proved it the rest of his life—till my father could say, "Uncle Grant could stick a Coca-Cola bottle in the ground and raise you an ice-cold drink by sunup tomorrow." And God knew I needed growing—I had mysterious convulsions till I was four, sudden blue twitching rigors that rushed me unconscious into sight of death every three or four months.) The best reason though would be that, having no friends of his own, he had taken to me, and there is a joke which seems to show that. One evening when I was nearly two, my parents left me with him, saying they would be back late and that he could sleep in an army cot in my room. But they came back sooner than they expected, and when they drove up under the trees, instead of the house being dark and quiet, there was light streaming from my bedroom and mouth-harp music and laughing enough for a party. In surprise they crept to the porch and peeped in. My high-railed iron bed was by the window, and I was in it in outing pajamas but not lying down—facing Uncle Grant who was standing on the floor playing harp music while I danced in time and laughed. Then he knocked out the spit and passed the harp to me, and I blew what I could while he clapped hands. And then they stopped it—not being angry but saying I had better calm down and maybe Uncle Grant shouldn't pass the harp to me in case of germs (I had already caught gingivitis from chewing a brass doorknob)—and that was our first joke on him.

It went on like that another year—him working the yard off and on and staying with me odd evenings—and then my father changed jobs (*got* a job after six years of failing to sell insurance to wiped-out farmers) and we left Macon, going west a hundred miles to Asheboro, still in North Carolina, where we lived in a small apartment. Uncle Grant of course stayed on in Macon—he still wasn't ours and we had no lawn of our own, no room for him—but before long my father sent bus fare to my aunt and asked her to put Uncle Grant on the bus (Uncle Grant couldn't read), and soon he arrived for his first visit. He spent the nights in a Negro boardinghouse and the days and evenings in our kitchen. There was nothing he could do to help except wash dishes (he couldn't cook), but help wasn't what my father wanted. He wanted just to talk and every evening after supper, he stayed in the kitchen and talked to Uncle Grant till almost time to sleep. I was too young then to listen— or if I listened, to remember the things they said. They laughed a good deal though—I remember that—and the rest of the time they talked about the past. My mother says they did but *she* didn't listen, and now they are dead and nobody knows why they sat there night after night at a hard kitchen table under a bare light bulb, talking on and on, and laughing. Unless they loved each other—meaning there would come times when they needed to meet, and they never explained the need to themselves. My father would just send bus fare through my aunt or there would be a letter from her saying Uncle Grant was ready for a visit and had asked her to say he was coming, and we would go meet the bus, my father and I—five or six times in the two years we lived in three small rooms.

Then we bought two acres of land in the country near Asheboro and built a house. Or began to. The land needed clearing first—of loblolly pines and blackjack oaks and redbugs and snakes—so Uncle Grant came and spent the weekdays supervising that. He spent the nights at the same boardinghouse and as far as we knew went nowhere and had no Negro friends, but he spent his Sundays with us. We would pick him up in the car after church—my father and I—and drive out to look at our land. He would tell us what trees had gone that week and beg our pardon for, say, sacrificing a dogwood that had stood in the carpenters' path. But what I remember about those mornings—I was five—are two things he did which changed my mind. One Sunday when the clearing had just begun, the three of us were walking around the land—I in shorts and what I called Jesus-sandals—and as we came to a pile of limbs and weeds, six feet of black snake streamed out. It was May and black snakes go crazy in May so he headed for me and reared on his tail to fight. My father and I were locked stiff in surprise, but before the snake could lash at me, Uncle Grant took one step sideways like lightning and grabbed the snake's tail and cracked him on the air like a leather whip. Then we all breathed deep and looked and laughed at two yards of limp dead snake in Uncle Grant's hand. The way that changed my mind was to make me see Uncle Grant, not as the nurse who sat with me nights or talked on and on to my father, but as a fearless hero to imitate, and I never saw him in the old tame way again, not for eight or nine years. Then another Sunday morning we were walking—the land was clear by this time and building had started, but there wasn't a blade of grass, only mud and thousands of rocks that looked identical to me—and Uncle Grant leaned down quick as he had for the snake and came up with a little rock and handed it to me. It was a perfect Indian arrowhead, and in my joy I said, "How in the world did you see it?" and he said, "I'm three parts Indian myself" which deepened the feeling I had had for him since the snake and also made our two rocky acres something grand—a hunting ground of the Occoneechees or a campsite or even, I hoped, a battlefield (though we never found a second head to prove it).

When the house was finished and we moved in, he came with us. There was one small room off the kitchen where the furnace was, and his bed was there and a little low table to carry the things he owned— in the daytime his shaving equipment and his extra shirt, and at night his precious belongings—an Ingersoll watch and a pocket knife. In the daytime he worked to grow us a lawn, and gradually, single-handed, he grew us a beauty. And once it was strong, he began to cut it—with a small hand sickle and his pocket knife. We had a lawn mower and he tried to use it but stopped, saying rocks were too plentiful still—the real reason being he could cut grass better, cut it *right*, by hand and if that meant bending to the ground all day at age about seventy-five and trimming two acres with a three-inch blade, then that was all right. It was what he could do, in spring and summer. In the fall he raked leaves, not waiting till the trees were bare and taking them all at once but raking all day every day. It was one of our jokes on him (a true joke—they were all true) that we once saw him run a few yards and catch a dead leaf as it fell, in the air, and grind it to dust in his hand. In the evening after us he ate at the kitchen counter and washed all our dishes and then went into his room and sat on his bed and looked at picture magazines. Sometimes my father would sit with him and I would fly in and out, but most of the time he sat in silence, thinking whatever his private thoughts were, till we gave him a radio.

That was Christmas 1939 and there wasn't much to hear except grim war news, but nothing we gave him ever pleased him more. Not that he had seemed unhappy before—I don't think he thought about happiness—but now he would sit there on into the night. I would sit beside him long as my mother allowed in the dark (the only light was the radio dial), hearing our favorite things which were short-wave programs in German and Spanish with Morse code bursting in like machine-gun fire to make us laugh. We didn't understand a word and my father who thought we were fools would step to the door and shake his head at us in the dark, but Uncle Grant would slap his thigh and say, "*Listen* to them Hitalians, Mr. Will!" *Hitalians* was what he called all foreigners, and "Great God A-mighty" was his favorite excited expression, the one he used every time some Spaniard would speed up the news or "The Star-Spangled Banner" would play so before long of course I was saying it too—age six. At first I just said it with him when he laughed, but once I slipped and said it in front of my mother, and she asked him not to curse around me and made me stay out of his room for a while. With me being punished my father filled the gap by spending more time in the furnace room, and it was then the jokes piled up. Despite all the war news, he would have a new joke every evening—my father, that is, on Uncle Grant. One night for instance after they had sat an hour listening, they switched off the radio to let it cool and to talk. They talked quite awhile till my father said, "Let's switch it on. It's time for the midnight news" so they did, and there was the news, waiting for them. When it had finished and music had begun, Uncle Grant said, "When does they sleep, Mr. Will?" My father said "Who?" and he said—pointing through the dark to the radio—"Them little peoples in yonder." My father whose work was electrical supplies explained about waves in the air without wires and Uncle Grant nodded. But some time later when they had sat up extra-late, Uncle Grant asked if it wasn't bedtime. My father took the hint but was slow about leaving—standing in the door, hearing the end of some program—so Uncle Grant stood and unbuttoned his collar, then thought and switched off the radio. My father said, "How come you did that?" and he said, "I can't undress with them little peoples watching, Mr. Will." So my father never tried explaining again.

Then after three years we lost the house and all that grass and had to move to another apartment in Asheboro. By then I had a year-old brother named Bill so again there was no room for Uncle Grant and nothing for him to do if there had been, and my father explained it a month in advance—that much as we wanted him around, we couldn't keep paying him three dollars a week just to wash dishes and that if he stayed on in Asheboro he would have to find someplace to sleep and hire-out to other people to pay his rent. He told my father he would think it over, and he thought that whole last month, asking no advice, sitting by himself most evenings as I was in school and busy and my father was ashamed in his presence, and giving no sign of his plans till the day we moved. He helped that day by packing china and watching how the movers treated our furniture, and when everything had gone except his few belongings, my father said, "Where are you going, Uncle Grant?" He said, "I'm sleeping in that boardinghouse till I get you all's windows washed. Then I'm going to Macon on the bus. I ain't hiring-out in this town." (Asheboro was a stocking-mill town.) My father said, "You might break your radio on the bus. Wait till Sunday and I'll carry you." Uncle Grant said, "I been studying that—where am I going to plug in a radio in Macon? You keep it here and if I wants it I'll let you know." My father said, "Maybe when I get a little money I can trade it in on a battery set," and he said "Maybe you can" and two days later went to Macon by bus, saying he would stay with a Negro named Rommie Watson till he found a house. But somewhere in the hundred miles, for some reason, he changed his mind and when the bus set him down, he walked to my aunt's back door and asked could he sleep in her old smokehouse till he found a place of his own? She knew of course why we turned him loose so she told him Yes, and he swept it out and slept on an army cot, coming to her kitchen for meals but not eating well, not looking for a house of his own, not saying a word about work. My aunt finally asked him was he all right, and he said, "I will be soon as I get my bearings." In about two weeks he came in to breakfast with the cot rolled under his arm and his bag of belongings. When he had eaten he said he had found a house at the far end of Macon—a one-room house under oak trees in the yard of a Negro church. Then he left and was gone all day, all night, but my aunt looked out in the morning and there he was, trimming her bushes, having got some sort of bearings, enough to last two years.

We had turned him loose in 1942. He lived on thirteen years and he never let us take hold again. We stayed in Asheboro three years after he left—two years in that apartment and a year in a good-sized house—but he didn't come to visit in all that time. I don't know whether we asked him and if we did, what reason he gave for refusing. He just didn't come and he might have said he was too old. But he worked for my aunt every day, strong as ever, still trimming what he grew with a pocket knife, and the only way he showed age was by not taking supper in my aunt's kitchen. In summer he would stop about six, in winter about five—before dark—and put up his tools and come to the back door, and my aunt would give him cold biscuits and sometimes a little jar of syrup or preserves, and he would walk home a mile and a half and spend his evenings by a kerosene lamp, alone. But that was no change for him, being by himself.

What *was* a change was that after he had been back in Macon two years, he fell in some sort of love with a girl named Katie. She was not from Macon but had come there as cook to a cousin of ours who returned so she had no Negro friends either, and though she was no more than twenty, she began to sit with him some evenings. My aunt didn't know if they got beyond sitting, but she didn't worry much, not at first. Uncle Grant was pushing eighty and it seemed at first that Katie was good to him in ways that made him happy. My aunt *did* say to him once, "Uncle Grant, don't let that girl take your money away," and he said, "No'm. Every penny I lends her, she pay me back." But then it turned bad. After six months or so Katie began taking him to Warrenton on Saturdays (the county seat, five miles away), and they would drink fifty-cent wine called "Sneaky Pete," and every week he would have the few hairs shaved off his head (to hide them from Katie as they were white). For a while he managed to keep his drinking to Saturdays and to be cold-sober when he turned up for Sunday breakfast so my aunt didn't complain but finally he slipped. One Sunday he came in late—about nine—walking straight and of course dressed clean but old around the eyes and with his hat still on. He said "Good morning" and sat by the green kitchen table. My aunt said the same and, not really noticing, gave him a dish of corn flakes. He ate a few spoonfuls in silence. Then he sprang to the floor and slapped his flank and said, "What is the meaning of *this?*"—so loud she could smell the wine and pointing at his bowl. My aunt went over and there was a needle in his food. Thinking fast, she laughed and said, "Excuse me, Uncle Grant. I was sewing in here this week and somebody came to the door, and I stuck the needle in the cereal box, and it must have worked through." That was the truth and, sober, he would have known it, but he stood there rocking a little and then said, "Somebody trying to kill me is all *I* know." My aunt said, "If you are that big a fool, you can leave my house" so he stood another minute and then he left.

That was in late October—he had just started raking leaves. His shame kept him home the following day—and for two months to come. My aunt reckoned he would come back when he got hungry but he didn't. What food he got he bought from his neighbors or maybe Katie sneaked him things from our cousin's kitchen, but he didn't show up at my aunt's, and every leaf fell and thousands of acorns, and she finally hired boys to clear them. He still hadn't showed up by Christmas when we arrived for three days. That was the first we knew of his shame. My father said, "To be sure, he'll show up to see me," but my aunt said, "You are the *last* one he wants to see, feeling like he does," and my father saw she was right. We had brought him a box of Brown's Mule chewing tobacco. He surely knew that—we gave him that every Christmas—and we waited but he didn't come. When we left on the 27th my father gave my aunt the Brown's Mule and told her to save it till Uncle Grant showed up. She said in that case it would be bone-dry by the time he got it.

But for once she was wrong. About two weeks later in a hard cold spell his house burned down in the night from an overheated stove. My aunt heard that from her cook in the morning and heard that he got out unharmed with the clothes on his back so she packed a lard bucket with food and set our tobacco on top and sent it by the cook to where he was, which was at some neighbor's. The cook came back and said he thanked her and that afternoon he came. My aunt was nodding but the cook waked her and said, "Mr. Grant's out yonder on the porch, Miss Ida." She went and told him she was sorry to hear of his trouble and what was he going to do now? He said, "I don't hardly know but could I just sleep in the smokehouse till I get my bearings?" She thought and said, "Yes, if you'll stay there without having company." He knew who she meant and nodded and spent the rest of the day cleaning the smokehouse and getting the woodstove fit to use.

He stayed there without having company, working on the yard by day and on the smokehouse by night. It was just one room, twice as tall as wide, with pine walls and floor. He scrubbed every board—cold as it was—and when they were dry, tacked newspapers around the walls high as he could reach to keep out wind. And as winter passed he kept finding things to do to that one room till it looked as if he took it to be his home. So when spring came my aunt hired a carpenter, and he put plasterboard on the walls and linoleum underfoot and a lock on the door. Then she took back the army cot and bought an old iron bed and a good felt mattress and gave Uncle Grant a key to the door, saying, "This is your key. I'll keep the spare one in case you lose it." But he never lost it and he lived on there, having got the bearings, somehow or other, that lasted the rest of his life.

We moved back to Warren County in 1945. My father got a job that let him live in Warrenton (or travel from there, selling freezers to farmers), and we lived in a hotel apartment, still with no yard of our own. But Sunday afternoons we would drive the five miles to Macon for supper with my aunt. When we got there we would sit an hour and talk, and then my father would rise and say he was stepping out back to see Uncle Grant and who wanted to come? That was a signal for me to say "Me," and for a year or so I said it and followed him to the smokehouse. Uncle Grant would have been waiting all afternoon and talk would begin by him asking me about school and what I was doing. I was twelve and wasn't doing much but keeping a diary so my answers wouldn't take long, and he would turn to my father, and they would begin where they left off the week before in the circles of remembering and laughing. Old as I was, I still didn't listen, but soon as they got underway, I would stand and walk round the room, reading the papers on the walls till I knew them by heart. (What I *did* hear was, week after week, my father offering to take Uncle Grant on one of his Virginia business trips and detour to Chatham so he could look up Felix his son and Ruth his wife if she was alive. Uncle Grant would say, "That's a good idea. Let me know when you fixing to go." But he never went. He rode with my father a number of times—down into South Carolina and as far west as Charlotte—but whenever they set the date for a trip to Virginia and the date drew near, Uncle Grant would find yard work that couldn't wait or get sick a day or two with rheumatism.) But a year of such Sundays passed, and I slowed down on the smokehouse visits. My father would rise as before and ask who was going with him to Uncle Grant's, and more and more my brother volunteered, not me. He was going on six, the age I had been when Uncle Grant cracked the snake and found me the arrowhead and we listened to Hitalian news together, so he stepped into whatever place Uncle Grant kept for me and gradually filled more and more of it. But not all, never all, because every time my father came back from a visit he would say, "Uncle Grant asked after you. Step out yonder and speak to him, son."

I would look up from what I was doing—seventh-grade arithmetic or a Hardy Boys mystery—and say, "Soon as I finish this," and of course before I finished, it would be dark and supper would be ready. But I always saw him after supper when he came in to eat and to wash our dishes—little fidgety meetings with nothing to talk about but how he was feeling and with gaps of silence getting longer and longer till I would say "Goodbye" and he would say "All right" and I would hurry out. (Occasionally though, he would move some way that detained me—by dropping the dishrag, say, and old as he was, stooping for it in a flash that recalled him reaching bare-handed for the snake to save me—and I would find things to say or look on awhile at his slow body, seeing how grand he had been and knowing how happy I could make him, just waiting around.)

It went on like that till the summer of 1947. Then we moved again—sixty miles, to Raleigh, into a house with two good yards and a steam-heated basement room—and as my father arranged, Uncle Grant followed in a day or so. He had not volunteered to follow, even when my father described the basement room and the grass and privet hedge that, since it was August, were nearly out of hand, so my father asked him—"Would you come up and help us get straight?" and he said, "I'll ask Miss Ida can I take off a week." She gave him the week and we gave him the fare and he came. He started next morning at the ankle-high grass, and by sundown he had cut a patch about twenty feet square and sat in the kitchen, bolt-upright but too tired to eat. My father saw the trouble and saw a way out—he said, "I am driving to Clinton tomorrow. Come on and keep me company in this heat." Uncle Grant accepted, not mentioning grass. And none of us mentioned it again. When they got back from Clinton two evenings later, he spent one night, and the next day he went to Macon for good. Busy as my father was, he took Uncle Grant by car and spent a night at my aunt's. Then he came back to Raleigh and at supper that evening said, "He is older than I counted on him being. He won't last long. So I bought him a battery radio to keep him company."

He was maybe eighty-two when he tackled our new lawn and lost. My father was forty-seven. Uncle Grant lasted eight years, working on my aunt's yard till eight months before he died (no slower than ever and with nothing but a boy to rake up behind him), spending his evenings with nothing but his battery radio (Katie having drunk herself jobless and vanished), complaining of nothing but sometimes numb feet, asking for nothing but Brown's Mule tobacco (and getting that whenever we visited, especially at Christmas). My father lasted six.

He died in February, 1954—my father. Cancer of the lung with tumors the size of bird eggs clustered in his throat which nobody noticed till he thought he had bronchitis and called on a doctor. It went very quickly—twenty-one days—and my aunt didn't tell Uncle Grant till she had to. Hoping for the best, she had seen no reason to upset him in advance, but when we phoned her that Sunday night, she put on her coat and went to the smokehouse and knocked. Uncle Grant cracked the door and seeing it was her (she had never called on him after dark before), said, "What's wrong, Miss Ida?" She stood on the doorstep— half of a granite millstone—and said, "Will Price is dead." The heat of his room rushed past her into the dark, and directly he said, "Sit down, Miss Ida," pointing behind him to his single chair. She was my *mother's* sister but she stepped in and sat on his chair, and he sat on the edge of his mattress. Some radio music played on between them, and according to her, he never asked a question but waited. So when she got breath enough, she said the funeral was Tuesday and that he could ride down with her and her son if he wanted to. He thought and said, "Thank you, no'm. I better set here," and she went home to bed. In the morning after his breakfast, he stepped to her bedroom door and called her out and handed her three dollar bills to go towards flowers and she took them. He didn't work all that day or come in again for food so she sent his supper by the cook who reported he wasn't sick, but before she left Tuesday morning for Raleigh, he was stripping ivy off the lightninged oak, too busy to do more than wave goodbye as the car rolled down to the road.

He just never mentioned my father, that was all—for his own reasons, never spoke my father's name in anybody's hearing again. My aunt came back from the funeral and gave him a full description, and he said, "It sounds mighty nice," and ever after that if she brought up the subject—remembering some joke of my father's for instance—he would listen and laugh a little if that was expected but at the first break, get up and leave the room. He went on speaking of others who were someway gone—Ruth his wife and Felix his son and once or twice even Katie—but never my father, not even the last time I saw him.

That was Christmas of 1954 and by then he was flat on his back in a Welfare Home near Warrenton, had been there nearly four months. Six months after my father's death, his feet and legs went back on him totally. He couldn't stand for more than ten minutes without going numb from his waist down, and one night he fell, going to the smokehouse from supper—on his soft grass—so he took his bed, and when he didn't come to breakfast, my aunt went out and hearing of the fall, asked her doctor to come. He came and privately told her nothing was broken—it was poor circulation which would never improve, and didn't she want him to find Uncle Grant a place with nurses? There was nothing she could do but agree, being old herself, and the doctor found space in the house of a woman named Sarah Cawthorne who tended old Negroes for the Welfare Department. Then my aunt asked Uncle Grant if going there wasn't the wise thing for him—where he could rest with attention and regular meals and plenty of company and his radio and where she could visit him Saturdays, headed for Warrenton? He thought and said "Yes'm, it is," and she bought him two suits of pajamas and a flannel robe (he had always slept in long underwear), and they committed him early in September—her and her son—as the end of summer slammed down.

We didn't visit Macon in a body that Christmas. My mother wasn't up to it so we spent the day in Raleigh, but early on the 26th I drove to Macon to deliver our gifts and collect what was waiting for us. I stayed with my aunt most of the day, and her children and grandchildren came in for dinner, but after the eating, things got quiet and people took pains not to speak of the past, and at four o'clock I loaded up and said goodbye. My aunt followed me to the car and kissed me and said, "Aren't you going to stop by Sarah Cawthorne's and see Uncle Grant?" I looked at the sky to show it was late, and she said, "It won't take long and nobody God made will appreciate it more." So I stopped by and knocked on the holly-wreathed door and Sarah Cawthorne came. I said I would like to see Grant Terry, and she said, "Yes sir. Who is calling?" I smiled at that and said "Reynolds Price." —"Mr. Will Price's boy?" —"His oldest boy." She smiled too and said he was waiting for me and headed for a back bedroom. I paused at the door and she went ahead, flicking on the light, saying, "Mr. Grant, here's you a surprise." Then she walked out and I walked in, and the first thing I noticed was his neck. He was sitting up in bed in his clean pajamas. They were buttoned to the top, but they had no collar and his neck was bare. That was the surprise. I had just never seen it before, not down to his shoulders, and the sight of it now—so lean and long but the skin drawn tight— surprised me. *He* was not surprised. He had known *some* Price would turn up at Christmas, and seeing it was me, he laughed, "Great God A-mighty, Reynolds, you bigger than me." (I was twenty-one. I had reached my full growth some time before, but he still didn't say "*Mr.* Reynolds.") Then he pointed to a corner of the room where a two-foot plastic Christmas tree stood on a table, hung with a paper chain but no lights. There were two things under the tree on tissue paper—some bedroom shoes from my aunt and the box of Brown's Mule my mother had mailed without telling me—and he said, "I thank you for my present," meaning the tobacco which he had not opened. I noticed when he laughed that his teeth were gone and remembered my aunt commenting on the strangeness of that—how his teeth had vanished since he took his bed, just dissolved with nobody's help. So the Brown's Mule was useless, like the shoes. He never stood up any more, he said. But that was the nearest he came to speaking of his health, and I didn't ask questions except to say did he have a radio? He said "Two" and pointed to his own battery set on the far side of him and across the room to one by an empty bed. I asked whose that was and he said, "Freddy's. The Nigger that sleeps yonder." I asked where was Freddy now and he said, "Spending some time with his family, thank God. All that ails him is his water." But before he explained Freddy's symptoms, Sarah Cawthorne returned with orange juice for both of us and a slice of fruitcake for me. Then she smoothed the sheets around Uncle Grant and said to him, "Tell Mr. Reynolds your New Year's resolution." He said, "What you driving at?" So she told me—"Mr. Grant's getting baptized for New Year. He's been about to run me crazy to get him baptized—ain't you, Mr. Grant?" He didn't answer, didn't look at her or me but down at his hands on the sheet, and she went on—"Yes sir, he been running me *crazy* to get him baptized, old as he is, so I have arranged it for New Year's Day with my preacher. I got a big old trough in the back yard, and we are bringing that in the kitchen and spreading a clean sheet in it and filling it up with nice warm water, and *under* he's going—ain't you, Mr. Grant?" Still looking down, he said he would think it over. She said, "Well, of course you are and we wish Mr. Reynolds could be here to see it, don't we?" Then she took our glasses and left. When her steps had faded completely, he looked up at me and said, "I ain't going to be baptized in no hog trough." I said I was sure it wasn't a hog trough, but if he didn't want to be dipped, I saw no reason why he should. He said, "It ain't *me* that wants it. It's that woman. She come in here—last week, I believe—and asked me was I baptized and I said, 'No, not to my knowledge' so she said, 'Don't you know you can't get to Heaven and see your folks till you baptized?' " He waited a moment and asked me, "Is that the truth?" And straight off I said, "No. You'll see everybody you want to see, I'm sure. Give them best wishes from me!" He laughed, "I'll do that thing," then was quiet a moment, and not looking at me, said, "There *is* two or three I hope to meet, but I ain't studying the rest." Then he looked and said, "You're sure about that?—what you just now told me?" and again not waiting I said I was sure so he smiled, and I reckoned I could leave. I

stepped to his window and looked out at what was almost night—
"Uncle Grant, I better be heading home." He said "Thank you, sir"
(not saying what for), and I stopped at the foot of his bed and asked
what I had to ask, what my father would have asked—"Is there any
little thing I can do for you?" He said "Not a thing." I said, "You are
not still worried about being baptized, are you?" and he said, "No, you
have eased my mind. I can tell that woman *my* mind is easy, and if
she want to worry, that's *her* red wagon." I laid my hand on the ridge
of sheet that was his right foot—"If you need anything, tell Aunt Ida,
and she'll either get it or let us know." He said, "I won't need nothing."
Then I stepped to the door and told him "Goodbye," and he said
"Thank you" again (still not saying what for) and—grinning—that he
would see me in Heaven if not any sooner. I grinned too and walked
easy down Sarah Cawthorne's hall and made it to the door without
being heard and got in the car and started the sixty miles to Raleigh in
full night alone, wondering part of the way (maybe fifteen minutes),
"Have I sent him to Hell with my theology?" but knowing that was just
a joke and smiling to myself and driving on, thinking gradually of my
own business, not thinking of him at all, not working back to what he
had been in previous days, feeling I had no reasons.

And went on till late last week—nearly seven years—not thinking
of him more than, say fifteen seconds at a stretch, not even when he
died just before his afternoon nap, the May after I saw him in December. Freddy his roommate told my aunt, "I was making another police
dog and he died"—Freddy made dogs to sell, out of socks and knitting
wool—and she and her son handled the funeral. We didn't go, my
part of the family (my mother had a job by then and I was deep in
college exams and my brother was too young to drive), but my mother
sent flowers and they buried him at Mount Zion Church which he
never attended, a mile from my aunt's, not in a Welfare coffin but in
one she paid for, in a grave I have never seen.

Yet because of an accident—stopping to buy postcards—I have spent a week, three thousand miles from home, thinking of nothing but him, working back to what he may have been, to what we knew anyhow, finding I knew a good deal, finding *reasons*, and thinking how happy he would be if he could know, how long he would laugh, rocking in his lacework shoes, if he heard what reminded me of him (a Hitalian face on a card—Amenhotep IV, pharaoh of Egypt in the eighteenth dynasty who fathered six daughters but no son on Nefertiti his queen and canceled the worship of hawks and bulls and changed his name to Akhnaton, "it pleases Aton," the single god, the sun that causes growth)—and him the son of Negro slaves, named Grant maybe for the Union general (a name he could not recognize or write), who grew up near Chatham, Virginia, and made his one son Felix on a woman named Ruth and left them both to go south to work and somehow settled in Macon near us, finally with us (claiming he could make things grow, which he could), and tended me nights when I was a baby and our yard when we had one and for his own reasons loved my father and was loved by him and maybe loved me, *trusted* me enough to put his salvation in my hands that last day I saw him (him about ninety and me twenty-one) and believed what I said—that in Heaven he would meet the few folks he missed—and claimed he would see me there. And this is the point, this is what I know after this last week—that final joke, if it *was* a joke (him saying he would see me in Heaven), whoever it was on, it was not on him.

TROUBLED SLEEP

"**H**ELP" was the first human thing it said after cracking down on me unseen and unnamed through the pitch-dark woods and the black honeysuckle and the snakes knee-deep surely on all sides, waiting to be waked up. "Help"—not crying or wanting but announcing calmly as if it knew what I needed most in all the world and was bringing it— to me, Edward Rodwell, nine years old, caught in terror in the August night alone with all around me noises I knew like my own name turned nameless new threats with dark for eyes and damp breaths that raked my bare neck and arms, and all because after supper I played Rummy with my cousin Falcon Rodwell on the porch while the light lasted and lost till I couldn't stand to lose another game and called Falc who was cheating as usual a Cheater, and my father turned round in his chair and said in that case didn't I reckon I ought to go to bed?—but not a word to Falc about wasn't he sorry too and he grinning in hiding behind his solemn face as I marched away to sit in my empty room long as I could with only the sounds from the porch of them joking and remembering and, once, my mother's voice calling out to Falc, "Falc, you look to me like a lighthouse." I leaned out quietly to see what she meant, and she was right—there was Falc charging back and forth in the evening, happy with himself as if I had never been born, reaching out a hand here and there, closing it on the air and adding one more lightning bug to the jar he held, swarmed already with gentle syncopated light. So I slipped out the back and walked the half-mile to this Dark Ring of mine and Falc's in the woods (for burying things and ceremonies) and sat down, thinking of nothing but ways to pay them back and win them back till full night came and caught me in dark close as gloves, and I could only wait, shivering in the heat for whatever would come to take me home where I was remembered no more or for the Devil to leap any minute into the Ring, dancing, or the Old Woman All Skin and Bones to lay a pale dry hand rattling on my shoulder and claim me for her own.

But the one word came again—"Help"—held out like a hard pear I could take or leave and, coming closer, sounds like "Who" and "Whoop," and I knew who it was and not seeing how or why, I thought things would get better from now on and that I could let loose the tears locked for fear in my eyes. They streamed down again hot as any acid, and I caught at them with my tongue and swallowed bitterly at the knot rising hard up through my chest and throat, laying all my misery at the back of my eyes because this was Falcon Rodwell, my cousin (though I had cause to wonder why) and my age, who had finally and under his own steam gone up to the bed we shared all summer and seeing I wasn't there, had known where I was and had broken through to me for reasons of his own that he might never tell, asking nobody's permission and coming in wide lost circles and seeing (and keeping to himself as his cross to bear) who knew how many things that never got into any book, the things he always saw the minute the sun went down and the reasons he never went out after dark without speaking The Shields nonstop—"Who" and "Help" and whatever else made him breathe out because with his warm breath, he claimed, came enough germs to hold off anything the night could offer—but *coming* and towards me, convinced of arriving in time to do what he had to do and not worried once at being the only thing on earth to need half an hour to cover the path between our house and this Ring, considering he and I and Walter Parker (a Negro our age that we blindfolded sometimes and took with us) had worn a path to the Ring so deep you could have found your way there in total eclipse if you had made us tell you there was such a place, and you couldn't have done that.

So he stumbled into the Ring, not by the one right ceremonial way but tearing through the round wall of bushes, breaking every rule we had made, stepping on the graves of two frogs who died from eating B.B. shot we gave them, and looking like the night because the moon wasn't up, black against black trees with only the pieces of light across his forehead that were the tails of lightning bugs stuck there still warm and pulsing. He stopped ten feet from where I stood and waited for his envelope of germs to clear, resting up for whatever he thought came next.

I wanted to speak to let him know I was there—that I hoped he hadn't come for nothing—thinking if I could make him say one word, I would know why he was here—whether to say my mother had just now passed on unexpectedly in her chair or my father had taken the first drink since the day I was born (when he went out to the woodshed, the only place you couldn't hear my mother screaming—I came feet-first—and fell down and promised to give it up if I lived and I did) or German paratroopers were falling on our house like butterflies or that he was sorry. So "Falc—" I tried and that was it. The knot filled my throat like dry bread.

"Nobody but Falc," he said and started in the direction of his name I had offered, holding out in front of him like somebody blind his arms that changed color as he came the way a crow's wings will in the day—black if he folds them but blue as steel in flight, leaving you glad you noticed him. He came on till his fingers touched my chest. Then slow and straight like an old Indian at a Last Council, he took his seat on the dry ground. I tried to make out the shape of his head but I couldn't yet, except that row of light—maybe it wasn't Falc? But what except Falc smelled like that, like money at the roots of his hair?—so I sat beside him, near as all my doubts and griefs would let me, swallowing hard at my full throat.

How long we stayed that way I don't know—not making a sound

and, as if wind was in our hair, our heads rolled back to the round hole in the trees over us that was the sky—but long enough for the stars, which were all the light we had, to begin doing what they normally did when I was that age and sad and looked at them long enough—wheeling down the sky to the left, slow, and when I almost shut my eyes, connecting up in the pictures I saw then wherever I looked—the elephant I prayed regularly to get and Johnny Weissmuller that I wrote letters to, asking if I could be Tarzan when he died, and a lot of people dancing—and the light left over fell down on Falc and me, so bleached and cool that all it touched—our arms and necks and folded legs—was like curved bones you find some days when you are out walking in the woods and bare bones laid neat in the leaves are the last thing you hope to meet.

But that went on in silence so deep my swallowing sounded like rock wrenched out of quarries, and we were so close I could hear Falc's body making its own noises—his slow heart and whatever else was inside him putting up a roar like the sea and the dry sound like feet in sand of a hand rubbing down the calf of his leg—and I kept thinking we would touch, he being all I had, not by reaching out our hands on purpose but maybe by thinking of it till magic took over. It takes two to work that though, and whatever Falc was thinking it wasn't on similar lines so we didn't meet. The only sign he gave of not being dead was— every time he could work one up—a long-range spit through the teeth though my mother had warned him to give up the habit or go hard and dry before his time like Mr. Coley Dickerson, a man we knew who spat in public and was dry as a used whisk broom already, at only middle age.

But I was improving—physically anyhow. My tears and my throat had eased, and that energy went towards making up hurt questions to say, hot and fast, such as "Falcon Rodwell, why in the world—if you are going to be my cousin and spend every summer with me and take what I give—do you do things like tonight?" But I never said it. Ask Falc a question like that, and you'd be in silence up to your ears. He didn't work that way—making up reasons for what he wanted to do. He did it and then if it was a bad idea (and nobody knew in advance what would strike him as a bad idea), he came and sat down where you were, even if it was the bathtub—not speaking or looking at you, but waiting to find his own way out of what he had done, and if that way didn't appear, well, waiting still like a box of Christmas oranges under the tree which if you don't open soon will sit till Doomsday, nailed shut and going bad by the minute.

The trouble was, my terror was gone and with it my joy that those sounds had been Falc's face and name, and I was left with only bitterness that wouldn't let me move—not first—and since moving first was my job, we might have stayed there all night if the sound of a plane hadn't started, out of sight in the back of our heads. We waited for it like our last hope, knowing the chances it had of crossing the hole in our trees were slim, and when we had all but given up, there it was for eight seconds—I counted them, I remember—with red and green lights answering each other back and forth like rhymes, taking soldiers most likely someplace they would rather not go.

So Falc spoke. He had found a way. "Where do you wish we were?" —meaning to get an answer, trusting I knew what answer to give.

"Dead," I said—the thing I had to say to start his game and the thing I meant, this night.

"Who do you know that's dead?"—meaning me to fill in while he made his plan.

All I could think of were two grandfathers and a grandmother I had never seen and Will Rogers and those frogs and an alligator named Popeye that was sent to me from Florida and lived for two years in my aquarium on lean bacon and was just learning to sing when we got hooked to the city water line with so much chlorine in it, and he stretched out and died. I told him those seven names that were dead, and he said that didn't sound to him such a wonderful group to be so anxious about joining so soon. But that didn't mean for me to stop.

"Where do *you* wish?" I said.

He knew. "Someplace with bears. Like Alaska."

"Yes, and we'd die there in five minutes."

"*You* might but I would go prepared and I would last. I would have a long knife and cut us out a house in the ice and make us a cave to sleep in, and I would peel the skins off of bears for us to wrap up in when the sun went down—except for one bear that I would save named Maurice who would be our friend and stick by us. I would give little birthstone rings and sun shades to every Eskimo we met, and they would come to visit us and drag up whales for us to eat, and I would make a pact with them about how if they did unto us, we would do unto them and vice versa."

"What if we didn't like eating whales?" I said because he was saying "us" and "we" as if he had carried me with him.

"Pemican," he said. "And the Eskimos would take us fishing, and we would divide up what we caught."

"And you would get two times more than anybody else."

"Well, if I did, it would be because I was working two times harder than you and Walter." (So Walter was with us, making it a three-man party. I liked thinking of Walter, black amongst that snow, cool for the first time in his life.) "And if you didn't like it, you could leave. You and Walter would have to go anyhow when winter set in, but I would stay on, making daily broadcasts to the *National Geographic* magazine about what my thermometer said and taking pictures for them, and if you wanted me to, I would play you a record of a song sometimes on Saturday nights and you could listen in. Then one night I would announce I was surrounded by blizzards and how even the Eskimos' blood was freezing fast and how I was alone with the dogs who were lying there staring at me, not bothering to hunt up any rabbits, just waiting for me to go to sleep. But Maurice would be at my side, and if I nodded or took a bath, he would slam off any hungry dog that got ideas—till the germs moved in and everybody started having fever. Finally there wouldn't be anybody left but me, sitting there with Eskimos and dogs dead and frozen all around me and even Maurice stiff as a poker at my side and my flashlight batteries gone, and then I would run out of sulfa medicine, and there wouldn't be anything to do but say The Shields till my throat closed up and I couldn't whisper 'Help!' The germs would know and close in by dripping from the ceiling onto my face and grabbing hold of my fur suit and holding me so I couldn't reach the radio to SOS or even make my will, and nobody would ever hear of me again."

He had told me that story, or one similar, a hundred times, and he always went that way—alone as Custer, staving off every natural foe for days, giving in to germs because you couldn't *see* germs. When we played cowboys, everybody else who had to die died of bullets or arrows, but Falc never died of anything but blood poison or brain fever or milk leg and even then only after he had called me over to where he lay and whispered his Last Will and Testament, leaving me his radio (the only one we knew of that you could get Hitler on, twenty-four hours a day) and making me give my oath to bury him in a copper casket and go to Sunday school and church weekly and turn into a great scientist and destroy germs. I would cry and offer to go with him if he would let me, but it would be too late, and presently he would stop whispering and lower that curtain he kept at the back of his eyes, and I would fall on his chest and listen for his heart (not knowing what a heart sounded like), thinking to myself, "No radio on earth will ever be what Falcon Rodwell was to me."

But no matter about me—Falc had finished his dying and sat quiet— not from sadness but as if the story was a grand bird he had made out of nothing, and when it breathed and spread its wings, there was nothing left but to sit back and maybe smile and watch it take off and circle and sail out of sight forever. Then he cheered up and said, "I am going home now"—not seeing he had left me worse than ever with his sad cold journey and his cheating and my father not trying to understand and the dark laid on me heavier than ice or what I knew about death.

He unfolded his legs and stood and waited. I was supposed to go first, but I sat still and "Falcon," I said, "we have got to lie down and die in real life." I didn't know what he would say, only that I could count on him not to say "Why?"—the thing anybody else would want to know. Falc knew.

"How?" he said and I thought he was with me, and *how?*, I thought, was the last problem we had, not noticing that my troubles didn't have to be his. All I saw were ways to go for good and take Falc with me.

"Blood Brothers?" I said, having tried two whole summers to make Falc cut his thumb a little and pass a few drops into mine and me into him, but every blade I produced he would look at and say "Not surgical enough" though any number of times he let me go so far as to cut my own thumb before he decided No and left me with blood wasting all over the ground—who knew? maybe the one drop of Indian blood my mother said we had—unless Walter was there to stand in. (After Walter had Brothered with me for the third time, he wanted to know, "When you joining the Niggers, Ed?" And I considered joining.) "Listen, Falc, we would just slice each other's thumbs real easy and lay them together and pass a little back and forth and let the rest run out on the Ring until we went to sleep and didn't wake up, and they would find us in the morning, lying on the bloody Ring, drained-out."

"There's one thing you forgot," he said—there always was—"your personal salvation."

"Oh no. Miss Ellie is in charge of that." (Miss Ellie taught my Sunday school.)

"What makes you so sure Miss Ellie is all that saved herself to go taking on a dozen others?"

"Miss Ellie is a saint."

"Saints don't grow on trees these days, and Miss Ellie wasn't any more baptized than you." (I was going to be a Methodist with my mother, but Falc was from the Baptist part of the Rodwells and knew all about how when Matthew 3:16 said, "And Jesus, when he was baptized, went up straightway out of the water," Matthew meant going *under*, head and foot, otherwise how could you come up out of it?) "So if we walk down to the creek, I'll give you Immersion and take it a second time myself to make sure, and we'll stay under and drown."

I felt that would be going back on my mother and on Miss Ellie who was the only person I knew that wouldn't call John "the Baptist" so I reminded him, "I'm a born floater and you know it."

"Then we could go to a field and start running and run till our hearts popped and we fell out." But Falc could outrun me by miles, and I could see in my mind Falc saying "Go!" and us starting out together and Falc tearing ahead, looking back every now and then, finally seeing me crumple to the ground, and running back and deciding it was his duty now to give up and go home and tell my father. I kept that to myself though, and it looked as if surrender was the one thing left—to feel our way home in our bare feet, knowing one of us was bound to step on a snail before we got there, and take whatever my father decided to give.

But then the moon came up, breaking into our piece of sky, looking the way it ought to look—the way people say it does—and giving us light enough to read the finest print. I turned and when I had seen Falc—really seen—for the first time in three hours, he spoke.

"That's how," he said, pointing up at it.

"How?"

"The moon. The moon will make you crazy."

And it would. Would Walter think of standing in moonlight? No— if ever he was playing with us after dark and the moon rose, he would spread his hands over his head and say, "I don't know about you all, but I ain't risking the sense I got out in this stuff" and leave and we wouldn't see Walter till morning. And didn't everybody know what moonlight did to Tom-Boy Thompson who got left in it by mistake at the age of six and rose up next morning turned to a general embarrassment who collected stray dogs that followed his bicycle in bony dozens and wore flannel rags around his neck in the scorching weather without offering a reason and threw cats down garden-house holes and was six years old every day of his life until he passed away, as a blessing, by the side of the road to Wise one evening when everybody was at prayer meeting and only his dogs, wandering into church and sniffing out his mother, told the tale?

"Falc," I said, "we will take off our clothes and stretch out in it and go to sleep and that will be the end of us."

"All right," he said—and I thought I had won—"but what if we don't die?

"We'll get enough to send us crazy anyhow which will embarrass Daddy and Mother when they take us places."

"And I could act like the lady that played tunes to your Daddy on nothing but the window sill." (That was something my father had told us from when he was eighteen and took a tour of the State Hospital in Raleigh and got cornered by a very fine-looking lady who said she was North Carolina's finest pipe organist and a pupil of Edward MacDowell and would anybody like for her to prove it? My father said "Yes" and she played "To a Wild Rose" with her long blue fingers—not singing or humming but silent, just on the concrete window sill that was an organ to her mind. And Falc partly lived for the day when he would be old enough to take the tour and see that lady if she was still alive and ask her to play.)

Then I pulled my sweat shirt over my head for what I reckoned was the last time and unbuckled my pants and thought and decided to leave them on so as to ease the shock on whoever would find us in the morning. I lay back on the cool ground and threw my arms straight back as if I was in water and watched Falc undress exactly that far and lie down too.

"Falc," I said—it was the last thing I ever wanted to know—"what will you miss most?"

"Mosquitoes' singing," he said as if he had settled it years ago for some occasion like this. Then he was quiet. He hadn't wondered once what I would miss.

The moon had turned the Ring around us to the image of the moon, and when we took our places to one side of the center (because nothing ever touched the center but fire and Walter who made the fire), the moon took our bodies, and I thought then we were two narrow boats left together in a silent bloodless world like those that Time Forgot where nothing ever moved or breathed but only quivered in the grip of that devouring light. Like that—together, I thought—we waited for sweet avenging death.

But I have never slept well, and before I had thought of closing my eyes, I could hear Falc's breath slow down with longer spaces between each sigh till there was no sighing at all and maybe no breathing. I said "Falc?" but there was no answer, and I raised up to see him. His head had turned away from me already, and I leaned over to find his face. Not a breath of anything came out of him, no more than if I had been in the valley of the Nile and struck the last blow at the sealed mouth of some great pharaoh's ancient grave and had centuries of dry nothing rush out to meet me. "Falc?" I tried again and took his shoulder that was hard beneath my hand and cool and shook it. But Falc had never been too strong on touching people, and I didn't want to touch him now he couldn't draw back.

Falc had gone ahead as usual and left me here no better than when the night began and with this body by me now, cold and stiff as Maurice our bear and those poor Eskimos, and the moon still pouring down. How was I to know that once you tried you could go as easy as that, so easy that your closet friend, one foot away, couldn't say what breath had been your last or next-to-last? All I knew was, I had to follow. I owed Falc that much and where else was there left to go? Again I fell back and closed my eyes and waited, but I saw things that wouldn't let *anybody* sleep—me finally dying and coming to in a golden field that looked happy, with ripe wheat and trees and a river and rafts full of laughing people and suddenly Falc standing at the front of the biggest raft by the white sail, talking to the boys all around him and joking, and every now and then one of them would dive in the water and circle the raft and shout up to Falc a name I had never heard and he would notice them. I ran down to the bank and called out "Falc—" and he turned just his eyes towards the sound of his old name, but they looked straight through me and on past as if I had never come all this way to join him. He turned back and the wind rose and the raft drifted on out of my sight till all I could see was the top of Falc's head by the mast, but that went too and those boys' laughing was the only thing left.

Seeing that, *knowing* that for the first time brought tears I had never wept before, choked out like iron that lay blue and cold on my cheeks and wouldn't fall or dry.

Then Falc stood up alive like fire—from sleep or from a game, I couldn't say—and said, "I am going to pee" and walked straight through the center of the Ring and the ashes towards a low blackjack tree by the edge that we always peed against to kill it, but he walked past that and took the path away. For a long time I could hear him whispering The Shields. They died out though and enough time passed for even Falc to finish, but there wasn't even the sound of him *trying* to come back.

So with all that long day lying on me, I gave up and fell asleep and didn't dream and wasn't dreaming when I felt a hand on the center of my chest. I was too much asleep to jump or shout, but I opened my eyes enough to see it was Falc, come back for his own reasons and feeling for my heart to know if the moon had worked. It hadn't and my heart was beating intolerably like a held bird but Falc didn't know where. For all he could feel and for all I showed him, I was gone beyond recall. He knelt awhile longer. Then he walked around the Ring twice, saying words that sounded old to him and suitable as a service, and I thought he would leave again, but next he was above me with his hands held out—first as if I was fire and he was cold, then with the palms turned up, and whatever olden rite it was to him, it was like giving to me. He stood that way whole minutes, turning every sad color in the moonlight, holding out with both hands what he wasn't ever going to give—his life that I had asked for. Yet thinking I would never know or thank him or ask for more, he found his way. He lay down near me, not too near and in the deadly moon but in half-shade a yard away, and tired as I was, I waited and kept my body quiet till he was asleep. Then I turned towards him and—not knowing what it was like to be Falc—I laid my arm on his chest which was the part of him in the light, and sometime—sleeping, I think—he took my hand.

When they missed us from our bed and my father came out at midnight to lead us home, walking straight as any judge to the bench, he found us in that secret place where he knew we were, and all he could see, he smiled at—me in troubled sleep in the full moon still and Falc dark and gone like he didn't mean to return, but in each other's arms at least and breathing slow.

GOOD NIGHT

I‍T WAS BRIGHT all day, so Gault worked the garden in late afternoon. And he almost thinned the strawberry patch before his knees and hips refused to bend. He was far past eighty—not sure how far—and he did as much as he did on the hope that Patsy Capps would visit tonight. She claimed twenty-four, looked sweet eighteen and came from a much bigger town than this—Goldsboro, some eighty miles on south. Saturday afternoon and evening were her time off; and deep in the country here, she had three choices—to stay in her own hot room, reading magazines, or hitch into Warrenton and sit with the colored in a stifling balcony to watch white cowhands kill each other or cross the tracks, walk a hundred yards to see Gaulton Walker.

Soon as Gault washed and put on clean clothes, he slipped the bottle of Brame's Oil of Cloves in his deep pants pocket. There by his leg it would warm in case this time Patsy mentioned it again. Gault hadn't prayed in thirty-two years or been near a church, since Noma left him; but he fixed the sight in his mind of Pat. Then he pressed on it steady to make her want his soothing hands, and his mind went to work.

So not long after full dark came, a hand was scratching soft at his door—"Mr. Gault, here Pat."

"Here Jesus" could not have pleased him more. But glad as he was when she stepped inside and sat by the lantern, he hoped for more. So

he kept his mind on the sight of her ankles, though his eyes could hardly see them in darkness.

In maybe an hour they'd pretty well covered everything fresh—their jobs, the people they worked for and lived with, scraps of war news (the new dead boy) and trifling memories. Gault almost slipped and told her he dreamed of his sister Anica—the day Mr. Lincoln broke their chains. But telling that now would tell his age. So when Patsy ran out of things to say and went off silent, gazing out the window at night, Gault was forced to raise the question he hoped all week she'd freely ask. He leaned slightly forward, not risking a smile—"Miss Pat, your ankles still swelling on you?"

Pat kept watching the empty window, trying to keep her face blank of meaning; but then a grin took her. Not meeting his eyes, she said "Mr. Gault, they killed me last night. Feel some better now."

He thought *Don't rush her.* But he said "They ain't healed?" That would give her a chance to stop him.

"I wish so but no sir, I doubt they healed."

Gault said "I may need to help you again."

Her smile was gone but her eyes moved toward him. And dim as it was by lantern light, with no word or nod, she might have meant yes.

They were seated on straight chairs, two feet apart. Gault knew not to stand—*Don't break your spell*—but he leaned to the bed, took the clean hand-towel, then found his bottle and pressed forward slightly. "Is it still this right one hurt you the most?"

Her face was still toward him, but her eyes had closed. She said "Yes sir."

The right one wore the gold ankle-chain he gave her last Christmas. It caught the light as he raised her right heel onto his knee. He'd planned to take it off this time for fear it would snap (the links were thin), but he feared again that the spell would break. So he took the risk and moved ahead. He opened the bottle, poured a pool in his hand and—gentle as if he planted the frailest flower known—Gault worked narrow circles with his bony fingers in flesh that began in the slow quiet time to pay him, rich, for all he'd lost.

In maybe two minutes his own eyes closed; and there again was his sister's face—Anica Jane with her gap-toothed laugh, rolling a rusty hoop toward the road, saying she meant to not come back: *Don't follow me, Gault. You a old-timey boy; I'm hunting a man!* And didn't she find one—what was his name? Hob Hampshire that slit her throat, ear to ear, for daring to laugh when some boy passed, and her with two babies dugging her still. Well, didn't she live, *live* and last? Doctor sewed her up for a dollar and Gault himself nursed her, for nearly a month till she sat up one clear sunrise and said "I'll preciate this, right into the grave" but was gone by noon, never seen again. Was she live now still, and where on Earth? A broke-down pitiful sight or strong? (her boys were killed in the First World War).

Gault set the right leg back to the floor, raised the left and renewed his oil. By then the smell of cloves in the heat had soothed them both; and though Pat still never spoke or sighed, she thanked this old man time and again in her own calm head. And when he had soothed her for what felt like the best part of a lifetime, she finally knew this was all he asked. There was no more harm in his hands than hate. So in her mind she saw herself with him at the beach (her white folks went to Virginia Beach two weeks every summer and Patsy cooked).

She pictured how she'd take Mr. Gault, maybe this next year. He'd help in the kitchen and yard by day, and then they'd wait till the dead of night when the place was swept of all but them. They'd sit in the dry sand, and she'd find a way—a whole new way that she'd make up—to help him on his natural path. Old as he was, she knew the path was bound to be death; so maybe she'd say "Mr. Gault, thank *you*" (he thanked her several times a night). "Now lay your head down here on Patsy, and do whatever you need to next." He'd shut his wide old golden eyes and soon be asleep, till sleep crept on to natural death. And she'd wait there till, well before day, a cool wave took his long bird-bones on out for good.

Part of her dreaming reached Gault's hands—not words or sights but the speed and kindness, the end she wished him. So he thought *I won't do this again till she asks me plain;* but far in the back of his easing mind, an old picture stood up to see. Some deed his mother told him about before Mr. Lincoln—how the Lord bent low to wash a man's feet in pure well-water, dried him gentle with a spotless rag and then got up and walked ahead to face his cross. Gault watched that sight till a meaning dawned, *You helping this child, you strengthening her. Now go your way and take your due.*

When Patsy left, a slow while later, they both part-knew they'd seen him through a last big door. Neither one gauged its height or width nor saw any name on its dark frame. But when Gault died past three o'clock in a clean nightshirt, his hands stayed warm for a good short time after both his mind and heart were cold.

AN EVENING MEAL

S AM TRAYNOR had got the reprieve two days ago—the five-year cure of his stomach cancer—and he'd spent both days in quiet pleasure, not unstrung but high on a joy he'd hardly known since boyhood. Because his parents were long dead though, and he'd lived alone since chemotherapy made him reckless for weeks on end, he had no close friend to tell the news. A woman who worked at the next desk over and the doorman in his apartment building seemed at least to notice a change. The doorman remarked on the tie Sam spent thirty dollars for, in celebration; the woman said "Sam, are you wearing blush?" (it was healthy color). And that was all, for human response. Sam wouldn't phone his aunt or her sons; they'd offered so little when it would have counted.

So after work that pleasant Friday, he walked ten blocks to eat at a diner he'd last visited the week before surgery, not even sensing a near ambush. It was not his favorite restaurant, then or now; but he'd planned this evening in further celebration—or the risk of one. That last visit he was also alone; but a new waiter was working the counter, a boy just off the plane from Amalfi and as good to see as any face that rushed toward Sam too fast to use, in his early days. The boy had accepted his invitation, turned up after the diner closed and—through a whole night—lent Sam his stunning body and smile, free as air.

And never again. When he left at dawn, he thanked Sam, saying "I liked you, sir." Sam stopped him there with a silent hand and fixed the moment in his mind where he knew it was safe as long as he lived. Five years later though, the boy wouldn't be there—surely not. His name was Giulio, called Giuli; and still his memory seemed worth the risk.

But there he was after all at the grill end when Sam took a stool up near the cash register. A few pounds thicker but lit with a heat that spread from inside him, the generous fearless eyes of a creature better than humankind anyhow. He was talking intently with an ancient woman in a genuine cloche hat, stained pink velvet. The one other worker in sight was a girl who served the counter and the booths by the street wall. Final daylight was strong at the windows, colored green by water-oak leaves.

Right off, Sam knew he'd give no sign. If Giuli glanced his way or walked by, Sam would look right at him but not speak first. That would test many things—how much the wait had changed Sam's looks, how deep his face had registered on Giuli that one dark night, what Sam's whole life might hold from here out: a whole new life. He was calmer than he'd expected to be and was halfway through a bowl of good soup before Giuli passed to ring the woman's check.

No look Sam's way; and once the woman passed back of Sam, blowing a dry old kiss at Giuli—and Giuli had actually turned to Sam and asked if the crackers were fresh enough—still no door swung open between them. Giuli grinned but in a general direction.

Sam knew it was strange, but he wasn't disappointed. The most he'd hoped for was some shared memory and the chance of Giuli's pleasure in the news. It was plain anyhow that Giuli's forgetfulness was real when their hands touched to exchange the crackers. The skin was warm as before and tougher. On the right ring finger, Italian-style, was a wedding band.

By the time his turkey sandwich was ready, Sam had agreed they'd touched near enough. They'd silently proved they were still alive and had asked for no more; but then Sam's mind set off on its own, watching a clear line of pictures that came from the night they'd shared nearly all they had. The same pictures had been a main help through the six hard months after surgery and X-ray—Sam's old skill as a home projectionist of well-kept memories. In lucky hours he could shut his eyes and play through a useful number of scenes, from minutes to days, in keener detail than when they were new, tasting individual pleasures and thanks strong as ever. There were twenty-some scenes from his adult years, eight of which were masterworks of time and light; and the scene that centered on the early Giuli contended for best. In the next half-hour, through his sandwich and tapioca pudding, Sam had again everything Giuli gave him and needed no more.

He believed that at least till he asked for his check and Giuli brought it, clearing the dishes in graceful ease—not a clink or scrape. But one more time their hands brushed; and Sam was startled by the wash of gratitude poured out in him—an unexpected need to say his own name, then allude to their meeting and tell Giuli what that memory had meant to a man condemned by a ring of doctors to die in a month. *It hauled me back*; Sam knew that much. At first a cold-scared hunkered patience of constant pain; then slowly an easier slog through time, dense at first as hip-deep seaweed.

Terrified and then edgy as the wait was, it came to feel better than what went before; and the new years turned out, of all things, celibate. In eighteen hundred ominous nights, however often Sam ran the scenes, he'd never once felt compelled to reach for another man near him. A bigger surprise by far than his cure; and he sometimes wondered if the X-ray had done it, burning out some nerve for longing. Or was it simply fear of more sickness? Whatever, Sam took the world through his eyes now. With no real blame and no regret, though he'd sometimes wonder *Am I dead and punished? Or maybe it's Heaven.* Alone on his stool he actually laughed.

Giuli turned from cutting a blueberry pie and seemed to nod toward a table beyond them—a nod and a frown to hush the air, then a dark-eyed sadness.

Sam hushed and tried to see a reflection in the glass pie-cabinet; it curved too sharply. So when he'd sat another two minutes, dawdling through the last of his coffee, he laid a small stack of bills on the check, caught Giuli's eye and said "Keep the change," then turned on his stool.

Four yards ahead—close to the door in a four-seat booth with the low light on him—a single man was huddled inward on himself as tight as if a blunt pole had pierced him, threaded his chest and bolted him shut. He might just weigh a hundred pounds; his rusty hair was parched and limp. His eyes hit Sam's a moment, then skittered.

It's Richard Boileau, already dead. Sam guessed it that fast; but since the man's eyes wandered to the window and watched the street, Sam stayed in place and tested his hunch. He'd last seen Richard in '78, the November morning after they'd proved through a long bleak night how well they'd learned each other's least weakness and how they could each flay the other with words. Then as daylight had streaked the roof, Sam suddenly found the one path out. He stood from the bed they'd shared for three years, picked up a few good things from the bureau— his father's gold watch, a comb of his mother's, his wallet and knife— and said "All right, the rest is yours."

The rest had literally been the rest—Sam's clothes, books, records, two years of a diary, a few nice pieces of furniture he'd more than half paid for. All well lost and Richard with it, the dazzling tramp hungry as any moray eel, cored-out by a set of monster parents. Through the years Sam heard second-hand of his whereabouts, always in town at a new address; but the two had never collided till now, if this was Richard.

For whatever reason, of Sam's old loves—vanished or lost—it was only Richard he'd thought of as dying, purple-splotched with Kaposi's sarcoma or drowning in lung and nerve parasites. Each day he'd read the obituaries, crouched against the name on the page; and while he chalked off friend after friend, Richard stayed inexplicably free. Even in Sam's own worst days though, when radiation seared his gut in third-degree lesions, he somehow knew he'd outlast the havoc inside his skin while Richard Boileau would certainly die in this new plague. And not from an endless hunger for bodies—scrupulous Sam could have picked a killer any calm night—but from some cold rage in Richard's mind to leave a string of his riders appalled.

But is this helpless scarecrow Richard? In two more seconds Sam all but knew. The worn blue shirt that swallowed the long neck was one Sam had left—a red *S.T.* still edged the pocket, sewed by Sam's mother. Had a stranger bought it at the Salvation Army? Sam turned away to steady himself.

By now Giuli was back by the grill, laughing with a cook that had just turned up, a rangy boy with a knife-blade profile.

Sam thought of quietly walking their way and asking if they knew the man in the booth—was he a regular; what was his problem?

But the young cook met Sam's eyes, gave a wave with his spatula, then kissed Giuli's jaw—their eyes were identical; they had to be brothers. Giuli called out *"Grazie,"* smiled at the whole room, took a short bow and scrubbed at his neck.

Sam stood up and faced the booth. The man was still pressed close to the window, though Sam could see there was nothing to notice, nothing Richard would have spent ten seconds on. The fact freed Sam; he stepped across, took the opposite bench two feet from the man's head and said "See anything good out there?"

The man turned gradually and, at close range, the skin of his upper face was transparent—that thin and taut on the beautiful skull.

Sam thought he could see a whole brain through it, a raddled mind, whatever it knew or had lost for good. But Sam stayed still till he'd drawn a direct look from the eyes—they'd kept their color, an arctic blue. Then he said "Is it Richard?"

No move or sign from the frozen face.

Sam tried a new way. "Bertrand? Remember?" In the early days he'd sometimes called Richard "Bertrand Le Beau" when nothing yet had dulled the shine.

At first the name seemed to penetrate. The eyes widened and the dry lips cracked.

But then a quiet voice said "You know him?" The waitress was there with a dry slice of toast and a cup of milk that gave off smoke. She set it by the man's right hand and spoke to him gently, "This'll warm you fast."

Sam took the risk and looked to the girl. "You know his name?"

The man might have been on the moon, engrossed.

The waitress smiled. "I know he's been bad off a long time. I know this is what he eats every night. But he's gaining strength now—aren't you, friend?" She touched the wrist that was nearly all bone.

The man faced her, his smile a ruin. He managed to lift the cup of milk though and drink a short swallow.

The waitress tapped Sam's shoulder lightly. "Sit with him some. He never sees people; make him drink his milk." As she left, she asked Sam if he was still hungry.

He shook his head No; but when she was gone, he saw she'd left an idle fork and spoon on the table, bound in a napkin. He took out the clean spoon, stirred the milk, drank a spoonful himself; then slowly over the next ten minutes, he fed Richard Boileau the whole cup.

BESS WATERS

1863

WHILE SHE chops cotton in the blistering field, her mother
has hid Bess Waters from the sun in a thicket of low trees and covered
her body with a clean sugar-sack. The child is awake now and pulls the
sack away from her face to watch the sky. With her mother's voice in
the field beyond her, Bess thinks the whole broad hoop of her vision is
all her own body, all hers to use—the white sky, leaves, a laughing
low voice beside her mother's in the hot safe distance, and her own
brown arms and fists above her. That knowledge will serve her all her
life, though she can't yet see she's a rickety baby that barely made it
through the past mean winter and will be the property of Mr. Cobb
Coleman for two more years, the last child born to his slave Nancy
before the Freedom.

Bess likewise can't know she almost smiles as her hand shuts lightly
on a carpenter bee that hovers above her, consulting the odors of milk
and syrup. The bee accepts the dark cupped palm and stills his hum.
Bess brings him down and sets him loose to roam her tongue. He waits
a moment in the damp sweetness, tests his wings and bumbles away.
Till the time her mother fetches her home, well on past dusk, Bess
Waters will seldom fail to smile when she's not dozing—the one good

gift she has from her father, a long-gone runaway whose name she'll hear five years from now and will then forget.

1889

THE EARLY fall days shorten fast, so Bess rises darker each morning to leave in time for the four-mile walk to where she works seven days a week in Macon by the railroad track. Mr. Jack Rodwell's new house is finished; and he and Miss Liz will be in the separate cook-house when Bess walks in at seven. Mr. Jack is shaving at a round mirror, and Miss Liz has already rolled out biscuit dough. When Bess says "Morning," Miss Liz says "Quick, go shake the boys. They're already late and they'll obey *you.*"

As Bess goes back through the morning toward the sleeping porch, she never thinks of the curious fact that, even at twenty-six, her body is still untouched by any grown man—black, white or brown. She's fought three strong men to earn that distinction (she cut one bad), so these two Rodwell boys she wakes are the only children she's been near since her only sister died at eight of whooping cough in a howling snow. As she scrubs the slats of the boys' thin sides with cold well-water, she says aloud "Thinking bout getting me some new young un. You boys know one I can steal or borrow?"

They both yell "Me"; then together "*Us, Bess.*" Warm and laughing as their mother is, they both resent their older sisters' airs and orders. And here last week in the bed they share, they made a pact to run away the day after Christmas and live back of Bess in a shed by the river. They're both under ten; they can barely carve their meat at the table, much less in the woods.

But they've already told Bess their plan, and she's all but promised to bring them whatever scraps she can from their father's pantry. She understands she's a piece in a game they'll never play; but more than once she's half-believed these two white boys could somehow wedge down into her life the way she lives it and stay nearby her one-room house, for all their sakes.

1916

MISS LIZ is on her hot deathbed, a late August day. Her kidneys have failed and her body's poisoned; nothing to do but try to cool her and ease the end. The boys, who are men now, have brought in three zinc tubs of ice to set round the bed. But through the hours, so many visitors have come in to kiss her or beg her pardon that the ice is useless; and nothing helps Miss Liz in her pain but Bess Waters upright by the pillows and steadily waving a palmleaf fan, muttering hope every minute or so.

Toward sunset the room nearly empties, and Miss Liz motions for Bess to lean down. At the delicate ear, an old-gold color that Miss Liz never noticed till now, she says to Bess "Say you forgive me."

Bess hears it's an order, however feeble; and she laughs a high note. "Forgive you what?"

"My whole life, everywhere I've been."

"You been no further than me, Miss Lizzie." Of all the white women Bess has known, Miss Liz has had the best disposition—she'd get right down and work beside you, tired as she was with her eight children—but still Bess can't quite find the word *pardon*.

So Miss Liz darkens around the eyes. "Help me, woman. I got to *leave*."

Bess bends till her lips touch the purplish forehead. "You do, Miss Liz; you leaving fast but I ain't your help. Ain't mine to give." Bess feels no taste of hate in the moment; she's never listed the wrongs of life to herself or others, not all in a row. She only sees the full truth, stood up there a little beyond her and Miss Liz both, like a man that just now strode through the door and waits tall and big-eyed, made out of flames. She points straight at him and tells Miss Liz "You ask the *man* to pardon you." It comes out reckless and bristles her hair.

But Miss Liz also sees the man; his eyes shine at her like a cat in moonlight. She says "Oh please" and ends that instant, partly grinning as her last breath fades.

1927

B E S S ' S O N E child, a skinny grown daughter, comes up to her at the well this evening, a mild mid-April. "Am I just dreaming you told me once that Derb was my father?"

"Em, you dreaming, day *and* night. I don't need to tell you nothing."

"But is he?"

"Why you need to know this late?" (Em was born when Bess was past forty).

Em looks at the blank air as if at a mirror; she's fine to see and knows it keenly. "Derb barking up my tree again."

Bess has hauled up a bucket of water. Slowly she bends and wastes it on purpose on the ground between them. "Derb old enough to be your grandpa." She feeds the bucket back down the well.

"Is that my answer?"

Bess nods. "—For this evening."

"Maybe you don't know."

Bess brings the new full bucket up and sets it beside her in young spring weeds. Then she turns on Em a face as fierce as a snake on coals. "I know every inch of your skin, mean child. I made it myself; no name on it *nowhere* but mine."

Em nods but has the gall to say "You won't be beating my head in the night then if Derb come round?"

Bess smiles. "Oh no'm. Tell him 'Come on, Derb.' "

"Can he eat here tomorrow night if I cook it all?"

Bess says "He can eat these pine walls down. Don't let me stop you. Just have him gone when I get home—it'll be past dark; they having a feast." She points through the woods toward where she works, still four miles away, for the Drakes now—the Rodwells' second daughter Ida, her husband Marvin and two strong boys. Ida is feasting her baby sister Lizbeth, who married a few months back and is home with her husband Buckeye, a drunk out of work but pitiful and funny.

It's Buckeye that takes Bess home from the feast at ten the next night. She's cooked and served a table of eight, washed every dish and scoured the kitchen ready for morning. Every separate bone in her long body hurts her; and when the car stops in sight of her house, old as she is, she prays a barely audible sentence, "Let this white man be tired as me" (Mr. Buckeye, she means).

He is. In a minute he's slipped her a quarter—serious money this terrible year, for the extra work he and Lizbeth cause her—and he's backing out the narrow track.

In the house right off, Bess knows she's very far from alone. Somebody's skin and bones press at her through stifling dark. She feels for a long match and lights the lamp. Before it reaches the edge of the room, Bess is forced down as if by hands; she sits at her table—this raw new company is crushing her mind. When her eyes are open to the dark, she can see the shape of two bodies, still but breathing, on Em's low cot. Bound to be Em and Derb Sweetwater; no other man will touch poor Em. But didn't Em swear she'd have Derb out of here? Now he's not just here and asleep, but his liquor jar stands on Bess's table in reach of her hand and less than half-full.

Her hand goes out and uncorks the bottle; in all her years she's yet to drink a drop of liquor. But her head falls back, and she drinks a half-inch of that pure fire. It goes down her so slow she feels its path to the pit of belly. Before it can reach her mind though she rises—her mind has got to be clear for this minute and maybe the rest of the life it leaves her, if any at all. On the stove Em has left one dirty skillet and one iron cooking-fork at least a foot long.

When Bess has stood by the cot a good while, she bends and touches a body through the sheet—no heads are showing, just shoulders and legs. Nothing moves. Bess says Em's full name—"Emily Waters"—in a normal voice. Nothing again. But two mouths are breathing; Bess hears the sigh. They're asleep, dead-drunk. Her hand feels out the line of a back. Broad and strong, it has to be Derb's. She sees a man's pants folded neat on the floor. Derb's good brown pants.

So Bess bends again and, calm-eyed as any mother at a cradle, she works the two strong tines of the iron fork through his left shoulder, from backward past his shoulder blade into gristle, then soft meat, then the rind of his heart. Slowly her hand comes off the fork handle; she takes a step back. Derb barely moves and never wakes, but his foul breath moans on a while till it quits in midair—a shot-down bird.

The rest of the night, Bess sits at her table. The lamp burns out before daylight; but she stays up, too tired to think. And when day breaks with Em still asleep, Bess barely looks to the cot but picks up a silver spoon (a spoon Old Mistress gave her mother) and tries to see her own face deep in the back of its shine. She's there unchanged but then at sunrise she looks again and sees, not herself but her mother's face. A face dead—Lord—since Bess was a girl. It's smiling though.

1938

EM'S ONLY child lives with just Bess now (Em struck out for Maryland, three years back, and has sent no more than a few postcards that Bess can't read but keeps by the stove). The boy's lean and tall, named June, aged eight; and Bess always says he's lucky to be here. Alive, she means. She'd stood over Em for most of a hot day's labor on the cot and finally hauled June out of her narrows by main force. "You come here spitting coal," Bess tells him; and June sees it literally—dry chunks of coal rolling out of his throat—when what Bess means is, before she could wash him clean of his mother, he chucked out a mouthful of coal-black tar that must have been old clotted blood.

Today in school June's drawn a picture of himself as a baby, sprawled in midair with nobody near him; and all around his scrawny body, he's set chunks of coal the size of his head. He brings the picture home for Bess and leaves it on the table near the lamp in case it's dark when she gets back and he's out hunting with his slingshot (he's caught a few birds but never a rabbit or squirrel, his main targets).

And when he walks in well after dark with one muskrat he killed at the pond, Bess is already there at the table, trying to see by low lamplight. As he stands in the door, she turns to him slowly. "June, fling that nasty rat in the woods." Her long hand makes a fling at the air.

"People say muskrat good eating, Mama."

"I ain't your Mama, and peoples died all over the Earth when I was a girl from eating such filth."

So June backtracks, hides the muskrat twenty yards from the house in a briar bush—he'll skin it at least and sell the hide if a fox doesn't drag it off in the night. By the time he's in the house again, he's forgot he's mad; and when he goes to stand back of Bess and feel her heat across a gap the width of his hand, he sees her dry face pressed to his school drawing, studying close.

At last her finger picks at the coal chunks round his picture. "They won't that big, you won't that skinny, but you was sure-God pretty to see. This baby here is *ugly*, child." Again her finger scratches the paper, the baby's face. She gives a dry laugh.

June's hand reaches toward her neck and waits in the air. He can smell her old thick blood through her skin. But he stops short of touch; they seldom touch unless she's scrubbing him or searching his hair.

Then, while she never turns back or looks, Bess says "Swear, June. Don't never leave me."

He thinks *I'll leave*, though it scares him to think it. He knows he loves her, strong as a blade; in his mind the feeling tastes long-lasting, a feeling he'll never say in words but will hold close for years. When he leans to turn the lamp wick higher, he sees that Bess is sound asleep, bolt upright in her ladder-back chair. She looks cold-dead. June knows death well enough to clamp his teeth and pray this old woman outlasts him.

1949

JUNE HAS killed a girl, a girl Bess warned him about years back when the girl's tan titties were flat as your hand but both her eyes were snagging on June already, *asking*. Killed her outdoors by the rim of the pond with a knife he bought from a store in Weldon. And dragged her wren-sized body deep down in the willows and reeds; then woke up Bess past five in the morning, "Mama, come on out here and help me."

Bess is easy to wake as a cat, but her joints seize up anytime she's still. (Eighty-six years old, she's long since lost real track of time. If white people ask, she honestly says she's "creeping on eighty." Black people are way too polite to ask.) Flat of her back she looks round the room. The lamp is lit so she lies flat and waits to see who's calling for help and from what world. Bess deals with numerous worlds here lately; what chance is there that this one is Heaven? Her eyes clear finally and show her June's face, all ashy and skewed in the mouth and eyes. "Oh Jesus. What you *showing* me?"

June says the flat truth—Mincie is dead and back in the bushes.

By the time Bess dresses and walks behind him all the awful way he leads her, the girl is cold but still smiling. Bess tries to shut the eyes but they stick.

The lids are frozen and the great brown pupils fix on June—life itself couldn't give her enough but she's happy now.

Bess takes June's hand and makes him touch his handiwork. "She eating you up, son. I told you she would." But once Bess works the eyelids down on the curly lashes, she knows the next move. She cooked for the Drakes till her eyes failed; the Drakes tend her still. Now she must send June to Mr. Drake, ask him please to call for the sheriff and lead him out here with his men and the funeral hearse.

When she says the words, June never looks up from Mincie's face—he can barely recall her, moving against him—but his head nods Yes.

If Bess can think of how to put it, she'll beg him now to find his knife and finish her too—they can't electrocute him but once, whatever he does. And she waits a long minute. When no more words volunteer on her tongue, she turns and heads on up toward the house. Everything she cared five cents about in the world is gone—worse than gone. Somebody got to cook some breakfast though and somebody eat it.

1951

IT'S A sweltering morning in mid-July, and Bess has walked every step of the way to Miss Ida's kitchen with a bucket of blackberries picked at sunrise. While Bess takes a chair by the sink, to breathe and clear her eyes, Miss Ida starts in washing berries.

"Bess, these are beautiful—where'd you pick them?"

"Just be glad you know me and eat em."

"—Well over a quart." Miss Ida's voice is light with the pleasure.

Bess gave up smiling twenty years back but she nods. "More to come."

"How much do I owe you?"

Bess looks out the window to the shady yard. What seems like a tall bear stands by the oak tree. Her mother had a picture of a bear nailed up on the wall beside her bed (something Old Mistress had thrown out as ugly); and through her mother's strangling last weeks, Bess had fixed on the bear to watch as something that anyhow wasn't in pain.

"What you looking at?" Miss Ida watches you like a hawk, though she treats you fair. She got the Public Assistance for Bess that's her only money; and Mr. Drake drives Bess to town every month or so if she needs salve, her one concession to the rheumatism that's clawed her hands.

Bess blinks, the bear is standing there, she knows not to say so—he can't be real. "Nothing. Cool shade."

They stay on quiet for a soothing while. Miss Ida covers the berries with a white cloth and sets them in the icebox. When she rises, not looking to Bess, she says "There hasn't been any mail at all." Bess's rare mail comes to the Drakes; they read it to her.

Bess takes a long time to say "No ma'm. I knew you'd bring it to the house if it come."

"I certainly would."

By now Bess feels her full strength back—strong as it gets. She looks again at the shady yard. "It was this morning, won't it?"

Almost too low, Miss Ida says "You know it was."

"Mr. Drake at the prison? I axed him to watch it."

Miss Ida stands, both hands at her sides like somebody's tied her. "That was too much, Bess—driving down there to Raleigh and watching that sadness. You didn't mean that. He sent the undertaker."

Still talking to the yard, the wide oak tree, Bess says "You know where my mama's buried?"

"On the Coleman place somewhere by the river, but that's just snakes and brambles now. You don't want June buried way up there. I spoke to your preacher; there's plenty room for June at Mount Zion. And I ordered the stone just like you told me."

Bess faces around, stunned past all reach. "June - Thorne - Fitzpatrick." She draws what feels like the shape of the name on the sweet damp air.

Miss Ida frowns. "You told me *Waters* was June's last name."

Bess eventually nods. "Ne mind, nobody but me try to read it."

1963

BESS HAS lain flat of her back all day on her own bed dozing, then coming to without getting up, talking in peaceful snatches to her mother, even thanking the dog for his high bark at what sounds like a car outside—"Keep at it, old gentleman. I'll feed you directly." She thinks she's said it, though it stays in her mind. She'll feed him extra when she gets up—all that buttermilk she can't drink, that Miss Ida brought her. She slides back to sleep.

A hand on the door—a soft knock, a wait, then three knocks louder.

Nobody Bess knows would knock this way; they'd call her name, "Miss Bessie, you there?" And they mostly bring her little somethings-to-eat, a pear or a handful of hickory nuts. No words now though but one more knock. Bess drags up slowly and, on her way, turns June's picture face-down on the table. No shame involved—just giving him shelter, wherever he is, though she hasn't seen his eyes in the picture for three years (her cataracts are ripe).

When the door's full open, it's a dark-haired white boy turning to leave. He halts on the top step. "I wake you, Aunt Bess?"

All her life she's never confessed to being asleep when somebody calls her. She bares her excellent teeth and says "Just lying, collecting my thoughts for church." She hasn't been to church in twelve years, can't get that near June's stone in the yard.

The boy—a man, thirty-one years old—says "Bess, it's Buckeye Price's son, Reynolds."

She weighs that claim against his face. "You got a heap more of your mammy in you—Lizbeth's eyes and Mr. Jack's hair. How they getting on?"

"Well, you remember my father's dead; and Mother's losing her sight but she's cheerful."

"*I* ain't seen a thing since before you were born." Bess waves a hand in front of her eyes and shakes her head, "Can't even see my own black skin."

"You sure knew me."

"I known you long as anybody left but your own mother. I was holding her wrist when you was born. Held her mammy's too the minute she died."

He's heard that before and, while she rises and moves to the door, he takes the memory as a sign her mind is clear enough. If he can keep her on track awhile, she may yet tell him all he needs (he's told himself that Bess is his hope of understanding what he can't pardon and passing that much on to others). One of her two chairs sits on the porch at the sunny end. He goes over, takes it and moves toward the shade.

"Where you going with my antiques?" She still hasn't laughed.

"I'm sitting you in the cool so you'll talk."

"You ain't still writing that book about me?" But she makes a careful way to the chair and lowers herself.

He sits on the top step, less than a yard of space between them. "I haven't started your book yet, no. I need your help." He waits and thinks he's lost her already—her eyes have lowered a curious veil across the pupils, a pearly haze—but he tries anyhow. "Start from the first, when you worked for Miss Liz."

Her eyes shut now. "That won't the first."

"But start there please; they were my grandparents."

There comes a long space when nothing on her moves; then her left hand rises flat on the air, a firm refusal. Her eyes are opening again and seeing; then they aim straight at him with a new peeled clarity as if his nearness has tripped something in her and reeled back youth. The hand stays up as she finally speaks. "The start was when my lips come open in Mama's belly and axed for light."

He says "I've got womb memories too—"

"You want this story or you want to talk? I'm near bout ninety."

He knows she's a hundred sometime this month (he found the month and year in a ledger from the Coleman farm), but he keeps it from her. He says "I want that story; tell on."

And honest to God, Bess tries to tell it. Her dry lips work and her mind sends words—she only recalls these scattered hours—but what comes out is dark shine and power from her banked old heart and the quick of her bones, dark but hot as a furnace blast with a high blue roar. It burns the boy first. Bess sees him blown back and starting to scorch; then it whips round and folds her into the light till both of them sit in a grate of embers, purified by the tale itself, the visible trace of one long life too hard to tell.

AN EARLY CHRISTMAS

BY SUNDOWN I knew I'd ruined the day, maybe even the rest of my trip. And I'd only got here three hours ago—Israel, the West Bank, the Old City of Jerusalem, December 24th 1980 and me almost at the Jaffa Gate on my way back toward a faceless hotel five hundred yards across the valley that anciently served as the model for Hell. I'd flown here on a personal whim, no work to do, no major plan. Fact was, I'd spent the previous Easter in Rome alone. And two days ago when I saw I'd be alone for Christmas, I thought I might try Rome again. My grown sons would be unavailable, my live-in lady friend had found younger company a few months back, and I was exhausted from the push to finish twenty pictures for an exhibition (I'm a landscape painter basically). So I had the telephone in my hand to book tomorrow's flight to Rome when I suddenly thought "No, Bethlehem."

With a change in Amsterdam, the flight was on time. My luggage was waiting in that low barn of a baggage room where a few years back a squad of arriving Japanese terrorists calmly opened their own slim bags, produced machine guns and mowed down dozens of passengers. I rented a car, then drove through a dry plain littered with burnt-out tanks and Jeeps from the '67 war, then up a spine of rocky hills till I reached Jerusalem in late afternoon—a ridge of light that was already strange and welcome as a rescue. I easily found my room, the size of a cigar box; then asked where I might get a ticket for mass in Bethlehem tonight.

The desk clerk lowered her lioness head in frank despair. "Nowhere, sir. You're weeks too late."

At that point a four-foot high bellhop—pretty surely an Arab—beckoned me over toward his stand, looked round conspiratorially and whispered that I should try an address ten minutes away by the Jaffa Gate inside the old walls, a Catholic agency for tourists and pilgrims.

I'd walked straight out in the still-warm sun down a valley path through dirt, weeds, more rusted car parts and up again through the western gate that stands by the ruins of Herod's palace—later Pilate's headquarters where Jesus was mauled. By the time I found the agency in its maze of trinket shops, the wide room was empty and dimming fast. Surely all tickets were long since gone.

But a bell had jangled when I walked in; and as I was almost turning to leave, a monk appeared through a green door. His brown habit was plainly Franciscan, but his English was almost comically French; and his livid dome and predatory profile sliced the air like a Grand Inquisitor's, hellbent to save me at whatever cost to life and limb.

I told him how I'd come without warning so had been unable to write for tickets by the November deadline. Was there a chance of a single, even standing room, in Bethlehem tonight? (Western Christmas begins in a Roman Catholic church adjoining the Greek basilica with its famous cave beneath the altar, the actual birthplace, a makeshift stable.)

Before he'd even heard me out, the monk's head slowly shook a firm no. But when I said I was sorry because I'd come as an artist for *Time* magazine—an instant lie—he gutted my eyes with his own ice blues, then asked for my passport. He took some time with the entry stamp, establishing yes I had just landed. And where was I staying? Who accompanied me? Did I have a car? Did I understand that Bethlehem was shut to cars till midnight tonight? The only way was on foot or bus, and I'd be body-searched by Israeli guards. When I switched to the truth—I was on my own with a rented car—he gave the thinnest frigid smile and laid his blackest ace between us. "Is monsieur a Catholic person?"

I have no quarrel with the Catholic church except for the fact that my sons' mother used her nominal Catholicism to keep the boys from me five bitter years while she refused to hear of divorce or any shared custody on grounds that the Church prevented her yielding when I well knew she had less faith than I in a storm, which was shakily little in those years. So the truthful answer was "No I'm not," but then I thought of the creed I'd repeated a thousand times in my childhood—*I believe in the holy Catholic church.* I met the monk's fuming eyes and said "Yes, Brother, Catholic."

He gave my passport one more look, comparing the photograph with my face as if I might have lethal designs on the manger itself. Then he vanished through what seemed a slit in space, that mute and slick. Through the glass in the outside door, I could see that the street was bright again even this late, a honey-colored gleam on the limestone.

A string of Arab schoolboys—all in blue smocks like midget painters—were scuffling homeward. One of them saw me through the glass and stretched his face in a monster grin, crossed eyes, fang teeth. Another boy cut a literal flip. He stood on his two feet, frowned at me deeply, spun through the air ass-over-tip and landed upright, laughing wildly.

I thought of the actual Bethlehem shepherds—local boys at leisure to greet the newest Babe with pet lambs, songs, their best rude pranks— and I took a step forward, smiled and waved. The monster boy was a twin to my younger son years back, and I started to open the door and speak.

But the monk was instantly on me—"Ah *non!*" He thrust a scattering hand at the boys; and then I saw that he held one ticket, printed large on heavy paper. When the boys were gone, he held it toward me. "Merry Christmas, Monsieur Boatner." Again his lips had frozen, smiling.

I took the ticket and reached for my wallet, not a tip but a seasonal gift for the poor (I assumed Franciscans still cared for the poor).

His eyes took offense and he said "Impossible" in English not French, then gave me the same dismissive wave he'd flung at the boys.

I must have felt a combination of shame at my lie of brotherhood with him and hot revulsion from his condescending hand. I thrust the ticket at him. "On second thought, *Ah non*, merci."

He was totally calm and accepted the ticket; this happened daily. He gave an Oriental deep bow with a wide arm-flourish—"As you say, Mr. Boatner"—and was gone again, uncannily fast.

Ten seconds later I was outside in a new damp chill, a purplish haze that had suddenly risen. The peddlers' stands were all shut down; the only moving thing was a beggar in a scarlet fez and a weird leather stump in place of one leg—the left leg showed from sole to knee with a palm-sized ulcer deep in the shin.

Thank God at least he was hopping briskly away and didn't spot me. I'd go to my hotel, drink malt whiskey and try to sleep through the glorious Birth till noon tomorrow.

Which was how I thought I'd ruined the trip.

I was very wrong, though if I'd plowed on bar-ward and bed-ward, I might well be a standing man now, a vertical painter, not a huddled gimp with unpredictable fingers that somedays blot out hours of work with a lunge. What bent my course was, again, a child—almost surely the one at the window who'd looked so much like my younger son. He was pale, black-haired, maybe eight years old, practicing soccer with a tattered ball and a limestone curb that faced the Arab Police Department and marked the line of Christ's real path from Pilate to the cross (the official Via Dolorosa is a medieval tour guide's invention).

As my normal gait bore down on the boy—five yards off—he spun, faced me grimly and suddenly fired his ball at my feet.

I hadn't returned a soccer pass in thirty years, but some vestigial trained synapse flared in my mind; and back the ball went, dead at his eyes.

He caught it, laughing, with both arms; charged ahead and up three steps, then turned to say "We give you tea."

He waited with his ball in the high door-frame beside a cafe till I took his next challenge and followed him up a winding stair into deepening dark. Young as he was, at the first landing, I had an apprehensive moment—my mind formed the sight of a *blade* and silently said the one word *knife*. But as we entered the dim apartment, I was quickly wrapped in the dense, amazing rough-haired mantle of Eastern hospitality.

The boy was named Jabril and was older than I'd first thought ("eleven and a half very soon"). He lived with his parents and older sister above the Citadel Cafe on the pocket square inside the gate; and in the time between sunset and Christmas dawn, they and their kinsmen served me tea and an unforeseeable strange lot more. His smiling mother was fortyish and stocky in a Western dress from 1950. The pretty teenage sister wore jeans and a starched tux shirt. The father was not yet home from work, but the women mustered round me with grins. They either spoke no English or wouldn't take the risk, but they made me endless tiny glasses of thick sweet tea with water boiled on a charcoal brazier in the midst of the room. There were also bowls of pistachio nuts, flat sesame cakes and small rice candies. Soon I was wolfing them down too fast; and again my exhausted brain repeated a word to itself—*poison, poison*—though my teeth chewed on.

I'd been seated right off on a sofa with Jabril beside me once he changed into cleaner clothes. His English was better than I could have guessed, and he reeled out normal boyish questions. Where did I live? Did I know Ronald Reagan? Why did he not help the Palestinian people? Was my wife sick? If not, where was she? How could I live alone? Was I not very sad? When would I go home? Was that near

Chicago where his uncle lived? Could he visit me soon? But the facts he truly cared about were where he lingered—"How much older than me are your sons? Are they very respectful?"

I said "They're more than twice your age—both grown men now—and one has a daughter."

"You will have many more grandchildren soon?"

I tried to explain how in America that wasn't my business—the children were up to my son and his wife.

It plainly failed to impress Jabril—he put up a finger to stop me short for a deeper probe. "Are they kind to you?—your grownup sons?"

I said they were, the times I saw them.

"But they have left you." His eyes were round and solemn as bronze coins, judging my sons.

For the first time clearly, I saw they were gone—really gone except for jokey visits—but I managed a smile.

Jabril's eyes refused to quit. "Why have they let you come here alone in the cold and rain?"

Bullseye and I saw he knew it. But I made up an answer about a commission to paint some pictures in the desert light southeast of here—the Dead Sea valley, an hour's drive. I tried to parry the rest of his serves with questions about his own friends, his school and with compliments on his resourceful English.

The mother and daughter stirred around us but never sat; and when I'd drunk all the tea I could hold and started drawing Jabril's head in a school tablet that had lain with his books, they silently disappeared from the room.

The boy sat still with enormous dignity as if he'd waited all his life for the man to appear who'd fix his likeness in history.

But given the night and day behind me (and the Franciscan creep), when I finished the line of Jabril's neck, I suddenly wondered if this were somehow irreligious—didn't Islam, like Orthodox Judaism, forbid a likeness of living things? I held out the drawing. "Is this all right?"

He faced me, barely seeing the tablet, and shook his head—a firm no.

I took that as a final answer, though what I'd drawn was a speaking likeness; and I started tearing the sheet from the tablet.

But again he shook his courtly head and stopped my wrist. He took the tablet, set it between us; then faced me again, graver still with eyes that had no need to blink.

Till now I'd seen only one Arab country—Morocco fifteen years ago—but I'd read and watched enough Middle East news to feel a twinge of actual fear. Here, unknowing, I'd made some irreversible gaffe—maybe worse than a gaffe. What would come down from the boy, the women, his invisible father, the nearest mullah or God knew who? My mind said *knife* a few more times, and I stood in place. "Please thank your mother and sister for tea. Good luck in school."

Jabril stood too. "You eat something now."

I realized that, in all my life, no other child had ever concerned himself with my diet. "Thank you. I'll go to my hotel and rest, then eat a good dinner."

"You eat with us." He stood as if a ready meal would rush in on us.

"Oh yes, thank you; the nuts were fine. The candy really filled me up."

He said "No. More." Then he reached for my right hand and said "We go."

The usual murk of jet lag, verbal imprecisions, vague anxiety and "What-the-hell" abandon overwhelmed me. I'd follow Jabril wherever he led.

It was back through the front door, down the stairs out into the night, then quickly back through the cafe entrance. At first the space seemed totally dark, but the boy led on, and then I saw what seemed a small alcove off the back. We turned in there and—ah—a long marble-topped table, Jabril's mother with her hair combed long, the sister now in a blood-red dress, an older woman with a prosperous mustache and two more men (one younger than me, one silver-haired). They'd plainly waited in this dim silence for our arrival. Once the younger man sat me at the head of the table, they all beamed on me and said "You are welcome" in various ways.

Then the older man called out for "Samir," and a stupefyingly bountiful meal slid into place.

Slowly the facts—were they facts?—emerged. This was Jabril's immediate family, not Muslim at all but Christian and Catholic. The younger man was the boy's father, a driver for the British consul. The older man was the father's father; the single woman was somebody's aunt who'd moved to San Francisco years back and was home for the week. The cafe seemed to belong to the family; and this was clearly their Christmas feast at which somehow I'd been expected and over which I half presided with growing peace and an appetite like none I'd felt since my days as an artist in the splendid highlands of Vietnam, drawing the beautiful terror for *Time*. Somehow the tablet with Jabril's portrait was rounding the table before the summoned Samir appeared with Scotch for me, the only drinker.

Samir was the waiter, the only one in sight this evening (the cafe was closed to all but us). He was a small man, maybe thirty, with one short leg on which he limped and a face so focused on his work that he threatened more than once in my sight to burst into flame—not anger but purpose. It was Sam alone who brought and re-brought platters of chicken with mountainous saffron-yellow rice, a flayed and all but grinning lamb with roast eggplant, endless mysterious bowls of relishes laced with yogurt and olive oil, endless bottles of mineral water and orangeade, more Scotch for me.

All the family ate with a hunger to match my own—with frequent sighs of satisfaction and cries of thanks—but no one ever spoke to Sam, not that I saw, not even the grandfather-owner-boss. And while Sam stumped his brisk way round us like a Levantine Tiny Tim at work with no real sign of resentful exclusion, he likewise never smiled or spoke; and he never met a one of our faces, not that I saw.

So as we neared the end of the food—and I'd exhausted all I could say to kindly people who nonetheless knew broken English or none at all (Jabril had long since donned the fathomless boredom of well-behaved children marooned in adults)—I found myself composing a history and home for Samir. Small as he was and lame in the leg, I thought past the present and saw him reared in the scapegoat wilderness south of Jericho, camped by white hot ruins or the lunar valleys of the Salt Sea shore (none of which landscape I'd yet seen except in boyhood Bible pictures). I pictured him herding the family goats alone in rain and roaring sunlight, yelling off packs of wild dogs or chased by older boys who stoned him for his withered leg.

The Scotch by now was kicking in; and when Samir passed my chair next, I beckoned him down and said a brief thanks. I figured that anyone waiting table this near the Old City's prime tourist route would know the word *thanks.*

But Sam drew back like a slapped child and said "Sorry. Sorry, sir."

Christ, who *was* I now? Jabril had someway refused my drawing, and Sam had thoroughly misunderstood a simple thanks. Since he was still balked there beside me, frowning darkly, I tried to correct myself with a grin and a toast from my glass.

At last Sam managed the ghost of a smile, but his eyes were already back at work in a fury of dread that he might yet fail the high occasion, and through the rest of the meal he plainly shunned my chair.

We'd started eating awhile past seven. By half past nine the tender lamb was a stripped white carcass staring us down from the midst of the table, Jabril was in his father's lap almost asleep, the lovely daughter had disappeared, the San Francisco aunt was dozing (even more jet-lagged than me); and Sam was bussing our plates away as if they mattered more than ever in his plan for the night, his feverish design, whatever it was.

The family had long since asked me to join them for their next round—a midnight mass beyond the Damascus Gate on the north edge of town—but I'd declined on grounds of fatigue. And now as the grandfather stood to organize a departure, I joined in a final round of handshakes, hugs by now, with thanks and vows to see them again "many times" before leaving.

As I turned, the father said "You can never pay to eat here, sir."

When I said "I may not ever eat again," Jabril's eyes widened; he raised a hushing finger and said "Now pray that does not come true."

Again this adult care from a child—but I took him seriously and nodded. Then I pulled the tablet from his hand. The drawing was better than I'd recalled. I liked it enough to write at the bottom, "Jabril at Christmas guarding his new friend, Bridge Boatner."

When the boy read it, he nearly smiled again; but I saw he knew I'd pierced his secret cover and thanked him.

Then I was out in the square again, bracingly cold and only a little disoriented. The Jaffa Gate was still twenty yards off, still dimly lighted. All shops were shuttered and most lights out—not a moving soul, even uphill by Police Headquarters—but I could see four pitch-black alleys yawning into the core of town. Though my map showed that Old Jerusalem was maybe the size of six square blocks of New York City, it was home to far more crucial deeds of humankind than the fifty states combined and doubled. Within the sound of my calling voice lay tangible traces of David and Solomon, Nebuchadnezzar's conquering hordes, Alexander the Great and the Maccabees, then lethal Herod and officious Pilate, Jesus, Peter, John and Paul.

A three-year-old on his first real hike could step from here in a quick half hour past the devastations of the Emperor Titus with the final razing of God's own Temple and the forced exile of all the Jews, through Byzantine mazes of power and murder to the actual rock from which Mohammed soared to heaven, then past that breach in the northern wall where the First Crusade poured through and turned these howling alleys to gutters of smoking Saracen blood. Not to speak of the scented gold remains of the Ottoman Turk and the swift return of Israel to its old home in pain and death. So, bleared and wobbly as I was and far from any visible home, it came down on me with serious weight—I was here upright and apparently strong in the compact thudding heart of a place as near to being *Homo sapiens'* ultimate socket as anywhere else.

That much memory left me thinking I'd pray for my skin and trot to my hotel the quickest way. I buttoned my jacket and turned to run. Then a voice cried out. I thought it said "Sir." And when I looked— God, no—there stood the beggar in the scarlet fez, some thirty yards off beneath a weak streetlight by one of the alleys. I looked behind me—nobody, nothing.

He had to want me; and when he cried again it was "*Sir*"—his arm was waving me toward him strongly.

In brief, I went, telling myself each step of the way that (1) I was tipsy (2) enough so to feel more than normal self-pity and (3) the lioness hotel clerk had assured me that Jerusalem, Old and New, was safer than "Your home on the range"—she'd actually sung a bar of the song which, if I'd thought, might have helped me guess I was in for a night of rules reversed.

As I got closer the beggar looked worse, a renegade from Rembrandt's etching of Jesus healing the sick and the poor. But he wasn't old and plainly not starved—mid to late fifties and reasonably stout with a scruffy beard. Besides the fez he wore a tan cotton smock with stains in all repellent colors. Ending just below his knees, it fully displayed his leather peg and the wound in his left shin. Closer up it looked like an ulcer bound to eat right through the leg soon—invisible parasites were gouging it deeper the nearer I got.

I moved up anyhow and then I saw a sizable box on the ground by his stump—black wood with an upright brass footrest.

"I will shine your shoes." That far at least, his English was clear, almost no accent. But this was surely no American Jew fallen on hard times, no Arab back from years in Detroit.

I said I doubted the shoes were worth it—old Cordovan loafers I saved for trips. I brought out a fifty-shekel note instead and held it toward him. "Seasons greetings."

Gently he refused my hand, never quite touching me but pressing me back with firm politeness. "Sir, I honor the name of your God; but I am not a Nazarene. I only thought to give your shoes a Christmas gift."

I thanked him, as much for the crusty words as his free shine offer. Then I set one foot on his box and asked to know his name.

"Sir, it is George." The West Bank still was stocked with men who'd learned their English from British officers staffing the Mandate. Despite his lack of detectable accent, George had surely worked for the Brits sometime in his life. In all his dirt and desolation, he'd kept that welcome blue-steel edge of command and no-nonsense. It sat on him like a cool addition to the Arab air of raptor force and the hot intent to do you enormous good or kill you—maybe both.

It was eerily like the air that hung round young Southern white men in my boyhood two generations past Appomattox, and soon I was feeling strangely at home. So I balanced on one leg in the dark while George spent ten minutes rehabilitating my shoes with only occasional grunts and cackles but no more words. When at last he said "Finished" and set my right foot back on the pavement, I fumbled again for my wallet to pay.

But his round face clouded, and his black eyes burned—"Never, sir. You did not hear me? I said it is our gift to you."

I might have asked who *our* was; but I offered my hand, half thinking I'd touch a leprous palm and win eternal credit for kindness. But George's skin was soft as kid-leather, and we shook on the gift.

Then he said "You come with me."

I might have bolted but at that moment the first two other humans I'd seen since dinner passed. They were young men, tall, alarmingly thin and dressed in the stark black suits and hats of Hassidic Jews. In the weak light their pure white faces and forelock curls looked far more vulnerable than any single cell of my body; yet they plowed forward, talking happily in what seemed Yiddish, and vanished down the largest alley. If a pair of humans defenseless as they could brave the night, who I was to balk?

When I looked to George, he'd slung the box across his shoulder and was waiting for me.

I said "Where now?"

He paused long enough to let me know he'd heard the question; then he gave a slow hook of his head and started toward the same black mouth where the Hassids vanished, David Street.

It was all downhill in long stone steps maybe five yards wide, with shuttered shops to left and right and only the occasional glow from living quarters above. No sound at all but my clean shoes, George's stump and the thud of the shoeshine box on his hip as he led the way. Or was he leading?

After maybe seventy yards, I paused alone at a cross street with a naked light bulb overhead. Both ways were roofed and plaster-vaulted twenty feet above. This was plainly the heart of a thriving market, and the faded sign said Christian Street. The streets seemed wider in both directions with a thicket of painted placards by the shop doors—jewelery, leather, mother of pearl, olivewood carvings, icons, Yemenite filigree, American jeans and a billion plastic bowls and jugs in every size and exotic shape.

Then I thought I could see George's shadow stumping onward to my left, at least the filthy back of his smock and his rolling gait. I took a few breaths to check for fear. In any other city, even this early on Christmas Eve, I'd have known I was crazy to tail a stranger through what by now seemed the stunned body of an endless giant we tunneled in.

But something new had freed me up. I thought the word *courage* and guessed this was it. In my past life I'd never been bothered like so many men by questions of my own personal guts—would I turn yellow under fire? I'd more or less always known I wouldn't, not because I was all that brave but as a direct result of an inborn painter's eye—I was mainly curious to see everything at whatever price, though except for the sights at my father's deathbed and once when I rescued my son Xan from the nearly perpendicular roof of an old garage, I'd barely faced a live-or-die test except for those months in Vietnam.

I'd watched enough Arab-Israeli news in the past forty years to have some sense of what lay round me. I even stood at the crossway long enough to weigh my chances—knives again, bombs, mugging at the hands of George and his friends, a slashed-out tongue or merely some innocent desecration of a Muslim shrine with consequent melee and twelve men shot, including me on tomorrow night's news for my sons to watch back home by the Yule log, guilty at last.

No, I felt as normal as if this were downtown Winston-Salem in my childhood, where the possible threats were terminal boredom or a fender bender from a cheerful drunk. In fact I felt a good deal better than at most winter solstices (I crave sunlight). Far from depressed by the Bethlehem failure, I could tell that now I was slightly elated, beyond the rewards of good food and Scotch. And it felt like a well-braced mood, no whim. Maybe I was bound for one of my rare but fruitful spells of easy solitude—those clear-aired plateaus when life seems nothing but fuel for work; and work ignites at the sight of canvas, like a frictionless engine with no upkeep.

Before I knew I'd made the choice, I was walking left on Christian Street and had gone a long way in the dark again before I thought to look for George. No trace of him ahead or behind; but when I'd walked another few yards, I heard a hoarse bark beyond me, then a long wail and furious claws on a dry wood door.

At another light bulb fifty yards on, what appeared to be George was waiting upright. His back was to me with one long arm out, bracing his body against a wall.

I trotted toward him but the closer I came, the more he melted deeper inward—a turn to the right, full dark again but I had the sense of space around me at last, level pavement under my feet. In another step I walked into something broad and warm, someone—George (by then I'd memorized his odor, not foul but high). I called his name, excused myself and took a step back.

He didn't speak. He came back toward me, found my right hand and drew me on through the new wide space maybe ten more yards. Then he said "Very slowly—slowly, sir—go down these steps. I will watch from here."

I could literally not see my feet, much less George behind me; but I felt a blank stone wall on my right; and I counted wide steps downward beneath me—eight, ten. By now someway I expected noise, the crash of something brass—huge cymbals—or a bass drum. But what came slowly was a feeble light to my left; then more, an actual shine. And then my feet were level again. A small square opened out to my left, the lighted open enormous door of a looming building, one man beside it. I looked back for George and called his name—no sign or answer.

Ten yards away from the open door, I could see the man was an Arab policeman standing at ease but plainly on duty. The light was strong, though it had the wavering feel of candle light, the thrill of torch light. On the plane I'd browsed through a 1910 British guide to Jerusalem with black-and-white pictures of holy sites and clear directions to the "sanitary fittings." But nothing here before me now matched any picture in the book. Was it another Arab Christian church?—then where were the people? Was it a mosque and did Muslims somehow mark the night? (Jesus after all remains a Muslim prophet.)

But then a second policeman approached from behind the door and stood by the first—the new man was younger, a half-head taller. I thought he looked directly my way; he even seemed to meet my eyes and he almost nodded. Then he and his partner lit cigarettes, began to whisper; and in ten more seconds, I caught a red glimpse of what was almost surely George in a ragged vestment, no fez now—the startling body was gone in an instant. But if it was George, the vestment had hung almost to the floor and hid his wound; and he'd shucked his wornout canvas shoes. Whoever, he'd swung what looked like a silver incense pot that poured blue smoke.

All right then, *Christmas*. The Arabs, if not quite "co-religionists" (as my guidebook called all Western white folks), were bent on my marking the night somehow; so I went toward the door. The police would stop me if I was trespassing.

As I neared them though—and then stepped past through the wide doorway three times my height—the younger man only said "Soon now," then nodded knowingly as if we shared a secret hope, then tapped his watch.

It was a church, yes. Just inside the door was a high stone wall with several gigantic sooty paintings of Jesus in various quandaries, ringed by the usual helpless disciples. By now apparently all alone in a huge roofed silence, I told myself not to hunt for signs but to roam here mystified till something or someone actually broke in on me crying "Death to the Infidel!" or "Step this way for perpetual bliss."

The silence deepened like night on a black plain. To my right I saw a curving set of worn stairs and decided to climb them—eighteen steps that opened on a wide low room maybe twelve yards square with a clutch of candle flames on my left. I moved toward them and was faced by an altar as cluttered as any schoolboy's room—tapers, modern Greek icons in toxic pastels of Mary and Jesus expertly boned, bloodless and cool. But the altar itself was an honest stone slab like a dining table on yard-high legs, and under the table was a low stone ledge with what looked like a broad disc in polished silver. It had an apparent hole in the midst, six inches across.

A voice said "Jesus - Christ - crucified - here"—a deep voice creaky with age or misuse and apparently close.

While my nerves still rattled, I looked round slowly. Behind on my left was a dark alcove.

An old man sat there robed like an Orthodox priest or monk—full bat-costume in dusty black with the standard Greek-priest mushroom hat, the full white beard with dried remains of recent snacks, the Santa Claus cheeks.

When I met his milky wandering eye, he gestured hard toward the silver medallion. "Reach in there. Stone - where - Jesus - Christ - crucified." If his voice went deeper, it would trip earthquakes. He held a fistful of narrow candles with a small cashbox on his bellied lap— you apparently bought your candles from him—and on the floor beside his chair was a roll of American toilet paper for his next john-call.

He'd yet to try to sell me a candle; but I found another fifty shekel note, laid it in his box and took a thin taper. I lit it from one at the side of the altar, set it up in a small tub of sand; then I briskly came as near to prayer as I'd come in years. I asked whatever might hear me for work—for my tired eyes somehow cleaned and strengthened, my right hand steadied, my pictures deepened and taught the old elusive facts again of how the world looks and what it's for. Then I bent to reach the disc. It ringed an actual hole, jet black; and one last brake in my mind said *no*.

But the monk said "Reach."

I was half bent over. I put my right hand into the hole up past my wrist. The air inside was decidedly cooler than the odorous room; but when I felt around in the dark, my fingers touched nothing.

The voice said *"Reach."*

My own mind told me to use my left hand—I must have thought I could spare that easier if the expected unseen jaw ground down. But again my wiggling fingers found nothing, far as they reached. I'd have to kneel to thrust in deeper—why though, for what? I glanced to the monk.

His hand was huge now and aimed me on.

So I got to my knees nearer the hole, then reached till my elbow vanished inward.

The voice said "Now. Golgotha - here."

Golgotha, Calvary—the Place of the Skull, the hill where Jesus bled to death in spring daylight. First my fingers clenched in fear—the mouth would scissor down this instant and take the arm I'd volunteered. But I knew this was a tourist stop; I had to be safe (where though were the tourists?). Then while I couldn't begin to see down that black hole, my fist spread open and my fingers moved. They found the chiseled sides of a socket in rough live rock maybe eight inches square—a neat chill socket.

The voice said "Cross was standing there - inside - your - hand."

I looked behind for human company.

The monk was in place, his piercing eyes, his tin cashbox, the roll of American toilet paper—a human at least, eight feet away. But he said it over, "Cross of Jesus Christ here now, here - in - your - hand."

My strong right hand, that had served me well but had started to tire these past two years, was rummaging now in the deep-hewn hole where a cross had stood. Like a reasonably sane and well-read man, I might have leaned back on my haunches or got to my feet and thought I'd check this out tomorrow in an up-to-date guide—what were the chances this was the place? (all but certain, I later read). But I stayed huddled, my whole arm reaching.

And somehow through that frozen groping in that tight place, my literal skin uncovered every sizable cruel act of my life—acts caused by me—and it fed them up the veins of my arm till each act stood, stark clear, between my eyes and the lip of a hole no bigger than the crown of a stovepipe hat. Each came as a face—none bloody or blue, no suicides or actual murders but each a genuine victim of me (though almost none had truly blamed me). The spotted dog I blinded with a slingshot when I was nine. The mother I let die more or less hardup and desperately lonesome. A wife I'd more than half deprived of the care a willing partner earns. Her willing but finally balked successors. Two sons for whom I'd set my bleak example of strength—a single rider, clear-eyed and generally well-intentioned to humankind but aimed away at his private pleasure and his taste for ease. And upwards of a hundred more, the beautiful line of bodies I'd used as personal fuel.

In under twenty seconds, still kneeling, I'd watched that set of human faces sacrificed by me to myself and now gone far past reach or repair. I stayed sane enough to know I was not the world's worst vermin nor other ravenous intentional beast; but maybe for the first time in my life, I saw the shape of all my crimes.

The monk was suddenly on his feet and rustling to fill a plastic bag with what looked like breadcrusts, his toilet paper and the shut tin box. I stayed in place but watched him work his stout old bones in silent pain and hoped he'd somehow look my way with the hope of mercy— I was that bad off. When he'd stuffed the bag and found an old umbrella behind him, his eyes stayed on the altar above me as he leaned to blow the candles out. Once he was done he stood behind me; and I waited to hear the voice again, saying *Leave* or *Stay*. But he laid a broad hand on top of my head—no word at all. I heard him shuffling back to his corner, then off to the stairs with his personal goods. When no sound came I looked around.

He'd stopped on the top step and faced me finally. It was not his Christmas (that would come later, Greek Orthodox Christmas); but he said "Joy - now"—that had to be it, just two clear words. Then he tapped a large black watch on his wrist as if joy lurked at the foot of the stairs and he started down.

Joy? Glory? Peace on Earth? I was not a church-goer. Most days in the past twenty years, I've barely been able to call myself a firm believer in any Cause-for-Visible-Things, any Cause that knows my personal name and maps my path. But when the monk's hat vanished downward—they had to be closing; hadn't the young policeman said "Soon"?—I saw no immediate reason, or way, to haul myself upright and follow. The weight of damaged lives inside me—visible faces, most of them live—was big and dark. And I knew I was neither drunk nor on the verge of a crying jag this far from home nor unrealistic. Every ounce of the weight I felt was *lead*, that dense and poisonous.

By then, again from childhood books, I'd recalled some sense of where I might be. Wasn't Calvary Hill long since enclosed in the ancient sprawl of the Church of the Holy Sepulchre?—the Emperor Constantine's attempt to join the sites of Jesus' death and his rock-cave tomb. Where though was the tomb? Since that one space had radiated sufficient hope of death confounded to spark Crusades and seas of blood around its door two thousand years, I thought one wasteful middle-aged man might give it a try, if time was left. I hauled my arm out and went downstairs in a quiet hurry.

The younger policeman was still at the door; and nearer me, with his broad back turned, was what I'd guessed was Shoeshine George in his ragged vestment—a priest or monk. I'd forgot poor George. He'd brought me here for whatever reason; was he done with me now? Would he know me here in this much light? I even thought "If his ulcer has healed, I'm leaving tomorrow"—not that I wished him any harm. I was just that far from giving in to the night itself and its uncanny air.

I walked toward the men; the policeman saw me; the man in the vestment went on talking, then also looked. It was nearly George but maybe not quite. I'd likewise never seen him well-lit; and since the vestment dragged the floor, it hid any possible wound or peg leg.

As he saw me the man came close to smiling but never spoke.

At least I could see that his robe was worse in several ways than George's smock—it had once been a heavy vermilion velvet but was mangy now, worn to the threads; and the gold braid had tarnished to bronze.

I asked the policeman "Is the Sepulchre here?" If time was up he'd just say no.

But he pointed in at the heart of the place, past the high wall with the sooty paintings, and again said "Soon."

The tomb stands free beneath the wide dome and is long since hid in a garish box that shields its live rock from the gouging hands of pilgrims (one mad Caliph all but hacked down the natural cave in 1009). By the one low door are twisted columns and, overhead, a crowd of oil lamps—mostly dark as I came near. But again I bent to look inside; and there beyond an anteroom maybe six feet long was an even older monk upright against the far wall—a whiter beard, gigantic eyes. I stood on the threshold, hoping he'd wave me in like George but he held still. I turned to see if I was alone. In a way I never stopped to question, it seemed very urgent—despite my nearly gone beliefs—that I be alone through whatever came next. I stood convicted of rightful blame for all my harm. The shadowy choir and the screened altar were empty and silent, close behind me.

So I ducked and entered the anteroom, not pausing to think who'd stood here before me—Mary Magdalene, Peter and John, Constantine, St. Francis and the gap-toothed Wife of Bath, Mark Twain, Herman Melville and T. E. Lawrence to start a list (is there any other place in which more world-famed figures have stood?). At once an unknown odor met me—not harsh but strong as a sweet narcotic, like amber warmed in oil of cloves. There was no smoke of incense, no visible source; the odor poured from the low walls around me, the trapped air of a distant planet or as if I were under a whole new kind of ocean water that let me breathe.

I took a deep breath, looked toward the old monk—still no signal— and entered the tomb. It's a small room maybe eight feet long by five feet wide with an eight foot ceiling. The walls and floor and the low shelf where Jesus lay are shielded by marble slabs again; and over the shelf is a big icon of the subsequent rising, with stunned onlookers— Jesus airborne over this space—and another forest of silver lamps. The same thick odor was all the air there was to breathe; and suddenly I thought I'd fall, hard on my face—if I didn't rush out.

But before I took the first step back, the old monk held out another candle. When my hand took it, he said "This is surely your Christmas, sir." A mild voice with again an echo of British officers decades past—

enormous patience, self-serene. When I kept my silence, he said "You are an American gentleman?"

I felt as gentle as a jackhammer pounding its way through granite in summer sun; but I nodded toward his imperturbable brow and eyes, then reached for my wallet.

His arm and hand were thin as a bird's leg, but he stopped me with a serious frown. "Your Christmas, sir—I know—is tonight." He pointed toward a few last candles burning by the shelf.

Somehow I needed to know his name. I said "Brother, my name is Bridge."

It pleased him and he thought it through; then he said "My brother, I am Anastos, which means 'Resurrection.' "

I saw the ludicrous irony of my whole life embodied here. In the warm promise of Christmas night, where had I come to mark the time?—the ultimate grave and me alone as any corpse. So sure, I'd take Anastos' offer. I'd have my Christmas at the core of death. I lit my thin free candle and set it in the circular stand at what had been the bloody head or feet of Jesus. And since I'd knelt upstairs on Calvary, I thought I'd balance off the visit and also kneel beside this shelf. It couldn't hurt me worse than the smooth cross-socket I'd rummaged in a few yards back upstairs on the hill.

Before I could move, Brother Anastos crossed himself, kissed his hand and reached to an icon on the tomb's back wall—the Virgin in grief.

I thought he was pointing it out to me, and I said some complimentary word. It was maybe twenty inches by twelve, deep under nineteenth-century varnish.

But Anastos tugged at its lower right corner; and the icon folded back, a small gate. Behind it, like some banker's home-safe, was a rough dark space—deep brown, nearly black. Then he took my wrist and guided it to touch the space.

Rock again, rough-hewn but worn like all these spaces by a billion hands. It was warmer than me and seemed to be the source of the air I'd breathed for two minutes.

Anastos said "The tomb itself."

His hand still held me; I still stroked the rock.

Then he met my eyes with a smile as joyful as any I'd known since my young mother's fifty years back. "Actual stone of Jesus' tomb." His palm pressed mine against the rock to print me indelibly with memory at least; then he let me go.

I took a step back and rubbed my fingers on tight dry lips. *Actual stone,* as though this were all the stone on Earth. That instant I felt it might have been—the breeding motherlode of rock. I didn't kneel but I bowed as deep as my spine would go, and I touched my lips to the old man's wrist.

When I rose he blessed my face with a slow cross dug in the air with just his fingers. He said "Your life commences now."

As real as the thrust of a hidden thorn, I felt a jolt in my right thigh— not pain so much as a muffled spasm, a doubling-up deep in the bone, the certain knowledge that something had broke and would never mend. I told myself it was tiredness, nerves; and when I'd turned and left the tomb, I made a quick way back through the church past both policemen (no sign of George) and somehow straight up the shadowy path toward Jaffa Gate. No soul in sight, no sound but the standard hum of bodies— thousands of bodies dreaming of rescue.

When I climbed out into the relative light of Jaffa Square, I checked my watch—ten forty-five. The square seemed empty like all the streets; and with what I'd undergone since my last sleep, I suddenly thought I'd never manage to spend the rest of this night alone. I knew I wasn't looking for skin. I'd gladly settle for one like creature breathing near me, not running in fright. Maybe Jabril's friendly kin were back from church? I looked toward the cafe—shut and dark. But I couldn't give up. I walked to the steps and faced the door. Behind the glass I thought

I could see a white shape move, face-high in the blackness; and then I heard dry scratching at the wood like cold rat's teeth. I stood my ground and the door came open.

"Christmas, sir. Good Christmas to you." The voice was light, almost a child's.

Maybe I'd been right—it was Jabril, already back and still heavily bundled.

But then he came to the forward sill. It was the waiter, young Samir alone and wrapped in a black parka that looked sufficient for Arctic hikes. He limped down the steps with easy speed and the same creased brow he'd worn through dinner. Then he shook my hand, searched my face and said "Sorry, sir."

"Sorry" again; he'd remembered his "sorry." What could he think I blamed him for? I said "*Not* sorry. You did a fine job. Are you finished now?"

"Finished?" The word seemed foreign to him. But before I could find a synonym, he gave his first smile. "*Very* finished, sir."

I was about to tell him "Good night" when something in his plucky face made me ask where he lived.

He pointed south. "In Tuqua, sir. Near Bethlehem."

I couldn't believe he owned a car, and surely buses had stopped by now. "How will you go?"

His smile hung on and he waved with a flourish down to his feet. "I am walking to Bethlehem very fast. Then I think my brother will drive me on. He has a taxi and I hope he is waiting."

I recalled Sam limping hours ago to serve our dinner, his steady frown. "How far is it to Bethlehem?"

"Sir, nine kilometers."

"And what if your brother isn't there?"

"I walk six kilometers more to Tuqua." No sign he dreaded the long prospect.

The night was dry but chilly by now, not quite freezing; and this man risked walking nearly ten miles? I asked him if he'd work tomorrow.

"Oh yes, I come at ten in the morning."

Well, here was a Christmas deed I could do—a first small payment on the debts laid out before my eyes on Calvary. I said "My car is in the New City not far from here. Please let me drive you."

"Oh *no*. You just arrived here, sir. You go to rest."

I guessed some member of Jabril's family had told him I was new in town, and again I heard the monk in the tomb say how my life began tonight. How though and for what? Whatever, for now I was bent on driving this lame exhausted man to his home before daybreak. I said "You will do me an honor, my friend." And for the first time, I heard my voice assume the formal music of Arab courtesy.

Sam paused to convert my words to sense. Then he said "Sir, thank you" and bowed. When I turned to lead us out of the gate, he fell in beside me with a burst of what was almost dancing, a graceful hop and spin on his damaged leg.

But my mind suddenly showed me one more face it feared I would harm tonight. Before we'd walked ahead ten yards, I felt the dread that someway now young Sam would pay for my reckless offer. I'd drive him deep into West Bank country; we'd be stopped and searched by soldiers. Out this late with a unknown American, Sam stood the chance of being shamed in public at least. I tried not to let myself see the worst I'd heard was possible for him; but then I saw my own cold body in a rocky trench, my throat cut through in a straight line—bled dry by smiling Sam and his kin.

No, we easily left the lights of New Jerusalem and were in the dark of open country in four or five minutes. At the first road-fork, the car lights struck a "Merry Christmas" banner strung above the way to Bethlehem—the words in English with minimal glitter. Just that first glimpse of normal Western holiday trappings eased me a little, and I thought of the lean Franciscan's claim that Bethlehem was closed to cars till midnight anyhow. I glanced at Sam. "Shall we try to drive on into town or leave you outside? Where will you meet your brother?"

Sam rolled his window down a few inches and smelled the air before he faced me—no smile, dead-level. "My uncle is certainly gone so late."

Not fifteen minutes ago he'd said his *brother* was almost surely waiting. Had I heard wrong? Was this the next rung down on the ladder to my unmanned confusion and ruin, a down I'd maybe triggered by telling a reflex lie about my faith and then refusing the ticket it won me? Commencement indeed. Or was I being steadily lured, on the stony skin of this dry land, to serve Samir in ways that CBS World News would know about by dawn tomorrow as I was sped toward a Beirut hostage cellar by the openhearted terrorist kin of Tiny Tim? Whatever, the next words came in hard through the crown of my head like inspiration; and while I understood they were wild, I said them fast. "If you'll just guide me, I'll drive you home."

Sam was looking ahead, intent on the two-lane white road before us. "Yes sir, now I am guiding you."

Right. "Will the soldiers be checking so late?"

"I know the soldiers. I will talk to them."

Right.

When we'd gone another half mile, Sam said "Perhaps no soldiers will find us."

I heard myself say "That would be fine."

Sam said "Very fine for me at least."

"They wouldn't harm you?"

He faced me squarely, drew out a worn Jordanian passport, opened the cover and held it to me. By the panel lights I could see what I guessed was Sam's name in Arabic and an out-of-date picture. With a finger he tapped at a circular ink-stamp under his name. The circle was black, the size of a dime, with a triangle in it. He tapped it again. "This sign here, sir, means 'Dangerous man.' The soldiers do not trust Samir."

Right. Danger. Of what and when? Yet I saw I was someway thoroughly right to be here now. I was on this spot, as I'd been elsewhere so many right times long years ago, for a keen clear purpose that would show itself if I watched and lasted—I knew that much. I'd wait to see the threat uncover its shape and smell and name its price. We drove on up the hilly road in deeper night past what seemed occasional fields and gullies but never a sign of human life, no lamp or upright moving shadow—man or sheep or heavenly host. I told myself I should feel at least the singular charm of nearing Bethlehem itself near midnight on Christmas Eve, led by nothing but weak starshine and a local boy in practical need. I only thought "No soldiers please. Nobody to slow us, wherever we go." But I said no more.

And Sam stayed entirely still beside me, breathing deeply at intervals that seemed inhuman—long silent waits like a creature with adequate private fuel.

Another few minutes and on my right far up the road, by a single light bulb high on a pole, I saw a squat building with a small white dome. At once from childhood memory, I knew it had to be Rachel's Tomb—Rachel, the favorite wife of Jacob, mother to Joseph and Benjamin.

Only now did Sam crouch forward and point to the right—"Here, here."

I noticed he'd started dropping the *sir;* but that discovery was swamped by a sight at the next road-fork—a sign saying left to Bethlehem, right to Hebron (Jesus' birthplace or Abraham's tomb, choose one but quick). I bore to the right as Sam indicated, for Abraham; and we picked up speed to pour ahead through deeper dark—if that could be—till whatever shine poor Bethlehem threw on the left skyline was well behind us; and nothing whatever faced us here but blackness unlike any I'd faced. Well, sure. Pour on. My work was done; I'd take what came.

Sam looked ahead and never turned, but he said at last "You will honor my home by visiting now."

I could hear it was not so much a question as a fact recorded. I thanked him and said I knew he was tired.

"You are my friend. You will visit my home."

"Sam, you're kind. You're my young brother and I'm truly honored but surely they're sleeping." There had to be a family waiting—not one Arab goes home alone.

He let a half mile slide beneath us. "They will wake to see my friend, believe me. You will drink some coffee and eat with me."

The whole lamb dinner was still aboard; I doubted I could eat a crumb. But I heard the arms of Eastern welcome lock around me once again; and I saw no way, nor wanted to, to flee politely. So we lapsed again and drove ahead.

Maybe two miles later Sam sat forward and studied the road close to the glass. "In fifty meters you will turn to the left."

I heard a feverish rise in his voice, and I might as well have been embedded in solid night, but I shifted down and slowed by half.

"No danger yet."

Yet. As we reached the turn, I could see the new road was only a little narrower and paved, though still there were no clear signs of life— no house or light. It was only when I'd taken the left that I noticed the sky, this far south, was suddenly lined with infinite stars so big they seemed like live faces too ardent to watch. "You specialize in stars down here"—I meant to sound easy.

"You have seen nothing yet." Sam was watching me but his hand came up and pointed on.

We rode on silent in the pitiful hoop of our headlights for another stretch that could have been either two miles or ten—I was that lost now, that certain I moved toward some hard trial, though my hands and mind were calm as in my steady youth.

At last Sam faced the road again. "I will tell you soon to stop the car." He leaned again to the glass intently. "Slow now and stop near that big stone."

The whole land was one big stone and ten billion pebbles, but I slowed and pulled to the rugged shoulder by a white outcrop.

Sam said "You drive very well, I think."

It seemed a solemn offering to me, the night's next gift. I even thanked him.

But he'd opened his door and was climbing out. The lights were still on; he crossed in front of them, waving me toward him with both strong hands as if I were some new pet he was breaking. As he moved, his limp was healing before me. His legs were level and he stood maybe half a head taller here.

So I killed the engine to join him in the freezing dark—it was much colder now—but when I stood upright on the road, Sam was already hid to my left.

"Come here to me." The *sir* was now completely gone. Did that make me his trusted friend or willing victim? I crossed the black space, and what was waiting was an open hand that fumbled for mine.

"I am leading you." The voice was almost surely Sam's; but the hand was larger, the skin was leather. Still I took its lead; and for a stretch, the ground dipped through a scrubby ravine; then a scramble up through thorns and grit. The hand dropped mine. I was on what felt like a broad flat rock. The stars burned harder overhead; beyond and up a long steep hill was a single flame—a lantern maybe (the light was yellow), though it held its place as firmly as if it sat on an altar, surviving change.

Sam's voice said "You are going there now."

The hand was behind me, then on my shoulder. It pushed me slightly and I climbed on in air so cold my lips were sealed in a thinner smile than the French Franciscan's. I longed to show his arctic eyes this outcome of his ticket-brush with one dazed Yank who refused to lie, and his power crowded the rest of my mind—him and the voice of the monk in the tomb, "Commences now." Let it then; I was ready to meet it, whatever it brought; and though I felt entirely alone—no sound of Sam—I walked the straightest possible line toward the rigid flame.

*

It shone from a wide door—open and lit—in a squared-off low house, white in the dark. And when I'd climbed the final slope and was ten yards off, I could see it was one oil lantern set on the inside edge of the front doorsill. A normal white plaster wall stood ten feet behind it, but there was no other sign of life. I looked around for Sam behind me—again no sign. I tested my mind. It had never been calmer. I walked toward the door, then stopped at the sill in reach of the lamp. It lit enough of an empty room to show four walls and a concrete floor. I heard a snatch of a song or whistle, and I looked behind me.

All below down the rough slope, the Earth was washed in blue starshine—only the ridge of rounded hills beyond the road was shaded now. I'd been in various deserts before, on mountains above the dirt of cities; but these stars burned with a whole new strength that was half alarming and showed me sights I'd failed to notice till my eyes adjusted. To my left the ground fell steeply away; the house was poised on a jagged lip at the rim of a pit. To my right near the road, there seemed to be a level field; and in the midst of a shrubby patch, a black shape moved like a purposeful dwarf.

It would crouch to the ground, then rise, shake its arms, move a yard or so, then crouch again and repeat the motion. At last it rose and started toward me—a tall man maybe, in powerful strides.

I looked behind me—the lantern still, no one in the room.

The man came on; both arms were burdened with heavy loads.

I thought the monk's main words again; and I walked toward the man, entirely reckless.

It was Sam very likely but firmer footed, barely limping.

As I moved down on him, he said "No. Stay. Go in the house."

I held my ground and when he was near, enough light struck him to show he held what looked like two dirty objects—rocks, maybe clods?

He came on at me and held them out. "We will eat these now."

They were some kind of tuber dug from the ground—giant yams? Turnips maybe, the first I'd seen since family meals in Depression days; and I asked the first normal question in hours. "You grew these here?"

"My mother," Sam said. He pointed behind me toward the door.

I looked and saw a short brown face, a five-foot body in dark robes of green and black that fell from the crown of her head to the floor, her small bare feet.

"My mother speaks no English, sir. She welcomes you."

Her brown face nodded beneath its mantle, and a wide smile spread. Two strong hands spread palm-open toward me.

Sam stopped beside me. "In, sir. Please."

Sir, the *sir* was back again.

His mother took the heavy lantern and stepped aside, nodding yes. So I took the last steps too and entered.

A half hour later by the round wall-clock, Sam and I were seated in sockfeet against the cold wall on the colder floor, exhausting our few common subjects—his boyhood friend who was now in Portland, Oregon (would I take him a gift when I returned?), the months that Sam spent last year in prison for "throwing one stone" at an army truck, the details of my sons again and the lives they led.

His mother had brought out thick wool cushions and a gray blanket with which she draped my shoulders and arms; Sam stayed in his parka. Then she'd vanished deeper into the house and silently made us scalding mint tea which she served in glasses iridescent with gold and shades of aquamarine like ancient Roman glass unearthed. As she bent before us, I'd seen the blue tattoos on her forehead and cheeks, at the ends of her mouth, on her upper lip and strong square chin—small marks grouped in patterns of three like a fox's track (I'd read they were charms against headache and the Evil Eye). Smiling, she'd left us and vanished again in the perfect silence beyond our room. We were still lit only by the lantern and whatever starlight fell through the door, still open on the freezing night. There was no other heat inside but the bright two inches of lantern flame.

And soon Sam asked me the first hard question. "Sir, why are you here, alone and sad?" His eyes were baffled. Who was this creature under his roof who'd chosen to wander the Earth alone, what fate had Allah struck me with, did I know why and how did I bear it? Surely soon I would choose a new wife and have new children, or my heart would dry—he used that phrase.

I gave him true but brief replies. I was a lifelong picture-painter; divorced with two grown sons, one married (I omitted the several gone companions); I had no present prospect of marriage and felt I was years too old for children.

Sam thought about it. "You will go back soon to live with your sons?"

How was I going to tell a young man, so plainly a part of the world's immense majority of clannish kin, that in America now an old-aged life among your children is more unlikely than universal wealth for the poor? I only said "Maybe when I'm very old, if I live that long, they'll take me in." I could feel I was grinning—the hope was wild.

"You are old now." Sam didn't smile but reached to touch my all-white hair as if it were some snow leopard between us.

I could see he meant me plain respect—I was old in a house where age was prized and kept at hand. His mother's hair had been a coarse brown for all her wrinkles—you knew such hair would make stout rope if you plaited it tight. I said "Are you here alone with your mother?"

"My mother is very old like you. She says she is more than fifty years, but all her life was spent in the desert—she does not really know these things like age and time. We are Bedu, sir. She still goes out in the spring with our sheeps." In this cold light Sam's face had grown younger. The forehead had smoothed; his eyes were somehow rested and cleared. Surely he couldn't be twenty-five.

I said "Will you try to marry soon?"

Again he held back. But then he grinned, his first real grin and wide as the door. "You see I am only a weak boy. I am safe at home for some more years." He made a childish blank face; then waved around at the room, the walls—only the clock, a pale framed photo of Sam airbrushed to near-extinction, a framed diploma in Arabic from Sam's school maybe, and the frozen air that now was seeping into my core. His home—safe, he thought.

I suddenly knew he wasn't safe; something waited to do him harm. I must have shivered under the blanket.

Sam's eyes went to sharp black points. "You are ready now?"

"For what?"

He faced the narrow door that led elsewhere in the house; then called one word in a near whisper, surely an order.

I watched the door as intently as he. Who or what would come and why?

A shuffling sound, a single thunk; and then the mother entered quickly, her feet still bare. She brought a round tray with china bowls and set them by us on the clean-swept floor. Another quick trip and she brought huge circular flaps of flat bread, moist and warm.

My relief at the sight of anything warm was so compelling, I was all but stunned; and before I could thank her and wonder how she'd summoned a meal in this cold hut without a sound, she left again.

Sam carefully told me the names of things—the turnips were sliced and lightly fried in olive oil, still hot and crisp on a bed of fried rice. There were olives, chopped greens in a piercing vinegar, thick goat-yogurt fierce with a high ammonia reek, and orange jam for the grainy bread. As he named each dish, he dipped me a taste on a fold of bread.

Odd as they were in combination, I ate them all like a long-lost sailor. "Does your mother wait for you here each night? Do you eat this late?"

"Sir, no. I eat in Jerusalem. All this is for you, our celebration for your first visit to our sad country."

"Your mother was sleeping?"

"Yes, since dark. She heard our car."

Ours. The car was parked a half mile off; but in this clean air, sound would carry far. "She was very kind to cook this much."

Sam waited as if to contradict me but then said "She is my mother—I told you."

That instant a barefoot child rushed in through the door from the night—a boy maybe ten in a man's army jacket that fell to his bare knees. He shot a hot stream of words at Sam, and his arm kept jabbing at the downhill air.

Sam leapt upright and slipped on his shoes. "The soldiers now are down at your car. I will tell them you are my friend and safe." I started to rise but he forced me down. "Not you, not now. I will let you know." Then he was gone with the child behind him.

The car had a rental sticker and license; my name was on the rental agreement inside the glove box, but I'd left nothing personal behind. Had some Israeli patrol decided I was lost or kidnaped, dead or a spy? (Sam had mentioned spies as we drove through the night. On two occasions he'd pointed out dark houses we passed—"This man is a spy. He will soon be gone; no one will find him, even the hawks." He pronounced it *spee*.) Had I got young Sam and his mother in dutch— an even more ominous stamp in his papers, his house blown up? Would the soldiers believe him or climb up here and grill me or worse? I'd after all plunged myself in the heart of the dark West Bank, scorched as it was—a land fought over these five thousand years, no sign of peace and maybe no hope.

Again I was calm, though in my mind I no longer saw my damaged kin, only Sam's hot face as it ran off to save me; and all I thought was *Son, son*—I must have meant Sam, with the leery soldiers in their hard light, another victim pinned at the edge of his turnip patch in sight of his Bedouin mother's roof—her winter quarters, this concrete tent. His face was white and slatted with moving shadows like bars. I stood and fumbled into my shoes; I'd fully explain myself to the soldiers and free us all or make loud Yankee protest cries.

But there again in the outside door stood the messenger boy, a little breathless. And dim behind him was a grizzled man in the checkered

black headcloth worn by every terrorist east of Gibraltar. The boy
stepped up to the still again and said "Oh please?"

I beckoned him in as if this were mine. And when he was in, I asked
if Samir was safe with the soldiers.

The boy only looked back to the man and waved him in with the
start of a laugh.

The man was my age, maybe older, with the terrorist's standard
three-day growth of beard on hanging jowls and neck. Wrinkled pants
and a tan suit jacket from the 1940s hung on him loose, two sizes large.

They both went to the far-end wall and hunkered there silent, fixed
on me.

Did nobody out here bother to sleep? The clock said nearly a quarter
past midnight, but hadn't it said that a long while ago? I tried again—
"Samir is coming?"

They faced each other; the boy nodded and the man laughed once.
"Samir, Samir." With two palms down he signed me to sit.

I took one long look through the door. Just since Sam left, the stars
had greatly multiplied. Broad clotted bands of light were laid from
zenith to ground, though still the car and Sam were hid—and the
soldiers, if any soldiers had stopped. I went to my place and crouched
again in the heavy blanket. By then its harsh clean animal smell came
like a welcome offer to shield me. When I looked again the boy had
lowered the lamp by half.

The room was all shadow, but he and the man were smiling now
and nodding at me. The man's hands went on in the air before him,
urging me down.

Some bread was left and a few cold scraps. I tried to wave them over
to join me, which was maybe a try at saving my neck—isn't it strictest
Muslim duty to honor the man you break bread with? True or not, I
clung to the hope like a signed safe-conduct.

Smiling still they refused the food. The boy cupped his thin belly to
claim he was full, though he looked half starved. The man put both

hands up by his cheek, closed his eyes and made the sign for peaceful sleep (or was it prayer?). When I looked puzzled he made clear signals— I should lie flat down.

I stayed upright and his smile quit.

With no more coaching the boy said "Rest" and smoothed the air as if to ease the line of my body.

I was bone-tired, so numb my frame felt nearly transparent. I felt I could punch holes through my chest with gentle fists; I knew my legs would refuse to stand if I tried to make a lunge for the road, whatever was down there or ever had been. Whatever was *here* with these two watchers posted beside me. I thought there was a serious chance my life would end if I obeyed them and lay down now. The tender sides of my throat were cringing at the real chance of a swipe from a long blade—my mind saw a black old-time iron blade with a dried bone handle. It could slice right through to my spine in an instant, almost no pain. In some entirely baffling way though, the serious question I thought of now was not my life or tortured death but the livest mystery of all—was any of this hour real, in this apparent outpost of hope or dream? *This hour?* What night and year was this, what nameless world, what target for light or black-hole dark?

I can only tell my next two moves—I can't explain or justify. Calm as a young lord, I tore a palm-sized piece of bread, sopped it in oil, chewed it slowly and swallowed hard. That showed at least I was human and helpless. Then I lay down long on my right side and faced the door, not seeing the boy and man (were they here?). A final thought cut through me, painless—*Christmas, Bridge: day's surely near.* In an instant I slept.

Next it was quiet and colder still, but my eyes opened on the door to the world. All the low air near the ground, all down the hill, was locked in dark. But the bands of stars were joining now and bending inward on themselves like grinding gates, broad slots of seamless pure white shine that poured from unimagined depths beyond the night. The man and boy?—there was only an empty wall where they'd crouched, though the lantern burned on lower still. I waited for what felt like a week, then raised my head for any sound. But the house might not have been around me—the only noise was a faint oiled purr as if those gates in the sky still turned. Yet what I could see of the sky was paler, a uniform unblemished bowl of gray (I was facing east; had I slept till dawn?). The clock was too dim, but I thought I could see it was snagged on midnight—a quarter past. I bit down on my tongue and lips; then dug a fingernail into my temple—I was feeling at least, one hint of life.

Right, then. I'd try to rise in silence, find my shoes and hope the hill still waited below me, not to mention the car. First though my mind recalled the hours since Calvary and the tomb at least—the guiding monks, the line of offended faces and names, my life commencing, the black and radiant dream I'd undergone with Sam and was held in now. Or was I dreaming; was this my life at last, here now, and all my crowded past was the dream? I knew only one word, honest *thanks*, though still I expected my death was near. Then I raised to my elbow, shook the blanket off my arms and sat upright with eyes I knew were truly rested.

To my left in the door to the back of the house, a new shape was standing; it trembled slightly on warmer air. I waited and saw it was Sam's mother, loaded with something—not food again. No, her arms were up at her chest and bearing another dark wool blanket, more cover for me. Then behind her, a whole head taller, was maybe Sam—a man at least, white-faced and grave.

I said "I must have fallen asleep."

They made no move, just the faint trembling like a thrill in the air.

I said "The soldiers left us alone."

Sam's mother turned back and smiled up at him.

He gave her no answer, her or me, though maybe he shook his head a little—maybe a no.

I said "You're safe though? Nobody's hurt you?"

"Sir, yes, I have been hurt very bad but not by you or those young soldiers." He pointed as though they were at the door.

"Sam, what can I do?"

"You have done it now. You trusted me."

I said I did and looked to see any blood or bruise on him, but his head was dim, and his body was hid. I said "I'm sorry, Sam—thank you both." My trained American-tourist hand went to my pocket; I'd pay at least for what I ate and the life they'd spared me. But my mind refused the tidy command. I must try to leave as clean as I came. I braced my arms to stand and slowly got to my feet—I seemed intact. When I turned to fold the blanket though, the buried spasm in my thigh repeated itself, this time like a savage tear at the bone. It threw me back, crouching in place; and I looked to Sam. "Sorry, I'm stiff."

"Not sorry, no. You were welcome forever."

I noticed the *were* and wondered if I'd spoiled his gift (whatever it was, I thought I'd received it—I was more than half wrong).

But then his mother came on toward me. Even upright her head was only a foot above me. She lowered her arms, shifted the blanket; and there was a child with wide dark eyes and strong black hair. How old—a month, two weeks, newborn, a boy?

It gnawed its fist and watched me with Sam's fearless gaze as if it already understood that children come as guardians for their older kin and are on duty always.

Sam had gone to the lantern, raised the flame and stood beside it, watching me.

Still unsure, I took the risk. "A fine new boy."

Sam nodded and moved to form a huddle with me, his mother, the watchful child.

Again I said "A son."

The mother's eyes were on me, beaming. However she smiled I had to be right—she was not the child's mother; this child was surely not born tonight; Sam was truly her son.

I wondered if his wife was still weak or, if young and pretty, was she hid from the sudden curious stranger? I said to Sam "Your wife is well?"

He took a long wait. "Sir, no. My wife is gone. Her name was Ayisha. She was twenty years old. I loved her since I was five years old. One month ago she died in here." He scrubbed at his chest with a slow flat palm as if she'd ended deep inside him.

My mind knew not to say the word *sorry*; sorry would cover nothing now. The child's strong head and learning eyes precluded sorrow and every other deep care but the *now*, his needy present. My hand went out and touched his firm warm cheek, then his forehead. I asked his name.

The mother finally spoke—was it "Hassan"?

The boy's eyes blinked; then came back to me, rapt again. I thought "His life commences now." How?—from *my* touch, this dim late moment in a feast not his, a foreign creed? "No," I told myself, "tired fool, go find your rented bed and sleep." When I stood I bent to kiss the child's fast-pulsing head, the fontanel. It was there I'd loved my own sons most in infancy, the cusp of death, warmer than me.

Sam faced me now with open arms; we clasped like long-lost biblical brothers, Jacob and Esau, friends at last.

I tried to say thanks; his dry hand stopped me.

He said "I take you now to your car. We have kept it safe."

We—who was *we*? "Where you and I left it?"

He nodded once and moved to the door.

"Sam, no, I can find my way. It's near sunrise, you've got to be frozen, you really must sleep." I didn't think that—shortly, if I gauged the time—he was due back at his limping job (or would he limp?).

He said "Bad dogs. I will take you past them."

I'd heard distant barks in the night, nothing close. Still I turned again to his mother to thank her.

She'd already taken my place on the mat as if to claim my body heat before it failed. And of course she watched the child, not me.

I could barely see the line of his profile, fixed on her, and his reaching hand that dug at her breast. He already knew who he needed and why, which was more than I'd known most years of my life.

Suddenly then Sam led the way out, limping again but stronger than back at the cafe all those eons past. One shorthaired black dog stood on a rock ten yards to our left but he looked harmless. Below us was one low tree, bare and gnarled—a dead olive maybe.

Sam silently went that far and stopped, then offered his hand.

It seemed important to give him at least a small return on a night this strange and somehow useful. Surely he'd take a gift for the child; I had one fifty-dollar bill.

Before I could reach in for it though, Sam shook his head and said "Bridge Boatner, you are welcome forever."

How did he know my full name?—I'd never told him, Jabril hadn't known, my passport still was deep in my pocket. *Leave it, Bridge. Don't ask. Leave now.* So I faced him then in the desert shine of another day, knowing that we were David and Jonathan in my child's Bible or Jacob again and his nocturnal wrestler—an apt farewell to one of the crucial nights of my life. I said "You're welcome in my mind, Sam, forevermore. You, your boy and any of yours." There in place that moment, I meant it.

He gave his gravest nod and bow, not quite an acceptance. He'd likely been struck too hard by death to trust anything not here in his reach and warm to the hand. He looked to the road. "Here, sir, *see.*"

I followed his pointing arm—there, whiter maybe (was it ice on the roof?) but apparently whole, was my actual car with doors and wheels. I felt outlandish gratitude.

When I looked to Sam though, he'd turned and started uphill home, no backward look at me or his desperate garden down the slope or the dawn in progress beyond this purple line of hills, the only brake between our bodies and the Dead Sea shore, Earth's nadir, the pit. Still he'd left his strong welcome in place.

Right. And he'd stay welcome with me. We'd managed to play our odd joint roles in one long curious Christmas Eve—played them *out* in fact, dead-true to ourselves and the world around us, the sky and light and other men's plans. For Sam the night would almost surely shrink to an early memory, an American visitor one winter evening near his first wife's death when his first son was fearless and eagle-eyed. For me it would literally be a commencement—the end of my first life, as I'll explain, and the start of a new. I told myself what felt like a law—I'd never see Sam's face again, never know his family name or his son's. Our business was done.

I turned the car, retracing our tracks; and the visible land lay as I'd guessed it—straight narrow pavement, an unmarked right, then on to the main road with its two choices: *Hebron* to left, *Jerusalem* right. I took the right, due north, and sped. The day leaked steadily in beside me. As I bypassed Bethlehem again—the unlit houses, two-story flats, littered and crumbling—my headlights struck a single shape on the verge of the road in a pocket of mist, a short man wearing a long full cloak. Another monk bound back from mass.

Only when I flanked him close could I see he wore a wine-red ground-length velvet coat with sheep's-wool trim on collar and hat and a straight white beard that reached to his waist—an Arab Santa Claus loose on the road; a mislaid player from a Dickens Christmas, hunting snow. In his fist a bell hung slack to greet the coming day or end his openhanded rounds.

I honked and waved.

He wielded the bell, then gave the final Asian bow I've yet to see. It was solemn as Sam's, and it looked deeply meant.

I stayed in Israel ten more days, avoiding every place I'd touched that first strong night, all avoidable faces—I'd leave them at that high dark pitch. I managed to see the Bethlehem church at five on Christmas afternoon. It was no disappointment; for all its gold and garish trim, the birth cave gives off that same primal force as caves where mankind sheltered ages past and left the shadows of their small hands and the beasts they worshiped, hunted and ate. Around the silver star in the floor that marks the birth-site (a star whose theft caused the Crimean war), I smelled the high iron odor of blood as if a girl had labored here not long ago; and I touched my brow to the points of the star as an Arab child had done just before me.

But afterward to balance my stay, I concentrated on the cooler Jewish and Muslim sites like the new dig south of Temple Mount where young King David's tiny city (1,000 B.C.) was being slowly peeled to light— twenty acres of bleached limestone with at least one obvious toilet-seat observing its imminent three thousandth birthday. In the Muslim dome on Temple Mount, I brushed the rock on which old Abraham half slew Isaac, where the Temple altar would later stand and from which Mohammed's horse soared to God.

Nearby were the walls of houses lit by Roman legions to fire the first Diaspora, then Solomon's cavernous underground quarry from which the Temple stones were hauled a few yards past that breach in the wall where the First Crusade would yet break through in howls for Muslim blood and lives. I took in all the right museums and the dome that covers the Dead Sea scrolls. But since in Poland twenty years past, I'd seen the remains of the camp at Auschwitz, I spared myself the modern shrine in New Jerusalem to six million dead at German hands, with our consent. The dead couldn't need a brief call from me; and after fifty years with myself, I felt I had very little to learn about the monstrous scope of my kind.

I did pass Shoeshine George a few times; his ulcer was drier but still looked killing. He never happened to look my way—or had long since done his part by me and let me pass—and that first free shine lasted well despite cold rain, so we had no occasion to speak. I even passed Sam's cafe close enough to see guests chewing hummus and bread; but Sam never showed at the window or door nor Jabril kicking his ball again in doomed Jesus' path.

*

Right at the end I drove east down the world's deepest rift through Jericho and its palm oasis, the oldest city, up past Gilgal where Samuel hacked Agag in pieces at Yahweh's ark; then on up the winding Jordan valley to Galilee, hearteasing and green—Bethsaida, Capernaum, Magdala, Nain, the beautiful harp-shaped lake herself (no "Sea" at all) with fishermen trawling in boats like Peter's family sloop, maybe eight yards long with a low mast and a wide red sail.

I made myself eat "Peter's Perch" at a lakeside restaurant empty of all but me and the waiter—another eager Arab boy with tragic eyes from over the ridge in Nazareth through the Horns of Hattin. On my used placemat he wrote me a fervent recommendation to his father back home (and the father fed me generously a half block down from where the girl Mary took an angel's offered deal, a child to be named Emanuel). The perch, by the way, were smoky but mild like none I'd tasted before or since—small and flat as baby flounder, clearly primed to volunteer for multiplication at their next chance (on Judgment Day?). In all the risks I took on food, I never got a tasteless meal nor any clap of "Samson's Revenge," the local brand of tourist trots; and all the cooks and waiters I met—Arab or Jew—were proudly dedicated men who understood their job was equal in use and dignity with priesthood, soldiery or medicine, not to mention art.

By the final night I knew my trip was more than over. I was well past ready to be in the home I'd made from my work. Right till then in the car alone, I could still mist-over at the thought of my sons and all the generous souls I'd lost, the thought of Sam's dead wife and his courage, his workhorse mother beaming her joy, the dark-eyed child already on guard. But for the first time in twenty-some years, I smelled the salt air of new work forming well beyond me, barely waiting—new from the naked white spine out and loyal anyhow to what I'd seen in this deep navel-core of the earth.

As I drove through pre-dawn dark to my flight, I crossed the plain of Aijalon where bully Samson romped his pranks on the Philistines till they sheared him bald and gouged his eyes. Dark as it was that long before day, my new eyes managed to see right into the fields beside me—thorny shrubs, with gray leaves small as a fingernail, that could outlast fire.

At the airport a gray-eyed security woman asked if I'd paid the West Bank a visit. When I confessed, she asked the names of persons I'd met. I gave her names from my childhood book of *Arabian Nights*. She accepted them, straightfaced, and asked if I'd been "given things" by any such person, a gift to take home or a package to mail. At the last moment Sam had handed me an olivewood carving of an old-time shepherd and a slip of paper with his boyhood friend's address in Portland—would I send it on? It was ten inches long and plainly wood, but what if it held a clever bomb to detonate at a given height? It was buried deep in my suitcase; so on the spot I chose to trust him. I told the woman I'd been given nothing but food and shelter for one cold night, which I chose to believe; she finally smiled and the plane did not disintegrate.

Home, I worked and, sure, it was new. Like a learning child with spellbound hands, I ran through nine large pictures fast—dreams of the trip, dreams of that dream, likely the strong work of my life yet. As I started the tenth, my leg began to pain me hard in that same spot I'd felt in the tomb and later at Sam's. Before the early pictures dried, I was partly lame and in some torment, denying my fears—cancer, leukemia, multiple sclerosis, curling arthritis: the reasonable night-mares of men my age who've spent a lifetime working in colors ground with lead, titanium and zinc.

It was none of those. I forced myself; and three days after I finished the tenth and final canvas, a doctor loped to where I sat marooned in strangers in a waiting room. He was far too young to know his powers; and his first line was "It's devastating," that frank and innocent, maybe that vicious (I've learned too much about medical sadists, or moral idiots licensed to cut, to err on the side of giving them leeway).

What I've got—what commenced that night in the tomb—is an astronomically unlikely mystery that has my flesh in unforeseeable hot revolts against itself, then long numb truces—bone and muscle slowly killed by their own blood, then left to cool before a new onslaught. The doctors said I might not have a year and added that, since I "worked in the arts," I might enjoy knowing that Laurence Olivier, the great actor, shared my "syndrome."

I've had eight full years, working most days. I think I know why—the work itself, the good it brings me, my live hope of a fair return to that band of messengers, from a thin-lipped monk and young Jabril to Sam's new orphan boy Hassan and a bleary Arab Santa at dawn on the Bethlehem bypass. And while I live in a wheelchair mainly with paid good help, my hands and eyes work on above the cooling ruins and make each day an art to match, in one respect, all art I know this side of Athens, Florence, Rome (Jerusalem proves how little art counts, being all but bare of intentional art). I match it, I mean—I'm not insane—in the driving will to show this world its visible likeness, front and back, crown to toe from where I've stood, in the clean new mirrors of honest pictures that mean to be guide lights usably placed in the frequent, sometimes permanent, dark. It's a shameless dare for one gimp painter to try so much, but it runs my life; and on rare days I've almost told myself I'm *there*—my destination, however hopeless. So pounded nearer the ground each year, I likewise match every face I've known in mainly pure ungrudging thanks—every gram of my fuel on fire, burning high.

REYNOLDS PRICE

Reynolds Price was born in Macon, North Carolina in 1933. Reared and educated in the public schools of his native state, he earned an A.B. *summa cum laude* from Duke University. In 1955 he traveled as a Rhodes Scholar to Merton College, Oxford University, to study English literature. After three years, and the B. Litt. degree, he returned to Duke where he continues to teach as James B. Duke Professor of English.

In 1962 his novel A *Long and Happy Life* appeared. It received the William Faulkner Award for a notable first novel and has never been out of print. Since, he has published other novels—*Blue Calhoun* (1992) was the ninth—and in 1986 his *Kate Vaiden* received the National Book Critics Circle Award. He has also published volumes of short stories, poems, plays, essays, translations from the Bible, a memoir *Clear Pictures*; and he has written for the screen, for television and the texts for songs. His television play *Private Contentment* was commissioned by *American Playhouse* and appeared in its premiere season. His trilogy of plays *New Music* premiered at the Cleveland Play House in 1989; and its three plays have been produced throughout the country as has a newer play *Full Moon*, his seventh.

He is a member of the American Academy of Arts and Letters, and his books have appeared in sixteen languages.